THE MODERN LIBRARY

of the World's Best Books

Lie Down in Darkness

Lie Down in Darkness

BY WILLIAM STYRON

THE MODERN LIBRARY · NEW YORK

The author wishes to express appreciation for permission to quote from the following songs:

"TRY ME ONE MORE TIME"
Words and Music by Ernest Tubb
Copyright 1943 by American Music, Inc., Hollywood, California

"DEEP PURPLE"
Lyric by Mitchell Parish / Music by Peter de Rose
Copyright 1934-1939 Robbins Music Corp. Used by special permission Copyright Proprietor

"GO TELL IT ON THE MOUNTAIN"
Arranged by H. F. Mells
Copyright MCMXLIX Handy Brothers Music Co.

"I'M THE RELUCTANT DRAGON"
Used by permission of Broadcast Music, Inc.

"THE TRAMP ON THE STREET"
By Grady Cole and Hazel Cole
Copyright 1947 by Dixie Music Publishing Co.

"WE COME FROM OLD VIRGINIA" AND "WHA-HOO-WAH!"
Used by permission of Alumni Association of the University of Virginia

"HAPPY AM I IN MY REDEEMER"
Words by J. E. March / Music by J. M. Henson
Used by permission of J. M. Henson Music Company, Atlanta, Georgia

"SATURDAY NIGHT (IS THE LONELIEST NIGHT IN·THE WEEK)"
By Jule Styne & Sammy Cahn
Copyright 1944 by Barton Music Corp. (Paraphrased by special permission)

"TONIGHT WE LOVE"
Lyric by Bobby Worth / Adapted by Ray Austin & Freddy Martin
Copyright 1941 by Maestro Music Co. Used by permission of the copyright owner, Maestro Music Co.

FOR SIGRID

Lie Down in Darkness

*Carry me along, taddy, like you
done through the toy fair.*

—FINNEGANS WAKE

AND since death must be the *Lucina* of life, and even Pagans could doubt, whether thus to live were to die; since our longest sun sets at right descencions, and makes but winter arches, and therefore it cannot be long before we lie down in darkness, and have our light in ashes; since the brother of death daily haunts us with dying mementos, and time that grows old in itself, bids us hope no long duration;—diuturnity is a dream and folly of expectation.

—Sir Thomas Browne
Urn Burial

One

RIDING down to Port Warwick from Richmond, the train begins to pick up speed on the outskirts of the city, past the tobacco factories with their ever-present haze of acrid, sweetish dust and past the rows of uniformly brown clapboard houses which stretch down the hilly streets for miles, it seems, the hundreds of rooftops all reflecting the pale light of dawn; past the suburban roads still sluggish and sleepy with early morning traffic, and rattling swiftly now over the bridge which separates the last two hills where in the valley below you can see the James River winding beneath its acid-green crust of scum out beside the chemical plants and more rows of clapboard houses and into the woods beyond.

Suddenly the train is burrowing through the pinewoods, and the conductor, who looks middle-aged and respectable like someone's favorite uncle, lurches through the car asking for tickets. If you are particularly alert at that unconscionable hour you notice his voice, which is somewhat guttural and negroid—oddly fatuous-sounding after the accents of Columbus or Detroit or wherever you came from—and when you ask him how far it is to Port Warwick and he says, "Aboot eighty miles," you know for sure that you're in the Tidewater. Then you settle back in your seat, your face feeling unwashed and swollen from the intermittent sleep you got sitting up the night before and your gums sore from too many cigarettes, and you try to doze off, but the nap of the blue felt seat prickles your neck and so you sit up once more and cross your legs, gazing drowsily at the novelty sales-man from Allentown P-a, next to you, who told you last night about his hobby, model trains, and the joke about the two college girls at the Hotel Astor, and whose sleek face, sprouting a faint gray crop of stubble, one day old, is now peacefully relaxed, immobile in sleep, his breath issuing from slightly parted lips in delicate sighs. Or, turning away, you look out at the pinewoods sweeping past at sixty miles an hour, the trees standing close together green and somnolent, and the brown-needled carpet of the forest floor dappled brightly in the early morning light, until the white fog of smoke from the engine ahead swirls and dips against the window like a tattered scarf and obscures the view.

Now the sun is up and you can see the mist lifting off the fields and in the middle of the fields the solitary cabins with their slim threads of smoke unwinding out of plastered chimneys and the faint glint of fire through an open door and, at a crossing, the sudden, swift tableau of a Negro and his hay-wagon and a lop-eared mule: the Negro with his mouth agape, exposing pink gums, staring at the speeding train until the smoke obscures him, too, from view, and the one dark-brown hand held cataleptic in the air.

Stirring, the novelty salesman looks drowsily out of the window and grunts, "Where are we?" and you murmur, "Not far from Port War-wick, I hope," and as he turns on his side to sleep some more you finger your copy of the *Times-Dispatch* which the newsboy sold you an hour ago, and which you haven't read and won't read because maybe you have things on your mind; and instead you look out once more at the late summer landscape and the low, sorrowful beauty of tideland streams winding through marshes full of small, darting, frightened noises and glistening and dead silent at noon, except for a whistle, far off, and a distant rumble on the rails. And most likely, as the train streaks past the little log-road stations with names like Apex and Jewel, a couple of Negroes are working way out in the woods sawing timber, and they hear the whistle of your train and one of them stands erect from his end of the saw, wiping away the beads of sweat gathered on his brow like tiny blisters, and says, "Man, dat choo-choo's goin' to Richmond," and the other says, "Naw, she goin' to Po't Wa'ick," and the other says happily, "Hoo-ee, dat's a poontang

10

town, sho enough," and they laugh together as the saw resumes its hot metallic rip and the sun burns down in the swarming, resonant silence.

Port Warwick is a shipbuilding city and the workers' houses begin where the marshlands end—the clean cheap clusters of plywood cottages springing out of the woods like toadstools—and now the men are going to work, their automobiles crawling eastward along the highway past more groups of houses encroaching suddenly upon the desolation of the marshland, backed up against the forest wall where in their tiny back yards the women are hanging up clothes to dry, turning pale faces slowly toward the train going by. The train slows down and the novelty salesman awakes with perplexed and fitful yawns and borrows your newspaper, and when you turn again the wilderness is gone, the suburban houses are rolling by, and the gray anonymous streets and the supermarket signs; then the freight yards and finally the slow shuddering halt at the station dock, which is the end of the line because beyond the dock is the bay, five miles wide and a deep salty green.

You get up and say good-by to the novelty salesman, who is going on across the bay by ferry, and you pull your bag from the rack and climb down off the train onto the station dock where the smell of the water is clean and refreshing after the flatulent warmth of the car and where, thirty yards away, your girl or your friends are waiting with expectant grins—"Oh there he is!"—and as you walk toward them you've already forgotten the novelty salesman forever, and the ride down. It's going to be a hot day.

At precisely eleven o'clock on a weekday morning in August of 1945, a black, shiny hearse, whose motor was so soundless that the effect was that of no motor at all, slid to a stop on the station dock at Port Warwick, followed by an automobile commonly known as a "limousine" in the mortuary trade—a Packard, and also highly polished. The driver of the limousine, Mr. Llewellyn Casper, was a slim, bespectacled man who wore gloves the color of house mice, and whose face conveyed a sense of alert and sympathetic awareness. It was a homely, lightly freckled face with the pale-blue, abstracted eyes common to most people who have flaming red hair such as his, and as he climbed from the seat and onto the dock and gently opened the rear door, he gave an impression of quiet, vigilant decorum—a man to whom one certainly, on a day like this, could entrust the cheerless details attendant upon the death of someone in the family.

11

He bent into the rear seat, saying, "We've got fifteen minutes before the train comes, Mr. Loftis. Do you want to wait in the station?"

From the back seat there emerged Milton Loftis, followed by a woman named Dolly Bonner, and by an old Negro woman dressed in black silk and white lace collar and cuffs. Her name was Ella Swan. "I think we'll wait on the dock," Loftis said.

"All right, sir. I'll be with you in a minute. Oh, Barclay!" He departed on sudden, noiseless feet toward his assistant, a pale young man in a baggy black suit who, bent over the hood of the hearse, was peering into the smoking engine.

The other three walked silently to the shadows beneath the station shed where another group of people had already gathered for the train. From somewhere beneath the dock, steam was escaping: it made a shrill incessant whistle. Above the shed the sky was clear and cloudless and a deep violent blue, the sort of sky that promises heat and vague languid activity all day long. The air, already humid, partook of the salty quality peculiar to Southern waterfronts: a brackish smell of creosote and tar and fish, touched faintly with the odor of something frying on a stove. Across from the dock, and separated from it by twenty yards or so of greasy water, a freighter lay tethered to its pier. Into the hold a gang of stevedores had begun to load a cargo of bauxite. From the pier came the rattle and hum of an electric crane, a scorched, galvanic smell of burned metal. A workman's voice from the hold, faint and sepulchral like the echo from a cave, cried, "Bring her over!" and a thick fog of dust started to drift from the ship, floating downward in an undulating cloud which settled gently on the dock beneath the shed and began to tinge everything with a fine sediment, faintly gritty to the touch. Most of the waiting people retreated into the station, pounding their clothes with their hands, but Loftis and the two women waited patiently beside the tracks while the haze settled upon them soundlessly, seeping into their clothes and encrusting the face of the old Negro in a dusty mask.

". . . and she wouldn't come. She wouldn't come at all," Loftis was saying. "I begged, I pleaded with her. 'Helen,' I said, 'simple decency demands that you come. This day at least,' I said. 'Don't you understand,' I said, 'it's our daughter, our daughter, not just mine. How can you expect me to endure . . .' I said, 'just how can you expect me . . .'"

His voice rose loudly on a note of taut and frantic grief and the two women, as if impelled by the same thought, patted him on the arms and broke out together in a flutter of tender whisperings. "Now don't you take on——" Ella began, while Dolly said, "Milton dear, you must be brave.

"Milton dear," she added softly, "do you think I should really be here? I want so to be with you, dearest. But Helen and all, and . . ." She was a woman of about forty, with a black dress and wistful eyes.

"I don't know," he said in a small voice.

"What? What's wrong, dear?"

He didn't say anything. He hadn't heard her and, furthermore, his mind was too occupied with his own bewildering sorrow. Yesterday he had been happy, but this sorrow—descending upon him as it had the night before—seemed to have confounded him beyond all hope, since, for the first time in his life, he was unable to cut his trouble adrift, to shed it like some startling and unwelcome chrysalis, and finally to explain it away as "one of those things." His face had become slack with grief, and as he gazed at the water his eyes wore a mildly astonished expression, as if he were watching the scene for the first time. He was in his middle fifties and had been good-looking in his youth (one could see that), and although some of the old handsome traces remained, his face had fallen into a limp and negligent disrepair: a young man's features distended into an unhealthy flabbiness, the skin over well-formed bones now full of big pores and deeply flushed. In his hair there was a patch of gray which had been there since childhood and which, far from being disfiguring, had added a flourish to his looks, a sort of focal point toward which strangers might direct admiring glances. About this patch he had been quite vain, and because of it had rarely worn a hat.

Ella Swan said, "Train gonna come soon. Peyton comin' on de 'leven-fo'teen. Po' precious lamb." She began to sob quietly into an enormous lace handkerchief. She had a wrinkled, wizened face, like that of an aged monkey, and while she wept her eyes peeped damply up over the folds of the lace and looked all around.

"Shh-hh," Dolly whispered. She laid her hand on Ella's arm. "Shh-hh now, Ella. Don't."

Dust sifted down, enveloping the dock like a fog; down the tracks two lone redcaps, hauling baggage from the station, trundled along, disappeared like phantoms, and Loftis, watching them, thought: I won't think too much about this. I'll try to occupy my mind with the water instead. On the ship a solitary figure, brick-red, trailing a cable, hopped along a catwalk and yelled into the hold, "Easy!" Perhaps, he thought, if I only think of this second, this moment, the train won't come at all. Think of the water, think of now. Just the same,

13

he knew he was too old, too weary for paradoxes, that he couldn't evade immediacy, and that the train would come after all, bringing with it final proof of fate and circumstance—words which all his life he had never quite understood, being an Episcopalian, nominally, at least, and not inclined by conscience to worry long over abstractions. It would come, bearing with it, too, evidence of all his errors and of all his love—because he loved his daughter more than anything—and the thought which suddenly struck him—that of meeting her this morning, silent, invisible within a coffin—filled him with horror. The train, he thought, is now on the outskirts of town and passing with a terrible rumbling noise over the last creek past the nigger shacks on the banks.

"Ah, my God," he said weakly.

Ella Swan turned her face toward him. She dabbed softly at her eyes, saying, "Don't you worry none, Mistah Loftis. Me an Miz Bonner take keer of things." Then she began to weep again. "Lawd God bless us Jesus," she moaned.

"Shh-hh, Ella," said Dolly.

Heartsick, frightened, he turned away, watched the water, listening. *I do not propose to convince,* his father had said (in the feeble light of a March afternoon thirty years ago, before the house was finally condemned, but not long before; when even the lightest footstep on the stairs sent a plaintive wooden squeal through the joists and beams, reminder not only of the swiftly aging house but of the passing of a finer, more tranquil age), *I do not propose to convince you merely through paternal advice which no doubt you in your willful notion of filial duty would abjure anyway, I only trust you will heed the warning of one who has seen much water pass as it were beneath the bridge one to whom I must admit the temptations of the flesh have been potent and manifold, and that you will perhaps in some measure renounce a way of life which even in its most charitable concept can lead only to grief and possibly complete ruination. I am an old man now. . . .*

So his father had somehow realized that his youth would rise up eventually to betray him, even though he couldn't have foreseen the final calamity—the son, middle-aged now and a bit flabby, standing here awaiting the symbol of his doom—any more than he could have foreseen that another and crueler war would level the earth or that long after his death, in some unbelievable way, the Democrats would take over—perhaps endlessly. His father. No more than a shadow. A wave of self-pity swept over him. He felt tricked and defeated and it seemed to him that the bigness of his sorrow was too much to bear.

14

Not just that, Papa. Other things. Life tends toward a moment. Not just the flesh. Not a poet or a thief, I could never exercise free will.

Besides . . . He watched the ship, the dust, three gulls swerving downward, seesawing on flashing wings. Besides . . . There *was* his youth. You forget your youth, that which, reckless, rises up to betray you. It's your youth, forgotten these years, that you ultimately regret—out of a life begun fifty-some years ago in a cluttered museum of a house in Richmond where his first memory was that of a sunny room murmurous with the sad, hushed sounds of Sunday afternoon and a parade outside with distant band music both bright and disconsolate, his mother's voice whispering, "It's music, Milton dear . . . music . . . music . . . music . . . listen, dear." The sunlight sifted downward through gently rustling blinds and somewhere infinitely far above, it had seemed, there was his mother's vacant, hovering face, unseen and finally unknown because she died before he could picture in his consciousness those features his father later said were refined and lovely. There were also walks in the park with his father and the damp, ferny smell of the woods and his best friend, a boy named Charley Quinn, who had a pale face and cheeks with famished hollows and a birthmark on his forehead like a brown-petaled flower, and who was killed at the Somme. *My son . . .*

Your first duty remember, son, is always to yourself (he was a lawyer, descended from a long line of lawyers, and until his death in 1920 he sported stiff wing collars and an Edwardian mustache) *I do not intend to presume upon your own good judgment, a faculty which I believe you possess in abundance inherited not from me but from your sainted mother, so as you go out into the world I can only admonish you with the words of the Scotchman, videlicet, keep your chin up and your kilts down and let the wind blow.*

But his father lacked the foresight to avoid spoiling his son and to realize that sending him to the University at the age of seventeen would produce the results it did: at nineteen he was a campus character known as "Blow," a sot even by fraternity standards who drank not only because whisky made him drunk but because, away from his father, he found the sudden freedom oppressive. He was talkative, he had a natural curiosity. They said he'd make a fine lawyer. And when he was graduated from the law school he was pleasantly surprised upon reviewing his record to find that he had performed so well, considering the time spent drunk and in the town whorehouse, which catered mainly to college boys: it was a mansion, he remembered, chandeliered, with University seals on the lampshades, and run by a fancy high-yellow named Carmen Metz.

He had been in the Great War, having made gestures toward joining the Army which years later he shamefully confessed to himself were trifling, having been greatly relieved when his father, through government connections, got him a commission in the Army legal branch. During the entire war he was at Governor's Island. There, by processes more simple than he had ever imagined, he was made first lieutenant and then captain—emerging from the war with that rank and with the colonel's daughter.

They met at an officers' dance on the island. Her name was Helen Peyton. Her father was a West Pointer, from an old Virginia family. Wasn't it a coincidence, she asked Milton as they danced, that her grandfather should have gone to the University, too? That night they walked along the seawall in a drizzling rain and when he bent over, unsteady, very drunk, to kiss her, the city lights drifted like embers across the darkness. Then she fled, the raindrops on her cape leaving a trail of trembling sparks.

Perhaps they were both too young to know better, but a few months later they were engaged to be married. They were both handsome people, and they were wildly in love. They liked parties, dancing; on Saturdays they rode horseback in Central Park. Yet she was strait-laced in many ways, rather severe: No, Milton. We'll have to wait till afterwards. And drinking. She loved a good time, but a sober good time.

"Now, Little Miss Muffet," he'd say, smiling, "don't be scared, a little one . . ."

"Oh, Milton, please, you've had enough. No. No. I won't!" And running off, unaccountably, weeping a little.

Now wouldn't you know? There's an Army brat for you. Crazy as hell, the unstable life caused it. Moving around always. But he loved her, God he loved her. For a long time he drank nothing. For her.

They talked bravely, brightly of the future. His father had a little money; he'd set Milton up in practice in Port Warwick, "a growing town," as the saying goes. They could have a good time there. It wasn't much money his father was giving them, but it would do for a while. They'd manage.

Then she told him. When her mother died she was due to inherit a hundred thousand dollars. "Oh, baby," he said, mildly protesting but elated, and so they were married with the bright hollow panoply attending such military affairs, the ceremony that disturbed him be-

16

cause of the untroubled thrill it gave him. The sweet excitement that came from the flags and the music, of which he was faintly ashamed, was not mere patriotism. It was rather the pride he had in his rank, which he had attained only through his bride and he knew it, but which nonetheless sent through him a fierce adolescent upsurge of exciting arrogance—the twin silver bars and the starched dress uniform, impeccably white. Nor was the feeling of sham and fakery canceled by the news brought by his father, now a diffidently mild, still doting old man in whom patience was no longer a virtue but a habit, who stood shyly in one corner of the officers' club at the reception, the ends of his once-proud mustache twitching sadly, and told him in an apologetic, mournful tone that Charley Quinn had been killed overseas, it was bad, too bad.

So the anger mounted silently in the younger man as he expressed a faint regret for the death of a boy he had lost track of long ago, barely concealing the resentment he felt at having been told such a thing on his wedding day—as if his father, in atonement for his ill-advised move in getting his son's commission in the first place, had passed the remark as a reminder that war was not all champagne and flowers and the tinkly laughter of officers' wives. And he had hardly restrained himself from saying something very bitter, archly insulting to his father as the old man stood there, the damp, feeble blinking of his eyes reflecting the weakness for which Loftis had felt all his life a quiet contempt. He wanted to get him out of there and on his way back to Richmond. He despised his father. The old man had given him too much. *My son* (he was living in a boardinghouse then; the old house had been torn down, a cigarette factory erected on the site, the steel and concrete walls impermeable to the lingering ghosts of a quiet and departed tradition or even to the memory of a dozen ancient cedars which had cast down a tender, trembling light upon that vanished ground) *my son, your mother was a joy and indeed a deliverance to me and I hope and pray if only out of honor to the blessed memory of her who brought you into life that you will as the Preacher said live joyfully with the wife whom thou lovest all the days of the life of thy vanity which he hath given thee under the sun all the days of thy vanity for that is thy portion in this life and in thy labor which thou takest under the sun. My son . . .*

A sudden, quick ache of pity and sadness came over him, he fumbled stupidly for a word to say, but Helen's face floated near, uptilted, offering him a kiss, and she led him away to meet someone. His father stood awkwardly in the corner then, groping in conversation with a

17

bored young lieutenant while he, the new captain, listened to the rhythmic wedding small talk of a general's wife, nodded, smiled, and thought of the pale boy with the blemish like a flower, the brother he had never had, and of his father whom he had never known. "Really, Helen," the general's wife was saying, "I think you have the pick of the Army. Such a peach!" And her laughter shattered the air like falling glass.

Think of now. From a boat somewhere a whistle gave a loud blast. Loftis looked up through the dust, the slanting frames of light. "Helen," he said absently, groping for her hand, but it was Dolly whose glove lay so consolingly on his arm and, turning to meet her eyes, he heard the train rumbling far down the tracks. "No!" he cried. "I can't go through with it!"

The hearse was parked near the coal elevator. Each time Mr. Casper bent over to explain to Barclay what was wrong with the motor, a gondola car was upturned on the tracks above them, and his words were lost in the furious roar of coal plunging seaward, swallowed up in a ship's hold with a hollow booming noise.

"Lyle," he would begin, "maybe the *fan belt isn't turning over. LYLE!*" Nervously he wiped dust from his cuffs, trying to keep calm. "Maybe the fan belt isn't turning over." Barclay climbed into the front of the hearse, let the motor run for a few seconds, but the fan was working. He turned the motor off.

"Did you check . . ."

Ree-ee-eep. CaaaaARWONG!

Bitter exasperation tightened like a knot in Mr. Casper's mind. He had had hardly any sleep the night before and the scene around him had a giddy and abstract air. "Now, Barclay," he said, "are you *sure* you checked the water?"

"Yes, sir," he said bleakly.

"Because I warned you the last time. This hearse cost nearly six thousand dollars, son, and we don't want anything to happen to it, do we?"

Barclay looked up from the engine. Mr. Casper smiled gently downward. About Barclay he felt warm and paternal, he had no children of his own. Lyle was slow, but a nice boy; nice but . . . well, slow. This was no day——

"Here," he said, removing his gloves, "let me look in there." On the backs of his hands there were freckles, large red ones lightly spired

18

with carroty tufts of hair. As he bent over a sour gust of smoke went up his nostrils. He groped forward blindly, smearing grease on his cuffs. Then he lost his balance and as he grabbed wildly for support his hand struck the radiator. Scalding pain ran the length of his arm.

"*Damnation*, Barclay!" He whirled, leaped away from the engine and clutched his hand. He looked fearfully downward where a blister was already forming: a small place, but it hurt, and the pain filled him with irrational anger. "Fix it, boy," he said softly, as softly as he could. "Fix that radiator. If you can't, I will."

Two Negro dockhands walked past, a length of clanking chain between them. Mr. Casper heard a chuckle. "Dead wagon. Man!" Mr. Casper was ashamed of his anger.

While he stood and sucked at the blister, Barclay found the trouble: the rubber pipe leading from the radiator had broken loose from its connection and most of the water had drained away. He stuck the pipe back in place. As Barclay went off to fetch a bucket of water from the Esso station, Mr. Casper fastened the hood and stood erect, wiping grease from his hands. He put on his gloves, heard a faint whistle up the tracks. He looked at his watch: eleven-twenty. The train. Above, a coal car slid down the incline of the elevator: a wild, descending lisp of steel on steel. The noise ground unbearably at his nerves. Damnation. Hurriedly he walked toward the group on the dock. A porter, emerging from the baggage room, laden with suitcases, bumped against him: " 'Scuse me, suh." He climbed the steps onto the dock, and a clean, cool gust of salt air struck his face. Then, breathing in deeply, he heard Loftis' distant, husky voice, high-pitched now and agitated, rocking tremulously on the edge of that sad hysteria he knew so well.

"I can't go through with it!" Loftis said, loud enough for a fat man passing Mr. Casper to stop and look back with questioning eyes. "I tell you . . . than I can bear . . . WON'T!"

Mr. Casper was a kindly man. Anguish communicated itself to him with the swiftness of light; learned, practiced in sorrow, he could easily distinguish between real and counterfeit grief. This was the real thing. He strode up and patted Loftis on the shoulder.

"There, there, Mr. Loftis," he said. "Buck up."

"No, I won't go up there. No, I don't want to see it. No, I won't. I can't. I'll just go . . ."

"All right, old trouper," Mr. Casper interposed gently, "you don't have to go if you don't want to. You just go and sit in the limousine."

The train rumbled ponderously onto the dock, sending down a vaporous white plume of smoke which swarmed and swirled about them. The engine shuddered to a stop, panting like a sudden and enormous beast beside them as the sunlight glinted brightly on a dozen greased wheels.

"Yes," Loftis said quietly, subdued now. "I'll just go sit in the car. I don't want to see it."

"That's right, old trouper," Mr. Casper replied, "just go sit in the limousine."

"Dat's right, po' ol' thing," Ella whimpered, "jes go set in de lemmosine."

"Yes, dear," Dolly added, "the car."

Loftis turned toward Mr. Casper with a look of deliverance, a wild-eyed and grateful expression that stirred Mr. Casper warmly and he repeated, "Yes, sir, you go sit down in the limousine if you want to. Everything's in my hands." And Loftis hurried off toward the car, murmuring, "Yes, yes," as if Mr. Casper's words had settled the issue.

When he had gone, Dolly burst into tears. "Poor Peyton," she wept, "poor poor girl." Her grief had a faintly dishonest ring, Mr. Casper thought. Of course, it was hard to tell about women: they were likely to be that way. He expected them to weep after all . . . but what was her connection with Loftis anyway? Something—a remark or a word he had heard—clamored for attention in his mind, but it was quickly lost. He had things to do. He walked up the tracks, peering through the dust for the baggage car, and a troublesome uncertainty plagued him. He had felt it somehow all morning and for a restless time last night in bed, but it was only the moment before—a funny look in Dolly Bonner's eyes?—that he really had begun to get uneasy. *Something*, he thought, *is rotten in Denmark*. Mr. Casper took pride in his work. The fact that Mr. and Mrs. Loftis seemed to be taking such a secretive—even un-Christian—attitude toward the remains of their own daughter shocked him profoundly and, in some obscure fashion, seemed an insult not only to him but to his profession.

He had received the Loftises' call the night before, not at his house but at the funeral home where—because of a stupid error he had made in his accounts the month before—he was going over the books with Mr. Huggins, the auditor for the Tidewater Morticians League. It was Mrs. Loftis' voice. He recognized it instantly, having had casual business with her from time to time in the Community Chest fund: the cultured, precise tone, polite but faintly superior. She told him the facts—which he jotted down in a notebook—in a voice oddly calm and devoid of feeling, and it was only after he had hung up, concluding with the usual condolences, that he remarked to himself and then to Mr. Huggins: "That was funny, she sounded so . . . *cold*."

Mr. Casper had no taste for the emotional congestion that usually afflicts women at times of great strain; often he had told Barclay that "a weeping woman is worse than a wildcat with wings," yielding to the boy one of his facetious epigrams, so carefully hoarded, by which, like the rakehell quip of a soldier before battle, he hoped to soften a little the austerity of their mission. But at the same time there was something within him—a feeling for dignity harmonizing with the nature of his work—that demanded that the bereaved, especially a woman, give some small token of distress, if only pale, drawn lips trying bravely to smile; eyes which, though dry, expressed endless grief. It was with great curiosity, then—remembering the tone of Helen Loftis' words, cool, heartlessly so—that he had approached their house that morning. She greeted him at the front door, her face as composed as if she were meeting the groceryman. True, he thought, her skin was worn. A fine tapestry of wrinkles had traced itself across the ghostly face. Sad, he thought, sad. But they—all those wrinkles and tiny little lines and convolutions—had been there before. They—along with the lovely hair, stark white, although she couldn't yet be fifty—belonged to some other sorrow. Then he remembered in a flash: something else a few years before—another daughter, a cripple. Who had passed away. Wasn't she feeble-minded? Barnes, his competitor, had handled . . . Lord almighty, he thought.

She made an attempt to smile.

"Come in," she said. "Mr. Loftis is upstairs. He'll be right down."

"Thank you, ma'am," he said, "I want to say——" Gentle words of consolation began to rattle in his head like dominoes. "I want to say——"

"That's all right, Mr. Casper, won't you come in?"

He entered the screened-in porch hesitantly, unnerved and bewildered. The morning sun was hot against his back. Around the porch hovered the odor of honeysuckle and verbena, bees, a couple of tiny hummingbirds.

"I would like——" he began.

"Please, Mr. Casper," she said with an impatience that startled him, "if you'll just sit here." She disappeared into the house silently, and her silk wrapper rustled weirdly behind her. He sank into the glider,

21

warm with the smell of leather, and he began to sweat. Through French windows he could see the dining room, shadowy, empty. Crystal and silver laid out on the sideboard reflected pools of light against the walls. Her work, he thought. Very neat and ordered.

Milton Loftis came out in rumpled clothes, with bloodshot eyes. He spoke softly, in a voice that was husky and tired. It was to be strictly private. No announcement in the newspapers—no, none at all. Flowers? No, they wouldn't be necessary. Yes, he knew it was all out of the ordinary but the rector had given his sanction. Yes (with a thin unhappy smile), yes, he was at the end of his tether.

"Don't worry, old trouper——" Mr. Casper began, but Loftis had vanished and Mr. Casper sat down again and felt the warm green leather beneath his perspiring hands. It was all so strange, he thought. He could see the bay, blue and waveless, resting in a sultry calm. Far out on the other side a tiny purple battleship, silhouetted, floated like a toy boat on a bathtub lake. An insolent gull squawked over the beach, soared upward and out of sight.

Ella Swan darted out on the porch. When she saw him she burst into tears and fled back through the door in a tumultuous rustle of ribbon and lace. "Lawd, Mistah Loftis, he's here!"

Mr. Casper heard voices floating from the hallway. Uneasily he leaned forward. Loftis was saying, "And so you aren't coming with me?" and she: "Why should I? I told you I'd come with Carey Carr:" and,

"Helen, haven't you even——"

"Please, I told you. I don't want to say anything else about it."

"But just decency demands——"

"Yes, decency. Yes, decency. Yes, go on and talk about decency."

"Helen, don't you realize——"

"Yes, yes, I realize everything. Everything."

"But I can't go alone. You said . . . you know yourself . . . what will people think——"

"Ha! What will people think! I know. What will people think! Don't make me laugh."

"Helen, just listen to me, please——"

"I'll listen——"

"I know it's useless to suggest now that we reconcile these terrible things. Well, it seems you'd do this one thing, not for me—but for Peyton."

"Milton, I'm tired. I'm going upstairs. I slept badly. I'm going upstairs now. There's a letter for you on the table."

22

"Helen, *please*."

"No. No." Her footsteps moved across the floor. "Why don't you take Dolly? Take your lover sweetheart."

"Helen, *please*."

"Ella's going, isn't she? She loved Peyton."

"Please, Helen, please——"

"No." The footsteps began to mount the stairs.

"Please, Helen."

"No."

Upstairs a door closed. *Lord almighty*, Mr. Casper thought.

"Please, Helen." From a distance.

"No."

With that, Helen closed the door. In her room everything was sunny and clean. A soft breeze shook the curtains; they trembled slightly, as with the touch of a feeble and unseen hand. Outside the window the holly leaves rustled, made thin, dry scrapings against the screen, and then this breeze, so familiar to her because of its nearly predictable comings and goings, suddenly ceased: the curtains fell limp without a sound and the house, sapped of air, was filled with an abrupt, wicked heat, like that which escapes from an oven door.

Downstairs she heard the screen door slam, a noise of feet on the gravel walk. No one said a word. The limousine and the hearse pulled away from the curb, almost inaudibly, and down the driveway. The house was quiet then, very still. Silence surrounded her in damp, hot layers, yet now, breaking this stillness, a single locust somewhere commenced a loud chatter: remote at first, threatening death and rain, shrill, ascending then, like something sliding up a wire, and scraping finally at a point, it seemed, not more than two inches from her ear— a menacing clamor, staccato, outraged and inane. The noise stopped suddenly and the enfolding silence was like an echo, a sound in her ears.

On the sheets of her bed there was a damp place where she had been sleeping the night before. She wondered: How many times have I or Ella let the beds go unmade this late? Not many. She sat down on the side of the bed and picked up the morning newspaper, the one which, for the first time she could remember, she, not Milton or Ella, had retrieved from the front steps at dawn. Vaguely it bothered her, for it had been an act quite out of keeping with the serene and orderly character of her life, and she thought: What did I do? Somehow I can't think . . .

Oh, yes. She remembered how odd it had been. Walking down the

23

steps past Milton in the hall, him who, fully clothed, asprawl on the couch, lay snoring with a soft, blubbering sound, and then standing on the porch as she peered out through the chilly dawn light at the deserted street, thinking in this queer, abstracted way: I have brought two children into life and I was a mother for twenty-three years. This is the first day that I have awakened knowing that I am a mother no longer and that I shall never be a mother again.

So odd of me. To get the

She began to read the newspaper. The Bomb again, a truce in the offing with the Japanese; a picture below showed a film actress, known for her legs, and an eminent café owner with a face like a mouse, wed yesterday in Las Vegas, Nevada. Married. Unable to concentrate, she laid the paper down. A huge emptiness began to creep over her, so familiar a thing, this easy, physical sense of languor and infirmity—as if everything had suddenly drained forth from her flesh, leaving her as limp as some pale jelly that floats in the sea. She arose and walked to the window, touching the sill with her finger tips. The locust was still. *How merciful that is.* Beyond the garden, the trellis and the swollen blooms of honeysuckle, beyond the dead azaleas, she heard a car pass on the road. The sound approached, faded, died.

Life, others.

She turned and stood by the dresser and examined her face in the mirror. An old woman's face, she thought, haggard and spooky: And I not yet fifty . . . half a century undone timeless like the memory of ruined walls. She swept back her white hair, pressing it against her head with hands that were pale, nearly translucent. Beneath the shiny skin of her hands the veins were tessellated like a blue mosaic, shining, like an intricate blue design captured beneath glass. Now she did something that she had done many times before. She pulled the skin of her face taut over the cheekbones so that the web of lines and wrinkles vanished as if it had been touched by a miraculous and restorative wand; squinting convergently into the glass, she watched the foolish and lovely change: transfigured, she saw smooth skin as glossy white as the petal of gardenia, lips which seemed but sixteen or twenty, and as unblemished by any trouble as those she had held up to another mirror thirty years before, whispering "Dearest" to an invisible and quite imaginary lover. She dropped her hands, turned away from the glass and, as if in afterthought, walked over to the bed and picked up the paper again. She scanned the page once more, neither with purpose nor out of any expectation, for she knew no notice would be there. Rather out of emptiness, remembering Milton the night before—seeing him for the first time in months—as he telephoned Frank Downs, the local publisher, saying: "Yes, Frank. My daughter, my little girl . . . yes, violent . . . so if you'll keep it out of . . . Yes, Frank . . . thanks, Frank—" and sobbing into the mouthpiece—"Frank, boy, she's gone, she's gone from me!"

He had come in the evening yesterday as she stood, after her solitary supper, in the hall. (Ella had said, "Kin I have de day off tomorrow, Miss Helen? Daddy Faith, he——" but Helen had said, "Yes," and Ella had gone back to the kitchen.) She had heard his car draw up and on the walk his slow and hesitant footsteps. It was nearly dusk. There had been a thunder shower before; the garden was wet and drooping. As he approached, a noisy flock of sparrows swooped up from the lawn like scraps of paper on a sudden blast of wind and disappeared into the boxwood, swallowed up, invisible, still cheeping raucously as the hedge showered down a tiny storm of rain. He stood at the door for a moment, his face flushed, bewildered, saying nothing; then he blurted, "Helen, Peyton killed herself," and entered. She made no reply, the sudden shock striking somewhere inside her chest like an electric bolt, flickering at her finger tips, numbing her cheeks, but receding swiftly as she remembered, thought *so, so, well*—receding even as swiftly as the storm which, passing, drifted with remote grumblings over the ocean, while unseen clouds cast into the garden a pink flushed twilight, swiftly fading. In the kitchen, amid the rattle of pots and pans, Ella Swan was singing a tune. About Jesus.

She could tell that he was already a little tight. They sat down across from each other, she on the sofa and he in his chair by the secretary, where the liquor was kept, unopened since he had left her almost two years ago. He poured straight shots from a new pint bottle of Old Forester—she watched his fingers, watched them tremble—into a dusty wineglass he had found on the shelf. Then he began to speak—a rush of words which he halted only long enough to drink, his face thrown back in the familiar mechanical motion, then bobbing forward as though by springs, ugly and distorted in a quick spasm of distaste as if even after all these years he were unable to cope with the smell, the taste of the stuff which had been for so long his balm and salvation.

"Harry called me at the club," he said. "Horrible . . . I don't . . ." He paused, bemused, and his eyes (she knew exactly what was happening) were not yet grieving but still perplexed, wearing the vaguely startled look of a man who is plotting a way out, an escape.

"I don't know why. I don't know!" he said, his voice swelling. "Why would she——"

"Hush, Milton, not so loud," she said quietly. She spoke to him twice that evening. This was one of those times, and she thought, even as she spoke: The suffering hasn't come quite yet. Not yet. It will take a while longer. He doesn't quite believe it, feeling with that certainty of selfish men that he will never come by misfortune. The suffering will come suddenly, though. And soon.

Night came quickly. The descent of darkness was almost tropical. Abruptly—like that—it was dark outside, and she arose silently and turned on a lamp. In the garden a lone frog made a shrill piping sound. She sat down again on the sofa, hands folded across her lap, calmly regarding the man who was no longer her husband and yet not a stranger, but something somewhere between the two. "Helen, I swear I don't know . . . Riding over here I was wondering what I'd say. Wondering because God knows we've lost something. Wondering because thirty years ago I didn't think all this would happen." He would halt, thrust his head into his hands for a moment, concentrating. Then, snatching the wineglass from the table in an awkward, greedy motion, he would drink, drain it in a gulp, and replace it on the edge of the table, from which it once fell unbroken and noiselessly to the carpet. He leaned over unsteadily and picked it up, saying, "I didn't think all this would happen." He paused. "You won't believe me, will you?"

She didn't look at him any more. She gazed through the window at the mimosa tree, bedraggled in the darkness, dripping rain. "You won't believe me but the first thing I thought of was you. You think I'm not telling the truth, don't you? You think I'm saying that because . . . You think . . ." He thrust his head into his hands. "Oh, God knows what you think."

The grief is coming now, she said to herself: He's beginning to know what suffering is. Perhaps that's good in a way. Even he. Perhaps that's good for a man—finally to know what suffering is, to know what a woman somehow knows almost from the day she's born.

He looked upward. He was silent for a moment. She heard him fumbling on the table with the whisky. Outside the mimosa seemed to come alive; the pink, mossy blooms groped at the air: something trembled, shuddered, sighed, although it was only the early evening wind. She heard the frog's throbbing voice, a late-summer sound of waning life, feeble and steadfast and unafraid. He spoke again: "Why don't you say something? What's the matter? Why don't you say something? What's the matter?" She could feel him bending forward in the chair, the voice coming as from a great distance—queru-

26

lous and half-drunk, very tired, "Answer me, Helen. What's the matter? Don't you feel anything? You haven't said a word all night." Again he ceased talking. She watched the mimosa, saw a glow from the kitchen and, faint among the distant pantry sounds, heard Ella Swan's tireless, patient lament. She said nothing. "Helen, say something to me. Helen! Now. Say something. Helen!"

Perhaps not yet suffering. Or grief. But quick. And soon.

She took a spoonful of medicine, swallowed it with water from a glass on her dresser: A cigarette. I'd give anything for a cigarette, but Dr. Holcomb . . . She sank down on the bed, on the damp place, and stretched out across the sheets. The sunlight in the room didn't fade; it glowed without shadow on the walls and ceiling. In a vase on her dresser four dahlias were withering. There were so many things . . . She had forgotten them. There were so many things . . . She shut her eyes for a moment. I must throw them out, she thought: the dahlias, I must throw them out before I leave. And in the darkness the fancied smell of old rancid water was sour and strong. She opened her eyes. By the dahlias light fell upon the figurine dresser lamps, upon those beribboned eighteenth-century lords and ladies frozen timeless and unaltered in some grave and mannered dance, the light and the heat and the silence in the house suddenly all becoming one, with form, it seemed, and with substance, inert and unyielding. She closed her eyes again, thinking: I must somehow get that fan fixed. And slowly thinking: Carey Carr is coming at noon. I must be ready. Not moving or stirring because of the weariness that had emptied her like a vessel. *I have always been so sick. All my life I have yearned for sleep.* Remote and apart from the silence in the house she was aware of faint noises outside: half-heard, half-remembered sounds flickered like shapes through her mind—a gull's cry, a car on the road, water sucking at the shore. She drowsed somewhere between sleep and waking, seeing the sparrows' wild fluttering swoop once more and the trembling drops of rain. ". . . killed herself," he murmured, and entered. Then he was saying, in the rapt and stricken voice, "Ah, she was too young. God! Too fine. How——

"Talk to me." In an agony, it seemed, of desperation, to communicate his distress, he hurried to the kitchen and told Ella Swan. "Lawd have mercy!" Soon then Ella went home, amid lamentations and wails, piled high with bags and boxes, kitchen debris, garbage for her pigs. She turned at the door, a black wraith with yellowed, aqueous eyes. "Lawd God, Miss Helen, caint I help . . ." but Milton teetered

27

past her, Ella was gone, and ne slumped back down in the chair. The bottle of whisky was empty. He couldn't find another, so, rummaging about in cabinets and drawers, mumbling to himself like a chronic and fretful old man in search of his pills, he finally came across an old bottle of sweet vermouth, from which he began to drink steadily, intent. For a long while he was silent, and then he said softly: "Humbly, Helen, with all the humid—" she watched him patiently as he tried to form the words, his tongue clutched to the roof of his mouth like a leech—"wiz all humility I ask you to take me back. We got each other now, that's all. I been an awful stink—" he paused, tried to smile—"I been an awful damn fool." His tone became suddenly beguiling, deprecatory. He waved his arm into space, toward God, perhaps, or an invisible witness, or nothing. "She doesn't mean anything to me. Honest. She doesn't mean anything. You think Dolly's been anything but a friend to me, a real good friend?" He leaned forward confidingly. "Lissen, honey, she and I've been real good friends, thass all. I know it's hard f' you to believe it. But thass all. Real good friends." For a moment he seemed to have forgotten Peyton; his face was absorbed and reminiscent, as if amid all the tangle of his desolation he were contemplating some brighter, happier place, more placid and reassuring. " 'Member, Helen? 'Member how we used to drive up to Connellsville in the summer? Marion and Eddie's? 'Member the time when Peyton almost got stung by the bees? 'Member the way she hollered, 'The bees, Daddy, the bees, the bees!' " He was laughing in thick little chuckles and, ceasing, his voice died in a faint wistful sigh, like wind through a shutter. "*Aaah*-hah . . . the way she came running down the hill hollering 'The bees, Daddy, the bees!' " And as he spoke she had a sudden glimpse, once more, of her brother's home in the Pennsylvania mountains where they had visited in the twenties and the thirties, too: safe and serene in the easy mountain sunshine and the easier money of the Mellons and the Fricks—the good life, the happy life, a hundred years ago. There were huge oaks all around, the house was spacious and wealthy; it stood high on a hill, and from the valley below, made faint by intervening oak trees, the sound of traffic ascended—the only reminder of a noisy other world.

" 'The bees!' she hollered. I can see her now . . . running . . . 'The bees, Daddy, the bees!' "

Can't you hear her, Helen?

Peacefully she drowsed, neither asleep nor awake. Sleep was like a light that trembled and died, swelled, sank back like waves on a shore,

28

fathomless upon lost drowned shoals of memory: she saw trees, sea-deep, cold light, a mountain pool. *The bees, Daddy, the bees,* and she looked up from the pool where tropical goldfish swam restlessly beneath green interlaced mountain ferns, looked up startled and then amused at Peyton who, fleeing out of the distant woods, fluttered mothlike for an instant on the sunlit hill, then floated down the bright mossy slope with abandoned, shrill cries of fear and delight—"The bees, Daddy, the bees!" *Why, the dear,* she thought, *she wandered up there all by herself,* and warm, shivery, she arose, her arms outstretched—*why, my dearest baby*—but Milton was running from his chair, intercepting her, tossing Peyton high in the air as the small prim skirt blossomed like a gaudy flower against the sky. And so, nuzzling his face against her neck, he bore her toward the porch, both of them giggling, both of them buzzing like bees.

Helen sat down again. The coffee on her breakfast tray was suddenly without taste, and for a moment she felt a helpless frustration. Milton was buzzing and Peyton was buzzing and her brother and her sister-in-law and the morose Polish cook converged all at once upon the veranda with mild fond murmurings of admiration and approval.

"Did you get bit?" Marion said.

"Come here to me, beautiful," Edward said, squatting down, and Peyton started to rush toward her uncle, but Helen heard herself speaking, without anger, calmly. "Come here, Peyton, let me brush you off. You shouldn't go up there by yourself. I've told you."

Reluctantly Peyton turned, sulking, toward her. "But, Mama."

"Come here, now."

"Go to Mama and let her fix your hair," Milton said. He was wearing white flannels, looking very handsome. "Go to Mama. Then you and Uncle Eddie and I will go see about the bees."

Peyton stood stiffly against her as Helen brushed and combed and groomed.

"It won't hurt her to go up there, dear," Milton said. "There's a fence, you know."

"I know," she said, lightly and without conviction. She felt vaguely foolish, and a hot embarrassed flush rose to her cheeks. Curiously she had the sense that they were all watching her, and with a small forced laugh she said, "Mama's darling got awfully dirty, didn't she?"

Peyton struggled and squirmed, reaching for Milton. "Daddy, let's go see the bees. Now, Daddy. Let's go see the bees." She held her tightly for a moment—"Keep still," she whispered—but she relaxed her grip and Peyton tugged away as Edward said: "There! I'd love to go for a walk with such a pretty girl."

Helen turned back toward the table and, with a quick shrug, pulled her coat up about her shoulders. She felt chilled and abruptly, terribly empty. The voices faded up the hill behind her. The Polish woman hovered near with a broom, between hoarse Polish wheezes muttering, "That child is spoiled already, Missus Helen. You and him spoil her something awful. You should take care."

"Yes."

"She grow up to be a lot of trouble. Me, I got five what got their bottoms spanked most every day."

"Yes."

"I got no trouble with them, neither."

"No."

"She's a nice little girl, though. Pretty. You got a pretty daughter, Missus Helen. Me, I love children."

It's not I, not I who spoil her—but the feeling she had, disappointment, bitterness, whatever it was, had passed away. She drank the rest of her coffee. Suddenly she wished she were back in Virginia, but that feeling, too, disappeared. How silly, she thought, how silly to imagine that—— How silly. Oh, how silly and absurd. Why, last night she crawled over against me on the bed—"Mama," she said, "do you love me?" And I said and she said . . . oh, how silly, selfish.

Maudie. But of course.

She got up quickly, spilling cream; walked past her sister-in-law picking tulips in the garden; hurried through the house with an anticipation that she did not and could not deny but, rather, exulted in, rushing up the muffled, carpeted stairs in a wishful greedy suspense like a child at Christmas and then, halting, tiptoed onto the shadowed sunporch where Maudie sat alone, her braced leg outstretched on a stool. Helen crushed the child into her arms.

"There, there, Maudie," Helen whispered, "Mama's here. There, Maudie-poo." *My first, my dearest.* She sat down with the child and soon contentment began to steal over her like a warm and loving flame. She felt peaceful and young, very strong, as if she could go on being a mother forever. She was twenty-four.

She was nearly asleep. Faintly she sensed cold streams of sweat on her cheek, once more the locust's alien chatter, threatening rain, the voice saying, " 'Member, Helen, 'member when we lived in Wilson Court? The apartment? 'Member the whistle, the way it used to

30

wake us up? 'Member, Helen, 'member when Peyton and Maudie came there was so little room? Remember how hot it was . . . Remember?" He drank again, draining the glass. "And remember . . ."

Remember. Oh, remember. How remember moments of forgotten time? Where is the way now (she wondered) through that dark upspreading wood? Leaf, locust, sunlight in the hollow, all those she had known, all had fled like years. Now silence sounds where no light falls, and she has lost the way. Rich. Poor. They were poor then, before her mother died, before the inheritance came. They loved each other. Not so much because they were poor, but because they were both still young and hadn't had to grow up to things. The apartment was backed up against the shipyard wall; a chill blue fog on winter mornings, rising from the river, cast an elegant mist over the streetlights outside; within, warm in bed, hearing people stirring in the halls around them, they felt propertied and secure; life like this, for all they cared, could go on forever. They slept late then. In the summer Maudie cried. (What's wrong with the kid? he'd say. She shouldn't holler like that.) What's wrong? What's wrong? The shipyard whistle blew, a weird wail, waking them up. Kick the sheets off. On summer nights his legs were long and white, faintly perspiring. Oh, my sweet, he'd say. *Oh, love* . . .

Now, gently drowsing, she remembers the whistle blowing. It surrounds space, time, sleepy summer evenings many years ago: a remote sad wail involving sleep and memory and somehow love. They'd fight on summer nights because it was hot and Maudie cried and the icebox made a dripping noise, and because the whistle blew. But they loved each other, and the whistle—now it's a part of sleep and darkness, things that happened long ago: a wild, lost wail, like the voice of love, passing through the darkened room and softly wailing, passing out of the sphere of sound itself and hearing.

"Oh, they were the days. And remember how Peyton . . . Oh——" halting, his face startled and distressed, as if he had had his hand in fire and only then had felt the pain. His lips trembled. He's going to cry, she said to herself: He's going to cry.

"Peyton."

He's feeling it now. Ah, that sorrow hurries like the wind.

He thrust his head forward into his hands again. "My little girl."

Yes, perhaps now it will be upturned, the chalice he has borne of whatever immeasurable self-love, not mean, yet not quite so strong as sin . . .

"My little girl."

Upturned in this moment of his affliction and dishonor to find there not that pride he would clasp to his heart like a lover, but only grief. Only grief.

He got up from his chair, weaving toward her with outstretched arms. He could hardly walk. The patch of silver hair lay bristling and disheveled. "Honey," he said, "oh, honey. Let's be good to each other. Just now. Let's be good to each other. Let me stay here tonight."

She arose silently and turned toward the stairs. "Honey, let me stay. At least just let me stay."

She didn't answer as she left the room and began to climb the stairs.

"Would you call Mr. Casper for me?" he said. "I can't. Will you call him for me? I just wouldn't know what to say." There was a moment's silence. "Honey, let me stay. Even if it's your house.

"Yes," he muttered then, "even if it's yours."

For an instant, as if conjured out of time and remembrance by the sound of music, those brief, petulant words made her conscious of a desolation she had never in her life felt before. It was as if through those words alone she had discovered the nature of their life together, and she felt closer to him for that moment than she had in years. Her eyes filled with tears and she blurted out, "Yes, stay, go on and stay if you want to!" Rushing up the stairs and standing bewildered above, shouting hoarsely back, "*Stay* if you want to!" and running to her room, weeping helpless, unfamiliar tears as the voice below cried, "Helen, honey! Helen! Helen!"

She stirred; the holly leaves scraped gently outside the window.
Oh, take me now.
She slept.

A breeze had sprung up from the bay. Huge iron-red clouds of dust blew across the station, swept upward from time to time on sudden gusts of air. Here, high above, the clouds shifted, spread against the sky in a translucent haze the color of rust. Through this haze the sun shone feebly and enveloped everything below—station, people, and all—in an immense coppery light, dim and horizonless as a Turner landscape, where even moving objects seemed to remain suspended, like flies in amber. The interior of the limousine in which Loftis sat now was fashioned in livid bluish fabric resembling the color of a bruise. In front of him was a folded-down jump seat, also draped in this cheerless hue, upon which he had thrown one leg, tapping his foot in time to music from a restaurant across the street. A guitar strummed. A plaintive juke-box voice, gentle and long-suffering, sang distantly:

> You know that you are free to go dear
> Don't worry if I start to cry . . .

And Loftis, intent above all to forget his terrible pain, tried to hear the words, humming along with them in a thin falsetto tenor. Past the window, which he had closed against the dust, a woman's crazy hat drifted, trailing pink cloth flowers on a veil; the woman herself, then, rear-view—big, bovine, in a motley of cheap and tawdry clothes, plump sunburned arms warding off the dust like snow or sleet, and the woman's countrified voice receding faintly: "My, my, ain't this a shame." In her wake Barclay followed, carrying a bucket of water. Watching him, Loftis felt a tug of nausea at his stomach. His head ached dully from the whisky of the night before. He leaped out of the door and walked toward the hearse, following Barclay, panting a little as he strode through the dust. "Hey! Oh, son! Son!" By the front of the hearse the boy turned and paused, wondering.

"Oh, son!"

"Yes, sir?" Barclay said. He was a pale slim boy of about nineteen. He had pimples and on his upper lip a fringe of timid pubescent hair, and he stood gaping in wonderment as Loftis bore down upon him, breathing heavily.

"Ah, well. Is it——" Loftis hesitated.

The boy said nothing. Although it was not his fault, he was afraid he would be held to blame for the broken radiator pipe. All morning he had worried: about whether he would please or not; about the fit of his brand-new black suit. He was conscientious and incorruptible and right-minded, a young man born to worry. Already the complexities of life, and of becoming a mortician, were oppressive and somehow unjust; he worried about these, too. The morning had given him no end of trouble. He felt that surely Mr. Casper was going to fire him and because he had worried about this he had scarcely let himself notice Loftis, even though he knew now that the man standing before him was the nearest kin to the remains he had driven all this way to fetch.

"Yes, sir?" he repeated hesitantly.

There was a faint grin on Loftis' face. "Uh . . . having trouble?"

The boy smiled back uneasily. "Yeah . . . Yes, sir. It's fixed now, though." He turned toward the engine and opened the hood. "The pipe here . . ." Poor guy, he thought: I reckon he is grief-stricken.

Loftis leaned over his shoulder. "You know these Packard motors are funny," Barclay heard him say. "They're funny. I had a Packard once back in thirty-six. Now I like Packards—I've got an Olds now—I like Packards O.K. But I had the damndest time with my feed line. I reckon I took that car down to Pritchard's five times before I got it straightened out."

"Yes, sir," Barclay said. He was pouring water into the radiator, the can held high, his elbow almost in Loftis' face.

"An Olds I like because of hydramatic drive. Here, let me help you there. . . ." He took the can and edged in front of Barclay. "Taller than you," he said with a little chuckle. The water began to slop over the engine and Barclay thought: Hell, I got to go get some more.

"Some people don't like hydramatic drive. I do. Pickup's slower and all, that's true, but if you drive around town as much as I do it's a pretty good thing." He put the can down. "My daughter was always after me about getting a convertible; a Packard convertible was what she always wanted. For herself, I mean. You know how kids are about cars." He looked at Barclay. "How old are you, around twenty? My daughter was a few years older than you she was——" He glanced at his hands. "You got something I can wipe my hands on?"

Barclay handed him a rag, thinking: the poor guy. He watched Loftis' hands tremble with a sort of palsied agitation, as he rubbed furiously at them.

The poor guy, Barclay thought, wondering: What would Mr. Casper say to make him feel better?

Then Loftis paused, looked around tentatively, aimlessly, as if he considered walking off toward town. His expression was neither of grief nor of fear. It was an expression, Barclay thought with sudden bewilderment, of absolutely nothing at all. He merely stood there, the rag clutched tightly in his hand, his face beaded with sweat but as blandly composed as a deacon's. I should say, the boy was thinking: I reckon I should say—— But Loftis' skin was suddenly the color of chalk, an incredible shade of white that Barclay didn't think possible even in a corpse, let alone alive: the face still composed and expressionless, but as drained of color as if color had never existed there, and Barclay watched in a sort of bewitchment as the dry, bloodless lips parted and said: "I'm sick."

34

Loftis said nothing else. Conscious only of a vague commotion around him—people walking through the dust, astonished voices like those of children caught in a sudden rainshower—he stood with one hand lightly, almost casually, resting on the fender, the other hand still clutching the rag. Then leisurely, in the methodical fashion of a sleepwalker, he let the rag drop from his hand and walked away through the dust. As he started off across the street his first thought was: I mustn't get sick here. I must get to a place where I can vomit—fighting back the nausea which surged up from his belly in hot demanding waves and then, in the near-deserted restaurant, walking past the juke box now mute and gaudy with shifting kaleidoscopic light, red and blue and green, and into the filthy toilet in the rear where in spasms, bending over an unflushed bowl, he was sick.

Afterward he went out and sat on a stool at the edge of the counter where he could watch the limousine—still shaken but feeling better as the nausea subsided, thinking: I've got to get hold of myself. I've got to be a man. A taxi driver who had been eating at the other end of the counter got up and paid and went out, saying, "See you, Hazel." Dully, Loftis watched him through the flyspecked window: strolling past, sucking on a toothpick with the poky, shiftless look of taxi drivers south of the Potomac—casual trifling ease. Then he disappeared beyond the window frame. Loftis, looking absently around him, found the place deserted except for Hazel.

"Hiya, what'll it be?" the woman said. "Ain't the dust awful?"

"Coffee," he said.

"Say, you look real sick," she said. "You must of hung one on last night." She went back to the coffee urn. There was a familiar sour odor about the place, neither clean nor particularly unclean: grease, stagnant dishwater, flabby, uneatable bakeshop pastries many days old. He gagged and thought he would be sick, and would have been had he not just finished being sick. He started to leave, rose halfway up from the stool, but the woman returned with the coffee, saying: "I seen you run back to the gentleman's room just now. I figured you was probably sick." He began to drink the coffee, saying nothing.

"Say, you got the shakes. What you need is a BC." He made no reply, thinking: If I can last out this day I might be all right. It'll get well before you're married, time cures all, must . . .

"I told Haywood—he's the driver just left—I told him you looked kind of green. I don't drink myself although I've always said what's good for the gander's good for the goose, to turn around an old parable . . ."

And Helen. I will bring her back to me today, cure her, make her well, tell her that our love never went away at all.

". . . deerlord knows a woman's heavy enough laden to want to hang one on once in a while. In fact . . ."

He was thinking: Quiet, just hush, quiet—knowing that at another time he would himself have broached any subject of possible interest: the weather, prices, even the God of the Baptists—anything to make conversation. He was a lawyer, he sensed a need for the common touch, and above all he wanted to feel accepted by a class of people with whom he naturally felt ill-at-ease. In his dealings, no matter how casual, with people whose station in life was palpably lower than his own, he felt embarrassed and guiltily mistrustful. Laundry people, gardeners, Negro handymen appearing at his back door with suppliant grins and appeals for cast-off clothes—all these caused him mild confusion. But long ago, through conscious effort which finally had become a habit, he had found he could disburden himself of any uneasiness by merely talking. And so he had talked, being indeed always the first to talk, even invoking subjects of the wildest absurdity—not only because he wanted to be liked by everyone, which was true, but because he liked to talk, because he liked the round meaningful shapes of words, and because he was afraid of being alone.

But now the woman appalled him, filled him with desperation, and he had a moment's fright because he didn't seem to understand a word she said. She seemed to be one with the anxiety and the dust and the nausea: a symbol, horribly purposeful, of all that can plague a man when he most needs peace and repose. She was a tall, raw-boned, sallow blonde of about forty with bulging eyes and pushed-in masculine features. She leaned slackly against a glassed-in case full of razor blades and stale cigars, gazing vacantly out of the window while she talked steadily, stridently and without enthusiasm, as if it made little difference that no one ever agreed with or listened to her—either Loftis now or that echoing, unlistening choir of taxi drivers and trainmen who, drifting in each noonday like flies, gave back to her across the counter what abstracted grunts they could afford between swallows of beer and the slow, indolent buzz of their conversation.

"No," she was saying, "I got nothing against drinking personally and as I say I can't see why a woman shouldn't drink, too, and it's a known truth that doctors often prescribe intoxicants for certain nervous disorders, ah, my sister-in-law in Newark had a chronic condition of the uterus and had to have it taken out and was prescribed by her doctor to take a shot of whisky each night before retiring . . ."

Peyton, Peyton, he was thinking; successful as he had been for many hours in forgetting all except the loss of her, she came back now to him swiftly, the thought of her exploding against his consciousness like a fist. A fly lit on the counter in front of him; numbly, he watched the black bearded proboscis probe against some sticky film and withdraw, iridescent wings fanning upward, downward, coquettishly. Somewhere an electric fan droned without end, in a still and constant minor key.

". . . that's the sister of my *helpmate*, if I might use the expression——" She paused and Loftis, languid eyes upon her, saw her lips compress abruptly in a look of derision and scorn. "You haven't seen him, I guess, since I rarely if ever seen you in here before . . . the *ninny*," she sneered, "well, pore thing, burdened as she was . . ."

Peyton—he saw her now: shape, form, substance; thinking of her in this way brought sudden fire to his chest. Lost now? Gone? Oh, that this moment should have never come, but would melt away like mist. My God, for a drink. Moving his arm upward, he became aware of a faint noise, as of paper crackling, in his breast pocket.

"Men," the woman said. "Men!" she was saying. Blind, headlong, she talked on and on exhaustlessly above the droning fan, above the sound of water slowly dripping. The fly pivoted, buzzed away.

Ah, yes, the letter—he had forgotten. Before leaving the house an hour ago he had put it away without thought, fearfully, and now fearfully, with trembling fingers, he withdrew it from his pocket, examining the envelope: a green stamp upon which a three-masted schooner rested at anchor, commemorating something, obscured by the postmark's sinuous inky lines. For an instant he laid the envelope on the counter, thinking: I just can't. But then he opened it, saw six pages of writing, the familiar feminine script. . . . Something wrung his heart like hands as, tremulous, irresolute, he began to read——

Dearest Bunny, today I was 22 and I woke up this morning in a thunderstorm feeling so old—really sick, I guess—and then the money order came with your lovely nite letter (those telegraph people must think you're my sweetheart) and I guess I feel better now. I went out and bought two quarts of milk and a Mozart concerto and I guess I feel better now. And I bought a lovely big alarm clock, too.

Bunny, you don't know how much I miss you, how much that long lovely telegram meant to me. You get stewed to the gills and you try to be modern but you're absolutely hopelessly conventional. Even so I love you and miss you terribly. I've really been so lonely

37

since Harry left (has the news *really* gotten around town? What kind of poison's being spread by the local you-knows? What has *she* said?) Dear Bunny, I suspect you're the only one who understands and doesn't too much care—from the gossip point of view anyway. Anyway, I *am* lonely, something I hate to admit but I guess it's true. After you've lived with someone for a time it leaves a huge gap in your life when they're gone—even if they're impossible (so you think) or downright horrible (maybe you just think that too). Just feeling that sort of vacuum and silence around you when you're cleaning the apartment or going to bed—that's what's so bad—even though if the person came back you'd slam the door in his face (not really).

So Bunny I just lay there last night and thought about you. New York is so beastly hot in the summer. I felt absolutely miserable. There's a bar downstairs (I remember you haven't seen this apt. since I moved up from the village) full of the loudest Italians imaginable. The juke box goes all the time full blast and of course it's worse in the summer with all the windows open. Then with a pillow over my head I almost drifted off to sleep when the Cecchinos (he's a dark and mustachioed (sp?) Latin type, a rather ominous young man) came in drunk—their apt. is across the hall—she shrieking at the top of her lungs and banging up against my door. So I just stayed awake until the bar closed listening to the busses go by and thinking thoughts. They weren't very pleasant thoughts—in fact they were very dreary and morbid and depressing. They've just started lately it seems, I've had these moments before, but never for so long—and they're absolutely terrible. The trouble is that they don't—these thoughts—seem to have any distinctness or real point of reference. It's more like some sort of black, terrible mistiness like the beginning of a disease, the way you know you feel when you're catching the flu. I try to fight against this feeling all the time but in it seeps, and I can't do anything about it at all. Thinking of you helps some, thinking of home—but I don't know, nothing seems to really help for long. I feel adrift, as if I were drowning out in dark space somewhere without anything to pull me back to earth again. You'd think that feeling would be nice—drowning like that—but it isn't. It's terrible. Then when I see the birds it seems [*something crossed out*]

Oh, Daddy, I don't know what's wrong. I've tried to grow up—to be a good little girl, as you would say, but everywhere I turn I seem to walk deeper and deeper into some terrible despair. What's wrong, Daddy? What's wrong? Why is happiness such a precious thing? What have we done with our lives so that everywhere we turn—no matter how hard we try not to—we cause other people sorrow?

I've never talked to you like this, dearest. I don't know why. I just want you to know these things. Please don't be embarrassed.

It's true. We've all been so unkind. I've been so unkind to people. It's [*something crossed out here*.] wings it

(Later) I hate this city, Bunny. Everything is so false and brutal and ugly. But maybe that's just *me* because I loved it so at first. The excitement, the students at the school—meeting Harry. He came back the other day to get some of his things. Everything was so terribly strained when he came in—I was in an absolute panic. I wondered—how could I have ever loved him? And yet I did love him once, I *did* very much. Wasn't it maybe I who had been unkind, who broke us up after all? Yet I couldn't admit it to myself at all—I just couldn't. It was a hot day and I suppose we both felt badly so finally we exchanged words. I called him something horrible and banged out of the apt. When I came back later that evening he was gone and I could have died. Do I still love him, Daddy? Do I still love him? I don't know. All I know is that something terrible is happening to me. Since I left the job I've been doing hardly anything, waking up late with the horrible hot noon sun in my face. I sit around and read and now and then I go for a walk. That's about all. Isn't it terrible, my telling you all these things? But I want you to know anyway.

Sometimes I see Laura—you remember her. We all went to the Vanguard that night. She's very tiresome, but I envy her somehow. Maybe that's the key to happiness—being sort of dumb, not wanting to know any of the answers.

I think of Maudie. Why did she have to die? Why do we have to die?

Oh, I miss you so, Daddy! I wish I could see you, talk to you and have you say nice things to me. I wish I could come home. I wish it were possible. Oh, Daddy, I wish I could come home! The birds are haunting me beyond all belief. Such wingless——

There was more but he read no further; it all became so crazy and confused. He placed the letter down gently, and gazed upward where a monstrous day-flying moth, crazed by light, whirled wildly around a dangling bulb.

"What's the matter, mister?" Hazel said. Loftis didn't answer her. "What's the matter, mister?" Hazel repeated. "Isn't there something I can do?"

He raised his eyes. "My daughter," he said, with a look of hopeless appeal.

"Why, you pore man," said Hazel.

Nothing now, he knew, could be changed at all. He put his head down on the counter and shut his eyes. Helen, come back to me.

"Why, you pore man," said Hazel.

Two

DOLLY BONNER descended the steps from the station dock, sidling down cautiously as if she thought high heels and tight jersey skirt might catapult her sprawling if she weren't careful, and then hurried up to Barclay, who was still tinkering with the engine.

"Have you seen Mr. Loftis?" she said. "Where is he?"

The boy looked up suddenly and raised a startled arm toward the restaurant. Dolly had given him a terrible surprise. "Over there. Over there, ma'am," he said. He closed the hood with a bang, for he had just seen Mr. Casper, standing by the baggage car with the remains, motioning him to bring the hearse over. The dust had lifted, although little eddies and swirls still lingered on the air; through one of these tiny clouds Dolly approached the restaurant, patting dust from her skirt. She heard the swollen notes of a mournful guitar; she peered in through the dusty window, shielding light from her eyes. Within, Loftis sat propped up over a cup of coffee, and the woman behind the counter opened and closed her mouth rapidly, soundlessly. Poor dear Milton. A rainbow of juke-box color enveloped the restaurant, a lovely spectrum endlessly shifting; a man with a deep, sad voice sang: "Take me back and try me one more time." Such a hillbilly song, yet it filled her with gentle, genuine sorrow. Poor dear Milton.

She wiped dust from her face with a handkerchief, powdered her nose, and looked briefly at herself in the windowpane. She was a dark and pretty woman and would perhaps have been beautiful except for a slightly receding chin which lent to her features an expression not so much of weakness as fretfulness, as if at any moment her jaw and lips might tremble in sorrow, like a little girl's. She had been much publicized for her social activities—Red Cross, the Women's Club, and the like—and her picture, taken shortly after her wedding, had been printed in the local papers sometimes as often as twice a month for over a period of twenty years until finally even she sensed the impropriety of the cloche hat and bangs which had given rise to idle and secret laughter around town. So she had had the picture replaced, regretfully, with another, newer one in which there no longer blossomed the youthful smile, but which instead recorded with precision the small puffy folds beneath her eyes and her neck, too, flaccid and slightly wrinkled. Now she gave her nose one last loving pat and entered the restaurant.

She laid her hand softly on Loftis' arm. "Dear, we'd better go now. Everything is ready and . . ."

"When the great Day of Judgment cometh," Hazel was saying in a level voice, "you and her will enter unto the golden streets together. Don't you worry, mister. That's what the good book says. John eighteen thirty-six, 'My kingdom is not of this world . . .'"

Loftis groaned, looking up at Dolly with frightened eyes. "You say everything's ready?"

"Yes, dear. Come on, now."

"This vale of tears," Hazel continued, "is like unto the veriest smoke . . ."

"How much do I owe you?" Loftis asked.

"That'll be five cents."

Loftis laid a nickel on the counter.

"My heart goes out to you, mister. It truly does."

"Thank you," Loftis murmured. Automatically he opened the door for Dolly. They stepped out together into the street, where the dust had cleared away entirely, and the sun now shone brightly. The jukebox voice, trailing them with remote sadness, sang: "Take me back and try me one more time." Far off, coal plunged seaward from the elevators, shaking the earth. Try me one more time.

Now, as they prepared to get into the limousine, Ella Swan labored down the steps from the dock and silently climbed into the back seat; the hearse came up, too, with sleek, privileged gravity and a dulcet honking noise, while pedestrians in its path scurried like beetles to the sidewalk. Dolly entered the limousine, then Loftis; the train, which was about to go back to Richmond, made a doleful blast on its whistle and Mr. Casper got out of the hearse and paused benignly at the limousine door, like a bishop about to consecrate something.

"All righty," he said, peering into the back seat. "Is everybody ready?" He smiled wanly. "Ah, I see. All right, we'll go now."

So they were off at last—Dolly and Loftis next to each other, Ella Swan on the jump seat sitting stiffly in black silk and rococo lace, her head bowed now in some old posture of contemplation or sorrow, saying nothing, and Mr. Casper in the front seat, starting the motor: Loftis could see his freckled brow and red hair in the little mirror. Yet they had gone no more than a hundred yards, trailing the hearse, when the hearse itself swerved toward the curb, stopped, and Barclay issued forth with a harried look, beckoning to Mr. Casper.

"Oh dear," said Dolly, "oh dear."

"What's wrong——" Loftis began, bending forward, but Mr. Casper had stopped the limousine, got out and walked to the hearse where, with Barclay, he began to hold parley over the engine.

"Oh, my God," Loftis said, to no one in particular. "Isn't it enough that I've got all this, without something else going haywire?" He thrust his head in his hand. "Jesus. It's more than I can bear."

Dolly laid her hand on his arm. "You've got to be brave, Milton," she said.

He raised his head without answering and gazed at the hearse. He turned away with a sudden shock, for inside, in that tasseled, becurtained gloom, he had caught a glimpse of the coffin, receptacle of all his love, which with panic he realized must today disappear forever. It was really, he thought, more than he could bear. He turned completely away from the hearse and craned his neck so that he could see the bay. Dolly murmured something softly consoling, harmless and incoherent; he ignored this, thinking: Jesus, she's getting on my nerves. Up ahead the motor in the hearse gave a sinister belch, throbbed feebly, and perished in an asthmatic gasp; for a moment blue smoke billowed through the limousine, then faded on the air. Jesus, he thought: This is more than I can stand. By the seawall, where he turned his gaze, overlooking the bay, there was a little patch of grass and a sycamore tree: beneath the tree a colored boy and his girl were tussling. She made a grab for him, laughing; her mouth was big, open; round with wild delight: "Git on!" the boy cried, and they tumbled together beneath a scrawny little bush, then lay still. Summertime. Light lay serenely over the bay. A herd of oyster boats was anchored far out; like cows they all faced in one direction: like cows, too, almost imperceptibly, they turned—with the changing of the wind. Above, around the vast circumference of the sky, a pale light was reflected, glowing in bright oblong patches against those clouds that hovered motionless on the horizon. It was a bright and sticky light, somehow menacing; it filled him obscurely with a feeling of storm and threat and coming destruction. Oh, God, he thought, shivering a little: What will I be doing tomorrow?

He must have sighed then, unconsciously, made a noise; perhaps he did, for once more he felt Dolly's soft gloved hand on his, the voice saying tenderly, "I'm with you, dear. I'm here. Don't worry, I'm with you."

He looked at her and tried to smile. "I don't feel very well," he said. He remembered the scene in the restaurant and his belly heaved. "This is the worst thing that ever happened to me."

"Dear," she said, "you'll just have to be brave." Her eyes glistened in sympathy, together with pure rapt adoration, the familiar expression which she wore, when near him, with mindless constancy.

"I was sick," he said.

"Oh dear," she exclaimed. "Oh, my darling."

"I vomited. Bile came up. I'd go to bed. Any other day."

"Oh, my poor darling." Again she rested her hand on his, and in a willful, irritable gesture he drew his hand away. In the past he would have devoured her sentiment, would have basked sunnily in this warm atmosphere of devotion. During the last few years he had relied upon her steadfast gaze of love and longing, perhaps unconsciously enough, as one among the assortment of props and crutches—along with all the whisky, and with Peyton—which supported him against the unthinkable notion that life was not rich and purposeful and full of rewards. That face, that gaze, that adoring glance, he had believed, were nearly reward enough. She was submissive and she worshiped him, and it was for those reasons that he had loved her. It had been that way from the beginning: he talked and she listened, while through this curious interplay of self-esteem and self-effacement there ran an undercurrent of emotion they were both obliged to call love.

Now, however, just as it had during the past few months, her presence had begun to worry him, depress him; each word she said somehow left him more and more unstrung. He wished he hadn't brought her with him. It had only been cowardice anyway, he reflected, that prompted him to go by for her this morning, when Helen had refused him. He had wanted company, that was all; he had needed so to talk to someone.

"What's wrong, dear?" she said. He glanced at her. She looked hurt, hurt because he had drawn his hand away.

"What's wrong?" he said. "Oh, God, now really . . ." He looked away.

"Yes," she said gently. "Yes, darling. Of course. I understand. I just wish I could say something to make you feel better." She groped in her handbag for a handkerchief and dabbed at her eyes. "There's nothing," she concluded, "that you can say at a time like this."

He didn't answer. It had begun to get fiercely hot in the limousine. Silently Ella Swan ran a hand over her forehead. A smell of salt and tar lingered on the air, rankly suggestive of sea, heat, stagnation. He crossed his legs, uncrossed them, and unaccountably sneezed: would they never fix that motor? There was a dim clanking sound; at the front of the hearse he could see Mr. Casper's rear, clad in shiny black, bent over the fender.

"Anything you try to say at a time like this," Dolly added, "sounds so inappropriate." She paused. "Somehow."

Please be quiet. Just hush.

A huge truck swung around the corner, roared past toward the station, heavily vibrating. On its side there were big red letters.

SCANNELL

Hogsheads of tobacco bobbed high above. The truck disappeared behind them, leaving an odor of tobacco, faintly acrid. Once more the hood of the hearse went down with a crash. Mr. Casper stood erect and wiped his hands. Barclay got in and started the engine; it made a fitful, hacking noise, like a dog coughing up a bone, then caught; an umbrella of blue smoke rose to the heavens and Barclay waved his arm valiantly out of the window. Mr. Casper returned with a distressed look and climbed back into the front seat. The hearse moved ahead.

"I'm terribly sorry," Mr. Casper said. "Terribly. On a day like this . . ." His voice sank into a murmur of vague, inaudible recriminations, and the limousine, too, began to move again. There were fields on either side of the road, full of marsh grass gently rustling in the sultry air; the first squat, unsightly buildings of the town loomed ahead. Gusts of air blew through the limousine, hot, laden with the odor of dead fish and rotting grass. From the shipyard, which lay not far away across the marsh, Loftis could hear the sound of metal falling, riveting hammers, the whistle of a train. They passed a little colored boy blowing on a tin horn; his eyeballs rolled back at the hearse, big black pupils wobbling in wonder. Loftis fidgeted, looked at his watch, crossed his legs again, thinking: Is not just remorse enough? Isn't there a way to set all this right? Isn't this grief enough? How long? What can I do? But haunting him still, his father's ghost, words said years ago: an old man in whom obscurity resembled solemnity often enough, and solemnity wisdom, but who nonetheless—through a stew of dogmatism and misinformation, through the scraggle of archaic Edwardian mustache in mild, uncomprehending protest at a world that long ago had passed him by—managed to say things which, if not precisely wise, were at least durable truisms, self-tested——

My son, never let passion be a guide. Nurture hope like a flower in the most barren ground of trouble. If love has fed the flame of your brightest imaginings then passion will perish in that flame and only love endure. . . . Son, listen . . .

Believe me, my boy, you have a good woman.

Loftis blinked, sneezed again. The old man faded, smiling with ghostly benevolence; the droop and tremor of unkempt, stained mustache withered away like smoke——

In his youth Loftis' attitude toward his father had been one of tolerance and of badly concealed impatience. The old man was fatuous and certainly, Loftis had concluded, something of a failure. Possibly as a result of this failure Loftis had never taken his advice seriously. Certainly, too, on the day of his marriage a quarter of a century before, Loftis knew he "had a good woman." And for the rest—those warnings which came back to him today with such a sense of doom fulfilled—those he had shrugged off quickly, although with a vague feeling of resentment, perhaps because he sensed they might come true. As for love . . . well, indeed, what about love? Passion had perished in that flame long ago, but at the time he had forgotten his father's reminder, and had thought that love had vanished, too. It wasn't true. With a surge of tender warmth he felt that love had never gone away at all.

Suddenly a horrid pain came to his chest, like unexpected fire. Peyton. *She is dead.* That's what Harry had told him. He thought of her crazy, wild letter.

Death by falling. Birds. Birds?

And now he couldn't remember when this passion had flown, leaving him so foolish and bewildered and astray: can any man?

On a spring morning years before, when the dew had nearly melted on the grass and Loftis, deep in the lawn chair and full of coffee, wavered mildly between the Port Warwick *Sunday Tribune* and contemplation of the early sunlight encroaching upon his private beach, he was aroused by a tumble of feet on the grass behind him, a small voice announcing passionately: "Daddy, Daddy, I'm beautiful!" So he had turned and with the attentive respect given young daughters by their fathers he had watched Peyton—standing in the grass beside him, age nine—while she gazed into a little mirror and said again, "I'm beautiful, Daddy!"

For a moment all this crushed his heart. She *was* beautiful. Perhaps it was the first cigarette of the morning, or the coffee, but he felt quite giddy. Anyway, he would always remember that moment on the lawn: picking Peyton up with a sudden, almost savage upwelling of love, pressing her against him as he murmured in a voice slightly choked, "*Yes*, my baby's beautiful," with wonder and vague embarrassment paying homage to this beautiful part of him, in which life would continue limitlessly.

". . . beautiful," he was saying; he held her awkwardly against his chest. Her long brown hair was in his face, blinding him. She giggled, pounded his back, and the mirror which she held fell silently to the grass.

"But you mustn't be so. vain," he said.

"No," she said.

"Come on, get up."

"No."

"No what?" he said.

"No, thank you, stupid."

"Is that nice? Come on, get up."

"O.K.," she said.

Now she was off his lap, spraddle-legged and barefoot on the grass, making faces at him.

"Don't," he said. "You'll freeze that way, you know. All your life you'll look like the wicked witch."

"I don't care," she said. "Let me see the funnies."

In his lap the papers lay hopelessly crumpled, printed with small dirty footmarks. He pretended not to notice, yawning, gazing up at the blue spring sky where dumpy clouds drifted past, melting at their

46

edges like smoke. The bay was very still, exuding a pleasant odor of salt. Past Peyton, with studied gravity, he gazed at the garden—his wife's—a turmoil of nameless color, roses, pansies, whatyoum'callits— he never knew. A mockingbird somewhere made a facetious chatter, crickets chirped in the flower beds, the scent of grass was hot, filling his nostrils with a coarse sweet odor—a spring day in Virginia. He yawned again, looking upward.

"Chances are it'll rain," he said abstractedly.

"Yes," said Peyton. "Chances are. Gimme the funnies."

"Don't say 'gimme'."

"Let me, then."

"That's better, baby," he said. "I'll give you the funnies on one condition. See that rosebush over there? Go and pick a rose and bring it to me. Careful, don't get stuck on the thorns."

Peyton ran off obediently and in a moment came back with a big red rose, trembling with dew. "Thank you, baby," he said. There was something mildly debonair, he thought pleasantly, in presenting your wife with a rose on a sunny morning.

"Let me have the funnies," Peyton said. She took the funnies without a word and sprawled out on the lawn beside him, reading Jiggs, plucking grass with her toes. In a lazy voice, as if in afterthought, she said, "Thank you very much."

He looked down at her. "Children," he murmured, "should respect their parents."

Peyton said nothing, with infinite languor turning the pages, while Loftis, legs outspread, leaned back and read the news—mayor admits, woman denies, something about the NRA; *Roosevelt*, he thought— well, he'd voted for him, but Christ knows what he'd end up doing. The blue eagle fluttering everywhere. A good man, most likely, a Democrat, but watch him. Paradox: youngish, well-to-do barrister Milton Stuart Loftis plans maybe legislative career, could be maybe junior senator (D-Va.), President (Nation Hails First Southern Chief Since Wilson). *Question*: Senator, what is your attitude toward the Common Man? *Answer*: Ah, since I'm a Democrat—— *Question*: Thank you. What is your attitude, Mr. President, toward the Common Negro? *Answer*: Ah, since I'm a Southerner—— *Question*: Thank you. Social Security? *Answer*: Ah, well . . . Thank you, thank you. (*My son, paradoxically enough . . . being a Southerner and a Virginian and of course a Democrat you will find yourself in the unique position of choosing between (a) those ideals implanted as right and proper in every man since Jesus Christ and no doubt before*

47

and especially in Virginians and (b) ideals inherent in you through a socio-economic culture over which you have no power to prevail; consequently I strongly urge you my son always to be a good Democrat but to be a good man too if you possibly can. . . .)

Paradox . . . but that was a long time ago and besides—well, the hell with it. He felt a curious desire for whisky—pleasant, way down deep. Now that was funny, he really shouldn't; he wasn't a morning drinker. . . . Just then, turning a bit, he saw Helen coming down across the broad upslanting sweep of lawn, leading Maudie by the hand. He hid the rose underneath the newspaper. They approached slowly together, mother and daughter, Helen guiding Maudie patiently, cautiously across the undulating, decorous space of sunlit grass until, at the flagstone steps slanting down a small embankment, Helen descended first; turning then, she reached up and with great care and tenderness held Maudie's arm as she limped down the steps, and so together again, twin red ribbons which they wore fluttering on a sudden ripple of breeze, they approached across the lawn, Maudie limping, looking from this distance very small and frail, and Helen gazing down with patient, tender eyes.

"Daddy," asked Peyton idly, "what does 'contraband' mean?"

"That means——" he began, but Helen and Maudie were in the little circle of lawn chairs and Helen, who had helped seat Maudie gently on the grass, sank down heavily beside him, saying, "Milton, there's a cigarette burn on the rug. Last night——"

"Which one?" he said.

"The Tabriz."

"Oh, God. Larry Ellis."

"No. Dolly Bonner. She's an impossible person to ask anywhere."

"Daddy," Peyton interrupted, "what does——"

"Hush, Peyton," Helen said, "we're——"

"Just a minute, dear," Loftis said. "Baby, you mustn't interrupt. Contraband means—well, it means something illegal—something that a policeman is empowered to confiscate . . ."

"Confis——" Peyton said, looking up at him.

"Now one thing at a time," he said softly. "Now contraband. What are you reading there anyway? All right, say that the U.S.A. has a law against foreigners bringing in perfume, or guns——"

"Or whisky," Helen said, finishing his sentence with a chilly laugh. She groped in the pocket of her blouse for a cigarette. "Whisky might be contraband."

He lighted her cigarette. "Whisky?"

"I see what you mean," Peyton said in a knowing tone, turning back to the funnies.

Helen stirred in her chair. "It's like when I ask your father," she said, "not to drink when the Appletons come and he goes out and buys another bottle. You might call that contraband."

A sudden flicker of resentment seized him at that—a moment's rush of blood to his face, ebbing even while out of the corner of his eye he watched her as she said, "You might call that contraband," smoke floating away from her mouth in little gusts, blue against the sunlight and the lawn, coiling away invisibly.

"Now——" he began angrily, but thought *Let it pass, let it pass* as Helen, sensing this irritation, gave his hand a light, nearly impalpable tap, murmuring, "All right, dear. Temper, temper." Now she was not even looking at him, he could tell, gazing instead with a smile at Maudie sitting on her pillow in the grass—frail, expressionless, staring up at the sky with sweet, insensible eyes.

The anger had gone. He watched Maudie, too, and a gentle feeling of compassion came over him, mingled vaguely with bitter distress. Right now—said the doctor, a kindly old man in Richmond, lisping hesitantly—she no doubt knew all she would ever know; too bad, one could never tell—the mystery of birth.

Great God in heaven, was it his fault! Well, whose? What?

There, there now, take it easy. No, no, certainly. The mystery of birth——

Tragic—it happened to any man, in the best of families. Be calm—that's what he had told himself to do. They had loved her, taken care of her, been good to her—that's what people said. "Oh," the older friends would say to him—sad, guileless women with gray faces and a sweet, elegiac air—"oh, Helen is a saint, she's so good to her. You're so lucky." As if, he would think bitterly, Maudie were a burden, even in her affliction, instead of a joy. Yet the child troubled him. He loved her, he longed for an affection that could never really blossom, but those eyes—those sometimes he could hardly bear. Until Peyton was born, bleak doubt assailed him. He looked at his wife's body with suspicion and his own with infuriate guilt. The mystery of birth . . . Poor dear gentle child. Now his heart went out to her yearningly. But there was no doubt that at times she caused him dreadful unhappiness.

Helen arose, knelt down and began to comb Maudie's hair; tenderly she cupped her hand beneath the child's chin, turning her face with great delicacy, like that of some fragile little china doll, all the while

49

making soft sounds, laughing gently, saying, "There, see!" or "Pretty!" Loftis got up and squatted beside them, extending the rose to Helen with a grin: "My love," he said, "is like a red, red rose," but Helen, preoccupied, turned her head and blinked at him, with a pale smile replying: "Oh." She put the rose on the ground. "Thanks." She turned back to Maudie. She had hardly noticed. His sunny, contented bubble burst and scattered. What the hell, he thought. He got up; passing Maudie, he bent down and stroked her hair.

She raised her eyes, grave, impassive, as brown and big as those balls that fall from sycamore trees. "Good morning, Papadaddy."

"Just Daddy, sweet."

"Papadaddy."

"O.K.," he said. He walked up the slope, panting a little, feeling a stitch in his side. The party last night: as usual he had drunk too much: Dolly Bonner . . . he banished it all from his mind. Sunlight lay brilliant around him. The grass, green and odorous, had been mowed just yesterday; it yielded springily beneath his feet. Small insects darted about, grasshoppers wildly fled his advance, and the house, toward which he turned his eyes, loomed above him freshly painted, substantial, invitingly open to the day. It was a big house, Virginia Colonial in style, an elegant house, although much too large for four people. They had had it built—thanks to Helen's mother, who had auspiciously died two years ago—at a cost of twenty thousand dollars. An immense surge of pride welled up in his breast as he drew near the house. Shingles on the roof glittered handsomely; a sprig of ivy had begun to climb one rainspout, coiling up from boxwood planted around the basement. Nodding there in the sunlight, this ivy seemed to lend a touch of permanence, possibly even of tradition, to the house. Loftis was filled with sudden elation: the novelty of ownership had not yet worn off.

He stood in the shadows of the awninged terrace, a bit dizzy from the climb: was that Helen calling behind him? He turned; the landscape, clockwise, swept before his eyes—trees, lawn, a gray streak of water, and Helen standing far below, calling upward.

"Church!"

Church? Oh, yes. Hell.

"No church," he shouted back. "Just take the girls to Sunday school! Take the car!"

"What——"

"No church——" he began again.

"What——" she seemed to say, but the words were blown back on a gust of wind. He flung his arm toward her, hopelessly, turning. In the living room he poured whisky from the decanter on the sideboard, half a tumbler full. Then he hurried to the kitchen where, bent silently over a table, Ella Swan was peeling potatoes. He struggled with an ice tray in the refrigerator, scraped his thumb, but finally extracted two cubes and dropped them into the whisky, tunefully clinking.

"Mmm-hh!" Ella said. A sigh of suspicion and reproach, of original sin apprehended and denounced, especially on Sundays. He had heard it before, he would hear it again. A score of them: old nigger cooks and nurses and laundrywomen from birth to death casting up eyes of blame and self-righteousness, in impotent reproach, across Saturday afternoon parlors, through the steam of Sunday stoves. He raised his glass happily, anticipating.

"Here's looking at you, Ella," he said. He took a large swallow, commencing to glow.

"Hmmph," Ella said. Downward toward the potatoes she bent her face—black and gnomish, a web of lines and wrinkles. "Ain't nobody lookin at me," she snuffled, "leas'wise not today. Know who's lookin at you, though. Good Lawd's lookin down, He say, 'I am de troof and de way and de life,' good Lawd sayin . . ."

"All right, Ella," he said. "That's fine. That's fine. No sermons. Leas'wise not today . . . for Christ's sake," he added deliberately, smiling.

"Dat's Beezeldebub talkin. See de cloven hooves and de monstern eyes. Should be ashamed of yo'self, praise Jesus sweet name."

Leaning against the refrigerator, he took another swallow; contentment enveloped him like a cloak. The kitchen, like all rooms, all scenes, began very slowly a sweet process of transfiguration: table, gleaming stove, Ella, white aseptic walls—all of these, as in some leisurely seraphic progression toward ultimate truth, began to take on the quality of perfection. Even the morning sunlight, flooding along the floor in bright pools and patches, seemed to be part of this wonderful house—his.

He walked to the little porch which adjoined the kitchen and stood there gazing out. On this side of the house there was a row of cedars which bordered his property, slanting downward toward the bay. Beneath them the earth was naked of grass, shadowed, cool-looking; as he had before, he felt a twinge of nostalgia. So much time had already passed: there were cedars like these at the school to which he had gone as a boy—St. Stephen's, faded brick buildings which overlooked marsh-

51

land. Beyond lay the river, flat and wide and blue, devoid of life on either shore for miles, except for the lonely school, so that sometimes standing there beneath the cedars, breathing the mingled odor of salt and evergreen, he would gaze out at the wintry river, at the endless miles of willow and cypress on the other shore, and imagine, as if in a trance, that this was not the Tidewater at all, but that these cedars and indeed all this wild and frigid sunlit space belonged to another country. Russia perhaps—the Arctic wastes he had read about in geography books, where the Lena and the Yenesei (he imagined) wound forever toward the dazzling sun of the Northern ocean, rimmed like this by cypress, willow and cedar, shores unpeopled, full of cold and silence. Once, too, it was to these cedars he went when in his last spring at school, in some fit of introspection rarely since repeated, he took biscuits from the kitchen and a book, poetry—Keats? Shelley?—and lay in the morning shade reading drowsily while countryside sounds rang out from every side, cows bawling, seabirds shrilling in the marsh, a boy's shout—until the bell rang lazily for morning service and he strolled off with the other boys to chapel, casting a reluctant glance behind to the place where he had lain, and at the river and the cedars, too—disturbed about something: loveliness vanished, or perhaps merely the sense that one bright instant of his youth would always, mysteriously, be bound up in the invisible and fugitive scent of cedar trees.

He smelled the cedars now; the odor filled him with a sense of time, things gone—things he didn't want to think about any more. So much time had passed.

Chapel. Church. Grimly he toyed with the idea of grace. If he didn't go to church, she would raise hell. No, she never raised hell, merely became quietly, bitterly unpleasant. Well, he just wouldn't go. Forget it. . . .

He turned. "Ella," he said archly, "would you care to join me in a drink?"

"Who?" She made a scandalized sound. "Not me. Not fo' a million dollahs. You gwan sin all you want. Ah don't keer. . . ." Somber denunciations followed him as he went into the dining room, to the sideboard, and poured another drink. Then he walked to the terrace where, startled, he met Helen and the two children coming up from below. Almost mechanically he thought to hide the drink but, thinking better of it, merely stood there in the doorway, glass in hand. "First today in my left hand," he said with awkward humor. Dammit, he thought, it was uncomfortable. . . .

Helen said nothing, returning his look with a quick accusing glance. Once on the terrace she shepherded the children to the door. "Peyton," she said briskly, "you take Maudie up and help her get dressed for Sunday school."

"Come on, Maudie," Peyton said gently. "Let's go upstairs. Come on, Maudie." They disappeared into the living room, Maudie's leg thumping—the sound receding dimly, ceasing, thumping again on the stairs above, ceasing once more. Helen turned.

"What's the big idea?" she said. He watched her face, taut with controlled anger. "What on earth's got into you?"

"Oh, listen, Helen——" He made a vague motion with his hand. Just like her, he thought. Get the children away—then get bitter, raise hell. Everything was going so nicely. . . . He took a swallow of whisky, a thin gesture of defiance. "Have a drink?" he said, and immediately regretted it. But now—— Oh, God, he thought. Her face softened; a shy look, quizzical, playful, almost tender, came to her eyes. She plucked at his sleeves, towing him to a couch. "Sit down, dear," she said.

"Look here," she began softly—sitting beside him in the shadows, she looked very pretty, pretty as she once had been ten years before, the cheeks pale, unblemished by age: a girl's face without sag or line or hollow, even beautiful once more, although maybe it was the whisky—"look here," she was saying, "you know you mustn't do this all the time. You know you'll ruin your health. Nothing moral or immoral about it, dear . . . just that you can't take the girls to Sunday school like that . . . you know we've got to go to church . . . we promised . . . you know that, dear. . . ." *You know, you know.* Now he wasn't listening. The same old thing. Jesus Christ, it was awful. Why did she put on the mother act? Why didn't she admit she despised him for his drinking, for everything? Instead of this cool, constant, silent bitterness and the desperate mother act, so obviously a fraud. Why didn't she for once make a scene, raise hell? Then he could explode heroically, get everything out of his system in one big blow. Oh, it was awful. Awful. Jesus H. Christ, it was awful.

But he wasn't listening. Just for a moment the elation returned, and as quickly collapsed within him. Past the edge of her cheek he gazed at the bay, resting in steamy doldrums. A few gulls circled lazily. Somewhere out of sight a motorboat coughed fitfully, died. In the winter, he thought, the bay would be gray and frozen, rimmed round its shore with snow, acres of frigid salt; warm inside the house, Peyton near him, they might gaze out and watch driftwood, gulls wheeling, a sky full of melancholy clouds the color of soot. He and Peyton . . . they would be together in the warm house—but that would be winter and he would be older, and not even on his way, most likely, to Senator . . . no, Judge.

He belched heavily. Helen swam toward him on a cloud of alcohol, filling him with sudden, intolerable discontent. "Look here, dear, you know you shouldn't . . . we promised so long ago . . ." Long ago.

He arose, looking down at her. "Now you look here yourself, my dear," he said, trying to keep anger back from his voice, "you might as well know I'm going to lead my life any good goddam way I please." She started for an instant, protest swelling in her throat. "Now wait a minute," he continued, "I don't mean to be nasty. I just want you to know a few things—among which is the fact that I enjoy taking Sundays at my leisure and the other is the fact that I enjoy drinking leisurely, too."

She sprang from the couch. "Selfish——"

"Hold on," he said, looking downward, unaccountably afraid of looking at her. "Wait a goddam minute. It's not a matter of selfishness at all. I don't want to corrupt anyone's morals. I'll go often enough so that the voting populace knows I'm not an atheist. I told you a long time ago about what religion or lack of it I've got. I'm tired of having my Sundays interfered with by a string of platitudes by Carey Carr—that . . ."

She said nothing, walking to the door, turning then with a murmur: "Voting populace. That's a laugh." She was quiet for a moment—a silence on the edge of tears. "Oh, Milton, Milton," she said in a despairing voice, and was gone.

He looked up warmly at the sky. He had told her.

Yet something interfered with this pleasure. A sense of ugly guilt crept over him. Now he shouldn't have said . . . Oh, Milton, Milton, she had said. There seemed a necessity for reparations, amends. But with a feeling of no more than weariness, he knew it was too late. The hell with it. He drank, hearing a voice. He peered around a corner of the awning; above, at a window, Peyton stood in her underwear, smiling down. "Hello, stupid."

"How's my beautiful baby?" he said, raising his glass.

Helen called, Peyton fled, the window fell with a crash.

That Sunday long ago had brought Loftis precariously close to an understanding of something: himself, perhaps. Ghosts of things done, things undone lingered on the lawn in that complacent afternoon

54

sunlight. Had he just turned soon enough he might have seen them and been properly frightened. But when he did turn it was too late, evening had come, and the moment for recognition was lost forever.

Now, "Would you be a saint," Dolly Bonner was saying delightfully across what seemed an acre of sunlit lawn, "and get me another drink, Milton honey?" Remotely a churchbell struck three. Shadows had begun to lengthen on the grass.

The way she said honey . . .

"Yes, yes, indeedy. I'd be proud, Dolly honey." He arose from the lawn chair uneasily—he was getting tight, too tight, and so would have to taper off with care; stepping over the legs of Dolly's husband, Sclater (pronounced "Slaughter," known as "Pookie"), for an instant using one of Pookie's knees as a sort of crutch—"Excuse me, Pookie," he said—he walked to Dolly's chair, smilingly took her glass with the faintest suggestion of a bow, and continued up the slope, feeling the glass a bit sticky, pleasurably warm from her hand. A few steps and he turned, contrite, looking at Pookie's and Helen's glasses: in his haste he had forgotten. But they were half-full; Pookie and Helen, talking, hadn't noticed him. He turned again, Dolly winked, smiled—gesture of some secret, puzzling, yet vaguely exciting *rapport*. The smile lingered on his vision even as he turned and the house above floated recklessly into focus.

A wild, random exhilaration had swept over him. Although perhaps now fogged by just one drink too many, his mind had been suspended for nearly five hours in a state of palmy beatitude. The scene of odious domesticity that morning had been changed, after Helen's departure and one more drink, into one of elemental significance, solitary enchantment. Secure in his misty Eden, he had wandered through the house: lace curtains billowed out like pale balloons, and he heard a hailstorm of gravel on the drive as Helen wheeled away; a horn honked, Peyton laughed in the distance, then silence.

Alone then, he had switched on the radio, a new and splendid one, an Atwater Kent he had bought six months before for three hundred dollars. There was a sudden belch of static; he leaped for the knob. A Sunday school choir commenced a falsetto chirping. Jesus loves me. Methodists, probably. He could almost see it: a row of maple chairs, young women with bad breath and half-moons of sweat beneath their armpits, a basement somewhere smelling of stale leaking water and moldy religion. A sad, shadowy place, where the timeless rattle of Proverbs and Commandments outlasts age and decay and even the dusty, pious slant, itself, of Sunday sunlight upon worn

55

hymnals and broken electrical fixtures and cobwebbed concrete walls. Methodists. They hated beauty. *Ah, God . . .* He yawned, took a drink, turned off the radio.

Bemused, looking at the floor, he saw on the rug a black scorched place where a cigarette had burned. Dolly Bonner. It could be re-woven perhaps. Dolly Bonner. Yes. Pale hands last night that went tap-tap-tap against a cigarette; ashes sprayed downward on the rug. He had brought her an ashtray, devilishly cajoling, obliging. "Dolly, shame on you for five minutes." "Oh, Milton—" her pale hand on his arm—"Helen. The Tabriz. I'm so sorry." Pale face, too, with a soft mouth downward drooping, lovingly, moist a bit from the last high-ball, daintily swallowed. Pale. "Why are you so pale?" he had asked. "Oh, Milton honey, I never go out in the sun. I'm so susceptible." Her finger tips on his made a little throbbing current of delight there. Like those buzzers jokers use to shock your hand. Then her laughter, almost inaudible, set her bosom all a-trembling: a pale tiny arc of breast peeped out, slyly.

He leaned back on the couch. Sunlight slanted through the room. Far off a dog barked, a man's voice—"Rover!"—and thin yelps fading off into a gentle Sunday silence.

"Mawnin, Mistah Loftis."

La Ruth, Ella Swan's daughter, shuffled through the room with a mop. She was a huge, slovenly Negro with steel-rimmed spectacles and an air of constant affliction. She came on Sundays to help out.

"Morning, La Ruth," he said, raising his hand. "How's your back?" She lumbered past, mumbling something about misery, toiling up the stairs with a sullen flat-footed sound, a great, aching hulk of a woman, moaning and groaning.

Well, Dolly, he thought. He settled back restfully. Well, Dolly . . . He got up abruptly and went to the telephone.

Now, balancing a bottle of whisky, ice and fresh glasses on a silver tray, he sauntered back across the lawn, intent that nothing should be spilled. Someone, the children, perhaps, had turned on the radio: a fragment of Brahms, a vast, unhappy whimper, swelled out behind him, then melted on the air. Beneath the cedars the children were playing. He lifted his chin at them, smiling broadly, and they waved back at him in unison. Peyton hollered, "Can we have some ginger ale?" He nodded, still smiling, and Peyton and Melvin, Dolly's little boy, scampered off toward the kitchen, leaving Maudie sitting sadly beneath the trees.

As he approached the lawn chairs Pookie arose and started forward.

"Let me help you there, old man," he shouted with oppressive fervor. He was short and balding and wore a lavender silk sport shirt through which there was somehow exposed part of a melonlike paunch, glowing pinkly. As he trundled toward Loftis he seemed to move through the grass with short, obscure steps of his own devising, like an inexpert roller skater. He was already quite drunk; one or two drinks always did it. Loftis despised him.

He fended Pookie off politely—"That's all right, Pookie"—and set the tray down beside Dolly. He saw Helen out of the corner of his eye. She was obviously still angry with him; her face was flushed, bent downward toward something she was knitting.

"Milton," Dolly was saying, "I was telling Helen if I could get Pookie some flannel pants like you've got on I might have to worry about some gal taking him away." She giggled.

Loftis leaned down beside Dolly, pouring whisky into the glasses. He could smell her perfume.

"It's not pants, sweetheart," Pookie said, sitting down. "It's my pussonality." Exploding on the air his laughter was wild and disheartening and the ensuing silence—since no one else had laughed—was rather horrible. Dolly filled the breach with a severe comment on the size of Pookie's behind, Helen bent toward her knitting, saying nothing.

"Aw, sweetheart——" Pookie said.

Dolly stirred in her chair—a sudden swell of hips, tightly draped in black. Even in spring, that excellent black . . . He stirred the drinks and eyed Pookie. How had she ever lived so long with such a jackass? He was a real-estate agent. Luck had been good to him: during the land boom just before the market crash he had made enough in commissions to drive a Buick and to get around to the best parties and to have his house redecorated by a stylish young decorator from Richmond. He also felt secure enough in his wealth to make several brash, futile attempts at joining the country club, and Loftis had always felt that Pookie's buoyant friendship for him was merely a badly disguised effort to have him speak a few good words to the membership committee. He and Dolly were Baptists. Dreariness and quackery. Loftis despised him. Despised him because he was loud-mouthed and had never been to college and furthermore . . . Because furthermore—God, it's true, he thought with a sudden shock—Dolly was the first woman since his marriage whom he had really considered making love to.

He served the drinks. Helen, it developed, didn't want any more;

she only drank to be sociable anyway, she explained with a pallid smile in Dolly's direction. It didn't agree with her. "I know what you mean, honey," Dolly said significantly. Helen returned to her knitting. For a while they talked aimlessly. Dolly spoke lazily of quilts and mattresses and bedspreads and the little town of Emporia, where she had lived as a child, and Loftis, sunk in his chair, thoughtlessly plucking at the canvas seat, would have been, he knew, bored to extinction except for the fact that Dolly *did* make him warm with desire each time, with a silken whisper, she crossed her legs. It was as simple as that and so Loftis kept his eyes on her legs; his mind, with unconscionable fascination, he kept upon bedspreads and quilts and the "funny little old peanut town" that Pookie had rescued her from. There was something common about her, Loftis thought as she paused once to drink, but she had a certain naïve, little-girl wit which wouldn't be too hard to take provided one weren't around her for too long. He pondered certain possibilities: he could get her off to Richmond somehow; people wouldn't have to know....

But what was he thinking? Good God, he had never had a thought like that before. His eyes drifted guiltily to Helen, back to Dolly's legs. He drank. Long, diagonal clouds formed above the bay. Over the cedars rested the sun, a faultless copper disk. The mockingbird, which had chattered all day, had fled now and no sound disturbed the quiet; nothing could be heard on the lawn save the easy rise and fall of careless talk hovering above the lawn chairs like bumblebees, a tatter of Brahms, unheard, that sighed down the slope, fading sorrowfully on the afternoon air.

He drank.

Pookie's face rose up like a ruddy, insubstantial globe, smiling. "What about this New Deal—" he walked past toward the whisky, his pants fluttering; Dolly's knees disappeared behind them, came back into view—"gonna give all the money to people who never worked for it, gonna give all the money to a buncha no-count niggers."

"Nigras," Dolly corrected.

"Nigras then." The pants fluttered past again, the big behind. "What about that, Milt?"

"The hell with it, I say," Loftis said over the rim of his glass, thinking: Now why did I say that? Far off, the churchbell struck four. Dolly's skirt was drawn back a little, exposing six inches of thigh, all the way up to . . .

God, he thought, looking away. Just like a schoolboy. A dirty, wretched little schoolboy.

"It's a trend, Milt. You can see it. Country drifting toward social-ism . . . kill off free enterprise. You know what, Milt? The National Realtors are sending a lobby to Congress already. You wait and see . . ."

Dolly arose, smoothing her skirt. "Well, if you all are going to start in on politics I guess I'll take this opportunity to go to the place."

Pookie looked up. "She means the little girls' room," he said with an explanatory wink. "Wait a minute, sweetheart. I'll go with you." He laughed his discouraging laugh, his little eyes lit up, and he took Dolly's arm with the air of one protecting an invalid. "That reminds me——" he began, and he embarked on a Chic Sale joke which trailed off eventually into pointless confusion. "Come on, funnyman," said Dolly languidly, pulling at his arm, and together they walked up the lawn, his hand pressed helpfully at her back, as if to keep her safe from all falls, all assaults. Loftis watched them until they disappeared, heard the children call beneath the cedars, laughing, screaming, heard, too, a rustle of paper beside him as Helen arose suddenly from the chair and stuffed her knitting into a bag. Her back was to him, he couldn't see her face; yet he knew from those quick, frantic motions that she was going to leave and that before she left she would say something withering, scornful and depressing. He didn't mind. He turned away. She said something. He turned again, in a carefree alcoholic haze through which somehow he perceived an enormous yellow butterfly, cedars, dying sunlight, and her face confronting him, red and unlovely, a lock of hair dangling—formidably full of out-rage and contempt.

"You're satisfied now."

"Why, Helen. What do you mean?"

"You didn't tell me that you called them, that you invited them over."

"Honey, I forgot," he said. A shambling procession of lies and excuses strolled through his mind. "I wouldn't have thought it was important anyway. Honest to God," he said amiably, "if I had known you wanted to be—to be apprised of the fact or that you wanted to be prepared . . ."

"Don't hand me that sort of thing," she retorted. "You know ex-actly what I mean." She ran her hand feverishly over her brow—a theatrical gesture, he thought—raising her eyes skyward. She's queer, he thought with an oddly pleasant feeling of solicitude: There is really something wrong with her. "Milton——" she said. She looked at him. Even armored by liquor he wanted to look away from her, and

59

did. "Both of them are beastly and vulgar and common," he heard her say flatly. "I know you hate him. Isn't it you just want to be with her? Isn't it? Well, isn't it?"

A moment of horror came over him. *She's not supposed to know.* "I'm not blind," she muttered, and walked away. He was alone.

Later there was twilight, and Loftis, far now from conscience or thoughts of Helen, told a funny story. Laughter floated across the lawn and up to the sky, blue shadows filled the air, and a faint breeze, stirred up by the coming darkness, made dry, hoarse scrapings in the cedar trees. *"Milton,"* said Dolly, "you ought to be *ashamed,"* but she and Pookie broke out again in laughter, and Loftis, rather pleased, smiled unobtrusively and turned away, watching dizzily a huge sunset that drained away in the west like blood. In the kitchen above a light winked on. He inhaled the sweet evening odor of roses and grass.

"That reminds me——" Pookie began, but there was a rush of feet down the slope behind them, and Melvin, who was nine and bore an embarrassing resemblance to his father, appeared at Dolly's side, saying, "Mama, Peyton hit me in the face." Apparently she had, for on his cheek there was a pink welt the size of a walnut, and now, having evoked attention, he clutched his mother's arm convulsively and let out a wail.

"That's all right, dear," she said indolently, "it'll be O.K. in a minute," and Pookie, in the midst of all these sobs and cries ringing out on the stillness, got up and knelt down beside the boy, saying, "That's all right, Buster, don't holler so."

The child stopped crying. He pressed his head against Pookie's shoulder and began a peevish, incoherent whimper. "Wanna go home, wanna go home . . . hungry," Loftis made out. Exasperated, Loftis poured himself another drink while Dolly, diverted for a moment, pulled a handkerchief from her purse and tried to wipe off Melvin's face. "O.K., Buster," Loftis heard her say in a voice full of irritation and boredom, "we'll go home in a minute," and for the first time in hours Loftis was aware of a bleak moment of depression. She would have to go, and then he'd be by himself. He dreaded the coming hours in the house with Helen. The goddam kid. Buster. Why didn't they have his adenoids taken out? He'd grow up an adolescent lout and most likely they'd have to send him to military school, to keep him away from growing girls. Wearily Loftis drank.

In an instant Pookie and Melvin had begun to climb up the hill toward the cedars—where the two little girls were still playing—in order to reconcile things; Pookie turned once—Loftis could see him—with a ridiculous smile gazing toward the lawn chairs, said something Loftis couldn't hear and proceeded on up the slope. Then, looking up from his glass to find Dolly regarding him gravely, Loftis returned her gaze, unsmiling, giddy, aware of something that made a faint summery humming in the air, fireflies flickering through the twilight like luminous raindrops, and of a hot, helpless desire.

"Are you happy?" he said softly.

She shook her head. "No."

"Why not?"

"Because Pookie isn't a handsome man."

"You don't mean that," he said.

"No, I mean because he's a funnyman," she said.

"Because he's a clown," he suggested easily. For a long while neither of them spoke.

"He's sweet," she sighed finally.

"The hell with that," he said.

Pookie descended the slope, flapping a cheerful arm in their direction. He passed them, heading for the beach. "Gonna take a look at that little old boat you were talking about," he called. "Gonna——"

Loftis lifted the bottle. "Have another drink!" he shouted.

"Thanks, no, old man," Pookie called back. From the distance his eyes were glassy, faintly perplexed; his face wore a befuddled grin. "I'm a man who knows when to stop!" Loftis waved merrily; Pookie vanished beyond the seawall.

"The hell with that," Loftis repeated to Dolly. "Somehow, somewhere, you got stuck."

They sat there for a few minutes in silence. Then Dolly stirred. With what seemed infinite tenderness she gazed directly at him. She was discontented, she had had too much whisky, and she was vulnerable to most any emotion, especially that of lust. "You're beautiful," Dolly whispered. "You're wonderful."

He walked toward her through the gloom. "Dolly," he said. "Sweet kitten . . ." he murmured, committing himself, he somehow knew, with foreknowledge and awareness, as if to an exciting and perilous journey.

Then all of a sudden, shattering the twilight, a wild, stricken scream came from above. He and Dolly turned toward the house together; Loftis heard Dolly give a startled gasp, half-rising from her chair, and he himself, hands still outspread, paralyzed in the gesture of

61

entreaty and affirmation, turned his eyes toward the terrace where beneath a tree he could see La Ruth, monstrous and disturbed, apron fluttering, hands to her face, making crazy motions on the brow of the hill like some black, outlandish bird. "Aiee-eee," she shrieked, together with long drawn-out cries of "Lawd!" and "Mercy!" and Loftis froze all over, trembling, so certain he was that someone had been killed. He was never quite sure how, in a state already befogged by extravagant emotion and by whisky, he gained the top of the hill, and yet he did, with the absolute speed of light, it seemed, leaving Dolly far behind—she who, horrified, too, cried, "Wait, wait!"—and stumbled up the flagstone steps and beneath the cedars where fallen branches almost sent him tumbling, and rushed desperately, afraid to think what might have happened, to the place where La Ruth stood cradling her face in her hands and lifting her eyes to God. "Now tell me——" he cried breathlessly. She smelled of cooking and of grease and she was speechless. "Now tell me, damn you!" he cried, shaking her, but she only rolled her great black eyes upward while a feeble peeping sound escaped from her throat.

He brushed her aside. There were voices from beneath the cedars and he ran there where, on the cool grassless ground, Helen and Ella Swan were furiously extricating Maudie from a mass of rope and twine. He bent down unsteadily to help, bewildered and frightened, but Helen said fiercely, "Get away, get away," and Ella, who with palsied fingers had begun to loosen a rope which bound Maudie's neck, moaned: "Dey tied her up, dey almos' killed her, de nasty things."

Now Dolly and Pookie arrived on the run, tripping on the roots of the cedar trees, and Maudie, who had had a handkerchief stuffed in her mouth and whose little face for a moment had been quite blue, began to breathe again. Her face turned a glowing red in an endless spasm of fear or pain, or both, and she emitted finally an agonized scream which, mingled with those of La Ruth still echoing hysterically from the terrace, gave Loftis a sudden sense of unearthliness. Helen swept Maudie up to her breast. The withered leg dangled pitifully and Helen began to walk about in little circles beneath the cedars, talking in soft muffled tones to the child who, becoming calmer, sobbed in a tortured, broken fashion against her mother's face. Vainly Loftis cast about for something to do or say. Somehow, as he stood there helplessly, the scene possessed a vast unseemliness, now that he knew Maudie was safe, and he wished that everything might suddenly vanish like smoke, leaving him in a lawn chair once more. Yet all that he could do, it seemed, was to stand there making futile motions with his hands and groping around in his pockets for a cigarette.

"Poor child," Dolly exclaimed, moving toward Helen with a comforting gesture, but Helen avoided her, turned away with Maudie and started toward the kitchen door just as Peyton and Melvin emerged from beneath a big hydrangea, four eyes in the shadows big with fright.

They all stood watching. Very gently Helen deposited Maudie in Ella Swan's arms, whirled then savagely and in silence before the sight of everyone—including a large chow dog that had wandered over from the neighboring house, his silly violet tongue lolling out—strode over to the place where Peyton stood with sudden-imperiled eyes and gave her a hard, vicious slap across the cheek. Then she spoke in a whisper, but they all could hear her. "You little devil!" she said and turned, head bowed, and took Maudie, who was still sobbing quietly, once again tenderly from Ella's arms and walked up the steps into the house. The screen door banged behind her, and Peyton began to shriek. Each of them watched this in silence—stockstill, rigid there beneath the bending cedars: Loftis and his guests and finally the two Negro women, who with shy and puzzled yet oddly comprehending grins had drawn near the others—each perhaps conscious of a clean spring twilight laden with cedar and the smell of the sea, and of something else, also: the cluster around them of quiet, middle-class homes, hedged and pruned and proper, all touched at this moment by a somber trouble; while each mind, too, perhaps turned inward for an instant, like the soul that forever seeks a grave, upon his own particular guilt. The bell, from afar, dropped seven jangling notes upon the stillness, and Peyton, weeping desperately, crept back beneath the hydrangea.

The door of the room where they stood, he and Peyton together, her hand in his, confronted the edge of darkness, like a shore at night facing on the sea. Beyond them in the shadows arose swollen, mysterious scents, powders and perfumes which, though familiar to both of them, never lost the odor of strangeness and secrecy—to him, because they stung his senses with memories of dances and parties in the distant past, and of love, always the scent of gardenias. In Peyton they aroused wicked excitement, a promise, too, of dances and parties, and—since she was still nine years old—hope that when the Prince came finally with love and a joyful rattling of spurs, the day would smell like this, a heartbreaking scent, always of roses. A breeze stirred

63

somewhere in the room, shook a piece of paper with a tiny clattering noise, like toy hooves echoing down a tiny road. He and Peyton stood still, listening; the paper chattered endlessly, small hooves galloping across the silence: the breeze died with a whisper and the paper, hooves, horse and rider, vanished without a sound, tumbled into some toy abyss. They listened, hesitant, somehow afraid, for now beyond them, floating up like crickets from the darkness, an alarm clock went *clickcluckclick*, a broken-down soliloquy, promising terrible things.

"Helen," he said softly. There was no answer.

"Helen," he repeated.

"Yes." That was all. A voice without anticipation or hostility, without anything. Silence again. They could hear her breathing, summoning up to both of them an instant's vision: the form outstretched, mother and lover, passionless, unfeeling, sick. What has happened to those warm, loving hands which once took care of us so well? But nothing stirred in the darkness. The hands were still. The alarm clock went *clickcluckclick*. So sick, so sick, so sick.

"May we come in, Helen?"

"Yes."

They crossed the room slowly, groping at the darkness as if they might be tearing cobwebs from some unseen wall. There were twin beds here, a small crocheted rug between, and they halted by her side still unable to see, yet aware through past acquaintance of things surrounding them in the night: rug, bedsteads, a score of little figurines and ornaments gazing at them, eyeless in the darkness; tiny bottles, too, medicine and pills, a little mirrored cabinet exuding a faint thin odor of sirup and chemicals. The sound of her breathing returned, close by, and as their eyes accustomed themselves to the darkness they sought out the place where she lay, a white-clad form gently breathing, hands across her body limp and unfolded like pale ghostly wings. Seabird wings.

"Helen," he said softly.

"Yes."

"Helen, I've brought Peyton. Peyton and I——"

They sat down on the edge of the bed across from her. A great blossom of fire suddenly illuminated the darkness; Helen lighted a cigarette, propped herself on one elbow. For a moment they saw her face, drawn and twisted with anger, sorrow—they really couldn't tell. She sank back again, blew out the match. The bloom of fire collapsed as darkness rushed in about them all: a tiny crumb of light flickered at the match end; then this also went out. Night enclosed them—night, fragrant with gardenia and rose, yet with a smell of medicine rising through the darkness, an unpleasant vapor faintly threatful, suggesting weariness and infirmity and disorder.

"Helen," he said slowly. "Peyton wants to tell you—that she's sorry . . . about Maudie."

"Mama, I'm sorry that I hurt Maudie. I'm sorry, Mama. I didn't mean to, Mama."

"Yes," Helen said.

They sat in silence, smelling the perfume, the medicine, the cigarette smoke, unable to see. High above, an airplane droned past; each of them stirred a little, listening: how far was it going, where? On the wingtips lights would flash green and red, demon eyes winking in the night.

"She's sorry, Helen," he said.

"I'm sorry, Mama," Peyton said again, a little breathlessly, as if she might begin to cry.

"Yes," said Helen.

"I'm sorry, Mama."

There was a whisper and rustle of bedclothes in the darkness. A hand reached out; she pulled Peyton toward her. "Oh, yes, dear. I know you're sorry. I know. I know. I'm sorry, too." And together, both of them weeping a bit, they made the soft, soothing sounds two women make when they try to forgive each other. Loftis sat idly by for a while, until finally Helen whispered to Peyton, "Now, dear, you go downstairs. Go and wash your face now. You must be awfully dirty. It's time to go to bed." Peyton stumbled past him—he couldn't see her—but he felt her fingers on his leg, trembling there like moths, plucking at his trousers. "Daddy?" she said.

"Just a minute, baby," he said. "I'll be right along."

Peyton left the room, bumping against footstools and dressers, and again Loftis sat in silence.

Finally he said, "She was really sorry, I think. It wasn't I . . . who prompted her. I just told her how to say it. I think she was really sorry."

"Yes. She was."

"Is Maudie all right now?"

"Yes," she said in a weary voice.

"I think she was just frightened," he ventured slowly.

"Yes."

Then he said something which he didn't want to say, it hurt his pride so, yet he knew he had to: "Helen, I'm really very sorry about today. Really I am. It was a very foolish business, the whole thing. I hope you really didn't get the wrong idea. I just shouldn't have done it."

"No."

"Invited them over, I mean."

"Yes," she said.

"Helen, I love you. Do you believe that?"

"I don't know," she said. She turned over on her side with a labored sigh. He couldn't see her, although he knew from her voice that she was still facing him. The words came without hesitation, in a tired sort of monotone, and as he listened he began to break out in a chilly sweat: "I don't know. I just don't think you do. I've tried to do the right thing. I've tried to humor you even knowing that when I humored you I wasn't doing the right thing. I just think you're a child. I just don't think we've ever understood each other. That's all. I just think we've got a whole lot of different values."

"Do you love me?" he asked quietly. It occurred to him that he hadn't asked her that in a long time, and the thought of what she might reply caused him a vague tremor of fear.

"I don't know——"

"How do you mean that, Helen?"

"If it weren't for Maudie. If it weren't for Maudie——"

"What do you mean?"

"I don't know," she said. "I don't think I'd be able to live with you anymore. I just think you're going to destroy us all."

He stood up. A surge of anger and futility rose up in his chest—and sudden shame, too, shame at the fact that their life together, which had begun, as most marriages do, with such jaunty good humor and confidence, had come to this footlessness, this confusion.

"Well," he said in a level voice, thinking *well, it's your money, that's the awful part*. "Well, I'm sorry."

"Yes," she said.

"We started everything and now we'll have to finish it."

"Yes." Her voice was cool, tired, full of indifference. She rose once more on her elbow, turned the alarm clock's luminous dial away from the wall so that a weird green halo of light was cast about her. Then she reached for a glass of water and swallowed a pill. He wanted to shout something at her. "Keep your hands off my daughter!" was what, with desperate urgency, he wanted to say, but for a moment he also wished to sit down by her and take her hand because there was something wrong with her—but he loved her, and she had to understand all these things. However, he really didn't know what to say, and so he merely turned and groped his way out of the room.

Downstairs he found Peyton twisted up in a chair, calmly reading *Winnie-the-Pooh*. He called to her and they went outside. They got in the car and drove for what seemed miles, out of town and through the lonely pinewoods, across wild swamps full of frogs that piped shrilly and, dazed by the headlights, hopped giddily onto the road and got squashed beneath the wheels. This excited Peyton but Loftis had a headache. It began to rain—a half-hour's steady drizzle which ceased as abruptly as it had begun. Finally, at about ten o'clock, Peyton announced that she was hungry and so, in a little fishing town up the bay, they stopped at a deserted restaurant and had deviled crabs and Seven Up. Peyton kept up an incessant chatter and told him to look at her: look at this new bracelet. Loftis had a beer. Then a red-faced woman, with a wen on her cheek, who seemed to be the owner of the restaurant, came up with sawdust and a broom and told them they would have to leave, it was closing time.

The car was parked on a dark wharf outside. They sat there for a long time, gazing at the bay. The tide rose, bright with phosphorescence, washing gently at the shore. It began to get cool and Peyton curled up beside him. "The more it *snows*-tiddely-pom, the more it *goes*-tiddely-pom . . ."

He looked down at her. "When you grow up, baby," he said, "you're going to be wonderful."

She didn't answer him. After a while, she said, "Daddy, I'm sorry Buster and me tied up Maudie."

"No," he replied, "that wasn't a very good idea. Buster and *I*."

"Buster and I. Why did Mama hit me like that? She never——"

"She was just feeling bad, baby." He put his arm around her and pulled her close against him.

"Yes," Peyton said thoughtfully. "I reckon she was feeling bad. I was really sorry to hurt Maudie like that."

"Yes," he said.

"Children should be kind to one another," Peyton said.

"Yes."

Soon Peyton fell asleep against him, and an offshore breeze sprang up, rustling her hair, bringing with it an odor of swamp and cedar, remembrance things, out of this season of love and rain.

Three

HALFWAY between the railroad station and Port Warwick proper—a distance altogether of two miles—the marshland, petering out in disconsolate, solitary clumps of cattails, yields gradually to higher ground. Here, bordering the road, an unsightly growth of weeds takes over, brambles and briars of an uncertain dirty hue which, as if with terrible exertion, have struggled through the clay to flourish now in stunted gray profusion, bending and shaking in the wind. The area adjacent to this stretch of weeds is bleakly municipal in appearance: it can be seen from the road, and in fact the road eventually curves and runs through it. Here there are great mounds of garbage; a sweet, vegetable odor rises perpetually on the air and one can see—from the distance faintly iridescent—whole swarms of carnivorous flies blackening the garbage and maybe a couple of proprietary rats, propped erect like squirrels, and blinking sluggishly, with mild, infected eyes, at some horror-stricken Northern tourist.

It was along about here, as the limousine, with its tires sizzling musically over the hot asphalt, proceeded into town, that Dolly began to have her premonition again. The day had grown hotter; greasy waves of heat swam up from the road. There was no wind at all now and the weeds on either side of the road, so hot and dry and motionless, seemed perilously close to flame. Trickles of sweat began to ooze down beneath her arms. The garbage piles swept past, emitting a nasty smell, and with a jolt the limousine had risen to the span of a small bridge. Below was a brackish creek, foul with sewage and hostile to all life save for great patches of algae the color of green pea soup, where dragonflies darted and hovered, suspended from the sunny air as if by invisible threads. She looked at the creek despondently: somewhere there had been a silly story about the creek—about a Negro convict who had fallen into the stream and been drowned and who, since the body, mysteriously, was never recovered, had reappeared from the creek at night on each anniversary of his death, covered with scum and slobbering horribly at the mouth as he prowled the town in search of beautiful white women to ravish and to drag back to the unspeakable depths of his grave. Pookie had told her the story each time they had ever gone past the creek, and although she didn't believe the tale, it had always caused her a pleasurable shiver of fear.

All at once the limousine gave a startling heave, dipping downward, and her stomach leaped up inside her like a balloon: this sudden jolt, together with the sight of the weeds and the garbage, and the boiling heat, gave her a sense of almost unbearable anguish, and so with a despairing little cry she sank back into the seat, wet and wilted, and clutched at Loftis' hand. She felt Loftis quickly draw his hand away: That's another time he's done it, she thought—and it was then, looking up at him, that she had her horrible premonition.

He doesn't love me any more. He's going to leave me.

The same premonition she had had last night, and now she had it again. The moment pierced her with hopelessness and she shrank into one corner of the seat, looking at him. He was gazing out of the window with misty preoccupation. A lonely willow tree swept by, and beyond, following his gaze, she saw half a dozen gas storage tanks, rusty and enormous, rising up out of the wasteland like the truncated brown legs of some awful assembly of giants. They were still far off but the car was approaching them steadily, and for some reason the prospect of nearing them, going by them, filled her with anxiety and horror. She began to weep a little, silently in the corner, engulfed in a bleak gray fog of self-pity; small tears drained slowly down her cheeks. It's true, she thought: the way he's been acting. He doesn't love me. He only came to get me this morning because Helen wouldn't come. Through a blurred film of melancholy she saw a brown wart at the base of Ella Swan's neck, unkempt strands of nigger hair turned gray.

Ugly. Oh, ugly.

She turned and stared miserably out of her window: He's that way not just because he's grieving for Peyton, but because he's rejecting me. I can tell. Two buzzards flapped soundlessly up from a junk heap, swooped toward the weeds, were gone.

Well, for that matter, she thought bitterly, she had felt all this, just a bit, for the past few months, although it had only been last night that she had really become conscious of something wrong. After all, he had left her once before to go back to Helen. It was his divorce this time, she knew. Backing out at the last minute like that. That was what he wanted to do. And last night. Last night had been just horrid, and as the remembrance—the recognition of the pure shock it had caused her, and of what that shock meant now—fled through her mind, a new, yet more crushing wave of agony and remorse swept over her and she began to sob in little stifled gasps, clutching the velvet tassel above her and rocking mournfully with the rhythm of the limousine as she watched the gas tanks mercilessly approaching, truncated and incomplete, like totems on a plain.

Oh, Milton honey.

Now late yesterday afternoon it had been very warm, and toward sunset she and Loftis had been sitting on the terrace at the country club. The club was on a bluff overlooking the James, a costly establishment, vaguely gothic in style, complacent and splendid. There was a swimming pool with sapphire waters near the eighteenth hole; a diver in shiny blue trunks arched against the twilight—they could see him from the terrace—and soared downward cleanly, behind beach umbrellas slanting like crazy sombreros, to break the water without a splash. Dolly and Milton were drinking martinis—this was his third, her second—mixed from his private bottles in the kitchen. Children in sunsuits, tumbling on the slope below, made pink pinwheel patterns against the grass. An odor of mint and pollen filled the dusk, and golfers wandered in from the course; their caddies trailed indolently behind, golfbags merrily clinking. There were perhaps a dozen other people on the terrace: lazy evening conversation, faintly heard, eddied, flowed, swelled downward toward the pool where a fat woman, sunbathing, lay on the grass sunless and asleep, absorbing the evening shadows.

"To D-day," said Dolly. It was their private joke. D-day was October twenty-first, when Loftis' divorce, the result of two years' separation, became final. Usually Loftis proposed the toast, but after Dolly had caught on she had managed to wear the joke a trifle thin, so now

70

Loftis didn't answer her but only forced a faint smile of acknowledgment and concentrated on the martini. A shiny red convertible slid to a stop on the driveway. White dresses issued from the doors like so much airy foam, and three young girls ran laughing up the walk, followed by three young men in tuxedoes, as solemn as crows.

"Dance tonight," Dolly said. "Dinner dance, it looks like."

"Mmm-hh."

"What are you thinking about, darling?" she asked.

"Oh, I don't know," he replied. "Nothing."

Oh dear, she thought. For all the years she had known him she had identified him with talk, speech; his talent in this direction was possibly the reason for their rather one-sided communion. She loved to hear him talk and was a conscientious listener, although often, in a dreamy sort of abstraction, she found herself listening not so much to the substance of what he said as to the tone of the words, the melodious, really endearing way he said them. The eccentric manner of twisting words into grotesque parodies of themselves, his supplications—"Oh, God" or "Oh, Jesus" when something went wrong—uttered with such profound and comical intensity to the heavens; and his own particular wit, the subtleties of which she often didn't get: to listen to that steady flow of words, the fine enthusiasms and the wry, damning accusations of things in general, so true, so commanding and intelligent—she could listen to all that forever. And usually she agreed with him. He had taught her so much.

But she was worried now. This air of preoccupation and mystery she had taken particular notice of in the past few months. It always worried her. It meant that shortly he would be rude to her, at least impatient, and she would be unhappy. She was determined to cheer him up. She took a sip of the martini; it burned clear down to the pit of her stomach—she had never decided whether she liked martinis or not, and only drank them because he did—but looking up past the flower centerpiece she took note of his brooding face and thought: Trouble trouble boil and bubble.

"Trouble, trouble, dear. What's the matter, dear?" she said lightly. "You can tell me."

"Nothing."

"You can tell me," she said. "Tell Dolly," she said, teasing.

"Nothing, dammit," he said.

She ignored this surliness, hoping by coy persuasion to make him be nice. "Now, honey," she murmured, "be nice." Just then, at a table near by, a woman with red hair and plump, exposed arms suddenly

71

leaned back in her chair and uttered a high-pitched, massive series of laughs. Detonating upon this casually genteel atmosphere, it had all the effect of a flock of geese set loose in church, and caused everyone on the terrace to turn with knives and forks hovering in mid-air, looking for the source. Then, recognizing the woman as a familiar character, given to such outbursts, they turned back to their tables with knowledgeable nods of their heads and patronizing smiles.

"Who's that woman, dear?" Dolly asked. Although their affair had been going on for years, it had only been lately that they had taken to venturing so easily together at the country club, and there were many people in the new, exclusive and beautifully exciting circle whom Dolly didn't know. Defined by Port Warwick protocol, Dolly had been "social," but never "country clubby." She had often come here as a guest, but poor Pookie had never been able to make the grade.

Loftis had looked, too. He was smiling a little, "Sylvia Mason," he said. He waved, " 'Lo, Syl." *"Milton Loftis.* How you?" A gentle, trivial greeting.

A waiter descended upon them with a happy grin and a metal tray, piled high with dishes, as big as the lid from a garbage can, impossibly balanced on four fingers. "Order, Cap'n Milton?"

Loftis looked up. "Hello, Luther. How you tonight? Clam cocktails. Steak dinner." The waiter left.

Suddenly he said, "I was thinking about Peyton." He drank the rest of his martini.

"Oh dear," she said. "Is she all right?" Actually she didn't care. Peyton, whom Milton dwelt on constantly, bored her stiff. And often when he spoke of her—although she strove to be understanding—she felt an emotion that, try as she might to call it something else, was nothing but wretched jealousy. To be known as "his mistress" by the children of the man you love is likely to cause worry and fretfulness and maybe broodings at night, and Dolly, who preferred things to be worked out simply, detested Peyton for her own sense of sin. She had avoided Peyton as well as she could during the past years—it was the only right thing to do—but even from afar she felt that the girl cast forbidding shadows across her tenderly hopeful destiny. *Milton and I.*

In the twilight he looked very handsome; the provoking streak of gray hair, the color of old pewter: a vulgar handsome man could never wear it with such grace. And soberly talking now; she loved him so much when he was sober, which was fairly infrequent: then his very spirit, so uncompromisingly aware of life, of the poignancy of their dilemma, so richly conscious of the fine things soon in store for them—

72

this sober, gentle spirit promised to envelop her like a flame, a tender flame radiating decent contentment just as the soft, temperate voice seemed to promise: "I will take care of you. You need have no worries now. I will show you what love is, and truth."

But he was talking about Peyton.

"There's something wrong with the girl. Ever since they broke up, she's been at loose ends. I get these letters, you see, and they worry the hell out of me. The poor kid's had a rough time. You see, what I advise her . . . take it easy. God knows I know that a marriage can be difficult. . . . It's a shame. Poor kid . . . I think I'll run up to New York next week . . . talk to her. . . ."

It was hard to concentrate; her eyes wandered to the other tables, to the Mason woman—on whose fat arms there were a dozen silver bracelets, jangling noisily as she ate—to tablecloths, silver, gay flowers, all imparting a splendid, important air of luxury and comfort. Inside, beyond the French doors, boys and girls in twos and fours strolled aimlessly about, waiting for the dance to start—the boys gawky and grave, wearing their new tuxedoes with grown-up unconcern, while the girls laughed and tugged at the boys' hands or, lifting their skirts off the floor, practiced a dance step or two. The band was tuning up. She lifted her gaze to a second-story window, where, screened a bit by a virile growth of ivy, was his room—the place where he lived, now that he had no home. His room. Inside there, drowned in shadows, she saw familiar things, faintly defined by the dying sun: a corner of his desk, the lampshade, the back of a chair where, sloppily draped over one wooden slat, was a white shirt he had worn, no doubt, that afternoon while golfing: something tugged tenderly at her heart. His shirt unwashed. And looking back at him now, at the grave, wide, honest, yet soberly comprehending face, she thought: He's so sweet.

"I don't think I'll ever get her back to Port Warwick," he was saying. "After her wedding she said she'd never come back here. Not that she should. She and Helen never got along and anyway I think she belongs up there. Poor kid. She's got a lot of talent, at least I guess she does. . . ." He was talking rapidly, with sudden, disheartening animation. She didn't like to see him like this; as images, thoughts of Peyton swam forth, a troubled glow inflamed his forehead; against the sun the lobe of one ear was transparent and a tiny pool of blood was gathered there, very red. When we're married, she thought, I'll have to make him stop drinking so much. . . . She had heard all this before. She was bored. She wished he'd talk about going to the Skyline Drive. From a glass dish she took a piece of celery, put it on her plate and began to nibble on a ripe olive. A bit giddy from the martinis, she tried to listen to him, but her thoughts, like dandelion seeds, strayed airily away: love, a marriage, maybe, in New Orleans, the Skyline Drive.

"She's had a rough time. . . ."

Oh, talk about someone else. Talk about us.

"Now she and Harry. Harry's a nice guy, but I think they resented each other somehow, almost from the very beginning. She should have taken more time! You go North—you become expatriated, exiled. You reach out for the first symbol that completes your apostasy— you become a Communist or a social worker or you marry a Jew. In all good faith, too, yearning to repudiate the wrong you've grown up with, only to find that embracing these things you become doubly exiled. Two losts don't make a found. Marry a Jew or a Chinaman or a Swede, it's all fine if you're prompted by any motive, including money, save that of guilt. My father told me when I went barreling off to the University, 'Son,' he said, 'you don't have to be a camp-follower of reaction but always remember where you came from, the ground is bloody and full of guilt where you were born and you must tread a long narrow path toward your destiny. If the crazy sideroads start to beguile you, son, take at least a backward glance at Monticello.' You see . . ."

She nodded, smiling vacantly. She had caught the word "Jew." It sent her mind astray again. Why doesn't he talk about us? Jews. How true. Like Milton she felt herself to be a liberal Democrat; about six years ago—soon after they had first made love, but before Loftis' political hopes had completely withered—he had mentioned something about her becoming National Committeewoman, if and when they were married. This had excited her terribly—even though she somehow felt the remark was meant lightly—during the mid-hours of one hot, sweet night at the Hotel Patrick Henry in Richmond. How lovely that had been. Their best, really their best. There had been an exquisite secrecy; untried as she was—for, though she had entertained many alluring fantasies, this had been her first out-of-town adultery—the knowledge of misdoing added enchantment to the night. The old Virginia drawl. "Miz Roosevelt, ah'm Dolly Loftis. How you? National Committeewoman from Virginia. Mah husband's tol' me so much about you and Pres'dent Roosevelt. Or shall ah say Franklin?" A neon sign winks shamelessly; red sinful splashes fill the room. She gets up, pulls down the shade, hiding her guilt beneath the darkness. Should I? Should I still? He's married. Stern pentecostal watchwords out of the gray November small-town past, making her sweat: Forswear adultery and other such iniquities. It passes. She crawls back into bed beside him, strokes his face, exalted, thinking: I don't care. He needs me. . . . "Milton," she says, "wake up, sweetheart."

He was still talking about Peyton, and now the evening started to get horrid. In filmy yellow waves, a bilious sort of despondency took possession of her; from the last martini, somehow swallowed wrong, a vaporous gas rose up in her nose, smelling faintly of juniper, and, looking out of the corner of her eye, she felt that two people, at least, were staring at her. She wished she might see a familiar face, for these, all strange to her, seemed suddenly to damn and accuse. A tawny light spilled over the grass below; through this light a motorized lawnmower, towing a sleepy Negro, moved like a boat across the green, showering a billow of bright grass before it. A man wandered out to the green and removed the flag; in the sunset the little red pennant had been so pretty, she was sad to see it go. The band began to play, and the sound of music, too, filled her with vague, remote sadness, and a fidgety yearning; hungrily, her mind sought old places, old events . . .

His room.

How can I talk about, tell anyone of this tender rapture? Loving a man so for all these years. Now untied from the tie that binds, poor Pookie gone to Knoxville, Tennessee, and Melvin at college, my tie is to him alone. Together we can never die. A farm girl from Emporia: what would Papa say now? I sophisticated and fancypants, vice-chairman of the Red Cross and member in good standing of the Tidewater Garden Club too. Sweet and ruinous, Milton says, with a soft sweet corruption about the mouth. I love him so.

Wanting him for so long, holding off, having to, sitting back on these hips he says drive him frantic, like a saint yearning for perfect communion. Holding off. Having to because he says we're both up-caught in the tragedy of a middle-class morality.

Still the gossip runs, but we go to his room, up there, now because he says he's free of that succubus which has so long held him in bondage, free now, legally and without error, and the hell with the paltry petty ruck of envious people who can't get shut of a virago or a jackass who holds them helpless, too. That's what he says. So we go to his room now, up there. I know it well. There is something dear and sweet about it. It encloses you with the scent or maybe just the feeling of him: a male smell like heather or tweed, his shirts unwashed and hanging over things, shirts I take home to the apartment to care-fully wash and iron myself. I love him so. Knowing he wants me, that's what's so good. . . .

He says I'm the dearest thing and age has made the fiber sweeter. And we are upcaught in the tragedy of a middle-class morality. We do not care, Milton and I, for that will all be over October twenty-first.

Sometimes I wish he'd get that faraway look out of his eyes. I worry. What is he thinking about? Sometimes I don't know what he's thinking about.

He says I'm the dearest thing. I think he loves me more than Peyton. Peyton is a bitch, although it's not his fault, but the fault of that succubus who treated her so badly. It's somehow Freudian, he says.

His room. We go there now and he pays the nigger a dollar to keep the hall door locked and because of this I can awake on Sunday morn-ing before he spirits me out as he says and feel the sunlight on my face and think well Dolly Loftis you've come a long way for a farm girl and think too as he says in the soft morning sunlight that there are miles to go before we sleep and miles more to go before we sleep. . . .

A waiter appeared at Loftis' side, mumbled something about New York on the phone.

"Thanks, Joe." He arose still talking, terribly feverish, Dolly thought, reluctant to be unchanneled from his singing flow of words. "Well, I've forgotten about becoming a statesman. Content with working on bond issues. Content with everything." A strand of celery had become caught in the back of her throat, dangled there itching against her palate. "Hell," he said expansively, "I might even start back to church. I might . . ." But he didn't finish the sentence for—perhaps because of the placid fading light, softening her face so that now, even more, she looked like a little girl—he seemed to understand that she had not been listening to him. Her wandering eyes, she sensed with sudden fright, had betrayed her, and he gazed down at her with an odd sad smile.

He must know. He must know.

"Milton——" she tried to say, but "What do you see in me any-way?" he had said, then turned, walked across the terrace and through the ballroom; she watched him until he disappeared behind a potted palm, and she lapsed back into her chair with a little groan, thinking: Oh something's happening.

76

A wisp of music unspooled from the ballroom, saxophone, drums; and thunderheads like Christmas snow rose in disordered piles high above: they would go over, she thought, over the city. People around her talked softly together, laughed in low, gentle tones; all of them, she felt, were watching her, but the band, the moaning saxophone, made her think of a dance right here, long ago. Peyton's birthday. The first time, after all the waiting, they had ever made love.

She waited. Then he came back and his face, gray as water, was full of agony and horror. He started toward her, but without a word he paused, turned and walked over to Sylvia Mason. The woman got up with a little cry, bracelets jangling, and put her great maternal arms around him. "Ahhh, Milton," Dolly heard her say. "Ahhh, Milton." People shuffled, turned about in their chairs; there was great confusion. "Ahhh, Milton," said Sylvia, "I'm so sorry for you," but Loftis said nothing, or if he did Dolly could neither see nor hear him, for his back, looming toward her, seemed to be slumped in pure despair against the whole vast evening sky.

Dolly arose. "Milton," she called, "what's wrong——" but they were already walking through the ballroom. And the Mason woman had her fat arm around his waist. Dolly sank down again. She didn't know what had happened, or where he was going. But she had the premonition. Funny little serpents, stars like minute flowers floated on her vision.

He doesn't love me any more.

She fussed miserably with her handbag, her hat. Then she ran to the edge of the terrace and saw him drive away, alone.

It was just her woman's intuition: Oh, please, God. Again. He's going back to her. Again.

Now here at the country club in August, 1939—the time that Dolly remembered, that first time—Peyton had had her sixteenth birthday which, to call back ancient history, was the day before the war began. There was talk about a Corridor—and what was *that?*—but in Port Warwick, attuned to a mood the papers all called "festive," thirty thousand people waved flags and cheered as the nation's largest pleasure ship slid down the ways, soon to transport well-to-do folks to Rio and France. There was prosperity on that afternoon in Port Warwick, and on the terrace where they danced a five-piece band was playing and Negroes in white jackets hovered in doorways, behind columns, as from any of a dozen scattered lawn tables one could hear the chilly laughter of beautiful young girls and the sound of distant, captivating music.

Helen went around and around, dancing with Milton in a dizzy blur of light, organdy, taffeta rustling about her, the young girls' perfume sweet and innocent on the summer air. "Oh, Milton," she said, "I'll sit this one out. I'm hot."

He smiled broadly. "But, honey," he said, "we just started."

She slid away from him.

"Don't be a——"

Wet blanket. That's what he'd say.

I'm so very hot. And tired.

Then he danced with Peyton; he danced with Dolly Bonner, holding her too close, and he danced with Peyton again. He laughed loudly, having, as usual, drunk too much. His fingers were pressed tightly against Dolly's back. He is not deceiving me. He nodded left and right to the young people who danced around him.

Nor is it, she was thinking, sheer coincidence that she should be here. Because of Melvin she is here. Indeed. Not sheer coincidence. He is not deceiving me.

She was sitting alone in a chair at the edge of the terrace. Above was a clear blue sky, below, waxed flooring, which had been drawn out for the dance, slippery beneath her feet. At the far wall of the terrace was a long mirror in which, past the bright dresses shifting constantly before her, she could see the young girls dancing, eying themselves slyly as they tried to catch sight of the gardenias pinned in their hair. She saw herself, too, and in a paneled glass door behind the chair her whole back was reflected from the mirror, and the effect was not of one, but of two. Helens sitting as if in a game of musical chairs, back to back. Sunlight fell upon her cheeks; she was a little past forty, but she looked much older. Somewhere long ago she had surrendered up most of her beauty, which had been considerable, to the passing of time, but a whisper of loveliness still lingered on her face. It was a face full of discontent and now, in repose, of sullenness, but there were fine lines in it, gentle arcs and swerves, prominences beautifully recovered into one agreeable symmetry. As she sat there, never allowing her eyes to stray above their level, but gazing only at waists, skirts and the mirror, her expression from time to time became unpleasantly clouded over: thoughts, ugly things, wrinkled her face. Yet now and then it would relax; a bright impromptu content would appear, and a sweet and casual loveliness.

And even now, as she looked up at the mirror, a waiter banged through the door behind her; the door swept to, flapping in and out, so that the twin-reflected Helens, blue-gowned, back to back in their

78

musical chairs, swung wildly out into space above and beyond the dancing forms, multiplied endlessly against the yellowing slant of afternoon light.

I must see how Maudie is.

A young boy with acne and a smirk asked her dutifully to join him in a dance. She refused, shortly. She was watching. Peyton, she believed, had been drinking. Her face so flushed, too happy. The boy protested, urged. She made a polite vague noise, gazing past him at the river. He left, smirking, and the band played beneath the trees.

> *When the deep purple falls*
> *Over sleepy garden walls . . .*

The terrace echoed to gay music, sad music, sad as a flute, and the air above, festooned with red bunting and white paper bells, was full of soft laughter and young sweet melancholy. She arose and walked through the dancing crowd. Milton went past, smiling down at Dolly—*he is not deceiving me*—but in the ladies' room an odor of powder lingered, and the colored girl looked up with a grin, saying, "Mercy me, Miz Loftis——"

"Listen," she said, "I want you to tell me if you see any of these girls drinking. Do you know my daughter?"

"Yes'm. I does."

"You tell me if you see, hear?"

"Yes'm."

"I suspect that some of them are drinking."

"Yes'm, dat's what I suspects too."

"You tell me, hear?"

"Yes'm."

The black devil. She won't tell.

She opened the door, went out, and music swelled around her like tropic air. She returned to the terrace, sat down again, and a woman named Mrs. La Farge, whose son, Charles, was here, came up and sat next to her.

"Helen, such a lovely dance! Such a lovely girl you have!" She was a jolly person with a wide, jolly face, and she batted her eyes from time to time, which somehow gave her an air of vague and intermittent wonder.

Helen turned to her with a cheerful smile. "Yes, it is nice, isn't it? But actually, you see, it's not my doing. You see, Peyton and Milton planned it all. I just stood by and took care of some of the little details."

"Oh, dear Helen, that's a storyteller!" She reared back and laughed, displaying on her chest a mosaic of sunny freckles which cascaded down into the vast privacy of her bosom. "Oh, dear Helen." She paused. "Charlie says Peyton's going to Sweet Briar next month."

"Yes." She wished the woman would go away. She wished she herself might leave. The club, the noise, the music, as they always did, filled her with anxiety. What? Where? She was feeling a bit dizzy, very tired. Dr. Holcomb: he says I mustn't strain myself like this. The word *thrombosis* made a resonant "gong," like a threatful bell, in her mind. If I should get a thrombosis—Gong!

"That's so nice," Mrs. La Farge was saying. "I played on the hockey team at Hollins. The year we played Sweet Briar——"

Helen was nodding, smiling, saying "yes," spacing these nods politely, and her eyes, she knew, were bright with interest. But she wasn't listening.

What? Where?

It would soon be twilight. There would be the birthday dinner and, afterward, more dancing and maybe swimming. She felt sick; heat rose oppressively from the flooring—huge, moist, asthmatic. There were sailboats on the river. A luminous glow brightened the calm; the sailboats, motionless, seemed to rest on quicksilver. At this moment a shadow rushed down the grassy slope; offshore, the river took on a chill dusky hue as the cloud passed over. The sailboats tilted. Sails belled out like wings but then collapsed desolately, all at once. Afternoon light returned to the terrace, insistent and humid, with the promise of rain. Milton and Dolly were dancing again. And Melvin dancing now with Peyton. Taffeta and silk and marquisette swirled about her and eight notes of music exploded from a trumpet, splintering the air—*boogie me, mama*—a boy's voice croaked and laughter, all young, all happy, settled around her in chill dwindling waves.

"We haven't decided—" Mrs. La Farge's breast heaved, shuddered; the sequins on her dress blinked like eyes—"decided . . . decided. Charlie's so young yet . . . he's such a steady, sober boy . . . V.P.I. most likely."

Milton and Dolly. They are not deceiving me. Dr. Holcomb said emotional disturbances past forty can cause physical complications, the menopause, you see, makes severe demands, hormonic readjustment. Estro—

genic. That was the word.

Oh! it was a brutal thing. She lit a cigarette absently, forgetting

Mrs. La Farge. "I'm sorry," she said, smiling, offering her one from a case, but Mrs. La Farge said, "No, thank you, dear, I never touch the things. We've abstained for Charlie's sake, both of us, Chet and I, because——"

Because——

Oh! it was a brutal thing. Because for six years it had been like this: Milton and that woman were having an affair. She knew. And did they expect her not to know? Just to be able to tell . . .

And what would she say? How?

"Mrs. La Farge, listen," she might say, "I've not wanted to tell anyone because—because I have children, too, and you know—— Listen, Mrs. La Farge, this has come to a head finally. Milton and Dolly Bonner. You might not have noticed. But I—it's a matter of divorce. Yes, you mustn't look so shocked, really. No, it's come to a head."

And then she might say—

"Oh, if you'd known the brutal things I've borne these years. Were you at the Lenharts' party Christmas two years ago? Yes, you were, weren't you? Yes, I saw, though you might not have. The way their hands met and the kisses, all in fun. It didn't matter that it was all in fun. I saw.

"I think they've met, too, in other places. I haven't any proof, but I'm sure . . .

"Were you at the Paiges' dance last year? In the vestibule I saw them, making their dirty plans. I know, and their eyes shining and the way their hands met there . . ."

But I shall never tell.

Mrs. La Farge giggled. "Oh, there's Chester. I'll have to go dance." She heaved herself up. "See you later, dear." Helen was alone. The horizon was full of black clouds, distant grumblings. Twilight was coming on. She felt sick, alone; no one since that pimpled boy had asked her to dance.

A frantic vision appeared to her, mingled all of a sudden with the music, the laughter, the day that seemed to be perishing with a gray and vanquished light all over the lawn: in bed at home, enfolded by darkness, she awoke to the sound of his footsteps. He stood by her bed, as he always did, looking down at her: Helen, Helen, this stuff just can't last—with his cool, facetious little laugh—I thought things were working out again.

I feel bad, she said, thinking: I saw, I saw them both then, yearning. The way their hands met there . . .

I feel bad.

And thinking: Oh I want to love him. **I do.** Again.

He left her without a sound. And as he left, in this familiar reverie, so real, yet somehow airy and strange, she collapsed back into bed, or rather into absolute darkness, knowing that by one word—Yes or Forgive or Love—she might have affirmed all, released all of the false and vengeful and troubling demons right up into the encompassing air of night, and everything would be right again. But she fell back into darkness, the door closed, sealing off the rectangle of light which had intruded for a moment into the room, her home, sealing off indeed all intrusions so that now, dreamful, drowsing, yearning desperately for sleep, she thought of the old Army days, the distant, shrouding sound of trumpets on a parade ground long ago, and her father's uniform, consoling just to touch, while longing in an endless sort of drowsiness to be surrounded by those strong and constant arms.

She looked up.

Peyton hurried toward her in a rustle of blue silk, sixteen, smiling. "Mother, Mother, don't be a dope. Come on, dance."

"What are you drinking?"

Blushing, Peyton looked downward. "Why, just punch, Mother."

"Come with me."

Peyton followed obediently and together they pushed through the crowd of boys and girls, through the smell of perfume, gay shouts of "Happy Birthday!" And in the powder room the colored girl, sensing something ominous, white folks' trouble, left discreetly.

Helen turned. "Give me that glass." She took a sip. Whisky. She wheeled about, poured it down a toilet.

"Your father gave that to you, didn't he?"

"Yes," Peyton said meekly. "He said that for my birthday——" She was beautiful, she was young, and these two things together caused Helen the bitterest anguish.

"I won't have it," she said. "I've seen your father ruin himself with liquor and I won't have it. Do you understand?"

Peyton looked at her. "Mother——" she began.

"Shut up. I won't have it. Get your things. I'm going to take you home."

For a moment Peyton was silent. Then she raised her eyes, gave her hair a wild, outraged toss. "I despise you!" she said, and was gone.

Flushed, trembling, Helen returned to the terrace. Milton smiled at her gaily. She turned away. A cloud scudded over the lawn, darkening the day like a shuttered room. Wind shook in the trees around the terrace, rustling the young girls' hair, expiring with a tender sigh as the day returned in a rush of light: the shadow swept down the lawn, vaulted the swimming pool, vanished. Below, in a patch of sunlight, she saw a familiar figure.

Oh, Maudie dear.

Down the slope she hurried, holding her gown up. Maudie sat alone in a chair near the pool, eating an ice-cream cone, glittering braced leg outstretched before her as she gazed impassively out at the river and the approaching storm. Helen drew near her, bent down and looked into her face, saying, "Come on, dear. Come with me. We're going home now."

Restfully Maudie looked upward, still serene, eyes still tranquil and unmoved.

"Yes, Mamadear."

"Come on now."

"O.K., Mamadear."

Helen took her hand. Over the river thunder broke with a crash, bathers fled from the pool, there were excited voices from the terrace as the first drops fell. The musicians scurried indoors, bearing aloft music stands and saxophones, and on the terrace Milton stood talking with Peyton.

She doesn't hate me. She doesn't. She doesn't. She just can't.

When Peyton pushed haughtily out of the ladies' room and into the lobby, Charlie La Farge was standing in wait for her.

"Peyton," he said, "where ya going? Peyton! Hey, beautiful!" He whistled.

Peyton hustled past and through the ballroom without a word, making for the terrace where music, borne on the wind of the coming storm, still echoed in bright brassy gusts.

"Aw, Peyton. What's wrong? Aw, beautiful!"

All the boys called her beautiful. She was beautiful. Her eyes were brown, always hugely attentive; like her mouth, they lent her face at once an air of thoughtfulness and of inquisitiveness. Her lips, which were just full enough, seemed always slightly parted in a questioning way, as if asking a softly tolerant "Why?" of all those young men who from the time she could remember had hovered about her, their vague, anonymous voices always busy like dozens of bees. Her hair was dark brown and generally cut short so that it closely framed her face, and by the time she had reached twelve she had lost track of the number of small boys who had asked her to marry them.

Now she took a short cut through the golf museum, the pride of the club—a spacious sunny room that opened on the terrace—where, neatly arranged in sparkling rows, were the mashies and niblicks and putters used by Bobby Jones and Tommy Armour in this or that tournament; and golf balls, too, like endless rows of pigeon eggs scarred and cut, with which people like Johnny Revolta won the Western Open way back in 1929. Peyton paid no attention to these; she brushed through the door and onto the terrace: a ribbon of green confetti snaked through space and fell quietly over her hair. Drops of rain like silver dollars began to spatter the flooring and Charlie La Farge, pursuing her, took her hand and said, "Come on, beautiful, let's dance one before it really rains."

She shook her head and withdrew her hand, looking around the terrace.

"Come on, sugar." Wistful, imploring.

She didn't answer. She walked up to her father who, glowing and smiling, was looking down into Dolly's face. "That would make a man rich," he was saying.

Peyton tugged at his arm. "Bunny," she said. "Come here a minute. I've *got* to talk to you."

Loftis and Dolly stopped dancing. "Why, what's the matter, baby?"

"Come on, Bunny, I've just *got* to talk to you. Excuse me, Mrs. Bonner."

Dolly's eyebrows arched dubiously. "Why, honey——"

"Come *on*, Bunny!"

"Excuse me, Dolly," Loftis said.

Peyton shrugged off a boy yearning to dance with her, and drew Loftis into the golf museum. It was dark here. There was a sporting smell in the place, of oiled leather, of tarnished trophies. She and Loftis sat down together on a sofa. Outside in the ballroom the musicians were setting up their stands, in order to proceed with the dance, and the boys and girls rushed in out of the rain.

"What's the matter, baby?"

Peyton began to cry. She let her head fall in his lap. "Mother says I have to go home!"

Well, goddammit, he thought. He had brought his drink with him from the punch table, a drink which he had kept spiked all afternoon, and he took a large gulp and stroked her hair before saying uneasily, "Why, baby? Why'd she say she wanted to do that?"

"Because," she said. "Because—because she said you'd given me a drink of whisky and I told her it was my birthday and you'd given me just one, and just a little . . . oh, Bunny!" She sat erect, clutching his arm, and the tears had disappeared as quickly as they had come. "It was a joke, wasn't it, Bunny? Wasn't it? Tell her so, Daddy!" she said angrily. "I can't go home. That's the worst thing I ever heard of!" She looked as if she might cry again, so he drew her toward him, feeling her arm against his leg.

"Well," he said reflectively, "I shouldn't have given you the drink. That was most likely my stupidest act of the week." It *had* been stupid, he thought. Whisky, of all things, was the perfect bait for trouble. For twenty years it had been a sufficiently extreme dereliction in Helen's eyes for even him to drink; now to allow her to think that he might be corrupting the morals of the young . . . oh, God.

Peyton drew away from him and put an arm on his shoulder. "Bunny," she said, "tell her something. Tell her we didn't mean anything. Tell her, will you?"

He took her hand. "O.K., baby. You won't have to go home. We'll see about that. Now smile."

Peyton didn't smile; she bent her head thoughtfully to one side so that her hair, in short brown waves, partly obscured her face. Then she said in a grave voice which, falling word by word upon his consciousness, made him stir inside with a grotesque and awful fear: "Bunny, I don't know what's wrong. It's absolutely a terrible thing to say and I don't know how to say it it's so terrible. But she's always done these things and I guess she means all right by it and all, but I can't help it, Bunny, I just don't love her." She looked up at him, paused and shook her head. "Bunny," she said again, "I just don't think I love her."

She arose and stood by the couch, her back to him. He got up unsteadily and turned her around and pulled her head down on his chest. "Honey," he whispered, "you mustn't say that kind of thing. Your mother . . . well, she's always been—well, nervous and high-strung and—well, she doesn't mean these things. She——"

"She doesn't have to take me home."

"No. We'll see about that. No. But, honey——" He held her close. A damp, morose fog, part darkness, part alcohol, part his own bewilderment, drifted across his vision. He felt that he loved Peyton more than anything in the world. He kissed her. As for Helen, well, to hell with this kind of business. He held his whisky, again, up to Peyton's lips.

"Now, honey," he said, "don't worry. You go back and have a good time and dance. You won't have to go home." Peyton drank deeply.

"O.K." She looked at him. "Oh, Bunny, you're such a darling."

She gave him a kiss, which lingered lightly as a raindrop on his cheek, and unsteadily left the room. He watched her leave; the door, braked by air, eased to with a hiss, and he was alone in the room, with the golf balls and the trophies and the mauve, descending light. He sank back down on the couch again.

For minutes he sat there, gazing out of the window. The dancing, after eighteen holes of golf earlier in the day, had wearied him; he was drunker than he should be, he knew, with the rest of the evening still to go, but his glass was empty save for two lumps of ice. He thought wistfully of replenishment. Through the doors he heard music, the sound of thumping feet. He imagined that would be jitter-bugging. The window, which was open, let in a cooling blast of air, but also a lot of rain, so he pulled it down, and the woolly athletic smell of the museum fell limply around him. The opposite shore of the river was completely covered by a wall of rain, drooping summer clouds as white as milk; the slope below he seemed to view as if through a piece of green quartz: a murky golf course, deserted, dusty with scudding wind and rain; submarine willows down by the river, so sedate and feminine in the daylight, now filled with tremblings and shakings, lifting their branches like frantic women's arms to the embrace of a rainy sky. An oyster boat moved soundlessly down the river near shore, and Loftis, groggy with warmth and too much whisky, must have dozed; just for an instant, though, because when he opened his eyes—or did he close his eyes at all?—the boat had moved but a few yards along the shore. Vaguely puzzled, anxious, gazing with heavy-lidded eyes at the river, he thought: What was that I dreamed? But drowsing off harmlessly once more, he saw fire, a pillar of smoke that hovered trembling on some remote horizon and grasslike shapes of windy rain, dissolving instantly into light. His eyes snapped open, it was nearly dark; the oyster boat had vanished beyond a curtain of tossing willows.

I need a drink. . . .

Down in the locker room he fished up a pint of Hiram Walker from his golf bag, had a drink, and was returning to the ballroom when he met Dolly on the upstairs landing.

"Why, Milton honey, I've been looking all around for you."

"How's it going, baby?"

"Why, Milton, what's wrong? You look like you just saw a ghost."

"It's Helen," he said. "She said she was going to take Peyton home."

"How silly!"

"Yes," he said.

"But why?"

"Oh, I don't know. I gave her a sip of whisky for a joke——"

"Oh, really. How silly!"

"Yeah." He sighed. "I shouldn't have given her——"

"No," Dolly said. "I mean how silly for her——" She halted, assuming an air of haughty indifference. "Well," she said with a little icy laugh, "you know it's really none of my business."

"No," he said. "I mean that's all right. It was silly. Silly of me, silly of her. But," he added after a thoughtful pause, "she's not going to take Peyton home."

"When did all this happen?"

"Just before it started to rain," he replied, "just a few minutes ago, I reckon. I reckon she suspected something."

"Yes," Dolly said with faint sarcasm, "I imagine so."

Loftis leaned wearily against the banister. "I made one over par for nine and par for eighteen this morning. It near about wore me out." He paused, and she came near him; he smelled her perfume, a sweet pungent odor, intimately coquettish, as evocative and compelling as the scents in those suave perfume advertisements—a fine, secular odor, suggesting undulance and flesh. It was always the same; he had come to identify this scent as peculiarly hers, just as, standing in vague, uneasy and often—later to his foolish surprise—unaccountable anticipation at a party, he would identify the abruptly thrown-open front door, the gay greeting, sometimes too noisy, but always enthusiastic and jolly and warm, with her alone; he sometimes felt that he knew she was nearby even before she entered a room.

He looked at her. She turned and leaned up against the banister, too. The sound of the party was distant, muffled by the walls. "God-dam," he said suddenly. "What kind of bluenosed moral . . . *crap* is that anyhow? Why do you suppose I've got to put up with that sort of thing? Why do you think——" He stopped in confusion. Never before, with Dolly, had he allowed himself to be so outspoken—outspoken, that is, in regard to Helen. Now he felt that for propriety's sake, or for the sake of some obscure sense of decency which prescribes that one doesn't reproach one's wife in this manner, he must

87

repair the damage. He said, "Well, hell—" he gave the banister a sharp smack with the flat of his hand—"maybe I *don't* know how to bring up children!"

"Oh, Milton," Dolly put in sharply, "don't be silly now. Really, it's none of my business but I think it's the craziest thing I ever heard of, her wanting to do such a thing. If I were you—of course as I say it's none of my affair—I'd just tell her what I thought. The idea!"

The moment seemed suddenly to Loftis to have assumed gigantic troubled proportions, of dilemma, of schism and heresy, and of moral strictures so subtle that it was beyond him, a poor lawyer, to plan a safe course of action. The music, from a distance, sent reedy and sentimental vibrations through the walls. The rain had ceased, a faint, tepid light seeped through the windows here, and far off he could hear the last remnants of the storm rumbling eastward, like a multitude of barrels tumbling off over the brink of night. Soon it would be dark.

"Dolly," he began (much too drunk for logic, he felt a curious exhilaration in succumbing to easy sentiment), "you're the only person who understands me, I think."

Her eyes swam up to the edge of her lowered lids, gazed at him tenderly and with what he knew to be understanding.

"I've been in Port Warwick for twenty years. I had great hopes when I arrived. I was going to be one hell of a politician. I was going to burn up the town, the state, everything. At the very least I thought by now I'd be Commonwealth's attorney. Look at me now— a goddam rotten failure, a bloodsucker using my wife's money to get just a little bit ahead, by which I mean to keep as well stocked with bourbon as the next hot shot in town, and by which I mean——" He paused. Confession was not his specialty, and although he enjoyed the mildly tragic sensation it gave him, it also left him a bit breathless.

"You're not," Dolly said passionately. She clutched his arm. "You're not! You're not! You'll become something great. You're fine and wonderful. You've got a terrific quality about you that makes everybody want to be your friend. They want to talk to you. You're positively—why you're . . . *radiant!*"

"Let me finish that for you," he said with a wink, reaching for her glass. Starry-eyed still, she yielded it up like a chalice, and he polished it off in one big gulp. In the little hallway it was getting warm, and he walked over and opened the window. He sat delicately on the edge of the sill, careful that he should get no rain on his pants. Dolly

88

trailed him, skirts rustling. She stood beside him and let her hand rest lightly on his shoulder.

"You know—" he looked upward—"you know, I believe this is the first time I've ever talked to you alone. Beyond nosey ears and eyes, I mean. We've always been so circumspect."

"What does circumspect mean?"

"Careful, cautious, coy."

"Why, Milton," she laughed, "don't you remember one time a long time ago at your place? We were alone then." She squeezed his shoulder, sending a pleasant nervous tremor down through his arm. "The first time you called me sweet kitten. I remember. Don't you remember, Milton honey?"

"Yes." He remembered. That was all a long time ago. A drunken and disastrous afternoon that lay chilled in his memory. He put it out of his mind and thought of Helen. Right now she would be gathering up her things, umbrellas, rubbers, and he would have to go out and face her—with an apprehension that approached terror.

I'm afraid of Helen, he thought.

He put his arm around Dolly's waist and drew her next to him. Her waist was most agreeably soft and through a little hole or gusset in her dress he intruded, before he knew what he was doing, his forefinger, and felt there, beneath the silk, a band of flesh, quite yielding and very warm. Dolly didn't seem to mind so he left his finger there and stroked at the silk while Dolly, silent, softly and a bit timidly at first, began to caress the back of his head.

"But by God," he said suddenly, embarrassed by the silence and feeling the need for some kind of assertion, "it's not that I haven't wanted to be with you."

"Or me either," Dolly said gravely.

It was dark outside, full of mist. A blaze of light illumined the swimming pool; in the woods beyond, a thousand frogs and katydids set up a shrill chaotic chirping. The stars appeared, and the edge of a summer moon, while the lawn tables, the shining Buicks and Oldsmobiles on the drive, all seemed engulfed by a ghostly, placid light through which the music, echoing from a distance, floated innocently out over the terrace and up to the stars. He groped idly, yet with a cunning sort of deliberation, toward the elastic of Dolly's pants; he thought *young, youth,* and "Milton," Dolly was saying, "I've wanted——" She stroked his cheek.

He arose and pulled her toward him. "Dolly," he said, "sweet kitten, I think I love you."

His arms surrounded her. He pressed upon her lips a long and despairing kiss.

Japanese lanterns bloomed over the terrace like swollen, pastel moons, painting the flagstones with an exotic light—orchid, lilac, phantom wings of midnight blue. On the tables crepe banners and paper hats lay strewn amid souvenirs, discarded favors and bricks of vanilla ice cream oozing messily away. The boys and girls had gone swimming. Loftis and Dolly and Mr. and Mrs. La Farge lingered over whisky and soda—at least Dolly and Loftis did, for Mr. and Mrs. La Farge, both of whom had originated in Durham, North Carolina, were teetotalers. The party had been a success; there had been the appropriate noise and disorder, and now three Negro girls went about, past the tables where other mothers and fathers sat drinking, and poked desultorily at the wreckage.

Mr. La Farge was saying, "You're Sclater Bonner's wife, aren't you? How's old Pookie? I haven't seen him in a coon's age." He was a runty, repetitious man with thinning hair and large, stained teeth. He owned a local wholesale grocery, played golf in the high eighties, and was completely overshadowed by his wife, who outweighed him by forty pounds and who was forever chiding him for his grammatical lapses.

Dolly nodded. "Pookie's in Richmond this week on a 'deal,' he calls it. Everybody's all worked up in real estate."

"The war——" Mr. La Farge began.

"Yes, the war, it's so awful," Mrs. La Farge broke in. "Everybody says it's bound to come almost any minute. Poor little Poland!"

"Poor us, you mean," Mr. La Farge said. He leaned back and swallowed part of his ginger ale, revealing in the process a row of stained and horselike incisors. "Poor us," he repeated.

There was a noncommittal silence, modulated by the distant sound of frogs and katydids, and faint shouts and screams from the swimming pool.

"Poor us," Mr. La Farge went on. He spoke in the flat, inflectionless tones of a Piedmont Carolinian, and Loftis, eying him sleepily— he had eaten and drunk too much and yearned to stretch out somewhere—felt that if he and Dolly didn't escape these people at once, he would perish of nervousness. Why was it his lot to be eternally hemmed around by inferior minds, by dentists and real-estate operators and expensive undertakers? To get off more often to New York and take in a musical, meet some interesting people, go to the Alumni

Club—that would be nice. Dolly nudged him with her knee. Take Dolly? But Chester La Farge was saying, "We should keep out of foreign entanglements. It's Zionist Wall Street leading us into war. International raspcallions."

Mrs. La Farge giggled. "Rapscallions, honey," she said.

La Farge made a vast, declaiming motion with his hand. "Rapscallions, raspcallions, it's all the same. The international Jewish bankers are conspiring to send my son Charlie into war, that's all I know."

Dolly and Mrs. La Farge responded in unison with a small interested hum of approval, while Loftis, bored, distracted, looked away. The swimming pool, infinitely far off, it seemed, trembled across his eyes with a filmy distortion, violently green, a cold and uncanny light into which young half-naked bodies seemed to be diving and tumbling with frightening abandon. "Yaaa-y, *Peyton,*" a boy's voice called, rising up over the dark slope along with a muffled splash, and without apparent reason touching him for a moment with a mild and uncertain sadness. He glanced at Dolly out of the corner of his eye: now this was an uneasy position, he thought; here he was sitting here with her, like this. Here he was, in full view of God and God knew who else: Millie Armstrong over there, for instance, who was one of Helen's dearest friends. Involuntarily, he thrust his neck down into his shoulders, as if to feel that they might imagine he was Pookie maybe, or Dolly's old uncle from Emporia—but just then Mrs. La Farge said with maddening directness, "What in heaven's name happened to Helen, Milton?"

"She had to take Maudie home," he replied easily, a bit startled at the simplicity of his lie. "You know——" He made a wan smile, turned the palms of his hands outward, and looked down solemnly at the table—all as if to say, "You know how these things are. This affliction, this burden. At least I know."

"Poor thing," Mrs. La Farge said, "poor child. She tires easily, doesn't she? Maudie, I mean."

"Yes," he said simply. He finished his drink, poured more from a bottle underneath the table, out of deference to a state law which prohibited public display of liquor. Dolly's shoulder brushed his as he bent over and just as this happened it seemed to him, with a vague sense of shame, that the long kiss still burned wickedly upon his lips. His mind drifted backward through the hours and he remembered: How quickly they had parted! It had excited him, that kiss, but it had startled and frightened him, too. Parted not because he had wanted to; feverishly, with all sorts of fumbling and satiny caresses, there as night fell completely, they had clung together: breaking apart for a moment, he felt his heart thumping, her hands on his, all over him—his cheeks, his hair—and gluey lipstick on his mouth. They had agreed in a concerted whisper: We've got to watch out.

"I'll see you later, my darling," she had murmured, and rushed upstairs.

Then the awful business with Helen. Perfectly awful. He had composed himself, thrown a stained red handkerchief down the stair-well and walked out, still unnerved, into the lobby where just at that instant, as he had imagined, she came flouncing out of the ballroom with Maudie and Peyton in tow.

"Hello, my dear," he said quietly.

All nerves, all agony, she was dressed in a black cape, arms full of paraphernalia meant for rain (as he had pictured it uneasily before)—umbrellas, two of them, Maudie's raincoat and overshoes and—the final sad touch—a bottle of aspirin clutched in her hand.

"Somebody sick?"

She pressed Maudie down onto a couch and leaned over, buckling the overshoes on.

"Maudie's catching cold," she muttered.

Peyton came toward him solemnly and wound an arm in his.

"Hello, Papadaddy," said Maudie, looking up with a smile.

"Hello, honey. Listen," he said, bending down and tapping Helen's shoulder; "Listen," he repeated softly, while the blood began to pound and pound at his temples, "let's get this straight, my dear. Peyton's staying right here."

She arose and turned with a wry and forbidding smile, while in a flash he saw her breasts heaving—this and, out of the corner of his eye, the assistant manager of the club behind the desk, a pale overfed man counting stacks of coins, eying the scene slyly through his bifocals, vacant discs of reflected fluorescent light.

She smiled, saying, "Right here with you so you can feed her whisky. Well," she went on smiling as she bent down above the overshoes, lifting, with accustomed tenderness, Maudie's braced leg and adjusting a leather thong, "you've got the wrong idea." A mo-ment's silence. "The wrong idea."

Ah, that's it, he repeated to himself: the wrong idea . . .

He stood there silently, hands in his pockets, watching her. No one said a word. Peyton clung to him, watching her, too, and Maudie, from her perch on the sofa, gazed down calmly at those hands flying over the buckles, straps and thongs. It was a fumbling performance;

she was in too wild a state to do with skill an operation which by all rights, having been for so long a matter of habit, should have required no skill at all. Futilely she tried to press one of the overshoes against the metal brace; it wouldn't go. Loftis, hesitant and afraid, made no move to help her. Or rather merely hesitant, no longer afraid, for he felt somehow, just for this instant, that he was taking part in a casual and unpleasant tableau which, like the tedious Sunday-school dramas he had performed in long ago, was unrehearsed and therefore a dismal nuisance because of the aimlessness, the uncertainty of the movements and the lines. There are these moments: when action is clearly indicated but impossible, and angry words, though desirable and urgent, just won't come; a baffling thing—one can't say these spiteful things and for unnamed reasons: maybe because on such occasions, in an atmosphere of hate and sorrow, there is still a guardian breath of love that hovers in the air.

Perhaps Loftis was too tight; maybe Dolly's kiss, after all these years, had destroyed and erased something. Sober, he feared Helen; for what seemed ages he had lived with her not so much in a state of matrimony as in a state of gentle irritation, together like the negative poles of a magnet, gradually but firmly repelling each other. But now, quite drunk, consciously, arrogantly superior to the situation, he watched Helen fuss madly with the overshoes and the straps of the brace, muttering beneath her breath with fierce, obsessed whispers, and calmly awaited his lines.

The moment came. Peyton's arm fell away from his. Helen arose and turned toward him with a smile while he, smiling too, drifted toward her and took her by the hand. "Now, dear," he said, "come in here with me." He led her into the golf museum with great dignity. As he closed the door he saw that the tableau had dissolved—all the waiting had been an illusion, past forever: there sat Maudie gazing out dumbly into space, Peyton beside her, sad and beautiful; even the assistant manager with his sly inquisitive eyes had turned back to ponder his stacks of nickels and dimes, and the music, which for a moment he hadn't heard at all, filled the night with harmless echoes, as it had before.

"You wait there with Maudie, baby," he called to Peyton, and closed the door behind Helen and himself.

He snapped the lights on. Beneath the self-satisfied photograph of a famous open champion she stood, her back to him, already lighting a cigarette. He sat down in a leather chair.

"Now listen——" he began.

She whirled to face him, outraged. "Now you listen, yourself——"

"Now, not so loud," he said, "least we can do is be ladies and gentlemen."

"All right," she said finally. Almost miraculously, making him uneasy, the tiniest suggestion of a smile appeared at the corners of her mouth, and she came over and sat down on the arm of his chair. There was, he thought, something still imposingly youthful about her in spite of everything—the complaints, the headaches, the moments of eerie and popeyed hysteria—and unaccountably he thought of her, just for an instant, riding a horse in Central Park years before. Where did all the rest of this come from? When?

"Well, now," he said, "what's the matter? What seems to be the trouble now?"

"Oh, Milton," she said, looking down at him, again with the disarming echo of a smile, "what did you give that stuff to Peyton for? Honestly, Milton, sometimes I think you've lost your mind. Tell me," she asked intently, "just why do you let her carry on like that?"

"For heaven's sake—" he groaned—"for heaven's sake, Helen, it wasn't anything. Christamighty, I just let her have a little bit. It's her birthday, for Christ's sake. It was a joke, a joke. What're you trying to make out of the girl, a nun or what?"

"Now don't be silly——" she began again. Her tone, soft and illogically persuasive, made him restless: he knew it well, and although he could somehow adapt himself to her tempers, it was this sudden change of mood that he felt he could never cope with. Here was Woman, with a capital W, tricky and awful, inconstant as the weather. But, "It's the principle of the thing," she was saying. "Don't you understand that? Don't you understand these fundamental things about decency and propriety? Don't you know that something like that, a little thing like that, as you say, can lead to worse things? You know——"

"My dear," he interrupted gently, conscious—though unable to do anything about it—that what he was about to say was cruel and unjust, "if you had ever got beyond Miss Whozis' finishing school you might have got another slant on morals and principles. Morals aren't picayunish little——"

"Milton—" she made an agonized little cry—"why do you talk like that? How can you say a thing like that?" She got up quickly from the arm of the chair—brow, cheeks, even her neck all creased and lined and indignant. She might begin to weep, now, he guessed. "What kind of talk is that? Insults! Insults!" She turned away from him and let her shoulders droop in a posture of humiliation and out-raged pride. "I love *my* God," he heard her say in a small voice, irrelevantly.

"O.K.," he said, rising. "I'm sorry for that. Forgive me." He sighed. "Forgive me."

She turned and said in chilling, ominous tones which from the very beginning, indicating an endless harangue, made him want to get out of there: "There are things that I can never forgive you for. There are a whole lot of things that no matter how long I lived with you I could never forgive you for. We've been building up to this. I love *my* God and you don't, that's one thing. You betrayed us when you stopped going to church; you betrayed not only me but the whole family. You betrayed Maudie and you betrayed Peyton who loves you so. I love *my* God," she repeated, drawing herself up proudly, "and you," she whispered, with a toss of her head, "you don't have any God at all."

"Listen, Helen——"

"Just a minute, Milton. I'm not finished. Let me tell you, too. Let me tell you. I know this. I know what sin is. I know what *sin* is," she repeated, and the word *sin* was like the cold edge of a blade sunk deep somewhere in his body. "I do. I do. In knowing that I'll al-ways be superior to you. *Hah—*" a little blister of a laugh, frightening him—"indeed I do!"

"Now, Helen!" he began to shout.

"Shut up. Wait. Let me tell you. Don't shout. Listen to me for a minute. Don't you think I know? Don't you think I know about you and Dolly? Don't you think I've been able to smell the dirt you've been up to with her? Do you think I'm blind?" She stared at him and shook her head slowly from side to side, accusing, condemn-ing. "Listen, Milton," she said. In her anger she had backed into a display case, and now with a movement of her hips she happened to bump and dislodge two golf balls, precious mementoes, which tum-bled to the carpet and rolled away. "Listen, Milton. I don't care what you do at all. You've spoiled Peyton rotten. You've forgotten Maudie. You've forgotten her! You've destroyed love, you've destroyed every-thing. Listen—" she paused again, lifting her hand—"listen, if you do one thing to harm Maudie, one thing, listen, that will bring shame on that child I'll——" She halted, peered for one terrible moment straight into his eyes as if, perhaps, to find there the ghost of a mean-ing for all this heartache and wretchedness, and then thrust her head into her hands, moaning, "Oh, my God, Maudie's going to die."

He wanted to comfort her a little, but he couldn't bring himself to do it. If it weren't for that kiss, he thought, I'd be in the clear, in the right. Guiltless I could comfort her. She was so wrong. She was so wrong, yet right too. Their paths, diverging in the wood, had gone limitlessly astray, and nothing could bring them together again. Both of them had lost the way. She stood weeping alone. He couldn't approach her. The kiss he had sealed upon Dolly's lips had sealed up for him, also, the knowledge of guilt, and there didn't seem to be any way of going back at all.

He followed her outside. She walked over to the couch and helped Maudie to her feet. Peyton, bending over, tried to help Maudie, too, but only seemed to get in the way, for Helen, shoving Peyton briskly aside, muttered, "Now don't you bother. Don't bother." She began to lead Maudie toward the door. Peyton stood stiffly by the couch, her cheeks flushed, saying nothing.

Maudie turned at the door and waved back at them. "Good-by, Peyton dear. Good-by, Pappadaddy."

Peyton waved and he, too, lifted his hand and watched them disappear, thinking: If only, if only . . . Thinking: If she knew what was true, if I knew what truth was too, we could love each other.

"Bunny, she wouldn't even let me help Maudie."

"She's pretty upset, baby."

She took his hand. "She didn't say anything about taking me home. She just left."

He smiled. "Yeah, baby. I talked her out of it."

She straightened his tie. "Buy me a car," she said, "for Sweet Briar."

"You're too young."

"Come on, honey, buy me a car." She pressed a big smear of lipstick on his neck.

"Gold digger," he said. "What kind?"

"A Packard," she said. "A big old sinful Packard convertible. Red-colored."

"O.K.," he replied. He turned toward the door, thinking that a breath of fresh air would clear his head. Outside, beyond the driveway, rain dripped desolately from the trees. "I'll think it over," he said. "Run along and dance."

Now, as he listened to Chester La Farge's gloomy discourse on war and the fate of the grocery business, it occurred to him simply and with the heady glow of discovery that in this world there was no way of telling right from wrong and, anyway, the hell with it. What had happened had happened and what might happen *would* happen and so he took a drink and let his knee rest against Dolly's, safe in the all-inclusive logic of determinism. The feeling of shame had vanished and the business with Helen seemed not nearly so awful anymore.

My son, most people, whether they know it or not, his father had said, *get on through life by a sophomoric fatalism. Only poets and thieves can exercise free will, and most of them die young.*

The hell with that, too. He had suffered, he felt. He took a drink. Beneath La Farge's unfaltering monologue came Dolly's whisper, "How are you, darling?" and he again pressed his leg against hers and looked into her eyes with a wide gaze of bright humor and longing, as if to indicate the sudden entrance into his life of love and contentment, in place of that huge void which had served in the absence of both these things.

"You might like the President," La Farge was saying, "but, by God, you don't have to like his fambly."

Loftis leaned back in his chair and laughed loudly. So did Dolly and Mrs. La Farge, all three of them in one hilarious accord, laughing, rocking against the flagstones like a trio of hobbyhorses.

La Farge exposed his teeth appreciatively and casually shot his cuffs. "Heh-heh, well——" he began, but far down the river a shipyard whistle made a long and soulless hooting.

"My heavens!" Mrs. La Farge arose. "It's eleven o'clock. Chet, we've got to go!"

"All right, doll."

"Charlie's still swimming, I guess," Mrs. La Farge said. "Would you be kind enough to see he gets a ride home, Milton?"

Loftis had got up. "Why, Alice," he said expansively, "I'd be glad to."

"Good night . . . night . . . night."

All the parents went home, some with their children, some merely with light-hearted entreaties that Loftis not allow Jimmy or Betty to come home too late, and he and Dolly were alone. The Japanese lanterns flickered and died. Violet shadows covered the terrace, his bottle was empty; the moon, big as a gold doubloon, clipped off at one edge behind a wandering cloud, dropped an insouciant light over the river, the lawn and through the strands, airy as spider webs, of Dolly's hair. They were silent. A whippoorwill called from the woods; they both slapped at mosquitoes.

"Well," Loftis said finally, "you just never can tell, can you?"

97

Dolly looked downward. "What do you mean, Milton?" she said softly.

He took her hand. "Funny," he said, "where you end up in this world."

She looked up at him. "How?"

"Oh, nothing," he chuckled softly, finishing his drink. "Sometimes I just wonder what we're here for. Sometimes——" He said something about "the deep," he said something about "the endless night," and Dolly, sleepy, restless, wishing he would kiss her again, reflected that Pookie would never talk of the deep or the endless night. She knew he would kiss her again. Night enfolded them with the odor of pine and grass, the smell of sea, a vast low tide beyond the forest, where shells, rocks and sea things, sad as the universe, lay drowsing beneath the summer moon. They walked together through the empty ballroom to an electric water fountain where each of them had a drink. He bent over and kissed her brow, swaying. In the dark golf museum, shoving her down on a couch, he managed—it was odd, for she was saying, "Oh, sweet baby"—to remember "the deep . . . the endless night," while the door again, easing to, cut off all light from the room, and from his faltering, only half-willing hands.

Charlie La Farge was just sixteen. He was of medium height, nice-looking, with the close-cropped hair that was the fashion among high-school boys that year. Through some happy accident of heredity he had escaped his father's tediousness, while retaining a little of his mother's jolly high spirits and humor. This did not make him anything special, but at least he was good-natured. It was his somewhat hybrid ambition at this stage of his life to be a lieutenant commander in charge of a submarine and to become a bandleader, combining the two so that the easy frivolity of bandleading would not contradict the other, austere side of his nature, which brooded often upon crash dives and the heroic terrors of depth bombs. He also gave women a great deal of thought, frequently to the exclusion of his ambitions, and sometimes his thoughts about women reached such a pitch that he knew his real and only desire was to lose his virginity. Breasts, legs, thighs and other things filled his mind with constant fleshy images, indistinct and maddening, the more so because he had no precise idea of what a girl felt like—although a fourteen-year-old first cousin named Isabel, from Durham, once let him rest one hand, lightly and on the outside of her dress, upon her disappointing little breast. On summer mornings he would awake in an ecstatic heat, half-frantic with the obscure and swollen dreams that lingered in tatters at the margin of his consciousness, and with a groan he would succumb to that private sin his father had vainly walloped him for at the age of twelve, watching the sycamores shake ever so gently, the sparrows that swerved in raucous, terrible haste against the sky.

A year ago he had fallen in love with Peyton. She alone among the pretty girls he knew remained unscathed in his morning despoilments; because he loved her, she alone stayed undefiled, unattainable. In a fashion he had fostered her remoteness, made of her something far apart from lustful considerations, and adored. He had had dozens of dates with Peyton, but he had never kissed her: he was afraid. He would leave her at night at her doorstep and drive slowly around the house—unkissed, balked and frustrated, peering up desolately at her lighted window in hopes of catching sight of her, she who, minutes before, standing at the door, had shown no emotion whatever at his aloofness and his self-control, but had merely said, "Good night, Charlie," touched his hand lightly and vanished into the house. At such times, toying with the idea of self-destruction, he would drive home and go to bed where, crucified, shaken, miserable with unfamiliar insomnia, he would listen to his sister's baby squalling in another room, and attend this solitary vision: He and Peyton had been happily married for some years now, but a trivial argument had come up; her back was to him; she was weeping. She was gazing from their penthouse window at the Manhattan spires and towers which lay below, as if drowning, in the movielike glow of autumn dusk. This light seemed to send tiny golden thorns through her hair. The radio, from distant hidden recesses in the room, played "Maria Elena," a recording his band had made before he went off to war with the submarine service. She wept, he couldn't see her face, and the climax was all simplicity and wonder: approaching her, he laid his hands on her shoulders and turned her about: "Peyton darling, you mustn't cry."

"Go away, you brute."

"Darling, I love you."

"Oh, no, Charlie, I mustn't cry," she murmured while, crumpled and acquiescent—realizing, as if by some transcendental power of autumn, of his strength, music, the power of love—she yielded herself up with a little cry, forgiving and forgiven, into his enfolding arms.

This, his most exciting vision, he turned over and over in his mind and ornamented and examined until it melted away and he fell asleep. The other dreams, fairly routine, concerned endless dancing, separate bedrooms in a Miami château and a good deal of problematical kissing.

Peyton looked slick in a bathing suit. It was made of tight red Lastex which glistened like a lobster shell under the arc lamps of the swimming pool. Dripping water, suntanned, she stood at the side of the pool, removed her bathing cap, and fluffed her hair out properly. A boy named Eddie Collins, standing with Charlie in the shallow end of the pool, was trying to persuade him to sneak off into the woods, where he had a pint of whisky hidden, but he shook his head absently, watching Peyton. There was a great splashing, a shout; some boy rose up like a seal at the side of the pool and heaved a rubber ball at Peyton's head. It bounced off. She laughed, threw the ball back and slid into a woolly robe. "Peyton!" he shouted, but the amplifier—playing music—the shouts, the splashes, drowned out his words, and Peyton, shod in rope-soled clogs, shuffled along the side of the pool and vanished up the slope.

He got out of the pool, dried himself off and put on a terrycloth jacket. He followed her toward the club, hoping to surprise her with a clap on the back or perhaps a horrible and chilling Dracula laugh, for which he had won considerable fame. She walked up the dimly lit front steps and started to go into the lobby but, drawing back suddenly, she paused there for a moment, watching. He halted and hid behind the fender of a car. Then he saw her go into the lobby, softly closing the screen behind her.

He crept up to the door and peeked in. The lobby was deserted, except for Peyton and a fat colored woman who staggered past under a loaded tray. An electric fan whined softly. A bug spanked up against the screen, clung there twitching, beneath his nose. The colored woman disappeared. Very quietly Peyton walked to the door of the golf museum and slowly tried the handle. She pressed downward gently, once, and again without a noise, but the door, it seemed, was locked. For two or three minutes she stood at the door; her head, cocked thoughtfully to one side, made him wince, it was such a lovely thing: he thought of kisses, of love.

She turned away and walked slowly toward him across the lobby. He drew into the shadows, ready to pounce. "Gotcha!" he cried as the screen opened; with a little scream she collapsed deliciously into his arms, then pulled back from him just as quickly, trembling, with a look of horror.

"Charlie!" she said. "Charlie! Oh!"

And fled down the steps and into the darkness.

What had he done?

It worried him enormously; never since he could remember—for he had led a quiet middle-class life, free from emotional extremes—had he seen on a girl's face, or, for that matter, on anyone's face, such a look of desolation. Then he knew. Standing at that door, he figured, she must have seen, or known, something frightening and terrible.

Later, when the other boys and girls had gone home, he searched for her, longing to offer his apologies, and finally found her sitting alone by the pool in the dark.

"Peyton," he said.

A flicker of moonlight crossed her face. She looked up. "Hello, Charlie," she said.

"What's wrong, sugar?" he said, sitting down beside her. "Look," he said painfully, "I'm sorry I scared you. I'm——"

"That's all right," she said quietly. "It wasn't that so much——"

"What's wrong, honey? Tell Cholly boy. What happened up there?"

"Nothing."

She lay back in the grass. He stretched out beside her, shivering a little, and put his arms around her, which was the usual thing to do.

"Nice party, honey," he said.

She was silent for a moment. "No," she said, "no, it wasn't a very nice party. It wasn't a very nice party at all."

"Come off it, kid. You're depressing. Get off this gloom kick, will you?" Kissing her, somehow, mainly occupied his mind, but lying there, feeling her hair brushing at his chin, he knew his head was too high, too far up. He edged down.

She was quiet.

"Honey——" he began.

"Don't," she said. "Don't say anything, please. Just hold me."

He shivered again. "O.K., honey," he said, "I can always oblige."

"Hold me," she said.

This was it, he knew. Desperate, yearning, bending his face toward hers recklessly, he hazarded, out of a year-long desire, the first kiss, coronation.

She turned her head away.

"No," she whispered, turning back to him.

With a shock he realized that she had been crying. He drew her close to him.

"Don't cry," he said, "I love you, Peyton."

"Hold me close."

That was all that happened. She put her arms around him, too, and they lay there like this for a long time silently by the abandoned playground, in the summer night.

The garbage heaps and junk piles have disappeared; the creek, down which the hearse and limousine traveled a parallel route, winds through a lovely meadow. Only the gas tanks, rising from the adjacent marsh, and the remnants of a deserted brewery, disturb the peacefulness of the scene. From here as far as the eye can see stretch the bay, the river and, obscured by a curtain of smoke, the distant sea. In the heat of midday, among the surrounding inlets and shallows, boys go hunting for shrimp; the marshgrass and cattails are motionless; the bleached ribs of a discarded rowboat lie half-buried in the sand, among driftwood, shells, seaweed like crumpled green banners. There is a tarry odor here, a strong smell of sea; above, the flaunting wings of seagulls tilt and recover, over the passing ships, the sound of bell-buoys and the sea itself, where dead men wash and turn and tremble and yield up to remote fathoms—perhaps on a summer noon like this—their inhabiting bones. The meadow is windless and peaceful, insects make a fitful drowsing sound; in August all the Negroes gather here with Daddy Faith, who drives down once a year from Baltimore, to find peace, redemption, the cleansing of the sea.

As the limousine rolled through the meadow Dolly watched the gas tanks approach; they frightened her, and again the monstrous thought rose up fearfully in her mind: He doesn't love me anymore. An act only of desperation, she knew—the way he had come to get her this morning, out of habit alone, maybe, and just because Helen wouldn't come. An awful dread seized her; the car dipped into a depression in the road and instinctively she reached for his arm, as if for support, but held her hand in mid-air, and let it fall on the seat. She closed her eyes: oh, please, God.

Most people in the midst of disaster have yet one hope that lingers on some misty horizon—the possibility of love, money coming, the assurance that time cures all hurts, no matter how painful. But Loftis, gazing out at the meadow, had no such assurance; his deposit, it seemed, on all of life's happiness had been withdrawn in full and his heart had shriveled within him like a collapsed balloon. He was not philosophical, he had never been trained that way, nor had he ever wanted to be. Emergencies had been things to get shut of quickly and to forget, and because in the past he had always been able to create some gratuitous hope, he had never had to believe in God. But hope. Yes: of course. Helen—she will come back to me. Faint, blurred as a mirage, he thought he saw columns of dust wreathing skyward from the farthest rim of the meadow; reflecting sunlight, huge, they ascended, spiraling: he saw weeds, sky, a ghost. I will cure her, make her well. Today I will tell her: our love never went away at all. Sweating, he narrowed his eyes, half-shut: a wisp of a smile flew across his lips—*My love*—and the gas tanks rose abruptly out of the marsh beside them. The air was full of coal gas, the odor of fish. The hearse slowed down, steam billowing from the hood. Then the hearse stopped and Mr. Casper, throwing on the brakes with a jerk, halted the limousine behind it. There was a barricade, distant confusion: music, singing, jubilation. A crowd of Negroes in turbans and white robes were milling around a glistening Cadillac convertible.

"What is it?" Dolly said.

Ella Swan leaned forward on her seat. "It's Daddy Faith," she whispered. Perched on a seat of the Cadillac, Daddy Faith was bestowing grace upon the crowd. He was smiling; his face, black as night, was greasy with sweat. He made a wide arc with his hand, half a dozen diamond rings spun and glittered, and his shiny opera hat and diamond stickpin made beautiful flashes above the throng. A sigh, vast and reverential, went up from the crowd—Aaaaah!—and a shower of dollar bills, nickels, dimes and quarters cascaded over Daddy Faith, over the car and onto the ground. A band began to play, brassy, jubilant—and a big bass drum.

"Happy am I!" the crowd was singing.

Thump

"In my Redeemer!"

"Happy am I!"

"I am so happy!"

Thump

"Those Negroes," Mr. Casper said, "are having some kind of revival or something. We'll have to detour down that road."

Hearse and limousine dipped toward the marsh, lurching over a cinder road. The Negroes rose up above them, unheeding, exalted, a mass of shifting robes, black arms lifted toward the sky, and Ella, peering out, said in a tone infinitely wistful as she turned, raising her hand to wave: "Hey there, Daddy."

The limousine heeled alarmingly. "Oh dear," Dolly said, "where are we going?"

Where indeed? Loftis thought: Does she always have to ask that? The brewery towered over them, brick spires and battlements tumbling into decay. Trumpet vines and Virginia creeper and honeysuckle trailed over the parapets. Loftis looked upward. Now on fine Saturday afternoons amid the damp odor of hollyhock and dandelion, the glow of sunlight on crumbling stone, small boys would throw rocks, shatter what windows were left after all these years and shout fearfully through the echoing, deserted halls.

"Where are we going?"

Where indeed. We are going to bury my daughter, whom I loved.

The gas tanks rose up enormously; the Negroes, all singing, vanished behind those lordly, rustling forms. The Negroes would reappear. The gas tanks were old; God knew how ancient they were. Venomous weeds grew here, and tatterdemalion flowers, white, blue and rose; among crevices in the rust and tangled ancient iron a lizard would peep out drunkenly at the burning sun. Loftis looked upward. Gas tanks as old as time, here in the marsh and weeds, seaward-facing, ageless, from the lovely Virginia shores.

Salt air blew through the car; from the floor arose a thousand motes of dust. The gas tanks swept past. The Negroes reappeared, singing.

> *Happy am I*
> *In my Redeemer!*

Oh, Helen, come back to me.

Four

ALL the way over to Helen's, indeed the entire morning, the Reverend Carey Carr had been thinking: Poor Helen, poor Helen. That and nothing more, for a predicament, overwhelming and hopeless, such as this one, couldn't be helped by piety, or prayers, either; it was the human condition alone that he must minister to, and by flimsy human means, and so it was nothing but poor Helen, poor Helen that he thought, over and over. He drew up near the curb beneath a stoplight. Downsloping, the highway reflected sunlight, shimmering heat, and his automobile, a Chevrolet coupé, began to drift across the pedestrian walk. He pulled the emergency brake, looking around him. There was a clock above a corner barbecue stand, neon-blue in the midday sun. It was after eleven-thirty, and he would be late.

Carey Carr wore spectacles and he had a cleft chin. At forty-two he still looked very young, with round plump cheeks and a prissy mouth, yet to people who knew him this air of cherubic vacancy and bloodlessness, at first so apparent, quickly faded; one knew that this face could reflect decision and an abiding passion. As a very young

105

man, he had tried to embrace all of the beauty of the world, and had failed. At sixteen he was a poet, convinced that the fact that he wasn't very masculine was still somehow tragic, noble even, and born of a fatal necessity. He was an only child. His mother, a widow, had fine liquid eyes, lovely skin which curved tautly over the fragile arch of her cheekbones and drew her lips outward and down, so that it always looked as if she were sorrowing a little over something. But it was really not sorrow. She was actually a sweet, thoughtful woman, with a certain old-fashioned gaiety about her, and she loved Carey more than anything. She encouraged his sensitive nature. When he was seventeen she packed him off to Washington and Lee where an old, famous poet was in residence. But it was a mistake. Beguiled to a certainty of his own genius, Carey wrote a sonnet a day for nearly a year and finally, hopeful but exhausted, took them to the poet—three hundred sonnets in a purple binder—not so much for appraisal as for admiration. What a mistake it was! The poet was a petulant and whalelike man who had resolved most of his problems in eating and in waspish, continual chatter about boys on the campus whom he suspected of perversion. He wrote poetry no longer, and had in fact developed a contempt for poetry in general, except his own, which he recited on Saturday nights to the half-dozen young men who sat languidly on the floor around him drinking sherry. He tried to be gentle with Carey, but only succeeded in brutally telling the truth: the sonnets, the boy knew finally, were miserably bad. He had staked too much upon them, and his failure shattered his health and his wits. He had what was then known as a "nervous breakdown" and was hurried off by his mother, who lived in Richmond, to a Blue Ridge mountain sanitarium.

Eventually his beleaguered soul took strength. He began to read the Bible, at his mother's prompting. The mountains soothed him; his mind soared again, but in a different way: he knew, with the same gathering ardor which had produced the sonnets, that God dwelt in the high slopes. He had had a vision which, it seemed to him in retrospect, had lasted many months. Feverish, his imagination took flight, lifted up into unearthly realms, high valleys smoky with the spirit of the eternal; a blaze of light enveloped him and he knew later it was a glorious thing, for this radiance, surely, had been the light of heaven itself. But then to earth, gently, he was borne on the billow of light—shaken, immolated and vaguely unsatisfied. He resolved to become a minister, to retrieve his vision through a life of hard work and prayer. His mother encouraged him. "Carey, darling," she would say, and her deep liquid eyes would grow soft and her mouth draw down, lovely and sad, "your grandfather was a man of the cloth and his father before him. Oh, it would make me so happy." Perhaps she thought that through the mysteries of theology she could get an even stronger hold on him, keep him for her very own. But here, too, she was mistaken. For when Carey got out of the seminary in Alexandria a few years later he was a changed man. He had put on thirty pounds and through a violent struggle had learned how to swim and play softball, and had in general cast out his womanish failings, even realizing, in this new pleasing maturity, a passionate affair with a girl who worked as secretary in one of the seminary offices. He married her quickly. A year later his mother died, crying in her last delirium that somehow she had been all her life tricked and cheated—of what, no one could presume to say—and imploring Adrienne, who was Carey's bride, to take care of him and love him, as she herself had done.

He had been in Port Warwick for eighteen years, as assistant rector and then rector of St. Mark's Protestant Episcopal Church. He had three daughters, to the youngest of whom, Linda Byrd, age five, he gave a moment's thought now as he paused at the stoplight, since yesterday had been his birthday and he could smell the odor of a shaving lotion which she had presented to him, rising faintly from his cheeks. And as he thought of the little girl—just for a moment intruding upon his thoughts, which all morning had been largely dark and full of melancholy—he smiled, and smelled the shaving lotion. Then he remembered Helen Loftis, and his face became solemn once more, filled with the same youthful, abiding passion—a passion which, though he hadn't ventured to think it such, was partly the strange and tragic sorrow he felt at never having been able to attain a complete vision of God, and partly devotion—devotion to his duty, a small thing, but which he performed as well as he could.

The light remained red for what seemed minutes. A laundry truck swerved out from behind his car and the driver, a youth with bare skinny arms and an underslung jaw, halted the truck with insolent dexterity beside him. The two of them exchanged listless glances and although Carey made the faintest beginning of a smile, the boy turned to study a clipboard with surly concentration. Carey turned, too, sweating, watching the light, still red, and the intersection where a suburban bus labored sluggishly through the heat, borne westward and out of sight as if upon the poisonous violet waves of its exhaust.

The light blinked "Go"; the laundry truck lurched forward, and with a peevish squealing of tires hurtled in front of him, past him, disappearing around behind the barbecue stand. He started forward; the air, circulating around his face, cooled him off a little, and, because of the heat, because of the urgency of the situation, he thought: I've just got to. And he began to speed down the highway at fifty miles an hour.

Carey lived at the opposite side of town from the Loftises. He rarely took this route to the section where the Loftises lived: although a faster way, if one wanted to speed, it was an ugly road, and he was partly conscious of it now: an asphalt highway traversing low marshland, neither industrial nor residential, but occupied by decrepit garages and hot-dog stands and the waterlogged tents of itinerant Madam Olgas and Doreens—palmists mostly—unhappily pitched between the visits of poor, inflamed, neurotic women, astray from God, and the monthly raids of the county sheriff. He saw such a tent now—set off in a grove of trees, with an old foreign woman in apron and spangled bandanna, turning beneath the pines with dim uncertain eyes to watch him. Then she was gone.

But Helen. What would he say to Helen? He feared seeing her, yet at the same time he knew that of all people it was he himself from whom she must draw the greatest strength today. Carey was confused by sorrow. Although he was certain that he felt and saw as deeply as any man, he *was* conservative and diffident by nature, and even after all these years he felt tongue-tied in the presence of those stricken by grief. He was made uneasy by unbraked hilarity and by extremes of sorrow alike, especially the latter; he preferred life to sail along pleasantly and evenly, and this, he knew, was for him a minor sort of tragedy. For, being so guarded and reserved, how could one ever hope to become a bishop?

Across the pinewoods the shadow of a hawk fled, a wraith, as black as smoke; the pines seemed to shake and tremble but the hawk vanished, sailing up over the roof of a filling station, a dusky shadow, wings outspread like something crucified. Carey looked at his watch: he'd have to hurry. He blew his horn, wheeled past another car recklessly, in spite of a third car, oncoming, looming ahead. His heart gave a leap but the maneuver was finished; the driver of the third car, which was not a car at all but a pickup truck, shook his fist as they passed and shouted something obscene. Trembling, he slowed down a little, thinking: That was close, and again: Poor Helen, poor Helen.

The day seemed plunged in horror. She would never cry; what had he been thinking? It was hopeless. She had lost the capacity for love

108

or grief, like a spring in some arid upland, drained dry by the sun. That was the worst of all. What had he been thinking? Lord, he thought, I must make her see the light. I must bring her and him together again. Lord, give me strength. Eager desire swept through him, his eyes became wet with tears. In Niggertown, past tumble-down shacks vined with summer honeysuckle, women in slow, aproned procession along the dusty roads, he slowed down, carefully, thinking of St. Bernard. "O love," he said aloud, "everything which the soul-bride utters resounds of thee and nothing else; so hast thou possessed her, heart and tongue." Wasn't there a way to lift her up, he wondered, make her whole? All the way through Niggertown he thought about this. He drove on. The idea took hold of him; he mopped his brow, pondering, turning onto a road by the shore where far out, alone in his skiff, becalmed, a colored fisherman mournfully evoked the wind—*Lo-ong comin Lo-ong comin*—in a voice like dying.

She had come to him six years ago, he remembered, on a rainy Sunday night in October when the leaves of sycamores lay upon the rectory lawn in drenched disordered piles and a gathering wind, blowing in chill and premonitory gusts from the river, had made him think wistfully of a new furnace and despairingly of his God who, he had prayed, would reveal Himself finally this year and preferably before Advent. It was a season for him of self-searching and vague, amorphous sorrows. The war had arrived and it was a difficult thing for him to speak of faith to people whose faith, so tenuous anyway, had evaporated upon the threatening winds of "a cosmic cataclysm," as he had put it that morning, in an amended sermon. There had been personal matters, too. Termites had eaten up most of the timbers in the basement, directly beneath the dining room; this he had only lately discovered, after a carefree, unwitting summer, and meals in the dining room had become fidgety and precarious, with the constant thought of repair bills giving him worry. Other bills were piling up: his two little girls were going through their year of childhood ailments, and had exchanged diseases in the careless way of children; he owed the pediatrician two hundred and forty dollars. In fact, it had been seeing the doctor on this particular night that had heightened his mood of quiet despair.

He had been standing at his front door; Adrienne had gone upstairs with the children, the younger of whom seemed to be coming down with something. "Nothing serious," the doctor said; "Don't worry." And he went down the steps. Standing on his glassed-in porch with a prescription in his hand, watching the taillight of the doctor's car recede into the night, it had occurred to him, as it had a thousand times before, that it was the most awful thing—you went through life expecting things to get better, hoping for the vacant, idle day when you would be free from worry, and although you were conscious of the folly of expecting a giddy bright time like that, you nevertheless went on hoping, sustaining your poor illusions: he groped for something meaningful—but his thoughts dwindled off into a prosy and confused prayer which he left half-completed. He gazed at his lawn, the seawall, the river beyond. The sycamores tossed nakedly; the faintest moonlight, yielded up through a rent in the clouds, outlined silver fish stakes, whitecaps, the masts and booms of sailboats upraised to the heavens like silver, suppliant arms. Cloud shadows fitfully crossed and darkened the moon which suddenly seemed too wild and ghostly for Port Warwick, and it was through this light, just as he was about to turn, that Helen Loftis approached him, alighting from her car, alone, and rushing up the walk in the rain.

He took her hand. "Helen Loftis," he said, "what brings you out in the rain?"

There was a constrained and agitated motion in the way she removed a green silk scarf from her hair, shaking it once so that the fine drops of rain scattered away, but she laughed as she stepped onto the porch, saying vaguely, "Well, I just thought I'd come."

He was surprised, mystified from the very beginning. But helping her off with her raincoat, he made casual talk, as if it were the commonest thing in the world to receive one of his flock—a lone married woman, at that—at ten-thirty in the evening, and he was worried about being in his shirtsleeves.

"Well," he said cheerfully, "this is a very nice surprise. Adrienne'll love to see you. I hope I can get her down here. She's upstairs with Carol——"

She touched him lightly on the hand. "No," she said intently, but with the same disarming smile, "you let her stay. I want to see *you*."

"Oh." He laid her coat on a table and, embarrassed, a welter of silence surrounding both of them, he led her to his study: a converted side porch, paneled in ugly oak, upon which varnish lay dark and shiny like lampblack, a place he had always considered both austere and cozy, because of the artful mingling of the secular and the orthodox; a Velasquez reproduction, for instance, dominated one wall, yet upon the adjoining wall there was the presiding bishop, handsomely framed and autographed. He could work here, shut away from the family, or just meditate. On his severe boxlike desk there was a silver
110

crucifix he had bought in Canterbury years before. Swiveling about in his chair, he might simply gaze at the pitilessly romantic stretch of waves and shore: deep blue and placid, but often given to wild moody squalls. Both crucifix and river, in their different ways, sometimes offered contentment and poignant, fugitive hints of another world.

He seated Helen and opened a window, to let out the stuffy air. He turned. "Will you have a drink, Helen?"

"No," she said, "no, thanks." Then brightly, "Yes, yes, I will. I'll have just a little whisky in a glass. Neat."

He smiled. "All right. I'll just be a minute. Let me get my coat, too."

"Don't bother, Carey," she said quickly. "All this formality!"

Something about her—her aimlessness, the way she stirred in her chair—made him uneasy, but he laughed elaborately and patted her on the shoulder, leaving her to thumb through a copy of *Life* as he went out to fix the drinks. In the kitchen he opened a drawer, poking about amid a heap of egg beaters, ice picks, spoons, for a bottle opener, and it was then, startled (for until that moment—perhaps because he was sleepy—his mind had been almost totally blank), that it occurred to him what Helen had come for. Not precisely. Because, even so, what would she want with him, to arrive so nervously at this hour of the night, and in the rain? But he thought he knew: there had been all that talk—scraps and hints and winks which he had taken note of at gatherings and which, as he had told Adrienne, set his teeth on edge.

They had begun just lately—rumors about the Loftises, rumors about "another woman," whisperings which disturbed him not so much because they concerned the Loftises—whom he didn't know too well, in any case—but because they upset his notions about the prevalence of human decency.

"Well, after all, dear," Adrienne had said—in the occasional brittle way she had, combing her blond, lovely hair at night with that brisk, self-assured, woman-of-the-world gesture which he had never dared tell her *really* set his teeth on edge, tossing the words over her shoulder—"well, after all, dear, you know extracurricular sports like that are not entirely new to the human race. If Alice La Farge let that fall it was because she talks too much anyway and she really should have had better sense in front of the clergy, but, after all, most everyone knows or at least should be able to tell that Helen Loftis is a *nest* of little hatreds. I can't say that I blame Milton much anyway. In France——"

But, "Adrienne!" he had said sternly, "I won't have that sort of talk," and then, mollified, sitting down beside her on the dressing stool, *patiently* telling her that he knew of course she was joking, that it was true this was not France, that, as he had pointed out before, the glory of this latter-day Protestantism was its liberality; however, she very well knew that the home was sacred, et cetera—of course she had been joking, they both laughed then—and so on and so on. That had been months ago, he had forgotten it; even so, for a while vague conflicting visions had possessed his mind: of Loftis, handsome, good-natured, talkative, for whom (since despite Carey's biennial urgings he had humorously refused to become a vestryman, or even to attend church) Carey had conceived a mild dislike; and of Helen—how could they be a match for each other? She had come prompt and obviously alone to Sunday school each week, herding the two girls, those amazing, dissimilar children—who *did* look feverish and unhappy and cold. *Cold* was the word; he thought of Loftis and of Helen, and then of Adrienne, who was really quite gentle, steadfast and full of the warmest and sweetest passion. And then he had put it all out of his mind.

He drew on a sweater and turned out the kitchen lights. When he brought in the drinks to the study—rye for her, a little brandy for himself—he was thinking wearily: If I had been a Baptist everything would be black and white, I'd pick and choose, either sinfulness or sinlessness. But Helen, standing at the window, turned to face him. She looked gently composed, casual, but he thought she had been crying. He tried not to notice.

"Sit down, won't you, Helen?" he said quietly, and took his seat behind the desk. "Now, what can I do for you?" Was he being too officious? "Business or pleasure?"

She took a handkerchief from her pocketbook and noisily blew her nose. Then she began to sip her whisky cautiously and with distaste. The chair squeaked and wailed beneath him as he leaned back to close the window; outside a gust of wind caught a pile of leaves, sent them whirling upward across the lawn. Finally she said in a shy voice which, if it weren't for the solemn way she was looking at him, he would have thought almost flirtatious—*cold though*, he was thinking—"Carey, don't you hate *hurt* women?"

"Why, Helen," he said, with a smile, "I don't think I know what you mean. What——"

"I mean," she broke in, "don't you despise women who are so insecure or stupid or something—maybe both—that they're always running around crazily trying to find something to hold on to. You know what I mean."

112

"No," he said, "I don't despise them. I think I know what you mean, though."

"Those kind of women," she went on, "are always *hurt* women." She paused. "That's what I call them." She looked away from him, out of the window. For a moment she seemed very grave and studious, calmly analytical. But there was nothing grim about all this. Indeed, she looked very handsome: he wondered how old she was. About forty—like some advertising man's idea of a woman professor, with impossible, lovely skin and placid, unprofessional eyes. It was a remarkable thing, for she never had seemed interesting to him before, and he suddenly had the impulse to make a joke—but she turned and said in a wistful voice: "Oh, Carey, I don't want to be a *hurt* woman." And then, brightening a little, "Can I tell you these things?"

He was not tolerant of her self-pity; his mother had had the same disease. Yet he said, "Go on, Helen, tell me what's the matter."

"I've wanted to come and see you for a long time, Carey."

And "Helen, you should have come," he replied.

"I would have come but I've been scared of everything. Scared of myself in a way, because I've been carrying these things around for so long, keeping quiet, keeping secret, you know, feeling that if I let them out, why I'd somehow be betraying myself. That understanding I've got, you see, which is so horrible in a way. I mean, knowing that the fault's mine partly. Not all, mind you—" her eyes were level upon him, and once more he had the impression that she knew exactly what her trouble was, but that the difficulty was in the telling of it—"not all," she repeated, accenting the word *all*, "but enough to know that if I stayed burdened with all this too long I'd go crazy. Dr. Holcomb——"

She paused, raised her hand with a sort of swift, harassed motion to her throat. "I won't tell names!" she said. "I won't tell names!"

"Shh-h, Helen," he cautioned, and Adrienne, in a bathrobe and hair curlers, peered in the door for a moment: "Excuse me—" with a cool nod to Helen—"Carol's all right now. I'm going to bed."

"Good night," Carey said.

"Good night, dear."

"Good night," Helen said. The door closed. "I won't betray anyone. No one at all," she said excitedly. He held out a match for her cigarette, the third she had smoked, in chain fashion, and which she held to her lips with quivering fingers as she bent toward him.

"Take it easy now, Helen," he said softly. "Finish your whisky."

She did as she was told. He watched her, and then, when she had put the glass down, he listened. She was calmer now. He turned his eyes away and looked out the window. A misty driving rain filled the night. From isolated branches the last leaves were falling in endless spirals of loneliness. He sensed a strange kinship with this woman: what was it? But, eyebrows cocked a little, attentive, he heard her say: "I couldn't put it out of my mind, the idea of them—Milton and this woman, Mrs. X—which I'll call her since I have no intention of betraying her, even in her guilt. I couldn't put it out of my mind. It was enough to drive you crazy. You see, I've known about the two of them for a long long time—six or seven years, at the very least. I'm afraid that all my life I've been very sensitive about right and wrong. My parents were Army people, and it was funny in a way: They were strict and severe with me, not a bit like some people might imagine Army people to be. My father was on Pershing's staff during the war. His own father had been a chaplain and Daddy was very religious. 'Helen,' he'd say, 'Helen, sweetheart. We must stand fast with the good. The Army of the Lord is on the march. We'll lick the Huns and the devil comes next. Your daddy knows what's right'—and go swaggering off in his jodhpurs and riding crop, and I thought he was just like God. The men loved him. He put the fear of the Lord in them, sitting on his horse (he was in cavalry then, and you've never seen anyone mounted so handsomely, so commanding. Really commanding). Fort Myer, with the beautiful woods and the river so full of the softest pastels—you could see them at evening parade. And Daddy on his mount—a silver gelding it was, named Champ, I remember. Daddy saying: 'I'll tolerate no misconduct in my outfit. We're marching like men to war, not like rummies and sinners.' They called him Blood and Jesus Peyton. And I standing by the parade ground, sixteen or so, watching him. The men just loved him."

Carey stirred uneasily and lighted his pipe.

"And severe and strict he was. But it was good for me. I learned what's right and what's wrong. We'd go to chapel every Sunday, no matter where we were. And when we sang hymns I'd watch him out of the corner of my eye—the way he sang so loudly in a lovely proud baritone and his mustache flicking in a stern and impressive way.

"Oh, but yes. You see, for a while we were happy, Milton and I. You'll never know. Then there were the four of us; we lived in an apartment up by the shipyard. We had an old broken-down Ford and on Sundays there'd be the four of us driving out to the beach, lying in the sun, picking up shells. Once the car got bogged down in the sand just as we were ready to go home, so we left it there until seven or eight that night, not caring, and went back and sat in the sand and watched the sun go down and drank chocolate milk, with Maudie and Peyton who were five and four then, I guess, respectively. Wasn't that a happy thing, to let your old broken-down car just stay stuck in the sand, while you went back to the beach and drank chocolate milk?

"But that was happiness, something else. I couldn't put this thing out of my mind. Let me tell you. . . ."

Long ago he had begun drinking. She had no idea what it was; maybe his need for her died, if Carey knew what she meant, or maybe it was Maudie, his disappointment and all that. An awful, awful thing, but it was that that she suspected the most—the last—though, as she said, it might have been both. Well (as Carey should realize), she was no prude, but he began drinking all the time—and it was then that he stopped going to church. Oh, she could see it all coming so very plainly. One has no idea what it is to stand by quietly and watch those bricks you've so carefully put together—safe and sound, you thought—crumble away, begin to topple off. It starts so slowly, takes you by surprise and sneaks up on you a little more month by month until then, at one point, you look around and discover that this whole structure you've so carefully built—and not yet completed— has begun to dissolve like sand in water, melted off with all the cruel underneath edges showing, so that you want to throw a cloak over the whole mess—your pride wants that first—and then, later, wanting not so much to hide it all but frantically to pick up those fallen pieces and by some shrewd, decorous masonry to repair, repair, saying, "Oh, please stop, please stop," all the while.

His drinking. And his way with Maudie—nothing obvious, Carey must understand, but insidious and unfeeling and utterly detestable. How could he do such a thing? And then the woman, Mrs. X. She was the thing, Helen said, which had torn off her skin of decency and reason, had stripped her naked with the meanness showing.

For six years (Helen went on)—long after she had reconciled herself to such a way of living, where her only hope was to recoup each loss as gracefully as she could, not fuss, but to supply her soul each day with new attitudes, new bulwarks, new hopes—for six years she had watched him turn to this woman, following his stupid progress as she might a fly in a spider's web, down in some ugly cellar—indifferent all this while, aloof, and only a little sad: look! they're apart, yet touching each other, antenna-wise—a lewd and diligent woman and her poor Milton who, fascinated, tries vainly to pry himself out of that awful mess. Flies and spiders, the underground chill. It was easy: though she couldn't see them, she sensed a trembling, acquiescence, the sweet convulsive entanglement. Done. How many times she couldn't tell. Victory for that other woman. And oh, her poor Milton.

Yet how could you really be sad about all this when sadness belonged to a long time ago, to memory?

So damn them both, she said. God please damn them.

It was a sinful thing, but she was righteous, wasn't she, wanting to see them swallowed up in their own filth? Carey would never know how hurt she was.

"Why can't a man stay with the wife who loves him so? You could see this injustice. It made me sicker and sicker; each night I prayed that this wouldn't go without reproach. But sin. Haven't I sinned, too? God, what is sin? Sometimes the logic of this life defeats me so completely that I think there isn't any reward here on earth, or vindication. Sometimes I think life is just one huge misunderstanding and God must be really sorry for confusing the issues so.

"Listen—

"Two weeks ago, after supper one evening, we were sitting on the lawn beneath the willow tree. It was the day before Peyton was going off to school, and I had been helping her pack all afternoon. The next day all four of us were planning to drive up to Sweet Briar. I had been tired and hot—I'd driven downtown that afternoon to get Peyton a new handbag and a hat, and I'd had to contend with the crowds—you know how it is. Then after the iced tea and coffee I felt relaxed. You see, a week or so before, at a dance I'd given Peyton, I had had a fight with her which had worried me for a long time, but we had 'come around,' you know, and weren't angry with each other anymore. We'd had so much fun, really, packing and all and getting excited together about going off to school, that I felt very happy— even along with that sort of sadness you get when you know your child's leaving you for the first time—and so I just sat there and watched the ships going out to sea and the hummingbirds in the flowers—things like that, you know. Maudie said she had a headache, so I helped her upstairs and gave her some aspirin and told her to lie down for a while and call me when she was rested. And she said, 'Yes, Mamadear,' and then she lay back on the sheets and closed her eyes and in a moment she was asleep. She has so little trouble in finding sleep, poor girl. . . ."

Carey thought: Come to the point. But he listened closely. She

116

went on, telling him how she had stood by Maudie's bed and watched her for a while. The sun had already gone down, leaving a foggy light around, filling the room with shadows. She could hear Ella shuffling on the porch below, Milton and Peyton talking together on the lawn, sudden laughter—that was all. It was still summer, but there was something of fall in the air; you can feel it at this time of the year— the moment's pause at sunset when the wind dies, when into this hollow of silence a cool breath rushes, and a single leaf falls from an oak tree—*tick-tack-tack* it goes, falling through the twilight—as if it had been touched by something perilous and final and strange. She had stood there smoking a cigarette, looking at Maudie and around her at the shadow menagerie on the walls—the pigs and kittens and ducks in sailor suits which stayed because Maudie still wanted them there; now they seemed to achieve a fragmentary sort of motion in the dusk and danced and jigged and nodded ever so slightly if she watched them long enough. But even as she watched, they began to diminish, first in the corners and then above the bed—pigs, ducks, kittens and all, silently dancing, receding one by one. Down below she heard Peyton, very gay: "Bunny! That's not *so*, silly."

The instant comes—a word, a color, a breath of wind—and there you are, thinking *Life is not bad, this peace will go on and on*—and pop! like starbursts such reflections scatter away and then come frightful thoughts of death and dying.

"Bunny, that's not *so*, silly!"

Maudie stirred and turned and slept. Helen went to the window. She could see them below beneath the willows, Peyton on the arm of his chair as together they looked at something—a paper or a catalogue; Peyton was stroking his hair. He was in his shirtsleeves; through the bars of the chair you could see the damp places beneath his arms where he had been sweating.

"She sat next to him," Helen said. "Her back was to me, too. She was in shorts; I could see her hips, the cotton drawn tight against them and shameful things occurred to me: that that body which I bore . . . no, I won't repeat it. Yes, then. That that same body which was part of mine (the way she was pressed against him now, you could tell already how not-so-innocently good she was at doing with men— you know, even though I don't mean with Milton) . . . I thought of it. Yes, I did. Stretched out in the woods at Sweet Briar, astray from home and unsupervised and all the rest. *So* vulnerable to some sleek boy from the University. And all the rest. You know. I'm her mother. I thought all this. And I kept on watching, hating too."

She couldn't remember how long it all lasted. Motionless in her hand, the cigarette burned down and ashes fell to the windowsill. Five minutes perhaps . . . and behind her she could hear Maudie breathing. What happened to her in that time? She felt that the devil stood by her side while she looked at them, while the cigarette burned down and this cold and threatening silence took possession of the house, the lawn, the dying sunlight, and each natural blade of grass and flower and bush around them: the hummingbirds had vanished, the trees were absolutely still. He said: *Look at them, look at their sin, look how they have betrayed you both: you and that feeble beloved heart behind you that must vanish soon. One has betrayed you through infidelity and one through vice and meanness: the ingratitude of a shameless child.*

So she watched them from the window and, as she did, it seemed that everything wrong and hateful in the world had gathered around the house and the lawn, drawn there in the evening for one brief moment and still more unbearable because she knew she was being evilly tempted, knew that their guilt was no worse than her own. Something happened then. During the instant she heard that voice it seemed that time itself had stopped: nothing stirred, no leaf fell; beyond the shore the incoming waves lay without motion in piled-up billows, suspended one behind the other in endless, furrowed procession around the bay, as silent and unyielding as if they had been carved from glass. The evening wind had frozen in the trees. Below, Milton and Peyton sat like statues together, and Peyton had one hand raised to a place where sunlight had gathered in her hair. There was no sound or movement anywhere, except for the furious quick beating of Helen's heart.

Something happened. Wind rustled in the trees again, a leaf fell, children shouted far off, and as once more the waves began to wash against the sand, Peyton's arm went around his shoulder, he looked upward, they laughed and turned their heads down to read—all as if her mind had been a film projector in which the film had stopped to offer her motionless detail of the scene before her, and had just then, at this instant, begun to move again. The anger disappeared and, she told Carey, her only distress was in knowing that she would feel this way once more—in five minutes, ten, a day, a week. How could she tell? But for the time she felt unburdened: the light was as gentle and lovely as it had ever been: the hummingbirds had returned to nod and bump around her flower bed; Peyton's voice, now teasing—"Well, I don't care what *you* say, Bunny"—filled her with pain and longing.

118

"I kissed Maudie and went downstairs again and sat with Peyton and Milton on the lawn."

Here Helen had paused, Carey remembered, and had turned away, confused, with the air of one who has said, "Let me tell you a story," only to stop midway because she has forgotten the way it's all supposed to end.

He leaned forward, clearing his throat, and said: "So you had a moment of real hatred—or evil and temptation, as you put it?"

"Yes," she said, after a pause. "Yes, I guess that's it."

"And you feel you've sinned because you yielded to that temptation with anger?"

"Partly," she replied, "it's partly that——"

"But, Helen," he said reasonably, wishing she hadn't stopped at this point where, to cover up the embarrassment of silence, he could only temporize, "Helen, that's not really bad, you know. All of us have shameful thoughts. Why, if the mind of the average person—*average*, mind you—were exposed to public view I daresay he'd be stoned to death in a minute. Of course, in the light of inward health it's no doubt a finer thing if one could control one's impulses, put them away before temptation really gets a foothold—did you ever read Montaigne?"

"No."

"Well," he said, thinking: Here's an intelligent woman and rather tragic at that—but actually it was the tragedy of frustration, probably sex, and if you could just humanize her and—well, what else . . .

"Well," he went on, "get his essays and read 'On Some Lines From Virgil,' on the advantage of casting out demons before they populate your mind. That's——"

"But listen," she interrupted. "Let me tell you! Let me go on!"

"Oh."

"Can't I tell you?"

"Why, yes."

She went on, and he relaxed again, looking at her thoughtfully. Really an odd woman. And how nice, a member of his church . . . and all that business about evil. It showed that perhaps they weren't all asleep. Of course, it was true: what he knew of psychology had led him to believe that too powerful a consciousness of evil was often the result of infantile emotions: hence primitive fundamentalism, especially the American brand, which he scorned. The cowardly Puritan, he had always thought, or the cowardly fundamentalist, unwilling to partake of free religious inquiry, uses the devil as a scapegoat to rid himself of the need for positive action: "The devil *forced* me," he says, instead of, "I turned my eyes from Christ's example," and by this process of negativism is enabled to perform any crime under the sun against humanity and reason. But this woman seemed different: in spite of her confusion, something strong and sincere and questing emanated from her, and he was moved to sympathy. She wanted no substitutes. No Montaigne. Really an odd woman—at least different. As for the devil: that still sounded like so much bosh, but let her have her symbol—at worst it was merely childish. His mind had been straying around; he thought of the neo-Orthodoxy, and he wondered sometimes if he wasn't in need of a symbol himself.

"I sat there for a while," she continued. "I was knitting. Ella came and went, carrying away cups and dishes, and then finally Milton folded up the card table and took it into the house. I looked at Peyton. She was curled up in a chair reading one of those information booklets that colleges send you when you're a freshman: where to come and who to see first and the rules and all that. I said, 'I think that hat will go well with the new suit.' Then she just said, 'Mm-hhh,' and I said, 'Of course, red will go well with it, too. The suit, I mean. It's a fall color.' And she said, 'Mm-hh,' again, just that. In that inattentive, sort of half-hearted way I've become accustomed to. Even with Milton she does it, although there's no wonder: he's spoiled her rotten. That hat, you see—at the last minute we remembered she needed one, and it was I who drove down in all the crowds and heat to get it for her. I picked out a nice one, too. She liked it right away. But her insolence. I put it aside in my mind: It's her way, he's caused all that, and besides I've always said, 'She's young, she's young.' I said, 'Remember, dear, like I told you you should change your sheets once a week. Put the bottom sheet in the laundry bag and take the top sheet and put it on the bottom. . . .' Silly details about going off to school, but I was concerned, you know. She looked up scowling, as she often does with me, prissy-polite, you know, and she said, 'Mother dear, for heaven's sake you've told me all about those things,' and turned to read without another word. That did it. I was only trying to help, but he's done these things . . . Never mind. I tried to keep the anger out of my voice and I said something like 'All right then, O.K.,' or something. Then I put my knitting down and got up and went to the flower bed."

She wished she could tell Carey how much her garden meant to her. Whenever the dreadful depression came back, she would fly toward her garden as one dying of thirst runs toward water. She'd pluck and

120

weed and pick, and as she knelt on the cool ground she felt, she said, absolutely rooted to something firm and substantial, no longer a part of the family. Now her back was to Peyton. Presently she heard Milton's footsteps on the terrace, then heard him as he sat down heavily next to Peyton. She heard the clink of ice, too, which meant, of course, that he was drinking.

He started to say something to her—"Helen dear," he began—but he said nothing else and she didn't answer. He talked to Peyton, they talked together—trivial, harmless things, father and daughter—it didn't matter what they said. For five or ten minutes she knelt there. The sunlight was dying fast, and to make the most of this contentment she had to hurry, plunging her fingers into the soil, pulling up weeds which she laid on a paper beside her, leaning forward from time to time to smell the blooms.

Ella Swan came out on the kitchen porch with her hat on. "Well, good night all," she said in her shy way; Peyton and Milton told her good night and Helen turned and called good-by to her. "Good night, Ella," she said. "Remember I'd like you early tomorrow morning." She watched her standing on the porch, partly obscured by the willows, old and bent and stooped-over, dressed fantastically in one of the cast-off gowns Helen had worn in the twenties, looking like a wrinkled ape someone had costumed for a side show in silk and tassels and clinging beads. She raised her hand to her eyes, squinting at Helen, although the sun was behind them.

"Mr. Loftis has to leave early to take Peyton up to school," Helen said then. She spoke in a bland yet not unfriendly tone—with what she hoped was just the right inflection—so that although her accent was impersonal it was also *excluding* in effect, making plain to Milton that somehow she had been insulted. The "Mr. Loftis" had done that, she hoped. And already, she told Carey, she knew that by those unfortunate words she had committed herself—knew that she wouldn't be going with Peyton to Sweet Briar.

"Because of her insult?" Carey said.

"I guess," Helen said.

"It didn't sound like much of an insult," he replied. "What Peyton said."

"Let me go on."

So Ella said, "Yes, ma'am," and hobbled down the gravel walk, *crunch crunch crunch* beneath the trees, and was gone. Helen continued her weeding; Peyton and Milton said nothing to her: she could feel their silence at her back, feel them even eying each other significantly, and because of this the same old bitterness came back.

I will not yield to this, she said to herself. *I will not yield to this . . .*

And struck through the earth with her trowel. She looked up, thinking *I will not yield to this despair;* saw waves, sky, clouds high above Port Warwick, where twilight hung like umber, or the most faultless rusty shade of gold. Her mind spanned forth, encompassing some small vision of the future. It was silly, and so easy: to think of a moment when time has run down like an old woman's heart, and the house on a sunny Sunday afternoon is full of grandchildren and, venerated, you rise to face the love of those who call you by name, being able to say then *accomplished, accomplished.* So that's what she thought. They made no noise now, but it didn't matter. She looked up past the beach, the bay, thinking: I will not yield. God willing, this sun will shine on me in the peace of my last days when Milton and I love each other once more, and I'll be old but happy then because Peyton loves me too; I'll have seen this through. . . .

But there it was. She looked down then, even smiling some, she recollected, prepared to get up at the sacrifice of pride and go sit and talk with Milton and Peyton; she looked down where her trowel had sliced through the earth and saw that it had cut a pomegranate root right in two. You could see it, she said, the buried ends exposed and green and moist, brutally severed.

"Carey," she said, "I wonder what these moments are that come to fetch us off into desperation. The pomegranate root. You see, I'd been on my knees trying not to yield, seeking God's help. *Teach me to love,* I'd been saying. I remember it all. I thought I could get up from my garden and decently, patiently, face those people who've harmed me the most. I'd show love and kindness. But it wasn't just that root, bleeding and ugly as it was; it was something else behind me. Peyton's voice. *So* undisciplined, *so* crude. Saying something like, 'Bunny, quit pinching me!' And the way he went on, 'Why, baby, I'm shocked!' and hers again: 'You're *mean*,' things like that, and the sniggering and giggling back and forth."

It was all these, she went on, but not alone: this other voice which she loved more than any on earth, floating through the dusk to touch her like hands: a voice, Maudie's.

At the window. She had wakened Maudie when she'd called to Ella.

Helen turned. Peyton said, "I'll get her, Mother," and was up and across off the grass before she could rise or even move. Then she struggled to her feet, her mouth open: "Wait, no!" she began. "As

122

God is my witness——" but only watched those smooth young wanton legs, limp-kneed, moving across the lawn and into the house, Milton sitting spraddle-legged in his chair, glass in hand, turning lazily to see Peyton disappear beyond the door, his red neck swelling, enlarging as Helen approached on the run, digging in with her heels past the lawn chair.

"For Christ's sake, Helen! What's the matter?" His hands on her shoulders, holding her.

"Let me go! She wants me. I won't have Peyton——"

"What's the matter with you? Get hold of yourself!" Shaking her now, his face red and frightened, one hand clamped on her shoulder, the other behind her neck, wet and cold where he had held the glass.

And she was shouting, "Let go of me! I'm going up there. It's my baby. I'll not have Peyton——"

But suddenly she was better, calmer—realized this craziness. The anger fell away: he was pressing her down in a chair, saying, "Helen, Helen, for Christ's sake." And then, more gently, saying: "Poor baby, you're all tired out, that's all. Take it easy. Take it *easy*, for Christ's sake. Maudie's all right. Peyton'll take care of her."

She sat there, not looking at him while he bent over her.

"You've got dirt on your forehead," he said, "right there." Touching her brow with his finger. She said nothing; however, she recollected, she supposed that at this moment she was thinking in an odd repetitive way: Yes, she'll take care of her; Maudie's all right. Not with relief or comfort, as she should have, because although she knew Peyton would take care of her, she still wanted to be up there and she couldn't get this wild false notion out of her mind: usurping my place, that's what; it's not enough that she play with Milton but now she goes to Maudie too. False, she knew, but she wanted to get up then and push Milton out of the way. She wasn't frantic about this; she wanted just to get up calmly and walk upstairs to Maudie. But she was afraid of revealing herself; the guilt was returning. She feared a new, ugly crisis with Milton: they had had too many arguments, too many.

Now he was gentle with her: "Let me brush it off, honey," pulling out his handkerchief and wiping her brow. She let him, sat there fidgeting, breathing in uneasy gasps. "There, it's all off," he said finally. "Now relax, baby." How could he be that way, so tender, pretending that nothing had happened between them? She wanted to get up then, started to, but thought better of it: I won't let him see; he's seen too much already. She sat back, avoiding his eyes. Night

123

was coming, and wind: the willows were tossing up and down. She heard Maudie's voice and Peyton's above her, then his, very gentle: "Well now, Helen, why don't you take it easy tonight? Just until she goes. Then she'll be gone."

That awareness. He knew. And to think that all along she should not have considered it: he knew. Part of a dream flitted across her mind: the gesticulating silhouette of a crazy female, no more than a shadow, which always came just before she went to sleep. Then she thought: how could he believe that Peyton hates me when—*I've been a good mother, I've done what's right.*

"There wasn't any reason for him to believe that, Carey, was there?" she said. Carey noticed she had almost ripped her handkerchief to shreds.

"There wasn't any reason for him to believe that Peyton hated me. Even I—and I've been close to her—even I couldn't think something like that. Wasn't what he said cruel, Carey? Wasn't it?"

"You mean," Carey answered, "that what he implied was that *you* hated Peyton. Isn't that what you mean?"

"I—I. No. I——"

"Take it easy, Helen. Go on." Carey's sinuses began to hurt. He blew his nose.

"Well, 'Yes,' I said to him. 'I'm sorry. I don't know what's the matter with me.'"

"And Milton said then—and he wasn't bitter—he said, 'Well, you're just tired, I guess.'"

But it occurred to her again what Milton had said. *Then she'll be gone.* What a rotten, rotten thing to say.

"Poor baby," Milton said then, squatting down beside her, "we have a rough time sometimes, don't we?"

She told Carey how she got up and turned away from him. "How can you say such a horrible thing? 'Then she'll be gone.' Just because all this packing and shopping's tired me out do you think I *enjoy* seeing my child leave from home? Do you think I like it? Do you?" She couldn't help saying that.

He put his hands on her shoulders again. "No——"

"Let me alone!" she cried. And she remembered that it was then, more than at any other time during the evening, that she wanted to say something about Mrs. X, the mistress, the snake, the despised woman of the shadows and dreams. "Let me alone, Milton!"

Neither of them said any more then, but both of them, she thought, felt that something was about to happen. It hung in the air, vast and extraordinary—a thin twilight humming like mosquitoes suspended above a pond, a noise indistinct, querulous yet violent. It approached, revealed itself: an airplane with silver wings, immensely fast, dipping overhead with a wild swoop toward the bay. The noise grew, night fell with a crash, and a gathering wind sent the willows tossing like a jungle of buggy whips. "Helen——" Milton called, but drowning out his words another plane appeared and slanted through the dark behind the trees, full of noise and flame and danger, and was gone behind the first.

She thought, *Something's happened to Maudie.*

"Helen!" Milton cried. "The fools!" And raised his fist to the sky. "You goddam crazy bastards!" His glass fell soundlessly to the lawn and the ice cubes which she stepped on, as she ran, glowed like diamonds in the grass. A light went on in the house. Maudie lay sprawled at the foot of the stairs, giggling.

"It doesn't hurt, Mama," she said. "Listen to the planes!"

Helen knelt beside her, stiff with fright.

"I let her slip and fall," Peyton said. "I'm sorry. It was dark. I didn't mean to."

"Mama, Peyton didn't mean to. Listen to the planes!"

She lifted Maudie up. Milton dashed in, and she heard his voice behind her: "Oh, good, thank the Lord! I thought something had happened."

She told Carey how another plane had joined that procession across the sky, the house rocking beneath this furious noise as if shearing buzzsaws had been brought earthward on the wings of some perilous bird. Then swiftly the noise diminished, the planes were gone, leaving only far out across the bay a receding and innocent billow of sound, almost musical, a tremulous twilight humming which faded, vanished, returned once, quavering, and became silent altogether. She looked up from where she knelt by Maudie. There was a bruise on Maudie's leg—a little place, but it appeared to her huge and awful. As in a dream, everything she had imagined had come true. A result, it seemed, of nothing more than some crazy mischief. She looked past Peyton—the shorts, the slim, tanned legs, her hips again. All these lost. Hers. She was going away. But something prevented her from saying the right words.

So, she told Carey, she yielded—to her pride, her hurt, her own abominable selfishness. She got up and put her arm around Maudie and said to Milton, quite without emotion: "Something *has* happened, Milton. Didn't I tell you? Peyton let her fall. I'll have to stay here." And she turned and went upstairs without a word more, to Peyton or anyone.

After Helen had finished that part of her story, Carey remembered, he had been inclined at first to say: so what? He hadn't wanted to make all these snap judgments, but his initial pity for her had been tempered by a strong irritation: here was a woman who had not been the dupe of life, but had been too selfish, too unwilling to make the usual compromises, to be happy. And although he didn't know her well, he would like to venture that she was also a complete prig. No wonder life had seemed a trap. All she had needed to do at certain times was to have a little charity, and at least measure the results. And he had told her so, trying to be objective, if, as he was later afraid, rather sententious. When she had paused, obviously miserable and overwrought, he had looked away from her and made doodles on his blotter, saying: "Was Maudie hurt bad?"

"No. At least, I really don't think so."

Then he had thought *ah, well* and had gone on to say weakly, "Well, like the adage, Helen: 'As the smallest leavening maketh bread firm, small kindness maketh love grow.'" Actually it was an epigram he had made up just that moment and a poor one; because he was never sure of the worth of his judgments he often quoted imaginary sources to lend an air of authority—a low habit but relatively harmless. And Helen had said then, after a long dead silence full of torment and indecision: "Well, I guess that's right. But I guess you're like all the rest."

"How do you mean that, Helen?" he had said gently.

"No. No, then. Not like all the rest. You're the first I've talked to."

"Well——"

"I sound terrible, don't I?"

"No."

"You say no because you're being kind."

"No, now, Helen, look here. I'll give you all the help I can. I'm not here to judge or condemn. I only said that because—well, suppose I take it back. I wasn't suggesting any lack of kindness on your part. I guess—— Well, maybe the way you told this thing to me has given me just the false idea that you've been maybe—selfish. At least this particular time. Or something." What else could he say?

"You mean that——"

"I mean that . . . Helen. Oh, I don't know——" he said hopelessly. "I mean that maybe it's not as bad as it might seem."

126

She closed her eyes and raised her fingers to her brow. "I thought that you maybe could help me," she said in a small voice.

Poor woman. It was a funny circumstance. In a day when a minister felt perpetually deserted, when the one thing one wanted most was to be able to offer spiritual guidance, here was a person who seemed to be in great need of whatever help he could give, and what could he say? Nothing really. So in the little gap before he spoke he concentrated heavily upon something up and beyond him and prayed, himself, for guidance. Finally he said: "Helen, do you believe in God?"

She looked up slowly, and said in a surprisingly self-possessed voice: "Yes. Or at least I want to."

"Then that's part of the fight already, and the better part of the eventual triumph. God has a strong adversary in the devil—" and he thought *yes, she knows that. She knows that. Which is all to her credit*—" 'his craft and power are great and armed with cruel hate' as the hymn goes—" of this Carey was sure—"God gives His greatest reward to those whose fight is desperate and whose struggle at the bleakest hour seems most hopeless. Because then one's only weapon is faith, which indeed often seems a flimsy thing, but unless you have it the struggle can avail nothing." And as an afterthought: " 'Say not the struggle naught availeth.' "

He leaned forward and suddenly felt unburdened, sensing so completely the truth of what he was saying, that he had to communicate this to her: "Does it sound funny I can talk to you like this in an age like ours?" She began a negative nod of her head, but he went on: "Excuse me for this, but you must—listen, Helen, remember that our age is only a moment in that time we can perceive as the timeless love of God. The devil, if you want to call him that, walks abroad today as he has before, but always he's been defeated and cast down. He rises with greater strength each time to try our faith. If our moment is worse and the devil seems more strongly armed, then it is our joy and our exaltation to seek combat: 'I have fought a good fight, I have finished my course, I have kept the faith: henceforth there is laid up for me a crown of righteousness.' Oh, Helen, there's nothing stupid or arrogant in such an affirmation, or nothing to compromise the reason; it's a tribute to the faith and strength and love of one's self, which becomes the love of others, and which is the timeless love of God."

"Who is He?" she said after a silence.

Could anything be more simple, or trite, or so hard to understand?

"God is love," he said, with a small feeling of triumph, and of sadness, too.

She looked away. "Maybe you've found him," she said, rather accusingly.

"I have," he said, lying, but not with any premeditation. He only felt that he *had* struggled for twenty years with simple, tangible evils. These, added up, were Evil, and they depressed him and in his dreams at night they gave him phosphorescent visions of earthly horrors and spiritual damnation. He could rationalize, he could say "These things happen to every man"—his gluttony, which kept his weight up and gave him gas, his petty parsimony—but nonetheless he knew that it was the little temptations which held him forever apart from true Christian peace, caused him to hurry through dark rooms at night and down the stairs, fearing even then, as reassuring light beckoned from the hall below, the clutch of a cold invisible hand. But he had struggled incessantly—against both the temptations and the vaguely mystical, idiotic fears; the struggle was the important part, and he felt that he could lie to Helen a little bit, if just to make her believe that anything might be possible through the grace of Jesus Christ.

But even this, he remembered now, had not given her a momentary contentment. She hadn't seemed to notice. She had gone on dredging the shallows of her despair, embarrassing him and, occasionally, touching him with her confusion. They had sat there until long past midnight—until Adrienne had called from upstairs in a muffled, cross voice: "Carey, Carey, aren't you coming to bed?"—but that had gone unnoticed. And Helen, never letting her voice rise now—she seemed to be getting tired—and pausing only to light innumerable cigarettes (even then continuing to talk so that the smoke came out in small voice-thickening gusts) had told him how she had gone to see Dolly Bonner the next day. It was all of a year afterward—when the gossip around town was unavoidable, even for a minister—that Carey learned who the woman was, because Helen persisted in calling her, with a certain charity, "Mrs. X." But later he was able to reconstruct the scene in his mind. Even though he didn't know Dolly, her ubiquitous smiling photograph had been in the newspapers every time the Red Cross or the Community Chest or the North Port Warwick P.T.A. had had the slightest excuse for a conclave: Dolly ("Mrs. Sclater Bonner") could apparently be imposed upon by her sister members to serve as hostess, or take the more arduous responsibilities. He remembered that picture. And later, when he learned "Mrs. X's" identity, he saw clearly all that Helen told him: the two handsome women facing each other at noon in a hot tearoom, each, through some propriety inbred or learned, controlling herself in a painful under-current beneath the gentle, ironic, hateful words, but ready at the first improper bat of an eyelash to do violence, even in public, to assert her claim upon Loftis, who by that time was fully halfway to Sweet Briar.

And Helen told him how she had gone upstairs with Maudie that night. She had turned brusquely and left the room holding Maudie's arm and feeling Peyton's and Milton's silence and their bewilderment, like a sheet of fabric laid upended in the partitioning doorway, almost palpable, motionless at her back. Upstairs she had examined Maudie's leg: there was a small greenish-blue welt below the knee where she had slipped against the newel post. Maudie giggled, as if she had no bruise at all.

It was then, bending over Maudie as she lay on her bed, that the shameful phrase occurred to Helen: *not inadvertent, not inadvertent.* The bruise was very small, and she had got out a poultice and iodine from the medicine cabinet, along with some aspirin, and perhaps it was this that further upset her—the dismal accretion of bottles and bandages around Maudie on the bedspread. Self-imposed, through some compulsion she had acquired over the years—this way she had of magnifying all out of proportion Maudie's tiniest hurts and ills— now her enormous solicitude sought not only a cure but, in a sort of panic, someone to blame for this bruise. Of course. Again Peyton, whom she had momentarily forgotten. And she had said to herself *not inadvertent, not inadvertent,* and elaborating upon it as she salved the bruise with boric acid ointment: *She by heaven was just going to show her independence, the little devil. Perhaps it wasn't intentional, but it was not inadvertent,* and here she drew a fine distinction be-tween the two by assuming something that, even as it darted across her consciousness, she knew was vicious and false: that Peyton might not have planned to let Maudie fall, but by some subconscious process let her fall anyway, for revenge, or to show her independence, or something. But instantly she thought *No, no, oh, no,* and in order to distract herself from this thought (which by definition, she told Carey, implied she had been a rotten and cruel mother to Peyton) she hurried to the bathroom and with a great deal of trembling soaked cotton in hot water for Maudie's bruise. Then she remembered that there was no need for hot water, the salve had already been put on, and so with a swift motion she threw the wad of cotton into the toilet, watched it spread and expand, and stood beneath the cruel, revealing bathroom lights gazing at herself in the mirror, the fading prettiness, and thought *Somehow I cannot concentrate.*

Oh, yes.

So then her mind was mostly blank. She walked back to the bed and undressed Maudie and put the brace in the corner and, after kissing her, slipped out and shut the door. She went to her own room and locked herself in. There was a strong chemical smell in here, and a heavy stuffiness, she remembered: she had sprayed Flit in the room just before supper, for now toward the end of summer the mosquitoes were active and venomous. She had watched them approach and had been prepared, patching up screens herself, arming the house with spray guns. The mosquitoes were big and brown, as big as mulberries, and they came in clouds at sundown, swarming out of the inlets and pools along the shore as if in one last onslaught before the advent of that deathly season already hinted at in chill, tentative winds, a subtle browning in the marshes. She snapped on a light and, holding her breath for a moment, threw up all the windows and then took off her clothes and slipped into a nightgown. Then she rubbed cold cream on her face, put up her hair, and got into bed. She lighted a cigarette and set the ashtray beside her on the coverlet.

All this time—it was odd, she told Carey—all this time she had been pressing back in her mind the confusion of the last hour, and it wasn't until she had pulled the coverlet over her and had arranged herself against the pillows, settling a copy of *Good Housekeeping* in her lap, that she realized what strain the effort to *not* think had caused her, and how tense she was: she could hardly read the magazine, it was shaking so. She put the magazine down: for minutes she had been gazing vacantly at a colored advertisement of hamburgers soaking in a repulsive red sauce, and it occurred to her that it was making her ill. And then—again it was so odd, she said—her next thought was this: that she had been behaving remarkably well, with dignity; recalling the events of the past few minutes, she believed she had been properly curt and distant with Milton when, at the bottom of the stairs, she had told him she would have to stay here tomorrow. All this, while she lay there in bed trembling, passed through her mind in a warm, satisfying wave, with the pleasant tingle that the remembrance of small triumphs lends to reflection. It was so odd, and indeed, hadn't this devil, or whoever he was, perhaps disguised himself in order to make her think such a vain mean thought? Although invisible, cleverly off-stage, wasn't he prodding her just the same? Nonetheless, she felt most satisfied.

And then (this, she said, she had pondered ever since and still had no explanation: maybe Carey would) then it was as if everything that had happened during the evening had come into focus, as if in the seesawing of her crazy moods she had slowly teetered and risen and fallen and had finally stopped, so that for one instant—did she have a fever?—all her thoughts rested at precise, unhurried equilibrium. She raised her hand to her brow, withdrew fingers watery with sweat; a pervasive scent like naphtha hovered in the air, and she sat stiffly upright in bed, scattering cigarettes, matches, ashes.

And thought: They don't think I was properly distant, dignified or anything. They just think I'm queer. And thought, thrusting her face into her hands: God help me please, I'm going crazy.

There it was: the suspicion tangible and outrageous and, for the moment, hardly to be denied. What could she do? She looked around her: at the familiar yellow-capsuled nembutal in a bottle on her dresser; she gave the bottle short, casual consideration: ten, maybe fifteen of those would fix things up forever—but the thought passed quickly from her mind. She wanted to scream but . . . how silly. And just as these notions fled through her consciousness, so, she remembered, the whole idea of insanity was forgotten as too difficult and too gross a thing to contemplate for more than an instant, and with a sigh she stretched out her hot legs so that sheet and coverlet enveloped her body in a soundless rush of air, like a tent collapsing. She lay silent for a while with her eyes closed and then, for no apparent reason at all, arose and walked barefoot to the window. Now for a moment she felt, as she put it, "normal." Most likely it was the fresh air, clearing her mind, but as she sat in a chair by the window the sweating and the trembling vanished. Below she heard music from the radio and laughter from Milton, vacant and loud and carefree, as if nothing had happened at all. Leaning forward with her elbows on the windowsill, she cupped her chin in her hands and looked down at the garden and the bay. Perhaps now, upon reflection, it was only the season that had made her unhappy: this tail end of summer, the September midpassage when the year seems sallow and emaciated like a worn-out, middle-aged countrywoman pausing for breath, and all the leaves are mildly, unsatisfactorily green. Everything then is waiting, expecting, and there is something in the air that promises smoke and burning and dissolution. One's flowers bloom gaily for a while, but September is a quick, hectic month, bearing on the air seeds for burial, and making people feel tired and a little frantic, as in a station just before the train pulls out. But it was lovely, too; it had its loveliness. Night had come, but over the sky was spread a pale-gray afterglow in which the evening star, rising over the bay, rested like a solitary gem on a sea of smoke; the earth below exhaled an odor of grass and flowers, the mimosas were shaking in the wind. Beyond these and the willows at the edge of the water, dark ships were passing slowly out to sea. War. And again a wind, faintly chill, pressed against her cheek, bringing an odor of salt and the cool imminence of fall, and huge mosquitoes, tapping futilely at the window. She blew softly against the screen. The mosquitoes darted up and outward against the sky and returned, settling heavily in the dying wind. A branch fell to the ground, leaves scuttled across the driveway and became silent all at once, an army felled in its tracks. Noise from the radio ceased, the sleazy female voice strangled in mid-note as if it, too, had perished on the wind's last dissolving sigh, and in the silence she thought of her imprisonment, her banishment.

The moon rose hot and orange, outlining the flower bed, serpentine and shadowy with nodding blooms, dark willows and, beneath the mimosa tree, two forms—Peyton and a boy. Helen leaned forward, watching. They approached each other and kissed, and the wind must have rustled in the branches once more, for there was a wild, long whisper and leaves fluttered down around them like the wings of birds.

"Good-by, Peyton."

"Good-by."

"Come back, Peyton. Come back soon."

"Someday."

"Good-by . . . good-by . . . good-by."

She turned away, again filled with unfocused anger. She went to bed and, face downward in a pillow, tried to pray—not for guidance, which seemed too vague and elementary, but rather that God please simply give her the logic to direct blame in the proper direction, for her own fear and anger: Dear Lord, I can't hate my own husband; dear Lord, I can't hate Peyton, my own flesh and blood—but she felt that something was wrong: as usual, her prayers seemed to be on a one-way line to heaven, and so, her ardor spent, she took two nembutals and finally sank into sleep, dreaming *Good-by, good-by* to the shadow-silhouette, the woman who flickered and vanished—while white blooms floated earthward, and through these she seemed to be bearing a letter: but to whom? She bent down close to see, saw marigolds, nasturtiums, poppies, shameful-red, and three black hairs which spelled out across her garden: SIN. She turned, frightened, but Milton said: "Here, baby, I'll mail it for you," and was gone with Peyton who walked in shorts beside him and held before her hips, as round as moons, the hat, a flowered crucible. "Good-by, good-by," she tried to say, but both of them were in the sailboat with Dolly Bonner, borne in a dark squall with sails awash, hurricane-swift far out to sea. A torrent of leaves filled the air, torn like feathers on a blast of wind past the house, garage, all reckoning, but there was a thump and the wind subsided: Milton with a smile reappeared in the garden soaked to the skin, pounding on a tree with her trowel: "Helen!" he shouted. "Helen, Helen!"

She awoke. Milton was knocking on the door. "All right," she called weakly, "all right. Just a minute." She climbed from bed and walked to the door, unlocking it.

"My God," he said. "What happened? I thought you'd fallen or something and knocked yourself out. How's Maudie?"

"All right," she said.

"You're all sweating, honey."

Standing there in the doorway. The two of them. Carey could see it all: the one shirtsleeved and fleshy, suntanned from a summer of golf, even now breathing a faint, pulpy odor of whisky as he looked with puzzled apprehension at the other, who was no longer overwhelming, but merely drugged and sick. Distantly, breakers swept up over the beach with a prolonged *waaas-h*, fell back silently into the night. And she was holding his hand, in a rare, voluntary caress touching him, trying through waves of nembutal to shake off fragments of dreams, gusts of wind, remembered rain, saying: "Milton, you musn't be unfaithful to me."

In a tone, most likely, that would unsettle any man.

And before he could reply, she went on in a flat monotone: "Everything's breaking up. If it takes all the strength I've got I'm going to see that we all stay together. Milton—" and she stroked his hand, which must have further surprised him—"I know what you've been up to and I'm not going to let it go on. 'Those whom God hath joined together let no man put asunder'"—a phrase recollected from the fathomless past, most inopportune at this point, Carey judged: that old litany of innocence which men forget and which women remember with the clarity of a nursery rhyme.

Then Loftis said, "What the hell are you talking about?"

"You know."

"What do you mean?"

"That woman."

He flushed, wheeled abruptly—"Oh, the hell with you anyway—" and walked down the hall. At the head of the stairs he turned. "The goddam hell with you anyway!" Then he was gone.

It occurred to her then that although he had been rude before, and had used foul words, he had never sworn *at* her. Never. Well, no matter. She sat by Maudie's bed for a long time, thinking. Maudie slept soundly. At ten o'clock the churchbell rang and she went into her own room and got into bed. Still a little later, as she lay there alone—determined to feign sleep when Milton came to bed—she heard footsteps on the stairs. She rose up on her elbow. "Peyton," she said aloud, "Peyton dear." But her voice was not loud enough; she had made the gesture at least, which, in the light of Milton's nastiness, was perhaps, she thought, of no matter either.

And this finally (the events thereafter, foreshortened, lacking detail, seemed confused, and Carey filled in the rest): sleeping in the morning, long after Milton and Peyton had gone, she heard children's voices breaking in upon her dreams like the chatter of remote, unknown birds, but loud, somehow appalling, and she awoke in fright. But it was just the sound of children after all: far off, laughter and the noise that bicycles make fading down a gravel road—and she sank back again with a sort of relief and gazed blinking through the clear oriole light at Milton's bed, gritty sand on the sheets: he hadn't washed his feet. After taking a Bromo-Seltzer to clear her head, she dressed Maudie, fixed breakfast, and then Ella came. Finally—it was ten o'clock by now—she made the telephone call, reflecting briefly in the process upon how calm and sure she was.

"Hello." (Helen knew the voice, which was lucky. To have to say, "Is this Dolly Bonner?" would be a forced betrayal of intimacy which, no matter how slight, she didn't want.)

"This is Helen Loftis. How are you?" And without waiting—"I wonder if you could meet me at the Bide-A-Wee at noon. I want to discuss something with you."

"Well, no, I really don't think——" The voice was more than hesitant: instantly shocked, defensive and afraid.

Helen broke in. "It's very urgent. I have to insist——" How formal!

"But no——"

"Then it'll have to be sometime else." Very decisively—the gauntlet thrown down. "Today would suit me best if you've got no other plans."

"I have to go to a——" Squirming.

"Then what day then?"

"All right, then. All right. The Bide-A-Wee?"

"Yes. I think—I think it'll be in both our interests."

"All right. Good-by."

"All right. Good-by."

So already she had frightened her. If nothing else, she had done that, gained an initial advantage, and she felt equipped to do battle. At eleven-thirty she instructed Ella about Maudie's lunch and then took a bus into town, to the Bide-A-Wee Tea Room.

By noontime a broiling heat had fallen over the town, and at the tearoom she took a seat in a secluded corner, beneath an electric fan which like a monstrous black flower turned its face from the wall in drowsy half-circles, dispensing puny hot puffs of air. From a distance the shipyard whistle broke the midday quiet, heralding the arrival of the office men who soon came singly or in pairs, wiping their necks with white handkerchiefs—"Je-*sus*, don't this beat them all?" But Dolly hadn't come and so she merely sat there, a little fearful that some man might recognize her, and draw certain conclusions when Dolly arrived. They knew about Milton and Dolly. They knew. Or did they? Men . . . An enormous Negro woman brought her water in a glass, with which she printed wet circles on a tissue doily. At last she arose, prepared to leave, but from the hallway, in the mirror of a walnut hatrack, she saw Dolly open the screen door and stand looking around, warm and unhappy. Helen smiled a little and beckoned, and Dolly came over and sat down, averting her eyes, with an apology and a guarded remark about the heat. The waitress appeared with typed menus, mopping her brow.

"What'll you have, my dear?" said Helen.

"Well, really. I'm not hungry," Dolly said, smiling uneasily. "Just some iced tea, I guess."

"Well, heavens, you have to eat," Helen said lightly, "especially in the summer. I've heard that a person loses so much that—waitress, I'll have the salmon croquettes and tea—that—what I mean is—" looking up—"you perspire so much, you see, that you have to eat to counteract that—the loss. Of course, that's only one theory."

"Yes," Dolly replied, gazing around in misery, "this sure is some day."

The waitress bent over. "You don't want nothin' else, ma'am?"

"No," Dolly said, "no."

"And how's your committee?" Helen went on. "I haven't been to the garden club in ages. I'm afraid——"

"Oh, fine. Oh, just fine."

By one o'clock they had neared the end of their road of mutual interest, and the byways had been fully explored; Helen, doing most of the talking, thought pleasantly of her particular hatred for this woman. Furthermore, she felt already victorious, deliciously regal: she could administer the *coup de grâce* at any time, and without the degrading preliminaries. She was hot now, but vaguely excited. She reflected that in the years she had known Dolly, no matter how casually and with what hidden suspicion, it had always been this way, more or less. There are people for whom, when you see them after a long time, you begin to hoard up mentally all of the stray scraps of information which you know might be of common concern, for after these are used up there is nothing left to talk about, and then inevitably the person will drive you to distraction. Such was Dolly, although now she didn't seem to be prepared to say anything at all—being fearfully ill-at-ease—and Helen, in mid-sentence, looked around her, watching the men drift out one by one, satiated, drowsy, scratching themselves, leaving behind in the room the fragile blue scent of cigars. She and Dolly were alone. The traffic, quieted during the lunch hour, began to flow again sluggishly up the street. She lit a cigarette.

"Oh," she was saying. "I remember Ellen Davison, she was the one whose husband left her, the Navy person, and it caused her all sorts of trouble. No one would speak to her. Well, she was truly a horrible person and you just might guess what it did to his career."

"Yes," Dolly said, and raised her head timidly, and Helen could see on her lip a faint beady mustache of sweat.

They were both silent then. Finally Helen said, "Don't you want some coffee?"

"No, thanks; no, really, I've got to be going. Melvin's going back to school on Monday and I've just got to do some shopping." She ventured the first part of a smile, as if Helen's suggestion about coffee had really indicated, marvelously, despite the telephone conversation, that this was a social visit after all. It was the smile of a reprieved prisoner, and it broadened upon her pretty face, and became suddenly a laugh of deliverance: "Honey," she giggled, "we sure do have a time with our children, don't we? Melvin's just like his daddy, the fat old thing. Sixteen, imagine that, and I got to get him size-thirty-six pants." She paused, smiled and looked at her watch. "Well——"

Now.

"Listen here," Helen said, bending forward. Again she couldn't

136

bring herself to repeat Dolly's name. "I want to talk to you about something serious."

Dolly turned, alert and intent. "Why, sure, what's the matter?"

"I'll get down to cases," Helen went on, not smiling, but not betraying anger, either—controlling herself. "It's my husband. Now listen—now I think you know why I wanted to see you. Listen—" she arched her eyebrows and, without raising her hand from the table, waved an admonitory finger—"I think really I've had just about enough, don't you? You see, I have a family, which is very important to me, a *very* important thing. Also, there's something else, the decency or indecency of the thing, if you know what I mean, and frankly—listen: Frankly, I'm tired of having these hints and rumors reaching me about the way Milton has been carrying on. Now, I know Milton isn't beyond reproach, he's got many faults like I suspect all husbands do, but I want to make it plain right now that I'm not going to let you carry on like this anymore." While she talked she knew somehow that things were not going well at all; she seemed to have lost the advantage of surprise, her face felt suddenly feverish and, besides, Dolly had not become immediately crushed, as she had intended, but was only returning her gaze with receptive, placid eyes, and with her lower lip tucked thoughtfully between her teeth. "You see what I mean," Helen went on in a level voice, "I'm not being vindictive. I'm right now offering you an opportunity to mend your ways and then we'll say, all's forgotten, live and let live, and so on. Do you understand?" What on earth had happened?

Dolly stretched languidly, all fear gone, as if now—having met the adversary—the apprehension, the pre-contest anxiety had vanished. Slowly she stretched, raising clasped hands to the ceiling, and made a small rude noise—like a belch—of apathy, of indifference. "Honey," she sighed, letting her arms fall, "I just wouldn't know what you're talking about."

"What do you mean—" Helen hadn't foreseen this: the fury—"what on earth do you mean? What do you mean—don't know what I'm talking about? I'll tell you what I'm talking about very well. You know exactly. For six years I've known about you and Milton. Six years. That's what. Watching you make a fool of him! Breaking up my family, that's what! And you don't know what I'm talking about! As God is my witness——" How disordered she had become, and how quickly her sure determination had gone astray! That subtle, secret weapon of Dolly's—of indifference, of smug, easy denial—had thrown her attack into wild confusion. Swiftly she said, in a loud clear voice:

"You see what I mean, don't you? You're breaking up my family because you're a selfish, immoral, vicious woman. For six years you've worked your way with Milton and now that my daughter has gone off to school I need him even more and I won't have it! Understand, I just won't!" She wagged her forefinger, then stretched out her whole hand, trembling, casting anathema through the Bide-A-Wee. Old Mrs. Prosser, who ran the place, appeared at the door with a bevy of wild-eyed Negroes. "I'll not suffer for six years," Helen shouted, "and then plan—look forward to spent . . . spending the rest of my life in human bondage to your dirt-smut."

Dolly had got up, collected her purse and umbrella. She looked down at Helen with a brief hard gaze. "You wait a while," she said softly, "just you wait a while. I'll put things right out in the open, which you'd never do. O.K. Listen," she whispered, bending toward her, "if I've done wrong with Milton—wrong, as you put it—it hasn't been any six years. It was two weeks ago, honey, at the country club at your dance. There, see, that's a confession. And we're going to keep on as long as Milton wants to. And I don't care how much or where, honey, or how much people talk. Because I love him and that's more than you do and you know it."

She slipped the umbrella straps over her arm, slowly, without effort, as if she were going shopping, which in fact she was. "Now," she said, "we're making all kinds of noise, and I'd better go. Don't talk about six years, 'my dear,' because it isn't true. Just remember that whatever Milton does it's because he's just been lonesome. Remember that." She threw a dollar on the table.

Then she wheeled and sauntered out with high heels disdainfully clacking on the linoleum, past Mrs. Prosser and the astonished waitresses, through the door. "Now——" Helen cried, half-risen from her seat, but her words fell emptily on the hot, still air, above the skittish noise of aprons and skirts and giggles, as the Negroes popped out of sight.

A few minutes later Helen boarded a bus at the corner of Twenty-eighth Street and Washington Avenue and, being deeply involved in thought, failed to notice that her nickel slipped past the coin slot and onto the floor. The driver glared at her briefly, but this, too, went unnoticed. She would just have to remain silent, she thought, as the bus bore her rocking gently toward home. There would come a working out. Of course, she herself had not been really sinful, she had only misjudged in too many cases, perhaps—been too impetuous. . . . Yes, remain silent, bear it all—and, above everything,

try to keep out of her mind the abysmal mistakes, like just now——
Oh, the shame! The humiliation! But then . . . forget it, forget it.

That night she was sitting in her garden alone when Milton returned from Sweet Briar. She told Carey later how Milton, after
putting the car away and disappearing into the house for a moment—
to go to the bathroom, she supposed—came out and sat down beside
her.

"Well," he said, shaking his drink, "our little girl's a college woman
now."

"Did everything go all right?" Helen asked quietly.

"Oh, wonderful. What a kid! She'll be the beauty queen. She
sticks out like a jool in a coal pile, like the nigger says. Already."

"Oh, that's nice," she said, "I wish—I really wish I'd gone. I was
sick last night. I really felt better this morning. I had a nice day,
really."

"That's good," he said, without much interest. "How's Maudie?"

"All right. We went over in the playground with the swings this
afternoon. She got a little tired."

"Mmm-hh."

They were quiet for a while. Then Helen said: "Did I hear you
talking to someone in the house just now?"

"Yeah," he said, "I was making a call."

"Oh." She paused. "I do hope Peyton makes good grades, not just
the beauty queen business. If she's going to be something——"

"Aw, Helen," he said with a little laugh, "she won't worry about
that for a while. You know that. She's got to worry about the boys.
First. She's a bright kid."

"Yes. I worry about that, too. The boys."

"She'll be O.K."

"I hope so." Again they stopped talking. Finally Helen said: "Did
she say anything about me—about me not going today?"

"Yeah, yes, she was mad. Hurt. She doesn't understand you. I
told her you were nervous—with Maudie and all. She knows all about
that."

Helen didn't answer, and was surprised in a way—for they rarely
came to her—that tears were running down her face. Milton stretched,
yawned, stood up with a faint snapping of unlimbered joints. "Well—"
he yawned—"I'm going to bed. I've got to go down to the C & O
tomorrow and see Peterson about that draft. What's wrong, Helen?"

She shook her head without answering and held out her hand,
which he ignored, or didn't see. "Good night, Milton," she said,

which was difficult, considering the swelling in her throat. "Forgive me."

"What for, Helen?" he said softly.

"Nothing," she said quickly, her heart pounding. "Everything."

"Good night."

Something in his voice told her that he was startled, even pleased, at her gentleness, her decency. Or just this weakness? But apparently, being surprised, there was nothing else he could say, and so he walked into the house. It was a very close moment, she thought, but not close enough for comfort.

Oh, how can he be that decent with me?

She blew her nose, a mosquito lit on her brow. She got up. Moonlight flooded her garden and the shadows sprang up, one by one, of dying flowers, the pomegranate, the patient, hovering trees. She knelt down by the flower bed. Even after one day, more dead petals littered the ground and she picked them up until she had a handful. She looked up. Above her the mimosa leaves were smooth, unhurried in the stillness, reflecting moonlight like pale hands of water: she thought of God—painfully—it was beyond reflection, like trying to picture your remotest ancestor.

Who is He?

From her hand the petals dropped away, dry ghostly husks; somewhere a door slammed and a bat, fluttering silently, swung down through the night and vanished among the eaves. *I will not yield,* she thought, *I will not yield.* Gray smoke from her cigarette in garlands, like hope, ascending eternally, rose through the darkness, and *I will not yield*—but it made no difference: the loneliness swept down around her, a mountain of withered grass.

Now, as Carey made a turn on the street, a row of houses facing on the bay appeared to the left of him. None of them were mansions but they were spacious and faced on neat lawns and here at midday, shaded by trees thick with the greenest of leaves, they all had the cool, withdrawn, silent look of nice houses on a summer day. The Loftis house was only a couple of blocks away and Carey drove on, hot and pensive and disorganized, beneath the shelter of the trees. Once the whine of a vacuum cleaner disturbed the silence, but faded, and somewhere a child, unworried by the heat, made a wild and momentous scream. Carey drove on, full of worry: what would he say to Helen? Now and then he looked at the houses, as if to take his mind off the matter at hand, but turned suddenly away, retaining only the small

140

vision of things well kept and drowsy and heavy with summer: an old man prodding at a flower bed, the huge white cat that lay sleeping on a coil of garden hose—and there was a woman with a rag about her head, who paused to wipe her brow with quiet exhaustion, looking hopefully upward between the fading wilted leaves.

What would he say to Helen? Yes, what could he say? What had he ever been able to say to her? Virtually nothing. And even through his sorrow—at the time of judgment, it occurred to him suddenly, the sun would shine like this all day, searching from an immovable apex, casting no shadows—he felt a sharp pang of resentment, and anger: she would *not* compromise, she would make no concessions. Which was bad, wrong. Yet he couldn't tell her that—not today. Not ever, perhaps. He had not been able to tell her so that night, nor on the other nights when she had come to him—cool, precise, reserved at first—repeating in essence the same tortured accounts of separate guilt, communal guilt, uneasy accusations, righteous accusations—differing only in small details: "I wrote Peyton three letters, Carey, and she didn't answer. It's Milton, I know; he's writing her, too, he's warping her mind——"

Did she really care? And was she crazy? No. He didn't think so. Obsessed, or something. But not crazy.

"Oh, no, Helen. Really, I don't believe that." Smiling a little. "Really, Helen, that's not a very nice thing to say. Why should he——"

Did she really care? he wondered.

Bending forward, she would look into his eyes, the reserve, the statuesque poise all going to pieces, as he had learned to expect it to, after an hour or so; and the fine, lovely mouth would quiver a little as she said: "Oh, Carey, what am I going to do? Should I get down on my *knees* to him? Is that what he wants? What in God's name does he want?"

No! Yes! He wanted to bang on his desk, arise magisterially, like a good confessor, being purposeful and stern. He wished to say both at the same time: No! Yes! No, my dear Helen, he doesn't want you to get down on your knees; that insults, at least embarrasses, any man. He wants only affection, decency, humanness, a woman's tender greeting. Yes! For heaven's sake, yes, get down on your knees not to him but to yourself: get down on your knees to that image you hate, be humble for one moment and perhaps your prayer will cast a light through the darkness around you; ask forgiveness for despising yourself.

Once he had tried that—"Helen, I think you have a low opinion of yourself—" but she had become disappointed and sulky. And once, irritated and rather bored, he had said shortly: "Helen, I can't help you, you know. I can only listen. You've got to look into your *own* heart and mind."

And she had wept, horribly, the only time he had seen her collapse. "You desert me, too! Even you!"

"No, Helen. Oh, no, listen, please don't get me wrong!" And after coffee and a talk full of stupid (he knew) reservations about a woman's right to happiness, all of which sounded vaguely like a soap opera, he had walked her to her car, a hand on her shoulder paternally—or in some fashion—saying, "I wish there was something I could do. Just hope, have patience. And pray, pray hard" (to yourself, he thought, love yourself), "this thing of his will wear itself out. It'll be easier for you then."

"And Peyton?" she said, absently.

"Oh, yes—" what could he say?—"I'm sure you'll see her soon. Don't worry about what she wrote Milton. I say she doesn't want to come home not because of you, but . . . you know how girls are . . . I think . . . they like to visit, go places." Fishing about hopelessly for words. Did she really care?

"Good night, Helen dear."

Sometimes she scared him a little, but she interested him; secretly he knew that it flattered his vanity to have her seek him out, talk to him: her visits, usually at night, averaged one every two or three months for the next few years. They became good friends, they talked about other matters; on one or two occasions she failed to mention Milton or Peyton—"her sorrow," as she put it once in an embarrassingly awkward attempt at irony. She seemed totally lacking in a sense of humor, but it really didn't matter: they talked of God, immortality, time and space, all in the enthusiastic, disorganized, eclectic way of high-school seniors, which Carey, being nominally, at least, and at the most unquestioningly, committed to Faith, hadn't employed in years, and which finally disturbed him so much that he guided the conversation back to the value of prayer. Then at times they would talk of Milton, of the sad vanishing of love and passion, and why, Carey explained, using Diotima's discourse as a point of departure, it was necessary, after the falling away of years and the dissolution of the object of love on earth, to search for the lasting, the greater, the eternal love. To *fight* for love. And this, being in the larger, abstract realm and therefore less easily available to effort or practical application, stirred Helen—partly because Carey was, he had to admit, a fairly persuasive

142

talker—and filled her, at least momentarily, with a sort of radiance: she was not, he figured, a highly intelligent woman but intelligent enough, if she concentrated, to be infected by the rhythms, the hard, pure grandeur of Plato's lines. And even as he finished—letting the book fall with a decisive plop upon the desk, trembling himself with emotion and, a little startled, hearing Helen say: "Oh, Carey, isn't that grand, isn't that true?"—a thin sharp blade of despair sliced across his heart because he knew it was true but that, true as the love of Christ, truth like this poetry lay on the mountaintops, a temple. But humanity never stirred from the valleys to seek comfort there, or perhaps it suffered too much to attempt the climb. Which was right?

All this was fine. The sweet intoxication of poetry and truths and heady generalizations lulled her mind and heart and for a while gave her an excess of peace, and finally he had to deny her so many visits, telling her over the telephone, as nicely as he could, that she mustn't, she really mustn't: remember what he had told her about mind and heart, self-reliance? Of course he was flattered, to know that he, a churchman, could give a little comfort to a sufferer, yes, a real sufferer: flattered, and pleased, too, that Helen had sought him out instead of a doctor—although sometimes he thought with vague suspicion that it was a doctor she really needed. Oh, how could you reconcile these things! He thought that he was enlightened, and he wanted to be, but this business of psychology and such matters was to him maddening and strange: that so potentially strong an ally should still possess no real Godhead and be so indecently inquisitive and expensive, and have no respect for the tender and infinite mutations of the heart.

So he was proud, flattered that Helen had come to him, and they were good friends as long as he agreed with her, admitted she was right. Only when, as now, he remembered how she would not compromise and how little they had accomplished during the past few years—the words, the poetry, prayers, the terrible inaction—did he feel misgivings and anger. The devil—or somebody—was still around. And God had not revealed himself. But I must make her see, he thought. I must bring them together.

"Never. No more," she had said, only a month before as he had left her house after a visit, hopeless, feeling that there was nothing he could do, "I'm alone now and there isn't any difference between laughing and crying. I can't do either." And shook her head, absolutely. She had killed, denied, the very thing she had come to him for in the beginning.

Now at the same house he drew up slowly at the curb, in the shade of the sycamores, and alighted heavily from his car, hot and sweaty and with a sort of hopeful despair on his round, friendly face, but with more despair than hope.

"Oh, please. Dear Jesus, wake up now." Some voice lilting and sorrowful, distantly arousing her from the hot solacing heart of sleep. And her shoulder. What was that trembling at her shoulder? Hot, too, the five-fingered grasp upon her arm, yet tender, drawing away the last rags of darkness, urging her to light, toward which she struggled, eyelids fluttering, reluctantly. "Wake up now, Miss Helen, oh, Lawd God, Miss Helen, I got de word about it . . . now there."

La Ruth hovered above, her face an enormous black ugly mask, suffering, shedding streams of tears. "Miss Helen, de reverend's downstairs waitin on to take you to de cemetery, he say." She stood beside the bed, Helen watching her drowsily—the hulking, misshapen form still bending forward in apprehension—watching her from the grief-filled bespectacled eyes to the huge, formless legs draped in stockings that had skidded about and hung in folds around the knees, and the transparent, water-stained skirt.

"Oh, Lawd, Miss Helen, I been pushin at you all dis time and you wouldn't rouse up, I thought you was dead, too——" And drew back then with a gasp, a cry of horror and grief. "God *knows*, Miss Helen, I'nt meant to say dat! Gret God, Miss Helen, Mama come home an' tol' me 'bout po' little Peyton last night and directly I fell down on my knees and spoke up fo' you, prayin fo' de divine intersection of precious Daddy Faith an' says wing down yo' angels to pick up de sperit of po' little Peyton and leave yo' chosen dearest one right here on earth to take keer of po' little Peyton's mama who——"

"La Ruth," Helen interrupted, sitting up, "go get me a glass of cold water." A raw feverish film covered her throat; her voice, these first words, came hoarsely.

"Yes'm. Oh, yes, ma'am." La Ruth stood there motionless, with grasshopper eyes, touched with dim, blossoming wonder at this victim of tragedy who, not once but twice now bereft of motherhood, could suffer so stoically and wake up from a hot day's sleep like this without hysteria. She herself had lost two of her three children and although she couldn't rightly place the father of either of them she could recall with what fright she had awakened for many days afterward, shrieking, blubbering crazily for God to send down his Apostle. Quick. To lead her not into paths of Belief (because she believed, anyway, with every part of her soul and body) but into paths of peace and grace, into Baptism, into the true waters that would wash and caress her worn-out body and flood away the various sorrows of her mind, which always sought dreamily for a man. And soon God had not just sent his Apostle, but had come himself, in a Cadillac, to make sure everything was all right no matter how much she had worked and sinned, no matter the children she had lost: Daddy Faith, who was the King of Glory, Wonderful, Counsellor, the Mighty God, the Everlasting Father, the Prince of Peace. That had been ten years ago, and all this time she had cherished him and loved him and, having contributed over four hundred dollars to his cause, had become an Outer Angel of the Port Warwick annex heaven, detached from Baltimore. Today was Daddy Faith's annual August Coming, and she had worked herself up into a fever of excitement, so perhaps could be excused for this sudden evangelism. Helen stirred, placed her feet shakily on the floor and looked up once more into La Ruth's stricken face that pleaded for understanding—that tried to tell her that she, Helen, too, was qualified for the million, billion, trillion, septidemicillion blessings, blessings flowing free for all that slaved and sweated and were acquainted with grief, or had ever just lost a darling baby child. "Po' Miss Helen," she said.

A car passed on the road. Helen looked at her wrist watch: it was just before noon. A hot odor filled her nostrils, a smell of body, crotch and armpit, like onions. "I just want a glass of water," Helen repeated in a weary voice.

"Yes'm. Po' thing. I sho' will git it for you. You just wait right there——" She hurried ponderously out of the room, and her huge flat-footed descent of the stairs, even from the distance, set the mirror rattling faintly, like the passing of remote boxcars.

While she was gone, Helen went to the head of the stairs and called down. "Carey! Carey!"

"Yes, Helen!" The voice floating up from the hall tried to be cheerful, lifted and fell in soft spaced syllables, rocking between professional solicitude and earnest, far-away sadness. "Are you—are you all right? Is there anything I can do? We'd better go soon. Is there anything I can do?"

Poor Carey, she thought. Such a dear, such a real dear, always trying to do the right thing.

"I'll be right down," she called. "I've got to get dressed."

In her room she spied the withered dahlias. She threw them in the wastebasket, then went into the bathroom and poured the stale water into the lavatory. As she dressed, the plodding elephantine footsteps echoed once more, ascending this time, and La Ruth appeared, with a glass of water isolated upon the vast expanse of a flowered enamel tray. "Dere, ain't dat nice?" she said. "All nice and cold and everything. You just set down for a minute and drink it all up—you look hot, Miss Helen."

"Thank you, La Ruth," she said. And indeed it was hot. Nothing disturbed the quiet; the holly leaves outside the window were motionless, reflecting brilliant tinfoil shapes of light. Beyond the trees and down the lawn the bay was slick and calm, without color, and in the sky, where only a solitary gull dared to soar through the heat, dusty gray vapor hung like a colossal balloon above the bay, threatening to unloose its dismal baggage of rain and wind. Helen powdered her face, covering up as best she could the lines and wrinkles there, and sat down—just for a breather, she thought—wondering if she could make it at all. The medicine, a sedative which she had taken two hours before, made her feel groggy and she was on edge, her nerves all raw. She longed for a cigarette—but Dr. Holcomb had said no. She sipped the water slowly and then, when the glass was empty, placed it on the window ledge, watching her frosty thumbprints fade and vanish, silver ghosts of snails contracting inward upon some sightless wonderland infinity. The floor creaked beneath La Ruth abruptly; Helen looked up.

"Miss Helen," she said, in an earnest voice, "I ain't got no mo'ning clothes. Mama she tol' me today befo' she come over here fo' me to git some mo'ning clothes from Sister Alberta Lemmon dat lives by de Bankhead Magruder place but when I went by there Sister Alberta she done left to go down to de Little Boat Harbor where Daddy Faith praise his name is holding preliminary ce'monies fo' de baptisin' tonight. Sister Alberta, she's an Inner Angel——"

"That's all right, La Ruth," Helen put in. "You don't need mourning clothes." She looked up into the scowling face, at the bulging eyes, which were bespectacled, still moist with a grief that seemed to embrace the entire world; the pink lower lip protruding a full inch outward, forever exposed to the wind and sun, ravaged by strange, livid runnels and gullies, now inexplicably filled Helen with something deeper than despair. She got up quickly. "You don't *need* mourning clothes," she blurted, with a sort of sob, and turned. "Oh, God, it's hot! What am I going to do?"

"I tried my best," La Ruth continued doggedly, in a pleading tone. "Mama she tol' me if'n Sister Alberta had gone on down to de Little

146

Boat Harbor to go by see Sister Moreen at de Crystal Auto Sto'——"

"Oh, La Ruth!"

"Yes'm."

"Just don't say anything else."

"Yes'm."

Helen sat down again, trying to summon up, out of her infinite weariness, strength, and the courage to face Carey: *he'll no longer tell me about God or Milton. I know now about it all. I know. I'll get by his silly, sweet persuasions. . . .*

"Get me my umbrella. It's in the closet where the luggage is."

"Yes'm." The enormous buttocks reared before her as La Ruth bent down, the faded skirt hiked high, revealing fat mahogany limbs and the sandy crater of a vaccination scar. "Seems like it's down here somewhere, if only I gets to it," the muffled voice went on, and then, triumphantly, holding up the umbrella, and easing gradually erect with pain and fitful, forgetful mumblings. "Dis yere one's black, too, like it should be. Mmm-hh, my back! Lookee yere, I'll wipe it all off for you right yere with dis old rag. Dis is a real nice umbrella, Miss Helen." And then down the endless tunnel of her mind, without tributary, where no thought could diverge or change, but only link with a sister-thought like elephants trunk-to-tail, she battened solemnly upon umbrellas and continued in a soft high voice: "Daddy Faith he got a umbrella dat he carries in his auto wid him ev'ywhere he go. Some folks say dat de stones on it's real diamonds. I don't know but——"

And moreover, she was thinking, he'll say that this is an inhuman, low thing, unworthy of my place in the sun, before God. That I should be so cold. And when he called me this morning he was shocked: Oh, Helen I don't know what to say. Oh, Helen it's the saddest thing. Oh, Helen I know about you and Peyton. Oh, Helen you must come today. Anyhow. Well, for my sake, Helen dear. Oh, Helen, have you thought of Milton? Oh, Helen he wants you now. Don't you see? Oh, Helen, salvation, it's all you have, don't you see? And oh Helen this and oh Helen that. And . . . oh hell!

Ha! Oh hell.

But what was this now? Somehow deflected from umbrellas, La Ruth had approached her, arms outstretched, miraculously contriving a new thought: "Lawd, Miss Helen," she whined, " 'deed if I knowed yo' misery I'd of come last night but Mama she didn't tell me 'bout it till real late 'cause I was washin' clothes over at Mrs. Massie's." She paused, swallowed hard. And now, shocking Helen, echoing Carey: "Oh, Miss Helen, Mama she tol' me dat what you

147

need is Cap'n Milton back. Fo' to keep you on dis lovin' earth, 'cause Mama say po' thing now with yo' chillun flown up to de bosom of God you needs to bide out yo' days with a dear sweet man. Gret God, Miss Helen—" her voice rose and descended on the hot air, like a cello—"Mama say 'take him back, take him back,' 'cause, po' man, bein a man he's de sinful kind and cain't help it, an' last night while she was here she heard de moanin and de groanin he made and it was de pitifullest sound in dis world, dat's what Mama say."

"La Ruth!" Helen arose, but the woman wouldn't stop, grasping her convulsively, and Helen could feel the scaly calluses of her palm.

"Mamma say ever since you come back from up there where po' little Maudie passed away, dat Cha'lottesville——"

Charlottesville. Oh, dear God, keep that out of my mind.

Still the hard callused clutch, and sweat—a Negro touching her. "She say ever since dat time you was fallin by de wayside yo'self and not seekin Jesus and all de jizzum run clean on out of you someways."

"Get your——" Helen, startled, tried to pull away, but behind those greasy spectacles the eyes, always so full of muddled despair, had in them now, beneath a film of blood-flecked moisture, the shine of revelation: "Lookee yere, Miss Helen, I had three men run away from me. All my life I done what was right and all dis runnin' away left me pretty near soured. Now come a day when my chillun flown off wid de angels and Gret God did I grieve, cryin' all de time and I couldn't move it was so hard on me, like I been clobbered on de head wid a hatchet. Den I would pray for de 'Postle and if'n dat didn't work for dear Jesus just to please send me my man back so's I could git me my lovin' even if dat was de onliest thing I could git."

She halted and let her hand fall away. Helen watched her. La Ruth was looking out of the window, breathing hoarsely, and the glow faded from her eyes then; this brief effort to make Helen understand about love and death and men and such things had been too much for her. No memory could stir her now; as if the familiar veil had been drawn over her mind and eyes, her face became relaxed and dumb again: now most likely the years could issue up only a remembrance of back-aches, fleeting spasms of love which meant nothing anymore, even in memory, the endless immolation. Almost. For her voice, this time in one last try, was wheedling and timid and high-pitched, and trailed off like water trickling down a gutter: "Mama says ever sence dat weddin' you wouldn't have no truck wid him. Like it was his fault or po' little Peyton's. Miss Helen, Mama says dat ain't right. 'Take him back,' she says, 'take him back,' for de Lawd's sake——"

148

"Shut up, La Ruth," Helen cried. "Be quiet!" And then, while the day itself seemed to be gathering huge, hidden forces at her back, like a tidal wave of heat threatening to pour over her, she rushed past La Ruth into the cooler hallway, saying aloud, "Oh, I can't stand this! I can't!" And again, "La Ruth, my umbrella!"

"Yes'm." La Ruth followed her downstairs with thundering footsteps, and, below, Carey was waiting with his white straw hat in his hand and on his face a horrid little smile.

"Helen." He held out his hand. "I'm so sorry. I'm——"

"Don't," she said. "Don't be."

"I don't know what to say."

"Don't try," she said, sighing. "Oh, it's so hot!" And thought, *Indeed if I consider Charlottesville that will be all. Which is worse, past or future? Neither. I will fold up my mind like a leaf and drift on this stream over the* Brink. *Which will be soon, and then the dark, and then be done with this ugliness . . .*

"Oh, it is hot," he was saying, behind her now, "I'm so sorry, so sorry."

"So sorry," she repeated, bending over to adjust her stocking, which Carey noticed was exposed far above her knee, the thigh blue-veined beneath, spindly. He turned away, blushing. *Oh, dear God,* he thought.

"Helen, dear," he said softly, "we'd better hurry. It's almost time." *How ugly she's become. After everything. Like a ghost.* "We'd better hurry," he said again, "it's almost time."

"Yes," she said. She let the hem of her skirt fall and stood up.

La Ruth handed her the umbrella. "Take him back," she said.

"I have an extra raincoat," Carey said, "you can use mine."

"Dear Lawd bless you," La Ruth whispered, weeping, "take him back, like Mama say."

"We'd better hurry, Helen dear, it's almost time."

Carey opened the door for her and she took his arm, clasping it to her side.

"By-by, Miss Helen."

"I'll see this through," she said to Carey sternly, and then, peering intently into his eyes as they went down the porch steps: "The end is upon us. There's no use to——" She didn't finish.

What? Carey thought. Against his wrist her hand felt thin and cold. Above them, as they got into the car, the sun, unwavering, passed its summit, sank toward the long afternoon.

Five

THE hearse and limousine had passed through the center of town and now, in the western outskirts, it seemed as if there would be little traffic on the highway which led to the cemetery, six miles away. This fact was a matter of considerable relief to Mr. Casper and to Loftis, also—though perhaps to a lesser extent. Loftis *had* to keep his mind off what was going to happen, and it was curious, he noticed, with what concentration he followed each stop, each turn of the hearse ahead as it passed the landmarks of the town, and with what dread he watched the hearse balk at the stop-lights, smoke spewing from the hood. If the hearse broke down Loftis knew that he'd be unable to bear it. He'd have to run away, through the streets, crying out his agony at the top of his voice or, if it happened later on the highway, through the woods, the marsh, perhaps falling down himself, finally, in some thicket, to hide his eyes mercifully from the sun. As a matter of fact, there had been a ghastly moment when in the midst of the noon-hour traffic the hearse did stop, completely. It happened just as the two vehicles had blundered into a long line of cars drawn up behind a stoplight at Thirty-fourth Street and Virginia Avenue. There had been no reason for this, actually, because Mr. Casper had told Barclay, not once but three times, to take the less-crowded route through Niggertown. But here they were, utterly stalled. Barclay ground away on the starter, but the hearse didn't move, and from all sides came the noise of car horns, irreverent and frantic in the noonday heat. At that moment an audible sound of despair had come from the limousine. It was as if the heat and the grief and the tension had all found a voice in the ferocious blatting of horns around them; and each person in the car also made a little noise. There was nothing maudlin about these sounds; they were too spontaneous, and they came from the very heart of pain: Dolly wept anew, Loftis gasped and covered his eyes with his hand, and Ella made a low sob or sigh, hard to define, which began low in her chest and built up on a soft, high, drawn-out note of grief ending on the word "Jesus."

As for Mr. Casper, he said, "Damnation," beneath his breath and got out of the limousine. Barclay emerged from the hearse, shaken and nervous, and a policeman came up, inquiring politely (he alone, it seemed, of all the pedestrians and motorists, had sensed the delicacy of the situation) as to what was wrong, and why, and could he help. It was fortunate, too, that he did arrive, for he was the one who got the hearse started. Barclay tried again, then Mr. Casper, and finally the policeman: it was an old trick, he murmured, that he had learned driving trucks with the Army in Italy. He was a young man, very sunburned and very efficient, and he merely depressed the clutch and pulled the hand throttle all the way out before pressing the starter, and the engine began to turn over nobly. Mr. Casper thanked him kindly, gave Barclay a dirty look and hustled back to the limousine.

Now on the highway things seemed a little better, and they rode on in silence. The pinewoods swept past; the sky was blue and brilliant, with thunderheads rising enormously on the horizon. Loftis had run out of cigarettes and he knew Dolly had some, but so much did he want to have nothing else to do with her—*nothing, nothing*, he kept saying to himself—that he refused to ask her for one, and only sat and suffered. Mr. Casper, it occurred to him, was not the type to smoke.

"Milton," Dolly said, between her sobs, which had become continual now, "Milton, say something to me, honey. Come on, Milton, it'll do you so much good to talk to someone. Say something——"

He said, "Shut up," which she did, partially, and now the only sounds in the car were those of her soft, moist sobs and the rustle of Ella Swan's skirts as she rearranged herself from time to time on the jump seat, her eyes raised to the roof as if in prayer. A fever rose at his brow, sweat soaked him as fast as the wind allowed it to evaporate, and he felt nausea rising inside, a green fountain. Like pictures strange thoughts burned in his mind, old stills from a magic lantern, and waves of weak, humiliating nostalgia, sad pictures that come at the edge of sleep: *Helen, Helen,* he thought drowsily, *my lost, my lovely, why have I forsaken you?* Visions white as sunlight, perfect as one flower, a gardenia, once remembered from a dance that never stopped till dawn, they came to him briefly, vanished, and he believed he slipped off for a spell, thinking of Helen dressed like a cat, bearing down on him with a knife: only it wasn't a knife, it was something else, a flower or something, and they were in Charlottesville, and there was Peyton too, her lips pressed to his, saying Daddy Daddy Bunny dear, the globe revolving monstrously out of night into day again, turning and turning . . . He opened his eyes. Dolly's hand lay wet and limp on his, her head was on his shoulder. The hearse had stalled. They were drawing up into a gas station and the sky was filled with smoke.

One Friday night in November 1942 Loftis had done two things which he had promised himself not to do. One of these was getting drunk. Had he known that the next day he was to make the drive to Charlottesville, he might have contained himself, although even this, he admitted later, was unlikely. A hangover, of the sort he had suffered from more and more during the past few years, tended to keep his mind, upon awakening, morbidly aloof from reality. On days like this, which was most every day, each object surrounding him (shoetrees, knobs on the kitchen range, his fearful razor) seemed to send out urgent, vaguely flippant tentacles of sight and sound which suggested that it was not *he* who existed at all: he was the inanimate one, listlessly humoring a queasy stomach, and these—tricky gadgets of metal and rubber—were possessed of thriving, noisy life and the power to drive one witless with anxiety. At the age of fifty he was beginning to discover, with a sense of panic, that his whole life had been in the nature of a hangover, with faintly unpleasant pleasures being atoned for by the dull unalleviated pain of guilt. Had he the solace of knowing that he was an alcoholic, things would have been brighter, because he had read somewhere that alcoholism was a disease; but he was not, he assured himself, alcoholic, only self-indulgent, and his disease, whatever it was, resided in shadier corners of his soul—where decisions were reached not through reason but by rationaliza-

152

tion, and where a thin membranous growth of selfishness always seemed to prevent his decent motives from becoming happy actions.

Here, too, like a sore, dwelt the perpetual consciousness of the failure of his marriage. Sober or drunk, he usually managed to keep this knowledge well back from the forefront of his mind; only in the half-death of a hangover when his mouth was a blister, his head stuffed with mohair, his guts an unquiet pulp, would this knowledge erupt and seep into his awareness and paralyze him with the sense of some evil trickery, of soul-disease, of secret nastiness. Nothing could help him then, not even a triple bromide; he could only wait for the sunshine or wind gradually to disperse his worries, and for his mind, like the slow expanding pupil of an eye, to think bright thoughts of familiar pleasures, familiar consolations—Dolly, for instance, or, more often, Peyton.

Fifty years had left him the appearance of a gratuitous, if somewhat dissipated youngness. His face was lean and florid, and just a little flabby around the jowls. His nose had a slight uptilt which he thought peculiarly aristocratic, and possibly it was, except that it exposed the hair sprouting in his nostrils—which Dolly would soon bring to his attention and which he would begin to clip. Otherwise his body was in good form: he thanked God for the co-ordination which made him a fine golfer—a gentlemanly winner in the Virginia tradition, he nonetheless loved to win, and he would never have taken up the sport merely for the exercise. Whisky, however, had begun to affect his game.

This lingering vitality was partly responsible for the resentment he felt at growing old, for the murky, suspicious resentment he bore toward Helen. "I am a fool maybe," he'd say to himself, or to Dolly. "She's right, you can't just uproot these roots. You know what it does to kids—" and passing quickly over this disagreeable thought—"but listen—I've got youngness in me yet. And she—her hair is getting gray, her face pinched with bitterness, or religion. That fruity preacher." Helen took no pains to conceal her new interest from him, and the fact that it should come to this—her becoming, after all, old before her time, obsessed, a little weird—sent him off into spasms of quiet, ineffectual anger.

He might have known; thirty years ago he might have guessed it, during their ambiguous, frustrated courtship; something might have informed him then, but he had been young and stupid, and it was too late now for recriminations. What else could he do, except stay married? What else? That they had lived so long together anyway, was, he often thought sourly, a matter for record; yet, because he was an idler of the most accomplished sort (this he was aware of); because, set out on his own, he could never earn enough, he knew, to maintain his self-imposed, patrician standard of living—he was still dependent upon Helen. And she, as she said, "for the children's sake," upon him.

Even though this was not all. Yes. This was not all. For though their supper conversation was guarded, and so chilly that it seemed their breath must turn frosty on the air, there yet had remained beneath the mistrust and suspicion that enveloped both of them the tiniest germ, some memento each of them had unconsciously salvaged, that cautioned them to keep their voices down and remember, hush: listen—the aerial melody of departed gaiety, as fragile as the smoke from burning dance cards, candles, midnight fires, might still be heard, very sad and distant, if you closed your eyes and let the years fall away. They had never closed their eyes, but the sense of something small and winking and indestructible remained; they had attended concerts together, and church (he on Trinity, Ash Wednesday, Easter and Christmas), exchanging valiant smiles and greetings with those friends who suspected all there was to suspect about them, but who turned away with frowns of doubt: "Oh, I can't believe there's any trouble there. Look at the way he laughed at her!" And then, hidden from curious eyes, they would drive home together in mountainous silence, say polite good nights and go to bed—she in her room and he in his—and on at least two occasions which they both remembered their forefingers touched and twined together, embarrassed and tentative and somehow disembodied, like little vines, but fell quickly away, while they marched briskly toward their separate rooms, pausing at their doors to turn, not looking at each other but still back to back, heads cocked to one side, listening for the aerial muted strand of vivacious music that was to both of them familiar but not ever quite heard, and so forever lost.

They stayed with each other. It was a perverse, heartless business. For a while everything would go along smoothly, considering the circumstances. Loftis would keep Dolly skillfully in the background, thus in a way managing to have his love and a certain serenity, too, for he noticed that whenever—by lies and disguise or, more often, merely by a large show of acting "naturally"—he screened his affair from Helen, she was almost pleasant again to live with. They would listen to the radio together, talk desultorily about the war, and often she fed him sandwiches and coffee, or supper, on the nights Ella and

La Ruth had off. But it was a heartless business for the most part, full of uneasiness and sudden, painful surprises. On certain days, either by a misstep, a revealing gesture on Loftis' part, or for no actual reason that he could figure out, Dolly would loom large in Helen's consciousness. He could always tell. Then she'd stop speaking to him and play with her garden, take Maudie for long lonesome drives in the car, or disappear at night (which gave him an opportunity for visiting Dolly) to see Carey Carr. Often she'd go to bed with an obscure ailment.

These times were for Loftis brutal and agonizing. They made him realize the precarious sort of life he was living and brought him closer and closer to the decisions he knew he would eventually have to face. And moreover, where these moments of confusion—as they often did—concerned Peyton, they left him shaken and furious, but even less able to act, like a bug wriggling upside-down on the floor. There had been last Christmas, for instance, in 1941, when Peyton came home from Sweet Briar for the holidays. That had been close to the end of everything, but not really. And why not? Lord, it had been those hats, he thought, those awful paper hats, which had made the season so grotesque and had finally clinched the issue. Crumpled tissue, purple and green, they had crowned Christmastime not with gaiety but with the sick hue of disaster, and long afterward they had given him dreams—floating about like gaudy sails in his consciousness. Actually it all shouldn't have been that way; at least it hadn't looked that way in the beginning. Here was Helen a few days before the holiday began, blithely energetic, hanging up wreaths and ribbons and tinsel bells. Fixing things up—she let it be known in an offhand way—for Peyton. Now wasn't that surprising? he had thought. He just couldn't figure her out. Maybe she was becoming normal again, for a time. But he was miserable for thinking it was odd: why shouldn't a mother want to make her daughter happy?

During these first several college years, in the summers and during Peyton's vacations, she and Peyton had managed to get on together with a minimum of friction: although they seldom wrote to each other, arrivals and departures were solemnized by kisses, they exchanged small gifts, and in general disguised their feelings, whatever they were, beneath masks of smooth feminine guilelessness. Loftis was aware that Peyton and Helen were not "close," but he knew that there was a certain love between them—an abstract sort of love, perhaps, but love nonetheless. My God, naturally. That they were not "close" he attributed just to the obscure quirks in human nature,

Helen's unfortunate neurosis, or, more probably, some furtive and unnatural sorcery practiced by Carey Carr. Anyway, he had been glad, if surprised, to see Helen exerting herself—so long as it was *really* true that she was preparing the house for Peyton's arrival on Christmas Eve. He had a few suspicions but he overlooked them. He glowed. Pearl Harbor had come three weeks before and was already half-forgotten: he felt that he could get an Army commission, perhaps a colonelcy, but that could wait. The season was filled with the odor of pine and cedar, as raw and heady as new-planed timber; there were eggnogs, dances, boisterous open fires; and old friendships, withered by the year's mercenary hustle, flowered anew, unless one was caught kissing another's wife too long beneath the mistletoe. His manner with Helen became fairly ingratiating, and he gradually forgot her; in the round of parties he even forgot Dolly, too, until she telephoned on Christmas Eve to remind him of his defection. He had instructed her never, never to call him at the house, but she had disobeyed—and at the wrong time. Ah, the horrible, chancy, luckless wrong time. At an eggnog party that afternoon, partly in honor of the new-born Christ and partly for Helen's brother from Pennsylvania, Edward, a bluff, red-faced man who had made the transition from coal broker to Army colonel with no noticeable loss of stuffiness. He was stationed at Camp Pickett. Loftis hadn't seen him for years and was peeved to note that he had got rid of neither his cavalier attitude toward Southerners nor his gruesome juvenile politics.

"Pearl Harbor was a surprise," he had been saying, "but we'll win this war. To think of those yellow apes climbing on an outfit as big as the U.S.A." Cold, erratic winds buffeted the walls, and windblown shapes of snow prowled around the house, swarmed at the windows, dissolving in a fine white shudder. The wall clock sounded five notes, borne above the rattle of conversation, through the mellow pine-scented air. By the dining-room door, unlistening and unconcerned, Maudie played with a doll, turned tired brown eyes sunward through the window, toward the ice-rimmed bay; Edward turned, too, and his eyes, seeking the sunlight, the far horizon, sparkled with tiny, propitious fires. "There'll come a time after this war when America will dominate the world scene. Then we'll seek military men for leadership. Five years ago I told you . . . you Southerners have a strange implicit faith in Roosevelt. . . . Mind you, this is no authoritarianism I preach . . , as Lord Acton said . . . but—when is Peyton coming?" On his neck a vein throbbed, a gentle convulsion passed through his throat while he drank.

It happened then. Helen, with a knowing look and a terrible mock smile, beckoned Loftis from across the room. He pushed his way through the crowd to the telephone. "It's a woman," he heard Helen say acidly. And then, furiously reproaching Dolly, he watched Helen disappear up the steps. She never returned to the party. Loftis said good-by to Dolly angrily. Yes, dammit, kitten; he'd see her soon. The afternoon wore on, dusk came; Loftis tried to keep the party going, but something heavy and vindictive hung in the air. The guests sensed this. Most of them knew of the Loftises' "trouble," and some of them, at least, had been cheered when they noticed that Helen didn't seem to be the withdrawn, tragic figure which gossip, for a long time, had made her out to be. But the telephone call had fixed all that. Nothing sends so chill a wind over conviviality as the knowledge of some approaching domestic unpleasantness; so the guests drifted out, leaving behind them, to sparkle with soapy rainbow hues in the twilight, their empty eggnog glasses.

It was at that moment, Loftis remembered, when the last guest (a young bachelor, very drunk, who had lingered to scrape moodily at the dregs in the serving bowl) had staggered away, that a wild sort of panic seized him. Where was Peyton? Why didn't she come? What had happened? His beautiful, gay party had been instantly shattered, like a Christmas-tree globe trampled by wayward feet. For some unknown reason, he was almost sober. He wanted to kill Dolly, but instead he said, "I'll be back in a minute, Edward," and with a curious irrational remorse went upstairs, passing the room where Ella, laced and ribboned, with a sprig of holly pinned to her breast, was putting Maudie to bed. He knocked at Helen's door; it was unlocked, and he entered. She was in bed. It was warm in the room and only a sheet covered her. There were no lamps on in the room; red fire, reflected from the snow, the sinking sun, had fallen upon the bed, and her folded arms seemed to gather this light to her breast like roses. Motionless, she lay in an attitude of death, a crimson marble sepulcher.

"You left," he said.

"Yes," she answered, looking straight upward.

"Why?"

"I don't know."

"Why?" he said, more loudly. "You could have been a little less rude, you know."

"I don't know. I think I'm catching a cold."

"Good God," he said.

"What?"

"Nothing," he answered. He sat down in a chair beside her.

"When is Peyton coming?" she asked.

"About now, I hope," he said.

"I want to see her," she said indifferently.

"All right," he replied. "Do you need any kind of medicine? Why don't you take a hot bath?"

She didn't answer him. Then, "Milton——" she began.

"Yes."

"Do you think we can ever forgive each other?"

"For what?" he said.

"For all this business. This misery."

"It's not misery, Helen," he replied, "unless you want to make it that way. I'm through trying to figure all this out."

"Oh, yes, it is." She stirred a little, and the fine red light poured in rivulets down through the folds of the sheet. "Oh, yes. No one will ever know what I go through. Isn't it funny? Here I work hard for a week and I'm happy and maybe I know that people say, 'Helen Loftis, look at Helen Loftis, look, she's become reborn.' Maybe they say that. But right now it's as if I had never been born at all, or ever wanted to be."

"Helen——"

"Oh, Milton, there's something wrong with me——" She sat up in bed, pushing the sheets down around her knees.

"What can I do?" he said, looking into her eyes. "I've said I'll go and you say no. I can't go anyway. Maudie——"

"Maudie," she said passionately. "Yes, Maudie. But not Maudie. Me! Here I've said to myself that it makes no difference anymore about love, or anything like that; we stay together like boarders or something and just hold together the formal things. All the rest doesn't matter. Be boarders together, that's all; all the rest doesn't matter." She paused, ran her hands through her hair, and coughed.

"Cover up——" he began.

"Wait." She laid her hand on his, and turned toward him, in the fading light, with her eyes moist and passionate. "I talk like that, you see," she went on, "but that's not thinking. I remember. Oh, listen——" She halted, drew herself close to him, and pulled the straps of her nightgown off both shoulders so that, noiselessly, it fell about her waist. "Look here," she whispered, "look at me." She placed her hands under her breasts and drew them up a little, and he was suddenly conscious of the smell of perfume. He gazed at her

158

and a sad, gentle wave of memory ran through him, and he reached out and touched one of her breasts. It was hot and soft, very smooth and familiar. She covered his hand with her own and pressed it strongly against her. "Feel that," she said, trembling; "haven't I got love down there, too? Once you held me in your arms and kissed me. I remember the apartment. How we talked to each other so much then. All the time talking. And at night, Oh, love, you said, holding me. That's what you'd say. Remember?" Her fingernails dug into his hand; swiftly she pushed his arm away and sank back into bed. Her breasts, still exposed, fell toward either side heavily, no longer youthful, rising and falling a little as with the effort of her breathing, and because she was shivering he covered her with the sheet. Again the crimson glow returned to envelop her, but it was almost night; light in the sky above the bay swam toward darkness, and so touched her body, the room, his still outstretched hand, with the softest shade of blue. He withdrew his hand and, leaning down, pressed his face toward hers, and even before their cheeks touched he felt the glow of her fever. "Helen," he said, "you'd better—— You're hot."

"Don't, Milton," she said. "That's all right."

From below there came a slamming of doors, young happy voices, and then Edward's laughter, too loud.

"There's Peyton," he said, drawing his face away from hers. For a moment they were silent. "She hates me," she whispered. He took her hand in his and held it tightly. It was awful. A note of music, stark and persistent, sounding from nowhere, but filled with the sense of indelible pain, hovered in the air, and he shook his head, as if to cast it away from him, thinking of his children, of that old ecstasy no longer his but lost now, and of Maudie dying in another room. Beneath his fingers he felt the web of veins which lined her hand, and he pressed it to his cheek. "Oh, no," he said, "oh, no, don't say it." But it passed. Sunk in resolute silence, she didn't answer; she pulled her hand away, breathing deeply, and the music vanished. His pain was snatched up into the night, as if by an unseen hand.

He would recall later how that moment had expressed for the last time the tenderness that existed between them. It seemed the closest they could ever get. Why hadn't something important happened, then? It was as if he—yes, she, too; how could he tell?—had just tried too hard. No one knows when the heart's eye opens; theirs had opened wide for a moment and had gazed each at the other, then blinked shut as quickly. It was too late now, he knew; anything might happen, and he was prepared for an emergency. He got up.

"Do you want to see Peyton?" he said.

"No."

"You said you did."

"A little later. I'm tired now."

"She doesn't hate you, Helen. It's you who hate things around here."

"She has said to me," she went on in a soft low voice, "she has said, I hate you."

"Don't be childish."

"She said that to my face."

It was no use. Damn Dolly anyway. Why had she called? And then it all came to him in a sudden bitter flash. He leaned over her, saying sharply: "Why do you have to take all this out on Peyton? Helen, what's the matter with you, anyway? You're not well. Let's go to that Norfolk man like I said. I just can't take any more of this."

She stirred, sighed, a thin ugly phantom of a laugh escaped from her throat, and she murmured: "Old innocent Milton. How thoughtful."

Yes. Good God, there was nothing to do. Some cold guilt crept up his back and he shuddered, saying quickly: "Helen, listen. Helen, I'll throw up all this other thing, you know. If you'd just not antagonize Peyton. Oh, God, it's so wrong! I thought this was going to be a fine Christmas, everybody saw how well you looked, and now see what's happened."

"All your fault, all your fault," she said sarcastically and because it was dark now he couldn't see her, but only heard the sullen rustle of bedclothes as she turned over on her side away from him.

That was all. He slammed the door as he went out, struck suddenly with a thought of his father's: *My son, pure frustration can lead to the highest understanding, pluck at those bare addled bones, sniff around, confront the awful truth and if you faint not, in the words of our Lord, and suffer in your hot desire then perhaps you will understand, patience, my son*; but Papa just didn't know. Papa could never realize that such talk was meant only for those who had no dilemmas anyway. He could never have foreseen this Christmas: how each minute that clicked past from the time he strode out of Helen's room seemed charged with a violent inevitability, beyond the reach of platitudes: Loftis felt he could have halted the outcome only by dynamiting the house.

And he recalled later how grown-up Peyton seemed, after a space of three months: she had let her hair grow and, sparkling with snow-drops, it fell in brown waves to her shoulders, somehow lending a new, saucy assurance to her face, which she held up to him for a kiss, grinning and breathless, and with winter's lovely glow inflaming her cheeks. She shook the snow from her coat and, holding his hand, said no, no, she positively couldn't stay for supper, Daddy, there was a dance at the country club in less than an hour, and she introduced him to Dick Cartwright, a slender, rather handsome young junior from the University, smelling of beer, who had a crew cut and an oversized pipe, which he ceased gravely sucking long enough to shake Loftis' hand, with the condescending air of juniors. In one corner of the living room Edward stood morosely nursing a drink and he bent down unsteadily and turned on the radio; having greeted Peyton and Dick, he had retreated to some grandiose world of his own, and Loftis, taking in this scene, had only time enough to turn and ask Peyton, "Are you going to stay till New Year's, honey?" before she had dashed up the steps, to dress, shouting back, "I don't know, Daddy!"

A heavy disappointment filled him (Why won't she stay home? he was thinking) and, with vaguely fearful, shadowy thoughts of Helen upstairs lying in the darkness, he turned to Dick Cartwright and offered him a drink, adding, "What branch of the service are you going into, son?"

The boy ran his hand through his cropped hair. "I think I'll get my degree and then go into the Navy. I'm in the Reserve." They all sat down.

"Better go into a man's outfit," said Edward humorously.

It fell flat. The boy made a nervous chuckle, swallowed part of his drink, and solemnly stuck the pipe back between his teeth. The lights on the Christmas tree cast a cheery glow through the room. Loftis tried to make conversation, but there were subdued sounds from upstairs—Peyton's and Helen's voices together, punctuated by silences, low and faintly ominous—and he found it almost impossible to concentrate. However, he did learn a few details about the Cartwright home on the Northern Neck, where Peyton and Dick had spent the first part of the holidays, and discovered that the boy's father was the well-known Harrison Cartwright, a wealthy automobile dealer who had strange, nebulous connections with the Byrd machine. The boy was nice-looking and had precise good manners, but with a sudden odd sense of possession Loftis began to wonder what Peyton thought of him, whether they had maybe . . . "Have another drink, Dick," Loftis said, and regretted the offer, for the boy already looked as if he'd had one too many on the road. Eventually Edward began to go on pompously and at great length about the coming campaign in the Pacific, and Loftis, hearing the voices grow louder upstairs, felt miserable, with a limping undercurrent of fury: *If Helen does anything, God damn her*—but then, taking the cue from Dick, he listened with polite resentment to Edward's speech, which had begun to compete successfully with the radio and the quavering, envenomed voice of Lionel Barrymore as Scrooge.

Peyton came down finally, but she didn't stop in the living room, and her evening gown made a soft diaphanous rustle in the hallway, then ceased as she stood, silent and mysterious, behind them. "Bunny," she called.

He got up from his seat and went to her. She looked beautiful and he took her in his arms, gazing down into her face. Oh, Lord, he thought and, aware of the answer, asked, "What's the matter, baby?"

She told him. He might have known. Helen had said, Peyton you must stay home. Had said, Christmas Eve is no time for parties, Peyton dear; Uncle Edward is here, you and Dick stay downstairs and I'll get up and get Maudie dressed and we'll all have a nice party right here. We'll open all the presents.

Or something like that.

Had said (As she saw that her words had had little effect, Loftis imagined, Helen's voice had risen a little here, and the old frantic glow come to her eyes): Peyton, dear, it's so nice to see you again, stay, won't you? You've already arranged . . . No, then? No? But really, dear—I'm so glad you've let your hair grow, it's lovely, dear— I've tried to fix things up so nice for you, and now . . . No, then? No? Oh, you've promised? (Sinking back onto the pillow.) All right, all right, have it your way then. (Turning to look at her for a moment, bitterly, then gazing away at the ceiling, perhaps with her breath now coming in long, pained gasps, or then again, naturally and easily, being mistress of her emotions.) All right then. I guess your father thinks it's all right. Go out, do what you want then. (Turning again.) Go on!

Dick Cartwright was assembling their coats and scarves in the other room, and trying nobly to pay attention to Edward. As Loftis held Peyton against him, she told him what had happened, in a remote wistful voice touched more with disappointment and regret than with anything else. She said, "I wanted to see Maudie, but—" and paused— "but I'm going, Bunny," she added, not angrily, merely with a sort of placid acceptance of the fact that she was a woman now, and that the age of eighteen was made for fun, while rather sadly, "It's too bad, isn't it, that everything has to be like this?"

Suddenly she became gay; she stretched out her arm, arched her wrist, and said in the tones of Tallulah Bankhead: "Richard, dawling, my coat if you please!" "Peyton——" Loftis began, and reached out for her with something like desperation. But she was gone before he knew it and he found himself standing alone in the hallway with the touch of her last light kiss upon his cheek, young laughter—in a way not really heartfelt at all—hovering in the air around him, as he blinked stupidly at the chill black night, the open door, the lopsided wreath, still trembling.

Pity had him shackled in frail impotence; he felt bound by threads of affection—or was it merely habit?—too thin to break. Even then, in the monstrous blush of pity which verged close to despair, he somehow knew that his vast pity for Helen was only a form of self-pity, and he cursed himself for an unmerry Christmas, for Peyton's unhappiness and his own bleak inertia. Perhaps, he later thought, he would have been justified at that moment in having a showdown with Helen, but it was Peyton who would suffer the most if there were a fight, and he knew that the longed-for phrase (mentally practiced with stern fury and gestures)—"I'm leaving now, Helen. Period"—would still only be a threat. Pity had him enthralled. Bemused by his *Weltschmerz*, he telephoned Dolly, but there was no answer. He nibbled on some turkey that Ella had left in the kitchen. Finally he went back to the living room and drank with Edward, and because he was lonely and full of pity he even warmed a little to the man's deplorable egotism, and they talked until past midnight when, to the faint sound of carols far down the street, they wobbled upstairs to bed.

So Christmas Day was ghastly. Pure hell. Waking with a headache, he knew by the sunlight that it was late, and by some dark residual sense of gloom that the day would have to be a cautious one, full of perils. The house was completely still; there were no festive shouts or excited murmurings—only silence. It felt like a house in which someone was lying gravely ill, and he got out of bed with a foul taste in his mouth. He looked at his watch. Helen and Maudie would be at church. Outside, the bay was partly frozen, but the exposed blue water was dazzling; the blues and the whites together were stark and monumental, like a day painted on a calendar, with no subtle colors anywhere. But far off in the north, clouds were gathering, promising more snow. He made a ticklish shave and dressed and tiptoed into the room where Peyton lay sleeping. He sat down on the bed beside her and roused her with a kiss. She stirred, stretched and pressed her head down into the pillow.

"God, I've got a hangover," she said.

He punched her in the ribs, gently, and leaned down and kissed her again. "Baby," he murmured, "what did you say?"

She opened one eye and then the other, wide, and, blushing, covered her head with the pillow. "Didn't know it was you" came the muffled voice.

He spanked her across the bottom. "Merry Christmas!"

"Ow!" She sat up, hair falling across her face.

"Who do you love?" he asked.

"Me."

"No," he persisted, "who do you love? Who's your sugar baby?"

She frowned, squinting into the light. Then she rested her head on his shoulder, and said sleepily: "Bunny. Anyway, it's 'whom' do you love. I think."

"Spell it."

"J-A-C-K-A-S-S."

"That's not right, but it'll do. Since you've got a hangover. When did you start hitting the bottle that hard? I thought *I* was the family disgrace."

"Oh, darling, I have the vastest capacity ever," she asserted, in a new sprightly voice, "I go with the KA's, you know. You should know. You're a KA yourself. I have really an enormous capacity. It's good for you. It clears the mind and allows the entry there of things of the in-tell-ect. I also have lots of other vices."

"What do you know about intellect? Or vices?"

"That's what Dick said."

"He's a nice boy. Do you like him?"

"Mmm. He's nice enough, I guess. He's in love with me," she said serenely.

A curious sinking sensation came over him. "Where is he now?" he said. "I thought he was going to stay here."

"He was, but when we came in this morning at the glorious hour of three-thirty he and Chuck Barlow just had to go to Chuck's house to finish drinking. Chuck's a KA too, you know—the Barlows live down in Hampton. So I told him to go on, it was all right with me, and I'd see him tonight." She paused, thoughtfully; her brow went up in tiny wrinkles. "I was a little scared, though. The roads are full of ice, you know, and everyone was most gloriously drunk. Bunny, you should have heard them singing—all the old songs—it was lovely. Oh, give me a cigarette, Bunny."

Now he would ask her. He held out a pack of cigarettes, saying, "Baby, aren't you going to stay until New Year's?"

She lit the cigarette, pushing the hair back from her eyes, and gazed toward the bay. "Are you?" he repeated, adding irrelevantly, as if he didn't want at all to hear her answer: "You've got to come down and open your presents."

"Uncle Eddie's gone," she said.

"What?" he exclaimed, surprised.

"When I came in he went out. They called him from camp. An emergency or something. He didn't want to wake you up. God, he looked lit. Mother was downstairs in her bathrobe telling him good-by when I came in."

"What would the war do without Edward?" he said, with a touch of malice and perhaps jealousy.

"What?" Peyton said, turning toward him.

"Nothing." He took her hand. "Are you going to stay with me a little while?" His voice was light but there was sudden pleading in it, and in order to hide his anxiety he added with a laugh: "Baby's got to quit running around the countryside all the time." The squeeze he gave her hand betrayed him and she drew it away, saying in the impatient, grown-up tone: "Oh, I don't know, Bunny. Now if you'll just get out of here—" kissing him smack on the mouth—"I've got to get dressed. I'm just most violently opposed to men watching my soft young baw-dy. Now go on, sweetie."

"O.K." He got up. At the door he turned and said, "Did she say anything else to you last night? When you came in?"

"Oh, I'm hung over!" Hard noontime light filled the room; it was a light which, from where he stood, dazzled and blinded, yet it possessed a cold transparency, a frozen lemonade color that brought to his eyes, still puffy with sleep, all the familiar, forgotten configurations of the room: the bookcase in fading childish enamel, red and green; tatters of high-school pennants still clinging to the walls; and in one shady corner a locker colored in naïve pink where still lay, for all he knew, in positions of blushing painted catalepsy, all the cast-off dolls. Here, framed in the sun's bright rectangle, she was already undressing, and along the arch of her back were drawn, like marks from a lash, the slatted shadows of the open blinds. Fascinated and confused, he watched this woman: she was shivering a little from the chill, and there was a final swift wriggle as the pajama pants fell from her waist.

"Well, are you going to stay honey?" he fairly shouted, in a broken voice, but she only called back over her shoulder, "Daddy, get out of here!" and, swallowing hard, he left the room.

The moment of excitement, confusion, whatever it was, lingered briefly but soon passed away, for when Helen arrived a few minutes later, pulling up the driveway with a sputter of tires on the hard-packed snow, the day began to gather quick momentum. Oddly, she put him off guard at first, not with a mere "Merry Christmas!" but with: "My, you should have seen the church, Milton. It was beautiful," smiling at him in an equivocal way, which made him turn his eyes aside, and still cautious, he started to make a general reply—"Well, nice!" or even, "Splendid!"—but she had deposited Maudie on a stool beneath the Christmas tree and, because Ella had been granted leave of absence to attend church, hurried into the kitchen to fix dinner.

He was not aware of the moment when the sky became overcast. He poured himself a drink; a smell of cooking drifted in from the kitchen, and in boredom, waiting impatiently for Peyton to come downstairs, he sat on the floor beside Maudie and picked out tunes on a toy xylophone. His gifts had not been opened: there was a large square package, probably a dressing gown, from Helen, another, smaller one from Peyton. Neither Peyton nor Helen had opened their presents—only Maudie, early that morning—and he sat amid a litter of tinsel string and wrappings plunking aimless notes from the xylophone, which was chipped and nearly bare of paint, a perennial. "Listen, Maudie," he said.

God knew how many Christmases ago Maudie had first seen it, uncomprehendingly pushed it aside, or how many Christmases, each Christmas, it had been revived by Helen to tie together the passing years, to perform its tinkling ritual of remembrance, regret and undying hope. Now, bending over him, Maudie inclined her head to one side and was pleased, perhaps, for she stared into space with brown rapt eyes which made him at least imagine she was pleased, as the hollow insipid knocking notes echoed plunk-plink-plunk around the room. *Si-lent night, ho-ly night.* There was an inept clashing of pots and pans in the kitchen, an undertone of furious, obsessed whisperings—was she talking to herself? "Helen!" he called dutifully, "can I help you?" No answer. He drank, looking up from the xylophone, and saw that the sun, like the day itself, passing with the merest unconscious flicker of a threat out of morning, had faded: a ghostly recessional of ocean-bound clouds hung over the bay, gray, portentous, billowing, enveloping the snow in an apron of dull dingy smoke.

Nor was he aware that Peyton had come downstairs, passing silently through the hallway, and was now standing in the door of the kitchen, saying, rather timidly: "Merry Christmas, Mother."

There was no reply. Peyton set her mouth firmly and went on: "I said Merry Christmas, Mother." Still there was no answer, only a flurry of mutterings that rose from the stove where Helen, her back to the door, was bending over a huge turkey. Helen's elbow knocked a pan to the floor with a clatter. She turned without looking at the floor and faced Peyton.

"Well," she said, "I suppose you're satisfied."

"What do you mean?" Peyton said.

"Are you *really* satisfied with yourself?"

"I—well, I don't know what you mean."

Helen leaned down and picked up the pan, wiping it on her apron. "Your Uncle Edward. He came all the way down from Blackstone on special leave to see us. He wanted to see you especially." She turned back to the stove, shaking her head. "Oh," she said loudly and paused, and in the silence that sound hung like an enormous zero between them. "Oh," she repeated, and turned again. "He was so shocked. Really, Peyton, he was so shocked. To see you coming in like that with that drunken boy. He wanted so much to see you before he left." She went back to the turkey, and her hands were trembling as she began to baste the bird with a spoon. Part of the turkey had been burned a little. "Haven't you got any self-respect, Peyton? Who taught you to act like that? To drink, to——"

"Shocked, my eye!" Peyton said.

Helen remained motionless, her back to Peyton still, the spoon suspended in mid-air, dripping grease. "Huh!" she said. It was almost like the first part of a laugh.

"Shocked, my eye!" Peyton repeated. "Uncle Eddie shocked! Why, dear, I've never seen anyone so polluted. Why don't you come out and say what you really mean, Mother? Why don't you? Why don't you say it was you who was shocked? What's wrong with you, anyway?"

Helen wheeled about, her mouth an oval, hovering on speech.

Peyton said, "Just a second. Don't give me that 'drunken boy' routine. He's my friend and I like him and what's the matter with you, anyway, Mother? Good God, Mother!" Her face was red with anger and she stood in the doorway, trembling, the two of them trembling, voiceless, both ready to burst into tears. The kitchen was littered in amateur disarray; a sweetish smoke arose from the stove, something was burning. From the living room, in thin inconsequential slivers of sound, came a carol on the xylophone.

"I've tried——" Helen began hysterically.

"Oh, nuts!" Peyton said in a low voice. "What's the matter with you, anyway?" She turned; the skirt of her bright red suit whirled about her knees; she stalked out of the room.

For half an hour they sat in the living room together—Peyton, Maudie and Loftis. No one said a word—except Maudie, who hobbled to her feet once and went to the window, remarking in low awed tones about the sky: the sun, what happened to the sun? The presents lay unopened. Peyton thumbed through a magazine; her face was still set in anger, and red, and she nervously crossed and uncrossed her legs. Outside, whirlpools of snow eddied down from the cedars; a fuzzy gray light filled the house. They waited. Wretched, and with another drink cupped in his hand, Loftis watched Helen's shadow, a brief pale reflection in its passage from the kitchen to the dining room and back, pass the hallway mirror: she bore plates and dishes to the table like a reluctant acolyte, votive, long-suffering, and there was menace in her hurried tread, in those footsteps so quick and determined and ceremonial. Like the trampling feet of some penitent no longer in love with penitence, but only rather tired, yet bound to see it through. Finally, in a flat, spent voice, she called, "Dinner's ready."

They went in. Just as, inevitably, they were eating Christmas dinner under a fog of hostility, so, as inevitably, and as a not really very ironic sort of counterbalance to the tension, Helen surpassed herself: the meal, except for a small burned part of the turkey, was impeccable. Everything was present, accounted for: clams, cranberry sauce, oyster dressing, a handsome centerpiece of ivy and holly. Yet Loftis knew there was pain and martyrdom in the precision with which the salt cellars were filled, in the careful fold of the napkins. All without Ella, all by herself. All by herself. For Peyton, perhaps. For us. For the family. God rest you merry . . . The day grew quiet. There was little conversation, and what there was of it was stiff and unconvincing. Helen, calm now, talked serenely of the weather: it looks like more snow. Solemnly Maudie thanked everyone for the fourth or fifth time, with a gentle nod of her head, for the presents she had received: thank you, Papadaddy, thank you, Peyton dear. Peyton tried to tell Loftis a joke, tried to eat. Glancing at him with a look of disgust, she let her fork drop helplessly, her plate still half-filled. A terrible melan-

in sudden mimicry, Maudie, who had started to cry. He alone was left sitting, with a feeling of paralysis, watching them. Above Maudie's frightened moans came Peyton's "Oh!" again, and Helen, the purple hat still slanted violently across her brow, her eyes growing wide with awareness, contrition or regret, perhaps just fear, put both hands convulsively to her mouth and began to sob. "I've tried to make——" she began. But no one was listening. Peyton tore off her own hat, threw it to the floor, and rushed weeping past Loftis out of the house. He was transfixed. It was many seconds before he was able to rise and shout, with lamentable rhetoric, "Helen, by God, this is the end!" But in the meantime she had run to the vestibule, dragging Maudie with her, and he could hear her frantic voice at the telephone: "Carey! No. Yes. May I speak to Mr. Carr?"

He grabbed Peyton's coat and his own, and followed her outside. It was frightfully cold; a path had been cleared along the flagstones to the seawall, and it was here, above the beach, that he found her. She was standing alone; he threw the coat around her shoulders.

"Baby, you'll catch pneumonia."

She didn't answer him, only nodded a little and shivered.

"Come on back inside now."

"No."

"Baby——"

"No, I tell you!"

"Baby, listen——"

"No."

"Baby, listen——"

"No."

"Look, baby, we'll get the car and drive down to Old Point to the hotel, have a drink, talk this thing over. It can't be this bad. Already she's sorry——" Frantically he contrived—anything to keep her with him—the weirdest blandishments. But it was no use. He turned her about and dried her tears, pulling her close to him.

"Look, baby——"

"She's crazy. Absolutely, Bunny. Absolutely off her head." She pressed her head down on his shoulder. "Oh, I can't stand it!"

"Yes," he said.

"I'm never coming back here again."

"No," he said hoarsely. "No, that's not true."

"Yes, that's true," she said, and her arms went tightly around his waist. It began to snow tentatively; past the frozen reach of ice the bay was as black as dusk, as despair, and a cruiser slid rakishly off into war and night: night would come soon on a day as bleak as this. He kissed her hair, her brow.

"Baby," he whispered, "don't leave me. I love you so."

"Bunny?"

"Yes."

"I've tried to do what's right. Do you think everything will turn out O.K. someday? I've tried, Bunny, I've tried. Do you think so?"

"Oh, yes, baby. Lord, yes."

"I'm a good girl, I think. All I've done is just what's normal. Oh, Bunny. I've——" She shivered. "It's cold."

"Shh-h. We'll get over all this."

But it was true; she was going, and he felt that she would never come back again. He felt it all afternoon when they sat alone in the living room. Helen remained upstairs. Friends of theirs, the Albrights, a youngish couple with eyes avid for refreshment, dropped in later on, and Peyton served them the rest of the eggnog. They lingered too long, talked too much, and ruined any chance he might have had to speak to Peyton; for when they left, still talking, they collided at the doorway with Dick Cartwright, who had come to take her off in his brand-new convertible. She packed her bag, avoiding Helen. She simply said that they were going back to finish the holidays at the home of Dick's parents on the Rappahannock. The snow had ceased. The air was damp and cold, and the houses up and down the street, with their dimly lit windows, had a subdued look, as if everyone finally were tired of Christmas. "Drive carefully, son," he said. "Write me, baby," and kissing her through the car window seemed neither sweet nor proper, but only the bitter farewell to a dubious season. "Come back soon," he said, and desperately: "Everything will be all right." But she merely gave him a sad grin, and winked. "Tell Maudie by-by for me," she said, and the pane of glass floated up smoothly between them, and the car eased forth down an arch of icy sycamores.

Inside the house, immersed in the glow of the Christmas tree, the presents lay unopened, including Peyton's. He poured a drink. If he could get off to war, he thought, get a commission, everything would be solved. . . . That lousy Edward with his cheap arrogance . . . Upstairs a light burned softly in Helen's room. He had four drinks in a row and went to the bottom of the stairs.

"Helen," he shouted upward, "you're a real horror, do you know that? Why, God damn your soul, I——" But what was it he was trying to say, and of what use? In place of anger, he felt only a vast, detestable pity. And at any rate, Helen made no answer. He turned on the radio: spongy sounds came out, a crooner's voice that sang of a white Christmas, and a choir of trombones shunting leaky, synthetic notes across the darkness.

He called Dolly, but she was out again. Finally, when Ella came at eight to wash the dishes, he helped her, getting soapy, getting drunk and filled with a sudden mawkish ecstasy: *Go tell it on de mountain*, they sang together, Ella disapproving. "Seems like you ain't cheersome with Christmas," she said, raising a withered arm to shove his glass out of the way, "seems like you just gittin' drunk." *Go tell it on de mountain*, he sang, loudly and bravely, *over de hill and everywhere.*

Dat Jesus Christ is born . . .

And "Good night, Ella," he said, "Happy New Year for you. Christmas Gif'!"—pressing five dollars into her hand, and finally groping his way upstairs past Helen's darkened room, the stertorous breathing sleep—dreaming what dreams?—and into bed, thinking of Peyton, close to tears.

That was Christmas. Peyton came home neither in the spring nor in the su.... when she stayed at the home of a classmate in Washington. Four times during the summer he drove up alone to see her. But from Christmas on, the memory of the holiday remained in a corner of his mind, inflaming his emotions, his affairs, and caused him to retreat from contact with Helen in almost any form. They lived like shadows together, indeed like "boarders," as Helen had said, but like boarders in some city rooming house who pass each other stiffly on the stairs, trailing behind them the warm air of suspicion and dislike and who, to show their real breeding, are each obsessively dedicated to keeping their radios turned down, the bathroom spotless, and their manners beyond reproach. They seldom spoke to each other, except on business. Loftis hated the business sessions—not merely because he was forced, with a sketchy show of politeness, to talk to Helen, but because, since money was involved, they made him conscious of his continued dependence upon her. From his law practice he received a marginal income, and the practice itself, involving as it did contracts and drafts and mortgages, was an increasing bore. Gradually though, and as if by a mutual unspoken agreement, his and Helen's daily life became so scheduled that they were not often faced with the ordeal of gazing into each other's eyes. Remorse for Peyton he knew she felt. He noticed that she kept Peyton's picture on her dresser, in a silver frame, along with Maudie's. That meant some-

173

thing, a little something, at least. And one hot, fearsome spring night he heard her call out her name aloud, while she slept: a lone startled cry—"Peyton!"—and lying in the muggy moonlit silence, alone in his room, he wondered about her dreams. When he left one week end in June for Washington, she astonished him with her shyness. "Tell Peyton I send my love," she said. He put on his raincoat; she kissed him on the cheek: it was like a feather brushing against his skin—the first time she had kissed him in over a year.

As for Dolly—well, all this time they had kept up a nimble romance, and it was an affair which should have, ideally, worked out all right on both sides, for at this point Dolly had begun to shuck off Pookie like an old cocoon, and Helen no longer gave Loftis any trouble—being generally silent and resigned and preoccupied with Carey Carr, and with Maudie. The only unholy note which intruded in upon their pleasure was Loftis' awareness that everyone in town knew about them. It wasn't because of Helen that he wished to keep it secret. He only wished to wear his rectitude like a topcoat, concealing from others what embarrassed him and made him feel not quite a gentleman. The nasty words of gossip which reached him clung thick as bats from the roof of his mind, and cast, to the very end, a bleak, secretive unpleasantness over their affair. People knew, as people in even middle-sized towns will know, their various ruses—artfully prepared, and sadly transparent: how on week ends he might entrain for Richmond—"to see Senator So-and-So," he would tell Helen, and perpetuating an unneeded deception; Dolly, in turn, would be in Richmond, too. Shopping. Everybody shopped in Richmond on Saturdays. Or Washington. Once in a while he and Dolly met in Washington, which was nearly two hundred miles away. Hell, they'd say in the country club locker room, you know how Milt's getting his. Everybody knew, bearing testimony to the fact that suburban vice, like a peeling nose, is almost impossible to conceal. It went all over town, this talk, like a swarm of bees, settling down lazily on polite afternoon sun porches to rise once more and settle down again with a busy murmur among cautious ladylike foursomes on the golf course, buzzing pleasurably there amid ladylike whacks of the golf ball and cautious pullings-down of panties which bound too tightly. Everybody knew about their affair and everybody talked about it, and because of some haunting inborn squeamishness it would not have relieved Loftis to know that nobody particularly cared.

But the war had distracted everyone a little bit. Loftis was an air-raid warden, instead of a colonel. When Pearl Harbor came, red pails of sand and coils of fire hose flowered on each front porch; the housewives, among them Helen, made bandages and learned how to stanch the flow of blood from shattered limbs; while the children, enjoying the pervading air of confusion, heard the warnings sound at night and watched their fathers, among them Loftis, rolling importantly up and down the darkened streets, shouting orders, stumbling over ash cans, and lighting up the sky with their flashlights. In the midst of all this, in November of 1942, Helen had taken Maudie to the University hospital in Charlottesville; it was a routine checkup, although this time a little bit more, too: she seemed to be getting anemic, her leg was hurting her when she woke up in the morning, and Helen, obviously, was worried. Loftis had always noticed a barometric sort of relation between Maudie's strength and Helen's disposition, and whatever winds chanced to cloud the little girl's health, chilling that small store of vitality—and *little*, he'd think, *little girl; my God, she's twenty*—also made Helen more grim and nervous than usual. It was his idea, or perhaps it was both of theirs, arrived at at the same time: Maudie and Helen going to Charlottesville for a while—for Maudie therapy of some sort, for Helen a rest, a change of scene, getting inland from all this war business. He talked to her like a doctor prescribing medicine. "Stay a while there, why don't you?" he said in a matter-of-fact tone. And she, with worried eyes on Maudie, said, "Yes, I will."

The memory of Christmas, of the vacant summer without Peyton, was still in his mind, and he was glad to see Helen go. Glad to get shut of her. With elation he drove them to the railroad depot, wondering a little at his high spirits, and finally—when they were gone—not sure at all of just what emotion he felt: how he had really sensed a genuine release at seeing them depart, and had kissed them both—properly, as a good husband and father should—but feeling the old momentary nudge of recognition in the way Helen had returned the kiss by a small squeeze, shy and nervous, almost speculative, at his waist. Yes, and the sense of regret—was it that really? It had passed so quickly—he felt when the two of them, Helen and Maudie, passed somehow through a mob of soldiers and sailors and then clambered awkwardly onto the platform of the train, the porter's voice above the babble to Maudie, "Come on, missy, that's all right, we'll get up here all right," and the way she finally turned at Helen's side and waved down at him through a blur of steam—"Good-by, Papadaddy"—smiling, looking homely and sweet and doomed.

At nine o'clock on Friday night a week later he was writing a letter to Peyton; a shorter note he had already written and sealed, telling Helen, in the standoffish, facetious tone which for the first time in his life he found himself using in a letter, that "everything is all right on the homefront." The wail of a siren suddenly filled the night and with war-inspired zeal he snapped out all the lights, fitted the silly tin helmet over his skull and plunged out into the darkness. It was a mild cloudy evening, promising excitement, and he wandered through his precinct for nearly an hour, virtuously refraining from smoking. But nothing much happened, as usual: the lights in the houses were all extinguished, the siren kept moaning, a dozen fighter planes arose gallantly to chase off the enemy, and got lost somewhere in the fog, and a spaniel ran out and snapped at his heels. When the All Clear sounded, he returned home, weary. He paused for a minute at a field adjoining his property, where the Army had built an antiaircraft battery (to protect the shipyard, they had said) and a row of barracks to accommodate the men. Night and day for weeks the air had echoed to the noise of civilian workmen hammering up the barracks, and there had been an uneasy few days at first when Helen's flower beds seemed dangerously close to ruin, while overalled figures hiked across the lawn to bother Ella and La Ruth for water. Now, with the floodlights blazing, the toadstool shape of the radar machine, humming, fanning the darkness, the field had a comfortable look of activity, and he turned toward the house with unabashed visions of glory: Colonel Loftis in Libya. It had begun to sprinkle, and when he rounded the corner he knew who had turned on the living-room lights.

She lay sprawled on the couch, smoking, reading a magazine, and she turned lazily and smiled at him when he entered the room. "Hello, honey. You been out working for Uncle Sam?"

"The word is volunteer, Dolly. When did you get here? When did you put the lights on?"

"I had the blinds closed. Until I heard the whistle blow just now."

"That doesn't make any difference, Dolly," he said peevishly, heading for the secretary. "You can see the lights through these blinds. What kind of impression do you think that'll give—the warden with his lights on?" He poured himself a drink. "Do you want a drink? And dammit if you don't mind my saying so I think it's fairly injudicious for you to come here, anyway. Not only that, but I asked you not to come. Do you want a drink?"

She pouted professionally. No, she didn't want a drink. She had been caught in a taxi during the blackout, on her way home from the bus terminal. The taxi driver wouldn't drive her any farther, but he agreed to bring her this far. That was all. My heavens.

"O.K. Now have a drink."

"O.K."

"That's better."

She drew up her legs and he sat down beside her, rubbing her ankle while he tried to form some sort of pithy maxim to brandish over her indiscretion. But he found himself rather pleased that she was here, and when she said abruptly, "Honey, do you want me to go?" he replied without hesitation, "No."

Then he paused. "But——"

"But what?"

"Oh, nothing. It's just that—well, what the hell. I told you over and over about this thing, not having to, either, because you should know anyway, about coming here, about the fact that even if Helen is away, she might come in any old time. . . . How did you know she wasn't here tonight, anyway?"

"Why, she's in Charlottesville, silly! Naturally——"

"You've been in Washington for three days," he put in calmly. "How would you know she hadn't come back?"

"Well," she hedged, "I just thought from what you told me Tuesday that from what she wrote you last week, it was pretty clear she wouldn't be coming back for at least two weeks more." And, as if she knew as well as he the illogic of this excuse—for he had told her no such thing at all—she added a postscript quickly, piously: "How's Maudie?"

"I don't know. Helen doesn't say much except that the doctors are running tests and so on." He paused. "Honey, why did you come here?"

She pulled her legs away from him and stood erect. "Well!" she sniffed. "I reckon it's fairly evident that it's bedtime. And *solus*, as you put it. Can I call a taxi?"

He sank back into the sofa. "Sit down, sit down, kitten."

Blinking her eyes at him, pursing her lips, she gazed down with painstaking reproach. And then she sat down again beside him and took his hand. "I guess I understand," she began apologetically. "I really should have known better. If you didn't want me to come——"

He kissed her cheek. "Hush," he said softly. "You know it's not that at all."

But it was that, precisely that, and her presence here made him feel uneasy and discontented. Not just because she had disobeyed him

177

and had come anyway, or because (although even now it was comfortable seeing her again) he had *really* wanted an evening alone, so that he could finish his letter to Peyton. Not just these. There was something else which he had carefully considered for the past three years, worked out in his mind with a conscious moral apprehension which surprised him, and which even made him feel a little self-righteous: that, by God, for your children's sake, or just for the sake of some ingrained gentlemanly ideal, you didn't go around making love to a woman you weren't married to, in your own house. *Your wife's house.* Yes. *Wife's house.* That was the loophole, the imponderable, the paradox—a trinity of troubles. For if it was your *wife's* house, and not strictly your own, if the greatest single burden of your life was not merely the loss of love for your wife, but the constant guilty knowledge of your debt to her—and your dependence—wouldn't the secret love-making here at home be a setting right of the score, a triumphant redemption? Frantic often, full of wild, witless indecision and mystified by the unreasonableness of a life which seemed to offer happiness only at the sacrifice of one's self-respect—thoughts like that would occur to him. And Dolly's apartment was cramped, tiny, smelling always of some invisible seepage behind the refrigerator, and it commanded a wide depressing view of the shipyard. Because of the war she could get no other place to live, and the passion that blossomed there seemed to Loftis degrading and unsatisfactory; whenever Helen was away with Maudie at the beach or in the mountains, he considered installing Dolly here at home. But—and this he knew was to his credit—such an idea he had always dismissed as cheap and vengeful, and the product of his weaker self; besides, the neighbors would see. The house would remain inviolate, not because of him, and now angrily again he began to form the words, turning to Dolly—*sweet kitten, goddamit now, you'd better go*—but here: she wound an arm around his waist, saying, "Darling, let's don't argue any."

He got up and refilled his glass. I'll ease her out nicely in a little while, he thought.

"How did everything go in Washington?" he asked. "You didn't pick up some hot young sailor for the night?"

She giggled. "I don't like youths much anymore," she said. "I like clean old men. Like you."

He raised his glass to her and smiled. "I'm the dirtiest old man you ever saw. Mentally, that is. All I thought about when you were gone was the incredible soft skin way up on the inside of your—

thighs, is it? Upper limbs, my aunt used to say. They have goose-pimples on them, most of them."

"Whose? Your aunt's?"

"No, a lot of women. They have little tiny goose-pimples all along the inside of their upper legs."

"You should know, honey. Who did *you* pick up when I was away?"

"I picked up three little girls and took them down on the beach and played Round-the-Rosy."

"Oh, hush, Milton."

He yawned. "I told you I was a dirty old man."

"No," she said with sudden brightness. "You're clean and youthful and I love you. And you've got a heart and a soul and you've got my heart and soul, too. So there."

It was very old stuff, but he was genuinely charmed. "Thank you, sweetie," he said. "Now tell me about the Grand Convention of the Apparel Buyers' Association of the Southeast or Seaboard or whatever the hell it is."

A flicker of disappointment crossed her face. "The Atlantic," she said touchily. "Goodness, I don't believe you care what I do at all."

"It bores me."

"I'm interested in your work. You tell me about your cases——"

"I don't have many cases," he interrupted, sitting down across from her; "they even bore me. I wish I had been a poet."

"Oh, you could do it, Milton," she burst out, forgetful of his slight. "You keep saying that. Why don't you do it? What would you start writing now?"

"Pornography. As befits a dirty old man. The way we make love, that's what I'd write about. The way I love it. The way——"

"Hush!" She got up and flopped down on the ottoman beside him. Grabbing his hand, she laughed and said, "You're a low, awful cynic but I love you. Kiss me." He leaned over and kissed her; fumes of whisky—his own, echoing back from her mouth, her cheeks, her hair—stung his eyes, and he drew away. He ran his hand across her shoulder. "I know it," he said finally with a sigh. "I *really* shouldn't be crude. I'm *really*, you know, a very sensitive person. Poetic. I'm sorry." The whisky was taking effect. "Now tell me, what did you do in D.C.?"

"I was a real puritan."

"Yes, I know that. But what else?"

"Well I had Thanksgiving dinner at my sister's in Alexandria and—— Oh!" She looked up at him. "Pookie's living in Richmond now. I wrote Melvin what hotel I'd be at in Washington and he wrote me there from school that Pookie came up to see him last week end. Isn't that funny, wondering all this time whatever became of the fat slob and then find that he's in Richmond after all! And—oh! the craziest thing—Melvin said that Pookie's *dating* the mother of one of his classmates, some woman who's divorced, too, I guess, and they rode down to Richmond all four of them like one big happy family. Isn't that the limit! Melvin might have a brother soon. All I can say is I hope the fat slob treats her better than he treated some people I know."

"Old Pookie isn't so bad," Loftis said leniently, "just kind of stupid."

There was a knock at the door. Dolly swooped up from the floor, eyes rolling white with surprise, and her dress made a panicky swishing as she fled, with umbrella, bag and hatbox, into the dining room. Loftis went to the door and opened it. An unshaven young man in workclothes stood there and asked him, in the slurred tones of Carolina, whether "they" might rip up a section of his fence.

"Who is they?" Loftis asked.

"Us."

"You?"

"Yep. Right over in that field." He thrust a hand out toward the darkness.

"Oh, you're from that construction crew. I thought you all had finished. When is the Army moving in? Did you ever sink that pump?"

"Naw. We connected."

"Connected with what?"

"The waterworks."

"Oh." He called over his shoulder, "It's all right, honey!"

"Can they rip up that section I was telling you about? Major Gresham says to tell you he's got orders. . . ." It was finally arranged; for some obscure reason the government wanted to remove part of his fence, which was all right with Loftis, since Major Gresham also wished to report that he would be paid—besides, anything to help the national security. In a surge of patriotism he offered the young man a drink and immediately regretted it, for the boy was completely uncommunicative, and dirty, and why wasn't he in the Army anyway? Glumly they drank together, standing in the hall while Dolly looked on curiously from the living room, and then the boy drifted off into the moist autumn night, saying, "Mighty fine," and with a lonesome wave of his hand.

Somehow the incident disturbed him. And why? Perhaps because it just brought back the consciousness of war: war was a young man's job and the young man got all the glory. But once long ago he had been young and had owned a uniform with shining bars. Nothing could ever persuade him that he hadn't liked his authority, because he had, and he wished he possessed it now. Not for authority's sake, really, but for romance: there is something about a soldier, and once he had worn his pride like a medallion past the pretty young girls, past Helen and the skirts that rustled—only that was long ago. Reflected in the window, a dozen searchlights bloomed against the clouds across the water. He heard Dolly say: "What did he want, honey?"

He thought of Peyton, the still unfinished letter.

"Look, kitten," he said, "let me do this letter and then we'll have another drink and then I'll take you home." He sat down at the secretary and, pausing, thinking, No, I'd better not have another, refilled his glass.

"But who was that?" she persisted.

"A guy." He explained about the fence.

"I don't want to go home," she said, and fell into a sulky silence.

An hour passed. Outside it rained; imperceptibly, but just as surely as his early resolution, his thoughts became untethered, and drifted buoyantly away on a flood of alcohol. Peyton, Great God, baby, come home—I miss you, I need you. Give the old man a break. Behind him, marooned in boredom, Dolly impatiently flicked the pages of a newspaper.

Now you told me [he wrote] that you're going to be in Charlottesville tomorrow. Well, baby, now I know you're going to have a good time with your young man and everything—who *wouldn't* be nice to my little girl?—but I do hope you go by the hospital. I know you want to see Maudie, but it would be the greatest moment in my life if your mother came back here and told me that you two had made up again. She loves you, baby, no matter what you think. Oh, I've been through all this so many times with you. . . .

What can I say? All I know is that it's pretty awful that this family should be like this. I do hope you went by and talked to her. If you didn't, please write her a letter. She's been so upset with Maudie, but I know what you mean when you say you feel divided and cut in half. That's the terrific part: I can see both the right and the wrong of this mess, but I don't seem to be able to do anything about it. Make an attempt, anyway, baby. Your mother's got a streak of pride a mile wide inside her, but I think she's changed now and is willing to go halfway—only it's up to you to make the first step.

It's not that I'm just concerned about the confusion that seems to reign in this family, although that's a lot in itself, but the fact that, honey, I just don't believe I can bear it if you stay away from home like this always. I know that you'll get married soon and everything, but until then it's not right for you to be running all around the country and calling other places home. You stayed away all last summer. . . .

Now. But he mustn't be like this, so depressing. He drank, full of dreams, and gay hopeful thoughts frolicked past through his mind like children's balloons. He would put things right. Dolly switched on the radio, filling the room with breezy music.

Listen, baby [he continued], it's just that I want you home more often that makes me ask you to make up with your mother. So please do this for me. But if something does happen and you don't get to see her, or if you want to wait a little while, come down here *anyway* next week end. Give the old man a break. I imagine they will both be still in Charlottesville then, so we'll have the place to ourselves and we can pile in the car and go have a picnic up at Yorktown or Jamestown or somewhere near the water. Bring along one of your young men, kid, if you want to. I think I can stand the competition. As for not coming home Christmas, well, honey, just don't worry, everything will all be straightened out by then and when Christmas Eve rolls around . . .

Christmas. Great God. Something sank within him. He remembered the paper hats, purple and green. He swallowed, filled his glass, and turned toward Dolly.

"Turn down the radio," he ordered.

She seemed to be a great distance across the room, propped up in an attentive haze.

"O.K."

"Goddamit, it's a dirty shame."

"What's that, honey?"

"Every time I think about Helen. What a lousy rotten deal she's given Peyton. Why do I put up with it?" He arose and strode about the room, enjoying his anger and theatrically slicing the air with his hand. "Why? Why do I take it? You'd think I'd have learned my lesson by now, wouldn't you? Jesus please us, is there really something so overpoweringly noble about my character that I can't just pick up and leave? How about it?"

Dolly took this as a cue and began to frame a reply, but the question was rhetorical.

"It's a shame," he continued loudly, "when you don't have the guts to get loose from an honest-to-God, dyed-in-the-wool, foursquare-gospel succubus. A real holy one, at that. Oh, God, what have I done to deserve this?"

She got up and went to him, placing her hands on his shoulders. Boldly she removed the glass from his hand and pulled him toward the couch. "Now, honey," she said, "you've had too much, don't you think? And you're tired and all and you'd better sit down over here and get calm. Sit down and rest now and tell Dolly all about it." It was moments like this that filled Dolly with radiance and desire, and like a good boxer she was pressing her advantage, even though the fact that it was not her, but Peyton, who had set off this violence, gave her a frosty pang of envy. "Please calm down, sweet kitten," she said.

"What's the matter, dear?" she asked, when he was settled on the couch and had retrieved his drink from the mantelpiece. "Tell Dolly."

"I've said enough," he replied sulkily.

At another time she would have lapsed into baby talk, saying, "Pooh, baby, Dolly fix," kissing him and soothing him, or concocting some blithe harmless entertainment to heal this *malaise*, but now the moment seemed filled with a dizzy and palpitant hope. Slowly she began, "Well, dearest, if you feel this way don't you think that now it's about time to make the break, before it's too late? It's awful, this stuff you have to take." She paused, twisting his ring: it was set with an opal and on the stone, in gold, was the seal of the University of Virginia. "Give me your ring," she said softly. But in the attempt to make the request seem partly a gentle mock command, partly a wistful plea, she succeeded merely in sounding childish, and he drew his hand away.

"Like last Christmas," he said. He hadn't been paying attention to her, and she was tired, tired, tired of hearing about last Christmas, about Peyton.

"Yes, I know," she replied. "That was just awful," and then quickly, "Oh, darling, why don't you do something about all this?"

"Oh, God, not now. I'm worried. I just couldn't, the way Helen would take anything like that now. Not even Helen."

"Yes, I know. Even Helen. Poor Maudie." There was a thought-ful pause. "You're just too good a person, I guess," she said sadly.

"But that's the way it should be. I can wait until the right time comes, I guess, but it'll sure be hard."

He wasn't listening. In his mind bitterness still perched like an ill-natured owl, blinking vengeance: Goddam. Rotten to treat my baby like that.

"I think you're right."

"What's that?" Dolly said hopefully.

"Nothing. Every time I think about things like that I feel just like letting the whole mess go to pot. Leave. Wash my hands of everything."

"What really happened, honey?" she asked, and thought, *oh oh, too late*. She had heard the story over and over again for nearly a year; now by some reflex, by some patient will to please, she had inadvertently asked to be bored, tortured. Anything distressed her—with a sense of exclusion—in which Loftis and his family, and not she herself, were involved. She didn't want to hear about Peyton again; she wished rather to have him caress her, ask her to spend the night, and she felt like kicking herself for this other encouragement. In order to divert him, then, she began quickly: "Honey, make me a drink . . ."

He surprised her. He seemed to have forgotten the story entirely, and he was drunk. Heaving himself to his feet, he didn't reply, but made an unsteady path to the secretary, where he poured out two huge drinks.

"Not that much——" she began.

He jerked about slowly, whisky slopping down the sides of the glasses, over his hands: it was like watching a puppet on wires, the way he turned. Now he was facing her, his mouth slack, his face red with whisky and anger, and eyes filmy, dilating, the size of quarters. He was breathing heavily; with each breath she heard a thin phlegmy string of noise escape from deep in his chest. Vaguely he frightened her. He stood there, breathing noisily, and she wished he'd clear his throat.

"More in fear and desperation," he said finally, "than in anger." He paused, smiled a bit, adding a genteel, "my dear."

"More in desperation," he repeated, "than in anger." Drunkenness brought forth the rolling periods, memory, his father. " 'My son,' my father used to say, 'we stand at the back door of glory. Now in this setting part of time we are only relics of vanquished grandeur more sweet than God himself might have imagined: we are the driblet turds of angels, not men but a race of toads, vile mutations who have lost our lovewords and our——' " He paused again, blinking thoughtfully, his head tilted to one side as if to hear anew, like peals from a distant belfry, the sour, defeated incantation. "I think," he murmured, "I think—I think he said, 'We have lost our lovewords.' "

"Yes, Milton," Dolly said.

"When he was alive I hated him. Now he's gone. That's all I can say. It's different. Different. He could remember Franklin Street in Richmond when Lincoln came in April, eighteen sixty-five. The trees were turning green, he said he was never so hungry in all his life, and all the niggers were running out hollering, 'Marse Linkum come save us like sweet Jesus himself!' He was nine years old, the trees were turning green and when he stood there in the sunshine Lincoln himself came by and his big old shabby stovepipe hat fell off. My father remembered that. He told me. How he came by, grave and thoughtful and tragic, my father this little boy nine years old standing there in the gutter, barefooted and hungry as hell, watching that hat go bang off a signboard over the walk and sail tumbling down into the street. And Lincoln bending down, unbending rather six and a half feet of agonized body even then only a week from death, unbending there right beside my father, picking up the hat with a little grunt. But pausing——"

"Pausing," Dolly said.

"Pausing. Looking into my father's eyes. These other eyes tragic and sweet and sorrowful: deep and old as time, my father said; it was like looking into two pieces of coal that had lain for ten million years in darkness. Pausing. Then he said, 'Sonny,' that was all. Unbending then, or rebending, straightening up and ambling on down the street like a great black giraffe. And my father, barefooted there, a little Confederate hungry as God knows what, remembering that face, those eyes all his life. As if he had looked into the eyes of Christ, like he said: the last angel, the last great man who ever walked on earth." He put the glasses down on the secretary. "We are a race of toads," and waved one hand ambiguously toward the sea, the war, adding, "The hell with their battles, anyway. I wouldn't be a colonel in their goddam cheap, mechanized war."

"Honey, you sound so bitter tonight. Being colonel——"

He waved his hand again, dismissing her. He was still standing by the secretary, and the unsteady, dangerous arc his shoulders described as they weaved about made Dolly, too, a bit giddy. "Sit down——" she began.

"Not bitterness, honey," he asserted loudly. "Something else. We lost our lovewords. Not the South or the North, or any of those old things. 'S the U.S.A. We've gone to pot. It's a stupid war but the next one'll be stupider, and then we'll like my father said stand on the last reef of time and look up into the night and breathe the stench of the awful enfolding shroud."

"Who will we fight in the next war?" she asked mildly.

"Canada."

Dolly turned fretfully away. "Oh, Milton, sometimes I think——" She looked up at him again, with a smile. "Now come here, darling; sit down. Don't drink any more."

"We've lost our lovewords," he went on wildly; "what are they now? 'I am the Resurrection and the Life.' What does that mean?"

"Milton!"

"What have I got? I'm perverted, religion's perverted—look at Helen. Look at how religion's perverted her. What have we got left? What have I got? Nothing! God damn her anyway!"

"Milton!" She had risen from her seat, her eyes wide and imploring.

He teetered slowly against the wall and said softly, "Go home."

"No, I——" She was close to weeping.

"Go home," he said thickly, "'M a gentleman. Morals. Not in m' own house anyway."

"Milton, what on earth? Oh, honey, you're so drunk. Just——"

"Please go home, sweet kitten."

"Oh, Milton."

He straightened up suddenly and smoothed back his hair. How handsome he looked, how changed! And how relieved she felt, watching him approach her now, the frenzy, by all appearances, gone: his eyes were tender, rather sad, and blinking a little. He opened his mouth once, made no sound; against the blackout gloom of midnight the curtains rustled, groped the air, and caught against his shoulder: capelike surrounding him, just for a second, they fell away then, and she was in his arms. His eyes were closed like a man in violent prayer. He kissed her on the mouth until it hurt. Pleasure and astonishment went down her back, and what a shock it was: chapped lips against hers saying like the old lost little boy she knew so well, "Oh, honey, no, don't go home. No, don't."

"Oh, my darling."

"You *won't* go home. Stay right here. I'll show her!"

"Darling, kiss me again. There."

"Oh, Jesus, I'll show her."

"Oh, darling."

The fear and worry she had wasted! All this was so simple: going upstairs hand in hand like lovers the first time (though pausing half-way, both of them, to descend silently and solemnly turn out all the lights), and swaying down the hallway, their arms about each other, to the door of his bedroom, the sanctum she had yearned for but had never even seen.

"Here, darling?" she was saying.

"Oh, Jesus, I'll show her." Over and over.

"Here, darling?"

He said nothing.

Then, "Wait," he said. He put his hand inside on her breast, paused, drew his hand away. He took her arm and guided her through the darkness to another room—a woman's, she could tell: perfume hung in the air, and a sharp smell of medicine. "I'll show her," he was saying. From the sea, wind brought the odor of salt and rain, but here all was emptiness, repose and promise, the silence of an abandoned room. Her heart beat faster and faster; she felt like a famished wanderer come back from a land where there wasn't any love: here, like all those other places, like the Hotel Patrick Henry in Richmond, or that funny little tourist camp—was it Chevy Chase or Silver Springs?—she could find, in the mystery of a strange and un-tried room, new passion, new annealment, as hot as desire, for their love, still so futile and lame. Two and three and her apartment, four places, and this made five. Poor Milton, such a lost little boy. He fumbled toward her and they undressed. In the darkness, taking his hand, with nothing troubling her secret glow of triumph, she lay down next to him on Helen's bed. Soon, "Have you?" she said.

"Not yet."

"Have you?"

"No. I can't," he groaned.

"Now."

"Yes, yes," he said.

It was a lie but she couldn't tell. In a moment she fell asleep, sleeping heavily, and she didn't wake when he stirred beside her: smothered by dreams of shame, he had been on a ship at sea, gazing toward a barren arctic headland. Beside him at the rail Peyton turned to face him, lips upturned for a kiss; but a breath of coldness, darkening the ship, sea and land, swept over them like a blast of hail. "I'm cold," she said, "I'm cold," turning her eyes sadly away and she was gone, and now it seemed to be the uttermost ends of the earth, this

187

land of rocks and shadows, walls sheering off to the depths of a soundless, stormless ocean, while far off on the heights there was a blaze without meaning, twin pyres that warned of a fear blind as dying, twin columns of smoke, a smell, a dreaming blue vapor of defilement.

Who is burning now?

Dolly slept. He turned from the sea, awoke, his head throbbing, and sat on the edge of the bed. He looked away from the sheets, the white, sprawling arms, and stared at the bay. Rain came down in torrents. Foghorns gave groans of warning all the way to Cape Henry, and searchlights prodded the darkness; the night was full of dizzy eyes. In the barracks in the field the soldiers slept. He thrust his head into his hands and thought of war and time, of headland fires and of great men, and of the shame of being born to such dishonor.

He could have died when the phone beside the bed rang, and the Western Union girl read, in weary hired tones: MAUDIE IS BADLY OFF. YOU MUST COME AT ONCE.

Even in autumn, season of death, time brings forgetfulness to thoughts of death, lost loves and lost hopes. Men (for instance, Loftis) whose fathers have lain for twenty years in darkness are often grateful that time has given them a dispassionate eye with which to view the hidden bones, the fleshless smirk, the hairless skull smothered among the roots and vines. Loftis could take refuge in time's conscience-obliterating flow just as easily as he could in whisky; as a matter of fact, it was a combination of the two—several incautious swigs from his bottle before he had driven as far as Yorktown, and contemplation of the fact that, no matter how bad things seemed, they would be over soon—which steadied his nerves for the entire trip. Death was in the air: he thought briefly of his father, of Maudie; but wasn't autumn the season of death, and all Virginia a land of dying? In the woods strange, somehow rather marvelous fires were burning: across the gray day, the road still shiny with last night's rain, gray smoke drifted, bringing to his nostrils the odor of burned wood and leaves. Ghosts of Rochambeau and McClellan, old campfires of earlier falls, with smoke just as blue as this, just as fatal. He thought of other things: a two under par he'd made last August, the thread of a song: what party was it, what dance? He drank.

He had taken Dolly to her apartment at dawn, kissed her good-by, miserably. She had said, "Oh, do call me when you get there. When you find out how everything is." He had hardly answered. "O.K., kitten. Good-by." The dawn itself was bleak, extraordinary: overcast, it spread against the western sky a pale reflection, more like dusk than morning. His head ached, he thought of Maudie. God, he thought, and all my life I have given such little thought to her. Now this . . .

And quickly he forgot her, pushed her rather, mercifully, out of his mind: a new vision appeared, filling him with relief and a momentary contentment—Peyton. For a while he had almost overlooked the sweet, glorious fact of the matter; now it came back to him with all the tender pleasure of finding, at the dry tag end of a party, four surprise bottles of beer: she would be in Charlottesville, too. He'd hunt for her, she'd be with that Cartwright boy. See, God: it is the law of compensation; for my fright you have let me still have this loveliness. Peyton, my darling dear . . . Thank you also for the C card; perhaps there'll be gas enough for both of us (even the Cartwright boy, if he wants to come along) to drive up to the mountains, to Afton.

By-by, Papadaddy. Oh, Jesus. From another pint, he drank. Past him a jalopy fled, carrying young people with pennants, bottles, celebrant smiles. Of course, he thought. The football game. Behind the receding window a girl turned, smiled and winked at him, and held up a pint bottle. He smiled back, and held up his own above the dashboard, but a curve took her out of sight, rocking wildly, enveloped by a boy's overcoated arm. In the drab county beyond Richmond— so poor, he remembered, that a crow flying over had to carry his own provisions—cornstalks prodded upward stripped and brown. Goochland? Fluvanna? All those funny names. He drank again, desperately. Among the pine woods beyond the nigger cabins smoke curled in the trees, drifted to earth: buzzards circled over, like homing angels swung higher and higher and vanished above him. Once he heard a shotgun, far off, and saw the rump of a panicky deer. *Just don't let her die, please,* he prayed to nothing, while he capped his bottle again; *for all of our sakes, just keep her alive, even* . . . Outside of Charlottesville a motorcycle roared past, a man and a woman in cowboy suits and airplane caps, and the woman turned blue, infant eyes in his direction and thumbed her nose. Choking with fury, Loftis gave chase, hitting seventy, but lost them, and at eleven o'clock when he drew up in front of the hospital he was soaked in sweat, hardpressed to find a parking space, and on the verge of getting sick.

In an upstairs corridor he walked aimlessly beneath the lofty gaze of nurses, and it was with an increasing feebleness of soul that he

189

inhaled the familiar hospital smell. Then, startled, he ran into Helen at a corner. He blinked at her stupidly, smelling her perfume, the medical vapor stifled beneath an odor of synthetic gardenias. He took her arms beneath the elbows. She looked awful, and she led him to a sun porch where they sat while she told him about Maudie. The sun porch was clean and uncomfortably warm and rather shoddy. The chair on which he sat was rump-sprung, and somewhere a radiator bore tuneless spanking notes through the corridors. He was very tight, and as she talked, filling his ears with a chant of medical terms too rapidly, too confusingly delivered for him quite to understand, he knew that it would somehow have been the decent thing to remain sober, at least for just this morning. November light, gray and depressing, covered the sun porch. His eyes wandered from Helen's face—what was it she was saying: an osteo-something, a tuberculous what?—resting briefly upon a pile of magazines, and now, fuzzily, he was gazing out over the college grounds, the leafless trees above walks where boys in overcoats hustled along, and the blue soaring hills. Absently he took her hand. "Yes, yes," he was saying, "I see," and looked back again at the sun porch: nearly deserted, it had a mausoleum air; hunched beside a window, an old man in a bathrobe hacked croupily and plucked at the antique blue veins of his hand.

"The doctors say she has a fair chance," she said finally, in a hoarse and wretched voice.

"That's fine," he said, "that's fine," and his words must have sounded as strange to Helen as to him—even while he was saying them—for she looked at him curiously, without a blink, her mouth open a little. It was odd, too, he thought, that his mind was on Dolly: nothing in particular—something she had said (to telephone her, wasn't it? Yes, but it wouldn't be really for Maudie, but only to talk to him), lingering in his consciousness—and instantly he thought how amazing, how amazing, the way she had seemed to take possession of his life, so subtly, perhaps, but totally. "Fine," he said again in a soft voice, without thinking, and feeling, at precisely the same instant, with a shock much as if he had been hit on the side of the head by a brick, that truly both of them had lost their minds. Through the gray light his mind floated into a semblance of focus, and he turned quickly to face Helen's startled eyes, and felt sweat beneath his armpits. "I mean," he said, too loudly, "I mean, Helen, what on earth happened? There wasn't anything wrong, much wrong with her when you left. Did something happen up here? What happened, Helen?"

She gazed at him for a moment. Her eyes were huge and red-rimmed, and it was obvious that she didn't quite believe what she heard. Then she closed her eyes and shook her head slowly back and forth, as if the idiocy of his question was just too much to bear. "Oh," she groaned, "oh, God." Behind them, framed against the chill sickly light, the old man was bent over the table as he picked through a pile of magazines, with one hand clawing at his crotch; Loftis shook his head, too, violently, striving for light and reason. He saw the old man's neck go suddenly up like a turkey's, Adam's-apple bobbing, as he gazed out, for no apparent reason at all, toward the hills. I *will* become sober, he thought.

"I mean, Helen—oh, you see what I mean. You say the doctors say she's got a chance and all——"

"Milton," she broke in, "I don't think I can stand this anymore. I can't stand seeing you like this. I just can't. I've just had enough. Don't you see what's happening?"

He looked at her for sympathy, in sodden distress, and he felt that he would have given all his wealth for the ability to pay one moment's sober penance. "Helen, I see——"

"Don't say anything. Just don't say anything. Your own daughter, as sick as she is, and you aren't even sane—yes, sane enough to know what's happening. You——"

Below, Halloween horns blew amid a garland of cowbells, a football sound, and the old invalid suddenly strangled behind them, horribly and obscenely, with a noise like the last gurgle of water sliding down a drain. They both turned; the man looked up, perfectly composed. He had a huge scimitar of a nose from which the skin had begun to peel away in flakes, eyes pressed so deep in his head that they seemed, to Loftis, like billiard balls sunk in their pockets. With a shock Loftis realized that the man had no hair on his body at all. And with the disregard for convention which is the privilege of lonely old people, he made no introduction but stared at the two of them from the caves of his skull and stretched a skinny, hairless arm toward the hills.

"Might as well be frank," he said. "I came up here to die. I came up to die near Mr. Jefferson. There he is—" he pointed toward Monticello—"there he is, up on the hill. On clear days you can see it from here. Yes sir, I sit here in the afternoon and look up at the hills and it takes a lot of the pain away to know you're near Mr. Jefferson when it comes time to shuffle off this mortal coil." His voice rose, thin, tremulous and old; Loftis saw a tiny flake of skin fall from his nose, but now there was a touch of color, too, on his cheeks, somehow rather dangerous. "I came all the way from the Eastern Shore to spend my last days here and Mr. Jefferson, if he was alive he'd appreciate it, I think. He was a gentleman. He was——"

A flicker of sunlight entered the room and at the same time a squat, officious nurse. "Mr. Dabney!" she said. "You know you aren't allowed out of that chair. Bad boy! Now it's back to bed with you." Mr. Dabney had no opportunity even to say good-by. He merely said, "Yes, ma'am," and humbly shambled out after the nurse, leaving behind the faint smell of rubbing alcohol.

"I'm sane enough, Helen," Loftis said quietly, turning back to her, "I'm sane. I'm sorry, too. Can I see her now?"

"No," she said, "she's sleeping right now."

"Oh." He hesitated for a moment. "Well, what are we going to do?"

She buried her face in her hands. "We've just got to wait."

It was painful, but they waited, saying nothing to each other. On the street below cars passed steadily, covered with streamers and Confederate flags, toward the stadium. Helen began to chain-smoke, glancing sightlessly through a *Reader's Digest*. Loftis tried to think of Maudie, but somehow his thoughts didn't seem to make sense: how, just how, was one supposed to feel now at a moment like this? Was this, after twenty years not of love but only a sort of sad, evasive fondness, all one felt—neither fear nor grief but just a wistfulness, a need to be left alone? It was cruel not to love or feel as one was supposed to. It was hell. And now it was even crueler, feeling as he did so anxiously the desire to say a sedative word, to know that he had already failed utterly in Helen's eyes and that she would dismiss his comfort as graceless or phony, and perhaps both. Yet he held out his hand, saying, "Helen, don't worry, everything'll be all right, don't worry," and with a mild shock he felt her take it by the finger tips, looking up at him with eyes sorrowful, almost kindly—as if for once, just for this once, perhaps—she was suspending from him the eternal crushing weight of her judgment.

"Stay with me," she said.

"Yes," he said. "Yes, I will, Helen."

"Stay with me," she repeated.

"Yes," he said.

"I've never felt anything like this in all my life."

"That's all right, honey, everything'll be all right. Just try to take it easy."

She took her hand away and said in a toneless voice: "You see, like we always expected, something happened. You see, don't you? I've told you how all my life I've been dreading this time. Remember what that doctor in Richmond told us years ago? How with her like she is you never knew what might come up to make her take a turn for the worse. Now this——" She paused. "But I know," she went on in a monotone, "I know. I know what's happened." She hesitated again, continuing in a voice more agitated: "Yes, I know, Milton. And I'm the only one that knows. Only if anything happens I'll tell you. Do you understand what I mean?"

"No," he replied, "no, Helen, I just don't see——" Listening to her, he could have sworn that for a moment she had gone mad, but now again she was clutching his finger tips, saying calmly, "Stay with me, Milton. Stay by me now. Stay with me, Milton."

"Yes, Helen, but what was it that——"

The same dumpy nurse appeared at the door with a busybody rustle and a tray bristling with thermometers and it occurred to Loftis that she looked like Mayor LaGuardia of New York City. "Mrs. Loftis," she said, "Maudie's still asleep, but Dr. Brooks would like to see you for a minute."

Helen got up quickly. "I'll just be a minute, Milton."

He rose from his chair. "All right," he said. "Don't you want me to——"

"No," she said, "that's all right. Dr. Brooks, he—he knows me and——"

Clumsily he took her by the arm. "Don't worry, honey," he said. "She'll be O.K. We'll all——" But she had left.

He walked to the window, thinking of the women in his life. He yearned for a drink, and wistfully his mind sought the glove compartment of the car. From below came the noise of moaning horns and a faint sad sound like distant tambourines, and people walked beneath the leafless trees. Against the hills a big blue kite rose and fell. Four young people passed in an open convertible, singing, waved an orange banner, and were gone, while behind him, borne through the odor of medicine, came a woman's voice demanding Dr. Hall, Dr. Hall in surgery: heavy the scalpel of him who cuts, heavy the knife, heavy the guilt. Professional men like himself, they knew the power of specious knowledge. He licked his lips; they were dry. He was a little surprised to feel a nerve twitching beneath one eyelid. What was it that Helen meant about Maudie? Or had finally just something snapped inside her? Poor little Maudie, he thought, just don't let her . . . The kite soared against the gray sky, swooped nervously and caught its

193

tail in a tree. Two boys went up after it, groping among the branches, but finally gave up, and the kite hung disconsolately among the topmost limbs, a splash of blue, like a jaybird snared in honeysuckle. Below it there was a lane, a row of houses, and the cottage, a seedy place, he remembered, but somehow redeemed even then, and that was thirty years ago, by the wild roses which grew around the porch, as in a novel by Gene Stratton Porter. They called it Sleepy Time Home, in the way of lovers who are eighteen years old; and eluding her father, who was a brakeman on the C & O Railroad and who despised University boys, was an exciting and dangerous thing. Late spring and Papa was away to Waynesboro or Staunton or somewhere, and they lay down in the darkness holding each other while she cried, saying: "Oh, honey, I just can't stand it. If Papa was to find out what happened he'd kill me, he'd kill me——" And bravely, resolute but frightened, and feeling even then desire like smoke rising between their bodies: "Don't worry, Audrey. Don't worry, honey, nobody'll find out, I'll get a doctor or something. . . . I know a fellow . . . somewhere . . ." How like that fear was this fear he had now, how long ago it was! He pressed his brow against the window, trying to remember. My God, Audrey—Audrey what? But he had been lucky; it had been so simple at that age to be cruel, since eighteen has no heart.

She had been lucky, too, had later told him, "I'm all right now, honey. I was just scared for a couple days, I guess." Asking him to kiss her again, like he used to. "No," he had said. "No, I'm going now." And her sorrow then, her horrible gasping enormous sorrow. "I'll kill myself." Frightened, he had replied, "Go on, I don't care," and had walked out into the swollen May evening, waiting for a shot, a shriek that never came, and disillusioned, for the first of many times, with love. At that age he was clear-headed enough to understand that he was not alone in a world of mismated passions: others betrayed and were betrayed, and got tired of loving. But his soul was romantic, and although he never saw her again he felt pity for her, and despised himself (just a little) for his misprision. Yet to have even *that* much conscience now, how noble it would be: he might have become a great man, a great lawyer, a poet. And pettishly, as he gazed at the kite in the tree, he tried to curse himself, but couldn't, and found himself cursing instead the obstinate female flesh which had destroyed his conscience even more brutally than time, and had brought him to these convulsive days and untidy evenings. He thought of Maudie dying, and of Helen, and he felt sick with fear and sorrow. The kite trembled in the wind, fell to another branch and then lay still. The row of houses looked gray and cold and shabby. That was so many years ago, she'd be nearly fifty, a woman run long ago to fat, with bad teeth and a house smelling still, most likely, of kerosene. He would walk up the steps, knock at the frayed screen door, watching the cottonwood tree, filled with leaves in spring, now bare and rusty, shaking in the wind: it would be taller now, bigger, arching heavy branches over the house. She would come to the door, a slattern in rags (Why, he wondered, did he snobbishly picture her like this?), with the odor of the milk of her grandchildren, and she would ask him, maybe nicely, what it was he wanted and who he might be.

He would tell her, then right off say, "Why did you betray me, girl? Why didn't you tell me what love was? You knew, you knew. You had the secret. The trouble we had, it should have bound us together: it only made me arrogant and cruel. You knew what love was, you could have told me. You betrayed me." And she would say, "Ah, no, honey, it was I who was betrayed. I gave you the secret, and that for the last time. Your last love was with me, and you never knew it. I tried to tell you that love wasn't in the mind or the heart or the flesh, either, but something that comes as easy as morning and never leaves. But you were afraid, even then——" And he would put in quickly, "But I was young then, and though I was cruel I guess I had more conscience than I do now. Have a little charity——" But she would say, "Charity, honey, don't talk about charity. You can't undo time. Go back to your life and stop thinking about what can't be retrieved and remember how love comes as easy——"

"Don't you see, though?" he would cry. "Don't you see? I want to know the secret——" Then she would be gone, the door would close, and he would be alone on the porch. He'd try to call out her name, but his voice would fail him and he would go too. He'd leave behind him forever the cottonwood tree, the bare withered vines, thwarted by longing: that woman's flesh should never become real, but reside only in memory, and that love should be just a sound which rose like a kite through long-ago darkness—a word, a laugh, a sigh, something like that, and the noise of sagging springs and the rustle of half-drawn blinds.

He turned from the window; his hands were sweaty and his face, save for a crescent of his brow which had been against the pane, prickly with fever. The sun porch seemed unbearably depressing, and he felt that he had to get out of there, go someplace, anywhere—anywhere to think things over. He went out into the corridor. There was no one in sight. A metal box, one of those vessels in which knives and such things are made sanitary, percolated briskly, sending up a cloud of steam. He was completely sober, but his eyes watered and his head ached and he was afraid. If only he could get to the car for a moment, if only he could go somewhere and concentrate and think things over . . .

"Milton!"

He turned. Smiling, Hubert MacPhail bore swiftly down upon him from the end of the corridor, or as swiftly as he could, considering his limp. Hubert was a Charlottesville lawyer and a KA, and he stood a good chance of being a federal judge if Harry Byrd would only die. Loftis liked him, in an unexcited way, but seeing him now for some reason was actual delight and he grabbed Hubert's hand.

"Hubert," he said, "what's the matter with your foot?"

"I stepped on a goddam roller skate," he said. "The thing was rusty and for a while they thought they'd have to take my goddam foot off. I've been on sulfa for a week now——" And so forth. They sat down on a hard bench for a moment, to rest Hubert's foot. He was a large enthusiastic man with fawn-colored pouches beneath his eyes and an indecisive mustache which looked as if it had been sprinkled on; Loftis had always got on well with him, although he remembered that when he drank he became smug and aggressive. They were still holding hands, and Loftis was embarrassed. And sad. When Hubert asked him why he was there, Loftis told him and felt his eyes blurring up with tears.

"Is it—is it bad?" asked Hubert gently.

"No, no," he answered, "it's not very bad. I don't think it is. The doctors——" His voice faltered. He hated the sympathy, but at the same time desperately would have liked Hubert to stay with him.

"That's goddam tough, Milton," Hubert said, shaking his head.

"Yes," Loftis said.

"God *damn* tough."

"Yes."

Hubert slapped Loftis' knee. "Look," he said, "let's go over to the house and have a drink. The boys are warming up for the game. It'll do us both good."

"No, thanks, Hubert. I've got to wait for Helen. She's with the doctor now." He looked nervously up the hall. It was airless and deserted. In an adjoining room a man groaned, and a fat, middle-aged woman came out, poking damply at her eyes with a handkerchief and calling feebly for a nurse. Panic seized him and suddenly he
196

thought of Peyton—finally, finally thought of Peyton. He turned. "Yeah, yeah," he said, "let's go over just for a minute. You got a car? I'll follow you in mine."

Hubert slapped him on the back and stood up. "Buck up, old fella," he said. "We'll beat this goddam thing yet."

In the KA house at noon there was an air of intense gaiety. Young people milled about on the portico, in the hallway and in the chapter room, and everybody said, "Hey! How you?" very loudly to one another. Although it was too early to drink or dance, everybody casually did both, to the noise of horns and saxophones, and the girls' faces became pink and lovely and excited, so certain was each girl that this day was meant for her alone. At the bar, in an atmosphere of calculated darkness, boys and girls stood drinking hot rum from Mason jars, and here a perspiring brother at the piano splashed happily through an improvised boogie-woogie. Couples drove up in polished automobiles, stayed for a moment, and left, but they would return in ten minutes, after a short drive to nowhere, like fledglings come home to nest. No one could remain away for long at an hour like this—not merely because gasoline was rationed, but because there was something in the air which demanded noise and companionship. Solitude, two lovers together—these were for another time, this evening, perhaps, and the football game itself was hardly mentioned: it was only a hurdle to be overcome before the real happiness began. So the piano competed thinly with the phonograph and there was a pleasant ripe smell of liquor everywhere and the girls' flushed pink faces passed from door to door, from room to room, sprouting like frivolous blossoms amid waves of laughter and the muted notes of saxophones.

Into these preliminaries Loftis walked, feeling old and somewhat out of place, with Hubert MacPhail hobbling at his side. There was a sprinkling of gray-haired men about, and Loftis greeted each by name and shook their hands, although without much spirit, because most of these fellow alumni he had seen not more than a month ago, at a football game in Norfolk. Hubert limped off to hunt for Buzz, his son. Loftis looked for Peyton, but she was not around and he was told by a scholarly-looking boy, who regarded him with a patronizing gaze and called him "Brother Loftis," that she and Dick Cartwright had driven downtown to fetch some ice. Loftis thanked the boy for the drink he gave him, and warily placed himself against the wall, between a velveteen drapery and a very drunk blond girl, waiting for her date, who eyed him coyly and was able, at his most casual word, to disgorge peals of high hysterical laughter. The mood of pleasing melancholy returning, he felt very fatherly toward her, and concerned, and he once tried to prevent her from slipping, in a spasm of mirth, down the side of the wall, but at that moment her young man came up to make a laborious rescue, and then their arms about each other's waists, the two of them weaved out of sight.

It was not quite one o'clock yet, but the mood had already become one of celebration, as if the game, a formality at most, were already won: at least no contest could be lost, encouraged as this one was by such dizzy rejoicing. Outside it was getting grayer and colder, but here, warmed by the nearness of other faces and the fraternal glow of alcohol, it seemed that every cheek was lit by a beautiful flame. The phonograph played louder and louder, the piano kept rattling in a persistent off-beat, and the half-dozen boys now dancing led their partners in ever-widening, ever more precarious circles around the room. Through a haze of smoke, wide-eyed girls with pennants and cowbells wandered, to pet, and be petted by, the graying alumni, and they cornered people in doorways and chattered breezily of *party-party-party*—in Richmond last year, or last month, or they couldn't remember. The boys in the meantime had begun to gather up their football trappings—blankets, raincoats, a flask to keep them warm—but the music went on, now a sad love ballad, dropping guitar notes on the air like silver dimes.

All of a sudden the door opened. A gust of cold wind entered, and Peyton and Dick Cartwright, flanked by two moon-faced boys who began to brandish whisky bottles.

We come from old Virgin-i-a, they sang, *where all is bright and gay* . . .

The crowd turned, a cheer went up, and the two boys, their arms around Peyton and Dick, led a brassy encore: "Are you ready? Get set!"

> *Wha-hoo-wah,*
> *Wha-hoo-wah,*
> *Uni-v, Virginia;*
> *Hoo, rah, ray!*
> *Hoo, rah, ray!*
> *Ray! Ray!*
> *U. V-a.*

"Peyton!" someone cried.

"The Body!"

"Lover!"

And part of the crowd swept past Loftis toward the quartet, laughing and shouting and holding up glasses, while Peyton and Dick and the moon-faced boys, smothered by the rush, disappeared from view. Loftis tried to catch sight of her, but couldn't. The two drinks he had drunk, both stiff ones, had clouded his mind and had heightened, rather than suppressed, his sense of fatigue: he remembered that he had eaten nothing since last night. Pawing through the crowd toward Peyton—"Excuse me," he was saying with a fixed smile; "I'm Peyton's father"—it occurred to him that there were two things he should be horribly worried over: well, of course, Maudie, about which he must tell Peyton right away, and the other: what? It made no difference. All that mattered was that he see Peyton, and what was all this commotion anyway, a joke, a ceremony? A boy's elbow glanced off his cheek and slowly, amid the press of bodies, amid yells and laughter, and with the silly set grin on his face, he was being squeezed, funneled toward a chill gray rectangle which was the open door. Someone's drink slopped over his shoulder, beneath someone's shoe his own foot was mashed—permanently, it seemed—and now, while a dark-haired girl with giddy eyes laughed up at him sympathetically, he was propelled, off-balance, out onto the portico. He stood there blinking. "Peyton," he called weakly, raising his hand. But she hadn't even seen him. Already she was with Dick Cartwright in a convertible, going down the driveway, and he saw her look out of the back window and wave an orange and blue pennant.

In the house Hubert MacPhail was standing next to a crackling open fire, warming his injured foot. Loftis walked up to him. "Hube——"

"Hello, Milt. Did you get a drink? Oh, yeah, I can trust *you*. Milt, this is my son, Buzzie." He unceremoniously nudged with his elbow a thin and pallid boy, faintly handsome. "Buzzie's not going to the football game," Hubert went on, without looking at the boy. "Buzzie's going to waste a seat on the goddam fifty-yard line to stay in where it's warm. Isn't that right, Buzzie? Buzzie doesn't like football, Milt."

The boy laid a limp sensitive palm in Loftis' and gave him a tortured smile. Although he made no reply to his father, his eyes, just for an instant, darted nervously, resentfully, and without any doubt at all they mirrored a very special sort of detestation. "How do you do, sir?" he said.

"How are you, son? Say, Hubert——" he began, but Hubert had

placed a hand on his shoulder and was talking. "What do you think of that, Milt? Wait three months for the biggest game of the year and find out that your own son has chickened out on you. I guess this generation's just lost the goddam Cavalier spirit don't you? Buzzie never was much for football though, were you, Buzzie? Lord knows what the goddam Army's going to do with him——" Throughout all this Loftis watched the boy shift uneasily from foot to foot, his teeth clenched over a miserable smile, and he felt sorry for Buzzie, and for Hubert a sudden thorough dislike, and yet something else troubled him, wretchedly: Peyton, Peyton, where had she gone, and why, and had this day indeed finally become the nightmare which he had dreaded so, and—by instinct, by some vague oppressive mood of fatality—had sensed would be inevitable? The music had ceased, the young people were leaving for the game—early, in order to get seats: pert and eager, with polished skin and shining eyes, the girls dragged the boys behind them, and the boys, though drunk, obeyed, for on this day and for this game you brought the girl you thought you loved. In an alcove, bent over a wash pail, a lone stag was getting noisily sick.

"Look——" Loftis turned to Buzzie. "Look, Buzzie, you know Dick Cartwright. You see, he's with Peyton. Do you know where I could find them?" He made a venturesome smile. "Gosh, I don't know what all the fuss was about just now. I saw Dick and then I saw Peyton——"

"Buzzie," Hubert went on querulously, "has always had what we might call an antipathy——"

"Wait a minute, Hubert," Loftis said irritably, feeling a little as if he were interrogating a prisoner: "Buzzie——"

Buzzie's eyes lit up and he smiled hesitantly. "Why, Mr. Loftis, I thought you knew. Dick and Peyton got pinned up last night."

"Pinned?" Loftis said.

"Yes, sir."

"Pinned?"

"Congratulations, Milton old boy," said Hubert with heavy gusto, "now you'll have a son-in-law with piles of jack, with connections, and when you're an old old man maybe they'll let you have Harrison Cartwright's mansion to die in, just an old shanty, you know."

"So she got pinned?" Loftis repeated.

"Yes, sir."

It had made him feel as abruptly old as anything since his fortieth birthday.

"Well," he said, "at least she got a KA." Not that it mattered. He felt utterly left out of things, and he drained his glass. "Do you know where she is, son? Do you know where I could find her? She pulled this vanishing act just now."

Buzzie was glad of the opportunity to say something. "Well, Dick's my roommate and I know that he said they were going to the game. He said they were going to meet Tommy Ames at the Virginian first, though, and I reckon that's where they went to just now."

"That's the same Virginian—the restaurant down at the Corner?"

"Yes, sir."

"Well, thanks." He turned to Hubert. "Hube, I think I'll run down to the Corner. I want to see Peyton, it's pretty important. You know——"

"Yeah, I know Milt. About the hospital?"

Loftis turned to go, pulling on his overcoat. Hubert called him back. "Look, Milt—" he paused, jerking his head contemptuously toward Buzzie—"since I've got to go to the goddam game alone, why don't you take one of these tickets and meet me there if you can. I don't want to sit there and freeze by myself."

"Thanks, Hube. I can't make it. I've got to go back——"

"Here, take the goddam ticket, anyway." He thrust it into a pocket of his suit. Buzzie had slunk quietly upstairs and Loftis left, too, with a hurried flap of his arm at Hubert, who stood alone in the chapter room, bitterly nursing his foot in front of the dying embers.

It seemed as if he blundered into noise and jubilation at every turn. But it seemed, too, that gaiety fled whenever he appeared: as quick as startled children, a herd of young people galloped from the Virginian waving pennants, blowing horns, and he was alone with a sinister feeling and his bottle clenched in one hand, listening to their cowbells vanish up the street, remote and tinkling, like the tiny bells borne aloft on the wings of Chinese pigeons. With a sense of frustration which not even one more long, long pull on his bottle could dispel, he was quite alone. He stood by the cashier's desk, looking up at the clock. It was 1:30. A half-hour more and the game would begin; a half-hour more and Peyton, too, would be there, her hand on Dick Cartwright's arm and her eyes shining and excited (he could see them) and a little tearful, most likely, from the cold. And oh, Christ, was all he could think, he had missed her again.

With a glass borrowed from a boy behind the counter, he sat down in a booth to think things over. Nothing, he reflected, was more boring than to drink alone, and that was a certain comfort, to be true: he was only rarely a solitary drinker. *Ah, but Milton, that's not true at all*, said his conscience, weakly calling like a drowning man from the flood of whisky, *you are a solitary drinker, a solitary man*. True? Was it true? How could it be? Yet there was something in it. Maybe. Something in the way he drank, even among crowds, to retreat within himself deeper and deeper and—rather than to talk—to sink into silence and morosely ponder the days that had vanished like last year's leaves. *Maybe! Not maybe. Surely. You are a solitary drinker.* He put a nickel into the juke-box attachment on the wall, struggling for argument, for words. Then he drank, hummed to himself and smiled, thinking of Peyton. Just at that moment a tall woman with a lovely vacant face came through the door, followed by Pookie Bonner, dressed in a shark's-tooth overcoat and carrying a huge Confederate banner.

"Milton!"

Loftis tried to hide, to turn away, to sink somehow beneath the table, but it was too late: Pookie was on top of him, abruptly and ferociously, bruising the air with preposterous cries of greeting. He slapped Loftis on the back and shook both hands, and in the pandemonium the flag, wet from rain, fell backward and enveloped the woman in a soggy crumple of stars and bars. "Milton, dammit, boy!" Pookie roared. "How long's it been since I've seen you? Why, doggone, boy, it's been a coon's age and I swear I don't believe you've changed a bit! Look at him, Harriet. This is old Milton Loftis I've told you about."

Harriet floundered out from beneath the banner and, smiling, gazed down at him with sweet empty eyes. "Pleased to make your acquaintance," she said.

"Won't you—won't you sit down?" Loftis said uncertainly. Surely this was worse—much worse—than meeting a cast-off lover, and he wished that he was in Pookie's place. With a diminutive gesture of fellowship—a faint wave of his hand—he indicated the empty seat. "Have a drink," he added, in a spiritless voice.

Harriet sat down smiling, elaborately tucking her skirts under, and Pookie slid in beside her with a thump. "We got to go to the game in a minute," he said. "We just came for some milk. I'm on the wagon now, Milt. I got ulcers."

"It started out with gastritis," Harriet put in quietly, "but Sclater just kept on drinking, anyway. Then he went to the Medical College

Hospital in Richmond and they did a gastroscopy and found this peptic ulcer just above the duodenum."

"Harriet used to be a nurse," Pookie volunteered.

"Well, it wasn't bad, really," Harriet went on, in her mild casual voice. Loftis looked at her again; she was all of forty, but beautiful. "It was very small, nothing more than a sort of tiny membranous inflammation. I keep telling Sclater there are much worse things to have, especially in the digestive tract. Colitis, for instance."

"Yep, that's right," Pookie said. There was a brief silence, and Loftis felt that certainly the ache of his embarrassment must reach out in some way and touch them both. The boy came up and Pookie ordered milk for himself, coffee for Harriet, while Loftis, saying nothing, drank again, now with a sort of violent determination to merge with his anxiety over Peyton, over Helen and Maudie (and some other fear, too: what was it?)—to merge with these his disgust, and the sudden maddening resentment he felt, for Pookie and this abominable Harriet. Slyly he raised his glass. "Here's looking at you all," he said.

Pookie, in return, toasted him heartily with his milk, and Loftis wished for anything—reproach, recriminations, surliness, even a fight— anything but this grin of Pookie's, and his docile, agreeable eyes. He was talking about Knoxville, Tennessee, a contract he had to build some houses there near a war plant, and wasn't it a swell thing, Milt, to have got in on the ground floor? How about that, Milt?

"Bully for you," Loftis said sourly.

And *oh God:* Pookie was saying it——

"How's Dolly, Milt?"

"She's—" he yearned to be three inches high—"O.K., I guess."

"What a swell kid!" Pookie went on. "Do you know what that kid said to me when we broke up? Listen, Milt. She said, 'Between us there's no bitterness, only sad recollections.' You know what she wrote? She said, 'Where'er you walk I'll think of you because there are miles more for both of us before we go to sleep.' Wasn't that a swell thing to say?"

"Yeah." *Dolly.* The cheap bitchy hypocrite.

"It's my feeling, too," Harriet put in, with sudden enthusiasm; "she must be an adorable girl. When Sclater and I are married, of course, there won't be any regrets or bitternesses. It's not the modern way, I don't think. I believe in *laissez-faire* very much." She risked an anemic faraway smile. "When we're married we hope to see a lot of both of you——" She stopped abruptly. The smile lingered on her face but the light had gone out of her eyes like a burst of scattered beads, and she regarded Loftis emptily, apologetically, still smiling. "That is," she added weakly, "that is—of course—if you're going to be married. . . ." The voice sloped off into a tedious little snicker. "Ha, ha! That *was* a faux pas!"

"Yes," said Loftis, "it was."

His remark went unnoticed, at least by Pookie. He broke in, "Listen, Milt, when you see Dolly tell her I send my love and all, and all's the same with me as far as I'm concerned." A clumsy, sheepish look came to his face and he looked down at the table and fingered his napkin. "Each month I send her her check I always write her a note, you know, to tell her . . . you know—but she doesn't answer."

"Sclater and I believe," Harriet added, squeezing Pookie's arm, "that a lot of life is governed by circumstances and a lot of these things a person just couldn't help. Isn't that right, Sclater?"

"That's right, honey," he said listlessly. The humor seemed suddenly to have gone out of him. He was pink and flabby with a bluish hue where he had shaved and a bottle-shaped nose which always leaked a little moisture onto his upper lip: Loftis remembered that and watched Pookie now, with pity and embarrassment, and struck speechless with a sort of maudlin regret. Of all days in time, should it have really happened that this day he meet one of the few people alive who could cause him such discomfort? Was this part of the plan, the nightmare? Unsteadily the room shifted; the juke-box music, which he hadn't heard until this silence, died with a sob and a flutter, and the Confederate flag, its staff kicked by one of his nervous, shuffling feet, slid ingloriously to the floor. He leaned over to retrieve it, thinking compassionately of Pookie: poor Pookie, nice Pookie with the hound-dog grin and the big be-hind, what had Pookie done to be in his fix, or himself in his own? It came to him swiftly: he hated Dolly. But it faded, and as he raised up he heard his own voice saying: "I'm glad to hear you're going to make big dough, Pookie."

The mention of money was like speaking of ice cream to a child. Pookie looked up, cheerful once more. "Yeah, Milt. I'm going to Knoxville next week. Then Harriet's coming down in January and we'll get married." Harriet squeezed his arm again, blushing tenderly. "What a deal I've got," he went on. "The whole thing's a prefabricated job on Army specifications, so my overhead'll be cut down so I figure by twenty per cent . . ."

"All this is secret, Milton," Harriet broke in. She intended faintly to reprove Pookie, but there was pride in her voice. "Top secret. Including the wedding."

"Aw, honey," Pookie said, "it's not a secret. The job, I mean. It's just restricted. The general told me it's just not the kind of stuff that's supposed to get into the newspapers. Anyway, the wedding . . ."

"Anyway," Loftis interrupted quickly, "anyway I'm proud to hear that you are doing . . . *so* . . . well. And my congratulations to *both of you.*" He extended both hands gravely across the table as he spoke, listening to the whimsical inflection in his voice, uncontrollable now, crassly insincere, he knew, and he watched—in amusement, chuckling to himself—the compliant, milky look of bewilderment come into their eyes. They were smiling, saying nothing. Harriet, he noticed, was not perfect after all—a sliver of gold sparkled behind one tooth. And he was saying, in a voice in which even a four-year-old could detect the tone of bogus good will, *this*—Great God!—*this:* "Old Pookie always makes out for himself O.K., doesn't he? Getting married to a sharp gal like this who loves you for love alone, not for your money. Just like Dolly. You know how she still loves you; my God, Pookie, that's why I'm having such a hard time getting with that woman. Why, God, man, don't you see, can't you tell, she loves you even now!" They were still smiling, with meekness and what seemed a little fear; each of them took one of his hands reluctantly, and beneath his skin theirs was damp and cool, ten fingers crawling nervously beneath, like round white worms.

"Why, man," he went on helplessly, "don't you see? You've got everything that the rest of us poor bastards don't have. You've got position, standing, real position, success. Everything, Pookie! You got what makes a woman want to love you. You've got a real touch. Everything you touch turns to gold. Just like old Prince Mildass. And listen, Pookie—" he bent forward confidentially, winking at Harriet and bearing down firmly on Pookie's hand—"listen, Pookie, don't let anyone fool you. Don't let anyone tell you that they marry you for your money, because they don't. They marry you because you're one hell of a . . . *grand* . . . *guy!*" He paused to drink, hating himself but exhilarated.

Their hands fell to the table. Pookie still smiled his doglike smile but Harriet, blinking her eyes, looked indignant. "Well, I never," she said. Pookie too should wake up soon, even Pookie, and Loftis waited, drinking: poor bastards, if they only knew how, by merely sitting there blowing platitudes like bubbles through the air (now, "Sclater, he's so drunk," she was saying), they had crucified him, had cut him, like two kids playing with a knife, right to his heart, poor bastards, they'd say: Let's leave him alone with his guilt, let's leave him now, Sclater,

205

Harriet honey. "Milt, dammit, boy," Pookie was saying, his eyes small and dark with sudden puzzled resentment, a look Loftis had never seen there before, "Milt, dammit, I don't know what you're driving at, but I think you'd better lay off that bottle——"

His poise came crashing ungallantly down; the bottle slid from his lap, fell to the floor and broke. Whisky crept across the linoleum and he watched it for a second, then turned to look at Pookie, who stared at the spilled whisky, too. It didn't matter—the whisky—it occurred to him, for in his overcoat there was another pint. But this: they had baited him, tortured him, no matter with what childish, stupid innocence. Tortured him they had indeed, and they were paying for it. Harriet pulled at Pookie's sleeve, saying, "Darling, let's go," and as he looked up Loftis caught his eye and rose from his seat unsteadily. Poor Pookie, simple bastard, he thought, gazing down into the puzzled, resentful face: oh, Pookie, blessed are the meek and the unaware, blessed are the ill-informed, blessed are you, Pookie, though a woman drain you dry, because your heart is incorruptible and you shall inherit the earth. He thought of the sun porch and of Helen waiting, and he shivered in misery.

"Pookie," he said, looking down, "you're one hell of a *grand* . . . *guy*. The only trouble with you is—the only trouble is . . ."

Harriet rose in her seat. "Tell him off, Sclater!" she yelled, but Pookie was hypnotized.

Loftis stretched out his arm in a wide sweep, gesturing for peace, amity and forbearance, and remembered just at that instant, through miles of drunkenness, his mission, still unfulfilled. Dear God in heaven, what was he doing here? O Peyton.

"The only trouble with you is," he said in a choked voice, "is that . . . oh, the hell with it." He turned and went out of the restaurant blindly, past Harriet and the dumfounded Pookie, bearing in his arms the Confederate flag, a trophy without honor.

With three sandwiches bought from a boy near the stadium gate, with a container of coffee, with a program he had bought and had not wanted, with his pint bottle of whisky, with a pillow he had rented and an umbrella, and an orange badge pinned to his lapel, with the huge banner that drooped from his elbow and trailed along the gravel—with these he was utterly overwhelmed. From the stands a yell went up, but he was still behind the barrier and he couldn't see. And at any rate someone was nudging him, shouting into his ear: "Ticket, please!" He asked the boy who was winning; the boy had very red cheeks and earmuffs, though the day was not that cold, and he roared, "We got 'em down on the ten-yard line!" Pillow and program fell from his arms: they had to, for his ticket was inside somewhere, buried deep in his pocket, among receipts, old letters, a railroad time-table. Another yell came from the parapet and a band, dismally off-key, played the victory song, while confetti swirled around him like fallen snow. "Already?" he murmured. "A touchdown already?" But the boy had disappeared.

Awkwardly descending the concrete steps, he found his seat, in a place conveniently athwart the student section where, he hoped, he might catch sight of her. The seat was in the center of a row and he sidled in, banging people with his pillow. There was another kickoff. He sat down. A wall of people, gray overcoats and pennants arose in front of him, behind, and on both sides of him. As he uncapped his bottle and placed all of his equipment on Hubert MacPhail's empty seat, it became clear that he, too, somehow must rise, for convention's sake. He peered down the row for Peyton, and got up, craning his neck toward the student section. "Sit down, Pop!" a boy's voice cried behind him, and he turned, his hair bristling at his neck, and found that he alone was left standing. On the field there was a time out: someone had been hurt on the last play. Everyone was sitting but himself. Who had called him Pop? But he eased himself down, half-way into the lap of a young woman with prominent teeth, like himself very tight, who wrapped an arm around his neck and called him "Dugout Doug."

"This is my husband, Arvin Lee Brockenborough," she yelled over the noise, for behind them someone had begun to blow a gigantic horn. "Isn't that a bearcat of a name?" She poked in the ribs a Navy chief petty officer, staring at the field, who was tanned and muscular and who, with huge hands propping up a gum-chewing jaw, pointedly ignored them both. "Arvin Lee, meet Dugout Doug!"

"Why do you call me that?"

"Because you look just like him! Or—do you? It depends."

"Like Mac——"

"Just like him, baby! Gimme a drink. Mmm. No, I don't really think you do."

Loftis took back his bottle from her, dipping the flagstaff, which he gripped in the other hand, in a jaunty salute. "Cheers, Mrs. Brockenborough!"

"Just call me Frances!"

"O.K., Frances!"

She smiled; there was a smear of lipstick on one of her large front teeth.

They drank. It was all very convivial, and shortly he became a friend in need to her. He told her of his troubles between the halves, when the tumult subsided except for brief sheeplike cries from the student section. A bottle bounced down behind them from tier to tier and finally shattered beneath their feet. "Ooo-h," she said, clutching his arm. She put the edge of her blanket over his knees. "My daughter," he said, "she's in the hospital over there." "Ooo-h," she said, "poor Dugout. Is it bad?" "No, no, it's very harmless, really, else I'd be over there, you see, instead of here." Her mouth hung open; there was a long silence, a toothy, wordless commiseration.

Gray light rolled over the stadium. Above, an airplane hung in the sky, hovering nearly motionless. A high-school band, gay with plumes, paraded out onto the field and nobody watched or listened. On the other side of the field the stands were gaudy with blankets and pennants, a patchwork quilt upended. Somewhere a siren howled and died, and on the sidelines there was a brief clot of people, a fistfight, but two fat cops ran up brandishing sticks, and the spectators scattered in all directions, like boys from a firecracker. It was a moment of suspension, of gloom even, although the score was tied: it had nothing to do with the game. It seemed merely as if all these thousands had been seized at once by the same numbness: gathered here between the halves, sitting idly, mainly silent now, it was as if, imprisoned by their boredom, they had been here since the beginning of time and would go on being here forever. Loftis munched on a soggy cheese sandwich, dividing it with Frances. Arvin Lee had gone to get a hot dog.

"You see maybe how severe my quest is," he said, wiping a crumb away, "what a trial it is to be so goddam drunk when—when, that is, when sobriety should be the password or watchword, rather."

"That's right, Dugout," said Frances, "the whole goddam thing's a trial, if you ask me. Arvin Lee's crazy about football; he played for Thomas Jefferson High School, and he drags me out so I freeze my fanny——"

"Oh, not that," Loftis broke in. "I love football. It's just that—that——"

"That it's a trial, it is. Poor Dugout. Is your wife pretty?"

"My wife is the most wonderful woman in the world. My family has—— My daughter——"

"Yes, poor thing. She's so sick."

"No she ain't. She's right over there. Somewhere."

"Who, Dugout honey? You said——"

"Peyton. My daughter."

It seemed as if he had been gently awakened from a long sleep. The corners of his mouth hung down, drugged and paralyzed, and through the gray light of this soft, new-born consciousness it occurred to him first, prime and foremost (*order, order,* he found himself pleading) that he was not properly articulating. Yes, without a doubt, that was of the utmost importance. This lack of ar-tic-u-la-shun. And he turned to Frances—watching the players gallop to the field again, the people rising in front of him—to say, carefully, distinctly: "It's her I've gots to find. My baby. I love her." He couldn't hear her reply, for there were renewed cheers, and the horn behind them again, loud, defiant, enormous; she blinked and smiled, shrieked something at him, and laid cold thin fingers beneath the blanket upon his leg. The awakening progressed slowly: someone, he noticed, had grabbed his Confederate flag, was waving it in great triumphant circles through the air, while his conscience, reviving from the brown depths of the day, told him that it was true: sitting here evading all, hiding his very identity among people for whom that fact, at least, was of no importance, he had committed the unpardonable crime. It was neither one of commission nor of omission, but the worst combination of both—of apathy, of a sottish criminal inertia—and it seemed that if he didn't rise at this very moment, become sober, strike boldly, act like a man—it seemed that if he didn't do all these things, his enormous sin would be advertised to the sky like a banner, and all these thousands would turn in their seats, the band silent, the players pausing to stand and face him grimly from the turf, even the drink vendors stiff and immobile in the aisles, all quiet, motionless, unblinking—to regard him with massive scorn and loathing. Even Frances. She squeezed down with her fingers on his leg, laughing furiously, and groped for his bottle. He looked at her without a smile, savoring this last minute of dereliction, and thought giddily of Peyton. Not to shelter her from Helen, from whatever catastrophe was in store for all of them today, had he wasted this last hour and a half, but only to anticipate seeing again that dear sweet face, only to make the meeting, once it came, more joyful by the long delay. Now no more of that. Ah, for a man to arise in me, that the man I am should cease to be. My father's line.

Peyton baby, you and I must grow older in a day, we must face this thing together.

He gave the bottle to Frances and got up unsteadily and bowed. "For you," he said loudly, "the sun, the moon, the stars, and this precious rationed pint of Old Crow."

"Thanks, Dugout," she said.

"Farewell," he said.

"Aw, come back, Dugout!"

He slid past her. "I shall return," he said, saluting, and then to Arvin Lee: "'Scuse me, Chief."

"On your way, Dugout," said Arvin Lee rudely.

He hunted for her until the end of the game, stumbling up and down the terrace of the student section, saying, "Do you know Peyton Loftis?" Some pointed in one direction and some in another, and he followed every lead, trying to keep out of people's way. Once, to an alarmed girl and her boy friend with horn-rimmed glasses, he muttered, "I got to find her before Maudie dies," and brought himself up short and turned away. There were tears in his eyes and the girl's voice, fading, said "Crazy," swallowed up in a roar as a long forward pass, which seemed to spin endlessly against the clouds, was caught for a touchdown. He bought a hot dog and an Eskimo Pie and refused drinks, in silver flasks which floated up to him out of the confusion, three times. Twice he stood erect and reverent when the Alma Mater was played, but he no longer knew the score, or cared, because of his desperate wild sorrow. At last, when the game had ended, he saw her far below on the field, surrounded by boys and girls, and he shouted, "Peyton! Peyton!" but he was being pushed upward and upward by the crowd, and he had lost his scarf. In the stands Frances still sat, now with her arm around someone else's neck. Loftis turned to yell at Peyton again: it seemed miles away and, besides, she was gone. Pinned! He had lost her. His banner was lost, too, his pillow, his program, his scarf, but on the way out someone handed him a red balloon.

Virginia had been defeated but, who cared? They trooped back to the fraternity houses in twos or threes, in delirious quartets, or in automobiles that glided slowly homeward through the mournful dusk. A few sang songs; others kept on drinking, and those who fell were not left to lie there, but were carried away between two friends, in the spirit of brotherhood. At the fraternity houses the colored men had built great fires and here the boys stood noisily discussing the game, while the girls, slightly tired, their faces blushing deep red, held out their hands to the flames and sniffled a little, for some of them had caught colds. It was five o'clock, a breathing spell. In the KA house a tall lean young man, who had slept the sleep of death all during the game, wandered down stark-naked to inquire whether it was time for the kickoff yet, and fled amid shrieks and yells, vainly trying to clothe himself with a drapery. Before it was dark the Boynton twins, daughters of a prosperous Methodist tobacco farmer from Chatham, quietly expired in their chairs at exactly the same instant and were put to bed upstairs, while everyone marveled that they should carry out the sister act with such constancy. At five-thirty the bar was reopened, the squeezes which the boys gave the girls lingered longer, less hesitantly now, and the sound of laughter and teasing voices, mingled with the throbbing saxophones, whisky, light from the logs, inflamed each cheek with a subtle fire.

Peyton sat on the bar, her legs crossed, drinking bourbon and soda. "Dickie boy?" she said, and ran her fingers through his hair.

"Wassamatter?"

"I feel very decadent."

"Why, honey?"

"I don't find myself very interesting here."

He touched her hair with his fingers. "You're beautiful here, darling. You look like a million bucks."

She stifled a yawn which brought a film of moisture to her eyes. "Money," she said lazily, "that's all you know."

"Quit giving me a hard time," he said, sighing. Two couples came up, spilling whisky and merriment. There were handshakes all around, toasts, and one of the boys, a pudgy Georgian named Ballard, kissed Peyton on the cheek. "Thank you, Alexander," she said. He began a long story, mostly incoherent, but anyway, he cried, his grandpappy fit with Mosby in the Valley and if there were any bloody Yankees around he'd vivisect them alive, give him a poleax big enough.

"I love you, darling," one girl said with a squeal, and Ballard hugged her, looking over her shoulder for approval.

"Don't be so chauvinistic," said Peyton, in a sophisticated voice, but there was a smile on her lips, and Dick hauled her down from the bar and they danced, very close, to a band playing "Stardust."

"I want to go somewhere," she said abstractedly.

"Where, honey?"

"Oh, I don't know. Anywhere. Everybody's so polluted here."

"I know. Bunch of bums."

"Oh, they're wonderful," she said, "all these guys. But I think everyone started out too soon today."

"Yes."

"And I like to drink, but——"

"But what?" he said.

"Nothing."

"We could drive down to the farm, honey," he said.

"Mmmmm-hh."

"What do you mean—mmmm-hh?"

"I mean——"

"Don't you like going down to the farm with Dickie boy?"

She pushed away from him a little, looking up into his eyes. "Oh, honey, *certainly* I do. It's just that—well, I've told you. I love it down there. I *love* that old place, and your folks. I just love it all——" She was thinking it over. "Oh, Dick, I just don't think it's right to go down when your folks are away. Besides——"

"Besides what?" he demanded gently.

"It's just that I don't think it's right."

"Prissy," he said. "How many drinks have *you* had today? I thought you were the Sweet Briar intellectual type with modern ideas."

"Don't be an ass," she said mildly. "If I'd had many drinks today, I'd be asking you."

"Do you love me?" he said.

"Mmm-m."

He stopped her in the middle of a dip, holding her close, their lips nearly touching. Past them a girl with an unattractive pale face and large breasts was being led sobbing, complaining of insults and Virginia gentlemen, so-called, and hoarse rowdy laughter filled the room. They hardly noticed. "Do you love me?" he repeated intensely. She looked up, eyes wide with astonishment.

"There's Daddy. Oh, he's bleeding! He's hurt!"

Having been lost, having left the game only to find himself wandering hopelessly down side streets, unpaved, dreary roads which he should have but hadn't remembered after all his early years in Charlottesville, Loftis had been possessed by the belief that all this was only a dream: his search, Peyton, even his fear and agony, were all part of an impossible illusion. He had sobered somewhat, by an effort of will so strong, so unfamiliar, that it had frightened him. And lurching through the cold gray dusk beneath the windless trees—listening to the bells and car horns far-off, receding from him, the fatigued departing sounds of half-hearted cries and bells signaling the knowledge, that, incredibly, he was going in the wrong direction, *away* from

Peyton, *away* from Maudie and Helen and the hospital, away from his colossal responsibilities—he had listened also to something being spoken in the air, and knew that it was his own voice muttering aloud. It came like a chant: I will be strong, I will be strong—above the noise of his feet scraping grittily across unfleshed fallen leaves and above the noise of the blood at his brain, pulsing a steady, somber, rhythmic voluntary, not of fear but of cowardice. His own cowardice had caught him unawares. Appalled him. And it was then, still murmuring, I will be strong, I will be strong, that he had turned about-face, as much as if he had heard a trumpet call, to strike out through the dusk back up the hill toward the KA house. He toiled uncertainly up the rutted road. This first part of the walk had taken a little over a half-hour, and perhaps, after all, it had been good for him. He had become more sober. At least he had regained a certain sensible balance, of reason if not of body. It was almost dark. He was in Niggertown. There was a variety of smells and all around him came a chorus of barkings while screen doors slammed and dark shapes came out to say, Hush, Tige, or Hush, Bo, for they knew, too, the dogs had sniffed a white man. Now no longer was he utterly lost. He felt calm, capable even, for the first time today in command of his senses, and although he was afraid for Maudie, still afraid, indeed, for them all, he forgave himself for the day's lapse of conscience. Strange things had happened; he had had strange dreams. God, if You are there, forgive Your foolish son. . . . It was at that moment that he fell into the culvert.

He was stunned, hurt; the sky, gray with clouds, was strewn with galaxies of capering stars. With blood flowing from a gash on his temple, he felt himself on wet concrete, and smelled weeds somewhere. He looked up slowly, groping for broken bones. He had fallen four feet off the road, although why and how he couldn't tell. Water trickled beneath him; there was a smell of weeds and sewage. Painfully and cautiously he picked himself up, holding on to some pipe, wet with scum, to steady himself. He pushed a handkerchief against his wound and moaned aloud, "Oh, Jesus, Jesus," trembling all over, while a black face peered over the culvert and said, "What's de matter, man?"

"I fell."

"Come on up here, man."

Strong arms offered him support, lifted him up: the man was a young, muscular Negro with a mean, mashed-in face and cheeks with scars pink and raw in the gathering darkness. "Hoo," he said, "you got a slit for sure." Loftis puffed as he dragged his feet over the edge of the culvert and stood erect, mopping the blood away.

"Do it hurt much?"

"No," Loftis said. "Thanks."

The Negro eased him down to a log. "Get you a portice and put on it," he said, "make you a portice out of some pipe ashes and some whisky and put in some lard so it'll keep de air out."

"Yes," Loftis said, "I will."

"Is you all right? Want me carry you up to Main Street?"

"No, thanks," Loftis said dizzily. "No, I'll be all right."

"You sure?"

"Yes. Yes. Thanks a lot."

It got dark, the Negro was gone, and the blood became matted in his hair. Lights winked on. Orange fires appeared in the houses, and shadow shapes flickered at the doors. It was getting colder. He pulled himself up. A dog snarled at his feet and he kicked at it feebly, hating all dogs forever. Surely this was a punishment, but unconsciously, perhaps mercifully so, he somehow made his way back to the house, concerned solely with the matter of not bleeding to death. There he was snapped back to life by the cool hand of the boy who had greeted him at noon, the priggish voice: "Ah, good evening there, Brother Loftis!" Exquisite warmth enveloped him. He saw Peyton.

"Daddy, Daddy, what happened? You're cut!" The music died; people turned and stared. Peyton took his arm and, with Dick Cartwright helping her, led him into a downstairs bedroom. He must have slept. Half an hour later he was bandaged, soothed, flat on his back in a bunk, and as his senses returned he heard Peyton say, somewhere far above him, that he was a perfect mess. She was sitting beside him on the bed. He turned his aching head and looked up at her. They were alone.

"Daddy, for heaven's sake, what are you doing up here anyway, and so stinking?"

"I—I . . . much better now."

"Does it hurt much?"

"Not much." He smiled, reached for her hand.

"It's not a bad cut, honey. Maybe you'd better go over to the hospital though and have them take a look at it. Bunny, just what on earth are you doing up here this week end?"

"I'm much soberer now," he said irrelevantly.

"That's not the point, Bunny——"

"I—I . . . Oh, hell."

214

"Why didn't you write me, darling? When did you get here? If I'd just known. Dick and I could have taken you to the game and——What on earth happened to you? Did you get into a fight?"

He rose up on his elbows. "No, baby, I just—I fell down. Baby, look here," he said earnestly, "I don't quite know how to say it. Something's happened today. I don't know. I don't know *what*. I just——"

"Bunny, for God's sake what are you trying to *convey* to me? I thought you were soberer."

"I am," he said. "Look, let me explain it. First there's Maudie, you know she's up here in the hospital. No, you don't know, do you?"

"Maudie? Up here again?" Her face became pale. "What's wrong with her, Bunny?"

"Wait a minute, baby; let me tell you." He paused and sighed, probing with a finger at his bandage. She pulled his hand away. Then he told her. All. About Maudie. About leaving Helen, and the party at noon and about Pookie, the football game and Frances Brockenborough and his disaster at the culvert and the drinking, drinking, drinking, and through all this about his mad unhappy homesickness for her, her alone; didn't she see: how she had fled him, persistently, impudently, and without any remorse, though of course (he smiled) she had really been unaware of it all the time. He held her hands tightly, grinning a little, asking her didn't she see, how it had been a torture for him all day: this pursuit of something which he had finally despaired of ever attaining, like the impossible ripe carrot on a stick beyond the donkey's nose; now here she was, he had found her, and wasn't that fine? And with a gay lie, the old panic returning, he kept on grinning and forced himself to say that he was glad she had been pinned to such a swell boy, and he hoped it augured good things, real things, for the future.

"But, Daddy, what about Maudie? Why on earth did you leave Mother? Why didn't you telephone over here instead? Oh, Daddy, honestly——"

"Yes, but, baby——" He hadn't foreseen this sort of thing: her doubt, this look of subtle, mild reproof. Not even that. Perhaps he had expected too much. He had foreseen her as jolly, popping with enthusiasm, as she had been when he had visited her last summer in Washington: then, when they had been together, alone in restaurants, in his car, at the evening concert on the river, they had seemed breathlessly close, indissoluble, perfect. That was as he had last seen her. Now her face was cool and grave, reproachful. Trustfully he had made

215

his confessional, told her everything—and look what had happened. He had even mentioned—in the oblique reference to Pookie—Dolly, thus putting on a conversational level a very adult and very tricky problem. She was no longer listening. He faltered, chewing on his words sourly and fatuously, like an old cow.

"Bunny, what about Maudie? We've got to go see her. Why didn't you stay with Mother?"

"Baby——"

"No, not for her sake. I don't give a damn about that. But just on account of Maudie. What prompted you to come out and get boiled to the eyes like this? Going to football games. When—when . . . Oh, Bunny, you're a mess, a perfect mess!" She got up and began to pace about, running her hands through her hair. "This whole family's nuts. Absolutely nuts!" She turned; tears were running down her face, tears not of sorrow but of anger and frustration and regret. "Why can't you stay sober once, Bunny?"

"Baby——"

"I don't give a damn about Mother——"

"Don't say——"

"I will say it! I don't *care* about her. I never have. But I'd think you'd have enough—oh, Bunny." She ran to him and threw her arms around his neck. "I'm sorry," she said. "I'm sorry, Bunny. For saying things like that. I love you. I just think you're a jerk." She sniffled against him, then drew back and dried her eyes. "Now come on," she said. "We've got to go over and see Maudie."

"All right, baby." He arose stiffly, once with her to go anywhere at all, to Abaddon, or limbo, or the bottom of the sea. Peyton went out to tell Dick she'd be back later. In the chapter room, still dazed, Loftis wandered through a conga line of pledges, seniors with paddles, and with his bandage threw panic through a gallery of simpering girls. From the door Peyton called for him to hurry up, which he did, stumbling a little, and someone pressed on him the KA grip, splashing whisky down his sleeve. Outside, in the brisk cold air, he knew he'd sober shortly: what the hell, in spite of mad things to come, he had found his baby—wasn't that enough?

They sat across from her on the sun porch, in the shoddy chairs. The place had not even the virtue of a gentle light; it seemed perfectly suited to weariness and waiting. Two bulbs behind scorched lampshades cast a bald white incandescence through the room; the lamps were set too high, with a studied and unerring miscalculation, and the light they shed denuded the room of all its comforting shadows, like the lights in courtrooms and bus stations or any place oppressive and temporary. In the hallway outside, nurses passed noisily, carrying away the supper trays. Here all three of them puffed on cigarettes; smoke floated in oily blue coils around the room. There was one ashtray, which Helen, standing at her vantage point by the door, kept to herself, and soon beneath the chairs lay a litter of smashed butts, some red from the paint on Peyton's lips.

"Love," said Helen in a quiet tone, scornfully, "love!" Her voice rose on the last word and she paused, staring at them violently. Neither of them returned her gaze. "Love!" she repeated haughtily. "Neither of you will ever know what that means!"

She sat down with a sort of swift, rustling fierceness, propped up rigid and tense and exact on the edge of the couch. "Now it's not the waiting that hurts so," she said more softly. "That I could stand. I have waited all my life, it seems, for things to happen, for things to come that never came, for one word, I guess, just one single solitary word to tell me that all this lonesomeness wasn't in vain—that my afternoons of waiting and silence and misery didn't add up to an eternity after all. One word and I'd be saved, a word that I could have said as well as you, it didn't matter, so long as we both understood: 'love' or 'forgive' or even 'darling,' it made no difference. One single word. If you only knew my waiting, all waits would seem to you like one minute, do you understand? But you don't know what love is— or waiting, either.

"So I could stand the wait all afternoon. I could stand the waiting. It was this other thing that mattered. All afternoon I sat right here where I am now, looking out at the hills. You never came, nobody came, but please don't think I suffered over that: the waiting I can stand. Nobody came. . . . Yes. The doctor came. He's a fine, nice man. It was miliary T.B., he said. I guess he saw I was alone, and he'd come and talk to me, pretending to be sociable, but that wasn't his real intention. He told me finally, very gently: that she probably wouldn't pull through—a day or two more or something like that—but never fear, there was always a chance. That gave me some strength. I sat here watching the light come down. Oh, what a dark day. I said to myself, be strong. That's what I said. I said, even if they don't know, well, Maudie knows, and that's enough. She knows! Want me to tell you about her, my dears?" She paused for a moment to gaze at them.

They looked back at her now with pity, with a sort of horrified tolerance, but with anguish, too, and guilt. And as if to reassure each other, they took each other's hand, conscious only of the moment's accusing silence and the treacherous, pervasive hospital fumes, in each corner confounding disease and decay. Suddenly Loftis blinked. His bandage had slipped down over his eye; with shaking fingers he reached up to adjust it. Past the door a colored orderly toiled, pushing a cartful of spoons; somewhere far-off, water trickled, murmurous, liquid, unceasing. Helen shifted a little on the couch, without lowering her gaze brought one finger up to the side of her nose in a quizzical, humorous gesture, but unconsciously, and then pointed a hand at them. Then suddenly she let her hand fall. Her eyes became gentle.

In a tender, reminiscent voice, she told them.

"Listen—I remember my afternoons . . . listen . . ."

In the summer they'd sit together on the porch, she and Maudie, watching the ships and the clouds and the bumblebees in the hollyhocks buzzing about, flying from light to shade. She'd sit and knit or read and Maudie would stay beside her, looking at the picture books. There would be a breeze from the bay, and clouds: they'd come over across the beach, edges dead-white, melting, with rain like dark stuff inside, traveling very low, and soundlessly bend the tops of the willows, trailing huge shadows across the lawn beneath; the wind would rustle Maudie's hair, the picture book and her hair, too. Then there'd be a sort of whisper and the wind would cease, the pages would stop fluttering and the sun return and make the lawn smell like grass again, very hot. They'd drink iced tea, Ella would bring it to them. They'd hear the screen door slam, Ella's feet limping on the gravel, to scrape then across the porch and finally stop behind them. Ella would lean down and stroke Maudie's arm, then put the glass in her hand and say something gentle to her, and leave. Helen and Maudie would be alone again.

Sometimes gulls would come over and Maudie would point to them and lift up her arms. Sometimes Helen would tell her about the battleships and freighters: they were anchored far out, and while they watched them the wind would change, the tide sometimes, and the ships would turn all facing the house, so thin against the horizon that they almost disappeared. Smoke hung above Norfolk; sailboats tilted against the wind: sometimes their hulls couldn't be seen, only the sails, so they looked like scraps of cloth being blown above the waves by something invisible.

Helen would tell her about Pocahontas and Captain John Smith, telling the mind of an infant, hardly even that, stories about people who hardly even existed. Were they still here, still alive? Maudie wanted to know. Helen would say, "Yes," because they were her friends: friends never died but always lived, and would live in her silent heart forever. She'd tell her of the ships coming past the house years ago, the Indian forest, and of the pagan who saved the Christian soul from sacrifice. Wasn't that nice, Maudie would say. Were they still here, she'd ask; where were they now, Mamadear? She'd say, "Out there, darling, now close your eyes and think and they'll return." And so they'd close their eyes, thinking; then Helen would squeeze her hand and they'd both look at the bay. So too, to Helen it would seem that all had changed: soon Maudie would say, "Yes, Mamadear, I see them," and below the scudding clouds it appeared that each stake and boat and scrap of sail had been swallowed up by the waves. The towns around the shore had gone; forests grew to the beaches. On the sand bars stood windswept trees. Even the house had vanished: from where the terrace had once stood they were peering through a sunny canebrake where insects darted and hummed; there was marshland beneath their feet.

Silence was everywhere: Ella, sounds in the kitchen, hammering from the barracks, the noise of bumblebees—all these had disappeared and they were sitting alone and quiet in the canebrake, waiting, hardly breathing. Sunlight streamed down endlessly; it seemed to come from another land.

Presently Helen said, "Look, Maudie, there they are," and they saw them: two ships, galleons with great pink sails. Then she said, "Listen, Maudie." They listened, heard high above like pipes the shrilling of a thousand gulls. She said, "Do you see them, Maudie?"

"Yes, Mamadear."

Then they looked through the canebrake and saw the sails dip and belly and pass on toward the river, twin flares of pink against the sky: no cities beyond, no smoke at all, no voices, only these passing galleons and the swell and dip of sails; they went away. They closed their eyes again, and she squeezed Maudie's hand. They looked up. "Yes, Mamadear," she said. Everything was as it had always been. Then they'd go to sleep.

Men were building the barracks next door. All summer long, and in the fall, they'd hear hammering and banging in the field. At first they could see the workers, but then the mimosas bloomed; it was hard to see. In the beginning those people didn't have any water, and Helen had Ella take them some every afternoon in a pail. They were rough men who talked loudly, profanely: they had tanned faces and muddy shoes; in the afternoons they could hear their swearwords and Maudie asked her what it was they said. She said, "Hush, Maudie dear, that's not for you."

So they'd sit and watch and listen. Ella would go out at three, carrying her pail. From the porch they'd watch her limp off across the lawn, slopping water over, with one hand shooing flies from her hair. Beneath the mimosas the men would flock like cows, leaning over the fence; Ella had a paper cup for each of them. After they had drunk Ella would bring back the empty pail. One day Maudie said, "Mamadear, can I take the water, too?" Helen said, "Yes, darling, if you're careful. If you go with Ella."

The summer passed. The leaves began to turn and all along the fence the mimosas bloomed; the bumblebees still buzzed around the flowers. Each afternoon Helen would watch them walk across the lawn together very slowly, Ella carrying the pail, Maudie the paper cups. Both of them hobbling along: it was, Helen recollected, a sight in this world to watch. Soon they'd disappear behind the trees and she'd look away and go back to her knitting or reading, thinking of the strange things that made Maudie happy.

Helen paused in her story.

"If you knew," she said. "If either of you knew just what tiny little things . . ." Her voice trailed off. No one spoke. In the silence she turned toward the window, her eyes musing steadily upon the darkness, upon remembered sunlight, remembered leaves, something: they didn't know. A smile came to her lips but vanished, and she turned again, pointing at them.

She said something about a man named Bennie. His name was Bennie. At least Maudie called him Bennie. Helen saw him only once. Sometimes they were gone for a long time, Maudie and Ella. She'd sit and watch and listen, waiting for them to return. Perhaps they'd be gone for half an hour. Helen would fidget a little and worry, smelling steam from the kitchen. Finally she'd get up and walk across the lawn to the path through the garden. Right here the mimosas were in bloom; she'd stoop down and pick up the leaves which had fallen in the flower bed, calling at first, "Ella, Ella." Then, "Ella, Ella," she'd say more loudly, "Ella, you'd better bring Maudie back; she's been standing up too long." Then she'd hear a man laughing, and Maudie's voice and Ella's and Maudie's again: "Good-by, good-by," she'd say, and the two of them would come stumbling with a crashing noise out of the bushes, like those wild animals in the movies, both of them laughing and giggling. And she'd hear Ella say, "Dat man sho' is some man," in a marveling voice.

Then, with Ella helping her, Maudie would come up to Helen, her face red from giggling, and repeat just what Ella had said: "Mamadear, that man is sure some man."

"What man is that?" Helen would ask.

"That man in there with magic," Maudie would say.

"That's nice," she'd say. "What's his name, darling?"

"Bennie," she'd answer.

Helen saw him only once. He was a thin little man of maybe forty, with a sad, dark, pock-marked face and black hair raked straight back from his forehead. He wore a red silk shirt and Ella told her he was part colored, part Indian: she could tell. Now each afternoon when they'd sit on the terrace she could hardly make Maudie rest long enough. She'd talk to her, tell her stories, but Maudie would stir and move about and ask her if it was three. Now it was always Bennie. So they'd go at three, Maudie and Ella carrying the bucket and the cups, and Helen would sit and wait as she had before. She was alone then. Maudie was happy. Stronger. The telephone rang, but Helen never answered it. Who, she asked herself, wants to talk to silly women with their silly games? Her life had been prudent and dark. She'd sit alone watching the clouds and the children yards out in the bay, wading, digging up clams.

So, as she said, she saw him only once, which was enough; along with him Maudie would always be remembered. Who would think that she whose lips had been so dark and prudent would not be one to die of pure anguish when she saw this thing, or not grind her teeth and beat her head against the trees? No, it was the other way around. Helen guessed Maudie knew what love was, which (and here she pointed at them again) was more than they would know in a lifetime of looking. Maudie *won*, she said, and thank God dying would be no more fearsome for her than going to sleep.

She supposed she should have been more careful, but she didn't know. After a while most of the workmen left, the barracks were up, and some of the soldiers moved in. But Maudie and Ella still carried water over, though no one needed water anymore: it was a kind of game with them after that, foolish and absurd, she thought, but so much fun for them that she didn't care. Often Ella would leave and come back alone, and Helen would say, "Ella, you'd better stay and watch," but Ella would wink and grin and say that it was all right, she'd go fetch her in a minute.

Once Helen waited for a long time. It looked like rain. She began to be worried. Across the bay the rain was coming down in gray wet sheets and the sailboats raced in to shore. The gulls were flying high above and over the land. She could hear the awning flapping; a piece of tarpaper tumbled end over end across the lawn; through the trees she could see the soldiers racing for shelter, eyes slanted back toward the sky. She got up and stood there for a moment, calling out.

"Maudie, Maudie," she cried, "come on back now; it's time, it's time," but there wasn't any answer.

She went down the steps and across the lawn through the flower bed, and stood beneath the mimosa trees. The wind was blowing hard, but there was no thunder. The blossoms on the trees were flung out pink and green like jungle birds about to fly. Finally they let go, whirling upward, and disappeared. She called again, "Maudie, Maudie," against the wind, but there was still no answer. She went to the mimosas, picking her way among the vines, the lilies that grew there, pushing away branches. The earth was spongy here; it smelled damp, and it was dark. She walked a little way down the fence until she finally saw them; then she stood behind a tree, watching.

He was doing tricks for her. He stood on the other side of the fence, a short ugly little man with a puny pock-marked face and black raked-back hair fluttering violently in the wind. His arms were raised above his head, skinny and straight and motionless like a man supplicating heaven and the sky; he made no sound, he didn't smile, only his fingers moved: swiftly they clenched and unclenched; gay blue balls appeared in his palms, seemed to dance there for a moment, and just as quickly disappeared.

Helen held her breath. Rain had begun to fall. She watched Maudie and saw her laugh and clap her hands, and saw her suddenly reach up and grope at the air, as if she were trying to recover those vanishing balls. He let his arms fall then and stood looking at Maudie with his sunken eyes sad and mysterious, his cheeks bulging like a rabbit's. Maudie laughed and cheered. He turned his head and peered up at the sky; gray light had fallen over the shore and as he turned, with the wind tossing his hair and with his bulging eyes and cheeks and with this sudden bitter look of annoyance, so comical but at the same time somehow alarming and fearsome, he looked like the greatest magician on earth. Maudie cried out something. He turned. "Again!" she cried. Then, one by one, the balls popped from his mouth with a little click and tumbled away along the fence.

And it happened then, this thing Helen had been talking about;

he did one more trick. He picked up the balls, scrabbling along beneath the fence; his red silk shirttail had come out, she remembered, and it flapped wildly behind him as he hopped around like a chipmunk picking up the balls. Then he turned and came toward Maudie. Up went the balls again; each vanished as he caught it: his hands were empty. They stood there looking at each other, and again there seemed to be something sad and mysterious in his gaze; he was like the old magician, old artificer from another country, and his eyes were black and tender: it was as if he had many secrets and somehow knew everything there was to know: not just those dancing balls but the earth and sky, leaves and wind and falling rain; he knew their sorcery, knew their mysteries, and he knew the secret heart of this girl he'd never even spoken to. Bennie. Could he talk? He never said a word. There was something in him that understood love and death, entwined forever, and the hollow space of mindlessness: he gazed at Maudie and didn't smile, only reached out his hand and made a ball come out of her ear, another from her hair.

Maudie knew maybe, Helen said; no, she *must* have known. There was that silent, sad, mysterious communion; God alone knew how she foretold the coming end. Something in his eyes, perhaps: the defiant glance toward the heavens, a violent look, or—afterward—the rapt, mournful gaze he gave her, that told her that such divine magic must come to an end like everything. She cried and cried. He put the balls in his pocket and stood there quietly, looking at her. She kept on crying, loud and unreasoning and anguished, and said, "No! No!"

Wind swept through the trees, and rain, plastering down her hair; Helen couldn't move. "No! No!" Maudie screamed. "No! No!" It was as if she had seen the end—not only of this afternoon but of all afternoons, of sunlight and the water she had brought, the dancing balls and of all and anything she had ever loved on earth. Of Bennie. She kept on shrieking. Helen thought she'd faint of horror.

"No! No!" Maudie screamed, and toppled weakly against the fence, stretching out her arms to him. But he didn't move; he merely stood there with the rain drenching his shirt, deepening the red, and gazed at her steadily and unhappily, understanding. Helen started to move toward her, but he moved first, swiftly. He walked to the fence and propped Maudie back up. He said nothing at all. She became quiet and looked at him with tears streaming down her face. Then he put his arms around her and kissed her once on the cheek.

That, mostly, Helen said, she would always remember: the swaying mimosas and the two of them, she much taller than Bennie, standing with the fence between, holding on to each other. After all these years she'd found it: a lover, father, magic—something. Helen didn't know. But Maudie had found it. He knew. Bennie knew. He stood erect finally and smoothed back his hair, looking at her. Maudie looked back, saying nothing either, only, with her eyes, imploring him to stay.

What could he do? Nothing, Helen knew. Just understanding was enough. He shoved his shirttail in and wheeled about and walked swiftly across the field through the rain and disappeared behind the barracks. Then she led Maudie back into the house.

"He never came back. Maudie never went back again. All October in the afternoons we'd sit on the porch again. Maudie never said a word about him or anything. I'd tell her stories but I don't think she listened. She sat beside me and rocked and looked at the bay. I suppose she thought about it a lot but I don't know. Maybe it was the thinking that made her so sick. I don't know. She became silent and peaceful; maybe she dreamed. Most likely she didn't even feel the strength flowing out of her like a dying flower. A dying flower. She was tired and her leg hurt her and she slept. I'd sleep too. We'd sit together and watch the ships for a while and see the gulls soar overhead and softly drowsing, close our eyes and let the picture books fall and hear the bumblebees. . . ."

It was as if Helen had suddenly awakened from a long, exhausting slumber. She crushed out her cigarette and stood up unsteadily. "So she's going to die," she said. "Now you know. About love. Why don't you go home? It's too late now to see her. Why don't you go home? You've had your fun. I've waited all day for you and now I'm through waiting and now I'm going to Maudie. Do you want some more whisky, my dears? You can get some at all the parties. Do you want your loving? Just try to get that too! Just try! I'll not wait any longer for anything at all!"

She raised her hands to her face and bent over sobbing tearlessly, without a sound. Tearlessly, that is, because from where they sat they could see, between her fingers, the harsh light shining on her cheeks, revealing no tears at all but only the tight-clenched eyes and closed, drawn-down mouth which held a prolonged and agonized inspiration of breath, like a baby's. They watched her shoulders shake and they both got up, hurt and a little awed by her madness. They were moved by guilt and by sorrow, but mainly by a sort of heedless, wanton love. For Helen and for Maudie, but for other things, too—for the memory of whatever had passed among them that had been proper and good, in spite of all the rest; for the memory of all that was now irremediable and beyond recovery. Loftis said, "Helen," and Peyton said, "Oh, Mother."

It was as if her vision still lingered and they were there, a part of it: of endless afternoons and soaring clouds, of mimosas that swayed and trembled, of a frieze of seagulls strung out immobile against the sky. There were bumblebees, too, and the magic, mind-haunted shapes of Indians. One juggled gay blue balls underneath the trees; the others, lunatic forms with knives, prowled around them in the canebrake. All of them, the shattered family, were home again, made briefly whole: they saw the swell and dip of galleon sails, at the prow a figure, breasting the mild summer storms of another century, who thought of conquest, thought of gold.

"Mother——" Peyton said again.

Helen looked up. "You," she said, "don't whimper at me. You're half the cause. Remember when you let her fall? I'll refresh——"

"But——"

"Remember?"

"Mother——"

"You don't care. About anything. And is that why you kept your father away from here all day? Guilty? You with your whoring around and your drinking."

"Helen!" Loftis shouted.

She turned and left the room.

"Dickie boy, let me have that bottle again," she said.

"Here, baby." Her head was on his shoulder, and with an arm around her he was driving with one hand. It was fairly awkward but the convertible was big and heavy, an Oldsmobile, and it clung safely to the curves which wound through the frosty night. Above, the sky was clearing. It was deserted, sleeping country, full of pines and swamps, puffs of fog which arose from the bottoms to envelop the road in dangerous gray swirls. The car, however, was an excellent one, built like a good ship to ride out any storm; indeed, the car did suggest some kind of boat: it was as spacious and padded and comfortable as any Doge's gondola and it took the bumps with the aggressive dignity of a ferry. They rode through a sea of mist and chill darkness; farms and fences, dark filling stations, a Negro church in a spooky grove—all these, lit up briefly by the headlights, were on a remote fantastic shore. Night was all around them, but they hardly noticed, encapsuled by steel and glass, warmed by a heater. The dashboard's green glow illumined them and they drank, safe for a while, listening mindlessly to music from a starlit roof over Broadway. Charlottesville was miles behind.

"And the thing that gets me," Peyton said bitterly, "is how still—after all that—she couldn't say a decent word at all."

"What a female. I wish I could meet her."

"No, you wouldn't want to."

"I'd like——"

"And the things she said then," Peyton interrupted. "It was awful. I went up to her but she turned away. Then she looked at me and said, 'It's your fault. Your fault. You let her fall, you let her fall.' My God, I didn't even know what she was talking about until she 'refreshed' my memory, as she put it. That time I was telling you about, heavens, a couple of years ago when one time I let Maudie slip——"

"And Maudie——"

"Yes! She wouldn't even let me see her. I left. I couldn't stand any more of it. I just left, not even knowing how Maudie really was, whether she was—dying or what, or how much of it had all been made up. For effect, you know."

"Jesus."

"She said, 'You with your drinking and your whoring around, you don't care.' That's the last thing she said."

"Jesus, honey, she sounds——"

"Yes. Crazy." She tilted the bottle and drank, and part of the whisky drained down her camel's hair coat.

"Careful," he said.

"Oh, Dick."

He comforted her, bending down to kiss her hair. On high ground, a straight, unfoggy stretch, he opened up, going very fast, and Peyton murmured, "I like to speed." He held her close to him. There were wide barren fields now, a patch of river to the south, the Rappahannock; this was territory that they knew, where one lane, one house or barn, gliding soundlessly past the car's vaultlike silence, only announced another house or lane or barn a few yards farther on, each more familiar as they drew closer to home. This was the Northern Neck, a land of prim pastoral fences, virgin timber, grazing sheep and Anglo-Saxons: these, the last, spoke in slumbrous Elizabethan accents, rose at dawn, went to bed at dusk, and maintained, with Calvinist passion, their traditional intolerance of evil. Most were

Presbyterians and Baptists, many were Episcopalians, and all prayed and hunted quail with equal fervor and died healthily of heart failure at an advanced age; destiny had given them a peaceful and unvanquished land to live in, free of railroads and big-city ways and the meretricious lures of the flesh, and when they died they died, for the most part, in contentment, shriven of their moderate, parochial sins. They were bounded by two rivers and the sky, and were as chary of the hinterland as of the deepest heart of Africa. A sturdy and honest curiosity filled their minds, provided the objects of such were not exotic or from the North, and the smell of sea filled their days; exacting in all matters, moral but never harsh, they lived in harmony with nature and called themselves the last Americans.

Only a great deal of wealth had the power, conceivably, to corrupt such people, but the Cartwrights, although oriented spiritually more toward the Farmers' Bank of Lancaster than toward the ancient parish church where each Sunday they offered their punctilious but rather sketchy devotions, were not corrupt. They were admired and respected and—because they were aware that they, too, were from common stock—the somewhat too-elaborate deference paid them by their neighbors embarrassed them and caused them to clothe their wealth in muted, simple gray. If they were parvenus, no one would ever accuse them of it; no one would snicker. Harrison Cartwright was an aggressive, quick-tempered man with a face like a bulldog, and he was blessed with the ability to acquire money as easily as a pigeon picks up popcorn. Each enterprise in that part of the state—banks, fisheries, automobile agencies, icehouses—everything, in short, that could produce a dime in cold profit was governed entirely or in part by Cartwright, and it was the natural result of this that he should act, too, in another, perhaps even more dizzily awesome sphere, as a sort of proconsul for Senator Byrd. Cartwright was a vigorous, domineering man, but like most real geniuses he had a grace and a sort of modulation of tone—a way of getting along with people—and he knew when to lower his voice. People who want a king nowadays want one with an aluminum scepter, preferably collapsible, homespun robes and a big, broad smile: Cartwright had all of these.

It is inevitable that men with such ambivalent natures should have strange effects on their sons. When Dick was six, Harrison Cartwright gave the boy a slap which tumbled him headfirst into thirty feet of water—all because his son was neither stout nor skillful enough to handle the sailboat's mainsheet. Equally vivid in Dick's memory were the sting of the blow and the dreadful strangling fear as he plunged downward and felt the rudder rake his scalp—and the effect all this had on his father: the remorse that tortured the blunt bulldog face as Cartwright hauled him dripping over the side, his mawkish, unmanly apologies and, finally, his tears. "Dickie, Dickie, Dickie," he groaned. "What have I done?"

His father baffled him, and as a child Dick was torn between love and hatred. In moments of calm, when his father was chastened and subdued and amiably playing the part of the tame country squire, Dick made fitful overtures and was ever surprised at the fondness and affection with which he was received. But there came foul weather, too, clouds and heavy sea; there were monsoon winds, smelling faintly of dollars, perilous transactions, heady enterprises to be sought on some distant hazardous shore. Then, relegated to a forgotten state, a grease monkey along with his brother and two sisters, he sought refuge in loneliness and with his grandmother, who had taken over the house upon her daughter-in-law's death and who suffered from arthritis and an excess of the Bible.

His mother had been an Episcopalian and although the family, out of deference to her memory and to habit, still attended the little church in the village, the old lady quickly modified this gentle, liberal influence, being a Reformed Presbyterian and a direct descendant of John Knox. At breakfast she took hot water, sweetened with sugar, for her bowels. In a downstairs bedroom of the fine old farmhouse where they lived, she performed each afternoon the stern offices of her faith, and it was here that Dick was summoned, a thin little boy with brown eyes, who leaned and drowsed against the slanting beams of light, spread his arms out to make the blood flow again, pinioned against the light by this gesture as if upon racks of stupefying boredom. Nodding, he would drowse, open his eyes again and watch the stern old eagle's face, the beak clapping endlessly over words of iniquity and damnation, intoned from a Bible clutched in an eagle's arthritic claws. There were pictures, too, conjured up, superimposed upon gentler, greener visions of the lane outside, the cedars, a grassy bank by the pond where crayfish crawled and scuttled down holes, and pollen from September trees made all the creeks run gold; these pictures were of heaven and hell, of the seven-headed beast, the vials of wrath, the woman, full of abominations and the filthiness of her fornications, who was called the mother of harlots; and the boy, like the divine author of the book itself, wondered with great admiration. Mainly, though, he thought of those combustible infants plunged to hell, who stretched out their tiny arms to a pitiless, fiend-faced Abraham and shrieked eternal baby cries of agony and burning. These haunted his heart. And later, stretched out belly-down beside the pond, he mused and dreamed, poked the mud with a stick, and saw them below beneath the streaming gold, children no bigger than his sister, drowned fathoms deep among clamshells and coquettish minnows—children who stirred and noiselessly screamed and were beyond touch of the pale redeeming waters. Because he loved his grandmother, because she treated him kindly and made him fudge, he suffered this treatment, not exactly willingly but with resignation, and so learned early in his life that candy was paid for by tears.

He grew up to be a tall blond youth—relatively unspoiled in spite of his wealth—with an average mind and good intentions. Three years at a small Episcopal prep school across the river served to obliterate his fear of God, and he discovered that being a rich man's son in a poor boy's school was a social asset, so long as he remained a regular fellow. A wide mouth like his father's kept him from being handsome, but he was attractive-looking, passably athletic and intelligent—no triple-threat man, yet endowed with enough of the natural graces for it to be unnecessary for him to make money his weapon. It was merely the badge of a mild superiority. He went off to the University, to study business, with an allowance of two hundred dollars a month, an unswerving faith, like all Virginia gentlemen, in whisky, and a need for sex which in him, he thought—as does every young man—was the most especially ardent and consuming in the world. In Charlottesville he found an acquaintanceship with alcohol easy enough, but one with women formidably difficult, and by the time he met Peyton, in the latter part of his sophomore year, his only sexual experience had been with an aging truck driver's wife who yielded herself up to him, along with five of his fraternity brothers, one hot spring night in a car parked behind a roadhouse.

With Peyton his desire was not removed in him, only suppressed, and he accommodated himself to the frustrating ritual of college "love" with as little pain as possible. Or tried to. Peyton filled him with delight: there was a way she had—a morose, wry humor, vaguely bitter without casting a pall, and more intelligently aware of people than his own—which made him finally conscious of his real love for her; and her beauty, that someday it might belong to him—not like his Oldsmobile but as a spiritual possession unqualified, imperishable, and beyond need of upkeep or repair—caused him to ache with longing to his very soul. Their life became one big dance, a kind of sea of music through which restrained words of tenderness floated like the sparkle of stars; they kissed, pressed their bodies close, and Dick became both contented and dissatisfied: was this the kingdom of heaven, so happy, and so painfully fruitless? "Peyton, don't you want—?" he'd say, and pause, and a tender desire would fill his heart, but he loved her and his was a protestant heart, and it rebelled.

Often, though, it was not these inequitable conditions of desire and decency which tortured him; it was Peyton herself. No one since his father had caused him such bewilderment, and occasionally he wondered—if and when they were married—how on earth he would handle her. He tried to determine what there was about him that she loved, or liked, or was fond of. She never said, "I love you," but that, he thought, was a technicality. He quickly discounted his money; once, when they had started to become serious about each other, she told him to heck with your money—and he believed her, because in logical matters like that he knew she was completely frank and honest. It was these other things that bothered him; he had an orderly and methodical mind, one which found an emotional balance at a fairly early age, and sought meanings: how, then, to reconcile these rages—weird, wild and unreasonable, always when she had had too much to drink, and generally directed at him—with her placid normal moments when, arms about his neck, she called him Dickie boy and kissed his ear with her tongue, and the smell of perfume in her hair made him so weak he thought he'd collapse in his tracks? A hundred times during the past two years, leaving some debauch which beforehand had charitably been described as a "little party-party," they found themselves alone, dizzy, miraculously safe after a frantic, moonstruck drive through the hills, woods—they hardly knew nor did it matter—where, parked amid thick deepening shadows, they felt each other, moist skin and hair, and were afraid to let loose their breath, so full were their lungs, such an unlovely, shuddering sound it would make. That year they played a song called "Racing with the Moon." It came not from some steel tower miles away, but from the depths of the car itself, and it was played only for them. Cramped, they lay side by side on the slippery leather while the dawn whirled drunkenly above them in a steam of light and the exclusive invisible music drifted up from the floor, drums, horns, and violins that glowed mysteriously, like phosphorescence, and touched their thighs and arms with a pale invisible fire. It was all very frustrating.

But there were other times, just as passionate, just as memorable, but awful. These evenings began—often, too, at the fraternity house—with the same gay, innocent intentions and ended up in a welter of ugly words, tears, misunderstandings. He could never tell what mood governed her heart; at the most he came to learn that she was somehow deviously tied to her home, her father, and that a letter from him or news from her family was apt to make her remote and unapproachable, or worse—after they had drunk and danced together for hours—to topple her off the wrong side of that emotional tightrope upon which she seemed always so precariously balanced. Then she was abrupt and baffling. Afterward in the car she'd accuse him unreasonably of neglect (he who had not, as well as he could remember, taken his eyes off her all evening), of lacking sensitivity, of general barbarities and poverty of feeling: how, she asked, could she be expected to marry someone who took all this fraternity business so seriously, whose whole life was already one big cliché? "Goodness, Dick, I like a good time, I like to party, but how could you stand there and laugh at the jokes that silly Tucker girl made, that whore? . . . Dick, I just don't think you'd be *gentle* enough, if we had children. . . ."

That sort of thing.

He'd suffer these abuses, knowing that they would be over soon, knowing that she would become tender and apologetic and kiss him. The fact that her bitter words did prick his modest self-esteem didn't really shatter him; he had already arrived at an evaluation of his attitudes, his sensibilities, and if Peyton, in spite of these irrational moments of outrage and suspicion, still loved him for his positive characteristics—whatever they were—well, wasn't that sufficient? She still confused him, but her moods contributed the seasoning to their romance, and gradually there became clear some of the qualities about him that she loved. It was partially that, being different, they complemented each other: in the midst of her wild outbursts he was aware that she yet knew he was strong and reliable, and that he would comfort her. Too self-respecting to be trampled upon, he still allowed himself to act as a sort of sieve for her emotions, knowing that, like him, she was tight and rather incoherent, and that she didn't mean what she said about him at all.

So, whenever he was away from her, it was the happy times that he preferred to remember. They were together as often as their studies allowed, which is to say almost constantly—every week end and on Wednesdays and Thursdays and even Tuesdays, when Dick would make the long afternoon drive over the mountains to Sweet Briar. Their meetings were casually executed, in the manner of college boys and girls, and even nonchalant, to other eyes; but all this was pure pose, for alone they allowed their arms to envelop each other, and threaded the hot cloak of their desire with kisses and frank hoarse demands, which neither of them expected, or really wanted, to be fulfilled. Once again they drank, drove for endless miles on black-market gas, and found themselves high in the moonlit misty hills, dancing to the radio turned full blast, in bare feet racing with the moon which Vaughn Monroe had evoked for them in soft thoughtless bars of harmony, and which, from these heights so fat and pale and benign, seemed, like the music itself, exclusively theirs. . . .

Now, toward dawn, they were nearing home. The pint bottle between them was almost empty. They passed wide empty fields, more familiar farmhouses, a creek, sluggish beneath a thin film of ice, with an Indian name full of *k*'s and *q*'s. A grass-green light had fallen over the earth but all was still sleeping and quiet and motionless, except for a yellow flame which flickered briefly at a window, or a trio of ducks which arose from the marsh, flew as swiftly as the car for a time, and veered out over the river. To the east the morning star faded, then vanished, and they emerged from dark sheltering woods in an explosion of light; across the fields smoke curled up from kitchen chimneys: the day had become officially Sunday.

"I told him I was going to quit school." Peyton had the hiccups and she paused to hold her breath while Dick counted nine. "There!" She took his hand again. "I told him I wasn't going to take any more of her lousy money."

"It'll be O.K.," he said, "don't worry."

"Maudie won't be O.K. Oh, Dick." She laid her head on his shoulder and he put his arm around her once more.

"It's only a few more miles, honey," he said.

They talked drowsily now, for neither of them had slept this night and only a short hour or two the night before. Yet their exhaustion was sustained by an undercurrent of excitement; it had been a tense and unsettling thing, what Peyton had gone through, but to people so young there is nothing final in disaster, the disaster itself often opening up refreshing vistas of novelty, escape or freedom. Dick had comforted her about Maudie: there was little else to be done about that except wait and see. In the meantime . . . In the meantime they had talked and talked—Peyton mostly—and because of the whisky, which had lulled and deceived their minds, their talk was repetitious and touched with a synthetic exaltation, and its sadness and its mood of fatality gave them a solemn sort of joy.

"And Daddy," Peyton murmured. "Like I told you. It was terrible seeing him the way I did before we left. Oh, you should have seen him. Really you've never seen such a sight. He was so lost he was just slobbering all over me, saying that this wasn't the end for us, to come back with him to Port Warwick." She sat up abruptly, looking at Dick. "Imagine that! He was so completely lost, she had so completely shattered him, that I really believe he lost his mind for a minute. Imagine him seriously asking me to come back with him, with her!" She paused for a moment, pushed the hair back from her brow. "The poor guy. He's such a dope. But I love him, Dick. I love him." She hiccuped again, and fished about in her pocket and came up with Loftis' ring. "Look, Dick, look what that old jerk gave me. Isn't it pretty? You know what he said? He said—he tried to be funny——" She gave a little laugh. "It was so pathetic with his bandage falling off. I fixed it for him. He took off this ring and tried to make a joke. 'Look here,' he said, 'if that rich young scoundrel can give you the pin the least you can do is accept this small token of affection from a broken-down wreck like me.' The dear. Oh, it was so pathetic . . . hic!" She sank back again, laughing helplessly, a small chain of indrawn breaths, linked by hiccups, that threatened to snap in fragments of hysteria. "Let me have a drink, sweetheart. To cure these."

"Poor baby. A bloody fine thing," said Dick.

"What?"

"All this." He turned his eyes from the road; his face was flushed and scowling, and he was having trouble with his tongue. "All this. I mean . . . oh, what the hell. I mean, don't quit school. Honey, we haven't got much time. Uncle Sam's going to get me. Let's get married. Today. We'll drive up to Maryland. Pop's got a lot of ration coupons lying around. We'll sleep a little first. Then we'll drive up to La Plata and get married. Honey, I'll take care of you for the rest of my life. Oh, honey, dammit . . ."

It was inconceivable that she wouldn't be listening. She was smiling. She said, "It would have been funny if it hadn't been so awful. Apologizing to me for that gruesome woman he's been running around with all these years. To me! Why would he do that? As if I gave a damn. I wanted to tell him that it was a fine thing, only why didn't he get somebody with a little sav . . . savoir-faire? Why would he apologize to me? I just guess he's got to apologize to somebody."

"Hey, how about it, darling?"

"What?"

"Going up to——"

"Oh, no, Dickie, not today."

"When? If we put it off——"

"I don't know."

"When? Tell me when."

"No, Dick. No! No! For God's sake, can't you see—— Oh, I'm getting so stewed . . . I'm getting——" She flung her head into his lap, squeezing his leg with her hand. He didn't flinch but looked straight ahead and said nothing as the car plowed through the mist, the green ineffable morning. A wood of oaks and pines appeared, two plain pillars of brick flanking the entrance to a gravel road; they turned off here. Half a mile beyond stood the house, deserted and silent. They passed over a small causeway which spanned the pond. Somewhere among the whitewashed outhouses, which had once been slave quarters, a rooster crowed. Huge oaks arched over the driveway, and as they drove up, the car caused terror among a flock of geese, which fled their advance in clumsy haste, emitting honks of dismay.

"Harvey must be up," Dick said, "I never saw such an energetic nigger." Peyton didn't answer, only raised her head a bit and let it fall again in Dick's lap. Her face was as pale as death.

With coffee they revived themselves a little. Still tense and nervous, they were too tired to sleep. It was five o'clock by the kitchen clock, but the clock had stopped and they wearily figured between them, somehow, not caring really, that it must be nearly seven. There was no one in the house but themselves, the family having gone—as Dick had explained before—over to King and Queen County, to visit relatives. The house itself was weary and still, and nothing disturbed the quiet, except for the infrequent crackle of timbers that stretched like a man's limbs upon awakening, warming to the dawn with a somnolent snapping noise as they had done each morning for nearly two hundred years. There was a musty smell about—the windows had been closed since Thursday—and they wandered aimlessly, not speaking, through the musty airless rooms, neither able to return to their conversation, nor to forget it. And it was as if their tension and their exhaustion—mainly Peyton's grief and lostness, her despair—had begun to communicate itself to the house. Amid those ancient rooms which carried even to this day, along with the radio, electric lamps and modern chairs, a sort of minor squalor of ancestral piety—old canes carved from a hickory, many years dead, long before the war began, and a pulpit-sized, rat-chewed Bible, and ante-bellum novels still dusty and uncut in their cases, and faded Christian lithographs of the Apostles and the Ascension and a swooning Susanna—amid all these they wandered, bearing with them, like an anachronistic odor, their peculiarly modern despair. . . .

They slumped down together on the couch, and agreed that they needed a drink. Dick got his father's bourbon and poured out two stiff ones. While Peyton was drinking hers, he went out and found Harvey, an old Negro who, a stereotype from his high-button Sunday shoes to his toothless grin and bleached poll, looked like Uncle Remus.

"I don't want you mention to Pop about Miss Loftis staying here," Dick said, somewhat thickly. Being worldly-wise and very old, Harvey understood and responded with a placid, "Yes, suh, Mistah Dick."

When Dick returned to the parlor he found Peyton standing by the window, a second drink in her hand. She had turned the radio on. He stood beside her for a moment, saying nothing. The sun had come up over the river. It was a beautiful river, broad and blue and serene, with no cities defacing its shore. There was something primeval about this river: with the woods crowding its banks, and the vacant tidal flats and the ducks winging southward through a blue, cloudless sky, it seemed as if the river had remained forever changeless, undisturbed by the tools or weapons of man, and would remain like this until the land returned to the sea, and the sea to the land, and the wash of tides would obliterate all—woods and seashells and homing ducks—and the river would roll on at the floor of some surging eternal ocean. Peyton turned to Dick and said, "They thought that they had had it."

"Who, honey?"

"Those people back in the Lost Generation. Daddy, I guess. Anybody who thought about anything at all. They thought they were lost. They were crazy. They weren't lost. What they were doing was losing us."

"Us?"

"Yes. They didn't lose themselves, they lost us—you and me. Look at Daddy, I love him so. But he lost me and he doesn't even know it." She took the ring out of her pocket and looked down at it. "The dear. I think we've got a Freudian attachment. The dear. He's such an ass. If it just hadn't been Mother he married, we all might have made out all right. She's been too much for him. So we're lost. He lost me and all of his friends lost their children. I don't know why, but they did. At least they had a chance to live for a while. But they didn't care and they lost you, too, and now you're going off to war and get killed."

"No, I'm not. I'm tough as hell."

235

"You're not tough. You're just like me, you don't know which way to go."

"I know I want to marry you."

"No, Dick, don't start——"

"Oh, honey, listen now, we could——"

It was as if his words had, with their persistence, hurt her physically, stirring up an agony of regret and memory and desire. She turned furiously upon him, and because she was drunk her voice was hoarse and the words confused. "Quit *talking* about getting married, Dick! Quit *talking* about it! You're selfish about me. And stupid. And if you want to know why I'm like this it's because I don't love you and I never have. Not because of you or anything like that but just because I don't love and I can't love and isn't that too bad. Isn't that too bad, Dick? Because I'm sick isn't that too bad? That you'll never——"

He knew she'd get over it. He took her in his arms, holding her tightly. She struggled for a bit but then became limp and because he loved her and understood her the kiss he pressed upon her lips was a devout one, sending a sort of holy delight through his soul. She said, "No," once, but that was the last word she said, for something had passed between them, a longing voiceless as air, and he led her into the bedroom. There was an old four-poster here, his grandmother's, and all day long they lay on it—the blankets pulled back because the room was hot and stuffy—naked and sleeping. The act of love had exhausted them but they slept restlessly, dreaming loveless dreams. The sun rose, began to descend, and afternoon brought a flood of light to the room. The radio, playing faintly from the living room, sent through their dreams a murmurous flow of intrusions: the war, a preacher said, was general throughout the world and at the smoky edge of sleep, between wakefulness and dreams, their minds captured words like Christ and anti-Christ, only to lose them and to forget, and to stir and dream again.

Sleeping, he took her in his arms; she drew away. A dog barked across the wintry fields. There was dance music and later, Mozart, a song of measureless innocence that echoed among lost ruined temples of peace and brought to their dreams an impossible vision: of a love that outlasted time and dwelt even in the night, beyond reach of death and all the immemorial, descending dusks. Then evening came. Arms and legs asprawl, they stirred and turned. Twilight fell over their bodies. They were painted with fire, like those fallen children who live and breathe and soundlessly scream, and whose souls blaze forever.

236

Six

CAREY drove cautiously, for now through the afternoon heat they had begun to come in droves—Negroes in turbans and white flowing baptismal robes. They came in busses and rattletrap cars and on the back ends of trucks; some came on foot. Out of dusty side roads they streamed, laughing and sweating, carrying between them paper banners—

DADDY FAITH BRINGS LOVE TO US

—and it was difficult to drive because of the children, draped in miniature robes, who ran out in front of the car. In fact, the confusion of traffic had become so general—the drivers of the trucks and cars passing each other, turning to shout greetings, with a kind of intoxicated recklessness—that for a moment he drew over to stop at the side of the road, beneath a grove of trees. They were stranded there briefly, run hopelessly aground amid a flood of surging robes, and Carey had a touch of panic: he felt that, with Helen, he was the only white person for miles, like a missionary isolated among hostile natives who tramped ceaselessly past, seeking some pagan redemption in the waters of the Congo. Then suddenly there was a lull; most of the Negroes

237

had vanished down the road toward town, leaving behind them a cloud of hot, powdery sand which swarmed in the air and fell, and left on the hood of the car a white film of dust. Helen coughed and wiped her brow. Carey started the car again and they drove on down the highway. Neither of them, since they got into the car, had spoken, although Carey had on one or two occasions essayed a tentative throat clearing. Now, however, he found himself talking, almost before he knew what he was saying: "What is it you feel now, Helen?"

There was a long silence. Past them rolled woods and swampland, gas stations, a seedy roadhouse. Finally she said, in level voice, "Fatigue."

"I mean, Helen dear," he went on, "I mean . . . about all this."

Out of the corner of his eye he saw her raise her hand and with two thin, blanched fingers pluck at the loose folds of her neck. It was an intense, ruminative moment, as if he had asked her something mathematical and involved and requiring heavy concentration. Then she said, in clear conversational tones: "I don't know, Carey. Is it possible to know when you've finally gone . . . haywire? You know what I mean? Years ago it would have been different. Everything was different then. I could feel things as well as another. But you know as well as I what happened when everything collapsed. Peyton and all. When Milton left. I told you about it then. I don't want to go on about it." She turned her face away, looking out of the window.

"You lost—" he began—"you deserted God."

"God deserted me. Before that. When Maudie died."

"No," he said, "God never deserts anyone," thinking, I won't go on about that. It's too late for that sort of thing. It's this other thing that counts right now, and we can talk about God later.

"Have you thought about Milton?" he said. "Have you thought about what I told you this morning?"

"I went to sleep," she said. "I dreamed. I didn't think about anything at all."

"What—what did you dream?" he asked hopefully.

"Lovely things. The way the beach was years ago. The sand. The fog in the morning. My garden, the way it was then, when I cared."

"Milton needs you and wants you," he said. "He's repentant. He's suffered enough."

"Yes, I've thought about that. Maybe he has."

Carey's heart beat faster, as if he had inhaled a thrilling breath of hope. "He *does* need you," he said quickly, "he *does*. And you need him. It's all you have. Don't you see, Helen dear? Don't you see?"

"Yes," she said quietly, "yes." But it was a faint tired answer, that really committed itself to no conviction at all, and Carey thought: Yes, maybe it's true, she's so far gone that nothing can help her. Not even God. So it's madness, after all.

And he thought briefly about madness, and this family, which had succeeded—almost effortlessly, it seemed—in destroying itself, and he became so overwhelmed by melancholy that his stomach rumbled and his hands and wrists became limp and trembled on the steering wheel. He thought of the wild evening after Maudie's funeral when, with Peyton absent and Loftis, he supposed, hiding upstairs, Helen had told him that everything was finished, there was no God, no anything, behold (with a nod upstairs toward Loftis, and which included, he gathered, Peyton, too) this breed of monsters. God, what words she had used! And then, at that moment, he had realized that it was impossible to believe otherwise: she had gone mad; how mad he was unable to say, but enough for him to understand, with an inward groan of despair, that she was too far gone for his ministrations to be of any use. And his own personal despair had arisen not completely from her tragedy, but from his: he had failed; all those years he had known her she had gradually become a sort of symbol to him, of every lost person who seeks Christ, no matter how fitfully, and is salvageable. But he had not saved her, he had not taught her faith enough to endure disaster; and that night, with the wind moaning through the weather stripping and Helen shivering in the cold of her house—and Loftis upstairs too drunk to fix the furnace—the sense of horror and failure had clutched his spine like the wet, wrinkled hand of a drowned woman, and he had become for a moment apostate, addressing a peevish, cruel prayer to the God who had still not revealed himself: *why, You God?* Yet he had tried, even after that.

Now this. Who was to blame? Mad or not, Helen had been beastly. She had granted to Loftis, in her peculiarly unremitting way, no forgiveness or understanding, and above all she had been beastly to Peyton. Yet Loftis himself had been no choice soul; and who, finally, lest it be God himself, could know where the circle, composed as it was of such tragic suspicions and misunderstandings, began, and where it ended? Who was the author of the original misdeed? Peyton, think of Peyton. Was she beyond reproach? Other children had risen above even worse difficulties. Maybe Peyton was the answer.

He jammed on his brakes. In his woolgathering he had almost run down a skinny colored woman who, bicycling, swaddled in the robes of her baptism, paddled away heedlessly, with a supreme look of joy.

"S-sorry, Helen," he exclaimed, and then, recovering himself: "I thought you had found it for a while, Helen."

"What?" she said listlessly.

"All that that you were searching for." He drove on. "For a while. After . . . after Maudie died."

"No."

"No—" he sighed in agreement—"no, you didn't." Then, "He needs you. You need each other," he murmured again, mildly and futilely.

"Oh, look," he said suddenly. "Look there."

In the driveway of a ramshackle gas station, which also seemed to be a roadhouse, the hearse was parked, drawn up ahead of the deserted limousine. Quickly Carey turned off the road, with a squeal of tires. He stopped behind the limousine and gazed around him. He could see no one, yet from somewhere near the hearse, and on the other side of it, where the hood was thrown up, came the low sound of voices. Something made of metal, a hammer or wrench, fell on the gravel.

"Well," he said to Helen, "they must be here."

"Yes."

"I wonder what's wrong."

"I don't know."

"I wonder what could be wrong," he repeated, but there was no answer. "Well," he said, "I'd better get out and see."

"Yes."

"Do you want to get out and go inside for a minute? It's hot out here. Sitting in the car."

"No."

"Are you sure?"

"Yes."

The afternoon heat bore in its embrace a drugged and heavy stillness; a truckful of Negroes passed on the road, and the sound died away to the east. Around them the sun-streaked fields were empty, wilted, almost blighted, as if by drought, and there was no sound of insects, no passionate flight and murmur among the weeds, and in the dark pinewoods behind them there was no sound of birds. Everything had flown the heat. Fumes of gasoline smoldered on the air, and Carey began to sweat.

"Helen. You don't want to sit . . . here."

"Yes."

He began to move toward the hearse, when she said something. "Wait," he thought it was. He turned.

"I don't want to see that woman," she said, in a flat, explicit voice. "Do you understand, Carey? She's——"

"What, Helen dear?"

"I don't want to see that woman. I don't want to lay eyes on her."

He returned to the car window and looked down at her. He felt angry and bitter and futile. "Helen," he said, in a mild, bitter voice, "why did you come today? If this is the way you feel about everything. Why? Only because it's the proper thing to do? Only——" He halted, trembling. "I'm sorry, Helen," he said.

She turned away and bowed her head slightly. "I'd give anything for a cigarette," she said. "Anything."

"I'm sorry, Helen," he repeated, and walked toward the hearse. She's lost love and grief maybe, he thought, but not hate. Not hate.

Over the motor three forms stooped—the garageman, Mr. Casper and Barclay. Mr. Casper stood up at Carey's approach, exposing his gums in the parched smile of his trade. "Ah," he sighed, "Mr. Carr. It's a bad day. A bad thing. A frightful thing. You came with the deceased's mother?"

"Yes. It's a terrible thing."

"Yes, it is. We've had some trouble here, but we'll have it fixed in no time. No time at all. I've called the sexton at the cemetery. Everything's been prepared. Oh, this is a sad thing, one of my saddest cases."

Carey agreed again that it was, indeed, a sad thing, and for a moment, with the sweat streaming off both of them, Mr. Casper, who in private felt himself as surely anointed as any of God's ministers, told Carey about the ways of the Lord, which are exceeding strange and move for causes unbeknownst to mortal men; and in spite of the heat, the blazing sun which threatened to burn holes through their identical white panama hats, they chatted for a moment, understanding each other.

But the heat really was dreadful, and Carey broke in on Mr. Casper—who, with his red freckled hands clasped together at his breast, spoke of the saving grace of a sanctified Christian burial—to ask where Loftis was.

"In there," Mr. Casper said, "with that woman . . . Mrs. Bonner, I believe." His bleak eyelids sank; over his face passed an ambiguous flicker, both roguish and disapproving, then it vanished. "In there," he repeated. "Please, sir, tell Mr. Loftis that we'll be ready to leave in just a few minutes. We've already been a half-hour, and the sexton——"

Carey hurried into the filling station. At the doorway he turned to look back at Helen. She was still seated in the front of the car, looking sternly ahead. Some puff of wind came, humming faintly in the pines; a curtain of dust blew over the hearse and cars, bearing with it dry weeds and cinders, but Helen took no notice: she gazed straight ahead at the barren fields, the wind in its diminishing blast still rustling, white curl by fine white curl, so perfectly waved, the ghostly shock of her hair. "Helen——" he began, and beckoned with his finger, but it was no use, she didn't see him. He went on in.

Loftis sat in a booth by the window, clutching a beer bottle with both hands, in a kind of sacramental embrace. A radio was playing hillbilly music. In another booth sat Dolly alone and sobbing, trying to find a dry spot in a wad of shredded Kleenex. There was a Negro, too, whom Carey knew—Ella Swan—who was squatting dismally upon a drink case in the rear, among an assortment of tires and oil cans, and who, when she saw him, arose with a little cry of recognition, but he put a finger to his lips and walked over to Loftis. Loftis didn't recognize Carey at first, merely turned his face dully upward. The streak of silver hair hung limply over his forehead. His cheeks were by now of a greenish color and his eyes, rapt and stunned and bloodshot, looked to Carey, who suddenly recalled a phrase, "like those of a man who has gazed so long into the abyss that the abyss has begun to gaze back at him." Without a word, Carey sat down across from him.

"Milton," he said, "I can't tell you how sorry I am. I want you to know that if there's anything——"

"No," Loftis said, with a wave of his hand, "there's nothing anybody can do." He tilted the bottle up and drank.

"I can help you," Carey said, "a little. I don't know how much I can help you and I know how you feel about . . . things. I don't want you to put your faith in me or even in God if you don't feel like it right now." He paused, very gently pulled the bottle away from Loftis' face, which was confronting him like a frightened baby's sucking on a nipple. "Look, I'm no jackass about these things, but why don't you put that away for a while. Today, at least. Listen to me for a minute, will you please, Milton?"

"I lost my girl," said Loftis.

"I know. I——"

Loftis looked away, resting his brow in his hand. "Don't tell me," he said softly, "that it's the judgment of God or any of that crap. I lost my baby. I got to——"

"Milton," Carey interrupted, "we haven't got much time. Tell me. Tell me, why do you want Helen back? Don't you see? That's the answer. You've got salvation in your hands almost. Helen knows it. She's still too proud. You've got to try and try again and make her see how completely you need each other now. Don't you see, Milton?"

"I've tried," he said listlessly. "I've tried. What else can I do?" His voice was weary and lost, but not without a touch of hope. He recaptured his beer and took a large swallow. "She's crazy. Sick. I've done my best. What else can I do?"

"Tell her now."

"I'm scared to."

"Scared of what?" Carey asked. "Scared she won't—?"

"Yes. Scared she won't say yes."

"Get this straight in your mind, Milton. Why do you want her back? You've got to be sure it's not just a reaction to all . . . all of this. Why do you want her back? You've got to look into your heart." Loftis said nothing. Around them, as if in woolen folds, hung the gigantic heat of the afternoon; two jalopies loaded down with Negroes toiled slowly past on the road, leaving behind a trail of greasy blue vapor which rose on the air currents, and fell, and vanished among the pines. A mockingbird began to sing in the woods, then ceased. At once they were aware of the sobs which drifted hoarsely up from Dolly's booth, but these ceased, too, abruptly. A four-bladed wooden fan revolved over them, and above its alternating flap and whisper came music from the radio, in a cheerless, sweet lament of religion and woe.

Only a tramp was Laz'rus that day
It was he who lay at the rich man's gate.

Blazing sunlight sloped through the window screen, busy with flies, and fell on Loftis' cheeks. He moved on the seat.

"Why?" Carey said.

Loftis thrust his head back into his hands. "Jesus Christ, man, I love her!" He looked up. "I've always loved her. You don't have to sit there, do you, and probe about in your smug, smooth way——"

"I'm not probing."

Loftis' voice broke, he looked away. "Sorry. You're doing your best. I just wish this day was over." He looked at Carey again. "There was a time," he said softly, "when I thought I'd found some kind of answer. God, we go through life fooling ourselves, thinking we've got

243

the answer, only it's never the answer really. I thought that being without Maudie would mean something to us. And it did, just for a while. It brought us together. I even stopped drinking. I broke down. I said to hell with this other kind of life. I thought there's something to be said for honor in this world where there doesn't seem to be any honor left. I thought that maybe happiness wasn't really anything more than the knowledge of a life well spent, in spite of whatever immediate discomfort you had to undergo, and that if a life well spent meant compromises and conciliations and reconciliations, and suffering at the hands of the person you love, well then better that than live without honor." He paused to gaze out at the fields, sweat pouring from his face. There would be rain soon; on the horizon a ridge of thunderheads churned and billowed, and a spasm of wind seized a grove of distant pines, rippling shapes of light across its surface like massive fingers. Loftis made a gagging noise, as if he were going to be sick, and at that point Dolly came up and stood by the table, dabbing at her eyes.

"Milton——" she began.

He ignored her. "So," he said, turning back to Carey, "I tried for a while again. I tried for almost a year. Honor. Then there was Peyton's wedding——"

Carey nodded. He remembered the wedding too well.

"I just couldn't take that. I left that day and now I'm sorry because I didn't realize that honor isn't given automatically, but you have to fight for it just as strongly as I guess you do for love. Once Helen told me you said that, that you have to fight for love. Today I know, I guess, but it's too late." He looked up at Dolly for an instant, and then back at Carey. "So I left and even then it was too soon, not realizing that that day was just one point along the way. I hadn't fought hard enough. I was impatient, at fifty-one years old I was impatient like a snotty-nosed child to rid myself of the only thing I had left in the world that was worth having—she who sick or not, weird or not, was the only person worth fifty-one years and more of living and was beautiful still—to me—a beautiful goddam rose blossom. . . ." He began to weep.

"I understand," said Carey. "I understand——"

The screen door slammed behind Mr. Casper. He came up and stood by Dolly, looking down at Loftis. "We're ready now," he said gently. "I'm terribly sorry. I've never had anything like this——"

Loftis rose to his feet with a groan.

"Milton," said Dolly, touching him. He paid no attention to her at all. Carey got up, too. A murmur of thunder heaved up faintly to the west. Light drained from the day for a moment, filling the room with green, cool shadows. From the cluttered corner of the room where Ella sat—or from where she arose now, an angular patchwork of lace and black mourning, to hobble toward them—the guitars surged and strummed, hoisting, as if by the palpable force of their wild woeful chords, a voice, a woman's, to a sort of tragic rapture.

> *But they left him to die*
> *Like a tramp on the street . . .*

The blaze of heat returned. Loftis walked toward the door, with Mr. Casper's hand limply consoling him on one shoulder, and with Dolly tagging at his side. Ella approached Carey just as he turned, and she made a baffled little salute and what seemed to be a curtsey.

"Please suh, Mr. Carey," she said, "is you gwine preach up dat po' chile to heaven?"

"Yes."

"Po' blessed chile. De onliest thing we got left to do is pray. Pray wid de sperit and pray wid de understandin' also, like Paul de 'Postle." She began to snuffle on her sleeve. "God have mercy," she moaned, "we done sho' seen de punishment, like de good Lawd say, de end of all flesh is come befo' me and de earth is filled wid vi'lence everywhere."

"Yes." He patted her on the arm, and led her toward the door. "The Lord," he said—as he bent down to her—rather wistfully, for the universe suddenly seemed intolerably empty and stark, "in His compassion and His infinite mercy will watch over all of us, forever and ever, be we among the living or the dead."

At the door he found Loftis standing alone on the steps. Dolly and Mr. Casper were already in the limousine, and Barclay was at the wheel of the hearse once more. The garageman, standing rag in hand at the foot of the steps, splashed into the hot gravel a russet stream of tobacco juice, upon which flies settled as soon as it landed. A cat crept out from beneath the garage, a mouse in its jaws, gave them all a discreet, slit-eyed glance, then loped away.

"She just won't look at me," Loftis said, "she just won't."

In the car Helen sat staring grimly in front of her, fanning her face with a road map. Carey put his hand on Loftis' shoulder. "Don't worry," he said, "afterwards. Afterwards everything'll be all right. Go on now with Mr. Casper."

"Yes," Loftis said, "afterwards. Yes. Yes."

Loftis went to the limousine with Ella. The breeze stirred again, hot, stifling. There was a sudden sickening odor in the air, sweet and diseased, pestilential, like that of burning flesh. Carey turned. By the pines the corpse of a pig lay smoldering in a barbecue pit. The weeds bent and trembled as a car passed on the road. Carey mopped his brow.

But there *had* been, Carey remembered, a moment in which a breath of divine grace had blown upon the family; in which, like a slender miracle, all their affairs seemed straightened out for a while, giving promise of improvement, if not of perfection. This was during the year following Maudie's death in Charlottesville. When he left the house after Maudie's funeral, recalling Helen's haggard distress (she had not said "good-by" to him, only muttered something about "waiting," "all my life I've waited"), he had expected any kind of violence: murder, suicide, God knew what all. Yet nothing messy or gruesome had come about. He had left her alone for a while, feeling, with a powerful sense of inadequacy, that his presence would only hurt her, irritate her, stir up memories of a time when, together, they had dwelt in a climate of hopefulness. So there was no God, that was that; let her find peace among her flowers, in the consoling heart of sleep which, he knew by now, she embraced like the breast of a mother; let her go to a doctor now, sick woman. That was that. He couldn't have foreseen the change in her, the change so emphatic—yet which came about with such seeming casualness—that his better senses should have run up a red flag of warning.

He visited her a couple of months later. Beforehand, there had been noncommittal phone calls; her voice had been placid, unhysterical, and at least, he figured, she was holding her own. Then he found them together one bright February afternoon, drinking tea. She arose from Milton's side to greet him—smartly dressed in what appeared to be a vague gray concession to mourning, with powder tastefully applied in a not too successful attempt to hide the rings beneath her eyes—and he could have been floored on the spot with a broomstraw. And grazing about upon the fringe of the conversation—which not once mentioned Maudie, or the stern hand of destiny, or anything depressing, for that matter, but which involved only certain changes to the house, plans for the garden in spring, a whole jumble of serene, practical matters—he had learned indirectly, and to his astonishment, just how matters stood. Loftis, it seemed, was accomplishing a personal revolt. It was happening, beneath an aura of exquisite torture, right before his eyes: while Helen spoke dreamily and with a faint, pensive hope of the good things in store for them, Loftis stirred restlessly and fidgeted, and his face wore a subdued, broken look as he gazed out the window and sipped the distasteful tea. Loftis, and not Helen, was the one who was achieving the impossible. He had begun to grab hold of himself. It was exhilarating to watch, and from one point of view vaguely disappointing—for what had taken place was not a matter of any mystical faith but apparently involved just guts, the revolt of a man against the pure footlessness which had held him in bondage for half a lifetime. Had he stopped drinking? Obviously. Now he was learning the pleasures of tea. Had he cut Dolly off? It certainly seemed so. What had happened? Had his guilt, like something monstrous and hairy and unutterable, prowled about his bed at night, filling his dreams with such thoughts of loss, of death, that he knew, upon awakening, that this ordeal was the only answer? Had it been pity for Helen? Or love? Or, in Charlottesville, had the bleak face of disaster so chilled him that he just fell on Helen, in a convulsion of necessity?

Carey didn't know, but the poor fellow was making a valiant try of it, and if he wasn't saving himself he had gone a long way toward saving Helen who, certainly far from happy but no longer sunk in the suicidal despair of a few months ago, said gently, over the rim of her cup, "Sometimes just the touch of a hand can redeem us, don't you think, Carey? Isn't that right, Milton dear?" And without shame, in a naked movement of intimacy, her hand had stolen out upon the sunlit satin pillow toward Loftis', lay lightly for a moment upon his pink, outstretched, unprotesting palm, and squeezed it until the skin became positively bloodless.

After that, Carey felt that he was through trying to figure her out. He had thought that Maudie's death would prostrate her, kill her. It almost had, he imagined, in the first few days, but he hadn't reckoned on the therapeutic powers of Loftis' conversion. His heart rejoiced at this, yet it was still faintly disappointing—that a death should accomplish overnight what all his talk about faith had failed to do in years.

Peyton's wedding took place on a Saturday afternoon in October of the same year. It was a brilliant, mild day, filled with the bluster of wind and leaves, and bringing from the water that same acute, clean, salty air which seaside resorts advertise as "salubrious." The wedding was to be at home (Carey had had, a week before, a genial

247

chat about it over the phone with Loftis, who had said that everything was "fine, fine" now, Helen sends her regards, we're both looking forward to seeing Peyton, and so on) and as he drove over that afternoon with Adrienne, it occurred to him, not very originally, that no ceremony in the Christian culture is more exciting, or grand, or awe-inspiring, than a wedding.

"It is the symbolic affirmation of a moral order in the world," he said out loud.

"Don't be so pompous," said Adrienne mildly. That shut him up. They drove on a way in silence.

Finally he said, "It's still awfully hard to figure out."

"What?"

"This understanding they've come to."

"Who?"

"The Loftises. Of course."

"Why?" she asked.

"I mean—I mean. Oh, so many things. I have a great deal of regard for Helen Loftis, but I can't understand why, considering Milton for what he is, he would stay with her. I wouldn't, I know. As a husband."

"Maybe," Adrienne murmured coolly, "it's because she's got the dough."

"That's not funny," he said.

"Why not?"

"As a poor man's wife you should know that money isn't the tie that binds."

"Sometimes it is," she said.

"Don't be cynical," he replied, "no man's that dependent. I mean—well, even if you are dependent, say financially, you still don't torture yourself crazy. Not for money."

"Maybe it's not torture," she said, "maybe he loves her. Or it."

"It. What do you mean, 'it'?" he asked, rather sharply.

"Maybe he enjoys being emasculated. Finally."

"Oh, Adrienne," he snorted, "honestly. You sound like you've been rereading one of those psychiatrists who simplify everything for the layman."

"No, dear. I'm just putting two and two together. After all, it doesn't have to be *it*. It could be love, you know. That's what we Christians are supposed to call——"

"Adrienne," he put in, "I *deplore* your flippancy in matters like this. I won't——"

248

She patted him on the hand. "All right, sweetheart," she said, smiling, "I was only fooling."

His sinuses hurt, and he felt that, for his own part, the wedding wasn't getting off to much of a start, but to keep things jolly he returned her hand pat and said, "I just guess it's what I get for marrying a Bryn Mawr girl, who is too much of this world." It was an old joke they had, and each of them made a mechanical, appreciative chuckle, and Carey, because he had quelled what might have developed into a nasty, day-long tension between them, felt as physically relieved as if he had taken off a wet pair of shoes. They talked no more of Loftis or Helen, but before they reached the house they had put Dolly to rout, agreeing that it was tough about her, but that it was her own fault really. Who else was to blame if she had to live like a Carmelite nun, practically a recluse, looking like a wraith with at least twenty pounds shed in her mourning for Loftis? Didn't that show you that the wages of sin is not death, but isolation? They wondered about Peyton, too, for neither of them had known her after she had grown up. And, in the light of the rumors which had floated about town concerning her reasons for leaving school, and her questionable conduct later in New York City, they agreed that it was a fine thing that she should finally be married here at home, where her roots were. Although Carey had to caution Adrienne about the faintly arch tone she used when she mentioned the husband-to-be—Harry Whatever-his-name-is—just because he was a Jew, "and a painter to boot."

"Why do you suppose they came back here?" Adrienne said. "After all this business between her and Helen."

He shook his head. "I don't know, dear," and was about to mention the touching, mysterious bonds that connect a father and daughter—for he had little girls himself—but he thought better of it and drove on. Life was strange.

The fact of the matter was that Loftis *had* been responsible for bringing Peyton home for the wedding, and when he awoke that day, with the early sunlight making a mellow, diagonal streak across the blankets and the frosty air, with its hint of distant blazing leaves, fanning his cheeks through the window crack, he felt happier than he had in years, and youthful and oddly hungry, with a deep, visceral, drowsy hunger such as he had not experienced since those days long ago at boarding school when, waking on Sunday mornings to the sound of a lazy bell, he had yawned and stretched, watched the myriad, swarming October light, stained with smoke and pollen, and yawned and stretched some more, inhaling the odor of fresh pancakes

249

from the kitchen downstairs, and felt an inexpressible and drowsy and luxuriant hunger—for precisely what he couldn't tell, perhaps the pancakes, perhaps a woman to crawl into bed beside him, most likely both.

Now he yawned, sat up in bed in order to belch more easily and, regarding himself in the window pane, found to his delight that he was still good-looking. Helen, he reflected, had said the same thing just last night during the recess of a Community Concert they had gone to, and it gave him pride to be able to confirm her judgment, by clenching his jaws and making his eyes narrow, so that the resemblance in the window pane was not too unlike Lord Mountbatten. A flaw in the glass, however, transformed him suddenly into a wasted, aging satyr, and he climbed out of bed, a trifle ashamed of his vanity. There was an air of readiness, of preparation in the house, and the sound of movement downstairs. Although it was only nine, there already stood on the drive below, underneath the sycamores, a caterer's truck, coy in pink painted doves and bridesmaids. This waking joy of Loftis' was internal and delightful and sensuous, the more intense because during the past few months it had derived from a sense of postponed disaster, like a mountain climber who has had fearful dreams of an avalanche, only to get up in the morning and emerge safely from his tent and breathe the vivacious alpine air. His joy was unrestricted and a bit overwhelming, and in a turmoil of good will he threw up the window and shouted down at Edward, who stole out from behind the caterer's truck in his colonel's uniform, drinking what looked like beer. "Hallo!"

Edward squinted upward, raised his glass. "Hallo, old man! Time to get out of the sack!"

"I am out. Isn't it cold out there for drinking beer? I thought you were going to Williamsburg."

"I'm supervising. Helen went up by herself. She said I'd do better here, helping out. Ha!" He drank, leaving a lacework of foam on his lip. "Ha! How much can a battle-scarred veteran help at a wedding? Woman's stuff." Edward had survived Guadalcanal, with wounds in the neck and what he insisted on calling his "tum-tum," and he took few pains to conceal the fact. He had arrived from Camp Lee late last night. Loftis refused to be diverted.

"When did she leave?"

"About an hour ago. She's going to pick up Peyton and her boy at that girl's house where they're staying and have breakfast before they come back. Helen called them on the phone. Come on down, old man, and have a short one. We'll start off this party and——"

Loftis smiled indulgently. "No, thanks, old man, I'm taking it easy." And pulled the window down, for the chill of the morning had begun to seep into his pajamas. The mention of something to drink sent a tentative cloud of gloom through his mind, for among his resolutions the one concerning moderation was number one. But the feeling went away; Peyton was coming, that was enough, and to the cadences of his own artless tenor he scrubbed himself in the bathtub, singing a Cole Porter song and thinking of life's rich promise, of discipline and fulfillment. He splashed childishly, making air bubbles beneath the washcloth, and a wreath of soapsuds among the hairs on his belly. And the remarkable thing, he thought—the remarkable thing was that Helen was not only wife, mother, *hausfrau* again, had not only joined with him to entice Peyton back into the fold again, but had actually volunteered to make the first welcoming gesture. Last night, back from the concert, Helen had been nervous and distracted; Loftis had had to soothe her.

"Do you think she'll be angry or bitter, Milton? What do you think she'll say? Should I . . . make the first motion? You know—kiss her? Tell me, Milton. Oh, I'm so worried. . . . Tell me, dear, if she's not still mad why did she stay up in Williamsburg instead of coming right home? Why did——"

He took her gently by the shoulders and went through it all over again: certainly she won't be angry. Hadn't her letters to both of them proved that? Hadn't she, Helen, herself been convinced of that months ago—after all the correspondence between them, at first so standoffish and halting, had finally become tender, tacitly forgiving, just as their letters had been in the old days? Yes, certainly, letters were no final proof, but weren't they sign enough, weren't they worth the chance? Don't be silly, Helen.

So eventually she had become calm and had agreed. In fact, he had succeeded so well in convincing her of Peyton's good intentions that she made a perfectly amazing suggestion. Loftis wouldn't go. She would drive with Edward to Williamsburg to fetch Peyton and Harry, thus proving to the girl that she wished only to greet her as a mother—solitary, loving, without Loftis, who might only dissipate by his presence the effect she wanted to give: of a woman, alone in the October sunshine, who is both contrite and forgiving and who, by her solitariness, is a symbol of humility and penitence and warm maternal love. It seemed to Loftis vaguely theatrical, but he knew that Helen was not beyond theatrics at times, and he said, "O.K., Helen, anything you think best." As for the reason why Peyton and Harry

251

had spent the night in Williamsburg (at the house of an old Sweet Briar friend), Loftis had his own ideas—maybe Peyton really was a little afraid of home still, and was trying to make her home-coming an easy, gradual thing—but he didn't let on to Helen.

Helen had gone to bed then. It was still early in the evening. He had been alone, and although he had been happy because Peyton was finally coming home, he hadn't, for some obscure reason, been able to define this happiness quite properly. He went through the rooms straightening pictures, flipped a bug out of one of the water-filled vases which stood around the house ready to receive the nuptial flowers. He wandered into the kitchen where Ella and La Ruth, together with La Ruth's son, Stonewall, were sitting around the table. Ella and La Ruth were making hors d'oeuvres, and Stonewall, who was four, was busy eating them. He was a skinny little boy with the pale, blanched undercolor of the white man who had fathered him, and his eyes were like chestnuts floating on twin pools of milk. When Loftis entered he turned these eyes toward him, in curiosity and in awe, and La Ruth gave him a rap across the fingers.

"Git yo' messy hand outa dere!" she cried. "Nasty thing."

"Well look at us," Loftis said cheerily. "How are we doing?" Stonewall slid beneath the table.

"Us is just dandy, thank you," said La Ruth prissily, looming large over a bowl of mashed olives, "just havin' de time of our life out here in de kitchen fixin' things up fo' de weddin'. My my, here is cheese an' green olives an' black olives an' florets of collyflower and Heinz's pickle party asso'tment and roe herrin'——"

"I presume you mean caviar," Loftis interrupted.

"No, indeed," La Ruth went on, "dat ain't what I presumes at all. Mama she tol' me——"

"Hush up," said Ella. She looked up at Loftis with a timid, snaggled grin. "Bet you a happy man, ain't you? Bet you feel de risin' in yo' soul, don't you?"

He agreed, nibbling on a piece of celery, that he was affected spiritually, and he went to the refrigerator for a beer when Ella, her face wrinkled with reproach, said, "Now, ain't you ashamed?"

"Just one, Ella? The last one before I lose my baby. One won't hurt, Ella."

She gave grudging permission with a little nod of her head, bent scowling down toward a pan full of bread crumbs, and La Ruth giggled softly. "Come on out from dere, Stonewall," she said. "He don't bite."

"Don't tell Miss Helen," he said, and walked to the back porch, with the beer bottle coldly perspiring beneath his hand. It would be his last, he thought, for a long while. It was very quiet on the water, and chilly, and the moon, hung like a pale lamp above the rim of the bay, seemed to shed only the coolest light over a crowd of fading, dusty stars. Drunken pilgrim, the earth reeled through a host of asteroids, and falling stars drained down the night like streaks of melted glass. In his veiled and perplexing happiness, Loftis could have wept a little, and for the state of tranquillity which, years ago, he never would have believed he could attain.

Helen had been right. The simple touch of a hand redeems us, and who knows, when fingers clasp each other and press to the white, invisible bones, what chemistry then? There is a decency in us that prevails and this touch, perhaps, only reaffirms it. The promises he had made to Helen he had kept and she, though she had no promises to make, had burst forth under the light of his transformation like the flower from which the shadowing stone has been rolled away, which unfolds toward the sun tender leaves of gratitude. It hadn't been easy for him, or for Helen. He had had to cure something in her, and because she was a reluctant patient, who had taken pains to nourish her suffering, his cure had been forcible, abrupt and highly emotional. Remembering the day in Charlottesville, he had become crazed with guilt, with the sight of the wreckage of their lives, and nothing was too violent for him, as long as he found some sort of equilibrium. Even his love for her, which was honest and deep, became subverted to this goal. He threw himself at her knees, in throes of Byronic remorse, wild-eyed, weeping, hair in his eyes, asking her to forgive him for everything, for Dolly, for not being a better lawyer, for his drinking—realizing, as the whisky fumes seeped up his nostrils and as she arose and moved silently away, the pity of it all: that, in order to convince her, he must cease indulging in the very thing which allowed him to be so grandly humble and contrite. The house was empty. Maudie was gone, and Peyton, too. Helen stayed in her room and slept, lulled by nembutal; she had Ella bring her meals on a tray, saw no one, read all the old *Geographics* and *Lifes*. She went to church no more.

One gray, windy afternoon in January—on purpose, she later told him—she took a small overdose of pills and Dr. Holcomb had to hurry around and lay a stethoscope over her feebly pulsing heart and stick her with a syringe. When Helen revived, the doctor left, telling Loftis, in a guarded, confidential voice, that he should take her somewhere for care. Because he was an old man, suspicious of progress, he used the word "alienist," and this archaism, coming from one whom Loftis felt should know what he was talking about, made him weak with a weird and peculiar fright. He went back upstairs to the place where Helen sat by the window, bundled in blankets. He took a lighted cigarette from her fingers. "He said you shouldn't smoke."

"Yes, I know."

He sat down beside her on a stool, startled by a hot water bottle, which he removed from beneath him. She let him take her hands.

"Helen," he said, "it takes a long time for a man to learn to believe in life. Some men, that is."

"Yes, and——" she began.

"What, honey?"

"Nothing."

"I guess it's taken me a long time. When I was a kid, even beyond that—when I got older—I thought I was living. I've just learned things—recently. I think it probably takes something terrible to happen to you before you learn how precious life is." It was the first time he had used words like these; he was aware of their inadequacy, and it was the first time that he—a man who all his life had been spendthrift with words—had become so intensely aware of the inadequacy of words in general. So he pressed down hard on her hand, stroked her fingers, to make up for his lack.

"Look how sober I am," he said.

It was as if she had been struck dumb forever. There was a statue of a woman, he remembered, left alone among the woods of his childhood somewhere—he could not remember—overgrown by ferns and laurel in a damp place where toadstools grew in a fairy ring. Time had not effaced its loveliness so much as rain, for it was made of a poor kind of stone, and it was a pity it couldn't talk, because with all its frowzy defects of ravaged eyes and storm-stained hair, it yearned, out of some monumental voicelessness, to sing a song or speak a word; its parted lips struggled for speech, it had a throat that lived. Loftis remembered, gazing at Helen. Was she trying to say something? He couldn't tell, because the light was fading from the room. She cleared her throat, something trembled on her lips, but she remained silent.

"Do you understand, honey, what I mean? Tell me you do. About what I'm trying to say."

Outside, there was no division between sea and sky; where the bay met the ocean, a foam-capped reef, breakers mounted into the gray, as white and as soundless as snow. He told her again, with love in his throat, how much she meant to him, how, after all his errors, he had come to realize that his existence was a fairly useless thing if she was not a part of it; Dolly was gone now, and for her, Helen, he had trampled upon his weaknesses; wasn't all this enough? He told her these things in a subdued, passionate, desperate voice. As he talked it seemed her lovely face took on more and more each second the lines of a sick and determined refusal, and by the way her jaw grew tight he knew at least that she heard him. Her hair, he noticed, had gray in it like streaks of milk. "Don't you see what I mean?" he said again, squeezing her hand, but she appeared, with eyes that still glassed in like watch crystals the hollow reflection of shattered nembutal dreams, an incarnate No—reasonless and mute. He got up; patience fled him.

"You're sick and I'm sorry," he said bitterly. "Well, God help me, what else can I do? I offer you myself and that's all I can offer. I say there are these things that can make us find a way, these things and nothing else, and it's like I was talking to the goddam bloody wind. You're sick. Certainly you grieve, but you're not the only one who's grieved, I've done my share of that. What makes you think you can afford the luxury of this particular kind of self-pity and self-hate? Why, by God? Helen, I've done my utmost damndest to make you see how much I care. How much I care to the extent of doing everything I know to make you see that I'm not the broken-down, unredeemable wreck you thought I was. I wasn't noble, either, about it, or self-conscious about it. I figured that along with all the crap I've put up with you I've done my share of the wrongdoing and I was willing to keep my mouth shut about some of the things I thought if only I could change your way of thinking. If only you could see that I who I admit am nothing great, I guess, was still willing to do anything to start things right again. God almighty, Helen, forgive me for saying this if you're as sick as I think you are, but what have you wanted from me, my manhood guts and balls and soul? What in Christ's name have you wanted? I've offered you everything I've got——"

He stopped, because when he looked down he found that she had turned toward him a little. Her face lost its hardness, and he figured that in her mind he must have stirred up, finally, memory or recognition, for something crumbled in her eyes. Her lips moved again but she said nothing.

He bent down once more, hopefully. "You haven't lost everything, honey. You still got me, if you want me. You've got Peyton. Who loves you. We'll write her together, tell her everything is O.K. now. She can go back and finish school next year, like she should. Honey, if you'd just realize that people do love you, you'd know that you've got years more of—Christ—grandchildren——" Caught up in his own hopefulness, a rich philoprogenitive vision came to him for an instant, of babies, dozens of them, frisky and pink against the green timeless grass. "Don't you see, Helen? Peyton doesn't hate you. She's the most understanding kid in the world. All we have to do is let her know how things are and then everyone'll be happy. Helen, you're all I've got, I'm all you've got. If you'll believe me, why, by God, the best years of our lives are ahead. I tell you Helen that we can defeat fear and grief and everything else if you'll only believe me and love me again. Honey, we can never die. . . ."

Somehow it had worked, his persuasions had touched her, and he marveled now, on the eve of Peyton's wedding, as much as he had then, nearly a year before. The bay was filled like a bowl with silence, and upon its surface, as if scraped off from the moon, lay a litter of careless silver. It was almost ghostly, this quiet, and if Loftis had heaved the beer bottle out over the seawall to break the water with a noisy splash, it could have fractured its silence no more abruptly than he finally had penetrated Helen's. He could only still wonder what he had said, which charmed word it had been to cause her to rise and throw off her blankets, to approach him with her eyes closed and her sickness still white and dusty on her cheeks like some fabled, lovely, medieval lady raised by potent magic from the tomb, and to put her arms almost weightlessly about his neck and murmur, "Oh my darling, you do understand me, after all."

No, he hadn't understood her, ever, but at that moment there had been no need of understanding: she was his once more, they were together and she believed in him. It was as if he had lifted by his self-abasement all the troubles from her shoulders, and afterward it was only when the desire for whisky became almost impossible to bear that he began to think glumly that he had let himself in for a hell of a situation. "Darling," she had said that afternoon, "darling, darling, you have learned, haven't you? You have learned what I need, haven't you? You have learned. I believe you. Oh, yes, together we can never die!" But later it was hard for him to keep his equanimity every day, knowing that he had, voluntarily and submissively, let her get the upper hand. His pride rebelled fiercely at times, but he beat it down, thinking of the good things yet to come—of a life lived soberly and honestly, yet partaking of the decent and rewarding pleasures, golf still and talk with good friends; Peyton coming home to visit them—with tragic thoughts and tragic events but safely behind, as in the minds of all real Virginia gentlemen. He had made wild headlong promises to Helen, and it was a struggle, but he didn't hold it against her that she expected them to be kept. He felt lucky when she said one day, "Don't be silly, darling, I don't care if you drink if you just use a little caution," and with a faint laugh, "Heavens, Milton, has it taken you all these years to find out I'm really no puritan?" So he drank a little, with caution.

Dolly, of course, might as well have been in Tibet. He saw her on two occasions after Maudie's death. The first time was when, with misgivings and fear, he ventured out of the house one night, a week or so after his reconciliation with Helen, and went to Dolly's apartment. He intended to put the situation up to her with as much honor as he could, but he failed wretchedly. No matter how little a man may finally come to feel for a woman, if over a long period of time they have been together and intimate, he will acquire a certain tenderness for her small deficiencies, and remember the dirty dishes in her sink—her third-rate books and queer tastes in music, the broken mirror she never fixed—with as much charity as her lips or thighs. Remembering these about Dolly, his mind had become enfeebled by the time he reached her door and, after coffee and cake, he got up to go with vague promises to see her soon. And when she asked, with a look of foreboding, "When, when?" he could only reply, "Soon, soon," and then go, haunted by the light in her eyes, which said, "Oh, you are leaving me."

But he was committed. Let him for one moment think of *this* particular betrayal, and he knew he would be lost. He tried to forget her, succeeded: she sank from his consciousness like one of those poor people encased in concrete who are heaved over the side and plummet to the bottom of the sea. She didn't forget him, though. Just when he had put her out of mind she began to call him, and, because he invariably hung up, to send him wistful, pleading notes in lavender ink, scented, and stuffed with humiliating souvenirs: roses they had picked during Garden Week at Westover, a postcard he had bought her on the Skyline Drive, two sticks from Popsicles they had eaten, with elaborate frivolity, at a Richmond fair. They shamed him, enraged him; it was these very things he had once told Dolly about Helen—the nagging, bittersweet memories—which made him frantic with remorse; how, having committed so much wrong, would he ever get out of life alive?

Dolly came to visit him one night. It was a rash thing to do, but she was lucky, because Helen had gone for a week's visit to her sister-in-law's in Pennsylvania. It was a terrible scene. Dolly flew in out of a rainstorm with her hair plastered around her face like serpents, clumsily threatened him with a candelabra, got sick on the rug, slipped up and fell in the mess and remained there, in a pale coma. It was the first time he had ever seen her drunk and so he hadn't known how to cope with her. He cleaned her up a little and drove her to her apartment, where he put her gently to bed and held her hand for a while, listening to her mumble an anguished fantasia of remembrances and longings. "Safe in their alabaster chambers"—lines he had once idly read to her from one of Peyton's poetry books, lines he had forgotten and could not tell how she remembered—"sleep the meek members of the resurrection." And she sank back into the pillows, like Camille, finally and mercifully unconscious, while he, sweat on his forehead and his heart wrung with regret, offered up to God or someone the first completely honest prayer of his life.

She troubled him no more. Because of that incident he had to make even more effort to forget her. Late in April he and Helen went on the train for a three-week vacation to a resort near Asheville, and there among the smoky hills, in the cool, ferny air where the sky seemed to be spread like a bottomless lake above them, they both calmed down. He turned her mind gradually away from Maudie and tenderly made her do healthful things, like swimming and riding, walking along the bridle paths. Her face was lined and worn, but her new bathing suit still defined a body receptive and warm to love. He made love to her three times, not particularly liking the act itself but afterward—as she drowsed peacefully beside him—smugly happy, proud that he was here rather than in bed with the vacationing Atlanta divorcee who had made a violent pass at him and whose perfect skin, resting like lacquer upon the pretty young oval of her face, looked as if it would crumble to the touch. Wistfully he thought of Dolly. But, "I love you, my darling," Helen said again and again; "how could we have wasted so much time? Forgive me," she'd say, clutching his hand tightly, as if to let go would set them adrift again, "forgive me, forgive me, forgive me, I've been such a fool." And when Helen talked like this, just as they do in the movies, with such conviction, he was unable to decide who really had been the fool, after all—he himself or Helen.

Evenings they drank weak, wartime beer with a Rotarian and his wife from London, Ontario. This man was named Malcolm Mac-

Dermott; he affected kilts and a crooked walking stick and to listen to him was like hearing water rumbling into an old washtub. There was no question, Loftis knew, as to who wore the kilts in the family, for he was the type of man upon whose conversation his wife waits in a sort of meek attendance, like a flustered maid, and when she spoke it was as if to rush in timidly and sweep up a crumb, and retire to the wall once more. She was in her early fifties, with a plump, bright-eyed, Canadian face. When Helen mentioned the recent death in the family, Kathy's swollen little lips grew tragic and she told Helen that she, herself, had suffered the loss of a child, but that she had found a diversion, and she blurted something about goldfish.

"Kathy girl," MacDermott boomed, "what's a mon to do with gold-fish ar-round the house? Nothing but a bother."

"For her, Malcolm——" she peeped.

"Goldfish!"

The subject perished then and there, but it did introduce a fascinating note into the conversation, for soon, unbelievably, Loftis heard Helen speaking of Peyton. "My daughter," she said; "she's my youngest, studying art in New York. She's such a dear although I guess I have a mother's prejudice. She hasn't been home in quite some time and you know the wallpaper I was telling you about last night, the pattern we're getting? Well, you know, I wouldn't have thought of getting it made without showing it to her first, she's coming along so well in New York. . . ." Loftis felt a crazy shock and later, in their rooms, the first thing he asked her was to repeat, please, what she had said to the MacDermotts.

Helen looked tired, but in her eyes was a look of solemn satisfaction, almost relief, as she came up to him and let her head fall on his shoulder, saying, "Wasn't it a fierce old lie, darling?" She sighed. "Peyton. We've hardly said a word about her, and now I've said it. Oh, darling, I do want her to come back home, for a while anyway. I do want to see her so. You do believe me, don't you, darling? Tell me how to write a letter to her . . . tell me . . ." She giggled. "Those funny MacDermotts. Tell me, darling. Let's go back home. . . ." He had let his head droop, too, softly, while around them the blue evening seemed to dwindle and die and in its smoky waning brought a dozen sounds he had not heard before: crickets and the nimble noise of children, footsteps in the hallway, soft good nights, and her heart and his, thumping like drums. It had been, by almost any standard, the most gratifying moment he could remember, and the night before Peyton's wedding he had retrieved it, the hearts' reunion, with a triumphant and savage ecstasy. A man so unaccomplished, he reflected, might achieve as much as great men, give him patience and a speck of luck; though his road slopes off to a bitter sort of doom—and the wind, blustering down the night through chill acres of stars, suddenly made Loftis feel cold, and his life a chancy thing indeed—he has had his moment, a clock-tick of glory before the last descent. You know this man's fall: do you know his wrassling?

Bring home the bride again, bring home the triumph of our victory.

Bathed, shaved and combed, attired in herringbone tweed and a checked waistcoat, he made his way across the living room, after shaking half a dozen outstretched, congratulatory hands. It was four o'clock, the ceremony was to take place in half an hour, and the house was filled with guests. They had come, the middle-aged men and their wives, the younger men getting bald at the temples and their wives, who were trying at thirty-five to retard a faint dowdiness of flesh, and the youngest of all, the boys and girls in their teens and early twenties who, grinning at everyone and holding hands, were trying to retard nothing at all save thoughts of gloom, maybe, for there was a war on and some of them must go away—all these had come to make Peyton's wedding a success. Many of them were friends of Milton and Helen, the younger ones were Peyton's friends from Sweet Briar and the University and Port Warwick. All the guests had settled into the variety of moods which a wedding brings forth. The younger married women were possessed by flightiness and rapture, with occasional brief depressions of the spirit, while their husbands puffed on pipes and cigarettes and eyed the girls in their teens. These youngest girls, the ones with the soft, virginal drawls and the moist, painted lips and little freckled bosoms that rose and fell elastically as they breathed, stood around twittering, trying to appear prim, but only succeeded in looking more and more excited as the ceremony approached. Among the gray-haired men there was an air of boredom, but though they were patronizing to the younger people they were always kindly, and their wives, who tramped off periodically to marvel at the wedding gifts, became speechless and sentimental and had trouble keeping back the tears.

Almost everyone had come; they spilled out into the dining room, both hallways, both side porches and—because it had become fairly warm—onto the lawn. There was Admiral Ernest Lovelace, who was the naval inspector at the shipyard; he had lost his wife in an automobile accident two years ago. There were the Muncys and the Cuthberts and the Hegertys. All three men were executives at the shipyard. Old Carter Houston himself was there, along with his wife, who remained a Virginia belle at the age of seventy and pronounced Carter "Cyatah"; these two sat in one corner and everyone paid court to them, for he was head of the shipyard. There were the Appletons and the La Farges and the Fauntleroy Mayos, who were F.F.V.'s; and the Martin Braunsteins, who were Jews, but who had been around long enough to be accepted as Virginians. Then there was a contingent of doctors and their wives—Doctors Holcomb and Schmidt and J. E. B. Stuart and Lonergan and Bulwinkle (they all smelled faintly of ether)—and there was Dr. Pruitt Delaplane, making his first hesitant public appearance after his trial and acquittal for criminal abortion. There were poor Medwick Ames, and his wife—who threw fits—and the Overman Stubbses and Commander and Mrs. Phillips Kinderman.

Among the younger people were the Walker Stuarts and the P. Moncure Yourtees and George and Gerda Rhoads, who were, everyone knew, on the verge of divorce, and a men's clothing dealer named "Cherry" Pye. The Blevinses had come, and the Cappses and the John J. Maloneys. Also the Davises and the Younghusbands and the Hill Massies, who had once won ten thousand dollars in a slogan contest; and a dentist named Monroe Hobbie, who limped. Those among the youngest group—most of the boys in uniform—were Polly Pearson and Muriel West and a willowy boy named Campbell Fleet who, it was generally rumored, had been expelled from Hampden-Sydney College for homosexuality; and the wealthy Abbott sisters— they were beautiful and blonde, and their father had made a fortune in Coca-Cola—and Jill Fothergill, who had arrived with Dave Taylor, and Gerald Fitzhugh. Ashton Bryce was in this group, and a fat boy named Chalmers Winsted, who had flunked out of Princeton, and Bruce Horner. These three were all in naval uniforms, as was Packy Chewning, who was a lieutenant (j.g.) and had won the Navy Cross in the Solomons.

Loftis found Peyton upstairs sitting alone reading a World Atlas, and looking beautiful and somewhat bored.

"Where's your mother, honey?"

"She went to the kitchen to tend to the champagne. Bunny, did you know that in all of Delaware there are only three counties?"

"No." He sat down beside her and kissed her on the cheek. "Baby, baby," he said, "I've had hardly any time to talk to you. Aren't you excited? You look wonderful. I've never seen such a beautiful, un-excited bride in all my life. What's the——"

"Virginia has a hundred."

"Hundred?"

"A hundred counties, it says so here. Texas has the most——"

He shoved the book away and swept her up toward him, laughing, kissing her helplessly. She lay tender and unresisting against his shoulder; he breathed the perfume in her hair, and was stricken by beauty at the sight of a gardenia pinned there, nestling just beneath his left eye. "Bunny," she said finally, pushing away from him, "you are such a demonstrative old bum. Come on, quit it now. I've got lipstick on your neck."

"I've hidden Harry," he said.

"You have? Where?"

"I've got him locked in on the sun porch with your Uncle Eddie and Carey Carr. Carey's briefing him on the service."

"That's nice," she said. "Poor Harry, he was in such a stew over the ceremony. He told me just a while ago that he had never seen so many Aryans under one roof in all his life. He said that when he saw Mrs. Braunstein it was like finding his mother at a meeting of the D.A.R." She chuckled beneath her breath, as if she were being tickled. "What a funny guy! All this business has given him a good case of the creeps. It's a good thing we're not High Church and he'd have to cross himself and all that rot. But I think maybe he's putting a lot of this stuff on. The nervousness, I mean." Peals of laughter came up from the lawn.

"He seems like an awfully nice boy, honey."

"He is," she said, and let her eyes stray musing upon the bay and the dappled blue sky and the windy lawn where all the girls stood chattering, in patches of red and blue. She looked down at her hands. "He is, I guess. I guess he's about the nicest person I've ever met—" and raised her eyes and winked at him—"except you, of course. I mean," she went on, "I guess he's got about everything a girl could ever want, if that doesn't sound banal. I mean there's something honest and right about him, and I can't quite describe those qualities without sounding a little silly. After Maudie died I wanted——"

He squeezed her hand and put his fingers to his lips.

"Yes, I know, I'm sorry," she went on, "I'm sorry, Bunny. We promised not to talk about that, didn't we? Well, by every letter in the alphabet I promise you that I'll forget." She paused and closed her eyes. There arose a tender blur of memories, phantoms, shadows, as he listened to her repeat the old hocus-pocus he hadn't heard in years; with her eyes closed and her lips drawn sweetly down she looked six or eight, just for an instant, and he could have hugged her to his breast. "So anyway, when I went up there I was ready to go absolutely wild. I guess I did for a while. All last winter and last spring I lived like a tramp, though I didn't let on when I wrote you. I lived like that, thinking I was worldly or something, and was miserable. Really, Bunny, you don't know how miserable I was. I think it was only the letters you wrote me which kept me going. And then even so I'd go out and drink too much with some of these horrid, awful people I knew—they were in the fashion business or they were interior decorators or they drew pictures for the expensive magazines, and all of them were slick and talked chic and none of them had any heart or soul—and then I'd come home with a funny feeling that I'd been betrayed, but only because I'd allowed myself to be betrayed, and then your letters for some reason didn't seem to help at all. They seemed stupid and silly and maudlin and rather futile—you were so far away and lost, too, and you didn't seem to understand me at all. And I tore most of them up, and then cried afterward, when I woke up the next morning, because I'd destroyed them. Oh, Bunny, you don't know how miserable I was then. I guess I hated everyone. I tried to pretend that I liked these new people, any people at all, but I didn't. I don't even guess I liked myself."

"Baby," he said, "you don't have to go over all those sad old things. Not today. All those things are buried and done with. . . ."

"I know, Bunny—it's just that I'm all worked up today." She laughed. "Here I am trying to be sober and sophisticated and modern and I feel like I was twelve again and back in Mr.—what was his name?—that pansy's dancing class. What was I about to say? Oh, yes, Harry. I was talking about Harry. Don't you think he's nice? He's so gentle, Bunny, and *real*. Does that sound like so much stuff to you, Bunny?"

"No."

"And he's going to be a great painter someday. Emily Genauer saw some of his work and she thinks he's got terrific promise. But like he says, Bunny, it's not so much all that business about becoming a great something or the finest this-or-that, it's being true to yourself inside. That's what he is, he's *right* inside—oh, damn, I can't talk without sounding like a fool."

He patted her hand. "I get you, baby. You don't have to explain to me. I know that any guy you liked would be——"

"No, Bunny, not any guy would be O.K. Just because I liked him. Remember that Lieutenant Timmy Washburn I wrote you about last spring? I liked him and——" She made a look of violent displeasure. "Oh, well."

"Incidentally," he put in, as he reached for her hand, "while we're talking about the life and loves of Peyton Loftis, just what happened to Dick Cartwright?"

Her eyes sparkled, grew wide with what appeared to be sadness and she dropped the subject hastily, as if she were brushing a bee away, with a quick, "Oh he was such a child."

"So—?"

"I don't guess brides can drink *before* the wedding, can they?"

"No," he said, "definitely not."

"An eentsy one?"

"No, now, baby——"

"Just a wee dram?"

Her voice touched him with worry, vague and somber, but because she was so beautiful, so fetching in the way she cocked her head to one side and repeated, in the soft supplicant voice, her quaint request, he got up—"Baby," he said, "we've only got twenty minutes"—and went to his bedroom. There, hidden amid a nest of mothballs in his dresser drawer, he found the cough-sirup bottle, a full half-pint. He uncapped it, stuck its mouth up to his nostrils and breathed deeply, thinking of Helen, satisfied that rye could be mistaken for terpin hydrate after all. He held the bottle up against the light, sniffed again, turned it about in his fingers. "No," he said half-aloud. He recapped it quickly, hearing footsteps in the hall, and stuffed it back in the drawer beneath a pile of shirts. It was only La Ruth. She frolicked in, graceless as a whale, humming the "Jersey Bounce." "'Scuse me," she said, "Miss Helen, she say she wants dem napkins up dere."

"Which ones?"

"Dem pretty ones dat come from de laundry, right dere on de bureau."

"What for?"

"Deed I have no idea, but I suspects dey's for de folks when dey start eatin'."

"That I'd say would be a logical conclusion," he admitted. If you were to peel back her skull, he thought, you'd find no convolutions at all on the brain, only a round, thoughtless, shiny sphere. She loaded her arms with napkins, transmitting shock waves of sound across the floor, shifting from foot to foot, her starched maid's cap on sideways, constantly mumbling. "My, dem folks is sho' gonna stuff dey guts today," she said, lumbering from the room, and he opened the drawer, closed it quickly. Below, the guests stood on the lawn talking together, moved from group to group; a balmy wind flicked the skirts of the Abbott sisters, who were scowling at each other, and he saw Commander and Mrs. Kinderman, bloated and stiff in their matching Navy blue. They talked to no one, and were borne staidly about upon gusts of scuttling leaves. He heard Edward's laughter somewhere, Edward who was already tight, with whom he had, for Helen's sake, enacted the most strained and touchy friendship, and for some reason the desire for a drink became hot and powerful. There were other footsteps in the hall, and he started, but they faded away; how silly to have this nervous, quarrelsome conscience, that resentment—yes, he had had it, just for a moment, at Edward's laughter which, in turn, had made him think of Helen and of the ridiculousness of her demands on him, demands he had paradoxically brought on himself—all in all, how silly to have to pussyfoot about like this on Peyton's wedding day, dredging up such ugly conflicts. Or was it silly? Well, my God, just one. He found two glasses, got the bottle out of the dresser and went back to Peyton's room, closing the door behind him.

"Oh, Bunny, you're so clever," she said, "all in such a cunning little bottle."

Loftis looked at her sharply. "Baby," he murmured, sitting down beside her, "do you really want a drink? Why don't we wait until afterwards? There's champagne——"

"Don't be a spoilsport. Make me a drink. This is just for my nerves." Obediently he poured an ounce or so into a glass.

"Aren't you going to have one?" she asked.

Why had he suddenly become so depressed? It was unfair of Peyton to seduce him like this, and he found himself saying, "You know, baby, I've found that when everything is going along all right you don't need anything to drink. When you're happy——"

But she broke in with a laugh, her face rosy with some sudden excitement, "Don't be so solemn, Bunny, this is for my nerves, buck up, sweetie. . . ."

He poured himself a drink and with the first swallow, his dark mood fading, he gazed at her, then past her—avoiding those eyes—to say, while the whisky taste began to seem unfamiliarly sweet and strong, "So anyway, honey, you're here and you're going to get married to a swell guy and that's all that counts. Isn't it wonderful?"

"Yes. I'm here. Thanks to you."

"It's not my doing," he said, "thank your mother."

"I've thanked her," she said wryly, looking away.

"Now don't——" he began, for it was wrong, unbearably wrong for her to bring up, on this day of all, the faintest suggestion of regrettable memories; those memories had indeed made this day poignantly perfect, childish in its brazen delight, like the day long ago of the circus or the fair, sweet from its apocalyptic dawning to the last, exhausted, bedtime end; all the near-ruined moments in the family had made this particular day even sweeter, but it was absolutely unfair of Peyton to suggest now that anything had ever been wrong one bit. The illusion of serenity would be swept away like so many dew-drenched spider webs leaving only the unsightly façade, the dusty plaster and all the bricks with their weathered holes. So *quit, quit* it, he was trying to say, softly but forcibly. . . . Ah, good, it didn't matter, she had been perhaps faking after all: "Bunny, what did you *do* to her? I could have dropped dead this morning when she came up to Williamsburg, with that really sweet smile on her face. Did you make her take hormones or something? Bunny, make me another drink."

"I——" She squeezed his leg. A churchbell far off struck the quarter-hour and he poured, helplessly, one for him, one for her, while Mrs. Fauntleroy Mayo's voice floated up from below in haughty, indistinct syllables, like fish bubbles bursting at the surface of a pool. Peyton's perfume was abrupt and sweet in his nose, with a certain knife-edge sweetness of exotic flowers he didn't know, perilous blooms of some jungle, and fascinating; his eyes swam a little as she hovered near—but was it the perfume at all, not the excitement, the day, the heat in the room? He arose and threw open the window wider; Mrs. Mayo saw him. Dressed all in patrician white, in jersey, she raised her gloved hand and waved her handkerchief, a speck of lace: "There's the lucky father," she cried, and everyone below looked up with a smile.

He ducked back in. "Baby, we should put all this away."

"What did you do to her, Bunny? I just couldn't believe my senses."

It was the whisky. There was no doubt of that: the rationed rot-gut which had filled his eyes with fuzz, made his stomach ache. It was like drinking acid. He put the glass on a table, banished a gnat from its rim. "I don't know, baby," he said, smiling down at her, "I don't know. It was you, you see. I mean, you see . . ." This was difficult. "I think she never knew how much she loved you until . . .

266

oh, what the hell, you know, baby, how confused she always was. I don't know, I just guess she figured too that once you get to a point where everything is on the rocks you've got nothing left, so you turn to what you started out with, the beginnings again. . . ." She was listening to him no more; with her glass in hand, she had got up and walked to the window, looking down at the guests. How could he have explained it to her anyway, convincingly and without embarrassment? How could he explain to this child a fact of life he hardly understood himself: a love which had been held together by the merest wisp of music, faintly heard only during unwitting moments when memory washed at their minds like breakers against crumbling stones; a love in which the principals involved might have dwelt at opposite rims of the universe, only to be drawn back always by some force he could never define—the impalpable, thin strand of music, a memory of lost, enfolding arms, or the common recollection of a happening very ordinary, but which had happened to them together—these and all the gardenias and roses, ruined scents that hovered in the air so many years ago, in the grass-green light of another dawn? A romantic old ass like him, as Peyton might put it, could never place his finger on any of these things, he could only somehow feel them; he could certainly not explain them to a child who, he hoped, still would not have to discover them so painfully for herself.

But she had turned to him from the window; she hadn't even heard the first part of what he had said. Her glass was empty, her eyes restless with a look that seemed to be neither anxiety nor excitement but just plain restlessness, and she said, in an abrupt, vaguely unhappy tone which startled him, "Daddy, please lay off of it a little bit today. Please do——"

"Why, baby, it wasn't my idea——"

"No, not the whisky. I mean—oh listen, Bunny, you're a dear and I love you but please lay off all the sentimental slop today. I like being back here—in a way I do," she added in a thoughtful voice, "with everybody trying to be nice again—but I feel that you're so worked up about it all that you're ready to just smother me. Please don't smother me," she said crossly, tossing her hair, "just don't *smother* me, Bunny! I wasn't doing you a favor by coming back here, it was a favor for me. I've had my time of wandering around. Do you think I've enjoyed being the so-called wild bitch, which I'm sure everyone has thought? Some girl I met in New York from school, she had been down here on a vacation, and she said that everybody thought I had been kicked out of school. How do rumors like that get started?"

"I don't—baby, now don't. It was——"

"Small-town crap, that's what it was. What makes older people love, just adore, thinking the younger people are hell-bent for destruction? They just love sitting around on their fat behinds figuring out some sort of new moral perversion that the younger generation is indulging in."

"Baby——"

"Not you, Bunny." She flourished both hands outward and down, in an exasperated motion, spilling drops from her glass. "I don't mean you. You'd love me half to death if you could. But don't you see, don't you see, Bunny? I come back here all sweetness and light trying my best to play the good sweet role, the prodigal daughter come back home at her parents' whim, seeing the error of her ways, back in the fold of the family. Well I'm playing it pretty well, aren't I? Kissing Mother back when she kisses me, pretending to forget everything. Don't you see, Bunny, I've got my own reasons for coming home. I've wanted to be normal. I've wanted to be like everybody else. These old folks wouldn't believe that there are children who'd just throw back their heads and howl, who'd just *die*, to be able to say, 'Well now my rebellion's over, home is where I want to be, home is where Daddy and Mother want me.' Not with a sort of take-me-back-I've-been-so-wrong attitude—because, Bunny, you can believe me, most kids these days are not wrong or wrongdoers, they're just aimless and lost, more aimless than you all ever thought of being—not with that attitude, but just with the kind of momentary, brief love recognizing those who fed your little baby mouth and changed your didy and paid your fare all the way. Does that sound silly, Bunny? That's all they want to do, that's what I've wanted to do and I've tried, but somehow today it all seems phony. I don't know why. I lied. I'm really not excited at all. Maybe I've got too many sour memories." She paused and looked at him, her eyes enormously sad, and he approached her, with the day in its crumbling promise going before his vision, tried to put his arms around her. "Baby——"

"Don't," she said, "don't, Bunny. I'm sorry." She held him off without even a look, for she was gazing down at the lawn, at the guests moving toward the house, all together, silent, but with a sort of giddy haste, like picnickers before the storm—holding him off as much by her silence as if she had finished erecting between them a curtain of stone, then said gently: "I'm sorry, Bunny." She looked up at him. "I can't figure where the trouble starts. Mother. She's such a faker. Look at this circus. Flaunting the blissful family. Oh, I feel so sorry

268

for us all. If just she'd had a soul and you'd had some guts . . . Come on now," she said, grabbing his sleeve, "let's go downstairs, sweetie. I'll put up a real good front for you."

He stood rooted to the rug, wishing to faint there forever. He had been bludgeoned half to death, not so much by these truths, he told himself while he drained the sedative glass, as by necessity.

"O.K., baby," he said.

The ceremony was carried out in fine style, although the living room was crowded, which made some people sweat a little. In secular times like these it is often the custom to get married in a hotel or in the city hall or in a vine-covered cottage across some state line, where an elderly JP waits in a soup-stained vest; one can get married there for as little as five dollars. Some people who are titillated by religion but who don't believe in it get married in a hotel filled with palms and ferns, with a friendly old judge in attendance, and have readings from a book of oriental poetry called "The Prophet." To most people it really doesn't matter how they are married, except to Episcopalians, who are often partial to the home and always partial to the poetic quality of their service. The service does have considerable poetry in it, and an observer at this wedding who happened to be keen on aesthetics would have been a little awed by Carey's performance. Among people he was no actor, and in his natural reticence he preferred to leave histrionics to highly charged individuals, the great Northern ministers in their marble and collegiate churches and such; he was not bishop material, but in his own mild and plaintive way he was a sweet singer of the liturgy, and could embroider upon the fabric of Christian poetry, already so rich in texture, the most exquisite designs. An altar cloth had been laid across a gate-leg table, and there were candles, and as he read from the service the flickering light covered his spectacles with orbs of fire and made him look—with his plump cheeks and small round chin and the deep furrow running from his nose to his pursed, budlike mouth—like a compassionate, brunet owl.

On the creaking camp chairs, rented for the occasion, the guests sat silent and bemused, and though the canvas of one ripped with a squeal beneath Mrs. Turner MacKaye, who was a large woman, no one noticed, for Carey's voice rose soft and sweet, insidiously compelling above the almost breathless breathing and the rustle of clothes and the distant bluster of the wind. It was a rich voice, slightly husky, in the middle register, and it became, as if singing, a strong, melancholy yet uneffeminate tenor upon the word "love," and mystically, caressingly baritone when it said, "Lord." Thus, in the fashion of an oratorio, this splendid voice seemed to express with each modulation of the text all manner of human longings—tenderness and love and hope—and cast a spell through the room that was at once celestial and erotic; it was a voice unique and compelling, and many women wept out loud.

Loftis hardly heard the words. Somewhere during the ceremony, the guests all arose. He stood in the front row of chairs, for some reason not next to Helen but next to Edward, who was visibly weaving, his breath coming hoarsely, pumping out with each wheeze a fruity odor of beer. Helen he could see from time to time out of the corner of his eye. She was standing stiffly on the other side of Edward, watching the proceedings with a look that was intent and thoughtful—almost analytical, it occurred to him; it was a look neither pleasant nor unpleasant as she stared at the backs of Peyton and Harry, or moved her head ever so slightly to get a better view of Carey. It was rather just a calm and studious expression, but touched with a curious, fleeting light of triumph, and Loftis had the sudden picture of some humorless philatelist gazing at a particularly valuable stamp. Why she should look like this he couldn't say, nor did he try to anymore, for he felt unbelievably depressed, and neurotic, and he had to go to the toilet very badly; yet he only faintly knew the cause for these feelings. There was no doubt about it: Peyton had been cruel, she had refused to become a part of the spirit of the day—he gazed up now at her back, to the place where her legs met her skirt, made of some green stuff that looked like satin, and she suddenly said, "I will"—and by not becoming a part of this spirit, which had really been just his joyful spirit, she had begun to destroy it . . . damn. He stirred. Harry said "I will," a deep pleasant voice with a New York inflection, and a woman snuffled somewhere in the room.

Why? Why this unbearable depression? Peyton's dress was drawn tightly against her hips; he could see them, the two crescent shadows that a tight girdle makes when you look at a woman's behind, joining above like a curved Dutch roof: it was too obvious, or something; she should have dressed more demurely. Now it wouldn't be long, the ordeal would be over, for Harry was slipping the ring over her finger. Carey suddenly said a few words which, though they escaped Loftis, seemed impossibly theatrical and hollow. Soon it would be over and there'd be the reception and of course by then Peyton's mood would have changed: he'd kiss her, she'd laugh, he'd shake hands with Harry,

270

they'd all be one big happy family while, with one arm around Helen and the other about Peyton, he'd nod to the guests and smile, tip bubbling glasses of champagne, and hear Peyton whisper, "Oh, Bunny, I *am* glad to be home." Yet before this, he knew, there were these last fading minutes and he was suffering boundless, inexplicable anxiety, and consumed by the same hunger he had felt so gluttonously this very morning. It was different. But this hunger was *different,* because it was inverse and oppressive and awful. He felt that the room had suddenly shrunk to the dimensions of a small hothouse in which the flowers and perfumes and powders and rouge, all the woman scents, had been compressed into one monstrous tropical odor; through this spongy stuff, above Carey's lilting words, across the slant of October sunshine, through the sound of sniffles and the brief, lecherous smacking of lips, through all these his anxious hunger groped like antennae, seeking refuge and escape. He let his eyes close, began to perspire, and thought of the blessed release whisky might give. Yet it was not only this; his eyelids slid open, he saw Peyton, those solid curved hips trembling ever so faintly; he thought desperately, hopelessly, of something he could not admit to himself, but did: of now being above—most animal and horrid, but loving—someone young and dear that he had loved ever since he was child enough to love the face of woman and the flesh, too. Yes, dear God, he thought (and he thought *dear God, what am I thinking?*) the flesh, too, the wet hot flesh, straining like a beautiful, bloody savage. He thought vaguely of Dolly, wondering why she was not here. Well . . .

No, it was not fair—and his senses returned just a little, and he opened his eyes—it was not fair of Peyton to ruin his hopes like this. It was most certainly not fair of her to shatter his dreams of a perfect day and he had the sudden impulse to rise and call off the whole proceedings, tell everybody here that the ceremony was postponed to a more auspicious time, when he and Peyton would have things straightened out. It was almost over. He saw Carey turn and face the altar; Helen bent forward, rapt and studious and without emotion, and pushed a strand of hair behind her ear. Edward coughed, rattling phlegm in the back of his throat, and Loftis groaned aloud, though nobody heard. And his hunger went forth again, sending fingers through the crushed, vegetable air; only this time, helplessly, his thoughts became flaccid and wet and infantile, and he hungered to go to the toilet more than anything else; in spirit he wandered down the aisle, mincing painfully past the lulled and turgid guests. They didn't notice him or, if they did, paid him no heed. Their heads would be bent in prayer—his too, in fact—but now he was standing in the downstairs bathroom, in fancy watching the mosaic of tiles, the immaculate tub, feeling all anxiety flow blissfully away, along with the lemon-clear stream. *My God*, he thought, *my God, my God, so far away*. Desire and hunger settled over him, and he thought of things past and passing, of all things fleeting, and of himself a child again standing above the ancient plumbing forty years ago; watching it then, that yellow jet, why hadn't he been made sick with the strangeness of the water flowing from him so promiscuously? Sick as he was now, stifled by roses in a strange room, and knowing that to be born is unbelievable.

"Let us pray."

He opened his eyes, closed them again, tried to pray. *Stand close, son*, his father had said, *hit the hole*.

From the tiny portable organ there came a volcanic burst of Mendelssohn, incredibly loud. Before he knew it, Peyton and Harry had vanished smiling up the aisle, the guests had dispersed in a noisy herd behind them, and Edward laid a paw on his shoulder, saying, "Felicitations, old man. Let's have a drink." Loftis shook him off, suggesting hurriedly, with a weak attempt at irony, that he go ambush some champagne. The effect of the ceremony had worn off somewhat, though he still felt dizzy and vaguely disoriented, and he took Helen's arm. Carey joined them. There was sweat on his brow, but he looked proud and somehow purged.

Helen looked up at him. "It was beautiful, Carey. Simply beautiful. You made magic out of it."

"Nothing, Helen," he said in a tone Loftis could not help feel was pompous. "I felt that I was joining those fine children in a union that was somehow . . . more significant and . . . meaningful." He paused with a smile. "I'm sure you know what I mean." He removed his vestments and stole with a chipper remark, which for some reason made Loftis squirm, about taking off his work clothes in order to show off his drinking clothes. Why, Loftis wondered, were these boys such hypocrites? He excused himself to go to the bathroom.

"Well, it was lovely, Carey. As I say—" and she touched him lightly on the hand—"you do have the magic touch." As a matter of fact, it was true: she had been held in thrall, as much as any of the dimmest and most susceptible of the women present, by the service and by Carey's artful mannerisms. Throughout the ceremony, she had forced herself to conceal her joy, revealing it, she knew, only in the light of triumph which flashed briefly across her eyes. It was a strange sort of triumph. Life until her reconciliation with Milton had been miserable and disappointing. In the past few months she had gone over her life in her mind, minutely, always trying to avoid thinking of Maudie. She remembered a time when she was young. She had wanted the future to be like a nice, long, congenial tea party, where everyone talked a little, danced a little and had polite manners. She had come to the party and it had been ghastly: everyone misbehaved and no one had a good time. Religion had been a toy, a trifle, and she had cast it aside in despair when Maudie died. But she had always been motivated by a stern, if misty and primitive, belief, and when she took the last nembutal, sinking not into death but into what she hoped would be an endless sleep, filled with only the friendliest of dreams, it had been with a prayer on her lips and a mysterious, whispered apology to her father. Milton had rescued her. She knew the limit of his patience and, in a sort of marathon, had teased his patience to the very brink. But she had got what she wanted. She had got Milton back, along with the chance to watch him plead and grovel and humiliate himself. What more, for one who had suffered a lifetime of indignities, of so much emotional privation, could be asked? Because she did love him; she loved him desperately, and although he had hurt her—and she was wise enough to admit (but only to herself) that she had hurt him, too—he had, by coming back to her, saved her from certain death. Saved her not only from those endless, drugged dreams but from death. Too many thoughts of Maudie would have driven her, she knew, quite insane, but Milton had saved her from all that. And there had been a period, in the first few weeks of their reconciliation, when her brain throbbed, intoxicated, and in her thoughts Dolly drifted like a vanquished corpse face-downward upon some swollen stream. It had been the first time she could remember that she had ever laughed aloud, privately—alone in her room swooning backward upon the bed, clutching her throat with nerveless fingers, in a spasm of soundless, hysterical laughter.

And this day had really been a triumph for her. No one would ever know. No one would ever know what electric fulfillment she felt, beneath the soft, tender dignity of her manner, behind the wrinkled, rather sad, but gracefully aging serenity of her brow. No one would ever know the struggle, either. The struggle to accomplish just this casual, collected air of the proud mother: the woman who has sacrificed, whose suffering is known to the community, but who, on the day of her daughter's marriage, presents only the face of humility and courage and gentle good will. It had been cruelly difficult to put on this act, and how she had connived, how she had falsified her true feelings! But she knew that any means justified *this* end, *this* day, and after she had murmured into Milton's ear, "Oh, darling, I do want Peyton to come home," she had rejoiced at the sincere and grateful look in his eyes; she could tell he didn't doubt her honesty.

Her honesty. Oh, what was honesty, anyway? After so much suffering, did a woman really have to be honest to fulfill herself? She felt that her marriage had been such a nightmare, she had endured so many insults—the weight of so many outrages had pressed so heavily upon her spirit—that she could discard honest intentions in order to make this one day come true. *Anything, anything,* she had said to herself these past months, *anything at all.* Anything that Peyton should come home. Anything that people should know Helen Loftis was a good mother, a successful mother. Anything that people should know: it was Helen Loftis, that suffering woman, who had brought together the broken family.

Now, in sheer, rash courtliness, Carey bent down and kissed her hand. She knew how Carey saw her: poised, gentle, smiling brightly. Who could tell, she asked herself—and certainly it wasn't Carey who could tell, in his dense, well-meaning charity—that this genteel sprightliness masked the most villainous intentions? Well they *were* villainous. Here a shadow passed over her mind, just briefly, but long enough for Carey to murmur, "What's wrong, Helen?"

"Why, nothing, Carey!"

They were cruel intentions, cruel feelings, and perhaps unnatural, but what could she do? She had suffered too much and too long not to feel them. Or it. This profound and unalterable *loathing* of Peyton. Poor Peyton. Dishonorable, sinful. Her own flesh and blood.

"Maybe I'll be seeing you in church again, Helen. Now that you've become reconvinced of my powers and all that." Carey was smiling down at her and she was about to answer him, but Milton came back just then, looking pale and harried. What was the matter with Milton?

"We'd better go into the dining room, honey. We're supposed to be in the receiving line."

"Oh, yes, sure, dear, I hadn't forgotten." Carey had walked to the hallway to hang up his vestments and she called back over her shoulder. "I might, Carey. I might at that. In fact I think I shall."

Loftis took her arm. "What's that, honey?"

She put her arm about his waist. "Oh, nothing." She looked up at him as they walked up the aisle: "What's the matter, dear? You

274

looked worried." Then she squeezed him, the soft, vulnerable flesh beneath his ribs. "Oh, Milton, I'm so happy."

Somehow most of the guests had managed to get into the dining room, although as before many of them overflowed onto the porches. Ella presided at the punchbowl, along with two colored boys in white jackets who were ready to pour the champagne. La Ruth had been put in charge of the hors d'oeuvres and sandwiches, the plates and forks and napkins, but before the guests had come in she had done so many things improperly—folded the napkins wrong, put the forks way out of reach on the table—that Ella had sent her to the kitchen to get her out of the way. When the guests entered to go through the receiving line, Ella and the two boys stood up in a sort of shy, awkward position of attention, punch ladle and bottles in hand. From time to time La Ruth peeked in from the kitchen, along with Stonewall, dressed in a blue coat and corduroy knickers, who got his fingers pinched in the swinging door and had to be silenced and soothed.

Helen and Milton had joined Peyton and Harry, and the guests streamed past, shaking hands, exchanging greetings. The older women—among them Mrs. Mayo and Mrs. Cuthbert and Dr. Bulwinkle's wife, who looked like a frightened little thrush and talked in gasps—had all been nearly wrecked by the ceremony, and were visibly affected. When they came to Peyton and looked at her each of them remembered her own vanished loveliness and fell on the bride in a silent, shaky embrace, each afraid to entrust words to her trembling lips. But the general air was that of exuberance and gaiety and joy. Peyton, everyone thought, was so beautiful and so graceful. She smiled at everyone and introduced them to Harry, remembering the right names. The older men, who thought she was beautiful, all right, and kissed her dutifully, had, nevertheless, seen so many children get married: their minds were on the champagne. Carter Houston, the head of the shipyard, was all gentility and breeding. He wore a pendulous, bleached-white mustache upon which there was not the slightest trace of a stain, although he chewed a pipe almost constantly. When he kissed Peyton he murmured, "My lovely," and his starched cuffs crackled and his fine old blue eyes sparkled romantically.

"So this is your boy," he said, turning to Harry, and halted, the only person in the room who might with impunity dally so long. He looked him up and down, courteously, gently, and turned to his wife. "This is her boy, Lissa," he said, as if she didn't know. "You must take good care of such a lovely child, Harry. And if you all don't stay in New York, why then you all must live in Port Warwick and come to visit us often. Peyton, you've stayed away too long. Isn't that right, Lissa?" He turned to the small gray woman clinging to his arm and smelling of Yardley's; she had the face of an aristocrat and an odd, perpetual smile. It had something to do with her eyes and the way her mouth went up at the corners, and all her life she had existed in an atmosphere of baffling good will, since because of this smile people could not help grinning back at her, even when she was, perhaps, sad. "Indeed it is, Cyatah," she said, "indeed it is."

"We will, sir," said Harry. The Houstons drifted off. The receiving line went slack for a moment, for Loftis, standing next to Peyton, had become involved emotionally with the crippled dentist named Monroe Hobbie. He once had had a dim-witted, handsome wife—a marriage abbreviated by the lures of a slick Italian seaman from Wilmington, Delaware, who owned a cleverer tongue than he, as well as two good legs—and at every wedding, in an effort to retrieve the splendor of earlier days, he became prematurely drunk and long-winded and pathetic. He looked up at Loftis and gripped his shoulder, muttering something about eternal youth, and then blundered speechlessly past Peyton and Harry, in a haze of forgetfulness. Loftis turned to Peyton.

"How's it going now, honey?"

"Insulted." She laughed.

"What's the matter?"

"Dr. Hobbie. He didn't kiss me. Poor fellow."

"Poor fellow is right." He looked at Harry. "Don't mind some of these people, Harry," he said in a low voice, and with a wink, "they're Virginians. Most of them are in a daze and—oh . . ." and he turned, because Helen had touched him on the shoulder, to say, "Here are the Appletons, dear."

So it went. The guests filed by, shook hands, kissed and were kissed, and made a decorous beeline for the champagne. There was whisky and gin, too, bottle upon bottle of it, for cruder palates. Helen had spared no expense for this, the blowout of her life, and Loftis, through his extensive social connections, had performed the necessary miracle with the ration board. The October sun shed a light like gold dust against the windows, but inside the air was all silver: silver of champagne and gin, silver of spoons, of the bars the young girls wore, tucked in their hair, and the silvery tinkling of half a hundred glasses, a gay and flimsy tintinnabulation. There was recorded music, something tender and Viennese, and it washed out onto the terrace, bearing with it a crowd of boys and girls, who began to dance, splash-

276

ing champagne in silver tracks across the piled-up leaves. The weather was mild and blue, thick with sunshine—one perfect day, everyone said, for a wedding; soon the windows were thrown open, mingling the odor of distant, smoky fires with that of perfume and flowers. In one corner a fat couple, the Cuthberts, both of them teetotalers, stood gobbling Smithfield ham; no one paid them any notice. Very soon Moncure ("Monk") Yourtee, always the joker, had lost himself in the spirit of things and began to kiss all the girls, young and old, until his wife, a tall stern woman, hauled him aside and calmed him down. Romance sprouted among the young people; there were promises, hand pattings, flattery. Someone brought Peyton and Harry champagne, and they kissed each other, while a man with a camera filled the room with a burst of light, and the German song, caught in its groove, went *Bist ein bist ein bist ein*, over and over.

"Somebody fix the record!" Peyton cried, breaking away from Harry and laughing. There were more toasts, more champagne, and the end of the receiving line at last: a girl named Winnie Byrd Taylor, who had grown up with Peyton. She was gaunt and homely, with no breasts to speak of, and she probably would never get married, and she embraced Peyton with a sort of whimper, letting her blotched face fall on Peyton's shoulder and crying a little, as if she could remember nothing but their childhood and the summer days beneath the trees.

"Thank you, Winnie Byrd," said Peyton, kissing her back, "this is Harry." Winnie Byrd touched him briefly, made an agonized smile and was gone. The four of them were alone together then—Peyton and Harry, Loftis and Helen; and Loftis, turning with his champagne glass in hand, looked at Peyton, and had a surge of relief. Everything seemed to have improved some. Utterly sober, he nonetheless felt a faint, tingling, pleasant intoxication: from the happy faces of the guests, the music, from watching Peyton. Mainly, from watching Peyton. There had hardly been a second since the end of the ceremony when he had taken his eyes off her: how happy she looked now, how excited, lovely, how much the glowing bride! And how wrong he must have been to have thought otherwise. Look: she had kissed him twice—saying, "Bunny, you dear"—in five minutes. His panic at the ceremony had been needless suffering.

Helen stepped aside for a moment to put her arms around some woman, an old friend, and over her shoulder Loftis saw Harry bend down and kiss Peyton again, right on the mouth. It was a private view he had, almost: one of those unaccountable lulls at a gathering during which the guests of honor, hastily ignored by the other people in favor of food and drink, seem to be completely and senselessly iso-lated. It is the mystery of a split moment in time, the instant when we could most logically ask, in our strange solitary state, even as guests of honor, "Life. What am I doing here?" For that brief instant one could remove all of one's clothes or faint dead away, and nobody would notice. Here Loftis was the only observer, and he sensed it, and as he watched them kiss he felt the same visceral, drowsy hunger he had felt this morning and at the ceremony; only this time it was neither pleasant nor unpleasant, but a little of both, partaking more of memory, really, than anything else, and causing him once again to recall a note of music only half-heard, sunlight somewhere, something irretrievable. Helen moved aside, a glass was lifted, there was the tinkle of laughter and the clatter of dishes; a lush fraulein voice sang *"tränen ins Auge"* above the remote whine of strings, and through the sphere of his glass, iridescent as a rainbow, which he raised to his mouth, he saw their lips touch and their eyelids drift close, and flutter excitedly, their arms about each other in an anxious embrace. No one saw, no one noticed, except himself, and he was split up the middle with a violent, jealous tenderness such as he had rarely felt before. Only a moment had passed. Bubbles of champagne rose sour and sweet beneath his tongue, and he watched in a sort of enchantment: Harry, dark and Jewish, handsome, blood gently pulsing at his brow, and Peyton, hair about her shoulders, eyelids so clear they might be transparent, drawn down, fluttering—her lips on his.

The spell was broken. Suddenly they drew away from each other, for Helen's back had loomed up in front of him. With one arm around the woman, she was saying, "Felicia, this is Peyton and this is Harry—don't they look good together?" Loftis moved in closer, about to say something, but someone touched him on the arm. It was Edward, blushing to the ears with champagne.

"Hello, old man, you aren't celebrating much. Here, take this glass." He had two.

"Thanks. I've got one," he said, raising his own.

"You're out." He put down a glass, removed the empty one from Loftis' hand, and replaced it with his own.

Loftis protested, then gave up. "I'm on the wagon, you know."

"Not today you aren't," Edward said. Loftis felt himself succumb-ing to his sudden, real urge to drink—partly to the authority in the voice—and he took a big swallow, hating Edward, for some reason, more than ever. He heard that voice behind a desk at some camp, saw himself for an instant a trembling lieutenant—"Not today you aren't"—how easily, under certain conditions, could that voice become a paralyzing command. Edward was at the stage of drunkenness in which the ego glows like a coal, and brilliant people become more inspired, but in which dull people, fired by the same inspiration, become only more dull. Loftis looked at the eagle roosting on Edward's shoulder. It would be nice, he thought with some envy, to have been a colonel and to have survived wounds on Guadalcanal (the champagne was working: he had a sudden vision of steaming jungles, heard the hollow rat-tat-tat *car-Wong*, as in the newsreels) but to have all that to be a man like this: no.

"Peyton's a honey," said Edward.

"Yeah."

"A real honey."

"Yeah."

"This Harry's a lucky boy. How'd he get hooked up with her?"

Loftis sketched in briefly what Peyton had written and had told him, the little he knew.

"He's Jewish, isn't he?"

"Yes, he is."

"He looks like the better kind, though. He must be, or that little sweetheart wouldn't've married him. He seems to be thoroughly O.K., you know, and I liked him from the very first moment I saw him. You know, when I was regimental exec on the 'Canal we had one on the staff. He was one of the best tactical officers I——" But Loftis was no longer listening. He had the funny sensation that, somehow, it was he who was doing Edward's thinking: he knew precisely what Edward thought, and this knowledge made him unbearably nervous. He swallowed some champagne. Well, so he was a Jew. Did it matter? No. Yes. No, thoughts like that were childish. It was remarkable, when you came right down to it, how blandly both he and Helen had accepted the fact, after Peyton had written them. He had been surprised but not shocked, as he might have been ten years ago, and he had been further surprised how placidly Helen, whom he had never thought of as intolerant but who had always been rather hipped on class distinctions, had accepted the fact. What had she thought? He hadn't asked her, and had forgotten all about it himself. Until this day. Yes, until this day. In the receiving line just now he had been soothed by Peyton's kisses—he could still almost feel them, warm on his cheek—and by the sweet, delectable noise of her laughter. They had held hands once, and it was as if by that touch, magically, she had erased his tension and anxiety, comforted him, made him think she was happy after all. Yet—and this angered him—it seemed that he was unable to exist for one moment without a worry; he preyed on them, or perhaps they preyed on him, took up a natural dwelling on his brain, like lampreys upon the belly of a shad. He had, frankly and ashamedly, worried about Peyton marrying a Jew, a painter and a 4-F at that. He was also rather old. Hell, he was almost thirty. So what? one part of him said, she's happy, look at her, isn't that enough? Yes, the other part of him said, but he's a Jew.

And why? Why did he worry? It infuriated him. That he should worry so about Peyton's happiness. That he should have finally these suspicions about a Jew marrying his *own* daughter, when all his life he had had no prejudice—perhaps because there were few Jews around, perhaps out of charity or good will—against Jews and only a little, for that matter, against Negroes. His suspicions had infuriated him, so that eventually he had laid them to a rather excessively solicitous attitude toward the guests. What did they think? Miller. His name was Harry Miller. It was one of those names straight from Yorkshire, like Harris or Palmer, which (so Loftis' New York classmates told him) many Jews claim for their own, so that in places like New York they evolve into names almost exclusively Jewish. What had the guests, having seen Miller on the invitations and thought nothing of it, most likely, thought of this Miller? Yes, he supposed that was what worried him the most. The guests. Well, if they had thought anything at all they had not betrayed it in their looks. They had been ladies and gentlemen. They had turned their bright, protestant eyes upon Harry's face, found it warm and gentle, and had shaken his hand. Perhaps they had said, "This is a special Jew. He is Peyton's boy." Perhaps they had. One way or the other, Loftis was pleased.

Edward smoothed back a sheaf of steel-gray hair, regarding Loftis with the puckered distaste of a bigot trying to be agreeable. "When I was a civilian there were New York Jews I knew in the coal business who were as nice a type——"

Loftis was peeved and bored, and he wanted to say something withering, but he only got up courage enough to put a finger over his lips and murmur, "Just don't you worry, don't you worry," with a wink he hoped was enigmatic, and strolled away. His glass was empty.

Now he found Peyton and Harry standing with Helen. The photographer was a nervous little man with the eyes of a dog who has been unjustly beaten. The light was all wrong, he complained, but the client wanted informal pictures: he'd try his best. He put Loftis between Helen and Peyton, made them all stand cozily together. "There," he said, "now stay still if you please will," and moved them about, adjusted lenses and plates, while the guests stood around in a half-circle, making comments.

"Smile if you please will."

"I'm trying my best." Peyton giggled softly. Beneath Loftis' hand her waist was soft, warm, though somehow Harry's wrist, which he touched, too, was hairy, and it intruded.

"Smile."

"Hey, Milt, grin like the day you tied Gene Sarazen," Monk Yourtee called. The laughter was general.

"Big smile, please. Mrs. Loftis, lift your chin up if you please will. That's the ticket."

There was a flash of light, another, one more; the session was over and the guests scattered back to the punch table, buzzing like flies over the pink tablecloth, already soaked with champagne. And more champagne was brought to the bridal party. The waiters were very careful about this. They came up grinning every five minutes, with loaded trays. After her second glass, Helen declined, but Loftis put his arm around her waist: "You don't mind if I have some more?" And she smiled and stroked his chin gently with her fingernail, saying, "On this day, dear, anything goes. I have lots of Bromo-Seltzer upstairs." In ten minutes he had three, accepting the colored boys' offering with thanks and indiscretion, remembering that he should tip them well, and soon he heard himself talking to Peyton and Harry—rapidly, paternally and lovingly. With Peyton's hand in his, he was saying the most gallant things imaginable. Youth was in the air, as much a part of it, indeed, as the music or the frivolous silver light, and he felt youthful himself and filled again with the curious, hungry ardor. "Don't get worried about anything," he was telling Harry, and he squeezed Peyton's fingers, "she's just like her mother here. There'll be a time when you just can't imagine how you ever got hooked up with such a fickle creature—they're always eying anything in pants, you know—but just don't you worry. You'll look into those big brown eyes and she'll laugh at you and what can you do? Take it from me, these Loftis women just make you helpless——"

"Oh, Bunny——"

"Milton——" Helen laughed.

"No, I mean it, Harry," he said over the rim of his glass, "I really mean it. It's from the Peyton side of the family. It's a family of warriors, you see. You've got to watch out for them just like you would some top sergeants. Now take a top sergeant I once had in the last war when I was in training. Now that guy could be as mean as he wanted to be, yet there was something gentle and—really sweet about him. He was an Irishman named McNamara——" And he had branched off, he knew, onto something irrelevant, perhaps silly. He had begun with an analogy and ended up with a tall tale, only to impress Harry. That's what wartime always did. You have to justify yourself, romanticize, if ever so subtly. But Harry's face, through the bubbly exultant light, was receptive, intent: it was a Jewish face, all right, dark and almost handsome, with eyes that looked as if they rarely condemned or, on the other hand, ever indulged themselves in factitious pity, and there was a deep, oddly patient, waiting quality about them which chiefly seemed to express a desire just to understand. Because of this expression, and partly because of the champagne, Loftis found himself liking this young man more and more, but it also made it seem that Harry saw right through his story, so he came back to the main point. "Anyway, Harry my boy, remember what I say, because I know. They can't beat you down for long. They really don't want to. It's all an act, like a top sergeant. They'll really love you to death if you give 'em half a chance. Love you like you was a darlin' little boy——" Then he kissed Peyton on the cheek.

It was obvious that he was not clicking, that he was lamely striving for a tenderly humorous effect—the reason for which he couldn't explain himself—and that he was failing completely. Along the line he had said something wrong. Harry was wearing an appreciative, courteous grin, but the smiles on the faces of Peyton and Helen—both of which he sensed, rather than saw, at the same time—seemed fastened on with paste, and concealed a tense and inner reproach. "Oh, Daddy," Peyton said—rather crossly, he felt—and removed her hand from his and drank quickly from her champagne. "Your father-in-law goes off the deep end at times," Helen murmured to Harry, still smiling the reproachful smile. Loftis struggled for words to correct himself, anything to unplug this awkward moment, but just then up came the Abbott sisters, looking exactly alike. They were eighteen and nineteen, and, with their erect way of walking and flossy, butter-colored hair which they each wore page-boy style around their faces, they seemed to have all the straight, stemlike grace of a couple of jonquils.

"We've had a nice time," they said in unison.

"You aren't going so soon!" Peyton said. "Oh, Evelyn, Jeanie!"

"We've got to go back to Chapel Hill," the one on the left said, "exams. You know how it is."

Peyton kissed them both. Everyone said good-by, and they walked off arm in arm. Loftis was grateful to them for the interruption, but when he turned back to the family he was conscious only of the fixed smiles and the almost shocking silence. What on earth had he said? The room itself was filled with noise. The ceremony had been the spring part of the affair, it had passed; that was all innocence and had withered like April. Then there had been the summer, season of nonchalance, easy acquaintance, the first mellow glow, through which the guests had drifted (alcoholically speaking) as through a mist of August sunlight. Now early autumn of the reception had come, and if you closed your eyes you could hear its sound: the loose, high, windy laughter of the women, the male voices filled with a sudden, hoarse bluster, like the rattle of leaves. Thus do all parties move toward the cold of winter and a final numb extinction.

Loftis was aware of the noise but for a solitary instant he felt—looking at Peyton and Helen and Harry—islanded in silence. And during this moment he again tried vainly to recall what he had said or done to bring on such a tense and obvious, such a mutual sense of uneasiness. *Ah, those smiles, those smiles.* Was it the kiss he gave Peyton?

Then all at once he had a flicker of insight and during this moment—so brief that it lasted, literally, one blink of Peyton's eyes—he knew what the smiles were about and he had a crushing, chilling premonition of disaster. Harry smiled politely, but he faded before his sight, for Loftis was watching Peyton. She held her glass in the air, touched it to her lips. But along with her smile there was something else he was conscious of, too: she had already drunk too much. Her face rubbed pink as if by a scrubbing brush, she glowed with a fever, and in the way her eyes sparkled, her lips moist and parted, he knew somehow, with a plummeting heart, that she was beyond recovery. It was a moment of understanding that came sharp and terrible. He felt that he had waited all of his life for this moment, this flash of insight to come about. He had just said crazy, unthinking, harmless words, but he had said words like "fickle" and "love" and "death," and they, in their various ways, had sent a secret corrosion through these two women's hearts. God help him, hadn't he known all along that they hated and despised each other? Had he had to spend twenty years deceiving himself, piling false hope upon false hope—only to discover on this day, of all days, the shattering, unadorned, bitter truth? Those smiles . . . of course . . . how Peyton and Helen had always smiled at each other like that! There had been words, too, attitudes, small female gestures which it had been beyond him to divine, or even faintly to understand.

And he had gone on for years deceiving himself—too proud, too self-conscious, maybe just too stupid to realize that it had always been he himself who had been at the focus of these appalling, baffling female emotions. Not anything he had done or had failed to do had made them hate each other. Not even Dolly. None of his actions, whether right or wrong, had caused this tragedy, so much as the pure fact of himself, his very existence, interposed weaponless and defenseless in a no-man's-land between two desperate, warring female machines. Now he had kissed Peyton, said the wrong words, and he had somehow hurt her. And the smile she wore concealed her hurt—to everyone else, at least—just as Helen's smile, echoing Peyton's, concealed only the wild, envenomed jealousy which stirred at her breast. What had she done? Why had Helen deceived him like this? Those smiles. He was chilled with a sudden horror. Those smiles. They had fluttered across the web of his life like deceptive, lovely butterflies, always leading him on, always making him believe that, in spite of everything, these two women really did love each other. That, deep down, there was motherly, daughterly affection. But no. Now he saw the smiles in a split moment for what they were: women smiles— Great God, so treacherous, so false, displayed here—himself between them—like the hateful wings of bats.

Oh, Peyton, I love you so. . . .

He reached out his arm, the smiles dissolved. There was a sudden squeal from the kitchen. In came La Ruth, scattering guests in every direction with her pushcart, upon which rested an enormous cake. Her face was a single grin; tramping forward, she made blissful little quacking noises, bowing left and right to the guests, who were convulsed. But something was wrong. In some way a chain of hot dogs had become tangled up behind her, in the strings of her apron. Oblivious, ecstatic, she trailed them after her on the floor—ten of them, at least—and she came on toward Peyton, whooping and shouting, shoving her cart, propelled forward by waves of high, hysterical laughter. Then, right in front of Peyton, she stopped and looked around her. "Here de cake," she said, her smile fading; "What I done wrong now?"

"Oh, La Ruth," he heard Peyton say, amused.

The room was suddenly quiet. Even the music had stopped, and the guests turned, peering over their glasses to see what would happen. La Ruth examined her skirts, scowling, looked behind her, but found nothing. There were titters from the crowd. Then this is what Loftis saw next: he saw Ella Swan push through the milling people, hobbling down upon La Ruth irate and frantic, her apron flapping. She flew swiftly through the crowd like an outraged black bantam hen, punch ladle in hand, a shriveled black Cassandra, muttering threats and doom. It was a scene that should have been avoided, but no one thought to halt it and Loftis, his head still giddy from drink and the slow encroaching premonition of disaster, stood stiff in his tracks, and saw Ella snatch the hot dogs from La Ruth's apron and hold them dangling before her. "Looka here," she yelled in a quavering, aged voice, "look what you done. Tol' you to wait. Git on outa here!"

"Mama, I——"

"Hush yo' mouf! Messin' up Peyton's weddin'! I'll knock you to yo' knees directly!"

"Mama, I diden'——"

"You hush up!" she yelled, brandishing ladle and hot dogs. "Draggin' dem weenies in here like dat. I oughta knock you in de head one!"

"Ella!" he heard Helen say, moving toward her, but it was too late: with her head buried in the folds of her apron, La Ruth had begun to cry. A great, agonized tremor of grief ran through her body; hair askew, hands over her face, she threw back her head and howled. "Ooo-oo, Jesus! I'nt mean to do it! Dey all got scritched up offa de table someways." And broke down again, incoherent, and hid her face in her apron, in a new convulsion of misery. Sweating, Loftis wondered how long all this could go on; it was low comedy enacted, it seemed—because of the horror which had seized him—upon the stage of high tragedy, and the foolish guests, egging La Ruth on with snickers, were unaware of the calamitous events about to proceed from the wings.

Then Peyton darted forward. He saw it in a flash. Saw her set the glass down on the table, unsteadily—she was tight, her cheeks were flushed, her eyes bright with glaze—and move toward Ella, calming her with a touch of her hand and a brief murmur. Then, lone in her command of the situation, she went up to La Ruth and put her arms about her shoulders with a little hug, saying, "That's all right, La Ruth. Thank you for the lovely cake. Everything's O.K., La Ruth." It was that quick. It took no more than five seconds, but immediately the colossal awkwardness of the scene had vanished. The music began again with a soggy lurch and the air was touched with the murmur of voices, the tinkling kiss of glasses. La Ruth dried her eyes, looked up gratefully at Peyton and trudged back to the kitchen. It had been a gesture neither lofty nor patronizing, but spontaneous and unaffected, and it afflicted him with such love that he hardly knew how to bear it. *Now don't be an ass*, his conscience said, but she seemed to be fading from him, vanishing in a powder of crushed-up dreams, and he found himself beside her, kissing her in front of everyone, much more than a father.

"Don't smother me," she whispered, and pushed him away angrily. "Don't *smother* me, Daddy! You're crazy! What will people think! Daddy, don't!" Beads of champagne rose up between them, a green smell of grapes, and she had indeed pushed him away furiously, where he stood witless with horror and desire, his heart pounding, a smear of red grease sticky across his lips. What had he done? "Don't smother me," she said again in a thick voice—for she had become suddenly and astonishingly befuddled. "Damn you, Daddy! You're spoiling everything!" And turned and weaved toward the cake with unsteady steps, the skirt about her hips shining slickly in the light. He stood shattered and bewildered in the center of the floor, thankful for the confusion which had hidden from other eyes his moment of madness. No one had noticed or heard, thank God. He turned . . . but yes, Harry had noticed. He caught Loftis' eye, looked away quickly, his dark face red with embarrassment. Harry had heard and . . . oh, Jesus . . . Helen, who stood in a bright oval of sunlight, staring not at him but at Peyton's retreating back, cruelly and with icy loathing.

Peyton and Harry had begun to carve the cake.

"Smile!"

There was a white blossom of light, cheers from the guests. The champagne hit him like a fist. Already he was hopelessly drunk. . . .

Six o'clock. Five minutes have passed since the first wedge was cut from the cake. There is a lull in the celebration, for it is the duty of each guest to have some of the cake, although cake goes poorly with whisky or champagne, and it is the last thing the guests want to eat. Few of them would care, really, about eating, but the guests have been to too many weddings. The cake has become symbolic of something and they have to face it: it must be eaten. Besides, it would be a pity to let that huge thing go to waste. Peyton and Harry have eaten the first slice; Ella, aided by one of the colored boys, is carving away the rest. The guests crowd around, their champagne put aside for the moment, and hold out plates. With its golden insides exposed and with white frosting crumbling softly around its edges, the cake looks like a great snow-covered mountain which has had one slope blown away by dynamite; at its peak, as if upon the top of Everest, stands a tiny bridal couple, embowered by pink sugar roses, whose faces have the serenely fatuous looks of store-window mannequins. Part of the groom has been chipped away. You can see through his morning coat to his guts, which are made, quite obviously, of nothing but candy. The bride's bouquet has become hacked off, too. It rests far below in the gaping crevasse. And now, while Ella chops perilously about the top of the cake, the couple becomes undermined by her knife; there is a rush of avalanching crumbs, bride and bridegroom tilt, totter, lean forward as if looking for the lost bouquet, and almost fall, but are halted by Monk Yourtee who, amid rowdy, pointed laughter, snatches them from the brink and gnaws off the bridegroom's head.

Outside, the sun sinks slowly behind a frieze of sycamores. A gentle breeze rises from the bay, filled with the faint, cool snap and odor of autumn. Leaves flutter across the lawn, troop up the slope and over the terrace and, one by one like vandals, begin to invade the room. The waiters close the doors and pull the windows down. Above the sound of music and the laughter the churchbell begins to strike six chimes, and one or two people look at their watches and decide that it's almost time to leave. Yet no one leaves. Not yet. The cake must be eaten and then there's space for more champagne. With cake-filled plates and reloaded glasses they scatter to the corners of the room. For a moment the conversation almost ceases. The mouths of the guests are full of cake. A brief contemplative sag has come; there's more thought than talk, and all good Episcopalian minds turn to thoughts of things done, things left undone, words said in an alcoholic fog, not more than five minutes ago, which would have better been left unspoken. Thus chewing, briefly ruminating, they pause to sanctify Peyton's marriage—the champagne its mystical blood, the cake its confectionery flesh.

Regard them now—Peyton and Harry, Loftis and Helen. Peyton is listening—appears to be listening—to Mrs. Overman Stubbs, who talks of her own bridal clothes, of Overman, of their honeymoon in New Orleans. Years ago . . .

She turns to Harry. "And your parents?" she asks, a woman with sweetness and solicitude engraved on every part of her plump and rouged, middle-aged face. Sweetness unadulterated, direct and without reticence, almost obsessed in its need to be spread everywhere, it leaves an odor behind her wherever she goes, like the smell that clings to one upon leaving a bakery. She is a good woman and on this day she feels an extraordinary tenderness. She has lived most of her life in Port Warwick, and Harry is the third Jew she has ever met. He's not strange at all, she thinks, he's handsome, with a sad sweet look in his eyes, and impulsively she wonders about his home, his family, the mysterious New York Jews, asks again, "Your parents? They couldn't come?"

"They're dead."

"Oh——" Almost imperceptibly her lips quiver, she turns blindly away: there, she's done it again. Her sweetness, her need to be nice. It so often makes her blunder. "Oh," she says, and looks up and smiles once more at Peyton, timidly, moving aside—"Well, congratulations again!"—bogged down by a swift confusion.

Peyton drains her glass and squeezes Harry's hand, then turns. Her face, upon which happiness has rested tangible and alive, making her eyes sparkle, suddenly and just for the briefest moment goes slack and angry, the gay façade dissolving like a film of plaster. "Let's go soon," she whispers. The churchbell chimes.

"What's the matter, honey?"

"This . . . all this——"

"What? Take it easy on the champagne."

"I don't like this," she said.

"Why, honey?"

"I—I don't know. I—oh, Tommy!" The happy look reassembles mechanically: she smiles, throws her arms about a young naval officer, who steadies her, because she is tottering a little.

Far off to the west the last chimes waver, die, fading seaward like great globes of brass borne upon a powerful and uncanny wind. The music ceases. There is a loud, drunken shriek of female laughter, cutting through the murmurous undertow of voices, yet above both of these, laughter and voices, the bell sounds roll toward the sea, return foreshortened on vibrating blasts, fade, return, and sink finally out of the sphere of hearing.

Loftis says, "Yes, yes." Monroe Hobbie has him clutched by the elbow, in a raw, anguished, dentist's grip. He speaks of love, of olden times, of lost ladies and one, in particular, who left him for a dirty wop. His eyes, bifocaled, reflect sorrow, his voice the memory of a vanquished love, but Loftis doesn't hear. Lost himself, his heart hollow as a drum, he watches Peyton through the crowd, thinking

288

not of vanquished love, but of chimes and bells. He drinks. The bells toll on through his memory. Seaward-borne, they strike reefs of recollection, shatter and recover, come back to smother his soul like something heavy and outrageous. *Time! Time!* he thinks. *My God, has it finally come to this, do I finally know?* And lost in memory, thinking not of Peyton but of this final knowledge—this irrevocable loss of her—he recalls the incessant tolling bells. With a steady, brazen certainty they had struck off the passing hours, marched through the house night and day forever. It seems that he had heard them for the first time, though they are silent now, motionless in their yokes. The guests reel giddily before his eyes, on his arm the dentist's clutch is raw and painful. *Those bells,* he thinks, *those bells.* Why now did they return to afflict him with such despair? *Count off twenty years.* The light in the room deepens toward gold, sending sandy threads through Peyton's hair.

A vision swarms through his mind, as sudden and as irretrievable as smoke. It vanishes. He looks down into the dentist's mouth, a fishlike opening, straining for breath like one who dies not for lack of oxygen, but of asphyxiation of heart and spirit, and the dentist's eyes fill up with tears: "For a dirty little sailor she left me," he whimpers. "Milton, man, she was the finest . . ."

The vision returns, and the bells. He sees the lawn outside, Peyton, summer. Peyton is a little girl with clean pink legs, a pink ribbon in her hair. Around them the grass grows thick and high and crickets jump through the spikelike weeds. Together they stand beneath the cedars, her hand in his; across the morning water flash gulls and sails, wings, waves sparkling like fire. She looks at her book, says, "Tiddely-pom," rubs her head against his arm gently, musingly, her long, soft hair falling on his knees. The air is full of heat, insect noises, the smell of summer and now, like the stroke of a pendulum, the first voice of the bells. "Bong," go the chimes, "bong," says Peyton, and turns, saying, "Daddy, tell me about the bells." He squeezes her hand, pulling her along. "Come on," he says. They go through the weeds out into the sunlight, across the lawn and up the new-mown slope, taking care not to slip; the dew is still cold and bright on the grass. They walk in silence, for, though Peyton talks incessantly, he has forgotten the words she said. Now they are on the gravel drive, walking past the house, the mimosas, the grape arbor drowsy with bees, the honeysuckled fence, and strolling together, her hand moist in his, down the drive and up the tree-lined street. So in this way, drunk with champagne, he feels, with his mind blank to the dentist's stricken words, blank to everything save the light woven through Peyton's hair, immersed in time: nine times the bells are tolling, birds sing in the sycamores, and he is with Peyton, holding hands.

Across a field they go, over the ditch they jump, and over a stile. In the houses, the proper, middle-class homes with the light meters shining in the light and the garages closed and the clipped, pruned hedges—in all these houses people are sleeping, for it is Sunday; no one stirs. Peyton's sandals flap-flap along the sidewalk, she talks of boys and cats and birds, and of bells; the chimes still ringing, a hymn now—*Jesus calls us*—they reach the church, gazing up at the ivy walls. The doors are open; they walk in, through the deserted, damp-smelling halls, past stained windows of Galilee and Capernaeum, reds like melted iron, blues the color of drowned men's lips, past parables and saints and miracles and the diamond eyes of Peter, intercepting the morning sun like lenses of a microscope. Now up the creaking stairs they climb, brushing a dust of plaster from the walls. Peyton sneezes, the chimes grow louder above them—

> *O'er the tumult*
> *Of our life's wild, restless sea*

—and then, emerging above in a burst of light, they stand at the belfry door, laughing together, deafened by the noise. In their arches the hammers draw back like bowstrings, leap forward, descend on the bell throats as swiftly and as wickedly as birds of prey. The timbers shudder and Peyton, frightened, clings to him. He shouts something back to soothe her but, squeezing the flesh of his leg until it hurts, she bursts out into a fury of weeping. Then suddenly there is silence, abrupt and shocking, louder than the noise: one high note quivers on the air, its vibration trailing seaward behind the deep ones, returns briefly, fades and vanishes, returns no more. Peyton continues to weep, silently, desperately, sobbing. He lifts her to the ledge and puts his arm about her, telling her not to be frightened. Beneath the eaves sparrows scuttle in their nests and fly off with a raucous sound. A twig falls from a sycamore. A car horn blows somewhere. He smooths dust from her skirt, saying, "Peyton, don't be scared," and then kisses her. The weeping stops. Beneath his cheek he can feel cool, tiny beads of sweat on her brow.

He doesn't know why his heart pounds so nor, when he kisses her again, in an agony of love, why she should push him so violently away with her warm small hands. . . .

Now in his memory the bells fade, finally die. The dentist snuffles, lifts up his bifocals to wipe his pink, inflamed eyes. Loftis says nothing. He has heard nothing. Across the room he sees Peyton break away from the young lieutenant, her arm crooked at the elbow in a curious, disjointed way, groping behind her for the empty champagne glass. It is a willful gesture, almost frantic, and though he cannot see her face, he imagines it: tense, glowing with artificial joy, like his own a mask, concealing the bitterness of memory. He wishes to go to her side, to talk to her alone, and explain. He wants only to be able to say: forgive me, forgive all of us. Forgive your mother, too. She saw, but she just couldn't understand. It's my fault. Forgive me for loving you so.

But at this moment, when he suddenly sees Helen, white with fury, throw a coat over her shoulders and go out onto the porch with Carey Carr, he knows that explanations are years too late. If he himself could love too much, only Helen could love so little.

Carey felt benevolent after three glasses of sherry, and he wasn't prepared for Helen, *or* her hysteria. He had been standing in a doorway talking to Dr. DeWitt Lonergan and his wife. Both of them were parishioners of his. He was rather fond of the doctor, who had a naïve way of thinking Carey liked off-color stories, which in fact he did as long as they stayed reasonably clean, but Bernice, who had big hips and wide-spaced teeth like the wife of Bath, and a mannered, nervous laugh, he found gross and somehow unwholesome, and he usually discovered, to his embarrassment, that he ignored completely what she had to say. She also had the habit of sprinkling her chatter with "You know's?" and "See what I mean's?" which, since politeness compelled him to make a reply, made his abstracted air all the more difficult, because he rarely knew what she meant at all.

And he was watching Peyton, with a dim, unaccountable feeling of sadness; he sensed something wrong, but he didn't know what. It had been the same at the ceremony. Watching her—yes, God knows she was beautiful—he had been troubled by the identical thought: sad, that's what she is. When she spoke the vows her lips parted not like all the brides he'd ever seen—exposing their clean, scrubbed teeth in a little eager puff of rapture—but rather with a kind of wry and somber resignation. It had been a brief shadow of a mood, just a flicker, but enough for him to tell: her "I will" had seemed less an avowal than a confession, like the tired words of some sad, errant nun. Not any of her put-on gaiety could disguise this, not even now when, from behind Bernice Lonergan's hefty shoulder, he saw Peyton turn from the navy uniform, wheel about and fill her glass, in a frenzy.

"I mean what with war and all I think people are more and more getting back to religion, see what I mean, Carey?" Awkwardly he looked up to meet Bernice's uncomplicated gaze. "I mean," she went on, "there's such a real need——" But at this point, just when he had about decided to go talk to Peyton, to calm her, Helen came up and grabbed him by the arm. "Can I see you?"

She excused herself to the Lonergans and, taking a route through the hall so they'd not be seen by the guests, led him outside. In silence he followed her across the lawn, all the way down to the sea-wall. It was chilly and he began to protest but at the edge of the seawall she turned and faced him, clutching his hand.

"Did you see it?" she said. Her voice was a hiss, like gas escaping from a bottle of soda.

"What, Helen?" he said. "What do you mean?"

"*Her.* What she did."

"I—I don't know——" He was appalled by her look, and a little frightened. Popeyed, trembling, she seemed so distraught as to be on the verge of some striking biological change, and her skin, in this fading light, was as colorless as the whites of her eyes. He shivered, drew his hand away. A dim sound of music floated across the slope, and crazy laughter.

"Didn't you see it?" she said again.

"No, Helen," he said sharply, "I don't know what you're talking about. And besides——"

"The way she's acting. Toward him. Didn't you see? Carey, you must be blind. You——" She took his hand again.

"Helen——" he put in sternly.

She went on, bearing down on his fingers. "She's behaving like the little tramp she is! Already she's drunk. Already! She'd been drinking before the ceremony, I could smell it on her breath! Now this. Didn't you see the way she acted toward him? Didn't——"

"Toward *who*, Helen? *Who?*"

"Him. Milton. Don't you see what she's doing to him? Oh, I can't stand this! Let it go on——" She drew her coat tight around her shoulders, and ran one white, bony hand through her hair. "After all I've planned and worked and sacrificed. Just for her and for him. Knowing how much she means to him, and how much he loves her! All this time I've been ready to forget that he's spoiled her rotten. That hasn't mattered one bit to me. I was willing to forget that as long as I knew it made him happy. To have her home again, I mean. It's pathetic, that's what it is, Carey. I mean, that he should love her so, when it's obvious she despises him. Hates him. Not just me. But him. After all we've——"

Less sherry in him and he might have reacted with considerably more intelligence, but all he could do was turn away, shocked and despairing, his eyes on a piece of driftwood bobbing below, his mouth opening and closing, struggling vainly for words. "Helen . . ."

"You mustn't look like that, Carey," she said, more calmly. "It's the truth I'm telling you. I've been willing to overlook that terrible fact all my life. That he's ruined her, spoiled her half to death. I've been willing to overlook that because I've loved him. With all his weaknesses and all his faults I've loved him more than you could ever imagine a woman loving a man. I was willing to overlook that woman and his drinking and everything. I was willing even to overlook the way he spoiled Peyton. And now, look. Look at what's happened!"

He threw his arms into the air, a vast stage gesture brought on by drink, and entirely inadequate. "What *has* happened, Helen?" He turned to face her. "What on earth *has* happened? What are you driving at? By heaven, I haven't seen anything! Yes, Peyton looks utterly wretched. But maybe something's wrong besides Peyton. Maybe——"

"There's nothing wrong with anybody except Peyton. Oh, the cruelty, the shame of having a child like that. And I've *loved* her, Carey, I've loved her! We've had our misunderstandings and all that sort of thing, but even when I knew she hated me the most I loved her. Loved her as only a mother can love someone. Only a mother——"

He took her by the arms. "Calm down now, understand, Helen? Listen to me. You've got to get hold of yourself. What are you driving at? Just what has Peyton done?"

"She's persecuting him, that's what she's doing. You can see it in her eyes. I planned this wedding just for her. And for him. Milton."

"How about for yourself? Don't you do anything for yourself?"

"I . . . I don't know what you mean."

"I mean, so you see a look in her eyes, hear a word, and you figure she's persecuting him. Just what do you mean by that? What did she say?"

"She said, 'Don't smother me!' in the most vicious, ugly way. She said—and she was drunk, too, when she said it—she said——"

"Wait a minute, Helen. What difference does it make what she said, or the way she looked, or how much she's had to drink? Just really what difference does it make? Good heavens, a girl comes home on her wedding day, to a house where relations, to put it mildly, have been strained. She's excited, she gets a little tight, her father is jolly and tight, too, and maybe a little bit too affectionate, and so she snaps at him. And you say she's persecuting him. Well, by heaven, I think you're dead wrong, and furthermore I think—— By heaven, Helen, what's wrong with you? How can you talk about Peyton like this?"

It was getting dark and cold. Some of the guests were leaving. At the top of the slope car doors slammed; there were farewells, the sound of wheels on gravel. Lights went on in the house. Helen drew near Carey, touching his hand again, lightly, tentatively. *How can you talk about Peyton like this?* That was too simple. How could she make Carey understand? He was such a sweet, stuffy, funny man, with his airs and his graveness and his suffering dark eyes. Although less than ten years separated them, she felt, close and alone as now, a strange, sweet pang: she wanted to mother him or something, fondle him, feel the rough, coarse fabric of his suit beneath her fingers. Such a dear, funny, stuffy man: how could she make him understand about Peyton and her troubles, her own misery and such things? Funny man. He'd ask her to come back to church or something. Now, when it was too late. Didn't he know she had found her God? Didn't he know that the devil had been slain, that Milton was her Prince of Light, come back all virtuous after befouling himself; once smeared with the sluttish filth of an evil woman, he had finally been won over: her own lure had recaptured him. He had been contrite, penitent, crushed with guilt. She, Helen, had raised him up, re-formed him in the image of decency, exalted him. Didn't Carey realize these things? Dear, honest, funny man.

A shiver ran up her backbone as she approached him, caught his blunt, honest fingers in her own. He was such a gentle, incorruptible type; perhaps, after all, she had been too violent in her attack. Perhaps softer, subtler words would win him over. And she found herself saying, "Carey, you must think terrible things about me. Don't you, Carey? But listen, honestly I've never been bitter toward anyone in my life without reason. You think it's unnatural of me to talk about Peyton like this, don't you—?"

She heard his voice, honest, gentle, incorruptible. He disengaged his fingers and thrust his hands in his pockets. "I think, Helen," he said, "that we'd better go in now. If you really want an answer, I think you're a very sick woman. I don't know whether it's proper to call a spade a spade in such a case, but you asked me. There's something wrong with you beyond curing, beyond anything I can do, anyway."

He was not looking at her. He was gazing straight out at the bay, blinking solemnly, his prissy mouth set in a small, grim line. And it suddenly occurred to her: how unfortunate. To have a funny, prim mouth like that, with such a fine mind, really a fine, noble mind to go with it: a mind that needed a big, wide man's mouth and a firm, manly jaw, too. But she felt the faint chill again and pulled the coat tightly about her, wondering. What had he said? She tried to remember. Oh, yes.

Sick.

"Carey," she chided him, "what a funny thing to say. Sick. Why, I've never felt better in my life."

He turned toward her. "Helen, I think we'd better go in," he said in a curt, sharp voice. "I have no intention of standing here listening to you revile Peyton. On her wedding day. Peyton has——"

Peyton. Carey's words floated off into the dusk. On some naval ship, anchored in the channel, a klaxon groaned, and a knot of sailors on the deck—she could see them, far out, as tiny as pins—scattered away like a broken cluster of pearls. Three ducks settled on the water, and the wind, in a sudden gust from the beach, brought a ripe, raw smell of sewage. She lifted a finger to her brow, in an attitude of deep thought, thinking: What is he trying to tell me about my sickness? "Furthermore," he was saying now, "I think there's something unutterably smug about your attitude toward Milton. I'm only saying this because I know you well enough, so be calm, Helen dear. That you should impute to yourself these strange, divine powers of healing is not only sinful in the abstract, but false and unjust, too. I should think you'd have a little more common humility. If I'm any judge of the situation, it's Milton who's accomplished the miracle, not you. What makes you think . . . as for Peyton . . ."

What was he trying to tell her? She stood listening to him, her eyes cocked, her mouth turned up in a bright, receptive smile. Yet she was really only half-listening to him: his words, angry, indignant, seemed to make not the slightest impression, and she felt suddenly that it was unfair, most *completely* unfair for him to be lecturing *her*, when it was she who had begun all this in the first place. And her mind sought back a few moments. She struggled to remember something, and memory fumbled through her brain like old yellowed fingers in a littered drawer: *I must make him believe me.* Peyton. Now he was talking of Peyton, saying, "From just the little I can gather, Helen, Peyton's had a pretty rough time of it. You asked my opinion and now you're getting it. In the first place, you'll have to admit that you never got on with her at all. Or she with you. You told me all that three or four years ago. In the second place, why should I (though don't get me wrong, Helen, I'm not attacking you) why should I have to accept your statement that she's just a little tramp? If as you say she's making a fool out of herself today, why do I have to believe that she's doing it because she's bad at heart? And even if that's true surely you can manage it without making a scene. So she *is* getting a little drunk. So she is! So, by heaven . . ."

Ah, she'd found it. This. Stupid Carey. Did he really believe for one instant it was the drinking, the vicious words to Milton, that mattered? How could he be so dull and stupid? Couldn't he see the deeper things she was getting at, trying to tell him? He was an angry man, all right. Listen to him, look at that plump, outraged face. All right, let him talk. She'd have her triumph. She'd always—though a whole array of ministers, doctors, men (*men!* she thought) protest her stubbornness, her wrongness—cherish the suffering of her life. What did they know of a woman's suffering? They should have kept their poor, inept men's fingers on *her* pulse all these years. How shocked they would be, what sober, pompous male mutterings would be heard, could they just feel the course of her pounding, angry blood. "How sick she is!" they'd say, and "ah" and "ahem" in their nasty male way, leaning over her bed with their coarse, male, armpit smells. "How sick she is!" they'd say. "Feel this pulse, Reverend, Doctor!" And she'd be repelled, but would delicately, graciously submit to their proddings, if only to see the light in their eyes—the wild, frightened light—when they darted swift glances at each other, saying, "The world has never seen a pulse like this. Has never seen such a sick woman. Feel, Reverend, Doctor, feel the pulse of the angriest woman on earth! How she must have suffered!" And she'd lie there drugged by the quieting nembutal, compliant, submissive, but with a sure, glad triumph swelling at her heart. For this would be an acknowledgment of a woman's fury, and (of course they'd realize it) the defeat of men in general. Milton might be there, too—poor Milton, whom she had loved, poor, blind, dumb Milton who had realized the error of his ways. Who had come back to her, as she had always known he would, literally on his knees, dragging his heels, remorseful, in tears. Milton she would excuse, of course. Milton had yielded to her. Milton had said, "I quit," had admitted she had been right all along.

Or her dreams. What did foolish men know of a woman's dreams? Of a woman like herself—despised, rejected, but always patient, reveling in the violent surge of her blood—whose dreams were always crowded with enemies, dreams bizarre and frantic, villainous beyond men's wildest imaginings? How simple-minded men were, after all! Carey there, puffing like a toadfish, round-faced and futile. What could he—with a switch now jerked from a bush, petulantly thrashing the seawall, saying "Now Helen, I insist that you leave that girl alone today!"—what could he know about the suffering that drenches a woman's life, soaks into her dreams like blood, makes her awake each morning with her teeth hurting, from all the gnashing and grinding while she slept? What could he know about her dreams?

Three enemies had always dwelt there, in her dream country, three enemies and a friend. Maudie had been sweet, like something musical, always hobbling near (looking past Carey's pink, petulant face she saw two gulls descend like scraps of rag across the dusk, and thought of Maudie with a sudden stab at her heart; thought, her lips trembling: *No, I mustn't think of Maudie now*), and Maudie she had always hid *behind* her in her dreams, hiding her from sight of the planetary, fearsome half-light, the fingering shadows, the enemies who, somehow, would rape Maudie first, then her. Maudie had been her friend. Then there had been the big enemy, once the most fearsome of all, now dead, vanquished, done with: Dolly Bonner. That bitch, that whore. Many times Dolly had died in her dreams, often by the knife that Helen wielded, grinning, but more often by disease. In this landscape there were always the vaguest outlines of a city, with many ornate towers, from which pestilence rose like smoke through the air. It was a city of corpses and a faint moldering odor which troubled her sleep, yet the odor was not of death so much, or putrefaction, but of an indefinable, musky rancidness, like cheap perfume or rotten gardenias. Through this vapor Helen strolled, clad in her party best, and always with a man. Though now and then the man was Carey or her father, it was more likely Milton or someone in a mask. The corpses which lay strewn about were faceless, iridescent with decay, soft in parts or part leathery, invariably female. So, fanning themselves, sedate, she and Milton or whoever he was strolled for infinite miles, it seemed, through this land of the female dead, offended by, and commenting upon, the musky, floral odor, but mutually delighted by one corpse in particular, faceless like the rest, head down in the shadows, with its legs—suppurating, clotted by a swarm of sucking, avid flies—unmistakably Dolly's.

If this was a vision more revolting than any she would tolerate when she was awake, it nonetheless possessed an adequateness, a rightness, which removed its nightmare quality and made her ghoulish stroll, in spite of the strange, sick smell, even pleasant. The more loathsome parts of the dream—the dried-up female organs, the yellowed, scabious flesh, which looked only too much like pictures she had once seen in a medical book—these faded away quickly upon awakening, leaving her with just the breath of the dream, the peculiar smell, and with a vague feeling of triumph. Yet she had remained fiercely discontented. That dream had come only in the past few years and, triumph or not, the ensuing days always seemed gray and bleak with a crushing guilt. She had never had such wicked, grim imaginings before and she asked herself: Am I going crazy? Besides, sometimes it was Maudie whose legs, outstretched and with the metal brace, were dead, and then she would wake up sweating and weeping.

It was so easy to defeat one's enemies in a dream. Dolly, a soldier in armor, she sometimes slew on the field of battle, the horse, white and named Champ, just like her father's, sinking its sharp hooves into Dolly's skull—the final blow. Sometimes Dolly died with stilettos in her back or in the electric chair, but always the corpse returned to its destined place in the plague-ridden city—disgraced, ugly, with sprawling, indecent legs. Thereafter, face-downward, she would float past on a sluggish stream and this time, with Milton at Helen's side murmuring sadly, "Too bad. I never loved the bitch," as they watched her drift away, Helen awoke cleansed and healthy, knowing she would never have to dream of Dolly, or of the city, again.

Sometimes the dreams became all mixed-up, and these were the hardest times of all. Then it seemed that *she* was the enemy, she was the one who threatened people, frightened them. Everyone fled her—men and women, everyone she had ever known—a whole army of them, until she stood on the moonlit, moonlike plain, alone and lonesome, crying out, "Won't someone please help me?" Then her second enemy, the Man, appeared: Milton, or Carey, sometimes her father, it made no difference—they all hated her, threatened her, asked her why she'd been so bad.

A terrible guilt fell over her. She watched Carey thrash the switch about, wanting to take it away from him. "If you'd just be calm, Helen," he was saying, gentler now, "you'd see that everything's going to work out all right. Look——" He approached her, trying to smile, but the smile was so forced and artificial, and he seemed so confused because of the wine he'd been drinking, that Helen felt he was losing

298

all control, that he was threatening her, too, play-acting, faking, and again she desperately wanted to take the stick away from him. "Look Helen, suppose you and I get another drink and go upstairs for a minute and calm down and talk this thing——" Ah, Carey, she thought, and she raised her hand a little, as if to ward him off. Did Carey know he was one of the Men? One of the enemy? Wouldn't he be surprised! To know how much a part of her he'd become, to know (and now she thought, *He really is weak and silly and doesn't understand, why have I had any faith in him and his silly, weak ways?*) how she'd dreamed of him, while he, no doubt, had been dreaming of silly, worldly things, furnaces and things, that silly wife of his, Adrienne, or of becoming a fat bishop with folds of fat covering up his tiny little worshipful you-know-what. How shocked and angry he'd be! And she recalled the dream again, with an inward, chilling fright.

Carey dislodged a stone from the seawall; it went tumbling onto the beach below, smacked sharply against the sewer drain, and the ducks flew up, the gulls, too, piping shrilly, leaving a floating waste of feathers. From the house came a renewed spasm of music, hoarse, Viennese, with the whine of an accordion, and she thought, *Silly ass, he doesn't know.* How naked to the waist he'd been one night, fat and pink with his belly button showing, pulling her along angrily after him through woods of fern and laurel, through her garden, trampling down the azaleas. She had screamed, "But, Maudie, she's gone!" and he had turned, threatening her with a big stick. Fat and pink, his titties bobbing with greasy yellow fat beneath, like butter on oatmeal. Threatening her with the stick, saying, "You must believe! You must believe! I am the way, the truth and the life!"

She retreated two steps backward along the seawall. Carey came toward her, brandishing the threatful switch. She had dropped her handkerchief, wondered if he'd be so much the gentleman enough to pick it up, but neither handkerchief nor switch seemed so important now as this matter of her enemies.

"You've been my enemy, too!" she said, only faintly aware of the choking in her voice, and of the big, salty tears which unaccountably had begun to flow down to the corners of her lips. "You haven't wanted to help me. You and your church! Honestly, Carey, how could you be such a hypocrite? Pretending to understand my problems all these years. Mocking me behind my back!" She groped for something crushing, annihilating to say, to this her enemy. "Your God God is a silly old ass," she said, "and my God . . . my God is the devil!"

"Hush, Helen, don't talk like that," he said gently. "You're all wrought up and nervous. Come on inside. Look, it's getting dark. We'll have something to calm us down and then you'll see Peyton. . . ."

Peyton! She wanted to shriek the name aloud. How could he be such an enemy! Wasn't Peyton precisely the one she'd been talking about for the past fifteen minutes? Did he think she'd been talking to the air, for a joke, for fun? She held up her hand. "No, don't come closer with that stick," she said hoarsely, sobbing, "you stay right there! Right there!" Carey stopped in his tracks. "Did you conspire, too? With that tramp, that little whore? Is she on your side, with my poor, weak Milton in the middle? You should die of shame! Don't you see what she's done to this family? Don't you see how she's used him right up to the very end? The shameless bitch. Excuse these words. . . ."

And she paused for a minute, to dry her eyes.

"Excuse these words, Carey. What else can I say about a shameless little seducer who's used her father's love to get everything she wants in life, who half-killed her own sister through negligence—did kill her in fact, she let Maudie fall! Who used her father's love, played on it like a sheer music box, rubbed herself up against him until he was half-crazy——" She lifted her hand again. "Don't come near me with that stick! I've seen it all my life. He was putty in her hands, sheer putty! She's drained him dry! *My* money, too, drained through him, my poor, weak Milton! You should die of shame for taking sides with a shameless bitch! After all my suffering, after all I've done for her. Now she comes home drunk, thinking so long as she's married she can get away with torturing him. Torturing my poor, weak Milton, who I slaved and suffered over to get back again. Comes home with a little Jewish artist she's been sleeping with for months! A little Jew. I thought I would overlook that, too, if just to make Milton happy. Anybody she was married to, all right, I said, even if he's not from Virginia and is from a mongrel family. Anything! Anything, I said! So long as Milton was contented once more. Now she gets drunk and lures him on with her sinful little tail twitching and then turns on him like a dog. 'Don't smother me!' she said, 'Don't smother me!'"

"Carey, don't you come near me with that stick!"

"Helen, poor Helen," he said, "you are mad."

A wave of agony swept over her. The air, the perishing twilight, thick with October leaves blown up from the lawn, was thicker with enemies. Something caved in on her mind: she saw Peyton, her gestures, her sinful hips, as round as moons. She saw Milton and Peyton together, and the tender, corrupt solemnity of their caresses: a multitude of red, soft lips, Milton's hair, Peyton's breasts, the torture of twenty years. "Damn you, Carey," she said, "damn you for not understanding me!" And as she spoke she knew that it was not Dolly's legs, but Peyton's, which had shone with the rainbow of decay, sprawled out so indecently in the dreaming, pestilential dust.

"Damn you!" she cried. "I'll fix her alone!"

"Do you mind an old man asking where you're going on your honeymoon? Or are you supposed to tell?"

Dr. Lawrence Holcomb was speaking. He was having a hard time getting attention because, tight as he was, with so little co-ordination, he found himself being squeezed aside by four or five young people who crowded around Peyton and Harry, laughing and shouting and spilling champagne. A bachelor at sixty-eight and an uneasy drinker, Holcomb was seized with an itchy, reminiscent lust whenever he drank too much, whenever young girls were around—the younger the better—and this fact saddened him. He was a scholar and a stoic; what temperate virtues he owned had been hard won, but still his eyes filled up with tears and he felt the old, burning lust at the sight of these girls—the slick, peach-skin little necks, the stuck-out, yearning breasts, the dozens of naughty perfumes which teased the air. There was one girl now, in particular; she looked up at him casually, impishly, a little blonde with a mouth like crushed fruit, and in his drunken, lonely desire he felt he could have borne her away on his shoulders, without one thought whatsoever. But no. Really, he thought. Really. And sadly, with the sadness of a man who has known all the crucifixions of the flesh, he repeated to himself the old Socratic prayer: "Beloved Pan and all ye other gods who haunt this place, give me beauty in the inward soul."

"What did you say, sir?" Harry had heard him, was shaking his outstretched hand.

"Peyton," he said, "I brought her into this world, I, the *fidus Achates* of this family for a quarter of a century, remain totally ignored on her wedding day, alone, unnoticed, unsung. I asked," he said, shaking his white, flowing hair in a parody of gloom, "a simple question, perhaps pardonable as the whim of a drunken old man, but my words are lost in the miasmal croakings of a horde of depraved children. I asked——" He put his hand on the blonde's waist.

"What did you ask?" said Harry, smiling, exposing a row of even white teeth.

"I asked where you might be going on your honeymoon. I asked——"

"Florida."

"Ah, Florida. Land of the mangrove and the simple-minded! Land of the orange juice and the palmtree and the brainless smirk! California's little sister, land of the waterskis and the muscles—congratulations, my boy." The blonde wriggled away with a chirp, and he succeeded in pushing toward Peyton.

"Hello, my love." He kissed her on the mouth, moistly.

"Doctor Holcomb, I haven't seen you for ages! You darling, you used to stick that cold piece of machinery in my ear! Here, let the bride kiss *you*." She smacked him on the cheek.

"Steady, my love. Steady." He cozied up to her, letting his arm steal about her waist. "I'll do the drinking around here. *And* the kissing. Where in hell's the champagne?" As if he had flourished a wand, a waiter appeared, tray extended. He and Peyton took glasses, but Harry, with a sudden frown, refused, and tapped Peyton on the shoulder. "Honey, you'd better go easy——"

"Young man," the doctor interrupted, "I am a physician. Disregard my last remark." His wrinkled face, with its beaked, talcumed nose and rheumy eyes and sagging dewlaps, became red with inspiration. " 'This day forever to me holy is,' " he warbled, " 'pour out the wine without restraint or stay, pour not by cups but by the bellyful, pour out to all that wull, and sprinkle all the posts and walls with wine, that they may sweat, and drunken be withal.' " Forever unmarried, he was touched to the heart always by marriage, and he thought of the unbearable tenderness of wedding nights and lovely, palpitating throats, nipples in the moonlight pink as unripe plums, and he ended the recitation with a dry catch in his voice: " 'The whiles . . . the maidens do their carol sing . . . to which the woods shall answer . . . and their echo . . . ring.' "

Peyton put her glass down and applauded. The doctor made a courteous bow and noisily blew his nose. Harry, in the meantime, had gone off for a minute, for a waiter had come up to tell him that Mr. Loftis wanted to see him on the back porch. "He drunk and ravin', man. You bettah hustle on out dere!" and the whites of his eyes had been wild crescents of doom, but neither Peyton nor the doctor had noticed all this. More of the guests were leaving now. They had said their final good-bys to Peyton and so, with coats and hats in their arms, they stood around in the hallway, ready to thank Milton and Helen for a grand time, but Milton and Helen were not in sight. At the punchbowl, though, there was still heavy business; in one shadowy corner, their champagne glasses recklessly upraised, slopping over, a young couple embraced. In another corner Monk Yourtee, abandoned by his wife, sang, "Friendship . . . friendship" with a very drunk girl named Polly Pearson; her string of rhinestones broke suddenly and Stonewall burst from the kitchen and scrambled to retrieve them, like a squirrel among popcorn.

Briefly alone with Peyton, the doctor turned and took her hand. "You look sad, my dear—you need wine and poesy. What's wrong?" A look of sorrow had come to her eyes; she put her hands over them, just for an instant, a curious, sweet gesture, thought the doctor, full of infinite distress, as if she were trying to wipe something away. "What's wrong, my dear?" he said gently.

"Ah . . ." she said in disgust.

"Tell Doc?"

"Ah . . ." She looked straight ahead, then gazed about the room, slowly, precisely, and it seemed to the doctor that she was surveying all this—room and windows, fading sunlight, rowdy guests—for the first, perhaps last time (there seemed to be little difference), through eyes no more dim with champagne than with some pure agony. It came as a troubling shock to the doctor, for not ten seconds ago she had seemed the very spirit of gaiety, and it sobered him. "What's the matter, my dear?" he asked again.

She turned on him her grave brown eyes. "Oh, Doc," she said in a hopeless voice, "if you only knew. If I could only tell you."

"You can tell me——"

She smiled. Her nose arched, her eyes sparkled, small pretty dimples came at the corners of her mouth; it was a classical smile, the doctor thought, and simply beautiful, but it was no good. It was a cover-up, and valiantly, through his whiskied brain, he tried to think: what could trouble the girl on this day? Epithalamion. But he couldn't make it out. Besides, she was going on about something: "I distinctly believe, Doc, that the race is headed for destruction. You know—" and she put one hand on his shoulder with a sort of drunken intimacy, making him feel ticklish inside—"you know what the trouble is, Doc? You know, it's not too much money at all. I have oodles of Communist friends in New York who'd make you believe that if they could. 'S not distribution of wealth or balance of population or any of those idiotic dusty things. You know what it is? It's time and remembrance, that's what it is. It's people having a little humble—humility about not what happens now, at this moment, but all the things that went before. In themselves, I mean. I mean . . . I mean, Doc, just little things like coming home. If you could just know how I love this place. I mean, the bay and the beach and the mimosa trees. Even this house, as Thomson, Howell, and Woodburn-architected as it is. Even this house——"

"Yes," he said, nodding his head. "Yes, I see, my dear."

"It's not old, this old house, is it? It's big and commonplace and middle-class, but I love it. I was born here." She raised her hand to her eyes again, in the same sweet, distressed gesture, and shuddered. "Oh, Doc," she cried, "I'm sorry. I'm sorry to talk like this. Do you see what I mean? Do you? Tell me you do, now, because I haven't got much time. I mean, not that someone should ever want to come home to stay, but that just to be understood for what you are, neither to be loved to death nor despised just because you're young. Do you understand me, Doc?" Her eyes were bright with tears and he patted her on the shoulder, thinking that indeed he did understand her—a little, at least—for at this moment, past her head and framed in near-by doorways, he saw them: Milton and Helen.

Ah, he thought suddenly, so that's what it is.

There they stood, so close together, yet unaware of each other because of the noise. In one doorway—the door to the kitchen— Loftis was struggling to steady himself, his face flushed and violent, talking to the bridegroom. The doctor couldn't hear what they said, saw only one of Loftis' hands propped tense and bloodless against the doorjamb, the other outstretched, describing desperate arcs in the air with his glass. But it was his face which was so startling, so troubling: limber-jawed, twitching all over with emotion, it seemed to be the face of a man making a last plea to some adamant, in-quisitional power, and it seemed further, to the doctor's mind, the face of someone on the verge of apoplexy. It was a wild and agonized face and the doctor, made suddenly cold sober, wondered what on earth Loftis could be talking about, for he was certainly not angry *at* the bridegroom, who listened intently, and with a worried look on his face.

Now at the other door, not more than five yards away, stood Helen. The doctor saw her pull the coat tightly about her shoulders, although it was stuffy in the room, even hot. On the phonograph there was a sudden blare of music, violently incongruous—"The Stars and Stripes Forever"—and from some of the loitering guests came a chorus of whistles, trumpetings, shouts for attention. The music fell on the room like boiling water; Peyton started, the doctor, too: he felt her squeeze his arm and he wanted to turn and comfort her, even protect her, but, his gaze on Helen, he felt stupefied by apprehension. He watched her suspiciously. She stood in the doorway without moving a muscle in her body. With her arms at her side stiff as sticks, only her head moved and her blue, crazy eyes: it was like watching an adder, thought the doctor; surely she was ready to strike. None of the other guests seemed to have noticed her, and this fact, too, increased his feeling of impending peril: of a snake which lies tranquil, cold as ice, save for its head motionless at the rim of some thicket, prepared as if by divine intuition to bite not the wary but the unaware. Peyton hadn't seen her. Nor did she see, as the doctor did, Helen's gaze dart and move once more from the walls to the punchbowl to the windows, linger momentarily upon the last fading light, and then fasten like teeth upon Peyton's back.

It can't happen, the doctor thought, it can't. And he knew Helen had gone off, knew it just as well as he had known for twenty years—having probed and prodded and palpated that tortured and self-torturing flesh until it was as familiar as his own—that there *would* come a time when all her fury and envy became unbottled—*poof!* like an avenging genie risen black as smoke from the confining, torturing lamp. Only, *not now*, he thought, *please, not now*. It was too late, he was too old, he had worked too goddam hard and long at becoming a man of good will to want to see a sweet, tender life such as this one smashed out like an insect. *No*, he thought, *no*, and he turned desperately to Peyton, to comfort her, to protect her, saying with a laugh: "Ah, my love, don't be sad." And he took her hand, feeling her new gold ring: " 'Her finger was so small the ring would not stay on, which they did bring; it was too wide a peck——' "

"Oh, that!" Peyton said. "How did you remember? I just love the seventeenth century! I——"

He saw Helen approach. " 'They are all gone into the world of light!' " he said. " 'And I alone sit ling'ring here . . .' "

" 'Their very memory is fair and bright,' " Peyton said. " 'And my sad thoughts doth clear . . .' "

" 'Either disperse these mists . . .' " the doctor said, tightening his grip on her arm. "Something, something, something, something . . ."

Peyton turned and saw Helen bearing down on them. "Yes. 'Or else remove me hence unto that hill, Where I shall need no glass.' "

Months later, when he tried to put in some sort of ordered sequence the events of the day, Loftis found himself hopelessly baffled. It was

305

as if he were trying to relive an experience in time, with the minutes all scrambled, an experience in which he was unable to tell whether one precise event followed, or antedated, another; whether he had talked to Harry *before* he developed the misery over Peyton, or afterward; when he had tipped the waiters, after Peyton left or before—had he tipped them at all? Whether, in fact, the reception had not preceded the ceremony; and for that matter had Peyton really come home? Had it not been all a drunken and terrible dream? When he came right down to it, he actually made little effort to remember the day; with its peculiar quality of dementia it seemed not a commonplace and civilized social event but a nightmare in vivid technicolor, with no director and clumsy actors, and wired—rather than for words and music—for one vast and febrile noise. Mainly, he recalled his anxiety: how, with his awareness of coming disaster, a fever had risen in his body, making him hot all over, and his underwear was drenched with sweat. This was the primary symptom—the fever—followed by a raw scraping in the back of his throat, which announced the arrival of a bad cold. It *was* a bad one, too, and it laid him low, prostrate and helpless, for a week afterward. Then there had been his crashing, outrageous drunkenness. Bad enough because of the frightful events—past, present and those he knew must come—his desire to drink, to drown himself utterly as in the sea or beneath sand, became even more powerful when, talking in the doorway to Harry, he found himself making a total, impossible ass of himself. At that point—by, most likely, an inaccurate count—he had drunk seven glasses of champagne, three shots of whisky straight, the Lord knew how much of the abominable pineapple punch. The whisky he had taken on the back porch alone, in a daze. And even then he knew that this course was perilous, not only in itself but because for eight months he had abstained, at least been moderate, and his poor, unsuspecting stomach just wouldn't be able to take it. Which was true. Because, talking to Harry, he felt not only the gradually encroaching symptoms of his anxiety—the fever, the itching throat, the sweating and the trembling and the dreadful weakness in his limbs—he felt not only these, but a new terror: the pains of his headlong flight toward helpless drunkenness: his stomach which, because he hadn't eaten (even a crumb of the cake), had already begun to protest, contracting in spasms that he imagined were worse than those of a womb in labor; his mouth, nervelessly, numbly drawn down; and this finally—the asinine, crazy things he heard himself saying to Harry. And although later he only faintly remembered what he had told Harry, he recalled himself standing

306

there wildly flailing his arms, saying things that were inept, maudlin, unhinged, and knowing then that these very words must drive him on and on toward newer, blinder, more helpless depths of drunkenness.

Yes, he could recall part of the moment, at that. He remembered at first his patronizing tone. He remembered saying something about Jews, how he liked them, something about a warm quality they had which Gentiles really didn't possess. He remembered Harry's eyebrows going up at this, remembered thinking *What the hell am I trying to convince him about?* But he also remembered that he couldn't stop talking about Jews, that he felt compelled to go on making Harry think he was a grand guy. Idiotically, gratuitously. And Harry remaining polite, intently receptive all along. He remembered saying, "Virginia has a lot to learn, but we like Jews down here as well as anyone else." Wanting to bite his tongue off at that, but compelled to go on and on laboring the subject more drunkenly each moment, a man tied to a runaway cannon.

And through all this, he later recalled, he had known that this wasn't what he wanted to talk about at all. He recalled standing there, watching Peyton from time to time out of the corner of his eye, watching her through the drunken mists of his own rising fever; she faded, sank back from his sight, wavered, as if he were regarding her as a double image thrown back through the waters of an aquarium. And he remembered then that she was irretrievable, lost forever, that he had no claims on her anymore. That she not only had rejected him, crushed him utterly, but that now she was owned by someone else. Him. Harry. The gentle, quiet, understanding Jew who stood before him, shifting his weight patiently from foot to foot, his shrewd, almond eyes seeming to understand Loftis' every gesture. And he recalled how his heart had been suddenly wrung with pain when he thought of this boy, and then thought of this boy and Peyton together. So then he had been about to say something, to reach out and tell this boy that he must take care of Peyton and love her always, for she was the dearest thing on earth. And it had been this precise instant that he saw Helen march across the room, ignoring the guests who got in her way, and walk up to Peyton and the old doctor and whisper something into Peyton's ear.

So then he knew it. It was a final moment, signifying everything. A whisper, no more, but a whisper of doom—brutal, unequivocal, in logic indivisible. How did he know? It needed no explanation. He knew it as well as his name, the fingers on his hand, the fact of breathing. He knew what this gesture spelled so well that it seemed to exist quite outside of time: he felt (and this was one of the few events of the day which later lingered clearly in his memory) that he could have predicted this scene—doctor and Peyton and the bending, whispering Helen—ten years ago, or twenty, it made no matter. It was just a gesture as inevitable as death. But he must have been paralyzed, for later, when he tried to remember what he had done at that moment, or had attempted to do, he recalled that he had been able to do nothing at all. Had he had a gun he felt he might have shot Helen then, watched her fall slain and bleeding among the guests and the shattered glasses and the crumpled pink napkins. Yet this was not really true, he realized, for, since he had not even made a word or motion in her direction, how could he have pulled the trigger of a gun? So he watched them in silence. Part silence, that is. Because, frightened to his soul, he couldn't tolerate it quietly. He had to turn sideways to Harry and say thickly, incoherently: "There've been too many nuts around here, son. You gotta take care of her and love her because no one's ever loved her right." He grabbed him by the arm, saying something like: "Harry, be good to her! For Christ's sake try to understand her——" But the last scene had begun. He turned and watched them leave the room together, Peyton weaving behind Helen past the glass-littered tables and the chairs and the bewildered guests, as compliant and submissive as Mary's little lamb. He saw them go upstairs.

Then Harry, too, was gone—somewhere, Loftis didn't know. Once he thought he saw him talking to the Cuthberts, or perhaps it was the Houstons; he was unable to remember how Harry had broken away from him, or why. As for himself, time and motion slowed down to the most creaking rattletrap pace, and from then on he seemed to be borne along through the festive rooms like something drunken and frightened and old. He kept up appearances, smiled, cheered the departing guests on their way with a chuckle and a hand pat and an occasional big hoorah, but all the time he was thinking, wondering, *What will they do to each other?*

At one point he met Cherry Pye, who had a fat rosy face and crumbs of hors d'oeuvres on his lips, which Loftis wanted desperately to wipe off.

"Betcha Poppy's gonna have a hot time inna old town tonight!" he mumbled through a mouthful of something, waving his glass.

"Yessiree!" Loftis said loudly.

"Yessiree *Bob!*"

"Drink 'er down, Cherry Pye, drink 'er down!"

"Drink 'er down, Poppy Loftis, drink 'er down!"

They embraced, singing, clinking glasses, and Monk Yourtee and Polly Pearson trotted up, joining them in a song.

Across the room six guests lingered to shamble gluttonously around the serving table. These were the eaters; the drinkers, most of them younger, gathered in clusters about the walls to talk, to make quartets of their own, and Loftis, singing in a quavering tenor—for the song was pitched too high—heard the high, hoarse soprano of Dora Appleton and suddenly broke away. "Come back, Milt!" shouted Cherry Pye.

He teetered across the room, warily, conscious of his grin, spilling champagne. Now in the embrace of new music, new friends, he put his arm about Dora, who, having been kissing publicly, had lipstick smeared on her face; together with Campbell, the strange, pale boy with eyes like violets and huge, transparent ears, they made a trio. Loftis had one hand on Dora's breast while they sang: " 'I'm the reluctant dragon.' "

"What a sweet voice, ol' handsome!" Dora yelled. Campbell simpered prettily, but it was Loftis she had shouted to, and he tickled her in the ribs.

"Such a cute girl," he said.

"Ol' handsome."

"Sweetie-pie. Give Poppy a kiss, too." Her face drifted toward him. In despair he kissed her, the rouged, smeary mask, and felt her tongue touching his, with the sweet taste of whisky. Blushing, aching with fever, he moved away. Darkness fell across the lawn. At the door he shook hands with Dr. Holcomb, who had his coat and scarf on; he heard—thought he heard—the doctor say, "Take care of her, Milton," while the old eyes watered gravely, and he wondered, *Take care of whom?* But the doctor had gone: the door shut to behind him, there was a swirl of chill air in the foyer, and Loftis, his glass fallen from nerveless fingers, looked down to survey the splinters and the whisky creeping across the rug.

His heart gave way. He sank weakly down onto a chair. There was no doubt about it, no doubt at all. He had to do something. Here alone he could hear the diminishing noise of the reception, weary laughter, weary songs: " 'I adore you, ba-by mine . . .' " they sang, and the winds of evening which rustled outside seemed to sweep the notes along like withered leaves. Two girls passed snickering down the hall. In the darkness they didn't notice him;

one stepped on his toe. Through the window the moon shone bright as a flashlight, and the evening seemed filled with a blue and shifting dust. On the water there were leaves and floating gulls, the wrinkled shadow of a breeze. Yes, there was no doubt about it; this was the time for decision. And he thought: So maybe all my life I've been wrong. Maybe I did cause all this. Then Helen was right. I killed with kindness the only thing I ever cared for, really. Maybe we're all just too highstrung, like Father said. They should have never put the idea of love in the mind of an animal. . . .

He was seized with a violent fury. "No," he said aloud, staggering to his feet, "no, goddamit!" He tramped through the spilled whisky, weaving toward the stairs. A blaze of light met him at the living room, shrill, weary voices, still singing, and then Edward, quite as drunk himself, who put a hand on his arm; Loftis went on. "Where ya goin', ol' buddy byddyroe? Le's have a smile from the old daddy himself! And a big, *big* han'shake——" And he threw his arm about Loftis' shoulder. "Y' know," he went on, "'s good thing I came to Peyton's nuptials. T' see all zeze people. Y' know if we were on a desert island you 'n I an' zeze people, why, you an' I'd be president and vice-president respectively. On accounta——"

"You just go straight to hell, Edward," Loftis muttered, shoving him away. He plodded on upstairs. In the hallway it was dark and silent. The sounds from below came up muted and indistinct. For a moment he stood at the head of the stairs with his nose in the air, sniffing, reconnoitering. He couldn't see a thing but in the darkness shapes and shadows reeled indiscriminately, and he had to steady himself against the wall. He felt his heart pounding, and a cold dread. He pulled himself together some and moved down the hall on precarious tiptoe, trying to avoid knocking things over. Finally from Helen's room he heard voices. A voice, rather: Helen's. He stole near the door. It was closed but not locked, and a thin wedge of light fell onto the hallway floor. He heard Peyton say, "Words, words, words—why don't you get to the point?" Later he was unable to recollect, because of the fog in his mind, just what came next, but it went something like this:

Helen's voice, unemotional, polite, but direct: "That's what I'm trying to tell *you*, my dear. No, I didn't expect you not to drink some. Do you think I'm a member of the W.C.T.U.? Certainly not. But my dear girl, it's this other thing that matters to me. Really, Peyton, after all we've done to plan this affair for you, do you think——"

Peyton's voice cut in angrily: "Do I think what? What? Will you please explain?"

"This business with your father. Do you really think you have any right to treat him like you have? After all he's done for you? I saw what happened just now. Really, Peyton, you needn't pretend that it didn't happen or no one saw it. Because I saw it. I *saw* it, I tell you."

"*What?*"

"Just this." Her tone grew short and harsh. "Just this. Lashing out at him like that. In front of everybody. I wasn't the only one who saw it. Chess Hegerty saw it, and the Braunsteins. Everybody. After all I've planned. After everything I've tried—not tried but *had* to forget about you, in order to make this whole affair come off right. I said to myself, 'Well, I'll forget everything that she's done.' For the sake of morality, for the sake of Christian principles. For the sake of everything decent I'll overlook the things you've done——"

"What things?"

"Never mind. I said I'd overlook them for the sake of everything decent. So you could be married properly, in your own home. The home you forsook easily, too. That was the irony. Anyway, for all these decent things, for their sake, I said I'd make this wedding a success. If it killed me. For your father's sake, too. Now see what you've done. Everyone knows you hate me. That doesn't matter. But for them to know you hate him, too! After all these years of your faking and your flattery and your seductions——"

There was a sudden thump, a creak of springs, as if someone had fallen abruptly back upon a bed. There was laughter, too, Peyton's, tense and somewhat hysterical but also muffled, the laughter of someone lying horizontal: "Oh, God, really. If that isn't the limit. Poor Helen, you've really suffered, haven't you? Poor Helen. You're a sad case, you know, and I really shouldn't be talking like this. I really should be silent and forbearing, charitable, really, but I just can't. You're such a wretched case I can't even feel pity——"

"You shut up. You respect your elders. Your parents who——"

"You can't even suffer properly," Peyton broke in, her voice solemn now; "You're like all the rest of the sad neurotics everywhere who huddle over their misery and take their vile, mean little hatreds out on anybody they envy. You know, I suspect you've always hated me for one thing or another, but lately I've become a symbol to you you couldn't stand. Do you think I'm stupid or something, that I haven't got you figured out? You hate men, you've hated Daddy for years, and the sad thing is that he hasn't known it. And the terrible thing

311

is that you hate yourself so much that you just don't hate men or Daddy but you hate everything, animal, vegetable and mineral. Especially you hate me. Because I've become that symbol. I *know* I'm not perfect but I'm free and young and if I'm not happy I at least know that someday I *can* be happy if I work at it long enough. I'm free. If I'd hung around in Port Warwick and married some simple-minded little boy who worked in the shipyard and lived in a little bungalow somewhere and came to see you and Daddy every Sunday, you'd be perfectly content. You'd have your claws in me then. I'd be obeying your precious code of Christian morality, which is phony anyway. But it's not that way. I'm free and you can't stand it——"

"You hate——"

Peyton's feet hit the floor; Loftis could hear them, the snapping, outraged heels. "I know what you're going to say! You're going to say I hate Port Warwick, Daddy, everything. Well, it's not true! I don't hate anything that you haven't forced me to hate and, damn you, you've forced me to hate you——"

Helen's voice rose on a high, hysterical wail. "You *tell* me these things and you don't know . . . you don't *know*," she cried wildly, "and you come here and make a mockery—with your—airs . . . and after all your sleeping around . . . you don't know . . . and your filthy little Jew . . ."

Loftis moved toward the door, but it was too late. The moment of silence which lasted between Helen's final word and what came next seemed to possess at once brevity and infinite length; this silence, so brief and so timeless, had, in its sense of awfulness, all the quality of a loud noise. Then Loftis heard it, a scuffling sound and a single, agonized moan, but he was still too late; he threw open the door. Peyton rushed sobbing past him into the hallway, down the stairs. He reached out for her, but she had gone like air, and he stood wobbling in the doorway, watching Helen. With her hands at her face she was moaning, but through her fingers ran trickles of blood and he looked at these, with a sort of remote and objective fascination, and paid no attention to her moans. He never remembered how long he stood there—perhaps half a minute, perhaps more—but when, sensing his presence, she removed her hands and looked at him, her lips moving soundlessly and her cheeks so dead and white beneath the raw, deep slits gouged out by Peyton's fingernails, he only said—making a bad job of it because of his perverse, whisky-thick tongue: "God help you, you monshter."

Then he went downstairs.

Did he call Dolly before Peyton left, or afterward? This part, too, he was unable to reconstruct with any accuracy, only there was a time, he remembered, some minutes later, when he was *holding* Peyton, holding her to his breast while she wept, saying, "That's all right, baby. That's all right, child. That's all right, baby." Over and over.

She had her coat on. Her bags were in the hallway beside her. When Harry, to whom he'd given the keys to his car, backed it out of the garage, they'd be ready to go.

The things he could think to say now were impersonal, futile. "Tell him to leave the keys with the man at the ferry. I know him. I'll pick up the car tomorrow. I'll send your presents."

She brightened up a little, erased her tears with powder from a compact. "O.K.," she said. "I'm sorry, Bunny. I'm really sorry, aren't you? Things'll be better someday." She gazed around the dark hallway with a lost look. "We don't have any whisky. Do you——" He went to the kitchen and got a pint from one of the colored boys. She put it in her bag.

He bent down to kiss her. She didn't move when he kissed her cheek, her ear, her hair. He kissed her on the mouth. "Don't——" she whispered, pushing him away. "Bunny dear . . . sober up."

Then he and she both, somehow, and Harry, were all propelled toward the porch in a shower of cheers and yells, falling rice. "Good-by . . ." everyone shouted, "good-by . . . good-by . . . good-by!" The car vanished down the driveway, followed by two frantic Chevrolets loaded with young people. He walked back to the door, almost fell down amid the slippery rice, but was caught by Monk Yourtee, who shrieked something about wedding nights, grandchildren.

"Go away."

Then, he remembered—and it suddenly all became clear—he was in the hallway, dialing Dolly again and again, a new drink beside him. He watched them from where he sat by the telephone: the last dogged guests—Polly Pearson, Monk Yourtee, Cherry Pye, the willowy boy named Campbell Someone doing an impromptu, lonesome dance, Edward passed out in a pool of champagne—and the anxiety drained away from him quickly and completely. Everyone was very happy. The music which was playing he didn't remember, but he hummed along with it, thinking of a new order in life, and when Dolly finally answered he said, "Kitten, guess who?"

"Milton!"

"That's right," he said, "it's all over over here."

"Oh, darling, what do you mean?"

"I'll get a taxi."

Unless you drive a car, to get to Florida from Port Warwick you must take the train in Richmond, which is far out of the way to the north, or go by ferry across the bay to Norfolk and take a different train from there. It is an inconvenient arrangement, and it is one of the reasons why many people of Port Warwick have become, in their geographic dislocation, perhaps more than ordinarily provincial; but it makes money for the ferry company and it is a pleasant trip, and everyone has become used to it by now. The ferry slip is not far from the railroad station, in fact adjoins it, in an atmosphere of coal dust, seedy cafés, run-down, neon-lit drug stores where sailors buy condoms and Sanitubes and occasionally ice-cream cones. The salt air is strong here. The wind rustles the weeds in vacant lots. Along the railroad track the Negro cabins are lit with the yellow glow of oil lamps, and in the moonlight a black figure appears to pull down the washing. The bus wheezes up to the ferry slip, takes on a group of drunken sailors and is gone. Silence descends. A restaurant door flaps noiselessly in the winds; water laps around the slip, and in front of the office, about the feet of some dozing, waiting passenger, a newspaper curls quietly. Occasionally a body is found in one of the vacant lots and, if the victim is Caucasian, the police begin their pogrom with sticks and flashlights and ominous sirens, causing nervousness and despondency among the Negroes.

Because it was not too cold, Peyton and Harry sat on a bench out in front of the waiting room, Peyton drinking whisky and water from a paper cup. The stars were out, and a big harvest moon. They had been sitting there for fifteen minutes, with only an old woman, who had a parrot in a cage, for company. Peyton and Harry said little to each other. Occasionally the parrot yelled, "My, my, why not!" in a cracked, sad voice, and the woman bent down and rapped on the cage with a withered hand, saying, "You hush, Spottswood, or I'll cover you." Peyton poured another drink.

A police car rolled slowly onto the slip, its siren purring adventurously and for no apparent reason at all. It halted in front of the waiting room. A puckered, elderly face and eyes blurred by steel-rimmed glasses surveyed them with cranky disapproval. The cop had a flashlight, too, which had been handed to him by his partner in the shadows, and this he turned on Peyton and Harry, although the area was flooded with light.

"You seen a big nigger around here?"

"How big?" said Harry.

"Six feet three," he recited, "light complexion, mustache, scar above the nose."

"Not lately. What's he done?"

"Slugged a old white man. Left him lyin' right in the middle of Warwick Avenue. Thought maybe somebody down here had seen him."

"Slugged him?" Harry said. "How do you know?"

"We got clues."

"What kind of clues?"

"All kinds of clues. Fingerprints. He left a footmark. Say——" He halted, regarding them suspiciously. "What are you askin' so many questions for? What business is it of your'n?"

Harry borrowed Peyton's cup and took a drink of whisky. "I'm a taxpayer," he said. "I'm interested in law and order."

"My, my," said the parrot, "why not!"

"Hush, Spottswood," the old woman said, giving the cage a crack.

Peyton poured whisky into another cup. The policeman's mouth became a severe and puritanical line. "Is that whisky you're drinking, young lady?" he said.

Peyton looked back at him unblinking. "If you'll take that silly light out of my eyes," she said, "I'll answer you."

The light snapped out. "It is," she went on, holding up the pint. " 'Old Overholt,' " she read from the bottle, " 'straight rye whisky, one hundred proof bottled in bond under government supervision at our distillery at——' "

"There's a law you know. Commonwealth of Virginia, Public Law number one fifty-eight," he said competitively, "prohibiting the display of intoxicants in a public place——"

Peyton yawned. "Oh, for heaven's sake . . ."

The cop looked at Harry. "What's your name? Let me see your draft and registration cards. I think I'll run you in——"

"His name is Harry Miller," Peyton said, rising to her feet.

"What's your'n?"

"Mrs. Harry Miller, nee Peyton Loftis."

"Nay what?"

"Peyton Loftis."

"You Mr. Milton Loftis' girl?"

"Yes."

"Well, bless my soul," he said with a wintry smile, "you must of

315

just got married. We had a special man sent out there last night, to take care of burglars. Bless my soul, you're right pretty, too."

"My, my!" the parrot croaked.

"Well," he said, "guess we'd better be shovin' along." And he waved his hand. " 'Gratulations!" The car moved slowly away, its siren moaning, vanished up the road.

"So there!" said Peyton and sat down.

He took her hand. "Loftis. Big name in these parts."

"I'm glad it's Miller now," she sighed. "*God*, I'm glad. I'd have settled for Lipchitz."

"Then you wouldn't have Miller."

"I know," she said, resting her head on his shoulder. "Then life wouldn't be worth living."

"Tut, tut, my dear, I'm not all that important."

"Yes, you are, too," she said. "Give me a drink." She sat erect suddenly, smoothing her hair. "Damn them," she said. "God damn them!" At this the old woman gave a leap in her seat, got up and moved off into the waiting room, muttering to Spottswood about liquor and profanity.

"Take it easy, honey," said Harry.

"I *won't* take it easy," she said. "I'm tired of taking it easy." She looked down at her fingernails. "I broke one when I did it. Look here." She wiggled her forefinger thoughtfully, displaying a nail broken near the end, with its red lacquer chipped away. "I went deep when I did it. I could have gone deeper if I'd wanted to, only I didn't have enough time. I could have gone right down to the bone——"

"Such talk," he put in, "you just forget about it all. Quit talking like that. You'll feel better if you just forget the whole thing——"

"I don't *want* to forget it. I want to remember it always. The blood coming out, the way the skin peeled away. I could feel the skin peeling away beneath the nail, then it broke——"

He turned toward her, gripping her by the wrist. "Now listen, Peyton," he said sternly, "you listen to me. I know how you feel and all that. But if you keep talking about it and going over it in your mind, you're going to make yourself miserable and me miserable, and the whole trip rotten——"

She turned away from him with a sniff, draining her cup. "Cut it out. You sound like Uncle Wiggly."

They sat in silence for a moment, fidgeting, suddenly chilled and testy. Above them Mars rose in its course, hung pink as a gumdrop above a plump and amiable moon. A few cars rolled onto the dock, nosing up like dogs against each other's bumpers. Across the water, silhouetted against the lights of Norfolk, the ferry approached, tooting importantly. Harry looked up at the sky. "What a wedding."

Peyton said nothing, poured herself another drink.

"Look," he said, "take it easy on that bottle. Part of it was nice, though, honey. The service, I mean. I liked Carey Carr. And that old fellow—what was his name?—Houston. And your old man."

"He's an ass."

"No, I don't think so. He was stewed to the eyes and confused. I think he thought you had attacked him, rejected him or something. He's not an ass, he was just sad——"

"He's an ass. He's lived fifty years in total and utter confusion, made a mess out of his life."

"Don't be too bitter, baby——"

"Bitter!" she cried, "don't be bitter, you say. How can I be anything else when I see where his kind of life's led him? How can I be anything else? Don't you see—he's never been beyond redemption, like Helen. That's the terrible part. Can't you see? She was beyond hope I guess the day she was born. But Daddy! He's had so much that was good in him, but it was all wasted. He wasn't man enough to stand up like a man and make decisions and all the rest. Or to be able to tell her where to get off. And that idiotic woman he's been messing around with all his life. What a farce! I'll bet he goes back to her."

"So——"

"What do you mean, *so?* So it's awful, Harry. That's what. I don't mean I have any righteous feeling about him and her. God knows she's better than that . . . that *harpy!* But isn't it awful? Aren't things bad enough in the world without having him crawl back to that idiot? Oh, I feel so sorry for him. Don't you see the trouble—?"

"Yes——"

"You do not. For heaven's sake, Harry, don't be so Christlike. Quit trying to spare my feelings. Tell me what you think of them. Tell me you despise them as much as I do! Tell me. Use your head, Harry. Go on and say it!"

"No, I——"

She jerked away from him. "Oh, honest to God, you're impossible." And with mustering despair he watched her getting drunk, frantic and unreasonable. The ferry came, warped into the slip with unhappy squeals against the pilings. They assembled their bags, paid a Negro fifty cents to help take them aboard. On the enclosed upper deck,

317

to which they ascended without saying a word to each other, there was a harsh light and an overheated smell. They sat down on the rattan bench, still without speaking. The windows were frosty with steam. Other passengers straggled in—a middle-aged couple, two sleepy soldiers, an overalled youth with pimples, the old woman with the parrot. Spottswood was now covered up, and as she passed by the woman glanced at them reproachfully; then she sat down at the far end of the deck. A juke box was playing somewhere, and behind a counter, selling soft drinks and hot dogs and souvenirs—*Come to Virginia*, the ashtrays read, *Cradle of the Nation*—stood a young man absorbedly picking his nose. He wore the air of overwhelming tedium people have when, though hardly stirring from their tracks, they move miles each day, and when Harry asked him for ginger ale, the bottle was warm.

"It's warm."

"It's all we got."

"But it's warm."

"Take it or leave it."

"Here, baby," Harry said to Peyton, "mix it with this. Or on second thought," he added, pulling the bottle from her coat, "maybe you'd better wait until we get on the train. We've got two hours yet, you know."

She looked up at him with red, weary eyes. "O.K. I'll just finish this one."

He sat down beside her again and she rested her head against his shoulder. He put an arm around her, murmuring "Sweetheart," but she said nothing. From beneath the deck there was a throbbing; the boat moved out of the slip, past an arm of the peninsula where the gas tanks loomed up bleakly in the darkness, past a light buoy with its winking red eye, and on into the bay. The juke box was playing "Frenesi." One of the soldiers sprawled out on the bench across from them and went to sleep. Presently Peyton said, "Harry. Where did you go?"

"When?"

"When she came and took me upstairs. Why weren't you there?"

"I was talking to your father."

"But I saw you talking to someone else, too. Just when I left. Some girl or other. Polly Pearson."

"She's quite a kid," he said. "She thinks the world of you——"

Peyton pulled away from him, digging into his wrist with her hand. "That's not the point, Harry! Don't you see—I *needed* you then. If

318

you'd been there maybe it would have been different. *You* could have done something. But you weren't there. You left me just like you always do. When I needed you. *Why* didn't you come and rescue me? Didn't you *see——*"

He made a soothing noise. "No, honey, now listen. Please don't give me a hard time about all this. I'm on your side, baby, believe me. Really. Just don't raise hell now; this is our honeymoon, unquote. If I had known, it'd been different, but I didn't know, I didn't realize——"

She snatched the bottle from his hand, poured out some whisky, drank it down savagely. She turned to him, her eyes inflamed, not very pretty, and with the old despair again he prepared himself for a harangue, thinking bitterly: And how about me? Was this wedding a picnic for me? It had been months since she'd been like this, and he'd thought he'd straightened her out, but no: now, as at all those early parties in the Village, she was taking out on him—when he had done nothing at all—all her grief. "Can't you keep your mind off these girls? Good *God*, Harry, on our wedding day! With all these other things happening, too. When I needed you. Do you think I'm just someone you can walk off and neglect and forget? You've done it before and you'll do it again, I know, and we're going to have a rotten, rotten time if you don't watch out."

"Peyton, don't be absurd."

"I'm *not* being absurd. It's all the truth. It's always when I *need* you like that that you——" But he was no longer listening; he shut off her words from his mind, neatly and completely, as if he had turned a switch. It was the only thing to do because, since there was, despite her claims, no truth to what she had been saying, he couldn't hope to combat her frightful illogic with phrases like, "Peyton, don't be absurd." He thought he'd had it licked, too, this kind of perverse, crazy talk, and now he felt weary and sad and disappointed. He stopped up his mind with pleasanter thoughts, thinking of Florida, watched the parrot woman nod and drowse and wake with a start. The horn blew, hollow and mournful, above them, and now Peyton, somewhat pacified by his quietness, was saying more softly, "All I want you to do is watch out for me. I'm not a nagger really, or a shrew. I'm sorry for what I said, darling. I married you because I need you."

He looked into her eyes. "Need?"

"I mean——" She struggled to say something.

"Need?" he repeated.

"I mean——"

"Need? Love?"

She said nothing.

"Love? Love?" he said bitterly, holding her arms.

She burst into tears. He let her cry quietly against his shoulder for a while, and held her hand. The middle-aged woman looked at Peyton doubtfully and, when Harry gave her a dark look, primly did something with her veil. The pimpled youth watched her, too, but became suddenly embarrassed and began to gnaw dreamily at a Hershey bar. Then Peyton stopped crying and dried her tears.

"I'm sorry," she said.

"That's all right, honey," he said gently. "You'll be O.K. when we get on the train."

"Yes."

"Now let's cheer up a little, for God's sake."

"Yes." She smiled and squeezed his hand. They danced then, after considerable persuasion by Harry, in a place secluded from the other people's eyes, a sort of passageway near the juke box, behind the lunch counter, where the souvenir pennants hung in gaudy rows and steam from the coffee urn got into Peyton's hair. It was cramped and crowded; occasionally they ran into the fire hose but when they did so, tilted off-balance, he bent down and kissed her, running his hand shamelessly, lovingly, up and down her thigh. She giggled and kissed him back with parted lips, the light making shiny sparks on her perfect white teeth. Once she nibbled at his ear and when it began to hurt he pinched her on the tail. The music, a sort of boogie-woogie, was full of trembling piano notes and a groaning bass; they played the record twice. An old Negro, a beggar with a coonskin cap and a mouthful of blackened gums, hobbled over from the colored section to watch them, to clap his bleached palms feebly in rhythm and to beg for a dime. Harry felt happy, gave him all his change, which was nearly a dollar, and received the blessings of Jesus. Peyton had another drink. They danced some more, this time to "Frenesi," and they were borne down the passageway like feathers on a gale of bawling trombones. The boat, hitting a swell, rocked beneath them, but of this Harry was not so much aware as of Peyton, sagging against him now, confused in her steps, her head heavy against his shoulder.

"What's the matter, honey?" He looked down at her, raised her chin. She was weeping helplessly and without a sound, her mouth drawn down in anguish.

"Oh, sweetheart——" he said.

She shook her head. He sat her down on a box full of life preservers. "Sweetheart," he said again, moving his hand against her cheek.

"They just never learned," she sobbed, "they just never learned."

But soon once more he had soothed her. She sat pale and shivering on the box, a little sick at her stomach, as she said. Harry had to go to the men's room. He patted her on the shoulder. When he came back she was gone.

He looked around for her, with a growing dread. He asked the middle-aged couple where she had gone; they didn't know. Nor did the sleeping soldier, who gazed up at him with one eye and belched. The boy behind the counter said she had gone out on deck. Harry tried to hide his fear—which was just nervousness, he began to tell himself, over and over—but at the end of the passageway he threw open the doors furiously, to be met by a salty and glacial breeze.

"Peyton!" he cried desperately. "Peyton, Peyton!"

The deck was empty. He ran to the forward part of the boat, bruising himself once on the davit of a lifeboat. Then he ran aft down the other side—filled each instant with a larger horror—to the stern, and it was here that he found her, standing placidly against the rail. He put his arms around her waist, squeezing it.

"Your heart's beating so," she said quietly.

"Yes."

"What's the matter?"

"Nothing."

Peyton was silent for a while. Then she leaned forward and propped her elbows on the rail, spitting over the side.

"Ladies shouldn't spit," she said.

"That's right."

"Look at it," she said, "it *is* dark and lovely. I wonder if it's cold."

"Don't you——"

"Don't what?" She seemed calmer now.

"Nothing. It's cold out here."

"Look there," she said, "there it goes." He looked up. From the rail they could see it—or imagined they could—among a chain of encircling lights upon the farthest shore—the house, surrounded like all the others by oaks and mimosas and willows. The streetlights, obscured by intervening, tossing trees, twinkled like stars. Harry rubbed the bruise on his arm. Then he leaned down and kissed her—sick and solemn as she was—on the ear, with as much love, he imagined, as ever a man had summoned.

"Which house is it? I can't tell."

"Oh, nuts, I can," she said. "They aren't all alike."

West of the cemetery great clouds rose up in the sky; they sent long shadows across the land and wind through the trees. A few miles away it was raining; thunder crashed over the cornfields and the highway, there was lightning, too, far off but menacing, a brief white streamer blown through the gathering wind: Dolly was aware of these things about the weather, these and the sudden chill she had, pulling her raincoat about her shoulders, plus the fact that there in the limousine, drawn up in front of a brick chapel the color of dried blood, she was quite alone. She was surrounded by tombstones. A hideous angel looked at her vacantly with oval, alabaster eyes, flourishing a wreath over the name of McCorkle. Against another tomb a bunch of brown, dead roses, propped up in a wire stand, gave a heave in the wind, and came down on the roadway with a clatter. Dolly jumped nervously in her seat, blew her nose into a wet piece of Kleenex and cried some more. No one now could assess her misery; how could he have been so rotten? And it had been so quick and cruel: "You just stay right here." Just like that.

There was a new groan of thunder, ending in a gigantic crackle. The very air seemed ripped apart. She jumped again, looking fearfully out of the rear window. The storm came on across the distant cornfields, sweeping before it dust and debris; borne on the blast a squadron of crows scooted frantically, wings flapping like windmills, filling the air with their dismal cries. In the farmyard two cows galloped clumsily for shelter, the chapel door began to swing, another wreath fell down in the road. Dolly hid her face in her hands, between sobs sucking for air, and clawed blindly for the handle to roll up the window. It was stuck. She moved over in her seat away from the storm: how could he be such a monster? She looked up at the chapel into which, twenty minutes ago, though it seemed to Dolly centuries, the party had disappeared. She could see nothing, hear no music, no organ or anything: would they never come out? Peyton's coffin, Milton, Helen looking like a ghost, the fat preacher, Mr. Casper, his stupid assistant, that old nigger—all of them had vanished into the place, leaving her behind and alone; it was, she thought, with an effort at fantasy, as if they had disappeared into the gates of hell. She felt rocked by dread, she was getting sick, although in some vaguely whimsical fashion one thought supported her in her suffering: she was the only one who was still sane. Helen was crazy, the

322

preacher was crazy, and Milton—how else explain the way he'd been acting? "You just stay there!" Violently, furiously, as if by her presence in there she'd be defiling the temple.

Now, as though shades were being drawn down in her heart, she was tormented by one single dread, and it became larger and blacker than the storm. Not that Helen would take him back—something told her that this could never happen—but that Milton wouldn't return to the car, today, to her. This, in its temporariness, was her greatest fear: she knew, or thought she knew, that Milton was going through a great, tragic crisis—hence his wild actions, his mean words, his hostility. Of course the poor darling was deranged, what with Peyton and all. She knew that when all this blew over he'd come back to her, would apologize for his brutishness today, and his neglect, and for making her stay out in the car. She knew his moods as well as her own. But that, still demented and crazy, or whatever he was, he wouldn't return to the car today, that he'd make her drive back to town alone—humiliated in front of everyone—with the stupid undertaker and the crazy nigger: this paralyzed her with fright. No, he just couldn't do it to her.

She wept softly, listening to the moaning wind. A few drops of rain fell on the roof of the limousine; one of them, huge and soft and cold, struck her on the cheek: she moved to the center of the seat. They'd had such fine times, too; she was getting in at the club, meeting better people, and his divorce was to come through on October 21. It was so sad—but no, he wouldn't leave her: then he'd have no one, no Helen, no Peyton, no little Maudie, no Dolly-pooh. Which was what he'd called her when, nights at the club, they lay awake all tired out and watched the ivy shake against the moonlight and she'd stick her finger, playfully, in his navel. Almost two years of bliss, free of that ghostly bitch. Now this. What would she do if he left her again? It was too much to think about. Now no more could she stay alone in her apartment listening to the radio, as she'd done those long months when he and Helen had been reconciled—an endless stream of Aldrich Families and Gangbusters and Contented Cows, mooing serenely only half-heard through the evenings filled with wistful tears, thrice-read newspapers, chocolate boxes empty and forlorn. The heartaches were too much, as were the times when she ventured out, to go to the bank or to her lawyer's for Pookie's criminally dwindling alimony checks, her face averted from the stares of those who might see, who might say: "Poor woman. Milton left her stranded high and dry." She'd have to leave town, go to Norfolk or Richmond, or back to Emporia and sit by her mother's bedside, watch the withered, wasting flesh of multiple sclerosis, look at her twitch and moan, change her clothes when her sphincter gave way; it was sad country, unsophisticated and dull and awful; she'd sit in the parlor and stare at the peanut vines stacked up in the fields like big brown thumbs, the peanuts and the red earth and in December the sad, rain-drenched cotton, looking as if it had already been used.

There was a crackle of thunder. She gazed up from her Kleenex. It was an odd sight. Emerging from the chapel, her hair blown by the wind, Helen stood cool and erect on the steps, one hand lightly resting on Carey's arm. Beside her—though Dolly couldn't hear his words—Loftis was saying something. His eyes had the horror-filled, yearning look they had had all day. Then—and a pang of grief such as she had never known before stuck her heart—she saw Helen turn abruptly and smile, with a word to Loftis. She couldn't see the rest. Carey got in the way; for no reason at all he made the sign of the cross, and far off to the east the thunder rumbled and rolled, came nearer. It began to rain.

Seven

POTTER'S FIELD for New York City is on an island in the Sound, half a mile east of the Bronx and just inside the city limits. The island is named Hart's, after a deer which, in the later days of the English settlement, was seen to swim out to the place from the mainland and apparently to establish residence there, among the scrub-oak and willow groves. The hart was later shot, so the legend goes, by a man named Thwaite who rowed out to the island in a skiff, with a big gun and a hankering for venison. It was this person, a gentleman of preternatural modesty, who named the island Hart's, rather than Thwaite's, and it was also he who made a tidy living for years by rowing picnickers out to the place; at that time there were sandy beaches there, woods, gentle groves—a perfect place, in short, to rest yourself, if you lived in the eighteenth century.

As the city expanded, however, it became necessary to find a newer and larger place to dispose of the friendless, nameless dead. Up until the middle of the last century, when Forty-Second Street was suburban and sheep still nibbled placidly around Columbus Circle, this purpose had been served by the old Pauper's Burial Ground, which occupied what is now part of Washington Square. The dead do not remain long dead in big cities, or perhaps they become deader; at any rate the markers were torn down, the square filled in with new earth and sidewalks laid across. They have become twice unremembered, those sleepers; once, though many bore no names, they had at least a sunny plot of ground. Now no one can mark them, and the nurse-maids strolling along McDougal Street, aware only of the birds and the boys and the dusty April light, cannot know even the fact of those who rest beneath the asphalt—their bones shaken by the subways—and await the resurrection.

The first person to be buried in the new Potter's Field on the island was an orphan named Louisa Van Slyke, who died in Charity Hospital in 1869. Many followed her; there close to half a million souls have been laid to rest, a lot of them nameless, all of them forgotten.

The island itself is bleak and unprepossessing. There are islands like this, serving all sorts of cheerless but necessary municipal functions, near every great city in the world—islands in the Thames and Danube and the Seine, and in the yellow waters of the Tiber. This one, perhaps because it is American, seems more than necessarily dreary. No blade of grass grows here, only weeds. On the south end of the island stands a sewage disposal plant. North of this is a city detention home, a great mass of soot-stained brick and iron bars, where derelicts and drunks and the less-involved dope addicts are "rehabilitated." Moss and flakes of pale green lichen creep along the walls. In the treeless shade of the courtyards, flowering in crannies below shuttered windows, are chickweed and ghostly dandelions. Still farther north of this jail, separated from it by a quarter mile of dusty, weed-choked rising ground, is Potter's Field. The glens and willow-groves are gone, the picnickers and the slain deer; if you stand here on the hill beneath a dead, wind-twisted cedar, the island's only tree, you can get a good view of the land—the sewage plant and the prison and the burial ground, each recipient, in its fashion, of waste and decay.

The towers of Manhattan are faint and blue in the distance, rising like minarets or monoliths; near by on summer days yachtsmen sail their boats out of City Island, and the patterns their white sails make on the water are as pretty as kites blown about against a blue March sky. Here in the field weeds and brown, unsightly vegetation grow in thick clusters, tangled together over the numbered concrete markers. There are no proper gravestones in the meadow. Rusted strands of barbed wire traverse the field, serving no purpose, preventing no intrusion, for few people ever visit there. It's an ugly place, full of rats and spiders, and crisscrossed, because of its prominence above the water, by raw, shifting winds.

To transport bodies from the morgue they once had a tugboat; painted black, a flag at half-mast on its stern, it chugged up the East River on Thursdays. When it passed, barge captains and sailors would uncover their heads, cross themselves or murmur a prayer. Now a truck is used, and the dead no longer receive this final benediction: who would salute a truck, so green and so commonplace? The coffins are made of plain pine and these—twenty-five or thirty each week—are laid four deep in the big mass graves. There are no prayers said; city prisoners are used for the burying, and they receive a day off from their sentence for each day's work in Potter's Field. The other dead must be crowded out—those who have lain there for twenty years. Now they are bones and dust and, taking up valuable space, must be removed. Not just twice dead like the relics beneath Washington Square, they become triply annihilated: the prisoners won't let them rest, remove them—bones, rotted cerement and rattling skull—and throw them in a smaller hole, where they take up one tenth the space they did twenty years before. The new coffins are laid in precisely, tagged and numbered; in this way many souls occupy, undisturbed, their own six feet of earth for two decades.

Then all is done. The grave is covered. The prisoners load up their spades and picks, climb back into the police van, and are driven away. On a promontory near the sea the old coffins are burning, for these too must be destroyed. They make a beautiful and lonely pyre; stacked high, they burn briskly, because the wood has become well decayed. Decay flowers in the air too, ripe and fleshy, yet it is a clean decay, as natural as dying leaves; decay is being destroyed. On the broken splinters flames lick toward the remnant of a shroud, and a garland of baby's hair, preserved as in a locket all these years, is touched by the fire, shrivels away in a puff of dust. Small bones, overlooked by the buriers, become charred and fall among the weeds. A rat peeps out from a burrow, sniffs the wind, then withdraws. The afternoon lengthens and evening comes, but the burning blue odor ascends, is caught by a breeze and sweeps down among the graves, curls about the monument. It is almost as if this monument were forgotten. Who put it there is a mystery; it bears the meadow's only epitaph. It is small and cracked and mostly covered by weeds; on it the graven eyes of Christ, weathered by many storms, still burn like the brightest fires. Below these the legend, obscured by brambles and the swirling blue odor of decay, can be read: *He calleth His own by Name.*

So the darkness comes on, covering the graves and the withered cedar and the nameless dead. Lights wink on around the Sound. Rats stir in the weeds, among the graves. The smoke still ascends in the night, clean and without guilt, borne like passion with the last dust of the nameless and the unremembered, upward and upward, toward the stars.

The police were not to blame. When they came for Peyton she had no clothes on. Then they went up to the twelfth floor and looked around, found her clothes but not a scrap of identification. What else, said the spinsterish-looking man at the Department of Hospitals, where Harry went later, could they have done? It had been a routine procedure. Wait for the prescribed length of time, to allow for identification, and then ship the "individual," as he put it—in a way that made him seem to smell of formaldehyde—on out to the island. Nobody had come to identify this individual. That was that. There was no doubt, then, that this photograph they had taken was of his wife? All right, then, there were papers to fill out and he could get an undertaker (of course, at his own expense) and retrieve—"exhume," he said—the body. Through all this Harry sensed the man's weary disapproval, as if Harry were just another negligent relative, but sick with sorrow, he didn't care.

He went out with his friend Lennie and the undertaker in a hearse. Harry had hauled Lennie, half-drowning, out of the Ebro on a spring day in 1937. It had been in the middle of the fighting; he had laid Lennie beneath a pear tree and had worked over him for half an hour before Lennie, groaning and with blood on his lips, had revived. They hadn't known each other. Later they discovered they had both been born on Caton Avenue in Brooklyn, had indeed both gone to Erasmus Hall. There had been nothing heroic about the rescue; concussion from a mortar had knocked Lennie into the water, and it was just lucky that Harry had been nearby. They were in different battalions, but after that they saw each other as often as they could. Not because of the rescue so much as because they simply liked each other. Most people, on being mustered out of an army, forget the names of their associates as quickly as they do the fact that the M-1 rifle is .30 cal., gas-operated, semiautomatic, and so forth, but when Harry and Lennie left the brigade they left together, and finally were graduated in the same class at N.Y.U. Harry was quiet, almost self-effacing; Lennie had a mass of carrot-red hair and was given to outbursts of temper and moods. In between these times, though, he was humorous and quick-witted and generous; somehow he and Harry made an amiable pair. Harry appreciated Lennie's sharp mind, his tart humor and his ability as an illustrator, which was considerable. Lennie had been crippled in the left arm by shrapnel, a bad wound, making that limb almost helpless. This had caused him to become bitter often, and cynical, and much of the time he relied upon Harry's cautious, quiet wisdom to straighten him out. They lived together for a while in an apartment on Cornelia Street in the Village. They managed very well. Harry taught classes at the University and Lennie had by this time begun to receive fairly profitable commissions from some of the magazines. When the Second World War came they were both 4-F, Harry with a spot on his lung, and neither of them cared much, or felt ashamed; they had had it, forget it, as Lennie said. Then Lennie got married to a bright-eyed, loving girl named Laura Abrams, and Harry—because he needed more room anyway; his canvases, according to Lennie, were becoming dismally heroic—moved uptown to a flat on York Avenue, in the east eighties. He and Laura and Lennie had big times during the first years of the war.

Then Harry met Peyton. It was at a party in the spring of 1943 at the house of Albert Berger. Albert was a young man of twenty-six or seven who subsisted on an annuity from his rich aunt's estate, and had bad eyes. He lived in an apartment in Washington Mews with a Great Dane and some excellent jazz records. He was thin and very white. He wore rimless glasses and carefully bedraggled tweeds and something about him—perhaps his dress or the way his eyes had a tendency to cross or get out of focus or merely to close and water helplessly—gave him the look of a sick, sexless person of forty. He was uncompromisingly generous, and was free with his whisky, but arch, self-consciously intellectual and prone to hazy dogma; he was not really very interesting. He did no work except to give parties every Saturday night, when his rooms would be filled with Hindus and anthropologists and floor-lounging people who talked desperately of Chelichev and Lenin and Reichian psychoanalysis. Everybody eventually came to Albert's. Harry didn't remember how he met Albert, but he liked a few of the people who came there, and it was there that he fell in love with Peyton. She was quite drunk, aggressive and argumentative. He didn't like her at all, but she was the most beautiful girl he had ever seen, and it was not hard to fall in love with her, in spite of not liking her. Presently, at about dawn, he found himself alone with her and Albert, who, his eyes closed, a nimbus of moisture soaking the edge of his lashes, told them that a certain new war novel was a finer one than *War and Peace*. "Aaah," said Peyton. Then, unaccountably, she burst into tears and threw her head into Harry's lap. Through the blue dawn he took her home, a one-room apartment near Sheridan Square. She clung to him, breathing whisky, and kissed him violently, disconsolately on the mouth. Although he wanted to, he didn't allow himself to go in.

The next day, a Sunday, he asked her why she had wept so; he was inquisitive and frank, but gentle: what's ailing you? he asked. She said she didn't know. They took a walk along Eighth Street. The sun was out, and the strollers with baby carriages and poodles; the fairies were in, rolling famished, swooning eyes behind the barroom windows. It was a beautiful day, but Peyton had a hangover. She described her feelings; she told him she felt as if she were walking undersea, as if she were surrounded by water. For some reason he remembered that later.

They sat on a bench in Washington Square and fed nuts to the pigeons. Peyton became happy after a while and he found himself holding her hand. They talked about whether Cezanne was greater than Goya, and Van Gogh greater than Paul Klee, arguing a little but not peevishly, and when Peyton said finally that the discussion was useless, that it was silly to "live by comparisons," he was surprised— remembering her attitude the night before—that she had become so subdued and sober. He agreed with her completely. Later she said she had left school, contemptuously remarking upon it as a "dancing class down in Virginia," but she wouldn't tell him why. There was something open and withdrawn about her at the same time; there seemed to be a part of her that he couldn't reach. She complained of a headache, said again that the day seemed filled with water; perhaps she was drowning, she announced with a pretty yawn, and let her head fall against his shoulder. "Did you ever read *Winnie-the-Pooh?*" she said, and he was about to answer, but a man with a broom came by, sending the pigeons aloft like feathered rockets, and Harry leaned down and said, "You know, you're beautiful."

"Yes."

"It's true."

"Yes." She paused. "Maybe I need to be analyzed."

He didn't know why he said it. "You just need me."

"Maybe so."

At first, like Harry, Lennie didn't care for Peyton either, and he told him so. Sober, she was pleasant enough, if quiet and vague, but get a few drinks in her and look what happened: *oy,* such perversity, such a sharp tongue. It was this, Harry knew, that Lennie responded to in the wrong way: two people, each with a wry, sarcastic turn, rarely get along. Besides—Harry had to admit it—Peyton had read more than Lennie, had a more acutely intuitive appreciation of Art, which she capitalized. And beyond this, too, was the fact that Peyton was from Virginia; Lennie, with all his virtues, was still the provincial New Yorker, often myopic, to whom everything south of Washington was ignorance and oppression: it was a prejudice left over from his early days, but hard to shake off. "You're still a sucker for hot lips," said Lennie, the second time he had met her, when Harry had come back to Cornelia Street after taking Peyton home. "Don't tell me you aren't staying the night with the lady?"

"She's tired tonight."

"She should be. Can't she ever turn it off?" The four of them had drunk sherry until late. An argument had begun. Laura had said something about an ignorant person she had met, from Tennessee. This had started Peyton off: why, she said, were there so many bigots in the North? Why couldn't they realize certain obvious truths: that the South was benighted, maybe, and the people filled with guilt, but didn't they see that this was the very tragic essence of the land, that it was still going through its upheaval, still shattered by conflicts, that it was improving, rising from the ruins, and that when it emerged it would be a greater place for its very ordeal? Couldn't they see that? Lennie couldn't see that: how romantic can you get? he wanted to know. They had argued some more, and the argument had ricocheted between Peyton and Lennie, while Harry and Laura quietly drank sherry. When Peyton spoke of Virginia, Harry saw passion glowing in her eyes, and love; she was so desperate to convince them all of the wonder of her lovely, lost land.

"You could have stayed in your sweet Arcadia," said Lennie.

Peyton had halted then, for the first time in the evening speechless, her mouth working nervously, trying to make words. "No——" she said, and more firmly, "No." It was as if she were no longer aware that they were in the room: she had seen something, past the walls, either saddening or frightening. She had lost the argument. She put her finger tips against her brow; she was tired, she said. Would Harry take her home?

"Yes I'll admit she's a nice-looking tomato," Lennie said later, "but she's confused. What kind of a job is she trying to give us? First all this talk about motion in Cezanne—all right, that made sense, she was sober. Then Marx, I've never heard anything so naïve. You'd think she had a card in the Comintern already. Then fill her with sherry and she's ready to lynch every——"

"It's not that, Lennie, don't be stupid. When something half-convinces you against your will you can't stand it. She's just . . . well, as you say, confused . . . but it's not the South. There's nothing intellectual troubling her. She's young yet. It's something else the matter."

"She's weird——"

"Oh, dry up."

"Are you getting yourself in love—?"

"Maybe."

"You *are*, aren't you, sonny?"

"Maybe I am."

Harry didn't know why he wanted so much for his friend to like Peyton, except that—unsure himself of the reason for his sudden, violent attraction and still bewildered by her—he felt an obscure need for Lennie's moral support. Lennie was a shrewd one and although it was his own love that was blossoming, and not Lennie's, he wanted Lennie to back him in his own shaky conviction: she's really not weird, Lennie, there's nothing screwy about her, she's just—well, as you say . . . confused.

But Lennie came to like her, too, even to love her after a fashion, and finally, when the marriage was breaking up, to agonize over her almost as much as Harry. It had been Lennie, rather than himself, who had noticed the change in her after the first few weeks of their "co'tin'," as Peyton put it. It had been Lennie who had said, "She's changed, son; she's really right nice," using Peyton's accent; "I do believe you're doing good things for her. Watch out, though; she's the dependent kind." It had been Lennie who had noticed how little Peyton needed to drink now (though Peyton had made the shy admission, too: "You don't drink like that when you're happy," she said, kissing Harry on the nose). It had been Lennie who had seen the sudden bad turn for the worse when they came back from the wedding, who told Harry two years later, "Those first six months before you got married were the best you two ever had." Lennie had been the one who drove Peyton over to Newark, to a special psychiatrist he knew; when that didn't last a month, when, right afterward, she went off for a week to Darien with a mystery writer, it had been Lennie who had comforted Harry in his suffering, saying, "I know you love her, son. Quit talking about nymphomaniacs. That's why you got to go back anyway and stick with her and show her that you're not her father, but just *you* that love her, son, just *you*." It had been Lennie who—when Peyton, after Harry left her again in desperation, came to Cornelia Street after him, drunk, hysterical and crying about drowning—slapped her across the face to calm her, then surrounded her with his good arm, kissing her like a brother, saying, "Now you just calm down, baby, and take a look at that guy. Can't you see he's crazy about you? He won't let you drown. You just take it easy." Now finally it was Lennie to whom he had gone in grief, to help fetch her back from the island.

The undertaker was fat and dark, an Italian named Mazzetti, whom Harry, not knowing any other, had found on Bleecker Street. When he spoke he was inclined toward obsequiousness, and he had fat, lewd lips, but for the most part he kept mercifully silent. It was a hot August morning, the drive up along the river and into the Bronx seemed interminable. The three of them rode in the wide front seat. Lennie knew just what to say, and when.

"You're not going down to Virginia?"

"I don't think so."

"I didn't think you would."

"You know why."

"Yes. I wouldn't think you'd want to have anything more to do with them."

On the ferry over to the island there was another hearse, driven by a portly Negro in cutaways, who grinned suavely at Mazzetti and doffed his Homburg in a sort of professional salute. He was accompanied by a young girl, a mulatto; she ogled them coyly from the front seat. Mazzetti made no sign of recognition. "They're always after insurance," he explained sardonically. "Which wunna you gen'lemen," he added, "will kindly identify the remains?"

"I will," said Lennie quickly.

Thank you, Lennie, Harry thought, for he couldn't bear to see that beauty dead.

In the field it was sweltering, swarming with gnats. A cloud of dust rose up through the heat. Three prisoners went to work on one of the graves. Harry saw the corner of a coffin and, without knowing why, could tell that it was Peyton's. He turned away. Lennie put his hand on Harry's shoulder.

"Buck up, son," he said.

"If I'd just known what was going on inside her. Why? Why?"

"Sh-h-h, take it easy."

"I could have stopped her."

"Cut out that talk."

Harry walked alone over to one of the other graves. More than anything at all he wanted to keep from thinking of Peyton and so, dazed suddenly by the heat and the horror of the place, he stood sweating and watched two prisoners, supervised by the Negro in the Homburg, disinter a coffin. A prison guard stood by, a pinched little Irishman with a bandanna around his neck, and a sawed-off shotgun.

"It's a terrible place," Harry said.

"I been out here for twenty years."

"God. You like it?"

"It's my job."

"It must be sad."

"Yes. Sometimes it is. It's the little boxes, the babies, that get me."

"I could have stopped her."

There was a sudden cry from the opposite side of the pit. Another coffin was open and the colored girl peered down into it, her eyes goggling. "God in heaven," she squealed, in a clear Brooklyn accent, "doesn't he look terrible!"

Harry turned away, his stomach heaving. He bent over and looked down toward his shadow, regarding the earth, weeds, a cloud of gnats. No, he thought, *I just don't know whose fault it is.*

Lennie squeezed him gently on the arm. "It's her, son," he said.

Oh that my words were now written oh that they were printed in a book. That they were graven with an iron pen and lead in the rock forever. For I know that my redeemer liveth and that he shall stand at the latter day upon the earth and though worms destroy this body yet in my flesh shall I

Shall I

Oh my flesh!

(Strong is your hold O mortal flesh, strong is your hold O love.)

"I don't have enough time."

I looked up from where I was lying, staring right into his eyes; he had eyes like coughdrops, the amber kind, and little blue freckles in the white part. "I don't have enough time, Tony," I said. "That's O.K., Peyton, I got lots of time," he said. "Besides I can't," I kept saying, "we can't do it today." Besides, I was thinking I'd still been dreaming. The clock said 2:25; the dots on it were as green as cats' eyes, even in the sunlight which slanted down through the blinds. He was standing there waiting, saying nothing, but I went on thinking, trying to think, because of the dreams: how many hours have I slept? I tried to subtract 2:20 from 3:00 but it wouldn't go, twelve hours and a half or eleven, well, it didn't matter. The dots were green and luminescent, shining like my conscience, though Harry said once I was sadly lacking in conscience, he said, "You have no moral censor," and I kept looking at them, not looking at Tony, listening to the whir inside. Once I'd had a dream: I was inside a clock. Perfect, complete, perpetual, I revolved about on the mainspring forever drowsing, watching the jewels and the rubies, the mechanism clicking ceaselessly, all the screws and parts as big as my head, indestructible, shining, my own invention. Thus would I sleep forever, yet not really sleep, but remain only half-aware of time and enclosed by it as in a womb of brass, revolving on that spring like a dead horse on a merry-go-round. I could hear Tony taking off his shirt. "I been sweating," he said, "I took a bath while you was sleeping," something about how a milk route is rough work, always that. "I'm tired," he said, but . . . "if a man don't get his lovin' he'll get sick." I was trying to recover my dream. I was stuck to the sheets from sweating; I stirred a little, my pajama pants made a little sucking noise where the sweat

335

came through, the sheets all wet and wrinkled beneath. Outside against the afternoon two pigeons came floating by, braking the air, landed on the ledge outside to send up a cloud of feathers and dust from their old droppings. There was noise below on the avenue, a bus, trucks, a subway train somewhere far below, rattling the walls. I tried to recover my dream and soon the smell came up, faint and blue from the bus, of gasoline. Then it was like this, I remembered: Harry was the man with the mask, rattling a garbage bucket. This was on the rocks in the park where we used to go walking, and I was below, looking upward. I said, "Harry, you come on down from there this instant!" but he took off his mask and turned his back so I couldn't see him, threw something—old newspapers, soup cans, a dead sparrow—into the bucket, shouting, "No, darling, no, darling, I can't!" A cop came up then, I know it was a cop, but the rest I disremember, as Ella used to say; he chased us off from the rocks, smiling, a happy Irishman, and then I couldn't find Harry. There were woods somewhere and the smell of ferns; I was lying with someone near a river, I don't know who, some woman dressed in a mother hubbard and sunbonnet like the grandmother I never saw, Bunny's grandmother; she was knitting a quilt, singing songs from Stephen Foster, saying, "Don't you fret, Peyton honey," and then the cop came up again and chased us away. We ran like birds and Grandmother ran like a penguin, waddling; she was crippled, Bunny told me once. She was a Byrd and very wealthy, but Grandfather spent all the money because he had no mind for figures. I watched the light come in through the slats; a drop of sweat rolled off my brow, then I could taste it. I didn't move, watching the pigeons stir and rustle on the ledge outside, sending up dust and feathers; they rumbled inside like fools, clucking away, and I could concentrate on what they were saying, I could make them say anything: mostly "How do you do, how do you do, how do you do," and then I'd make my mind click, like you do when you know the sun's in the west but imagine that outside on the street it's morning; I'd make my mind click like that and the pigeons would say, "Look at the fool, look at the fool," or "Wanna big screw, wanna big screw," like Tony sometimes. His belt buckle clinked behind me, the same one I knew he always had on—A.C.— Anthony Cecchino, my Tony. A woman came out across the avenue, waving a mop on the fire escape; I watched the dust fly up; an air current caught it, scraps of paper and gobbets of lint, bore it higher and higher against the skyline, against a cloud dozing peacefully in the sky like a huge white rabbit. Bunny always used to whistle through his teeth when we were playing croquet, and sort of waggle his head seriously but there was a light in his eyes; with three beers he could play better, he always said, and would pat me on the tail when I went through two wickets. The dust disappeared, leaving blue sky, and the rabbit became a duck with feathers drifting off its back. There was a duck in the dream, too, either big or small, floating somewhere on that river, some kind of bird. I could feel myself smiling. Bunny always said that his grandmother took snuff; it was all right for ladies to do that then, she stuck it under her lip and during Lent she ate like a pig, but she gave up snuff. She was a dear woman, he always said, and I always knew it and held up the mezzotint to the light and kissed it once it was so beautiful; she was dressed in lace and I could imagine the snuff beneath her lip and there was a dear loving look in her eye as if, when you climbed into her lap, she would hold you and tell you stories about little girls in the War between the States and rock you to sleep. Tony was humming something. I turned my head, watching him naked in the middle of the floor. He turned, too, sideways, hands on his hips. He said, "Look, baby," but I didn't look, turned away, and watched the white fluffy duck fade against the sky, become something else—by the mass, said Polonius, like a camel, backed like a weasel, but very like a whale. Tony said, "All for you, baby." I said, "Yes, but I can't" and he said, "Why?" and then I rose up on my elbows, feeling the sweat suddenly cool against my back. "I just can't," I said, "I can't, Tony," and then I felt it: the cramp exploding in my womb as if everything inside of me, heart, liver and lights, had been squeezed aside and I was all agonizing womb, crying aloud, gasping like a fish. "What's the matter?" he said. He came near me. I wondered if I was bleeding yet. "No," I said. He said, "You done it last time. What's the matter?" I sank back again, watching the clock: 2:30, it said, and I could hear the almost silent whir, see the words BENRUS Swiss movement, U.S.A., in a crescent around its rim. I said, "No" again, with a thought for the clock: inside, it would be filled with clean chrome, springs and cogs all working quietly; in there I could creep and sprawl along the mainspring, borne round and round through the darkness, hear the click and whir, my only light a pinpoint where the alarm button comes through, shining down on the jewels and rubies like a shaft in a cathedral. A cockroach ran along the windowsill, wiggling its antennae. It stopped and I moved a little, then it went down a crack. Tony saw it, too; he ran his hand through the bluish hair on his chest. "Cockroaches," he said, "I hate cockroaches. Why don't you put powder down? I hate cockroaches." I could feel another cramp coming on; it was not there yet, resting superimposed on the nausea I had like a big hand with claws ready to strike. Then it struck; I was all womb again, gasping silently. I lay quiet, watching Tony run his hand through his chest hair, scratching himself; then the claw retreated, went away. "Get me my pills," I said. "What pills?" "Pills for this pain," I said, "they're in the top drawer." I lay trying to get my breath; there were dots on my eyes like drifting sparks projected on a screen: on the other side of the screen Tony fumbled through the drawer, hair on his tail, small red pimples, hair on his shoulders too. He came back with the pills and a glass of water. I took them and lay back again. He unbuttoned my pajama top and put his hand in on my breast. The sparks still floated on the screen. There were tiny, opaque spots, too, of water; these shifted always outside of my vision, along with the sparks: I couldn't concentrate on them long; instead I watched the rooftop across the avenue where a man shook a stick at pigeons. They seemed to rove around the blue like a flurry of slate-colored leaves, noiselessly with flecks of light against their wings: I became afraid of something, I wanted to go to the bathroom and get sick because of the fear, but Tony put his hand between my legs and played with me: it hurt and I felt the cramp coming but it didn't come, and I thought of all the Byrds I'd seen: there was a one-eyed condor they had stuffed in Lynchburg that had lice in its feathers and Dickie Boy said, Look at the final irony, he that preyed nobly in the Andes is preyed upon by Virginia vermin, which was real insight for Dickie Boy, and then there was an ostrich we saw in the zoo in Washington that stuck its head in the sand and then its tail feathers went straight out like an Indian warbonnet. He said, "Come on baby, take 'em off," and I said, "No, I can't, Tony, I just can't," and he said, "Why?" again. "Because it hurts me!" I said loudly and he bent down with a smile and kissed me; I closed my eyes, I wouldn't open my teeth and his tongue went shooting off into the side of my cheek. "No," I said, "no," but when I said it his tongue went in: he smelled of milk. He couldn't get it off, he always said, even with all his baths: now so close he smelled like a dairy or a nursery or a soda fountain where they haven't been clean, milk enveloping me like the heat. I was sweating now. The kiss would be long, I knew, with the tongue like that and the constant smell of milk; I thought of Byrds. Grandmother was from Lynchburg, too; she had the face of an angel, Bunny used to say; he said she used to make hermits and call him Bunny so when I heard him tell it I started to call him Bunny, too: how lovely and exciting, I thought, to be your father's grandmother and have him

338

climb up on your knee, pink-faced like he is now, I guess: I wondered
if that lock of hair was there then, silver as cigarette ash, dangling:
but Tony ran his hand up my side, milky hands. The tickle they
made ached and didn't tickle; I had a fever, maybe my skin was
yellow, I thought, like the time I had jaundice, for the fever was the
same and Tony's hand ached and didn't tickle. I felt his tongue now,
the slick underpart and the strip of flesh beneath, loose like the comb
of a rooster; so I let him: I told Tony once he was like Pride, like
Ovid's flea: he could creep into every corner of a wench, sit on her
brow like a periwig, kiss her lips like, what was it? Feathers, birds.
Fie, what a scent is here! I remembered that part, but he didn't understand it, or that I meant milk. He stopped kissing me, looking
down at me, his eyes amber as coughdrops, freckled blue. Once I
cried when Harry took me to the river and said that I was fairer than
the evening air, clad in the beauty of a thousand stars. "Come on
now, goddammit," Tony said. He took off my pants, lifting me underneath. I thought of feathers, birds, and when he went in it hurt, but
no more than the other pain quiescent in me now like the claw of
some bird waiting: I put my arms around him, feeling the hair. I
could hear the clock whir so near me it brushed against my ear:
tick-tick-tick, that minute hand making its perfect orbit in space,
bearing us like freight through the sky, Harry and I sprawled along
the springs and drowsing there to yawn and stretch and turn and
watch the revolving diamonds, rubies red as blood from the cut throat
of a pigeon, set perfect and complete among the precisely ordered,
divinely ticking wheels. Sheltered from the sky like drowning, only
better: the sun within submarine, aqueous, touching the polished
steel with glints and flickers of eternal noonday light; so we'd have
our sun among the springs and our love forever. When it was over, I
was weeping. "What's the matter, baby?" he said. "Nothing," I said.
"Well, quit it," he said, "you'd think we didn't know each other. You
gonna say, 'But I don't know you very well'? Is that what you're gonna
say?" "I don't know you very well," I said. He said, "Oh, for Christ
sakes, you gimme the creeps. You're about as much fun as a stick." I
turned over on my side and watched the clock, not crying anymore. I
heard Tony running water, washing himself, humming again, and
I tried to remember how long I had known him, a month maybe, a
week, it was hard to say: only the first time there had been something
about the incinerator in the hall, and then we drank beer, talking
about birds, and when I woke up I was feeling the nest on his shoulder, where hair. Birds, I mean; there was something confusing going

339

on, I knew that. I pulled the alarm button up and looked down into the hole, but all I could see was one small white band of metal: that would be the dome where light seeped in: outside, the hands, the luminous dots—all these would be my conscience, and Harry and I would be hidden from that, thank God. Lenin said there was no God, and Stalin said collectivization + electrification = Soviet power, all working like a clock, tick-tock, and when Albert Berger said that, his eyes watered as if he'd been gassed and there was no God, he'd say, save Him in the spirit of the creatively evolved, in the electrons of a radar screen or in the molecules of DDT. Yes, Harry said, but DDT is death, God is life-force, love, whatever you will, but not death. And how do you know, said Albert Berger, and I said—remembering something I do not know, I was drunk I guess, with what Harry always called an alcoholic, facetious desire to shock—I said For now is Christ risen from the dead, the first fruits of them that sleep. Too loudly, the wise, quizzical, psychoanalyzed faces turning toward me from the floor, the martinis in mid-air pale as mountain water, all quiet, puzzled, expectant, and I said it again: The first fruits of them that sleep! and slipped off the couch to bruise my behind. I don't know why I did it. I thought of Carey Carr. Outside the pigeons chuckled and rustled, throats swelling like bladders, iridescent, throbbing; if you cut them with a knife the blood would rush out; Dickie Boy couldn't ever get big after the first time, he was afraid and sometimes he'd sob he was so frustrated, his bird was so small and futile, but he had warm hands and when we lay down in the darkness I felt his ribs. Tony walked across the floor, I couldn't see him but he had his shorts on; he always did, with a bottle of beer. "What are you lookin' at the clock for?" he said. "You give me the creeps." I heard myself answering him. Strange. To answer like that, I thought: the voice disembodied, directionless, coming from nowhere, spoken to the pigeons or the whole wide blue air: "I am having communion with dead spirits." I could hear the clock whirring against my ear, perfect and ordered and eternal. "Ah, you funny kid. Come on, honey, give us a loving kiss." He pressed the beer bottle against my spine, I should have known: it went through me like a blade, only the blade was made of ice and it routed out that horrible claw: the cramp came groaning up through my womb and I cried out loud. "Oh Christ!" "Aw, baby, I didn't mean to." I lay back holding my belly, kneading the skin, wishing more than anything on earth for a hot-water bottle enormous and limber, as big as the room and so hot it would scald the flesh, and I was about to ask Tony—but I remembered, the bottle I had

340

was busted. "Just get me a hot towel," I said, "please, Tony, get it for me." "I'm sorry, baby," he said, leaning over; in the hair on his chest there was lint and one of my hairs, long and brown: I saw these as he bent over me, and the Christopher medal, dangling, trembling at the end of tiny golden links: the baby half-strangling the Christ-Carrier with His small brazen arms, the sea and the wind and the darkness—*Travel Safely*. Jesus Saviour Pilot Me. The pain retreated once more toward the skin, tenderly, mercifully, and I thought: it's a wonder our insides aren't all destroyed. "That's all right now," I said. "I'm goin' next door," he said then, "I gotta get some sleep. We'll stay up all night tonight, huh?" "If you want to, Tony," I said. He kissed me on the cheek, lifting my breast up in his hand. I could smell the milk again, rancid and sour; then he stood erect, singing, "Saturday night is the *happiest* night of the week. Soo-o they say . . ." "Just let me rest for a while," I said. "O.K., baby." I don't know when he left, that part is hard to remember; the door clicked sometime and I was alone sweating, sprawled out, listening to the whir of the clock. I lay there for a long while, listening; a fly buzzed somewhere in the room, heavy as slumber, stopped buzzing when it landed. I could see it in my mind: blown in off the fruitstands its feet sticky with oil from bananas, a long proboscis which moved in and out like a pump, legs hairy as a mink and strewn with microbes; I had left an orange on the table and I wondered if the fly was there sniffing around. In my clock Harry and I would be safe from flies forever; they'd drum about overhead blackening the sky, trying to get in, poking their noses through the skylight; we'd see the bearded prisms of their faces, the scowls: we'd be secure forever, guarded by chrome and immutable timeless steel. Something came down from above, a Wrigley wrapper fallen from heaven: it joined a bunch of dust, whirled away across the street, over the housetops. I rose up on my elbows, thinking, listening to the tiny whir of the clock. A subway train roared out of the South, went below somewhere shaking the building, was gone. I tried to think. There were birds in my mind, landbound birds whirling about, dodos and penguins and cassowaries, ostriches befouling their lovely black plumes, and these seemed mixed up with Bunny. Maturity and age aside and after all you are beyond the age of discretion, he'd said; at twenty-two a young lady should know her own mind, the letter went (or did I remember rightly?), maturity and age aside, my lovely one, you must try to settle this thing with Harry, as a lawyer I can tell you one thing, as a father another—let me tell you as the latter: having suffered heartbreaks enough for ten men I can assure you that the love which you know in your heart to be true *is worth every struggle*, though I'm a fine one to talk, stranded as I am now as it were upon a drifting raft from which the dear remembered shores of an earlier, better love seem to recede ever more ceaselessly into the mists of time. And I've tried to be good, but I just don't know, I just don't know: when I lay down in Darien with Earl Sanders he had a drink in his hand, and I shouted, "No, no, I'm a good girl, I was brought up right," sounding like a child, but not knowing what else to say. On his shoulders there were liver-colored spots the size of silver dollars and I wept like a baby thinking: if Harry saw me, thinking of St. Catherine, of Orestes and Iphigenia and her knife: *my life hath known no father*, she screamed, *any road to any end may run*, and outside cars went serenely on the gravel springtime roads and I could hear children call beneath the trees. I pushed the alarm button down and sat up on the side of the bed. The pigeons fluttered off in a cloud of dust and feathers. I thought of Bunny's letter and then of a letter I had written him: but I'd sent it home instead of the club, I remembered, and *why?* That scared me, but I thought about it anyway; perhaps she'd send it on to him, and then again perhaps she wouldn't. Then I forgot about it. I walked naked to the stove and put water on for coffee. Things were better now for a minute, I sat down on a chair by the stove and watched steam rise from the saucepan, thinking things were better. Dormant, cautious, watchful, like that condor with one waking eye, the pain left me alone inside, lying somewhere beyond my womb; the pills held it off, and I put my brow in my hand and closed my eyes, listening to the hiss of the gas. There were moas now, and emus, big birds with arched gobbling necks and skin beneath their legs, as big as stilts, and prissed around in the sand, yet these, along with all the other ones, stood flightless in my mind, and noiseless, leaving me alone: I felt better. I put some Nescafé in a cup and poured water over it and sat down again. It was almost three. A subway rumbled underneath, I turned on the radio: this bomb they dropped yesterday, the man said, is big, 20,000 tons, 100,000 lives, which would save Dickie Boy, way out in the Philippines with his landing boat. Dickie Boy had a sweet lovely face but his mind was a sheet of paper upon which no thoughtful word had been written, and he couldn't get it up, but it was so beautiful on the river and I wondered if I hadn't been wrong: something flowers like time in my soul and I would be a child again and have Dickie Boy lead me along the beach and pick up shells; on the Rappahannock the dawn came up as red, and I remembered I was bleeding and I went into the bathroom and fixed myself. It was my last one. I scrubbed my face and brushed my lovely hair, for I must be pretty for Harry: he would have scolded me for forgetting. "You are always out of things, darling," he'd say. "What's the matter, don't you think of tomorrow at all?" Or, "Come on now, I'm *not* nagging at you, but is it too much to ask, too much to ask, that you clean beneath the bed?" Or, "They say that jealousy is the meanest of emotions but what the hell was the big idea tonight?" That hurt the most and I thought *damn Harry, damn him,* and I stopped brushing my hair, for I was angry, I would *not* go, in spite of all the resolutions I made last night. I thought *you* just come back to *me,* but here: reason came on like a light in my mind, there was a flutter of wings, the birds fled across the sand, swiftly as a gale toward the horizon, and I smiled at myself in the mirror, feeling clean for a moment, and well. "It was always you," he said, "who complained so bitterly before we got married. About this and that. About my neglect of you and the way I ignored you, none of which—" and he smacked his hand with his fist—"I've ever done. Now this. Who's degenerating now? *Who's* gone off the deep end?" That hurt the most—then—when he said it, because he was right, but he didn't know about my plan for the clock, I couldn't tell him—then—I didn't want to, I was mad because he was right and when I lay down in Darien with Earl Sanders I was beneath him, sweating in the afternoon; I could see light through the fake chateau windows, a green million leaves, and I bit him on the ear pretending it was Harry I hated, until he shrieked: I liked that because it was Harry I bit. When it was over he turned on the Philharmonic; then I could hear the children call beneath the trees and I thought of Mozart dying in the rain. I put the brush back in the cabinet, Harry would think I was pretty. But I knew I must try not to think of Earl Sanders: that made me feel sad, and confused about Harry; besides, the birds came back and things shadowed over some—it seemed that a lot of light went away from the day and the birds came in a scamper across the darkening sand, surrounded me once more, in the bathroom, behind the confusing mirror. I turned out the light and got dressed, backwards: I should have waited until afterwards to comb my hair. My coffee was cool but I drank it anyway, and ate a doughnut. Grandmother made doughnuts, too, Bunny said: I should have dearly loved to see her and to crawl up into her lap. Then I washed the cup and the two saucers; Harry would like it, when we came back tonight, for everything to be clean: I'd show him. I went around straightening things,

343

dusting the bookcase and the books and the shelves. He'd taken all of his paintings except one, of me. Green-eyed, beautiful, in the style of Renoir—but better, he'd said. That was two years ago. I dusted it carefully, looking at my eyes: they were tender, like I was then, I guess, and he hadn't taken it because he didn't want to remember me as I was: too goddam painful, he said, to see something all vivid on the canvas when you know it still lives, somewhere apart from you now, all lost and destroyed. I tried to explain to him about the clock: didn't he see? But he said I was drunk and depraved. "I've tried my best to help you, Peyton, but I can't do any more." I watched my eyes, light went down across them like morning. I rubbed them with the rag and the dust came off clean. Nagasaki, the man said and he spoke of mushrooms and Mr. Truman: there were atoms in the air everywhere, he said, and he explained, but I couldn't make much sense. My eyes came off clean, globed from the atoms falling slow or swift, I remembered, I see the suns, I see the systems lift their forms. Lucretius had a heart as big as all outdoors said Harry, but he, too—empires, lands and seas—he too, like these, went soaring back to the eternal drift. I knew I had to get out of there; it was hot, I could feel sweat rolling down my back. I cleaned out the ashtrays with a paper napkin and stacked them up neatly in the sink. Far below in the airshaft a voice rose, round and Sicilian, female, thick as juice from a tangerine: "Vi-to!" To-to, the echo went, up through the barred windows, past the crevices and the cool, soot-stained brick, the cracked, frosted bathroom windows, the drainpipes and the radio wires and the walls. "Vi-to!" It became still, a truck passed outside; I wondered who Vito was. I threw the doughnut wrapper in the garbage bucket, turned the radio up; sinfonie conzertante, like something ordered and proper and of another earth, morns by men unseen and a far fantastic dawn, but not very clear: there were Negroes on another station, remote, faint and blurred between the fantastic flutes and oboes and the ascending strings: "Heal dem, Jesus, heal dem!" and distant hallelujahs bare and absolute as a nigger church stuck out in a sunlit shabby grove. "Heal dem, Jesus!" I turned the radio off; I had a sign or something, and with all my sleep I was tired; the pain stirred, came up in my womb, but it was not much of a cramp. The place looked clean, and this would please Harry. I went to the door, but I remembered: I went back to the windowsill and got the clock. I cupped my palms around it, looking at the dots and hands, which shone with a clear green light in the darkness: we have not been brought up right, I thought, peering down into the alarm hole:

there in the sunny grotto we could coast among the bolts and springs and ordered, ticking wheels, riveted to peace forever. Harry would like to know: rubies he'd love and cherish, in that light they'd glow like the red hats of Breughel dancers. I could hear the serene and steady whir, held it closer to my ear for the ticking, an unfitful, accomplished harmony—perfect, ordered, whole. Then I took the clock and stuffed it in my handbag. I opened the door and went out into the hall: there was a smell here of something cooking, spaghetti and heavy garlic, but a shadow passed over the day again, a tin can clattered down the airshaft, and darkness ran down the walls like a thicket of vines: I watched my hands darken and I trembled a little, thinking of home, yet I knew that this I must try not to think about too. I closed the door, heard a rustling: they followed me, I believe, the flightless birds that I couldn't see, with a feathered rustling and sedate, unblinking eyes: here they came across the sands, peaceful and without menace, ruffling their silent plumes: I wanted to cry. This mustn't. Yet I walked down the stairs, thinking not of home but of Grandmother again: she had snuff beneath her lip. "You gotta pay da rent?" said Mrs. Marsicano at the bottom of the stairs. "I will, Mrs. Marsicano," I said. I smiled at her. She had a mustache and two moles, and she smelled sour and rank, like raw, faintly tainted veal. "I'm going to get Mr. Miller right now. We'll be back tonight. He's coming back to live in the apartment and he'll pay——" But she said, "You tella me these things alla time. What I got to believe? Mr. Miller he been gone fa two months. You all the time say he's gonna pay. How do I know? The check you gimme she bounce, you owe me one hundred and eighty dolla——" "We'll pay you," I said, still smiling at her. "Don't you worry, Mrs. Marsicano, I'll make that check good——" But "Ah, you makea me sick," she said and turned to waddle away, scratching her arms, and her dog, a black mongrel with red-rimmed eyes, lifted its leg up and watered the stairs. I heard her tramp down the hall, saw her disappear into the darkness, the dog scuttling after. She was right and I knew it and the birds rustled somewhere in the hall: I listened for their noise but Harry would take care of me, I knew. I couldn't think for a minute, thinking that the bank was full of money, my money, but then I remembered: all that which Bunny sent me on my birthday I'd spent, and I remembered the phonograph I had bought, and all the records, and the Benrus clock, my womb all jeweled and safe; it cost $39.95. Too much for a clock but I just knew it had to be a good one, and pretty, with fine turning hands: somewhere in the play someone said the bawdy hand of the hour is on the prick of noon. I peeked into my handbag; Harry's was just right. Once he asked me who took my maidenhead and I said a bicycle seat named Dickie Boy: when we lay down that afternoon I heard Papageno singing in my sleep and I dreamed of dancers on a green fantastic lawn and sand and pyramids; it was the first time I ever dreamed of birds, they came sedately across the sand, and when we woke up Dickie Boy couldn't get in. I looked; my clock was safe. I walked on down the hall and onto the sidewalk. A great wave of heat smoldered up from the concrete: you could see it smoky and transparent against the tenement walls and it pasted the dress against my back with sweat. Charles Marsicano was an imbecile and he looked at me with empty brown imbecile eyes and with sweat on his face like a layer of grease. Always his lips were open, they became chapped and peeling, and he spoke: "Where ya goin', Peyton?" "I'm going up to Cornelia Street, Charles," I said. "What for, Peyton?" "To get Harry," I said. "Wan' me to take your garbage down, Peyton?" "No, thank you, Charles," I said, "wait till Monday." "O.K., Peyton." I left him standing on the stoop, sweating in the heat and the sun, working a yo-yo. He had eyes just like Maudie's, and Dr. Strassman in Newark said, "Be calm. Be calm. That's what we're supposed to work out together." But, "I don't think I like you," I said. The place was just like I imagined, antiseptic, therapeutic, clean, with metal venetian blinds, and Dr. Strassman's nose was red from a cold. "But you see, I think I'm more intelligent than you," I said. "Perhaps so, but certainly less stable," he said. "Perhaps so," I said, "but certainly more aware of the reason for my trouble." "Perhaps so." "Perhaps so." But we went on for a while, and he said, "I wish you wouldn't quit. I wish you'd have more patience——" and then I forget what he said, he was stupid and ignorant, wouldn't he like to know about my clock, but he *did* say that: it's not any guilt you feel about your sister, it's something else and apart from that. When I let Maudie fall I saw the bruise come greenish blue with tiny broken veins, but she didn't cry much. Once Bunny and I went for a walk with Maudie and we got into an argument about birds: it was a thrush, I told him, and he said a mockingbird: it was dead and its eyes were closed, a boy had shot it with a BB gun and Maudie picked it up and stroked its wings. Strassman said I was confused and insincere; you are dangerously abstracted but what was this about birds? He was interested; I wouldn't tell him. I walked up the avenue; shadows slanted eastward from the buildings and within these shadows I walked, holding the clock and bag close to my breast. "Did you hear about the bomb?" some boy said, and he ran off shrieking into a café where the old Italian, palsied and pale, sold lemon ice. We drank espresso in there each Sunday night; there was no clock then, or need for one: the walls were bare, the chairs were made of wire, and Harry spoke Dante in English: now hearken how much love did honor her (looking into my eyes) I myself saw him in his proper form, bending over the motionless, sweet dead, and often gazing into heaven for there the love now sits which (when her life was warm) dwelt with the joyful beauty that is fled. Blessed Beatrice. And I said, "A prophecy?" And he took my hand and the Italian came up to wipe off the spilled espresso with a palsied hand, and Harry said, "You will never die, you are the love that moves the sun and other stars." I thought of death and slumber, and I took my hand away from his and thought I heard behind the walls the serene, peaceful rustling of flightless wings. Why did Harry come to say I couldn't love? He should know about my clock; I walked into the awninged shadow of the café and took it out of my handbag, holding it up in the light. "Why you lookin' at that clock?" said the little boy. His face was potty with soot, streaked with moist yellow from the lemon ice. "Because I just bought it," I said, "and it's beautiful." "How much did it cost ya?" "Thirty-nine ninety-five," I said, "federal tax included." "Where'd ya get it?" he asked. "At Macy's," I said. "My ma——" he said, but I wasn't listening: the light didn't seem to come properly through the hole. Perhaps it would get dark after all in there, like day and night, the alternating light and blackness: we'd see dusk and dawning, too, sprawled out drowsing on the springs, darkness blacker than the blackest carbon around us, and stir and dream and touch hands across the constant, clicking, oscillating wheels. At night there'd be no light; because of this the flutter of the wheels would seem louder, more comforting, lulling us to sleep: the dawn would fill it with red sunlight and an azure sky and Harry would kiss me awake. Maybe we'd have babies there: he said, "In your state you not only don't want the natural things in life; you deny them completely. All right then, we won't have children," but I thought I was anyway and when I went to that doctor on Sutton Place he stuck a tube with a warm light up inside me. He was a Hungarian, and when I squirmed because the tube made me feel hot he said, "Does it teekle? Dot's allride, only pwobing," and he probed some more and I got so hot I could hardly stand it, looking at the powdered Hungarian face and flicking mustache and insolent, thoroughbred flesh: then the birds all rustled in the sand, their legs unhinged, necks craning, round, unblinking, incurious eyes and I lay down somewhere in the desert topography of my mind, only it was his couch, and he was holding my hand while I trembled in dread and guilt, and said, "Dot's allride, dawn be ashamed, it's a naughty leetle instrument." I put the clock back in my bag, horizontal now, beneath a green silk handkerchief. From under the subway grating came a puff of smoke, sulphurous, scorched, inexplicable. I thought: Something is dying. And I watched the smoke come up and the little boy scuttled away through the fumes, dropping ice behind him in a lemon spatter. Far off some chimes tolled, reminding me of home, but I knew I must never think of that. I walked on up the avenue, looking downward and scuffing my heels, in a way showing of nothing—this was very hard. There were seagulls in the air, and through the heat, the smell of sea; I saw the gulls winging southward toward the river: one had a fish in its mouth which fell; the gulls flew on. I was thirsty and I thought of going into a bar: then I was more than thirsty and I knew that I would dearly love to drink more than one. Even though: if I drink more than one I will be drowning again, here in the heat, and the heat and what I've drunk will not sweep over me thunderously, like a seawave, but will immerse me gently, dreadfully into the drowning day, like an octopus in a tank. So I thought very strongly I must not, I must not, to avoid the drowning feeling and also because of Harry: he must see me as I am, sober, gay, respectable and lovely. And I must not, I thought, passing the theater: inside 20° cooler, said a blue banner with icebergs, while the cashier, cozy in her air-conditioned box office, gazed at the heat in a chilled reverie, like an orchid inside a florist's icebox. I must not, but the sign said BAR and I pulled open the door. Two colored boys came out carrying a wooden plank; I could hear hammering inside and I passed the colored boys, stepping aside: "Dat man he always want me to go runnin' around in de midday sun," said one: he had a smile and a mustache, the color of his skin. I could smell him, sour like wild onions growing in the shade: I wanted to touch him. She always said I must never call them ladies, but women, and when Bunny and I drove the laundry over to La Ruth's, chickens pecked around in the twilight dust and I smelled that smell inside, looking at the chromos: they had blue skin, I thought how strange they'd have pictures taken. The door swung back, another one opened, and I was in the bar, not 20° cooler but 30° or 40°, and I sneezed, the sweat fading off my back. The bar was almost empty. I shivered in the cold, sneezed again, and the bartender, with a trout's face, said nothing, wiping

348

the bar. "A dry martini, please," I said. I sat down on a red leather stool, which wobbled. They were hammering in the rear somewhere; I could smell gin. The radio was on about the bomb but I didn't listen, thought they'd play music maybe *Schlage doch, gewünschte Stunde*, when the voice goes up and up tragically as a night without stars: thus Harry and I—and I felt the clock in my purse, ran over its form in my lap touching, with my fingers, the necessary buttons and levers to operate. And I thought: Could we not get one wound up forever? Suppose as we soared dozing across the springs the wheels, the cogs and levers, all these should give way, run down; then our womb would fall, we'd hear the fatal quiet, the dreadful flutter and lurch earthward instead of the fine ascent. Then I looked at my face in the quivering martini, and then a soldier came up and sat down beside me: no drowning, I thought, that was for the old days. And he said, "Ain't I seen you around here before? Don't you live near Prince? I think I seen you around here before." He was dark and handsome but when he opened his mouth his teeth were rotten and he smelled of garlic: I was trying to think, I didn't answer, looking at him in the mirror. The first sip made something happen: it rose up in my womb. When I was a little girl I thought it was diarrhea and she said read that in the Kotex box. Then I went out and sat on the porch with Maudie and looked at the bay, thinking about dying. He said: "Ain't I seen you around?" I turned and said, "Yes, I live right down the avenue." "Where you from? You sound like you came from down South. I was stationed at Fort Bragg. That's in North Carolina." "No," I said, "I'm English. I'm from the southern part of England. Dorset, to be exact." "You sound like you had one of those accents. Just a little bit." He put his hand on the bar; he had dirt under his nails, I wondered how he could be in the Army with such teeth. I said, "No, it's an English accent." "You cold?" he said, "you're shiverin'. You want to wear my jacket?" "No thank you," I said, "I'm perfectly comfortable." I drank more of the martini, feeling water come up beyond my eyes: no, I thought, no. "Ain't I seen you around with Tony wat's his name? Cecchino? Me and Tony went to P.S. 2——" But I said, "No," turning to him, "no," I said, "I don't know any Tony Cecchino. I'm just a stranger. I'm from Dorset in England and I'm visiting with my aunt and uncle the Lacorazzas." "You don't look Italian," he said. "You look more like you was from Ireland maybe or Germany." "I'm from Tuscany," I said, "they have light complexions there. I was from Perugia and then when I was four my parents moved to Dorset in England."

"Perugia ain't in Tuscany," he said, "besides Lacorazza, that's Sicilian." "Oh, pooh," I said, turning away, "the little you know." He put his hand on mine, but I drew it away. "Don't gimme a tough time, baby," he said nicely, "ain't I really seen you with Tony Cecchino? You know Tony." But that seemed to be all again: the water came up, and a rustle of wings. For a moment I couldn't think. What? And when? Perhaps he could see my fingers shake and God, I thought, don't let me suffer so: they came so serenely across the darkening sand, my poor wingless ones; how could they bear to ruin this day? They rustled behind the walls, staid and unhurried, with plumes useless as hair. I trembled, thinking *no, no* and there were words unsaid which I'd tried not to say or think all day: *and will he not come again? and will he not come again?* no, no, he is dead. There was confusion. But all I could say was, "No. No Tony. I don't know any Tony." But Bunny wasn't dead! A rustle of wingless feathers, flightless wings, they all pranced staidly through the gathering dusk: "How can you be this way, Peyton?" he'd said to me. "Don't you see what you're doing to us? Don't you see? What do you want me to do? I'm not your handmaiden. This is co-operation, not your dependence versus my so-called stalwart, solacing strength. Sometimes I think you're as nutty as the so-called fruitcake." What did I *mean* by saying he goosed that girl, that's what he said. And I just couldn't bear it, having first this: at Albert Berger's we were drunk and I felt drowning in the summer night, and Albert Berger snuffled, wiping his glasses, saying Ernst Haeckel, have you never read him, pretty one; beside him Spencer is an ass, a coward and a midget: who else but old Ernst knew the absolute—God is a prayer automaton, a gaseous vertebrate? I felt drowning underneath the heat and gin, yet there were chimes inside my brain and I remembered: how long, Lord, wilt Thou hide Thyself forever, shall Thy wrath burn like fire? "Remember," I said to Albert Berger, "how short my time is." And got up and walked through the room smoky and submarine with chattering, eyeglassed faces, to find Harry. He was kissing a refugee girl in the kitchen; her name was Marta Epstein and he had his hand on her tail and I hated all Jews. And he said Forgive. Forgive me, he said. On his knees he said it, but the chimes were still in my brain and I was drowning and I knew something was wrong on earth. Something in me that was wrong refused to forgive, and I thought forever; I said, "You did it while I was drowning, that's what makes it so awful. I'll never forgive you." And I was drowning; the heat that summer was hotter even than this one, and it came up to my

350

neck: I could have died when I saw his hand on her tail, yet not to forgive—was this not worse? He said finally, "Things that shatter you like that, well, they aren't the things at all, it's in you, if you hold such bitter vengeance." And I knew he was right—"one defection so small," as he put it—it should never have hurt so much. He was right and I hated him for his rightness; how I used it inside as a bludgeon, not to wound him so much as myself: his hands played out against her shiny black satin ass, I could see the hair on his knuckles sprung out tense like whiskers on a butterfly, and those fingers lay on my mind night and day. If I just hadn't been drowning I wouldn't have hated, I would have forgiven, but the heat and the gin: later I even kissed a sleepy-looking drunk while Harry watched, though he was queer, I think; we both were blind from drinking and I stuck my tongue in his mouth, I think. That was what had me in the bar—not Marta Epstein but the drowning. I couldn't think and the soldier said, "What's the matter, baby?" but the feathers were rustling once more, and the long feet scuffing the sand placidly, carelessly: I couldn't think, only remember, and I remembered when I lay down in Darien with Earl Sanders we stretched out naked on the terrace; we talked about Dorothy Sayers and we had a quart jar full of mint juleps: then he didn't wait until I was ready, and hurt me, and it was the first time I saw the birds, alive, apart from dreams, crowding stiffly like feather dusters across the lawn beneath the maple trees. I shut my eyes to close out the ugly Connecticut sun and I knew I was paying Harry back for his defection so small, I drowned on the terrace and when I slept afterwards I dreamt of drowning too. Now I had signaled, one forefinger outstretched wiggling, and the bartender brought me another martini. "Let me pay, kid," said the soldier, breathing garlic. "No, thank you," I said. "Aw, come on . . . tell us your name, kid," he said. "My name is Mary," I said, "Mary Ricci." "Glad to know you, Mary." "The same," I said. "My name is Mickey Pavone." "Glad to meet you, Mickey," I said. "Where you goin' tonight?" he said. "I've got to go meet Harry," I answered. The martini hurt my teeth; somewhere hammers were knocking and plaster slid down between the walls. I was beginning to drown some: the water not so much within me as if swallowed, but around me, not touching me, with the shimmering quality of vagrant but surrounding thick light. It seemed to lap at the windows, the mirror, making the air opalescent and somehow milky; yet it was not this water which threatened me so but my own mind: the water remained, like the birds, detached and even aloof, upon the boundaries of my consciousness a submarine wall persistent, but without menace: I wanted to not think about it. "I've *got* to go meet Harry," I said, as if he'd kept on asking me the question, which he hadn't. "I've *got* to go meet Harry." "O.K., baby, I believe you, take it easy. Who's Harry?" "Harry's my brother," I said, "Harry Ricci." "Yeah? You got a brother?" "Yes, I have three." "I got five," the soldier said. "What does he do?" "He's from Philadelphia. He's very rich. He's a stockbroker." "I once lived in Philadelphia," the soldier said, "it's a dead dump, you know. I lived in Darby. What part of Philly does this Harry live?" "In Shaker Heights," I said, and thought *no*, closing my eyes to the water. "You can't kid me, baby," he said, "I worked in Cleveland before the war. Shaker Heights is outside of Cleveland." "I know," I said, "he is *in* Cleveland now, he was *from* Philadelphia." "Aw, baby," he said, "come on, what're you tryin' to cover up? Come on, let Mickey in on it. Now tell me, if this Harry works in Cleveland just what building does he work at?" I turned away thinking, from the black gums, the sawed-off teeth; I was very confused: "Now you lie about it, persistently, and outlandishly, Peyton, why did you say Greenwich now when I know damn well it was Darien"—and I turned back to the soldier. I don't know why, I wanted to cry again, but I thought *no*. "He works at home, he doesn't work in a building, and besides——" I paused. "Besides what, kid?" "Besides, it's hardly any of your business." The soldier leaned back and laughed, smacking his leg: I watched the orifice glinting with stubs of ivory, shredded black gums, quivering, upraised tongue: "You kill me, kid. You're a real story-teller!" "Yes," I said, and I swallowed the rest of my martini whole and burning, "and now I must be off to meet Harry." He was still laughing. "Harry! That kills me, baby. I'll tell Tony Cecchino you're two-timin' him." I opened my mouth: "You'd better not"—but I didn't say it, and I remembered I had forgotten Tony. Guilt is the thing with feathers, they came back with a secret rustle, preening their flightless wings and I didn't want to think. "Tonight, baby." He had hair on his shoulders like wires. Harry, I did it because we loved each other, once we lay awake all night and he said blessed Beatrice, he said Lady I saw a garland borne by you, lovely as fairest flower. "Now why are you crying?" the soldier said. "Turn 'em off. I won't tell on ya." I stopped right away, looking up through the water. "You'd better not, Mickey," I said, "please don't." Then I thought: Well, it's all right, when Harry comes back it'll be all right about Tony. Only. Only we'd have to move away, because Harry and Tony wouldn't get along, living next door. And Mrs. Marsicano: Harry would pay the rent, and I was glad the place was so pretty and clean. Only. "Yes, tell Tony," I said, "if you want to. Only——" "Only what, kid?" "Only wait until tomorrow." "O.K., kid." I got up to go, holding my bag and clock close against my breast: this always gave me a certain peace. I thought I could hear it ticking there, a clean, ordered multitude of jewels and springs, above my heart. Globed from the atoms, I hadn't heard: such destruction, the radio said, has never before been seen on earth. "What you standin' there for, kid?" said the soldier. "I'm listening to the radio," I said. "I'm communing with the spirits of the dead." "You're nuts, I think," he said. "Good-by, Mickey," I said. "So long, Mary," he said. I went out the door, it was like walking into a kitchen where the oven is on and all the burners: colossal and suffocating, and thick with smells—of a bakery somewhere, caramel popcorn from the theater, gasoline and factory smoke and drains. I tried to think: here it became very odd, for it took me a long time, half a minute maybe even a minute, to decide on going left or right. A thousand times at least we'd walked up to see Lennie there; I knew it was somehow north, yet I felt that the bar had been in another country: had I not already walked too far north? I had to ask a girl. She had her tongue wrapped around an ice-cream cone, black insects on top, sprinkling off: "That way—" pointing north—"second corner." "Are you sure?" "Sure, I'm sure." "Thank you then," I said. So I started walking again, looking down at the concrete and scuffling along. Surrounded by water it was hard this way, but the pain had retreated far down inside me and out of sight: it was lucky this month with small nausea and no headache. Then I thought: Even if I begin to drown completely and the day comes down on me like all the oceans as it did last time, then still Harry will keep my head up above: that was my pride and joy and just to hell with Tony anyway. Past the drugstore it smelled of Coca-Cola and medicine, cool, but I went on: in the window, hung amid soot-coated blue and white crepe streamers, a sign said LAXA-TEEN—Conquer Irregularity Forever. Albert Berger had piles. But then I stopped, moved in under the awning, and thought. Oh Harry. I thought. Oh. No. Because he had said just that. Oh Harry. "You're asking the completely impossible. Something you inherited from your mother, only in reverse. You're a Helen with her obsessions directed in a different way. Talk about my irregularly oriented mind, how about yours: you want to lay anything in pants, that's all——" Only I said then (it was two months ago, couldn't he see how close I was to drowning?) I said, "Oh, Harry darling." I said to Lennie, "Make him come back, Lennie. I promise. I'm drowning." Only they couldn't see, they just couldn't see—"Go on back to your Italian friend," Harry said—I just couldn't make them understand: that with Tony it was different, that the heat and the gin and the drowning. We dumped some trash in the incinerator and then I could see the Christopher nestling in his hair: it was gold or something, and I had drunk all the gin, then he pressed up against me and made me——— That sober part of me shrieked in dread, yet the shrieks—oh Christ!—they wouldn't go through the water, and then he had his hand inside: couldn't Harry understand? "There was no defection so small," he said; "there's a big difference between a pat on the tail and a quick roll in the hay with the milkman." Couldn't he see? "I'll never do it again!" I hollered, "I'm drowning! I need you!" Couldn't he see? But he said, "You're just drunk. I've given you every chance in the world. You said the same thing when you came back from Greenwich or Cos Cob or Darien or wherever you went with that writer slob and so to hell with you." My poor Harry, couldn't he understand? "*Need, need,*" he'd said, "I refuse to be needed unless I'm loved too and so to hell with you." Beneath the awning it was cooler. Two fat nuns in summer white fluttered past, mumbling secretly in French: *Monseigneur O'Toole . . . la la . . . gras comme un moine*—they were sweating, they vanished around the corner, white-pleated butter churns. Chimes in my drowning soul: oh, no, God, I thought, he'll come back with me. And I thought, lifting the handbag to my ear, the clock ticking inside precise and steady as before: here all our guilt will disappear, among the ordered levers and wheels, in the aqueous ruby-glinting sun. Then I said, "Please help me," and the druggist, sunning his sallow face in the light beside me, said, "What's the matter, young lady, you got an earache?" He was an old man, a tiny one with hair sprouting from his nose. "Yes," I said. It was hard to *orient* now, as Harry would say: the man wanted to help me because I'd asked. "Yes," I said again, "it's in this ear." I pressed the bag against my head. "Right here." "You'd better see a doctor," the druggist said, "that's dangerous. It can get in your brain and kill you dead." "Yes," I said, "it hurts terribly." "You just wait here," he said, "and I'll get you a couple of aspirins." He went off into the store. I stood there in the heat, the bag against my head, listening to the tick and whir of the wheels: oh, he'd come, I knew, and I tried to think of anything, music or poems or the clock—music and poems *within* the clock—anything but Tony and lying down in Darien with Earl Sanders and all the bad things I'd done. He's soft and tender, I thought, is my Harry, and how does it go: bind him with cowslips and bring him home. But it's decreed. It's decreed that I shall never find him. When I was a little girl I had the earache and Bunny held my legs and Mr. Lewis up the street held my arms and Dr. Holcomb stuck a thing in my ear to puncture it; I'd scream out loud it hurt so, and she said poor Peyton poor little Peyton, but did it really hurt so much, did you have to scream: then she and Bunny got in an argument: I went to sleep then with a fever and I dreamed of a fat woman sitting down on me and then of a little boy in a field picking a violet. "Here you are, young lady. You just take these and then go straight to a doctor. Hear me?" "Yes," I said. I took the pills with water in a cup which he brought. "You go straight to a doctor, understand? Let that infection spread and you'll get mastoiditis. A doctor'll take care of you." "Thank you," I said. "Thank you very much. Which way is Cornelia Street?" "Two blocks up, you just go straight to a doctor." His nose quivered like a rabbit's. "Thank you," I said, "good-by." "Good-by, young lady." I walked on up the avenue, holding my clock and bag. I was sweating, and that I knew wouldn't be so nice for Harry, I wish I had remembered to use the O-dor-o-no: saves your clothes from stains, does not rot dress. But my dress was pretty—silk, cream and blue in stripes—clinging nicely: wouldn't Harry be glad? From the corner, waiting for the light to change, I could almost see the end of Cornelia Street and Lennie's place, but Jeanette MacDonald, famous star of stage, screen and radio, held up a cigarette on a stripped and peeling billboard: boys played baseball in the shade beneath, one of her arms was amputated: it lay on the grass below and the boys sat on it when they rested. I leaned outward so I could see past the billboard, but only one window was showing three flights above, the green curtain hanging limply: I couldn't see Harry there. And then I thought: what would I say? The clock would come last, a sort of surprise gift. Perhaps he'd be alone. First the buzzer, then the long climb upward; I'd hear his voice from above: "Who is it . . . is it?" I wouldn't answer, but wait. Then panting some, I'd knock at the door, and he'd open it: *Hello*, I'd say. *Hello. I'll bet you're surprised to see me.* And he'd say, *No, I knew you'd come.* And I'd say, *I'm sorry, Harry,* and then I'd say, *I love you, Harry,* and then we'd lock the door and pull down the blinds and lie there through the heat and the afternoon darkness, watch dusk come late, lie down and sprawl on the springs and drowse awhile, touch hands across the incessant, ticking wheels; this darkness is as perfect as the center of the earth, only with the glow of rubies and diamonds, shining with a self-luminous light, flawless and divine: blessed Beatrice, man at that light, said Harry, becometh so content that to choose other sight, and this reject, it is impossible that he consent: once he took me upstairs in Richmond, I was home rocking upward in his arms, and then he laid me down on a strange bed, and I called out, "Daddy, Daddy," for I didn't call him Bunny then. Yet. I knew I mustn't think of this: I clutched the clock to my breast, and stepped down off the curb, looking toward the window. Then there was a monstrous and agonized shriek of tires behind me, so close I could almost see them—sparks, tortured asphalt, peeling rubber—and I turned, saw it approaching, the grille of a truck with a metal face smiling, and the onrushing, enlarging, threatening word—halting not two inches from my eyes: CHEVROLET. "You nuts? You wanna get yerself killed!" He stuck his head out of the window, a man with a mashed-in nose like a spoon that's been stepped on, and bulging outraged eyes. He hadn't shaved, there were rough red patches beneath. "In plain sight!" he yelled. "You nuts? You seen me comin', I seen you look up!" "I most certainly did not," I said. "Please don't shout." But he went on talking, and I stood there holding my clock, while cars began to honk behind him: "People like you oughta have theirselves examined. Suppose I'da knocked you down?" "Don't holler at me," I said, "I'm not deaf," but then a policeman came up, and I watched the sweat run purple underneath his shirt. "Now just what goes on here?" "Ah, this nutty dame, she walked against the light and I almost run her down. People like her gimme a pain in the ass." "Now you mind how you talk," said the cop: it was a voice of Mayo or Down or Antrim, I thought of green things suddenly and a far, fantastic lawn: "Now tell me, miss, how fast was this fellow going?" "Fast as the wind," I said, "faster." "Faster than the wind you say now?" "Yes," I said. He looked at me shrewdly, perspiring and with suspicion. "Well then, tell me now, miss, just how fast is faster than the wind?" "I don't know," I said. I held the clock and bag close against my breast and I wanted to cry again, but I didn't. "I don't know," I said again, "very fast." "Well now, miss, you know you must be more careful. You can scare the bejesus out of a man doing that." The horns persisted up and down the street, growing louder, a chorus of chromatic moans. The cop motioned the truck on, and the driver went off with clashing gears, scowling at me, still pale with fright. "You must watch your step, miss." "I will," I said, and I held the clock closer to my breast. He looked down at me, sniffing. "Haven't you been drinking quite a bit,

miss?" he said. "Yes," I said. "I had two martinis at the Napoli Bar."
"You don't have to be afraid of me," he said, "I won't hurt you.
Might I ask where you're going?" "I'm going to see Bunny," I said.
"Bunny?" he said. "I mean—" I answered—"I mean Harry." "Well
now, miss, sure that's fine, but what I meant was could I help you
find your way? You look a bit like you're lost." "No," I said, "I'm
going up to Cornelia Street, right up there." He walked across the
street with me, holding my arm. I could see water rising up across the
avenue, luminous but clear, my drowning: I felt a cramp coming on.
"In this city you must watch your step, miss, they drive like the divil
himself." "Yes, they do," I said. "They don't drive like this down
in Virginia." "Ah now, that's where you're from?" "Yes," I said,
"Port Warwick. Harry's my uncle from Port Warwick. He's visiting
with Lennie on Cornelia Street." "Ah now, so, and who's Lennie?"
"Oh, he's a cousin of ours." "And might I ask, miss, what you're
holding so careful in that purse?" I looked up and smiled at him.
"Harry and I robbed that bank on Ninth Street last week. They don't
know. This is all money." We were on the curb, he threw back his
head and laughed. "Aw, sure you're a fine one all right!" He patted
me on the back. "Now you take care, miss." "I will," I said. "Thank
you very much." "Good-by." "Good-by." Then I had the cramp
again, walking down the block to Lennie's: it was all I could do to
keep from getting sick, and I leaned up against a light pole, getting
rust on my hand; and then I couldn't think of anything again but
becoming immoral, the birds came rustling around me through the
silent, luminous water, fluffing up their wings, and a cloud seemed
to darken the day and chilled, like a fan, the sweat on my back: I
leaned there while the pain worked awhile on my womb. One drop
of anything, I thought, would save the life of poor damned Peyton,
for it had all been so immoral, and maybe, after all, he would say no:
"No," he'd once said, more filled with grief than myself, "no, I don't
understand it. I've heard of men turning queer in a year or two, but
never a girl so good and decent and with such fine ideas just to collapse. That's what I can't see, Peyton, can you? What's *happened*
to you?" Yet he didn't understand about my sudden drowning, these
birds, I never told him about them. Harry didn't know about the
birds, or how I felt about Marta Epstein, his defection so small:
couldn't he forgive me for not forgiving him, and for what I'd done?
Couldn't he understand how I suffered over my own hatred, and in
my own despair? He could never see that or anything: or when I lay
down in Darien with Earl Sanders once we were standing up, in the

shower stall, and then the wings and feathers all crowded through the yellow translucent curtain: so I slumped down against him in the pelting spray and I thought oh Harry, I thought *oh my flesh!* I thought poor thing that hungers, poor inch of God, poor man. The cramp went away. I stood up straight from the lamp post, then I took my bag and walked on down the street. The light had sunk more behind the housetops and people were sunning themselves in doorways, slow-stirring and torpid like dozing cats; I wanted another martini but at Lennie's building I forgot about it. My heart was pounding so. I paused. A woman shook a blanket above, in a thicket of fire escapes, sending down a dust storm, and a baby howled somewhere; the street was deserted mostly and peaceful: I knew I mustn't think of home. I went into the hallway and pressed the button, heard the bell ring above; it was so quiet here, like a distant telephone chiming in your sleep—once and twice and one more time: on the avenue trucks passed mumbling, and a bus, I could hear it: the hiss of an opening door, another hiss as it closed, and the motor's labored, ascending roar, fading away. On the avenue; then I was on the bus myself, packed in sweltering among all the shoppers, smelling the fumes, the sweat-stained leather seats, borne uptown and away from all this misery and my pounding heart, with a throttled, hushing roar. Only now, the bell rang five times at least, I was still in the hallway, sweat streaming down my face, and alone. I rang once more but no one answered. And I thought: oh Harry. And sat down on the ledge by the door and took the clock from the bag, but no: then I felt that I was humoring myself, like a child: too much of a good thing was bad, even my clock, so I refused—refused to think even of this the consoling cool darkness and the ceaselessly moving wheels. That I'd save for Harry. But Harry. Oh Harry. *And will he not come again?* I put the clock back in my bag, feeling it from outside, all the levers and buttons to operate. There was a patter of feet outside the door, a flurry of heels, two puffs of light on tossing hair, and a woman's voice: "Children . . . come back . . . Dorothy . . . Tommy . . . come back . . . children . . . come back . . . come back." I sat there quietly, hardly moving, and I thought as surely as my lost love: oh God, I must die today, but will I not rise again at another time and stand on the earth clean and incorruptible? I tried to pray without weeping but when I prayed I wept, for I couldn't tell what or whom I was praying to. I said there is no God. God is a gaseous vertebrate and how could I pray to something that looks like a jellyfish? So I stopped praying and took a paper napkin out of my purse and dried my tears;

I would be a good girl, like Bunny always said: once in school we had a play and I was the Spirit of Light and I had a silver gown on that you could almost see through, then he took me in his lap and when I jumped up I saw his face: it was red and tense like a baby's when it goes off in its diapers. You must be a good girl, honey; don't mind what I do, don't mind what she says. Just remember what Grandmother said, there'll be pie in the sky for them that keep their pants on: it's what he said she said, and once Bunny and I went sailing, I trailed seaweed in my hand watching crabs scuttle in the shallows: then she spanked me with a hairbrush or something. It was all very confused, but she spanked me because I made Bunny cut my lovely hair short, like Marlene Dietrich, and then we went sailing, my hands filled with bubbles, periwinkles, and I thought of Grandmother with snuff beneath her lip. *Schlage doch, gewünschte Stunde.* The children had returned: they came back past the door and dragged their heels, looking solemn. The boy had a toy tin watering can; scowling handsomely, he carried it beneath his arm. Outside pigeons whirled giddily in the sunshine, and a garbage truck came by with a clatter. I couldn't think what to do. I tried to pray: lighten my darkness, I beseech you, oh Lord, and make me clean and pure and without sin; God, give me my Harry back, then, Harry, give me my God back, for somewhere I've lost my way: make me as I was when I was a child, when we walked along the sand and picked up shells. Amen. Then I opened my eyes, and then I saw the note: a folded-up piece of paper hanging out of the mailbox. It said "Laura," and I opened it, read in Lennie's scribble: "Gone to A. Berger's for what we don't know except we're bored. Harry says if P. comes to tell her he's gone to Peru love and kisses." I read it three times, just to make sure: my salvation. At least I knew exactly where to look. I refolded the note carefully and stuck it back in the slit in the mailbox, and the door slammed: in came Tommy Givings in tweeds, with his pipe, with kindly blue eyes, a very parfit gentil Hingleshman. "I say, what are you up to, Peyton?" he said. "I'm reading a note," I said, "I mean I was reading a note." He had a bald spot, over it he smoothed back nervously a twist of kinky gray hair; expatriate like myself, a happy scholar gypsy. "Dear gull, what's the matter? You look like you've been having trouble." "Nothing," I said, "I was just reading the note." "Ayess, I see." He chewed on his pipestem, looking at me gravely. "I was hunting for Harry, but he's gone out," I said. "Ayess." He pulled out a huge linen handkerchief. "Now you have smut all over your face. All amongst the tears. Tommy wipe." He wiped my face, humming some tune, smelling of tobacco. "There now. How's about a drinkie up at my place? You can wait for Harry boy there." "No, thank you, Tommy," I said. "I've got to go right now over to find him. He's gone out with Lennie." "Dear gull, do you think you'd better? You look all whacked, you know. What on earth have you been doing? Now come on with me——" "No," I said, "thank you, Tommy. I've got to go find him." I backed down the hall past the mailboxes, holding the bag at my breast, watching him: the pipe in his hand now, eyebrows up, and a smile on his lips, perplexed and concerned. He put out a bony hand. "Dear gull——" but I pulled open the door and went out into the street. Heat smoldered in the air like a living flame. The children had gone, and the mother. Pigeons clucked and rustled on the rooftops. A little old Italian staggered past, perishing beneath the load of an armchair, groaning, sweating; far down the street a hydrant burst in a fountain of silver water, and three boys in shorts scampered in and out, and darted and retreated like slick brown bees toward a silver blossom. Shrill cries in the air, and a plane muttered overhead, but the rest of the street was silent. A taxi came slowly by, I stuck out my hand. He opened the door for me, reaching back with his arm, and I said, "Forty, Washington Mews." I put the bag down beside me on the seat, kept my fingers on it. His name was Stanley Kosicki, 6808 behind the dust-smeared glass, and he said, "The man on the radio says that bomb'll finish up the war inna hurry." I didn't answer. I took out my compact and put powder on the tear-streaks, then painted my lips. "I was in World War One. In France. Argonne, Belleau Wood, Shadow Terry. You know how many times I was wounded? Take a guess." "I don't know," I said. "How many times?" "Take a guess," he said. "Oh," I said, "three times." I looked out the window; we were on the avenue, halted at a stoplight, and I watched those who crossed by: a Western Union boy poking along; twins in a baby stroller and their mother, drinking a Coke; a Jewish woman, fifty maybe sixty, with red pancake makeup and a lavender veil thick as a fishnet: she wore a look of anguish, and all of them, sweating, including the wilted, sun-prickled twins, were trailed by two lesbians in trousers, who loudly flaunted their tough, sad voices on the suffocating air. The light blinked green, we went on; he said, "Three times! Guess again." "Two," I said. "*Four times*," he said, "more than any man in my outfit." "That's nice," I said. "I seen it all," he said, "Argonne, Belleau Wood, Shadow Terry. A buck private I started out, too. Guess what I ended up at?" "I don't know," I said. "Take a guess."

"Oh," I said, "major." Sweat oozed out in beads behind his ears, through the bristles of his gray hair. "*Major!* Guess again." "Oh," I said, "I don't know. Captain?" "*Captain!* Naw. Master Sergeant. I went in buck private and I rose up higher than anybody I joined up with in my outfit." I couldn't think. I was tired from praying, and from weeping, too, and I was ashamed Tommy Givings had seen me: why was it when I thought of prayer I thought of home: why these two things always together, giving me grief? So for a moment thoughtless I glided up the avenue in content, cooled by the breeze, listening to the driver. He talked of Shadow Terry then, we passed Fourth Street, and I thought—it came fast as light, this thought, I surrendered—of Harry meeting me, once more, at Albert Berger's door. *It's me,* I'd say, *it is I, Peyton your darling, come home to the land of the living.* Well, there would be that hesitation, only natural, in which his face would darken some, he'd shake his head, but it would be only the puzzled prelude to a smile: he'd take my hand, move out into the hall. *Land of the living indeed,* picking me up and whirling me around in that way, so that my heels would go clacking against the walls. *Land of the living indeed!* Maybe we wouldn't go back in; no, we wouldn't go back in to Albert Berger's and his gang of lost moral libertines, as Harry used to say. No longer the air-conditioned carpet, the dry martini, the wet Freudian soul, as Harry used to say. *Let's get out of here, baby,* he'd say. And I'd say, *Let's go where there's grass.* And he'd get Lennie's car and we'd bump through the dusk toward grass and trees and rocks—perhaps to Long Island, to his uncle's house, or maybe Connecticut, where there was an inn we knew. Yet the clock first, in the hall. Yet again, perhaps later, in the darkness: *Darling, I bought us a present, much too expensive, it cost $39.95 but you don't mind.* And so it would be just that way: globed from the atoms in the whirling night, among the springs and jewels and the safely operating, bright celestial wheels. Our bed transformed, a spring coiled, softer than the feathers from a dandelion, sheltered by steel from the threat of hell or anything. Yet lying. And we could hear the sound of katydids among the trees as we always did, in the pine-smelling, frog-filled Connecticut night. It happened at the inn, where Harry and I. Yet lying. And only I knew it wasn't Harry at all, and the taxi driver, peering back at me through green sunglasses, must have heard the noise I made in my throat, for he said, "Watsa matter, lady?" only I knew it had not been Harry at all. Remembered that: when I lay down in Darien with Earl Sanders it hadn't been Darien the second night at all, but the inn, outside Torrington, and the night was filled with the smell of pine, and the noise of katydids: then he pulled back the sheets and said, Baby, you're good at this, and I smelled woodsmoke in the air and felt his soft, fat flesh; there was the juke box from below: To-night—we—LOVE (while the moon is): then in my drowning soul the birds pranced solemnly across the plain and their feathers rustled flightless in the evening, but with a noise, like the chill, fretful chatter of katydids. *How long, Lord, wilt Thou hide Thyself forever?* "Watsa matter, lady, you sick? You shakin' like a leaf." I looked straight into his mirrored eyes. "Remember how short my time is," I said. "You wan' me to stop at a drugstore? You look like you got the colic," he said. "No, that's all right," I said, "I'm all right. I just don't have much time." He swerved past a bus and turned down Eighth Street. "Don't you worry none," he said, "I'll have you there in two minutes. Flat." He hocked something up, spat it out the window; in the fading afternoon two young men strolling along, one with an earring, both in silk verdigris pants. *Shall Thy wrath burn like fire?* I couldn't think again, then thought flooded over me with a rustle of feathers, scraping, katydid wings: suppose. Yes. Suppose it was not like that at all, but that he should say you just go to hell. Suppose that turned out to be. Then I should never go home, south again, but always uptown like this, always north: and he shall never come again. I couldn't help it, with Harry going: once at night at Uncle Eddie's in the mountains, it was summer and cold and upstairs alone the katydids scared me: she closed the door, sealing me in blackness, with only my child's fearsome conscience—the alarm clock at my bedside whirring away, bright with greenly evil, luminous dots and hands. I knew nothing about birds then, or guilt, but only my fear: that I should be borne away on the wings of katydids, their bewhiskered faces that nuzzled mine and brittly crackling claws that pinched my flesh, a hum of wings overhead carrying me outward and outward and outward into the alien northern night; more I couldn't know—only perhaps to land among the rocks and the trembling unfriendly ferns, swooning in the darkness, serf-child to the katydids forever. So in my bed I cried but voiceless, afraid to call really (afraid of her anger), the words strangled in my throat. Instead, I covered up my head with the pillow and peered out at the clock: friend and enemy: I knew that once past my conscience, those wicked, luminous dots and hands, I would find my peace amid the consoling wheels. Yet *alas*, and I knew *alas* for it was what they said in the fairy books, I was thwarted by those evil, luminous eyes; they wouldn't let me go into my clock, and the gathering shrill wings of the katydids scared me so that I called aloud, "Mother, Mother, Mother." And she came in her slip, a lovely silhouette against the door. Shame on you, Peyton. *Shame. Shame. Shame. Shame.* Then the door closed and I was alone. Then Bunny came up from the party below, weaving through the furniture: I could smell the whisky and the sweat beneath his arms, he lay down in the darkness beside me and told me about the katydid circus, never be afraid. Then he went to sleep and I put my hand on his chest, and felt his heart beating and heard him snore: could there ever be a love like ours? "Now, lady, you just stick with old Stan Kosicki," he said, "I know this city like the back of my hand," and we had drawn up at the corner of Fifth Avenue, another stoplight. I could see the entrance to the Mews down the street, I wanted to get out now. "I'll just get out——" I began. But he raised his hand and curled his lips, grandiose, in complete command. "Now you just wait, lady, and we'll go right there. You look sick. Just leave it to old Stan Kosicki." So we waited, and I tried not to think of home, but. Oh, I tried not to think that way, yet if Harry. So we waited. I looked out the window; the afternoon had grown later, yet nothing had seemed to cool. On the corner a man in droopy, stained white sold Good Humors from a cart: two little girls in sunsuits held out nickels for orange ice, and there was a woman in slacks, with a pointed, insolent face like the Afghan she held on a leash, who bought an ice-cream sandwich: she held it down to the dog and he devoured it with a greedy pink tongue. Heat-worn people, moving languidly through the afternoon, fanned themselves with newspapers; I began to get thirsty again, and I thought of home. Albert Berger had said, "Of course you suffer over that, you have revealed more than you know to me, my pretty; after all (his eyes watering), I am a student of people; it is symptomatic of that society from which you emanate that it should produce the dissolving family: *ah ah*, patience my pretty, I know you say symptomatic not of that society, but of *our* society, the machine culture, yet so archetypical is this South with its cancerous religiosity, its exhausting need to put manners before morals, to negate all *ethos*—— Call it a *husk* of a culture. It's a wonder, my pretty, you weren't put out at the age of six, like certain tribal children in the d'Entrecasteaux, to dig grubs for yourself alone." "Yes. Yes." That's what I replied. But I remembered grass, and gulls. "All right, lady," the driver said, pulling up in front of the Mews, "old Stan Kosicki brings you to your destination safe and sound." The meter gave a last click; he stopped it, pulling up the flag: 0.50. I felt in my purse but I counted only thirty cents. Terror. This would mess me up with Harry, and I remembered him, before it really got bad: "I hate to bring it up, darling, but you'll have to be more careful with the dough, I hate to say it, darling, but it all becomes part of the syndrome, along with the dirt beneath the bed, do you understand?" "I only have thirty cents," I told the driver, and my heart was pounding not because of him but of my Harry: what would he say when he had to pay? But then I said, "But just wait a minute, and I'll go get some." "Sure, lady, old Stan Kosicki is patience incarnated." He stuck up his hand, lit a cigarette and leaned back. Or was it, I thought, sitting on the edge of the seat and retrieving my bag, or was it—— It was Strassman who talked about the syndrome: you are dangerously abstracted, he said and he wiped his nose, you do need my help you know. "Oh pooh, you're crazy," I said aloud, and the driver turned and chuckled: "That's right, lady. It's a crazy world. Sometimes I wonder if even old Stan Kosicki ain't crazy." "Not you," I said. I got out of the cab. "Just a minute," I said. Then I walked across the asphalt drive to Albert Berger's, the first door painted white, with a bronze phallic knocker from Spanish Morocco. A skinny Hindu answered right away, before I had time to think. Of Harry coming or anything. His name was Cyril Something: he had an accent both Balliol and Indian and a perpetual leer, he had a martini in his hand. "'Allo, Peyton," he said. "Hello Cyril," I said. "Is Harry here?" "You mean Meestah Harry Meelah?" "Yes," I said, "Harry Meelah. Is he here?" He stood wobbling for a minute, looking at me and thinking, with a wrinkled brow and blue, pouting lips. "Naw," he said, "I'm rawther afred not." I couldn't think: I stood watching him, then I turned sideways toward the avenue and saw a flight of sparrows come from a tree, sprung out of the foliage like a swarm of wasps, chattering shrilly, disappear over a housetop. A bus passed south, six people on the top deck absorbing the sunshine: I couldn't think. Then I thought: oh Harry. I held the bag to my breast, bent my head down, heard the patient steady click and whir of wheels. You, swiftly fading. Where had he gone? "Why, Peyton, why do you weep?" Cyril said slyly. "I'm drowning," I said. "Drowning?" "No," I said, "I mean I'm not drowning. I mean I'm crying because I'm so happy. Because the war is over and we have saved the world from democracy." "Queer girl. Won't you plis come in? Albert will be delayted, you know." "Yes." I wiped the tears on my bag, and the powder came off, too. I stepped inside, my reflection in the hall-way mirror: a perfect mess. Cyril opened the other door; he wobbled slightly. He put a hand on my waist, propelled me forward gently: "We haven't seen you for *such* a time." "I know——" I began, but then I thought, why am I here? With Harry not. And I turned around, clutching my clock: "No really, Cyril, I mustn't come in." "And why not, mayt I ask?" He had wide-spaced teeth, his fleshy lips surrounded them like blue rubber cushions. I said, "Because he's not here." "Who?" Puzzled again, the mystified East. "Harry," I said, "Harry!" "Ah," he leered, "Meestah Harry Meelah. Well, stay a bit, p'raps someone will provide you weeth info'mation." "Perhaps," I said. He turned me around again, pushed me into the room: an air-conditioned seacave with strangled sick sunshine and darkness infringing upward, where cigarette smoke curled in milky wreaths and Albert Berger, like Poseidon and his trident approaching me through the gloom with a cocktail shaker, sidestepped the rocks huddled on the floor. "Ah, Peyton," he said, "my pretty one, you've come back to us." "Yes," I said, "where's Harry?" "Oh, my dear, you'll have to ask Lennie. He's in the study with La Baronesse du Louialles." "Oh," I said. He hovered over me with a caved-in chest, eyes watering allergically behind his glasses, skin white as a turnip. "And Harry isn't here?" I said. "Oh, dear no, he left almost as soon as he came. Something about work, poor drudge. Come sit down by me, pretty one." His voice was high and hollow, sexless, ageless, almost extinct, like the empty clacking of a metal bird. "Come with me, my pretty," he said, and he took my hand with fingers chilled by the cocktail shaker and by something else cold and internal, too, as if his heart pumped not blood but frigid, dark, subterranean water. Thus I passed with him through the room, my clock clutched tightly, thinking of home. I saw their faces in the darkness: Daphne Gould, who had once taken on a pony; and Mario Fischer, the millionaire's son; Dirk Schuman and Louis Pesky and Schuyler van Leer, the anthropology students; Pierre Liebowitz, a rich florist who dyed his hair; two soft-voiced Negro boys I didn't know; Pamela Oates and Lily Davis, who were in love; Edmonia Lovett, who once almost suffocated to death in her orgone box; four stray soldiers—all these gave me a swift darting glance, and turned away. Then Albert and I were sitting on the window seat; I had a martini in my hand and he spoke: I half-listened, watched the beautiful day begin to expire outside with a final gush of yellow light; across the alley the slate roofs of the houses were in sunshine, the walls in shadow: soon the roofs, too, the gables, birds' nests and crawling ivy, would be in shadow, and in darkness. A cloud above drifted slowly eastward, fluffy, touched with pink, shaped like Africa:

lands I will never see, the far coasts, flamingo evenings, the yellow, rotted jungle dawn. I said, "It's been a lovely day." And Albert Berger said, "Pretty romantic one. Have you thought of forests and wonderlands and fairy books like you used to? Have you been thinking of all the impossible things?" I said, "I've been thinking of morns by men unseen. I've been thinking of a far fantastic dawn . . ." and I had a cramp, bent over, heard in the dizzy, spark-speckled darkness one single voice hoarse and arrogant, somewhere on the floor: "Malinowski! How can you say that? Old Bronislaw?" I pressed the bag and clock to my belly, trying to push back that pulsating pain: worse this time than ever before: I bit my tongue. It went away. "I'm sorry," I said. "I should be at home." I sat erect, not looking at Albert Berger but outside, at the sunshine. "Poor pretty," he said, "even the loveliest must wear the duodecimal disgrace, bear the catamenial anguish. I should write a book of sonnets about the poor lost lovelies; perhaps Cleopatra used a wad of crushed roses, you know, and I suspect that Helen——" But I couldn't listen; I watched the sunshine, thinking of Harry: first Helen, then blessed Beatrice, sweet Helen, make me immortal with a kiss: once I squatted beneath the rosebush by the kitchen. It was summer, too, and I heard Ella singing in the pantry and the constant buzz of bees; then I saw water trickle on the ground beneath me, a rivulet flooding toward the garden, and Helen snatched me up among the smell of roses: *you mustn't mustn't can't you be proper. God punishes improper children.* I could smell roses and I heard the bees buzzing in the heat; then Bunny came and we sat out on the seawall and he read me James James Morrison Morrison Weatherby . . . "So it must be difficult, pretty one," said Albert Berger. "What's not proper?" I said. "What?" he said; his skin seemed to get paler and paler in the sunlight. "What's not proper?" I said. "My dear girl," he said, "such a feckless wandering mind you must have. I didn't say proper, I said difficult." "Oh," I said. "I said it must be difficult for you?" "What's difficult?" I asked. "To live in this distressing world—alone now as you are—with no real intellectual supports to put your mind at ease. Have you heard about the bomb?" "Yes," I said. He leaned back on the seat and made a weak sexless laugh. "Cool!" he said. "Man's triumph. I've been predicting it for months and months. To Louis and Schuyler. Now they're appalled, such lovely boys but soft-minded, unwilling, safe in their bosom of *social* anthropology—*social*, mind you: the science is getting so cluttered with offshoots that it begins to look like Medusa's hair—unwilling to accept the historical determinism, tragic as it is to the spirits of neo-humanists, the historical determinism—may I not even say propriety, to use your word?—they are unable to accept the pure *fact* in all its beauty. Man's triumph! Jaweh! So up in bloody pulp go the children of Nippon . . . and yet . . . and yet——" His eyes watered, he sipped daintily at his martini. "And yet," he went on in a sudden sad tone, "even Louis and Schuyler, they don't *have* to agree. My view of the universe is harsh and brutal. In each act of creation, be it the orgasm of the simplest street cleaner or the explosion of atoms, man commits himself to the last part of the evolutionary cycle; by that I mean death, frosty, cruel and final. Thus I do not ask you any more, my pretty, to believe with me that the evil in man is both beautiful and preordained. Socially, I'm catholic and I have the most tolerant of minds. You just stay as pretty as you are, safe in your land where a whimpering Jesus gently leads Winnie-the-Pooh down a lane of arching plum blossoms. You will always—why, pretty one, you have tears in your big brown eyes." "Yes," I said, "remember how short my time is." He put his hand on mine, like some polyp from an arctic sea. "Oh dear," he said, "I'm very sorry. Really, Peyton, I'm very sorry. Is there anything I can do?" I looked into my bag for something to blow my nose on, saw the clock, covered it up quickly. Albert Berger handed me a handkerchief, I blew my nose: a young man leaned back against the rug, rolled his eyes up at one of the soldiers: "But you see," I heard him say, "I'm *happy* in my inversion. I have found but a perfect relationship with Angelo, but a perfect one." "Yes," I said to Albert Berger, "you can tell me where Harry is. That's how you can help me." "Pretty one. You're such a lost child. You *do* want your Harry back, don't you?" I said, "Yes. Yes. Oh, yes." He snickered. "Such a brave new girl. You *do* expect a lot. May I make a suggestion—of course it wasn't Harry but little Laura who told me, who finally impels me to suggest this to you—might I suggest that you rid your house of dairymen much as you might cockroaches; then I have no doubt that your Harry could take a different stand. As it is, Harry is such a lovely boy, I've had *such* hopes——" *No*, I thought. Across the room Edmonia Lovett heaved to her feet, dumpy in winter sack tweeds, preening her henna hair. "Why does he go out with her," she shrilled, "when he can go out with an analyzed dame like me who can reach a climax?" I watched her lurch to the phonograph, put on a record, the Wang-Wang Blues; yet I watched her through water for a moment, my drowning, the submarine cave, the dwarf shapes floor-sprawled, all immersed in transparent aqueous light. The voices came up as from the bottom of the sea: Albert Berger, he said I must exorcise my dairymen, yet he didn't know, nor could he hear, as I did somewhere among the draperies behind me, the fidget and stir of flightless wings. Albert Berger, I must say, can't you ever know what it is when you lie down in a strange bed and with a strange man and in a strange country; there is no menace in their tread, which is so cruel: across the darkening sand they come stiff-legged craning their necks, stately and regal, ruffling their lovely plumes. So even clutching his hot hostile flesh, you can't find peace in the dawn but hinge your eyelids down tightly, feel his Christopher against your breast and then even then they pursue you across the plain, incurious and bored like feathered kings: Albert Berger, O my God! I would cry out, don't I know my own torture and my own abuse? How many times have I lain down to sin out of vengeance, to say *so he doesn't love me, then here is one that will*, to sleep then and dream about the birds, and then to wake with one eye open to the sweltering, joyless dawn and think *my life hath known no father, any road to any end may run*, to think of home. I would not pray to a polyp or a jellyfish, nor to Jesus Christ, but only to that part of me that was pure and lost now, when he and I used to walk along the beach, toward Hampton, and pick up shells. Once he took me in his arms and gave me beer to drink and I heard her voice from behind the mimosas, *shame, shame, shame.* "For shame, pretty one," Albert Berger said, straight through his martini. "Why do you cause that lovely boy such trouble? Did Strassman say merely that you were dangerously abstracted or that you were psychogenically incapable of sexual fidelity——" "You just hush," I said. He raised one finger whimsically aloft, pale Ichabod Crane ready for a pronouncement, but Lennie came up then, shirt sleeves rolled up over his pink sunburned arms. "Hello, honey," he said nicely. "What's the matter? You look all done in." "Lennie, tell me please where Harry is, please do," and I took his fingers, my handbag falling to the floor with a sudden frightening, jangling bell: all the eyes goggled up through the water from the floor bottom through wreaths of smoke like trailing seaweed, alert and popeyed as startled fish. Still the alarm clattered on, muffled some by the bag, but loud. I groped for it, hearing through the room a slow-rising chorus of laughter. Then I found the button and turned off the bell. Lennie sat down laughing beside me. "What have you got in there, honey?" he said. "A time bomb?" "No," I said, "a clock. For Harry and me. It's a present." "Oh," he said. The smile faded; he looked at me kindly, but with suspicion. "Are

368

you going to give it to him today, Peyton?" he said. "Yes," I said. "Tell me where he is, Lennie. Please do." Through the room the laughter dwindled, then died out: the bespectacled faces regarding me with interest. Someone whispered. Someone said, "My God," looking at me—they who have no God, less than mine, a prayer auto- maton, less than mine, who dwells in some land I shall never see again. Albert Berger moved away through the water. "Listen, Pey- ton," Lennie said. "Why don't you go over to Cornelia Street and stay with Laura for a while? You look positively awful. What have you been doing? You look like you've been on a two weeks' drunk." He paused. "I told Harry I wouldn't tell. It's that simple. You go stay with Laura——" "No," I said, pulling at his sleeve. "No, Len- nie, please tell me where he is. Please do." "I can't." "Please do." "I can't. You look like you need something to eat. Go tell Laura I said break out the bacon and eggs——" "But Laura doesn't like me anymore," I said, "so I can't." "She *doesn't* doesn't like you," Len- nie said. "She's just disappointed and irked with you like everyone else——" "Oh, no," I said: but *no*, not even Lennie, he didn't under- stand. So I would say Lennie, behold, I tell you a misery: "I'm sorry, Lennie, for what I've done, today I'm trying to exorcise my milkman and my guilt." Couldn't he see? But then I said, "Please, Lennie. I'm drowning." He took my hand and looked me in the eyes: it was a disappointed look, past irritation but not quite disgust: "Peyton, honest to Christ, please don't give us that again today. Really, Pey- ton . . ." "But I am, Lennie," I said. "Can you blame him," he said, "can you really blame him? He's done everything he could for you. He's worried himself sick, he's lost weight, he's nearly had a break- down. Every time you've come back he's listened to you, he's agreed with you. Then you begin all over, with your bad checks, your Tony, or that guy Sanders. You wouldn't even stick with Strassman. And the terrible part, Peyton, is the fact that in spite of all you've done he still loves you. But he just can't take it——" Lennie would always be the first to understand but now he wasn't, nor could I tell him all, the *reason*: when I lay down in Darien with Earl Sanders I hated it; on the terrace, lying on that blanket, I could hardly hear the swol- len, rustling plumes for the other things that bothered me: I was sorry in this way I'd punished Harry for his defection so small, and then there was the smell of paint on the terrace railing and I thought of summers long ago. Once we went down where they were painting a boat on the beach: I remembered Bunny's hand, and the way the sand came up between my toes, the paint chemical and hot on the swarm-

369

ing summer air, swimmers beyond and gulls floating in the blinding blue: then he squeezed my hand and I remembered remembering *I will remember this forever.* But at the door something knocked and the Hindu Cyril answered, just then, letting in a rectangle of light. That driver, Stanley Kosicki, stood there; he said, "That's the dame. She owes me fifty cents." I had forgotten. "Lennie," I said, "I forgot. That taxi driver. I owe him fifty cents but I only have thirty. Here. Could you pay him the rest?" Lennie looked at me, the disappointment disgust. "Christ, Peyton. You take a taxi when you don't have hardly subway money and then you make the guy wait. What's the matter with you?" "I'm sorry, Lennie," I said. "I really did forget. Here, please take this thirty and pay him the rest. I'll pay you back." "Oh, nuts." He got up, walked to the door, his shoulder finally obscuring the driver's scowling, muttering face. So desperately I tried to make my lips work, to say, "I'm sorry," to the driver; the door closed. I sat there saying nothing, listening, with my bag uptilted, to the ticking, ordered wheels: then across the room I saw Albert Berger's mouth yawn with noiseless laughter like a shark's, say: "Coo! And the irony is this: with the revulsion we humans have for the body, the secretions and juices and, as it were, plasms, the weakest still lie down in the moist and odorous conjugal embrace. Coo! And yet——" And yet now more strong than before something in me stole into the clock: we lay there together, Harry and I, in the safety of springs and the order of precisely moving wheels, like sleeping to exist in some land where we were young again, and dream of meadows or such consoling visions that come at the brink of sleep, dogs that barked once in the September woods, ducks across the sky, and the way he carried me up and upward—oh Christ!—when I was the Spirit of Light. "Now please do what I told you," Lennie said, looking down at me. "Go over and tell Laura to feed you. You look starved. Then go home. I'll talk to Harry later. Maybe——" I said, "No, I can't wait. Please tell me where he is. He's going to come back with me. And the clock." "What?" he said. I didn't answer. "What is this about the clock? What are you carrying it around for?" "Nothing. I just bought it," I said. "Oh," he said. "Well now, you just——" I got up. "No, Lennie," I said. "Please listen to me. You've *got* to tell me where he is." "No," he said. "You've *got* to," I said, "you've just *got* to. If you don't——" He put his hands on my shoulders. "*Shhh-h,* honey, take it easy. If I don't, what?" I turned away. "I don't know," I said, "I'll——" "What?" he said. "I don't know," I said, "kill myself." He grabbed me by the arm. "Look, baby. I think you *are* in a bad state. Look, my car's outside, I'll call Strassman and we'll get Harry and drive over to Newark——" "No," I said, "he's crazy. Strassman. He has a cold." "A what!" Lennie said. "Nothing," I said, "I mean—I mean just tell me where Harry is." I turned and pulled him by the sleeves. "You've *got* to, Lennie. You've got——" Lennie put his arm around my waist and led me toward the hall, past the people squatting like rocks, through the submarine drowning light; the Wang-Wang Blues petered away and the young men rolled their eyes like agates through seaweed wreaths of smoke. So in the hall then. "All right," he said, "but if he won't see you, promise to come here or go to Laura's. You need somebody to take care of you." "Thank you, Lennie," I said, "oh, thank you. Please forgive me, Lennie. Do you think I'm bad?" "No," he said, "no, honey. You just need straightening out. Why do you——" "Why do I what?" I said quickly. "Nothing," he said. "Why what?" I said. "Why do you act like you do? Why did you have to run off with that Tony guy that last time? That's what got Harry. It'd get me, too. Why? Why?" His voice was gentle; though I tried, how could I speak to Lennie, when behind us in the foyer, at his words, prancing harmlessly with speckled, flightless feathers, came across through the polished regency chairs—the brasswork, the spotless mirror—my poor, despised, wingless ones: how could I explain that? Or when I remembered: *Harry doesn't love me else why would he have hollered at me like that about the checks unpaid and the dirt beneath the bed and lying down in Darien with Earl Sanders, my agonizing vengeance . . .* That would be difficult to explain, indeed: that I couldn't *have* Harry holler at me like that, so I must lie down with someone, perishing in my hatred, hearing the echo in the night: "What do you *mean* I don't love you, Peyton? I love you more than you'll ever know. I'm just not your father. I'm not supposed to put up with these things." Thus an echo in my guilt and feathered darkness; how could I explain this to him? "I don't know why," I said. "I don't know." "Don't cry," Lennie said, and he took out a big red handkerchief and wiped at my tears. "Don't cry, honey. Now look. Harry's painting. Marshall Freeman lent him his studio this afternoon. Harry's there. It's right around the corner, on University Place. Look, I'll put down the address." And he took out his wallet and a slip of paper and began to write down the address. "There," said Lennie. "Now promise me. If he won't see you, you promise to come back here or call me, or go over and see Laura. I can't guarantee——" "Oh, that's all right," I said. "He'll see me. Soft and tender is my Harry." "A new line, huh?" said Lennie. "Yes," I said. "Thanks, Lennie." He closed the door behind me; I was sweating again, standing in the hot, still afternoon. I walked east. The houses across the alley were drowned in shadows; even on the rooftops there was no light. Way off in the river, so faint they seemed like car horns, boat whistles moaned: it was high tide, I guessed; they'd be pulling out to sea. At home high tide too, or thereabouts, and between the seawall and the water not more than two feet of sand, where we'd walk carefully along, kicking the driftwood and shells; Ella Swan would come out for the washing in the afternoon August heat, raising her hand to shield her eyes, to look at the ships passing out to sea: thus once Ella and Maudie and I—we proceeded slowly across the grass, listening to the bees in the rosebush, smelling the sea. Thus once. Only I couldn't remember, but just *know* the mimosas near-by, and that was another time. Thus she brought it up: *when you let her fall when you let her fall*. And the mimosas in the heat fingering the air, pale strands like hands of water: *when you let her fall*. And Strassman said, "Birds?" And I said, "No birds for that," for birds were for another time, another guilt, when I lay down with all the hostile men. "No birds," I said. "Then what?" he said. Then I couldn't remember, couldn't tell Strassman of this separate despair hidden beneath the smell of mimosas and sea somewhere beyond my reckoning: *you let her fall*. But I didn't. "Perhaps you didn't but you are still dangerously abstracted." Then he was toying with me, that bastard psychoanalyst. I said all hope lies beyond memory, back in the slick dark womb, and he said, "That's what I mean, your abstraction," yet couldn't he see, too? Why was it when I thought of her I thought of blessed Beatrice? That was what I'd like to know, Dr. Irving Strassman; please to remove that Kleenex from your silly nose: was it because once when we were blown like petals through the years of our innocence he said twin heroines have I: one fairer than the evening air, clad in the beauty of a thousand stars, the other blessed Beatrice, O Light Eternal, self-understanding, shining on thy own. Something like that. But mixed-up. And when he said, Sweet Helen, make me immortal with a kiss. Then I cried. Then Strassman said, "But there's no connection." How could I tell him about the mimosas, the light at home coming down and the bees sailing plumply about in the salty air? *You let her fall*, Helen said. Then I walked down alone on the seawall; then Bunny came up and took my hand: we saw darkness fall across the bay and I thought of Grandmother with snuff beneath her lip. *Schlage doch, gewünschte Stunde*. "Are you sick, dear?" I was leaning with my head up against the gate, and the old woman came out—she had a dog on a leash—tapping me on the shoulder. I didn't answer. "Can I help you, dearie?" I looked up. She had a wide, cheerful face and blue eyes. "Are you sick?" she said. "Yes," I said, "I have a headache." "Poor dear," she said, "hold Buster and I'll give you a piece of Aspergum." I took the chain, holding it along with my bag. "It's like chewing gum but it's got aspirin in it. Here, now just pop it into your mouth. Why don't you go home and rest?" I stuck the gum in my mouth and began to chew, tasting peppermint. "I will," I said. "Thanks very much." "Not at all," she said, "you just go home and rest. Here, I'll let you out of the gate." The dog sniffed at my heels, I stepped out onto the street. "Now do what I say," she said, smiling through the fence. "I will," I said. "Thank you. Good-by." I spat the gum into the gutter: WIFE HACKS LOVER, WATCHES HIM DIE, the scrap of tabloid said against the grating; a puff of breeze caught it, pushed it along. I crossed the street with the green light, the wind flicking my skirt; but it was a hot breeze, filled with some suffocating vapor and the odor of a bakery, and I sweated more; then the breeze died. I looked at the address Lennie gave me: it said 15, and I walked south down the block gazing upward at the—21, 19, 17—descending numerals. Then I came to 15 and then I thought: suppose the clock again. Suppose the blessed, wonderful, enclosing, warm clock. Suppose he should fail to realize the value and the sacrifice: $39.95, our womb all jeweled and safe. Suppose. Just suppose. But I didn't want to think about that. I climbed three brick steps, pushed open the door and went in: FREEMAN on the mailbox, first floor rear. I pushed the bell and waited, but I waited even less than a time to think, for the buzzer went off right away, clattering beneath my hand, an imprisoned rattlesnake. I went in and down the hall, past a frieze of tiles, a table littered with mail, a mirror in which I saw myself—shocked, with circles under my eyes, and disordered hair: I passed on breathing, from behind chrysanthemum wallpaper, the stench of other peoples' lives. My drowning. I paused: please let him say yes. Then I walked on, and then I reached the door. I pressed the bell, heard it sound inside somber chimes—*bing bong bong*—staid and solemn, churchlike, outside my soul. "Who is it?" I didn't answer, stood with my head against the door and listened to my heart's fearful pounding, the clock ticking too, against my breast, all ordered and safe. "Who the hell is it?" Then footsteps across the creaking timbers. "Yes?" he said. I didn't answer, for fear he. Suppose he.

373

Couldn't he understand the miracle of my invention, the soaring dark soul-closet, lit only by jewels through the endless night? I confess an ecstasy at that: thinking, while he stood separated from me for one second by the thinnest panel of oak, of us untroubled through some aerial flight across time, the ticking like music, only better, sheltered from the sun and from dying, amid the jewels and wheels. "Who is it, dammit. Speak up." I held my breath, But yes. He threw open the door, stood there silent when he saw me, tense and grim: I saw a vein pulse at his throat. "It's me," I said, smiling, "come back to the land of the living." "You've got the wrong house," he said. "We don't want any." Past him in the room an easel and a painting, windows thrown open to the fading light. There was a streak of blue oil across his brow, and the sweat stood up on it in tiny globes, and he said, "Why don't you go away?" Yet this I had prepared for too; I said, "I brought you a present." "You mean a bribe?" he said. "No," I said, "a present. Can't I come in?" "No," he said, "I'm working." He started to close the door, and the fright came up in my throat; I said, "I won't disturb you. I'll be very quiet." "No," he said, "go back to your Italian friend." "I'm drowning," I said, and I took his arm; he pulled away. "Oh, Christ," he said, "go see Strassman or somebody——" "Harry," I said, "listen to me, please——" He let me in, turned his back on me and walked to the easel; the door slammed behind, I strolled across the floor, holding my clock. He was painting an old man. In grays, deep blues, an ancient monk or a rabbi lined and weathered, lifting proud, tragic eyes toward heaven; behind him were the ruins of a city, shattered, devastated, crumbled piles of concrete and stone that glowed from some half-hidden, rusty light, like the earth's last waning dusk. It was a landscape dead and forlorn yet retentive of some glowing, vagrant majesty, and against it the old man's eyes looked proudly upward, toward God perhaps, or perhaps just the dying sun. "That's a beautiful picture," I said. He didn't answer, took a brush and painted a gray stroke across the ruined city. "I think it's wonderful," I said. Still he didn't answer, painted on, his shoes scraping on the floor. I sat down on a chair and watched him. Outside in the garden the paradise trees stirred almost imperceptibly in the stifling air; sparrows rustled among the leaves, chirping, and the yells of children came from afar, like something out of memory. I said it then: "Come back, darling." He didn't answer. "Come back," I said. "I'm sorry for what I've done." Still he didn't answer; the ruins came closer, faded beneath his touch, soundlessly. He painted on. I thought of the clock, took it out of my bag. "Look, darling, look at the clock I bought us. You were always complaining that that old clock wouldn't keep time. Now look." He didn't say a word. "Look, darling," I said, "all jeweled and safe," then wondered: why safe, why that? He turned, held the brush in mid-air, dripping a bead of blue oil. He looked at the clock. In the silence we could hear its ticking, along with the sparrows, the far-off children. "You got it at Macy's," he said, "and it cost $39.95. Right?" "Yes," I said. "And you paid for it by check," he said. "Yes," I said. "And the check bounced higher than a kite," he said, turning back to the easel. "Thank you very much for the present, which *I* paid for out of our joint quote bank account unquote. Ex-bank account, that is: there's nothing left." "Oh," I said, "oh," listening to the words over his shoulder and not knowing how his face looked, except the words: bitter and angry and full of disgust: and in the clock, for one brief moment plummeting earthward, he and I crushed and ruined amid all the fiercely disordered, brutally slashing levers and wheels. Yet "Oh," I said, "oh." Then I said "I'm sorry, Harry, really I am. I didn't know. It was a present for you. I'll get some money from Bunny." Safe again, the clock upright, soaring through space, Harry and I: it was a close call, I thought. "Why?" he said, and turned angrily, clutching the brush: "Why, why, why? *Why*, Peyton?" "Why what, darling?" I said. "Why do you do these things? Deliberately, without the slightest twinge of guilt? *How* can you do it?" "I don't know," I said. "I forgot." "So you say your Bunny'll pay for it," he said. "Well, somebody better had. I had to borrow from that ass Berger to cover the check. What's the matter with you?" "I'm sorry," I said. "It won't happen again." "No," he said, and he went back to the easel. "No, it certainly won't happen again." Then I walked past him to the window, and the dread began to move up inside. I couldn't think: the paradise leaves rustled ever so slightly, turning up their bleached undersides to the dying sun. A cat crawled along the fence and a woman called to it—"Toby!"—from where she stood huddled, a shawl around her shoulders, in a garden, among phlox and roses and crimson zinnias. I couldn't think, the evening had crept part way up the walk here, and I thought I heard thunder in the distance, but it was something else, a subway train, or a truck or remote, fantastic guns. So I said without thinking then, "Come back with me, Harry." Over my shoulder. "The three of us?" he said. "That would be cozy. We could get free milk, though. I'll bet." And I said, very slowly, "But don't you see, darling? Tony is nothing, nothing at all. I'm sorry, I really am, and I've told you so. I was mad at you because you were right, you know. That I *was* depending on you for everything, and being a spoiled child and everything. But I was mad because that was the truth, don't you see? And I took out my little vengeance that time you left in a huff. It was cruel to do it that way, I know, but I'm sorry——" "You've told me that," he said, and I heard his voice become more tense, more angry and bitter. "Look, Peyton, I'm trying to work while I've got the light. Why don't you just go?" "No, Harry," I said, and I turned. "We could have children——" "Those tears won't help a hell of a lot with me, baby," he said. "We could have had children a year ago, but that was the time you said I was so unreliable that I wouldn't know how to be a good father——" "That was the time——" I started to say. "That was the time," he said, "when I knew the truth and told you so: you are absolutely incapable of love. Oh, to hell with it anyway." He threw down the brush. "Now will you kindly——" he began, but I said, "Children, Harry, we could——" no sooner than saying it, than remembering again, with a rustle somewhere behind the fading plaster walls and water-stained ceiling, through the stacked-up empty picture frames, of flightless wings. They came across the sand. Out loud I said, "Protect——" but didn't finish, remembering that guilt, for the second time, which I had not even told Harry: the doctor, probing, the instrument, the merciless, inside twitching. "Oh, Harry," I said, "I'm sorry for what I've done." "Protect you from what?" he asked. "From milkmen, from mystery writers?" "No," I said, sinking down on the windowsill, "from me." He was gentler with me now. "Where did you pick up your strange code of ethics?" he said. "What's happened to you? If I could remember you as you were once, that would be fine. At least I could keep my temper. But I don't think I can even remember that time. When you at least had a few ideals that weren't product of myth or fairy-book fantasy. That time when you modeled for me and I was fool enough to say to myself that a girl with a face and body as lovely as yours could never be anything but beautiful inside, too. What happened to that time, my lost lady, my blessed Beatrice——" "Don't," I said, "please don't say that, darling." "I guess I was a fool," he went on, "with all the suspicions I had, too. Inside. I ignored them. When you'd nag and nag and nag at me for my so-called attentions to other women. Just when you were so Goddamned beautiful that it made me itch just to be in the same room with you. How could I convince you that I had no designs on some other dame, that idiot Epstein girl? I couldn't. Well, by God I've

376

had designs in the past two months. You can bet your sweet life I have. You want to know how many times I've got laid——" "No, Harry," I said. "Don't, please." "Weep your head off," he said. "The shoe is on the other foot. Isn't that the metaphor?" "Yes," I said. He was silent then, shaking a bit and playing with a brush. I tried to think as I watched him, both of us silent for no more than five seconds: couldn't he see, couldn't I convince him of, instead of joy, my agony when I lay down with all the other hostile men, the gin and the guilt, the feathers that rustled in the darkness, my drowning? Then I would say: oh, my Harry, my lost sweet Harry, I have not fornicated in the darkness because I wanted to but because I was punishing myself for punishing you: yet something far past dreaming or memory, and darker than either, impels me, and you do not know, for once I awoke, half-sleeping, and pulled away. "No, Bunny," I said. That fright. I spoke: "Please don't stay angry with me today, darling. I won't be able to stand it. Bunny'll pay for the clock." "Clock, schmock," he said. "To hell with the clock. It's paid for. What I want to know is do I still have to pay the rent for you and Tony?" "No," I said. "No, don't talk like that." "I don't like to talk like that," he said. "I'd much rather talk about other things. I'd like to sit around like I think I remember we used to and talk about color and form and El Greco or even just which drugstore sold the best ice cream. Like we used to. Blessed Beatrice——" "Don't," I said. He went on, "There are a lot of things I'd like to talk about. Do you realize what the world's come to? Do you realize that the great American commonwealth just snuffed out one hundred thousand innocent lives this week? There was a time, you know, when I thought for some reason—maybe just to preserve your incomparable beauty—that I could spend my life catering to your needs, endure your suspicions and your mistrusts and all the rest, plus having to see you get laid in a fit of pique. I have other things to do. Remember that line you used to quote from the Bible, How long, Lord? or something——" "Remember how short my time is," I said. "Yes," he said. "Well, that's the way I feel. With your help I used to think I could go a long way, but you didn't help me. Now I'm on it alone. I don't know what good it'll do anyone but me, but I want to paint and paint and paint because I think that some agony is upon us. Call me a disillusioned innocent, a renegade Red, or whatever, I want to crush in my hands all that agony and make beauty come out, because that's all that's left, and I don't have much time——" "I'll help you," I said. "Oh, Harry, I'll help you." "Balls," he said. "If this had been the first time, maybe so; I'd still be a fool. But it's not, it's the fourth or fifth or sixth; I've lost track." "It's a beautiful picture," I said. In the dim light the tragic face still looked heavenward, amid the junk and the rubble, through the final, extinguishing dusk, proud and unafraid, my Harry. Who knows our last end, thrown from the hub of the universe into the dark, into everlasting space: once he said we are small blind sea things pitched up wriggling on the rock of life to await the final engulfing wave, yet my Harry: who can tell the eyes of man gazing ceaselessly upward toward his own ascending spirit? "It's got belief," I said, "or something. It's got——" "It's time for belief," he said. "Don't you think? You should know." "Yes," I said, "once I had belief. When we walked along the sand and picked up shells." "Who?" he said, "you and Sanders in the cabaña. At Rye?" "No," I said, "Bunny and I." "You and your bloody father," he said. "Yes," I said, not thinking all this time. Then I said this: "I wish you'd take the clock. Even if you bought it. Inside there—did you know?" I took him by the sleeve and drew him closer, smelling the sweat and the paint, the blessed flesh. "Look here," I said, and I pointed toward the alarm hole. "Look, you know? You know what? We could get inside and float merrily along." I laughed then, very loudly, not knowing why. "Harry and I among the springs and wheels. It'd be so safe there, to float around and around on the mainspring. The man said there were jewels in there, too, fifteen of them. Wouldn't it be glorious, Harry, to——" But I felt his hand on my arm then, gripping it tightly; he said, "Peyton, don't say any more. What's the matter, honey? Look, there's something really wrong with you. You're trembling all over." "Yes," I said, "the clock——" Only, "Sit down," he said. "Sit down here and wait a minute." And he pushed me down in the chair. "Marshall has some phenobarb around somewhere. Wait a minute——" He started to move away, but I took him by the hand. "No," I said, "that's all right, darling, I'll be all right. I was just afraid." "Of what?" he said. "I don't know," I said. "Have you been taking dope?" he said. "No," I said, "that's one vice I haven't mastered." "Well, you just rest for a minute," he said. Then he said, "Awful, awful, awful!" his voice behind me loud and anguished, his worried pacing heels, too, on the floor that creaked: I sat trembling and with a cramp now and the pain rising inside to claw aside every organ, kidneys and stomach and whatever else, and I bent over suddenly, watching the light deepen, turn purple outside above some shingled water tower, the furious pigeons wheeling around: far off there was the sound of thunder, or of guns. "Awful,"

378

he said. "What?" I said. The pain receded, went away. "What's happened to us," he said. "That's what's awful. That's what." "I should see Strassman," I said. "I think so," he said. "Why don't you let Lennie take you over again? On Monday." "That'll be too late," I said. "What?" he said. He sat down and took my hand. "I mean," I said. "Oh, darling, that's not what I need. I need! I need—— " He squeezed my hand. "Take it easy, darling, take it easy." "All right," I said. And he said, "I'm with you, baby." He said, "I'm with you, baby," again, like that, and rubbed my hand. "I've got the curse," I said, yet even with this—"I'm with you, baby"—I felt the same despair, no better or worse, and it was strange: I had not anticipated this, but only had foreseen some blossoming joy, where we'd kiss or something, swoon into the clock, and everything would be without fear or dread or pain. The light waved in the sky, sent shadows across the garden, where the cat sprawled asleep in the dusk and the woman came and went in her shawl, picking flowers, carnations. A young man walked out and yawned, looking at the sky, cleaned his spectacles, then went in. The air was hot with guilt; I sweated. Then, Harry, I would say, why are you like this to me? Not for your defection so small, really, did I do my petty vengeance, but just because always you've failed to understand. Me. Oh yes, it started out with your hand on the ass of Marta Epstein, so then lying down there was a sweet thing for me. Yet the guilt that always followed: oh God, haven't you been able to tell how I've suffered in my own torture and my own abuse? Why haven't you understood me, Harry? Why? Why? That's all I've worried about, really: not that you should accept what I've done. Of course, no man. But that, once it was done, you should try to understand me, for it lies past memory or dreaming, and darker than either, and once when you were angry at me because these was no toilet paper in the john I could have pitched myself out of the window, so lost did I feel and homeless, and everything. So that when I would come to you screaming about my drowning, and you'd never understand, then I'd have to go back and shriek at him, smothered by the odor of milk. Oh, I would say, you've never understood me, Harry, that not out of vengeance have I accomplished all my sins but because something has always been close to dying in my soul, and I've sinned only in order to lie down in darkness and find, somewhere in the net of dreams, a new father, a new home. Bother the birds, they were not half so bad as your not understanding. I took my hand away from his. "You've just never tried to see my side of the matter, have you?" I said. For a moment he said nothing,

nothing at all. I thought he might not answer. Then he said, "What do you mean by that?" Then I wished I hadn't said it: like always my mouth opened to speak peevish words my consciousness hadn't thought of, only thought of by that part of me over which I have no authority: my guilt. "What do you mean by that?" he said again in a flat voice. "I mean," I said and I knew I had to go on, yet even now still was there no escape? "I mean, Harry, don't you see? All of this, as bad as it is, is just reacting to the fact that you've never understood me. You haven't tried." He got up. "Haven't tried?" he said. "What are you talking about? Haven't tried, my eye! That's all I've spent two years doing, trying to understand you——" And I thought: oh Christ, I said it and didn't mean to say it, now there's no retrieving myself, yet I had to go on: "I mean, darling—don't get angry—I mean every time I've gone off like this it wasn't entirely my fault, don't you see? Remember Marta Epstein——" I could feel myself shiver at my own words, and then at his groan. "Oh, really, Peyton, you make me ill. Is that all you came for, to give me a tough time about that?" "Oh, no, darling," I said quickly. "No, don't get angry. Please don't. It's just, I mean that you—that I've been at fault, I mean, but that I never did it unless you gave me some cause to. When I felt I couldn't rely on you, or when you got cynical——" "Cynical!" he cried. "Who's cynical? Are you trying to tell me now that just because on the few occasions when I didn't obey your tiniest whim or spoil you half to death, you had a right to cuckold me, and almost in front of my eyes! Why, God damn it——" "Harry," I said, "don't get angry. Please——" "Awful!" he said. "No, it's true. You just can't love. You come up here on a pretext that you're sorry and contrite when all you want me to do is to tell me that I'm the one who should be on my knees, begging *your* forgiveness for sins I didn't commit. Isn't that right, Peyton, isn't that right?" "Yes," I said. "I mean no. No, Harry, please believe me——" But he said, "Why don't you get out? Get out." "Oh, Harry," I said, "you just don't understand." "You can dry your tears, baby; they don't work on me. Get out." "No," I said. "Get out," he said, "get the hell out of here, you slut." "Oh, Harry," I said, "there you go again. I'm not that. If you just had any understanding——" "I've got plenty of it," he said. "Right at the moment I understand that you want me to go through the same routine you've wanted me to go through for months. To take you on my knee and put my strong arms around you and tell you that I was wrong because there was dirt beneath the bed, that I was wrong for calling you on your extravagance, that I was wrong for not letting you ruin us both by being the spoiled, willful child that you are—now you have the wrong idea. Now get the hell out of here." I put my arms out to him. "Get out." Across the margin of my mind they came, the wingless birds, the emus and dodos and ostriches and moas, preening their wings in the desert light: a land of slumber, frightening me, where I lay forever dozing in the sands. Would he never come again, protect me from my sin and guilt? I saw them prance staidly in the far corners of the room, at the edges of the walls, through the piled-up picture frames, all grave and unmenacing in the drowned and stifling dusk. Outside the sparrows chirped and fluttered; someone called distantly; I held out my arms. "Get the hell out," he said. "I'm drowning," I said. "Help me, Harry." "Get out," he said. I got up. "I'll never be able to come again," I said. "Good," he said. I walked past the easel, past the ruined city, the dusty twilight, the tragic upraised eyes. "Don't make me go," I said. "It's a beautiful picture. I'll help you." There was no reply; he stood at the door, unconsciously stiff in a gesture he himself would be the first to think funny: one hand on the knob to the open door, the other arm outstretched and pointing downward toward the hall, classical and stern, the cartoon father to the prodigal, pregnant girl: Go, and never darken my door again. "Get out." His face was red, fierce, unremitting. "It won't do you any good," he said. "I've tried. I've been through this too many times." "O.K.," I said. My pride. Then I said, "It seems that you'd try to understand. I never did it except when——" He took my arm and pushed me toward the hall. "That's enough," he said. "Tony'll understand. Tell Tony. Or tell your old man; he'll take you on his lap and tell you what a good girl you are. As for me, I've had it to my——" And the door slammed behind me. I was standing in the hall holding my bag, his last words—"to my very guts"—muffled, deadened now by the walls. I blew my nose on my handkerchief, stood listening to his retreating, creaking footsteps on the floor. Then the footsteps came back again. I held my breath. He opened the door and said, "Here, take your clock." I felt it cupped in my hands, the rounded, polished metal, the levers and wheels to operate; then the door closed, the diminishing footsteps, he was gone. I pounded on the door: "Harry, let me in! Let me in!" And until I scraped my knuckles. "Let me in, Harry. I'll be a good girl!" He didn't answer. I walked down the hallway and out onto the sidewalk, walked along north, past a florist's, where red cannas were set out like flags in the dusk. The lights were on inside and I bought a daffodil for a nickel and pinned it to my breast. The woman was small and dumpy, with freckled arms. "Don't you want to use my comb?" she said. "No, thanks," I said. Then I walked outside, with everything gone, including the clock: this I took to a drain near the curb. I bent down and pulled it out of the bag, holding it close to my ear: I heard the last ticking, all my order and all my passion, globed from the atoms in the swooning, slumbrous, eternal light. Then I threw it into the drain, heard it rattle below against the accretion of gravel and litter, and vanish far below with a splash. I stood up: to my very guts. I thought I saw an old man fishing in the twilight, his line limp in the shimmering, mirrored water, but it was a string he dangled into a basement grating and groped for money; the bum tipped his hat to me as I walked by, and he smelled foul and of whisky. I had twenty-five cents left, and I gave him two dimes. "God will praise you for that," he said. "I know," I said, and walked along. I got sleepy, the brother of death haunting me with a dying memento: Bunny would understand that, perhaps he would understand my going: undivorced from guilt, I must divorce myself from life, in this setting part of time. I would go back to Bunny, but she would never permit that, or understand. I walked along, turned the corner at Fourteenth Street and went down into the subway. I had a nickel left for the turnstile; I pushed through. They followed me, prissing along with their stiff-legged gait and their noiseless, speckled wings. I turned. "Go away," I called, "go away," but they came on, and a woman passed giggling, said to a man sweating underneath a tower of packages: "Drunk as she can be." "I am not drunk——" my mouth working, but I didn't say it, and walked down the stairs. A train came by with that frightful noise; I put my hands over my ears, watching it in a blur of vanishing light, heading south, a forest of up-thrust arms, all tilted as if by a gale. And I thought: it was not he who rejected me, but I him, and I had known all day that that must happen, by that rejection making the first part of my wished-for, yearned-for death-act, my head now glued to the executioner's block, the ax raised on high and I awaiting only the final, descending, bloody chop: oh my God, why have I forsaken You? Have I through some evil inherited in a sad century cut myself off from You forever, and thus only by dying must take the fatal chance: to walk into a dark closet and lie down there and dream away my sins, hoping to wake in another land, in a far, fantastic dawn? It shouldn't be this way—to yearn so for dying, or for that chancy, early fate, when I'm young yet and lovely and braver than you think, my God, and my heart beats stronger than a pump: then too I want to be bursting with love, and not with this sorrow, at that moment when my soul glides upward toward You from my dust. What a prayer it was I said; I knew He wasn't listening, marking the sparrow but not me. So to hell. I was thirsty enough but even hungrier. I wanted to drink water, gallons of it, but I was hungrier first. So I looked into my bag again for some money, hoping. But there wasn't any. Then I put my hand in the pocket of my skirt and found, covered with lint in the seam, a zinc penny. There was a machine with chocolates in it, four kinds and a mirror: I stood aside from the glass so I wouldn't see myself. In it I discovered bittra and nut and bittersweet and plain and I decided on bittra, putting in the penny and pulling the plunger: nothing came out. I pulled it again, but I got no chocolate. Then I tapped the machine but still nothing came out; besides, the subway trains pulled in, red and green lights burning port and starboard like ships at home, and I got on then, thinking about the machine. I sat down next to a Puerto Rican reading a newspaper; he smelled in the heat but no worse than I now, most likely, and the headline read—*traficante marijuana:* I turned away, thinking of gallons of water to drink, thinking of home. So proceeding north on the Lex. Ave. Express to Woodlawn Ave., where I'd rather not go, but home: if Grandmother lived now, had not dwelt in some jasmine time of long ago. That was hard to remember, that house in Richmond: it was very old, Bunny always said. There were oaks all around it; I remembered those and the hollyhocks: thus in the sweltering summer noon I was carried upward in his arms to lie down in murmurous, strange light, on the damp, strange sheets, napping, hearing along the cobblestones the staid clipclopping of a horse, and a Negro's voice far off—*flowahs! flowahs!* I saw him even then, when I was three or four or five: he luxuriated in my drowsing fancy, and my mind went forth, half-dreaming: I saw him below hunched behind his sleepy mare, coal-black, and with a switch for the flies, sweat pouring off his brow as he sourly frowned at the horse's coarse, flourishing tail: behind them both begonias and lilacs and larkspur nodding beneath an umbrella, cool in pots of clotted moist earth. Then the cry again—*flowahs! flowahs!*—and the fading hooves along the cobblestones, beneath the sheltering cedars, vanishing flowahs flowahs into my dreams, in a strange bed, in a strange land. And I thought then, oh Bunny, what has happened to me that I hate myself so today: Albert Berger said that I was blocked up in my sexual area but I know something else and so, Bunny, I would tell Albert Berger a misery: behold, we have not been brought up right and my memory of flowers and summer and larkspur is conjoined equally with pain: that all my dying. That when I lay down in Richmond in Grandmother's bed I saw her picture on the wall so benignly smiling, even on that day I heard the flower man clipclop along beneath the cedars, moved and peered at it in my slumber through half-closed eyes; a face that once brushed Longstreet's beard preserved behind the nacreous glass, still smiling and with a bulge of snuff: and I reached out my arms, cried *mother mother mother*, to that image even then twenty years before turned to bones and dust. The train stopped at a station; this last car deserted, save for the Puerto Rican, who moved away. Then it went on rocking down the tunnel with rails, with darkness, with winking red eyes. I put my head in my hands, thinking of thirst, thinking of gallons of water to drink and cool dew somewhere, resting on a lawn beneath the mimosa shade to hear the distant trumpeting of gulls or thunder or guns. I couldn't think; the train rocked on, bearing me north, and I prayed, though my prayer in the sweat and fever and sudden cramp, which made me almost sink to the floor, seemed addressed no longer to God but to Albert Berger, a gaseous vertebrate with eyes weeping strange red tears all over the windy universe. The train stopped at 125th Street; I got off amid a crowd of shoving Negroes. I pushed up the littered stairs, dropping my bag. "Hey, lady, you drapped yo' bag." I didn't answer, climbed on, came out into the twilight, where a theater marquee blossomed capering globes of red and blue, and Van Johnson, twenty feet high, sent a smirk across the evening. And then I walked fast up the avenue, past the throng, into the shadows where there was little noise. I turned. Sooty buildings towered all around me. I turned again, facing the street: I thought I could see them still, prancing up the avenue, a whole flock of them flightless, wingless, borne floating through the aqueous twilight like feathered balloons caught upon strings. I said, "No" out loud, and an old colored woman paused at my side, with round, white, curious eyes. I turned and ran a bit but it was too hot: I began to wheeze and to sweat and the pain returned in my womb: I thought, oh Christ, have mercy on your Peyton this evening not because she hasn't believed but because she. No one. had a chance to. ever. I stopped running then and calmed myself down: Have mercy, I said. There was a loft building here, facing an alley: the door had swung open. You had to climb three steps for the door; these I walked up gingerly, holding onto the rail, and the steps sagged and creaked, giving off an odor of dust. In one corner there was an elevator; inside and beneath a dimly glowing bulb an old Negro dozed on a stool: moths fluttered around his head. I tiptoed past him toward the stairs. Then I climbed and while I climbed I thought that only guilt could deliver me into this ultimate paradox: that all souls must go down before ascending upward; only we most egregious sinners, to shed our sin in self-destruction, must go upward before the last descent. I climbed seven flights and rested, propped up against a wall fanning myself with my hand: the hall smelled of some fabric, a cutting room where Negroes worked: everything was deserted, and over the darkness and the desertion hung that odor of lint and dust and the strong sour odor of sweat. I stood erect: Did I have a companion? I felt that someone was watching me, myself perhaps; at least I knew I was not alone. The birds had vanished for a moment, and around me hung that idea of someone watching me in the darkness: friend or enemy from another time, male, female, it made no difference, even perhaps a dog—some presence huddled in a corner of the cutting room, among the presses and frames silhouetted against the city lights, looking at me with mourning eyes. I turned and walked up again, past walls peeling plaster, crayon marks and water stains, upward and upward through the pervasive sour smell—like a pantry I knew once where La Ruth used to change, an odor of pickles there, and lemons, resting mingled and palpable on the heat, yet through it all this smell, of a land lost from me, unvisited, irretrievable. Bulbs hung at every landing and around them, as if borne back ceaselessly to the light of their beginning, fluttered a cloud of moths: more than I had ever seen before, rich and plump from the woolen lint and scraps of cuttings, beating at my face upon each landing like a bleached storm of windblown petals. I reached the top. "Finish," I said out loud. Oh, let me die. I walked down a long corridor, in the darkness stumbling over piles of jackets: I could feel the touch of woolen arms, knew the smell again—of blankets and lint and wool, enfolding me forever. Then I came to a door. There was enough light to see: it said WOMEN. I threw open the door and went in, touching a row of tiles. A toilet gurgled somewhere in the darkness and I groped toward the window. I sat down on the radiator beneath it, looking out on the starless sky fired red as an oven from the city. Then I stood up, heard far below one furious, continual honk of a car horn; some mortal insanely attuned to noise: it blatted on. Now all this blessed relief, taking off my clothes; my dress first: I carried it out to the loft where I'd seen an ashcan, ripped the silk up so that it looked like so much scrap and shoved it down into the can beneath a pile of cuttings. Then I walked back into the washroom. I went to the window again, took off my other things and threw them on the floor. Afterwards, I kicked off my shoes and stockings and stuffed them beneath the radiator, stood up: I was naked, clean if sweating, just as I had come. Something seemed to hurry me through space, I heard that thunder again, on the remotest horizon, guns perhaps, something: above Java or palms on the Laccadives, in the profoundest sunlit seas. Something hurries me through memory, too, but I can't pause to remember, for a guilt past memory or dreaming, much darker, impels me on. I pray but my prayer climbs up like a broken wisp of smoke: *oh my Lord, I am dying*, is all I know, and *oh my father, oh my darling*, longingly, lonesomely, I fly into your arms! *Peyton you must be proper nice girls don't. Peyton.* Me? Myself all shattered, this lovely shell? Perhaps I shall rise at another time, though I lie down in darkness and have my light in ashes. I turn in the room, see them come across the tiles, dimly prancing, fluffing up their wings, I think: my poor flightless birds, have you suffered without soaring on this earth? Come then and fly. And they move on past me through the darkening sands, awkward and gentle, rustling their feathers: come then and fly. And so it happens: treading past to touch my boiling skin—one whisper of feathers is all—and so I see them go—oh my Christ!—one by one ascending my flightless birds through the suffocating night, toward paradise. I am dying, Bunny, dying. *But you must be proper.* I say, oh pooh. Oh pooh. Most be proper. Oh most proper. Powerful.

Oh most Powerful

Oh must

It was as if all the air had become an ocean. It was not rain, but solid water, which came down over the cemetery and Carey's last glimpse of the place before he darted back into the doorway was of flooded tombstones, grass plastered down by the torrent, and finally, in the limousine, of Dolly, sealed with round, frightened eyes behind the streaming windows like a guppy in a fish bowl. There was a crackle of thunder; lightning struck nearby in the woods. Carey thought he heard the crash of a falling tree. He turned. There was a short corridor here, smelling of damp concrete, a depressing place, ill-lit and lined with empty niches. At the end of the corridor Mr. Casper and Barclay had taken refuge, along with Ella Swan, who stood against the door leading into the chapel proper, and wept desperately and audibly into her handkerchief. A chill had arisen with the rain, and Mr. Casper turned up the collar of his coat; now and then he rubbed his hands together and looked up piously toward the thunder.

Loftis had dragged Helen into a little anteroom nearby. This had happened when the storm broke. Carey had seen it all: the compliant look on her face, her smile. She had even put an arm around Loftis' waist as he drew her along with him. But when, closing the door, he had gazed back at Carey for one confused moment, his face wore the same look of agony. A minute had passed, certainly not much more. Carey heard Loftis' voice, high, hysterical, tormented, muffled by the walls. He couldn't hear Helen's at all. Then the door broke open, and Helen came out, followed by Loftis with outstretched arms and bright, glazed eyes.

"Why have I wanted you?" he shouted. "Because you're the only thing left! That's why! My God, don't you see? We're both sick, we need to make each other——"

She rustled up and took Carey's arm. "Can't we go now, Carey? Milton," she said over her shoulder, "don't make a scene. Please don't make a scene."

Loftis approached them wildly, his hair flying, and clutched her by the arm. Carey felt his bowels give way somewhat, in fear and in horror: the place seemed touched with a violence greater, even, than the storm. A spray of water swept beneath the door.

"Scene! Scene!" Loftis shouted. "Why, God damn you, don't you see what you're doing! With nothing left! Nothing! Nothing! Nothing!"

"Would she want it that way?"

"She?"

"Yes," Helen said.

"She? Who? She?" he cried.

She removed his hand from her arm. "Yes," she said softly, "I imagine she would."

"She would?" he yelled.

"Milton, I've told you that anything you need or want from me you can have. Except—" she paused, still smiling—"except—— Well, we've been through it all, haven't we? One has pride——"

Then Carey saw something take place which he could never have predicted—much less, he later said to Adrienne, thought ever could happen at all, among civilized people of a certain maturity. Whenever he told Adrienne, usually with a pipe, usually with something to drink, sherry perhaps, or a drop of bourbon, he told it with sorrow, slowly and thoughtfully, and with a sort of grave wonder. Yet secure in the rectory, though he tried, he could never retrieve—in a vicarious, not really too worthy attempt at excitement—the same horror, which had made his guts moist and his limbs paralyzed and futile, and which had caused something in his brain to say, at the moment it happened, "Oh, my Lord, You shall never reveal Yourself!"

Loftis pulled Helen about so that she faced him and began to choke her. "God damn you!" he yelled, "If I can't have . . . then you . . . nothing!"

"People!" Carey cried. "People! People!" He couldn't move.

"Die, damn you, die!"

It was over as quickly as it had begun, one red flash of violence spread out like momentary lightning against the storm. Loftis relaxed his grip on her neck, stood trembling and weeping in the hallway with its fading, ugly light, its smell of dampness and rain and death. Helen slumped against Carey, heavily, without a sound, and distantly within the chapel, where Peyton's body lay, something stirred, moved, a piece of falling slate perhaps, a rain-blown gutter pipe—who knows? Carey said later, with his pipe and bourbon, except that the noise seemed ghostly then, somehow fatal, and altogether quite shattering to his mind, fevered as it was with such hot wild winds of ruin and godlessness. But it was over. Loftis lifted his hands to his face—a sudden, angry, almost childish gesture, as if he were striking himself in the eyes with his fists. Then he turned and ran out into the rain. He didn't pause at the limousine. He did give Dolly, it seemed to Carey, a brief glance as he hurried past the car—but here Carey might have been mistaken. The last he saw of him was his retreating back, amid all the wind and rain, as he hustled on, bounding past wreaths and boxwood and over tombstones, toward the highway.

Then Helen steadied herself against Carey, and she pressed her head next to the wall. "Peyton," she said, "oh, God, Peyton. My child. Nothing! Nothing! Nothing! Nothing!"

Toward the end of the day, when it was nearly dusk, Ella, La Ruth and Stonewall stood on a corner in North Port Warwick, waiting for the bus. The sky had cleared, the storm had passed, rumbling far off eastward; near them the trees dripped water, roses on a trellis bore round white pearls of dew. It was cool and quiet on the highway. The evening star had risen in the west, one ornament in a blue, cloudless sky—this and the pale rind of a tilted new moon. Ella and La Ruth both had on their white baptismal robes, and white turbans wrapped around their hair. Stonewall was dressed identically, and in miniature, except for the turban: he wore none, which allowed him, from time to time, to reach up and scratch his sparse, kinky hair. There were no tears now, no grief or lamentation, at least outwardly exposed; Ella's face wore the passive look of one who has seen all, borne all, known all and expects little more, of either joy or suffering: she was too old, and if occasionally the wrinkled serenity of her face became a touch grim, it was because her outlook on life was basically tragic, and not because of any passing anger or bitterness. La Ruth's face was formed in one huge pout: she had missed out on Peyton's funeral, and this had left her with a vague, empty feeling, of a grief that had been stifled, that had not—since no one had let her go to the ceremony—reached a proper climax in her heart; and there were a number of other lacks and disappointments stirring about inside her, none of which she could define or very well understand. Now and then she began to moan, to press Stonewall against her belly, and to rock backward and forward in a lumpy expression of anonymous, uncomprehending woe, but Ella would always touch her on the arm and tell her to stop. Stonewall was lost in dreams. "Mama," he said, "Christine say she want to frig wid me. Do dat mean——"

La Ruth gave him a crack on the head. "You hush yo' nasty face," she said. "You gonna need mo' dan baptism to save yo' dev'lish soul."

She began to moan again, rocking back and forth in the twilight, and pressed Stonewall against her: "De Lawd he'p us, Mama, Satan is fo' sho' stalkin' around de proppity dis day. Seem like de Lawd jes shet de door on His people——"

"Quit moanin'," Ella said, grabbing her arm, "trust in Him."

The bus, marked "Special," came clattering over the hill; they got on. They dropped two nickels in the box.

"How old is that child?" the driver said, turning cold blue eyes on La Ruth.

Three steps down the aisle La Ruth turned. "He's five years and 'leven months old, six come September."

"Are you sure?" the driver said.

"Yes, suh, 'deed I is. Mama she said always tell de troof when de man asks. Dat child ain't but——"

"O.K., O.K.," the driver said.

The bus pulled away from the curb; the three of them moved to the rear, joining a group of Negroes on the back seat.

"How do, Sister Ella? You do look fine," said a small plump woman with tan skin. Her robe had arms of lace, with beads; these she rattled noisily and obviously, tucking the hair beneath her turban. "I do hear, though," she said solemnly, "from Sister Moreen. She said you had sorrow in yo' fambly today."

"'Deed we did," Ella sighed, "de Lawd plucked off de prettiest creature in dis world."

"When de Lawd plucks, he *plucks*." A thin little man had spoken; he was very old, with a mangy gray mustache, but spry. When he spoke he clapped both feet on the floor, for emphasis. He fanned himself with a bandanna.

"'Deed he does, Brother Andrew," Ella said mildly. "De Lawd plucks fo' sho'. When he plucks."

"Ain't you grievin'?" said the other woman.

"Done grieved all I can," said Ella. "Can't grieve no mo', Sister 'Delphia, can't grieve no mo'."

"Dat's right," said Sister Adelphia. "Daddy Faith, he say grief is a wellspring and a fount, dat when it run dry den it's time to lift up yo' heart and praise Him fo' His blessin's, dat it's time fo' thanksgivin'——"

"And de blood offerin'!" Brother Andrew put in, snapping his heels.

"And de blood offerin'!" said Sister Adelphia.

"Amen," said Ella.

They rode on through the twilight, past fields and woods and dirt roads. At each road the bus stopped to take on more people, until finally it was crowded with passengers, all Negroes except for one white man, a railroad worker, who stood up in front and seemed nervously out of place. The air generally was that of expectancy and hope and jubilation; they jostled one another, stepped on one another's toes, sang hymns. One old woman near the back door became prematurely hysterical, began to wail and to clutch rapturously at the walls, until the driver slowed down and, standing up, told her to quit it, because she was ringing the bell. Soon they were in Niggertown, on Jefferson Avenue; the street outside became a parade, filled with robed and turbaned figures streaming eastward toward the water. Some blew horns; a band could be heard somewhere in the distance, brassy and loud, with celebrant trumpets, xylophones, and a thunder of drums. The bus halted in the jam, waited, lurched on. La Ruth began to moan again. "God he'p us," she said. "Dem po' people! What dey gonna do? Po' Peyton. Oh, Lawd, Lawd, Lawd . . ."

Ella rubbed her hand gently across La Ruth's knuckles. "You hush now," she murmured. "It's all done and finished with. God will provide in heaven."

"Amen!" Brother Andrew put in.

"Dis day I am with you in paradise," said Sister Adelphia, nodding her head certainly. "De Master hisse'f said dat. Ain't dat enough fo' you, Sister La Ruth?" She rattled her beads; there was a trace of a sneer on her lips, one that indicated she had no use for doubters.

La Ruth hiked Stonewall up higher in her lap. "I know," she said, "but de po' chile, Miss Helen crazy an' all, God knows I don't know . . ." Her voice trailed off, and she gazed out the window; the river could be seen from here, a motionless silver patch at its junction with the bay: on the distant shore, behind a stretch of trees, the sun was setting, a violent half-circle of yolk-colored gold. Nearby was marshland, cattails and sawgrass standing up straight and without motion in the windless dusk. It was high tide; the smell of sea was borne through the windows, salty and faintly sulphurous from the rot of the marshes, but clean. At the railroad crossing the white man got off. The bus moved on, faster now; black hands waved wildly from the windows, toward the sky, toward nothing, in rapture; faint from across the bay there was a final groan of thunder as the storm passed out to sea. Ella sat up stiffly in her seat and rocked with the motion of the bus, her eyes glued together: it was as if she had become suddenly oblivious of the noise around her, the prayers and the laughter and the singing; it was an expression neither grieving nor devout but merely silently, profoundly aware: of time past and passing and time to come, a look both mysterious and peaceful. "Gran'ma," said Stonewall, tugging at her robe, but she said nothing and rocked tranquilly along with the motion of the bus.

Finally the bus turned off onto a dirt side road winding through the marsh. It crossed the railroad track again. They went slowly; there were watery places traversed by corduroy logs; and the bus heaved and lurched, scraping up cattails beneath the fenders. A cloud of mosquitoes swarmed through the windows. The people slapped at them, leaving streaks of blood on brown skin. "Happy am I," someone began to sing, "in my Redeemer," and by the time the bus reached the beach everyone had joined in, except for Ella, who kept her eyes peacefully closed, and Stonewall, who didn't know the words. They ground to a halt, bogged down in the sand. Then everyone piled out. La Ruth came last. Here there were scores more people standing around on the beach; some sat in the loose, dry sand near the marsh, eating watermelon and fried chicken and green sour grapes as big as plums. A railroad trestle arched over the creek nearby, and long tables had been set up in its shadow: they sagged with food, and around them the juice from discarded melon rinds ran like blood in the sand.

But most of the people looked at the raft. They stood around in clusters, watching it, discussing it. It lay anchored offshore in the shallow water, bobbing gently in the waves. On it had been erected a sort of stage, surrounded on four sides by a golden damask curtain; embroidered designs—dragons and crosses and crowns, Masonic emblems, shields, bizarre and unheard-of animals, an amalgam of myth and pagan ritual and Christian symbology—all these glowed against the curtain in green and red phosphorescent fabrics, literally hurting the eyes. At the corners of the curtain were tall golden rods, and surmounting each was a transparent globe, through which an electric bulb shone, giving outline to painted red letters, which said simply: LOVE. Three or four elders, in black robes and black monks' skull caps, tended the raft, and the water came nearly to their waists, although they had little to do except to keep the raft from rocking in the waveless shallows, and to send occasional self-important glances toward the throng on shore. Now many of the people crowded up close to the water's edge; at least a thousand had come: they milled about in the sand, some still with chicken in their fingers, shoving each other, trying to get a better view. Ella and her family stood with Brother Andrew and Sister Adelphia at the rim of the shore. Stonewall was wading; he was eating a deviled crab. La Ruth sucked noisily on a bottle of pop.

"It sho' is pretty," said Sister Adelphia. With an air of careful insouciance she thrust her arms out, to display her rattling beads.

"It sho' is," said Ella. "It's de prime sanctua'y, de alpha and de omega, where all mysteries are revealed."

"Amen!" said Brother Andrew, with a nervous skip on the sand. "Dat's what he say."

La Ruth belched. "Stonewall," she said, "come on in here outa dat water! Put on dem sandals, boy. You gonna snag yo' feet on a oyshter."

Stonewall complied, scuffing meekly back up the beach, dragging his robe in the water. He had found a playmate, a little girl of about four, who had jam smeared around her mouth and who, when Ella bent down and said, "What's yo' name, child?" told her in a tiny faint voice, "Doris."

"Where's yo' mama? You lost?"

She giggled, stuck the hem of her robe in her mouth and refused to answer.

"Well den," Ella said, "you jus' stick wid Stonewall. He take good keer of you. We find yo' mama directly." They all looked up again at the raft. Something seemed to be about to happen; a dark hand poked itself out of the curtain, beckoned to one of the wading elders: he climbed up on the raft and disappeared into the sanctuary. There was a murmur up and down the beach; the crowd pressed closer, buzzing, speculating.

"He gonna make de 'Pearance any time now."

"He sho' is. I kin always tell."

"How come *you* know?"

"I kin always tell. When de elder goes in, it's almos' time."

"De band gotta come yet."

"Dat's right. Wonder where dey is?"

Then, as if it had been given a key, a trumpet sounded in the marsh behind the crowd, one loud clear note, massive and prolonged. The people turned, gave way in the center, and the band, twenty or thirty male musicians in bright scarlet robes, strode down the beach, made a precise military turn, and waded out into the water. A gasp went up from the crowd; everybody applauded, some people cheered.

"Gret day, don't dey look swell!"

"Mmm-*hh*. Talk about a band!"

Sandaled and robed, the musicians struggled toward the raft in hip-

393

deep water, balancing themselves with outthrust trombones and cornets: these glinted in the twilight, sending muted gold reflections across the water. Then the band turned and slowly arrayed itself in two groups beside the raft. An immense quiet fell over the throng; there was not the faintest whisper, except among the children, who got their ears wrung, or were poked, by their parents. It was a moment of supreme expectancy. Down the shore a ferryboat pulled out of the slip, tooted, and the sound drifted across the water, lingered, then faded. Small wavelets lapped against the shore; someone groaned with excitement, was hushed, and an airplane buzzed unheard across the sky: above, the air grew pink and then darkened to a deep crimson, flooding the bay with a sudden burst of fire. Out behind the raft a croaker leaped up with a silver splash of fins; La Ruth began to rock and moan. "Oh, Jesus, po' people. What dey gonna do? Po' Peyton. Gone! Gone!" Ella jabbed her in the ribs. "Hush up now!" La Ruth sobbed quietly, clutching Stonewall by the arm, but Ella gazed at the raft, again, with the look of peace and mystery. There was a flutter behind the curtain, a quiet gasp from the crowd, and a man appeared at the edge of the raft. It was not Daddy Faith. It was his majordomo, announcer, Gabriel, chief lieutenant: a personage with a stern, muscular face, and glassy, bulging eyes. He seemed to come from finer, rarer stock, with his aquiline profile, both views of which he displayed without modesty, almost contemptuously, and with his thin, straight-lipped mouth. None of the crowd had seen this man before; they stood watching in wonder and in humility. His robe was blue, caught tight at the neck like a vestment; above his heart, embroidered on the robe against his hard, visibly muscular chest, was a silver escutcheon of obscure design. He stood for perhaps a minute, stockstill except for his arrogant, turning head, on astonishing display; a small breeze came up, flicking the hem of his robe. The raft rocked gently. Then he raised his arms slowly from his sides.

"Lift up your heads, O . . . ye . . . *gates!*" he cried.

There was a pause. The voice was like no voice ever heard before—orotund, massive, absolute, like the sound of thunder, or the voice from the whirlwind; it possessed a quality of roundness that was the roundness of the infinite—terrible, majestic and beautiful. He still paused, his arms outstretched, glowing like sun-scorched ebony in the dusk. Then he spoke again. "Lift up your heads, O . . . ye . . . *gates*." Another pause. "And be ye lifted up, ye *everlasting doors!*"

A murmur ran through the throng once more; people turned to one another in a flurry of whispers. "My, listen to dat man!"

"Don't he talk right?"

"Hush, man. Listen at him."

He spoke once more. "And de King of Glory shall come in!" Then he lowered his arms slowly to his sides, so slowly that they seemed to descend upon invisible cords. Water rocked the raft, but he stood stern and erect and unperturbed, his robe a blue splash against the red shields and green prophetic talismans and crawling dragons. Then something seemed to change within him; it was not that he appeared any the less regal or stern: he still wore the bulging, hot look of arrogance and contempt. Rather, it seemed that this first majestic, almost unbearably imperious tone which he conveyed through his voice, dissolved; now tempered, even with a touch of gentleness, the voice spoke again.

"Who *is* dis King of Glory?"

It was a question. No one replied. The crowd remained still, quietly stupefied, and with a shaky reverence. Ella stood with her sandals sinking into the beach, bemused and peaceful in her rapt look of mystery, tears streaming down her wrinkled face. Her lips moved over her gums, but she said nothing. The voice came again across the water, majestic and beautiful: "Who *is* dis King of Glory?"

Then Ella said it—the first—shrieked it aloud, her arms flung up to the dusk, her eyes rolling toward heaven. "Daddy Faith!" she yelled. "Daddy Faith! Oh yes, Jesus, He de King of glowry! Daddy Faith! Yes, Jesus, oh yes!" It was like the first firecracker on a string, and it set off an explosion of yells: everyone took up the cry. It was as if Ella's shriek had been all they needed, and they began to shout too. "Daddy Faith! Daddy Faith, He de King of glowry! Come on out now, Daddy, come on, Daddy!" Then a hush gradually settled over the throng, for the man had motioned for silence; Ella was one of the last to quiet down: she kept crying it over and over again until her voice was a squeak—"Yes, Daddy Faith, he de King of glowry, yes, Jesus!"—and until Sister Adelphia, herself almost hysterical, calmed her somewhat, saying, "Hush now, sister, we gotta lot mo' to go!" So she became quiet, her breast heaving, plucking at her robe, her turban askew, and with tears still coursing down her cheeks.

Then the man's voice came across the water once more: "He *is* de King of Glory!" He gave a short nod of his head, a furious, quick gesture; and with a flourish of his robe he stepped down the ladder and into the water. For him it seemed a token of abject and complete humility, to descend in this fashion; had he at that moment sprouted wings and soared up into the sky, no one would have been startled, so utterly

395

possessed he had seemed of the absolute and the miraculous. But, in spite of his majestic voice and bearing, he was only the prelude to the coming wonder; thus his sudden descent seemed not humble, but only proper. And the ensuing wait, which felt like hours but was actually only a minute or so, was even more dramatic in its effect than the appearance of the man in blue. They all stood around for a moment, whispering. "Man, dat was some show!"

"De way he talked!"

"Look at him standin' dere!"

But gradually it occurred to them that Daddy Faith had still not made his entrance. "Why don't Daddy come?" They quieted down, fidgeted; the time passed. Gulls circled overhead and a crab scuttled toward the shore, stuck out one glistening blue claw, and retreated toward the shallows. Ella gazed steadily at the raft, at the elegant dragons, the crosses and cruciform-embroidered trees and bizarre crouching lions; she said nothing: her eyes, yellow with rheum, reflected a perfect peace, a transcendent understanding. Stonewall ran his empty crab shell through Doris' hair, and she whimpered; silently La Ruth took the shell away. "Where's Daddy?" someone said.

Then it happened, with the sound of a trumpet. A robed, scarlet arm went up, and a single note rang across the water. The arm descended, the curtains parted, and Daddy Faith appeared. The crowd stirred and grinned among themselves, but remained respectfully quiet. There he was: a round tub of a man, as black as black ever could get, dressed, like all the rest, in a simple white robe. He stood at the edge of the raft, smiling, benign, avuncular; had he been white he might have been mistaken for a senator, with his quizzical, shy yet friendly eyes, and his benevolent smile. He had no turban, his head was as devoid of hair, and as shiny, as a bullet; his hands were small, not much bigger than a child's: he put these out in front of him, gently, more in entreaty than command. Then he spoke. The words were hoarsely spoken, but sweet and soothing, and they poured over the crowd—touching them, palpably, so that one could almost hear the people shudder—like some liquid from paradise, caressing and divine.

"Comfort ye." Softly.

He paused, gazing at them with a smile, and with benign, twinkling eyes. "Comfort ye," he said again, in the raw rasping voice, but the words were gentle, borne across the water with infinite tenderness. He paused once more, raised his arms outward and toward the sky.

"Comfort ye, my people!"

396

Then he struck himself on the breast with the flat of his hand. This too seemed a gesture not so much lordly or pompous as merely fitting, self-evident and in perfect harmony with his benevolent grin. The thump echoed across the water, and he spoke again.

"Saith your God."

He dropped his arms to his sides for another moment silent and contemplative, with gentle, twinkling eyes. The people stood rigidly still and expectant, waiting for his next words. The band stirred uncomfortably in the water; the elder in blue, hip-deep beneath Daddy Faith, surveyed the crowd with flashing, scornful eyes. Then Daddy Faith spoke again. They knew what he was going to say, watched him stand there relaxed and benign, and his words, a question, were hardly out of his mouth before they were crying the answer.

"Who loves you, my people?"

"You, Daddy! Daddy Faith! You loves us! You, Daddy!" Ella joined in with the rest, her arms outstretched and with blissful weeping eyes, as if she could gather him by pure force of will, and across that stretch of water, into her arms. "You, Daddy! Yes, Jesus, you loves us!" But Daddy Faith motioned politely for quiet, with a sweep of his hand. He was chuckling out loud; they could hear him, watched him put his hand slyly to his chin and chuckle happily, all the time regarding them with his friendly, humorous eyes.

"Dat's right," he said.

He paused, still chuckling.

"*My*, dat's right."

He ceased his laughing, but a smile lingered on his face, and he shook his head, in amusement and with a certain wonder.

"Dat *sho'* is right!" he said. And everybody laughed again. Far off the horn of a freighter blew; darkness would be coming soon. The red fires had disappeared from the water, now it had only the green of dusk in it, and the palest pink from the vanished setting sun. Daddy Faith straightened himself up. His approach at first was direct but friendly, almost like that of an uncle or a raconteur engaged in conversation with children. Once or twice he paused to look at his wrist watch, and only gradually did his voice lose its soothing, intimate tone and work up to its true grandeur, its native triumph. The crowd listened, stood shuffling in the sand, and while he spoke some old women, including Ella, closed their eyes and prayed. "We seen a tough time, my people," he said, "all dese years. We done had de wars and de pestilenches and de exiles. We had de plagues and de bondages and de people in chains. Isr'el has suffered in de land of de pharaohs and de land of Nebucherezzar. And de people have laid down in de wildness and cried out loud: Woe is us fo' our hurt, our wound is grievous, and where is now our hope? Dey shall go down to de bars of de pit, when our rest together is in the dust. And de people have wept out loud, My Lawd, my Lawd, why hast Thou fo'saken me? De people have been sore hurt and dey say, our inheritance is turned to strangers, our fathers have sinned and are not, and we have bo'n their iniquities. And de people have wished to see de pure river of de water of life, clear as crystal, proceedin' outen de throne of God and of de Lamb. Dey stand in de streets of desolation and dey say, Lawd, show me dat revelation where dere shall be no night and no need fo' candle, neither light of de sun. Show me dat, Lawd, for our hurt is grievous and our way is fenced up so we can't pass, and dere is darkness in our paths.

"Now de people of Isr'el done gone off to war," he went on, propping himself against one of the golden rods. Above him the lamp flickered LOVE in the dusk; Ella, rapt and with her eyes closed, moaned a quavering, "Amen!" Somewhere in the crowd a woman echoed, "War. Amen! Yes, Jesus!" and the words drifted shrilly across the darkening marsh. "Now de people done gone off to war and dey sent down de atom bomb on de Land of de Risin' Sun and de sojers come home wid glory in dey th'oats and wid timbrels and de clashin' of bells." He paused again; his eyes grew sad, caressing the throng. "Well, my people, it do seem to me dat we got a long way yet. De hand of de Lawd is against de sinful and de unjust, and de candle of de wicked is put out. But mo' time to pass yet and de eyes of de people shall see His destruction and dey shall drink of de wrath of d'Almighty. And dey shall see a time of hate and a time of war, like de preacher said, and dey shall hear de sound of battle in de land and de great destruction. 'Oh, Lawd,' dey'll go on and cry still, 'Oh, Lawd, I am oppressed, undertake fo' me! I mou'n as a dove, my eyes fail wid lookin' upward! Hear my prayer, Lawd, and let my prayer come unto Thee! Don't take away my freedom again, Lawd, don't take away dat!'

"Dey gonna holler 'O God, de proud are risen against me, and de assemblies of vi'lent men done sought after my soul! How long, Lawd, wilt Thou be angry fo'ever, shall Thy jealousy *burn like fire?*'"

In the twilight came a hoarse "Amen! Oh yes, Jesus!" Shadows from the sheltering marshland lengthened over the water, and there was a long wild moan, a woman's tortured wail, "Oh yes, Daddy! You *right!*" Daddy Faith put out his tiny black hands, a motion of compassion and tenderness.

"Comfort ye," he said softly, "comfort ye, my people. Do you not know dat I will sprinkle clean water upon you, and ye shall be clean, and a new heart also will I give you and a new sperit will I put widin you? If it were not so I would have told you."

"Oh yes, Daddy!"

"Hallelujah!"

Then there was a vast sorrow, one somehow proud and proper and just, in his voice, as he spread his arms to heaven and lifted his round face toward the dusk. "Be not afraid, my people. De voice said, Cry! And he said, what shall I cry? All flesh is grass, and all de goodliness thereof is as de flower of de field. De grass withereth and de flower fadeth, because de sperit of de Lawd bloweth upon it . . .

"Sho'ly de people is grass."

He paused, gazing with benevolence upon the throng. "Sho'ly" he repeated tenderly, "sho'ly de people is grass."

"Oh, Daddy!"

"Praise him! Praise him!"

He quieted them again with a single wave of his hand, tapped himself gently on the chest, and smiled. "De grass withereth, de flower fadeth," he said, "but de word of your God shall stand forever."

When their baptizing was over, drenched and exhausted, Ella and La Ruth climbed back up onto the beach, dragging behind them Stonewall and Doris, who still hadn't found her mother. They walked up the sand a bit, to the camp tables beneath the trestle, and here they sat down. Ella still trembled with the fever of the ritual, remembered the bubbles, the salt water in her nose as she went under—yet, more than this, half-swooning when he smiled at her, as her place came in line, and the divine delight of the touch, on her turban, of his hands. She squeezed the water from her robe and then nibbled on a piece of fried chicken. She shivered with the cold and the memory of his hands. "Dat was sho' some immersion," she said.

La Ruth didn't answer. She had her face in a piece of watermelon.

"Gret day, dat was an immersion," Ella said again.

Sister Adelphia and Brother Andrew joined them, together with a light young girl who seemed to be Doris' mother. She snatched Doris up from a sandpile, where she had been playing with Stonewall.

"Runnin' off like dat!" She slapped the child and then, when she began to scream, kissed her until she became quiet. "Crazy little fool," she crooned, half-sobbing herself, "runnin' off from me. I thought you

399

was drowned." Then she said, "Thank you, Sister," to Ella, and vanished with Doris up the beach.

Sister Adelphia crushed out the water from her robe and sat down on the bench next to Ella with a bottle of Seven-Up. "Whoo-ee, Sister, I seen 'em all now."

"Amen!" said Brother Andrew.

"Dat was *one*, all right," said Ella. "It was in dis world." All sins washed away, her warfare accomplished, her iniquity pardoned, beneath the touch of his hands, in the flooding seas.

La Ruth let the melon rind drop from her fingers and began to moan. "I don't know," she said, "comin' around to thinkin' about all dat time an' ev'ything, po' Peyton, po' little Peyton. Gone! Gone!" She thrust her head in her hands and spread out her legs, snuffling into the wet sleeves of her robe. "God knows, I don't know . . ."

Sister Adelphia sniffed scornfully, rattling her beads. "Ain't you been baptized, Sister?" she said.

Twilight fell around them; the evening became sprinkled with stars. Far off the band tooted triumphantly, around the illuminated love-lamps, amid the flare of blossoming torches. Ella thought of the touch of his hands, the sin-destroying seas. The spell was still on her, and she got up. "Yes, Jesus," she said in a soft voice.

"Dat's right, Sister," said Sister Adelphia, clapping her hands together.

"Yes, Jesus!" Ella said again, louder. She began to shake all over. "I seen Him!"

"Amen!" said Brother Andrew.

"I seen Him!"

In the distance a train rumbled, approached the trestle, setting saucers in a rattle on the table. Ella whirled about in the sand, a black finger upraised to the sky. "Yes, Jesus! I seen Him! Yeah! Yeah!" The train roared, trembled, came nearer. It was a ferocious noise. Stonewall stuck his fingers in his ears; the others turned their faces toward the sea. "Yes, Jesus! Yeah! Yeah!" The voice was almost drowned out. The train came on with a clatter, shaking the trestle, and its whistle went off full-blast in a spreading plume of steam. "Yeah! Yeah!" Another blast from the whistle, a roar, a gigantic sound; and it seemed to soar into the dusk beyond and above them forever, with a noise, perhaps, like the clatter of the opening of everlasting gates and doors—passed swiftly on—toward Richmond, the North, the oncoming night.